THE TERRARHEA CYCLE

PART 1:

"WOLVES AT THE DOOR"

BY mic LOGAN

The Terrarhea Cycle, Part 1

Wolves at the Door

First Paperback Edition March 2022

First Digital Edition March 2022

Cover Art by Patrick Ventura at www.artstation.com/pxvx

ISBN 978-1-7378979-0-3 (paperback)

ISBN 978-1-7378979-1-0 (digital)

ZIRCUITOUS

zircuitous.com

DEDICATION

To my Mom and Dad, who instilled in me a love of fiction
from a young age and never stopped me from following my
dreams, even when they probably should have.

CHAPTER 1

Sitting cross-legged on the floor of his room, Jamie stared at his reflection in the mirror.

His reflection stared back disapprovingly.

Back when Heather had liberated that battered mirror from a closet door in their old home, she had said it might make a useful addition to Jamie's new lodgings. Lately, it had become more of a distraction than anything else. After all the drastic changes that had come along these last few months, it simply didn't seem possible that Jamie still looked exactly the same as he had before. The dour expression he currently wore was certainly seen more frequently these days, but even that was hardly new, just more prevalent.

Sighing, Jamie fell onto his back and pushed the long bangs out of his eyes. The cracked plaster overhead was a dingy shade of white with a large brown stain in one corner where the roof had long ago leaked. All the ceilings in Heather's tiny little house looked pretty much the same, which meant they were a perfect match for the walls and the floors.

The real estate agent assured Heather that the leak had since been fixed. Almost everything Jamie owned was in that one room, a lot of it still packed up in salvaged cardboard boxes, but he had a hard time caring if a leaky ceiling ruined any of it or not. What was the point of getting emotionally invested in anything when life would just swoop in and take it all away without a moment's notice? Jamie hadn't saved much from the estate sale, either his own things or those of his parents. It was just stuff after all, and no simple reminder of happier times would do anything to ease the fact his parents were gone.

"Jamie, get up!" Heather called from down the hall. She was trying out that authoritarian voice of hers again. It would need a lot of work before she became a real parent. Most of the time, Jamie still thought it sounded like she was joking.

"You're gonna be late for school!"

Jamie pinched his eyes closed. "I've *been* up," he said to the ceiling.

"Well, in that case, get your ass in here and eat something." This time, she assumed her easy-going, older sister tone, a role which came much more naturally to her.

"Yeah. I'm coming."

Jamie rolled to his feet. There wasn't any reason to make things harder for Heather than they already were. This had been tough for both of them.

1

Again, he looked at himself in the mirror. The smile he forced onto his face looked so fake he let it drop.

He found his sister at the dining room table, scanning through the socials on her tablet with one hand while eating from a bowl of cereal with the other. "Morning," she said. Heather always dressed nice for work but the dark gray blazer she currently wore was something she only pulled out when she wanted to look especially professional.

"Another presentation?" Jamie said, the words falling from his mouth as he crossed into the kitchen. "If you're not careful, your co-workers are going to realize that's the only blazer you own."

Frowning as she looked down at herself, Heather brushed a piece of lint from her sleeve and straightened the coat. "You think? I guess I have kind of been wearing it a lot recently. I should take a look around on eBay to see if I can find anything nice."

'Cheap' was what she really meant. Maybe Jamie's comment had cut a bit too close to the truth to actually be funny. Bantering with his sister used to come as second nature but now it felt like such a chore. When he opened one of the cabinets, the door nearly fell off right in his hand.

"I really gotta update the hardware on those things one of these days," Heather said, peaking over the gold-flecked countertop that separated the two rooms. "And maybe slap on a fresh coat of paint."

Jamie simply grabbed a pop-tart and fitted the door back into place. From the look of the cabinets, they had already seen about twenty or thirty too many coats of paint. And a few new hinges weren't going to help either. The entire kitchen needed to be gutted, along with every other room in the house.

Jamie went into the adjoining living room and retrieved his book bag from the couch. Heading for the front door across the matted orange carpeting underfoot, he said, "I'll see you tonight."

"I can drop you off on my way to work if you want."

"No, it's a nice day." He needed to get out of that house right now. It felt like he was about to suffocate. "I'd like to walk."

"Well, okay. I'll see you tonight then."

The doorknob rattled in Jamie's hand and it took several tries before it actually turned. This house was going to fall apart around them before Heather would be able to get it fixed up. Jamie froze with the door open only a crack.

"You know," he said without turning to face her, "I really wouldn't mind getting a job to help out with things around here."

Even before the words finished leaving his mouth, Jamie knew he should not have spoken. Hearing Heather sigh, he closed his eyes and tapped his forehead against the door jamb. He should have left when he'd had the chance.

"We've been over this before," Heather said. "Money's not *that* tight. If you want a job to earn a little extra spending money for yourself, that's one thing, but fixing this place up is on me. I'm not gonna make my little brother pay for it and I'm certainly not gonna charge you rent either."

But Heather's finances certainly weren't enough to fund all of her grand plans for this house *and* pay for Jamie's needs as well. He did his best to help with chores; washing dishes, mowing the lawn, doing the laundry; but that hardly offset the drain he put on Heather's pocketbook simply by living here.

"You're never gonna be able to flip this place if you don't remodel it," Jamie said. "If nothing else, a job would give me something to keep my mind off everything."

Heather's chair screeched as she pushed it back from the table and her heels clacked across the dingy linoleum floor. "Jamie, you're only a kid once in your life. I'm not gonna let you waste that by becoming an adult when you're barely even sixteen. If you want to take your mind off what happened, why don't you start by getting out of the house once in a while instead of just moping around your room all the time? You should be out there having some fun, making new friends. What about those two guys from school you told me about: Alex and Eric? Why don't you hang out with them once in a while?"

Jamie rapped his forehead against the door jamb once again. "Derek," he said, correcting her on that second name. Those two had been some of the few at Jamie's new school who had actually made an effort to be friendly to him. Unfortunately, no matter how many times Jamie tried to convince them otherwise, they still seemed to think that just because he knew who a few obscure comic book characters were, he was a fanboy of their caliber. Now they wouldn't leave him alone.

"Well, what about that big neighborhood Halloween party coming up?" Heather said. "I've heard it's quite the event. Last year, it looked like everyone had a lot of fun with it."

"Yeah, I don't really think so."

"But you love Halloween! You and Jack and Kristie always used to put so much work into your costumes."

"Jack and Kristie aren't here, are they! They still have their old lives back home! And just how the hell are either of us supposed to be having any fun when Mom and Dad are dead!"

Heather stopped short at the edge of the living room and Jamie knocked his head against the door jamb a little harder. He shouldn't have snapped at her like that. She was only trying to help.

"Jamie, I miss them too, but you have to deal with these things. If you don't face them head-on and just keep looking back over your shoulder all the time, you're going to end up running into a wall." That sounded just like something their dad would had said, but the last thing Jamie wanted to hear right now was Heather inelegantly parroting one of his timely, Zen-like quips. "You can't keep hiding from what happened."

"I'm not hiding from anything!" Jamie threw open the door and stepped outside. "I couldn't hide from it even if I wanted to!" He almost slammed the door behind him, but instead settled for merely closing it with slightly more force than it usually took to keep it closed. Stalking across the front yard, he adjusted the backpack strap on his shoulder and set his sights on the sidewalk beyond.

Even though they were brother and sister, sometimes Heather didn't understand a thing about him. The age difference had never helped the two of them connect, but even when their parents had been alive, Jamie never quite felt like anyone in his family could relate to him, not entirely.

In this case, there wasn't anywhere he could go or anything he could do that wasn't a constant reminder of what had happened. Every aspect of his life had changed because of his parent's death. Having to live with Heather, that dingy little house, Jamie's new school, this whole city: each one of them underscored that fact with singular intensity.

At least it really was a nice day for a walk. In the sunlight, the air was warm. Majestic old trees lined the wide curving streets of the neighborhood, their leaves just starting to show the first hints of fall color. Even though more than a few of the other homes along the street were in the midst of full-blown remodels, things were usually fairly quiet here. Heather had been lucky to get her own little piece of this neighborhood before the current round of gentrification had driven real estate prices through the ceiling.

Regardless of how empty the streets and sidewalks might have looked that morning, this neighborhood was only one in a sea of hundreds. Jamie could barely even comprehend the enormity of the greater metropolitan area he'd unexpectedly found himself living in. Back home, he'd been able to walk from one end of town to the other in half-an-hour. This one suburb alone made his hometown look like nothing more than a wide spot in the road.

He'd only gone a few blocks when the smell of dumpsters, more than any visual clue, alerted him to the fact he'd reached Walter's Café, a local fixture for more than thirty years, or so the weather-beaten sign out front claimed. That meant he only had two more blocks to go until he reached the school. He wished the walk could have been longer; or that he didn't have to go at all. Jamie plodded to a stop when he heard a loud caw from a neighboring yard.

There at his feet, a large black crow strutted back and forth across the wet grass, its feathers shimmering blue in the morning light. It wasn't all that uncommon to see them digging through people's trash, but they usually flew away before letting anyone get that close. Squatting down, Jamie held out his hand. He still had a few minutes he could waste before he had to get to school. Dragging its wing and flapping awkwardly, the crow hopped into the branches of a nearby shrub.

"Hey, are you alright?" Jamie said, moving nearer. "Did you hurt your wing?"

The crow eyed Jamie's hand as it inched closer, first cocking its head sharply in one direction and then the other. Then, without warning, it lashed out at Jamie, raking the tip of its beak across the back of his hand, and deftly took to flight on a pair of perfectly functioning wings, cackling all the way. Jamie pulled his hand back with a hiss.

"Yeah, very funny!" he called after the bird as it flew out of sight. The crow's beak hadn't broken the skin but it had left a long red scratch that was already starting to itch. Jamie glanced up and down the length of the street. Fortunately, the only person in sight who might have witnessed that exchange was a wizened old street person in the alley behind Walter's Café who seemed far more interested in digging through the trash cans than in any of Jamie's antics.

Jamie couldn't help but stare for a second or two. At one time, the old man's clothes might have been quite nice, but they were now just as ragged as the grey beard hanging halfway down his chest. His hands and face were dingy and worn and he kept muttering to himself as he went from one trash can to the next. If things had turned out just a little differently after the death of Jamie's parents, could he have ended up in a similar situation?

Jamie thought about offering the old man the last few dollars he had with him but didn't know if an unsolicited handout would be appreciated or not. It would have been so much easier if he was still back home where he never had to consider matters of etiquette like this. From the way the old man continued muttering to himself, maybe it would be best to simply leave him alone.

Jamie was just about to get underway when he noticed a small object lying on the sidewalk just ahead of him. Unable to take his eyes away, he stepped closer.

It almost could have been a large smartphone but even a very old model wouldn't have been that bulky. The whole thing was a deep shade of black so shiny it almost looked wet. It was also completely featureless, without any buttons or markings of any kind, its sinuous skin flowing from one plane to the next without so much as a seam or even an angle. Jamie had never seen anything quite like it before.

"Um, excuse me," he said to the old man. "Did you drop this?"

The old man mumbled something and seemed to almost turn in Jamie's direction but instead pulled the lid off another trash can and began rummaging through its contents.

"Hey," Jamie said a little louder, stooping down to retrieve the strange black object. "Are you sure this isn't...yours?"

He trailed off the moment his fingers touched it. The surface was so silky smooth it almost felt like liquid in his hand. At the same time it was firm, with an almost rubbery feel. Even more bizarre was the way its mirror polished surface remained unnaturally cold after having been lying directly in the sun. His fingers didn't even leave any marks where he touched it. It was also quite heavy for its size, as if there were countless intricate mechanisms packed inside that seamless casing. The elegantly curving lines of the concave sides and the convex ends drew Jamie in, his eyes tracing the swirled reflections across the surface from one to the next in an ever-shifting mass of colors reminiscent of gasoline floating on water.

With a startled cry, Jamie fell over backward when he suddenly noticed the street man looming over him and staring down with strangely lucid eyes. Just how far had Jamie let his mind wander? He cleared his throat and swallowed hard, his mind racing.

"Um, it is yours then?" he said, again offering the object to the old man. This time, the old man took it and slipped it into one of his coat's gaping pockets. His expression then became distant once more and he stumbled down the alley, mumbling as he went.

Jamie didn't move from where he'd fallen. He just kept staring at the old man's back until he disappeared out of sight at the far end of the alley. It didn't seem possible that a lumbering old man like that could have crept up on him so stealthily. The strange black object had certainly been interesting, but it couldn't have held his attention that fully, could it? A quick glance at his cell phone, however, revealed that it had been nearly ten minutes since he'd stopped to pick it up. That had to be wrong. It couldn't have been more than thirty seconds at most. Unfortunately, he couldn't chance disagreeing with his phone if he didn't want to be late.

CHAPTER 2

Jamie made it to school before the first bell rang, but he still had to get to his locker, and then to his first class, all in less than three minutes. Just setting foot inside those choked halls slowed his progress to a standstill. The place was so much bigger than his old high school. He'd been attending classes here for nearly a month now and he still hardly knew any of these people; mainly because none of them wanted to know him.

He wasn't smart enough to be a geek, he wasn't handsome enough to be popular, and he wasn't athletic enough to be a jock. He wasn't even enough of a rebel to be an outsider. To most of these people he was simply invisible. That suited him just fine most of the time but not when it meant he couldn't get past anyone because they wouldn't even acknowledge his presence.

Jamie had just managed to round the last corner before his locker when a heavily muscled body slammed into him so hard he went over backwards. On the way down, his head struck a old cast iron radiator with a hollow clang. Maybe he'd have to accept a tardy after all.

As his fellow students stepped around and over him, Jamie sat up, rubbing furiously at the back of his head. It didn't seem to be bleeding but he could already feel a bump forming. A short distance down the hall, a small crowd of jocks was moving in the opposite direction, talking exuberantly amongst themselves but none seemingly aware of what they'd just done. Probably just an accident then. Jamie climbed to his feet as the only two people in the entire school who had taken notice of his fall came rushing forward. Alex was short, plump, and pale, while his friend, Derek, was tall, skinny, and dark. If it wasn't for their marked physical differences, Jamie might never have been able to tell them apart.

"Hey, are you alright?" Alex said. "That was a pretty good fall."

"Yeah," Derek said, adjusting his glasses. "When we saw Seth knock you down, we thought you might have cracked open your skull."

If it was Seth who'd pushed him, maybe it had been done on purpose after all. Not that it would have changed his decision to ignore the incident. Jamie merely rubbed his head again and made his way down the hallway with the other two following at his heels.

"I'm fine," he said, entering the combination to his locker.

"God, I hate Seth," Alex said, glaring down the hallway at the backs of the boys who'd pushed Jamie. "Just the other day in gym class, him and some of his goons were roughing me up so I took a swing at him!"

"And you missed," Derek said.

"Yeah, but I was the one that Mister Hansen sent to the principal's office for fighting."

And why was that news? Seth was a star athlete on some team or another, so the administration pretty much let him and his comrades get away with anything they wanted.

As they were speaking, the first bell rang, and the halls began emptying instantly. Jamie dumped most of his things into the bottom of the locker, grabbed a textbook and a notebook which would hopefully be enough to get him through pre-calc, and slammed the door shut. With Mister Fisher's classroom all the way on the other side of the building, he'd have to hurry.

"I'll see you guys around," Jamie said, hoping for the exact opposite.

"Oh, hey!" Alex said. "Are you doing anything Friday night?"

Jamie could have pretended not to hear and just kept walking, but for some reason, he lingered half a moment. "Um, why?"

"The Raven's Castle is hosting a big Magic: The Gathering tournament. We were wondering if you might want to come along. It should be quite the shindig."

The only reason Jamie knew what they were talking about half the time was because Kristie had been an even bigger comic book geek than them. If he wanted to change his social standing quickly, over-association with these two would be a sure way to do it, but not for the better.

"Um, I've really got to get to class right now, but I'll, um, think about it, okay?"

"Sure, man, no problem," Derek said. "Just let us know."

Jamie didn't quite make it to class before the second bell rang but, with Mister Fisher standing in the hall chatting idly with a fellow teacher, he was able to sneak in without risk of recriminations. Unfortunately, his entrance hadn't gone completely unnoticed. Standing in the aisle right ahead of Jamie's desk was that black-haired skank, Lorrie. She and April, the blonde who sat right in front of Jamie, glanced at him as he took his seat and shared a few whispered words between their laughter. If Mister Fisher hadn't been such a stickler for his assigned seats, Jamie would have rather sat at just about any other desk in the room.

"Cutting it a little close, aren't you?" Lorrie said. "You know Mister Fisher likes everyone to be in their seats before the bell rings."

Jamie glanced across at Lorrie's own unoccupied seat, but the irony was obviously lost on her.

"Oh my god, would it even be possible for him to have any more wrinkles in that shirt?" she said to April. "Isn't that the same one he wore yesterday?"

Now that it had been brought to his attention, Jamie did have to admit his shirt was pretty wrinkled. He hadn't quite worked out all the finer points of doing laundry yet, which is probably why Heather wouldn't let him touch any of her good clothes. However, it wasn't as if either of these two were qualified to criticize Jamie. April seemed incapable of putting together any outfit without including something pink. Today it was a pleated skirt in pink plaid. Lorrie meanwhile couldn't have picked out her own clothes without first consulting the latest fashion blog.

"You think he'd be able to get here on time if he doesn't even bother to change his clothes," April said to her friend.

The girls shared another laugh and Jamie rolled his eyes. He had quickly discovered that retaliation wasn't a good idea when dealing with these two. One of them seemed to be Seth's girlfriend and after the first few times Jamie had actually bothered to counter their asinine jabs, Seth had come after him looking for blood. Jamie managed to escape that first confrontation without suffering more than a verbal putdown, something easy to ignore when delivered by someone of Seth's rather limited mental capabilities, but it had been backed up with the very believable threat of physical violence should Jamie continue standing up for himself. Thus, it had become easier to simply ignore them. Today, the girls apparently had more important things to worry about than finding new ways to taunt Jamie, however.

"No, it's like I was telling you," Lorrie said to April. "You don't need a pocket watch at all, just something to focus on. I read all about it on a website last night. Here let me show you."

Sitting down on the edge of April's desk, Lorrie began waving a pen back and forth in front of her friend's face. "Just listen to the sound of my voice. Let everything else melt away. You can feel your body growing heavy, heavy, heavy…"

"I don't think it's working," April giggled.

"That's because you're not relaxing. You have to -- hey!" Suddenly Lorrie fixed Jamie with a venomous gaze. "Were you just looking up my skirt!"

It would have been easy enough to do; if Lorrie's skirt had been any shorter, it would have been a belt. However, Jamie had been trying his best to ignore her, right up until she felt the need to draw his attention to her lacy yellow panties. As he rearranged the notebook on his otherwise empty desktop, he simply muttered, "I'm not Mister Fisher."

"What did you just say!" Lorrie leaned forward, trapping Jamie's notebook under her palm and putting her cleavage on display instead.

Laughing, April had apparently heard Jamie clear enough. "That is the only reason she's passing this class!"

Lorrie broke into a string of obscenities, either directed at April or Jamie, it was hard to tell which, but abruptly cut herself off at Mister Fisher's belated arrival. She threw herself across the aisle and into her own seat, pretending as if she'd been there the whole time.

"Alright class, let's begin," Mister Fisher said, feigning ignorance of Lorrie's display as he dropped his books onto the front desk with a thud.

In that same instant, Jamie's entire world changed.

Gone were the desks, the school, and even the other students. With legs extended, as if in mid-sprint, Jamie seemed to be floating, scenes of a dark forest drifting past on either side. Was this a dream? Had he fallen asleep in class? Was he still sound asleep in bed? Or maybe even in his old bed back home, just down the hall from his parent's bedroom?

A split second later he crashed to the ground. His forward leg crumpled from the impact and catapulted him into a chaotic end-over-end tumble. Loose dirt and dry twigs flew away in his wake. His senses were nothing but blurred impressions of motion, earthy smells, and flailing limbs. It was impossible to tell how far he rolled before he finally came to a stop. To his disorientated mind, it felt like miles.

With palms flat on the ground and eyes open wide, he pushed himself up, spitting dead leaves out of his mouth. This didn't feel like any dream he'd ever had in his entire life. His thoughts were perfectly coherent and his senses were somehow sharpened to the point of distraction. Rendered in such startling clarity, it almost hurt to look at the freakishly large trees which surrounded him and supported a fledgling spring canopy of leaves hundreds of feet overhead. Late afternoon sun angled down through the trees and fell in mottled patches on the spindly shrubs growing in scattered clumps on the forest floor. His ears rang from the crystalline chirping of insects and birdsong coming from the creaking branches of the trees. He could practically taste the earthy mist that hung heavily in the air and feel the thick smell of rotting vegetation against his skin.

He sat up with a start only to find his arms and legs entangled by some mass of tattered red fabric hanging from his shoulders. The jeans and tee-shirt he'd been wearing moments before were gone, replaced instead by a single tailored garment of pliable brown leather that perfectly contoured his body. On his feet were a pair of heavy, thick-soled boots. The gloves on his hands left his fingertips exposed so he could see all the dirt and oil that had been ground into his skin from performing some activity he couldn't remember doing. The red cloth appeared to be a poncho, though most of the countless rips and tears it sported looked like they'd been there since long before his current tumble. Dressed like that, he must have looked like some bizarre cross between a motocross racer and an old west drifter.

The lengthy gash his fall had left in the ground stretched back nearly fifty feet, but he didn't appear to have suffered so much as a scratch from it. The spongy loam must have absorbed the majority of the impact. It was only once he started thinking about it that he realized that same ground seemed to be shuddering with a rhythmic vibration suggestive of approaching footsteps.

"Don't move!" a tinny voice boomed through the forest. "By the authority of the Finttiranos Military, you're under arrest!"

Jamie twisted around and his eyes grew wide. Looming into view over his right shoulder came a colossal humanoid form standing at least thirty feet tall and constructed entirely of metal. In its hand, it held a massive sword over half as long as its wielder was tall. Its hulking shoulders were not even remotely within human proportions and the tiny head set down between them stared unblinking at Jamie from its glowing yellow, v-shaped visor. It must have been a robot of some kind, but unlike any machine Jamie had ever seen, its movements were just as fluid as if it were a living thing encased in armor.

"Sir, you got him!" a second similar, but slightly different, voice said. Jamie turned to see another of the giants approaching from the other side. Nearly identical to the first, it carried what could only be a rifle nearly as big as a car. Both of them spoke with a strange accent and strung their sentences together differently than Jamie was used to, sometimes using words he'd never even heard before, but none of it was quite so strange he couldn't grasp their meaning. "Damn, but he was moving fast! How the hell was he doing that?"

"Corporal, take up a covering position," the first giant said. Its voice seemed to come from no one place on its anatomy, but rather from a series of vibrations coursing all through its metal armor.

"You don't suppose that's him, do you?" the second giant said. "We'll get a commendation for this!"

"Now, Corporal!"

"Ah, yessir."

This couldn't possibly be a dream. If it were, the logic of the dream itself would let Jamie know where he was, what these things were, or at the very least, what he should be doing. Instead his mind remained frozen.

"Don't even think about moving," the first giant said.

Keeping its sword pointed steadily in Jaime's direction, it took a knee. That thing was huge. It could probably crush a car under its foot. Jamie didn't even want to think about what it might do to him. The thought of dying at the hands of giant killer robots while tangled in a poncho would almost have been funny under different circumstances.

Jamie drew back when a hiss of steam escaped from either side of the giant's head. Momentarily, the top and bottom halves split open along the line of its glowing yellow visor, one rotating down and the other back. From inside rose a uniformed man, the segments of his articulated seat lifting his shoulders above the upper rim of what must have been a cockpit. In his hand, he held a pistol which he pointed directly at Jamie. With his free hand, he gripped a cable mounted alongside the cockpit that lowered him to the ground.

His uniform's knee-length tunic had an authoritarian cut and was the same shade of dark green as the robotic machine he piloted. Dark grey trim emphasized the military-style patches on each arm, the silver bars on his shoulders, and the black starburst-shaped pins on his high collar. Jamie couldn't imagine him belonging to any military he had ever heard of.

Likewise, Jamie had never seen a gun like that before either. It looked like it was made of brass with a polished wood grip. The front end of the barrel flared downward sharply, giving it something of a hatchet-like appearance. Most strange of all was the faint yellow glow apparently coming from the many bizarre symbols etched into its surface.

"Hands where I can see them." The man advanced like a hunter wary of wounded prey; though how anyone could fear Jamie looking as he did was ridiculous. "No sudden movements."

Face drawn taught, Jamie couldn't take his eyes off the barrel of the gun. After having spent countless hours target shooting with his friends and family, he'd developed a healthy respect for firearms of all kinds. Having one pointed at him like this was something he'd never experienced before. All it would take is one single pull of the trigger and he'd be dead.

"What's going on?" Jamie said. "Who are you? How'd I get here?"

"You're under arrest for trespassing on a military compound and assaulting military personnel," the soldier said. "If you are the Red Rogue, I'm sure there will be more charges down the road."

"What's a Red Rogue?" Jamie said. "Please, I think you've got me confused with someone else. I didn't assault anyone and if this is an army base, I'll leave. I don't even know how I got here."

"You left the base miles ago," the soldier said, not easing his stance in the least. "Now what's your name! National affiliation!"

"National affiliation? I-I-I'm from the U.S."

"U.S.?" The soldier brandished his sidearm more forcefully in Jamie's face. "What the hell is that supposed to mean!"

His arms still tangled in the red poncho; Jamie cringed. How the hell had he gotten into this mess? "The United States of America! I'm an American!"

"What kind of nonsense is that! Are you working for Secotia? Thieradoon? If you're just another stupid bandit, I swear I'll shoot you dead right here and now. Why were you trying to break into the Yarzak Depository? Are there more of you?"

Geography had always been one of Jamie's better subjects in school, but he was relatively certain he'd never heard of any of those places before. Of course, having a gun pointed at him wasn't making it any easier to think.

"Please, I just want to go home."

"And I told you to raise your hands!"

Maybe it wasn't the bravest thing to do, but if surrendering to these people kept them from killing him, it didn't seem like such a bad idea. Wherever he was, they must have been the authorities. Surely, once they heard his story, they would be able to sort all this out. However, with the poncho still tangled hopelessly around him, the simple act of raising his arms with any degree of speed or elegance proved impossible.

The soldier stepped forward, nearly pressing the barrel of his sidearm into Jamie's face. "Hands in the air! Now!"

Seeing the conviction in the soldier's eyes, Jamie pressed his arms skyward, ripping the red fabric of the poncho as if it were nothing more than tissue paper. He hadn't expected it to tear so easily. It must have been even more threadbare than it looked.

What transpired next almost seemed to happen in slow motion. The unexpected ripping of the poncho threw Jamie off balance just enough that he stumbled forward. Startled by the abrupt motion, the soldier's finger pressed down on the trigger. Jamie's eyes could make out a rotating disk of glowing symbols appear in the air directly in front of the weapon's barrel. From the center of that strange phenomenon shot a bolt of pale blue energy that tore into the ground where he had been just a split second before.

He didn't know how he'd gotten out of the way. He'd seen the weapon going off and so he reacted, springing to his feet before the soldier even seemed to be aware of it. Jamie could have fled, but having his assailant's gun right there within reach, disarming the man completely seemed like a much more permanent solution. The pistol twisted out of the soldier's hand with relative ease, as if he barely had a grip on it. Jamie tossed it away and was just about to try reasoning with the man when a sound like the sizzling crack of a lightning bolt filled his ears.

Looking up, he saw a bright flash streak over his head, briefly illuminating the dim forest with a brilliant sphere of light as it traveled quickly out of sight. The second robot had taken aim with its gigantic rifle and fired. More shots followed in quick succession; each discharge accompanied by a twin row of blazing red symbols projected down the length of the barrel on either side a split second before an angry ball of white-hot lightning shot from the end.

The speed at which the lightning traveled left no time for evasion. The second shot impacted the ground nearly twenty feet away and threw up giant clods of steaming earth. The third streaked past close enough that Jamie could feel the intense heat radiating from it. Another ripped into one of the gigantic trees, leaving half of its trunk nothing more than a twisted mass of jagged splinters. A final blast struck the open cockpit of the first robot.

As if finally realizing just how haphazard his shooting was, the second robot ceased fire abruptly, its stance betraying a very human sort of chagrin. However, the damage had already been done. A series of explosions spilled from the first robot's cockpit, quickly building in intensity.

Jamie didn't like the sound of that one bit. He tried running in the opposite direction, but his legs didn't seem willing to cooperate, instead shooting out from under him with more speed and power than he could comprehend. He tripped over his own feet and fell, carrying both himself and the solider to the ground just as the entire burning machine exploded. A massive fireball washed across their backs and the accompanying shockwave pressed them flat to the ground. Jamie clutched handfuls of dirt in his hands and closed his eyes. Never in his life had he ever considered he would die like this.

CHAPTER 3

As the flames dissipated, Jamie could hardly believe he was still alive. The solider lying on the ground next to him had survived as well, though from the glassy look in his eyes as he shook his head, he had been badly stunned by the explosion. In contrast, Jamie felt just fine, entirely clear-headed and not even the least bit singed.

Behind them, a savage fire burned through the underbrush around a pair of kneeling mechanical legs; apparently all that remained of the soldier's machine. Whistling purple flames spewed from the dismembered hulk, growing steadily more shrill. As Jamie stared, a jagged shard of metal fell from above and imbedded itself in the ground only a few short inches from his face. The soldier's eyes grew wide at that and both of them scrambled to their feet as fast as they could.

This time, through sheer force of will, Jamie kept his legs under control, but every step was a struggle not to fall yet again. He and the soldier ducked behind the trunk of a particularly large tree, instantly casting them into the shadow of the searing heat from the flames. The other machine rushed toward the inferno but even it couldn't get too close to the heat.

"Lieutenant! Lieutenant!" the second machine cried out in its tinny voice as it danced frantically at the edge of the flames. "Lieutenant, are you alright!"

"Corporal! Over here! Don't let him escape!"

"Are you insane!" Jamie cried. "He almost just killed us both!"

"Just surrender now," the soldier said, taking hold of Jaime's hand and twisting it behind his back as he clamped his other arm across Jamie's throat. "Things will go easier on you at the trial if you do."

"I told you I didn't even do anything!" Jamie wrenched his hand free and pulled the soldier's arm away from his throat. He could feel the soldier's muscles straining to maintain a hold, but Jamie wasn't even trying, and he was manhandling this full-grown adult like a child. The moment Jamie broke free, the soldier came at him again and threw a powerful right cross that caught Jamie squarely in the jaw. It should have hurt, but apart from forcefully twisting his head to the side, Jamie felt little else. In fact, the soldier looked more shaken from the blow than Jamie did.

It must have been the adrenaline.

"What is wrong with you people?" Jamie said, grabbing the solider by the front of his tunic. He shoved him back against the tree as if he weighted next to nothing, actually lifting his feet right off the ground.

The back of the man's head bounced off the tree with a resounding thud and the air instantly went out of his lungs, his whole body going slack. Jamie hadn't meant to push him that hard -- he shouldn't even have been able to. Something wasn't right. "Oh man, I'm sorry, I didn't mean to -- oh crap..."

"Get away from the lieutenant!" the second giant cried as it bore down on Jamie, one arm drawn back, its hand balled into a giant metal fist.

Jamie pushed the soldier out of the way and jumped in the opposite direction. His legs uncoiled with unprecedented strength, driving his feet in the soft loam. When they found purchase, he didn't simply jump out of the way, he somehow launched himself clear. Several tons of metal fist hit empty ground with the force of an explosion. Clods of dirt and splintered tree roots pelted Jamie as he sailed through the air, only coming to a jarring stop when he collided with the trunk of another, somewhat smaller, tree. He flopped to the ground, dirtied and disorientated, but without so much as a scratch. Something was definitely wrong.

"What the hell kind of freak are you!" the robot said, charging after Jamie. "Why won't you just die!"

Die? Hadn't they been trying to *arrest* him? Jamie got to his feet and ducked a second swing of the giant's fist. This time, it ripped a sizable gash through the tree which had just stopped his fall. The whole trunk shuddered fiercely and numerous branches, each the size of a large tree themselves, rained down from above. Several bounced off the robot's armored hide, doing little damage but throwing the machine off balance. As the pilot concerned himself with fending off that assault, Jamie ducked between the robot's stomping feet. The sheer power necessary to move such a machine as smoothly as it did was impressive, but its shifting joints still groaned in protest to the sudden movement. In the end, gravity and momentum won out, forcing the entire machine to stumble backward frantically in order to stay on its feet.

In the confusion, Jamie dashed away from the carnage, planting his feet carefully with each step in order to avoid another fall. Though his body still did not quite feel like his own, practice made control a little easier.

Finally regaining its balance, the robot took aim with its rifle yet again. Jamie heard the angry hiss of lightning and dove to the side just as a bolt of blazing white energy ripped past him. That had been too close. Just a split second slower and it would have vaporized him for certain. The ground shuddered as additional shots riddled the surrounding forest floor with shallow craters. Jamie slid behind a tree and crouched down, covering his head. He needed to get out of there. Unfortunately, the robot had him pinned down and the forest appeared largely devoid of concealing vegetation or topography.

As the robot continued firing indiscriminately, repeated blasts struck the tree behind which Jamie had taken cover, quickly reducing its trunk to splinters. The top half swayed drunkenly for a few moments, listing dangerously before finally toppling through the branches of its neighbors and ultimately crashing to the forest floor. Jamie didn't care if the robot was still shooting or not, if he stayed where he was, he was dead for certain. Running through the falling branches, the deafening explosions, and the searing heat, he dodged wildly until he finally found cover behind another tree which had largely escaped the robot's barrage unscathed.

Over the sound of the explosions, Jamie could make out the dismounted solider shouting for his subordinate to cease fire, though Jamie was quite certain it was not done out of concern for their target's wellbeing.

"Did I get him?" the tinny voice of the robot said once its rifle finally fell silent.

The first soldier sighed with exasperation. "Go check! But if you didn't, he's probably long gone by now. Just try to keep your finger off the trigger for a second or two!"

"Um, yessir."

Jamie pressed himself in tight against the tree. If he hadn't been standing there listening to them, he probably could have escaped just as they'd suggested. Now that they were focused on finding him again, he wouldn't be able to make it very far without being spotted. He needed a place to hide. And with the terrain being as flat as it was, the trees were the only things big enough to offer any kind of concealment. However, the lowest branches had to be at least twenty feet overhead. Logic told Jamie that he'd never be able to reach them, but events had so far made it clear there was nothing logical about any of this.

Jamie considered the space he needed to clear. He'd already managed one jump of at least such a distance, so it stood to reason that there was nothing preventing him from doing so again. The thunderous stomp of the giant robot urged Jamie into action. His legs tensed and released, sending him skyward. Not only did he reach the branch he'd been aiming for, he actually overshot it. Only through a frantic thrashing of arms and legs was he able to grab hold of another. With the giant robot rapidly approaching, he had no time to find a better spot. Hoping that his pursuer would not look up, Jamie hung from the underside of the branch like a sloth, holding himself perfectly still while the machine passed underneath.

Each step it took caused the entire tree to shudder, but apart from that, the machine moved in virtual silence. The only sound which could have been attributed to an engine was a faint hum that Jamie felt more than heard. Even the heavy smell of oil seemed to be coming from its softly groaning joints and not from any kind of exhaust. The overlapping plates of metal shifted as it moved, offering Jamie brief glimpses of its complex inner mechanics. Etched into every surface, both exterior and interior, were artistically arranged symbols written in a language unknown to Jamie but clearly similar to the ones imprinted on the soldier's sidearm. Earlier, he'd thought the way these symbols glowed was an illusion created by the setting sun, but now in the deepening twilight, he could see for certain that this unearthly radiance was not coming from any outside source. Whatever these machines were, they must have used some form of advanced technology unheard of back home.

All Jamie needed was another few seconds until the machine passed him by. He felt as though he could have held onto the branch for hours without growing tired if need be but the outer layer of moist bark and lichen kept crumbling away from under his fingers, forcing him to readjust his grip every few seconds. The more tightly he tried to hold on, the faster it rolled away.

Then, all at once, his hands slipped off entirely and he dropped back toward the ground, lunging hopelessly for the branch which had already passed beyond his reach. If this fall didn't prove fatal, the robot would just need to step on him to now bring this chase to a close.

His back hit first, but it was not with a soft thud on the forest floor, but with a loud metallic bang. Jamie rolled across the angled shoulder of the robot, reaching for anything at all to arrest his fall and only managing to finally find a grip as his legs dangled over the edge. The robot came to an abrupt halt and its shoulders rotated violently, the centripetal forces pulling Jamie horizontal. If he allowed himself to be flung off, the ground might have offered an opportunity for escape, but with the frantic stomping of the robot, it was probably safer to remain right where he was for the time being.

"Get off!" the tinny voice from the robot boomed as it flailed its arms about and carelessly tossed its rifle aside. The giant weapon crashed to the ground a short distance away and somersaulted toward the burning wreck of the first robot. Now, with both hands free, it began swatting at Jamie like he was some kind of insect. Giant metal hands scraped across thick armored plates with an angry screeching sound. Reacting purely on instinct, Jamie let go of the robot's shoulder and slid across onto its head-like cockpit.

"I said, get the hell off!" the robot said, this time one of its hands coming down right on top of Jamie. It would have hit him for certain had he not dropped down the back of the robot, only barely grabbing hold of a seam in the armor at the last second. The fist that had been intended for Jamie instead glanced off the side of the cockpit. Metal crunched under the impact and the glowing yellow visor splintered into thousands of angled shards.

"Oh shit," the robot said, its projected voice now mingling with a very human one coming from below the smashed hatch.

That was enough. This guy was clearly nuts. If he wasn't stopped soon, someone was going to end up dead, more than likely the pilot of the robot himself. Using the momentum of the still thrashing machine, Jamie swung himself onto the front of the cockpit and braced his feet against the machine's angled prow.

Through a large gap in the twisted metal, he could see into the cockpit. It was a curious affair, outfitted with more instruments and switches than a fighter plane but all fashioned from bronze and crystal like some Victorian antique. At its center sat a wide-eyed pilot staring back at him. The military-style haircut and pressed green uniform didn't do much to disguise the fact that he couldn't have been much older than Jamie himself. If anything, it only emphasized the fact he was just a kid -- just another bully throwing his weight around. Gritting his teeth, Jamie grabbed one side of the hatch in each hand and wrenched them in opposite directions, his fingers digging into the metal. Crystalline instrument panels shattered, and the thick armor folded back like sheets of tin.

Adrenaline alone couldn't account for that, but Jamie was past caring about how impossible his actions had become. He reached through the gaping hole he'd just created and pulled the pilot out of his seat with one hand. The sidearm the pilot had been reaching for fumbled from his grasp and rattled down to the bottom of the cabin.

"Would you just cut it out already!" Jamie said to the terrified soldier.

"Pl-please don't kill me," the soldier said. "I don't want to die!"

"I'm not trying to kill anyone! You're the only ones doing that!"

The fierce expression on Jamie's face faded as a distinct tingling sensation welled up in the pit of his stomach. The robot had never gotten its feet firmly on the ground before Jamie had removed its pilot from the controls. Now the entire machine was starting to tilt sharply.

The soldier let out a high-pitched wail as Jamie took hold of him and jumped. A moment later, the robot toppled over completely, the massive hulk of metal crashing to the ground with a thunderous impact that shook the trees and sent the first solider stumbling.

The pilot cried out a string of curses as he and Jamie fell quickly back to earth. They landed hard, Jamie's legs crumpling and the unbalanced weight of his passenger sending him into a roll. Not knowing what to expect from either of the two soldiers next, Jamie came to his feet in a flash, the whistling flames of the first fallen robot burning uncomfortably close behind him.

The solider Jamie had just pulled from the robot was writhing about on the ground. "My leg! You broke my fucking leg, you bleedin' git!"

"I just saved your life!" Jamie shot back.

"You're still under arrest," the first soldier said, stepping forward and staggering slightly. "Just turn yourself in before things get any worse for you."

He couldn't be serious. Jamie glanced around at the devastated forest, smashed machines, and injured soldiers. How could things possibly get any worse? Night had fallen completely since the start of this madness. Outside the glow of the flames, the forest appeared pitch black. What other dangers could still be lurking out there? Were there even more of these robot piloting maniacs waiting to descend upon him?

"Look, I didn't do anything wrong," Jamie said, skirting along the edge of the flames as he backed away from the two soldiers. "I don't even know what's going on here."

As Jamie started to turn, the whistling from the burning wreckage grew even more intense. The first machine's warped frame, no longer able to hold itself upright, tumbled over all at once, landing directly on top of the other machine's discarded rifle.

The first soldier threw himself over his comrade, pressing them both flat to the ground. "Get down!"

Caught in mid-step as he turned, Jamie was buffeted by a deafening shockwave that lifted him off his feet. A blistering wall of heat engulfed him and everything around him became fire. There could be no doubt about his fate this time, he was dead for certain. He shouldn't have left Heather the way he had that morning. Now he'd never have a chance to tell her how much he appreciated everything she'd done for him.

CHAPTER 4

Singed and smoldering, Jamie crashed to the ground, pushing up a small berm of dirt in front of his limp body. He should have been dead. At the very least, he should have been broken and bleeding. However, though his clothes were somewhat charred, he himself had somehow escaped injury yet again.

Where the two machines had been, there was now nothing, not even the gigantic trees which had been standing nearby. The flames were more fierce than ever, sweeping through the underbrush and igniting anything in their path the least bit flammable. In the distance, silhouetted through the flames, Jamie could just make out two figures, one helping the other scramble clear.

After everything that had just happened, Jamie had no interest in sticking around for even another second. He was already on his feet and after a few steps, broke into a run, quickly gaining speed, his legs carrying him farther with each step than any top athlete could ever hope to match with three of their best.

Jamie didn't know where he was going, he simply ran, the huge ground-eating strides quickly becoming natural. He fell into a rhythm of floating through the air after each step, his toe only touching the ground long enough to send him off into another long arch. The darkened forest flew past. Even on a moonless night like this, his eyes could still make out every obstacle well before he reached it. He bounded over fallen trees and dodged around small stands of bushes without slowing. The topography remained relatively flat, interrupted only by an occasional rolling hill or clump of mossy rocks protruding through the loam. Wherever he was, it was starting to look like he was in the middle of some vast, uncharted wilderness.

Now, with his whole concentration no longer required just to stay on his feet, his thoughts drifted to other matters; like where he was, how he had gotten there, and how he was able to do these incredible things. No matter how hard he tried to convince himself it was just a dream, his hyper-acute senses wouldn't let him believe any such thing. Every last detail of everything around him was just too clear, too sharp, and too real. There was no way his mind alone could have fabricated all that on its own.

That kind of logic would seem to argue against the possibility that this was just taking place inside his head. If so, could he cross off dream, mental breakdown, and drug-induced hallucination from his list of possibilities? Without those, he was left with what: alien abduction?

Maybe he was dead, and this was some madman's version of hell. A quiver passed through his body that nearly broke his stride.

Slowly, he drifted to a stop, not even slightly winded after having traveled what must have been several miles at least. His overly sharp eyes couldn't even detect the slightest hint of firelight from those burning robots he'd left behind. His chest felt tight, but not with fatigue. Part of him wanted to drop crying to his knees right there. How was he ever to make sense of what was happening to him?

He stumbled on for a while longer, not quite ready to give up just yet. The mists rising from the forest floor grew steadily heavier, dampening everything just as thoroughly as if a rainstorm had just moved through. Off in the distance, a thin glint of moonlight could be seen starting to rise through the trees. His mind alternating between utter despair, convoluted theories that tried to explain his situation, and complete blankness, Jamie found himself ambling through a gigantic clearing before he even noticed the sudden change in his surroundings.

This wasn't a natural clearing, however. All the trees that had once been growing there had been cut down, each stump neatly sawn off about a foot or two above the ground and surrounded by piles of fresh sawdust and the butts of countless hand-rolled cigarettes. Boot prints covered the ground, having stomped all the loam down into a claggy mud. Hoof prints nearly a foot wide and narrow wheel ruts also crisscrossed the area, most of them angling away to the far side of the clearing where a path could be seen snaking its way into the forest. Despite all the activity that had obviously taken place there not long ago, the ones responsible were nowhere in sight.

Off to his left, Jamie heard the sound of trickling water. Slowly, he headed in that direction and soon came to a small creek which meandered past one edge of the clearing where the large trees growing along its banks had been spared the same fate as their neighbors. Fat, swollen roots crowded the little stream and threatened in some areas to nearly choke it out of existence entirely. Jamie stepped up to the edge of a pool created by one such dam of roots and stared down into the placid water.

For a moment he almost didn't recognize the face staring back at him: skin caked with dirt and soot, hair singed and disheveled. A few handfuls of water helped clear away the worst of the grime and returned his face to something more closely resembling the unchanging visage he had become so familiar with. His cheeks may have been a bit more hollow and his muscles slightly more defined, but otherwise, whatever had happened to him hadn't changed his outward appearance much at all.

Once again, Jamie racked his mind for some explanation but, try as he might, he couldn't remember anything between Mister Fisher's precalc class and suddenly appearing in this strange forest. Running his fingers through his hair, he couldn't even find any trace of the bump he'd suffered from his fall back in the school hallway. Had he experienced a trauma so horrible he'd blocked out all memories between then and now? Weeks, months, or even years might have passed without him knowing. What might have become of Heather in all that time? Was she worried sick wondering what had become of her little brother? Was she even still alive?

Jamie closed his eyes and swallowed hard. This had to be a dream. There couldn't be any other explanation. He was probably still in Mister Fisher's class, head down on his notebook, drooling while everyone laughed at him. All he had to do was wake up.

Kneeling there at the water's edge, he imagined himself regaining control of his comatose body in the real world, forcing first a finger to twitch, then a toe, sliding his foot across the floor, lifting an arm. When he opened his eyes, however, the scene remained the same as before he'd closed them.

The silvery arch of the moon had since risen high enough that it could now be seen more plainly over the edge of the nearby clearing. Catching sight of that, Jamie's mouth dropped open and he stepped calf-deep into the pool without even thinking about what he was doing.

Instead of the perfect luminous sphere he had been expecting, this "moon" was a chaotic mass of angled fragments that formed a large ring. A secondary halo of smaller glittering bits tapered away at the edges and reached out toward the opposite horizon without quite reaching it. The entire formation seemed so close he could almost reach out and touch it. It looked so wrong suspended there against the blackness of space, as if all those fragments were too heavy to stay aloft by themselves.

"Come on, wake up," he said, placing his palms flat against a nearby tree and resting his forehead between them. "Just wake up."

He pinched his eyes closed and thumped his forehead against the tree. He couldn't end up like this, trapped on an alien planet; lost with no way home. It had to be a dream. It just had to be.

"Wake up!" he said, knocking his head against the tree with enough force that his teeth rattled inside his skull. "Wake up wake up wake up!" He bashed his forehead again and again, harder with each cry. Something gave way under the continued impacts and he felt a thick fluid running down his face. Maybe beating himself unconscious would bring an end to this madness. At the very least, it didn't seem like it could have made things any worse.

With one final blow, he sank to his knees in the water, his body racked by tearless sobs as he dragged his uninjured forehead across the splintered pulp he'd made of the tree. He just wanted to go home and live a normal life. First the death of his parents and then the move to live with Heather and now this? Why did these things keep happening to him?

With a single heaving breath that did nothing to stop his jaw from quivering or loosen his throat, Jamie sat back on his heels. If he really wanted to find a way out of this situation, he couldn't panic. He had to look at the facts as rationally as possible.

Despite how much he wanted to believe this was all just some dream world concocted by his over-imaginative psyche, it still felt too real for that; more real than any dream he'd ever had in his entire life, far more real than most of his waking life had become as of late. Even if it was a dream, it didn't seem like he was going to have any luck snapping himself out of it. And trying to reason his way out of a fractured mental state would probably only be an exercise in futility. He had to assume this was really happening to him or he'd likely end up driving himself truly mad with all the possibilities.

But even if he had been abducted, violated, and given these strange abilities, it still couldn't explain his surroundings. That left only two real options as far as he could see: either he was no longer on Earth, or some disaster had befallen his homeworld to which he was somehow oblivious. That meant his top priority had to be finding out where he was. The rest could wait until later. What he needed to find was someone he could talk to who wouldn't try to kill him on sight.

The loggers who'd created the clearing might be a possibility but if this country was ruled by those robot-piloting maniacs, they might be just as likely to turn Jamie over to the authorities as they were to attack him themselves.

Pulling himself out of the water, Jamie stepped up onto the bank of the stream and sat down on one of the large tree roots arching out of the ground. As he sat there, weighing his options, his thoughts slowly turned inward and focused on a strange and slippery nagging sort of feeling rattling around in the back of his mind. He couldn't quite put his finger on what it was -- almost as if it were no more than an idea that had been all but forgotten, except for the memory that something *had* been forgotten. When his attention was elsewhere, it could be overlooked with ease, but much like a scab that one can't resist picking at, it was always waiting right there to draw his interest should his thoughts start to wander.

A distant clang of metal-on-metal echoing through the forest pushed such abstract thoughts to the side and had Jamie on his feet in an instant. Had those robots tracked him down already? But then, he realized that he'd probably been stranded in that forest for several hours already, if not even longer. He scanned his darkened surroundings but even with the fragmentary moon now illuminating the forest just as clearly to his eyes as if a full noonday sun were overhead, he could see nothing except more trees.

Jamie was starting to think that he might have imagined the sound when a second clang echoed in the distance, this one accompanied by a dull thumping roar. It almost sounded like a cheering crowd. Could there really be people that close? The noise was coming from roughly the same direction those tracks led away from the clearing. Tentatively, Jamie began walking toward it, careful to keep the largest trees between him and the metallic bangs which continued sounding at random. Maybe these people would turn on him at first sight, but if he wanted answers, he could not keep running from every shadow he saw.

CHAPTER 5

The land began to rise steadily, and after cresting one shallow ridge, Jamie found himself climbing another far steeper one. Beyond it glowed a steady illumination which left Jamie thinking that it had to be coming from powerful electric lights. The slope had been stripped nearly clear of vegetation save for a few lonely trees and spindly shrubs. With each step, dead leaves and half-rotted vegetation slipped out from under his boots, slowing his progress considerably.

The closer he got to the top of the ridge, the more that roaring noise did, in fact, sound like a cheering crowd. The clangs had become more distinct too, as well as growing far more frequent and increasingly chaotic. Jamie crested the ridgeline just as a particularly savage clash rang out, followed immediately by a swelling of cheers. The sight which met Jamie's eyes stopped him in his tracks.

The ridge dropped away on the other side into a shallow ravine but quickly rose once more to abut the base of a towering wall. Built from neatly sawn timbers of gigantic proportion and masterfully riveted metal panels, this manmade barrier stood at least fifty feet tall and ran along the very top of the ridgeline, curving away out of sight in both directions. The top was crenellated and covered, presumably for the protection of sentries, though none appeared to be on duty at the moment.

Across the ravine from Jamie stood a double gate. It was probably big enough to accommodate those giant robots he'd faced in the forest, and at the moment, it hung open wide to reveal glimpses of the many distinct roof peaks on the other side. The cheering crowd that Jamie had heard, a mixed group of men and women in equal number, most of whom had drinks in their hands, surrounded a crater-like depression at the head of the ravine. Illumination for the event they'd gathered to watch was provided by what Jamie assumed to be some kind of helium-filled globes that floated on tethers above the crowd's heads. The event itself appeared to be a fight between a pair of man-shaped vehicles, each circling the other at the bottom of the crater like two metal gladiators. Jamie didn't even think to take cover, he merely stared.

Standing no more than twelve feet tall, these machines were more utilitarian in design than the last ones he had seen. Their blocky, angular frames had been painted a drab yellow, but had since become marred by patches of rust, mud, and numerous scuffs, scratches and dents. With nothing more than a sturdy roll cage to protect them, the two pilots were clearly visible inside their machines' squat torsos.

Even watching from a distance, Jamie cringed when one of them punched the other so forcefully it knocked his opponent right off his feet. The crowd went wild, frantically cheering on the pilot who'd delivered the blow. He raised the arms of his machine overhead in triumph as he marched around the perimeter of the makeshift amphitheater, soaking in the applause right up until the other robot tackled him from behind. Both pilots could be seen laughing heartily as their machines rolled across the ground, each of them trying to outmaneuver the other. The audience, laughing and wagering with gleeful abandon, seemed to be enjoying themselves just as much.

Apart from the way they were dressed, the spectators all appeared normal enough. Natural cloth and leather in plain colors seemed to be the standard fashion hallmarks. Some of the women wore dresses or skirts, but most were attired pretty much the same as the men in rugged, utilitarian pants, shirts or tunics, and heavy leather boots. Most of the spectators looked like they'd just come from a particularly grueling day of dirty labor, but a few were more respectable than the rest. Their garments were neater, less soiled, and more colorful, decorated with silk cravats, enameled boot cuffs, metal braids, and intricate embroidery. Many of the spectators also had strange-looking handguns strapped to their hips, swaggering along like they'd just walked out of a western, though no one seemed overly inclined to use them at the moment.

Though the general style of everyone's clothing was decidedly archaic, there was no single regional or societal influence that could have been used to describe it. Even the people wearing the clothes didn't seem to share any common ethnicity or race; features and colors were shuffled about to such a degree that it was impossible to even guess where any of them might have originated from. With that much variety, Jamie probably wouldn't stand out at all -- provided his actions didn't gave him away.

Letting out a long sigh, he trotted down toward the activates. If he wanted answers, he couldn't wait for them to come to him. Down the center of the ravine ran a dirt path, wide enough for an automobile, but from the look of the ruts and hoof marks preserved in the half-dry mud, seemingly only used by heavily-laden carts, gigantic beasts of burden, and maybe an occasional giant robot. Jamie followed it right to the head of the ravine. With everyone focused on the match, most didn't even notice him. Those few that did spared him no more than a fleeting glance.

A slightly overweight man with a simple steel helmet on his head, stood guard just outside the gate. While his pants, boots, and shirt were ordinary civilian attire, the bedraggled jacket he wore over the top had a number of official-looking pins and patches that seemed to indicate some bureaucratic institution. Though it was the same dark green as the uniforms worn by the soldiers piloting those robots, the cut was distinctly shorter and less tailored. Whatever his authority, he wasn't offering any hindrance to the steady trickle of people coming and going through the gate. In fact, with a blunt-headed spear in one hand and a drink in the other, he was cheering on the match just as exuberantly as the rest of the spectators.

Now that Jamie had gotten closer to the floating lights scattered around the area, he could see that his first impression of them was completely incorrect. Instead of helium-filled balloons with a lamp inside, they were actually glass spheres partially surrounded by an intricate bracket of metal bands. These bands were etched with rows of convoluted symbols reminiscent of those which had covered the giant robots, and at the center of each sphere hung a glowing crystal that appeared to be the actual source of the light. He could see no cables for electricity or pipes for gas, and the spheres looked far too heavy to keep themselves aloft without aid, but that's exactly what they were doing, floating in the breeze just like balloons. The globes weren't even connected to the metal brackets or the crystals to the globes. All three seemed to bob to their own independent rhythm, the only thing keeping each light from floating away entirely was a thin piece of rope, tied to the metal bracket on one end and staked into the ground at the other. It must have defied countless physical laws, but yet there it was, right before his eyes.

However, looking over the spectators once again, he could now see these floating globes weren't the only such oddities present. Everything the least bit mechanical in nature seemed to be covered with variations of those eerily glowing symbols; whether it was the giant robots that moved as nimbly as a person, handguns that could shoot energy beams, a pocket watch that projected a hologram-like diagram into thin air, a pair of telescopic goggles, or even a simple heated mug. For every piece of equipment in sight to be adorned in such a manner, the markings had to be more than just aesthetic.

"Eh, wha'cha up to there, boy?" a man said from a short distance away. "You look like a borrang in an opera house."

Hoping that he wasn't the one being addressed, Jamie turned, only to have his fears confirmed. Two men in shabby work clothes leaned against each other, laughing through gap-toothed and yellowed grins as they took turns gulping clear liquor from a flask they passed back and forth.

Jamie gulped as well. He should have known better than to try blending in so casually with these people. Unfortunately, running at that point would only raise more suspicion.

"Oh, pretty lights," one of the men laughed as he looked up at the floating spheres and swayed precariously. Their accent sounded a lot like the soldiers' but the way they slurred their words made their strange manner of speech almost unintelligible.

"You're not from around here, are you?" the first man said, leaning forward and holding onto his friend to keep from falling.

Jamie's eyes darted back the way he'd come. The path was still clear. He could probably be out of sight before either of these drunks even knew what was happening.

"Of course he's not from around here!" the second man said, slapping his friend on the shoulder. "Look at his clothes!"

Jamie pulled the tattered red poncho across his tight-fitting leathers. It didn't really help him retain that much dignity, but it was better than nothing.

"He's just a traveler," the second man continued. "They all dress like that."

"Lord knows we have enough of those coming through these days." The first man grinned at Jamie. "So you probably don't know the real fun's in town."

Jamie's mouth moved in wordless reply.

"More fun than watching mecha-wrestling or staring at gloworbs all night," the second man said, chuckling. "Whiskey, hookah, and Raven-Slaves! It don't get much better than that!"

His friend wrung his hands and quivered with exaggerated anticipation. "Gavrin has the best damn Raven-Slaves for rent in this whole county!"

"He's got the only Raven-Slaves for rent in this whole county!"

"Ha ha! Too true!" the first man said, raising his eyebrows knowingly. "And I'm gonna get me a cute little one tonight!"

They both cheered uproariously and shared another drink. Most of it was coughed out in laughing sputters but they only grew discouraged when they realized the flask was empty.

"To the tavern!" the second man said, pointing toward the gate with theatrical flourish and swaying dangerously.

"To the tavern!" the first man agreed, doing his best to imitate his friend's gesture and nearly falling to the ground in the process. Once he regained his balance, he turned back toward Jamie and waved for him to follow. "Come on, boy, I'll buy you a drink!"

"You can regale us with tales of the wonders beyond our dreary little Tavnic!" the second man added.

If Jamie was on an alien planet, those two couldn't have been any more human. And even if he had only marginally understood what they were talking about, they had invited him to come along. If they wanted to talk, maybe Jamie could get some answers out of them. He swept his gaze across the cheering crowd one last time and then stepped through the gate, trying not to look too much like he was avoiding the guard.

Inside the wall, the land dropped away into a large oblong depression completely encircled by that towering barricade. Packed in tight against the far side was a collection of buildings, all constructed of stone, timber, or stucco, topped with tiled or thatched roofs, and arranged on a rigid grid of streets. The central street, running perpendicular to the long axis of the village and neatly paved with cobblestones, was by far the widest and most formal-looking. The rest of the streets had to make do with a paving of brick, though their state of repair decreased considerably toward the edges of the village, eventually giving way to a stretch of undeveloped ground covered with scraggly trees and wild scrub growth that extended right up to the inside of the wall where Jamie stood.

Off to his right, the buildings had a distinctly industrial character to them, dwarfing the majority of the others which stood only two or three stories tall in most cases. These smaller buildings looked like homes to Jamie, most with fenced-off areas in front or behind for flourishing gardens but there were almost no lawns anywhere to be seen. More of those odd lamps lined the streets, though these were permanently affixed to the tops of wooden posts instead of being allowed to float freely.

A damp sawdust clung in varying degrees to nearly every surface in the village like some malignant yellow fungus. That was probably the source of the musty wooden smell which hung just as heavily in the air as the acrid wood smoke coming from the chimneys and the dense evening mists drifting through the streets.

Undeterred by any of the grime or medieval smog, groups of people on foot made their way through town, some laughing and singing, others looking deadly serious. There were also others who wandered the streets dressed in what could have been variations of Jamie's own hard-wearing garments. In a few cases, they looked even more lost than Jamie suspected he himself did.

The two drunks from the gate seemed to have all but forgotten about Jamie so he meandered along several paces behind, trying to look like he knew where he was going. He had even been doing a passable job of not gawking too much at all the strange sights right up until they arrived at a sort of improvised civic square at the border between the residential side of town and the industrial one. There he stopped dead in his tracks.

Though the plaza beyond stood at the outer edge of town, with one end open to the undeveloped stretch of land at the base of the city wall, it was easily the largest center of activity in the entire village, filled with scattered groups of revelers, all drinking, singing, and dancing. A long warehouse boxed the plaza in on one side and a row of open-fronted shops did the same from the other. Meanwhile, a single massive building dominated the far end. It rose four stories high in a cascading series of stone walls below and timber balconies above, all capped-off by arched tile roofs, each one covered in green moss. A wide porch along the base of the building created a transitional space between the revelry in the plaza and the far more lively carousing that could be heard from inside.

Jamie let the drunks go on ahead, singing and kicking up their heels as they went into the far building arm-in-arm. Above the front door hung a large wooden sign, adorned with the image of a bird in flight. The words inscribed below it were written in a language Jamie could not read. Some of the letters looked familiar, but others were completely foreign. Regardless of what the sign actually said, the place certainly looked enough like any earthly tavern Jamie had ever seen. Provided no one carded him at the door, it didn't look like he'd have any problems getting in either.

All he had to do was act like he knew what he was doing. That would have been easier if the strange sensation in the back of his head had gone away. It was still more of a feeling than a physical malady. And it was hard to tell for certain, but it had possibly grown more persistent since he'd first noticed it. In his mind's eye, he was starting to imagine it like a rubber band looped around his subconscious and pulled tight, leaving him on edge while he waited for the moment it would snap back and sting him.

Pushing it out of his thoughts, Jamie strode across the square, maneuvering around the small knots of people gathered there and stepped up onto the tavern's porch. The smooth deck under his bulky boots felt strange after having spent the majority of his time on this world running through the forest and walking over uneven roads. The patrons on the front porch of the tavern lounged about on benches or gathered at tables, all of them far more interested in the dark beer they drank from big wooden mugs and the lithe young women serving it than in Jamie's awkward gait, however.

On this warm night, the double front doors hung open and the hazy clouds of smoke that drifted out seemed almost to reverberate from the steady cacophony of laughter and merriment that accompanied it. As Jamie grew near, his pace slowed to a shuffle. Seeing the inside of the tavern, he was no longer quite so sure he wanted to risk going in.

Men and a smaller spattering of women packed themselves into the cavernous room inside, filling every seat and even crowding into the aisles as they sang, danced, and laughed uproariously. Several arm-wrestling matches could be seen, while elsewhere, deadly serious card and board games were being played with equal amounts of money being wagered on each. The small alcoves around the perimeter of the room were filled to capacity as well, but in this case with blurry-eyed patrons lying on pillowed cushions whose dangling fingers wrapped loosely around elaborate hookah pipes.

Of those patrons who did not seem hypnotically unaware of their surroundings, nearly all the rest drank heartily of that same dark beer which flowed freely from the stoneware pitchers of the serving girls gracefully flittering though the crowds on bare feet. While everyone else in town seemed so unique in appearance, these pale-skinned girls with black hair all looked so similar that they could have been sisters. They even dressed alike, in blacks and dark grays with long, flowing skirts, tight corsets, and dangling sleeves.

In all this madness, where was he even supposed to begin? The drunks he'd been following were nowhere to be seen, having already been swallowed up by the chaos inside.

"Um, excuse me, could you...?" Jamie asked of one of the people pushing his way around him to get inside. The man ignored him and kept walking.

Jamie tried again with another, but the heavy-set, bearded man merely snarled in reply and gave Jamie a look that suggested he might very well kill anyone who tried to delay his entry into the tavern for even a moment.

Letting the man go on his way, Jamie turned sharply on his heel and headed down the length of the porch as if that had been his intent from the very beginning. There had to be some better place to look for answers, preferably ones that didn't involve navigating a room full of drunken lumberjacks. The rest of the village appeared mostly quiet, but the street lights were still glowing warmly. There had to be someone out there who could help him.

CHAPTER 6

Now that Jamie took a moment to think about it, that niggling feeling in the back on his mind had definitely become more pronounced, almost to the point of intruding on his thoughts now. He blinked hard in an attempt to push it aside, but it remained, just as clear and maybe a touch stronger than it had been a moment earlier.

As he walked down the length of the porch, considering his next move, a large man stood up from his chair directly in Jamie's path. Jamie had to sidestep frantically in order to avoid a collision. Meanwhile, the man continued on without even noticing the near disaster his carelessness had caused.

Not wishing to make an issue of it himself, Jamie turned back in the direction he had been heading and instead ran right into one of the serving girls who was going the other way. She let out a panicked yelp as she tumbled over, trying desperately to regain control of the large pitcher which had already slipped from her grasp. The occupants of the table it careened toward jumped back at the prospect of being soaked with drink but Jamie shot forward with that frightening speed he now possessed and managed to catch not only the girl but also the pitcher as well, spilling only a few drops of beer in the process. A chorus of laughter and cheers rose up from the displaced men, but Jamie didn't hear a word of it.

Staring at the girl, his breath caught in his throat. It was impossible to guess her age, maybe still just a teenage girl, maybe already a young woman. Her pale skin glowed vibrantly like fine porcelain and this contrasted sharply with her short fingernails which were an oddly alluring shade of pearlescent black. Her long, straight hair was also black but it flashed with a bluish iridescence in the clear lantern light. Strangest of all were her eyes. He couldn't be sure it if was just a trick of the light or his own imagination, but in the one brief moment she glanced up at him, they appeared to shine like amber.

Jamie's rough fingers pressed against the soft, warm skin of her bare midsection. With something of a start, he jerked away, only then realizing that he hadn't let go after catching her.

"S-sorry," he said.

"No, *my* apologies, sir," she said in a small yet crystalline voice as she gracefully disentangled herself from Jamie. "The fault was entirely my own."

Jamie wished she hadn't lowered her eyes so quickly; he would like to have gotten just one clear look at them. But then, brushing a strand of hair away from her face, she turned and retreated through the revelers gathered on the porch. Though her steps were not hurried, she moved quickly on her bare feet, gliding around the swaying patrons without coming close to colliding with any of them.

Jamie knew he shouldn't stare but he couldn't help himself. If only he were better at talking to girls he would have wrangled her into a conversation by thinking of something clever to say instead of merely apologizing to her like some bumbling half-wit. Sometimes he was so stupid. Any excuse to talk with her a little longer would have been good enough. He sighed, the heavy jug in his right hand pulling his shoulders down.

He hadn't realized he was still holding that either.

"Hey wait!" Jamie called after the girl.

With something of a halting start, he set off after her, dodging around the other patrons with considerably less skill than she had displayed doing the same. Fortunately for Jamie, all the men he bumped into had already drunken enough that none saw fit to protest with more than a few gruff words of warning or a slurred curse.

The girl had reached the edge of the porch and was just about to step down into the weed-choked alleyway beyond when Jamie finally caught up to her.

"Hey, wait up!" Jamie tried again. "Please!"

She stopped with one bare foot on the first step, her skirt fluttering around her legs as she turned. Her eyes wide and her shoulders tight, she looked first from Jamie to the darkness of the alley and then to the trampled foot path which wrapped around the side of the tavern. Then her shoulders stooped and she fixed her gaze on an empty spot several inches in front of her toes.

Jamie slowed his pace as he approached. The porch was nearly abandoned here, and the thick walls of the tavern kept the majority of the noise from inside to a minimum. It made their surroundings suddenly seem very private. Illuminated only by the faint lantern light which spilled this far, the girl stood tall and thin and pale, like some shuddering angelic vision projected against the darkness. Jamie had to work some moisture back into his mouth before he could speak.

"Um, it's okay," he said, holding out the jug of beer as he inched his way forward. He tried to smile warmly but knew it looked ridiculous when combined with the dopy expression that had to be plastered across his face. "You forgot this."

"I..." she took the offered jug in both hands and hugged it to her chest, her eyes remaining downcast. "Thank you. I must apologize once again for being so clumsy."

Jamie smiled. She was anything but clumsy. And while her voice did carry that same accent as everyone else, she spoke in a slower, more deliberate manner that made her sound more poised than the rest. "You don't need to apologize. I'm the one who ran into you. It was my fault."

The girl looked up with a quizzical expression through the fine strands of hair framing her face and then quickly away. "That...is very kind of you to say, sir, but entirely unnecessary. I should have been paying more attention to my surroundings."

"Seriously, you don't need to apologize for anything." If he gave her a chance to reply, the two of them could have spent hours trying to lay claim to which one of them was responsible. Not that he would have had a problem with that -- the sound of her voice alone made his smile broaden -- but that would have been a terrible waste of time spent with a girl this intriguing. Besides, there were things he wanted to talk to her about.

Like...

He couldn't think of a single thing to say to her.

"Your...eyes," he said at last. He wanted to tell her how beautiful they looked but thought that sounded too hokey. He could have asked her why they looked the way they did but thought that sounded too much like he was accusing her of being a freak. All he really wanted was just one more chance to see them again. Unintentionally, she granted his unspoken request when she tentatively looked directly at him for the first time.

If it had been difficult for Jamie to speak before, now the task became almost impossible. It really wasn't just a trick of the light that made her eyes look the way they did. He could have gazed for hours into those two brilliant orbs of striated gold and yellow, the color stretching from the vaguely oblong pupil in the center all the way to the edges without any trace of white to be seen. Instead of looking freakish, they merely added to the rest of her otherworldly allure. She smiled uncertainly and dropped her gaze back to the floor. If he didn't say something soon, she was going to take offense, or even worse, leave. Hastily, Jamie averted his eyes as well.

"I'm sorry," he said. "I didn't mean to stare. It's just that you're...so beautiful."

Jamie mentally kicked himself. He'd gone and said it anyway.

"We Raven-Slaves are accustomed to such...attentions, sir," the girl said

"Raven...Slave?" Those two drunks had mentioned something about that. Jamie had never stopped to consider that such a thing might actually be a person though. And especially not one like this. "You're a slave?"

The girl looked at Jamie as if he had just grown a second head. "Yes...I am of the Slave Races."

Jamie glanced over his shoulder and for the first time noticed that all the serving girls had those same yellow eyes. That, along with their other shared features certainly did set them apart from everyone else. But as slaves? It didn't seem possible. "All of you?" he said. "Your whole...race?"

The girl paused before answering, her head tipping sharply to the side in a vaguely avian gesture of puzzlement. "Yes."

Jamie knew that slavery still existed in backward corners of society, but that sort of thing was so far removed from his everyday life it might as well have been some urban legend as far as he was concerned. To come face-to-face with it like this made his stomach lurch.

"Sir? You look pale." Hastily, the girl set the jug aside and touched Jamie's bare forearm. Her fingertips sent an electric tingle through his skin.

"Yeah, maybe..." Jamie said, allowing that faintest touch of hers to guide him down to a seat on the top step of the porch. She joined him, sitting close enough that he could smell the faint herbal scent of her hair. She certainly didn't seem like a slave, not that Jamie knew how a slave should behave, or even what being a slave might mean here, wherever here was. "So, do you live here?"

"Yes, I have lived in Tavnic all my life." Wringing her hands, the girl said, "Up until recently, I had been owned by a young couple, acting as their household servant. When they moved away, they could not afford to bring me with them so they sold me back to Master Gavrin. I have mostly been working here in the kitchens ever since."

"That's horrible." And not just to know that such an entrancing young woman had been treated like a piece of furniture but also to hear her speak about it so casually.

A hint of melancholy touched her face, but she managed a thin-lipped smile. "I do miss my former masters and their children, but few Raven-Slaves can expect to avoid such circumstances forever." Smoothing the folds of her skirt across the tops of her knees, the girl said, "My name is Alaida."

Jamie felt like kicking himself all over again. That's how he should have started this conversation: by asking her name! And now she'd beaten him to it.

"Alaida..." A pretty name for a pretty girl. "I'm Jamie."

The girl, Alaida, almost snickered, though it took an effort on her part not to. "I am sorry," she said. "I have never heard that name before. It..."

"What?" Jamie prodded, finding himself snickering along with her.

"It...sounds like a girl's name."

Unlike when girls usually laughed at him, Jamie merely shook his head and smiled. "It can be a girl's name but in my case it's short for James."

"Jamie. James. Jamie," Alaida said, as if both names were strange to her. "It does not sound any shorter."

"I guess they *are* about the same length," Jamie had to admit.

"Forgive me for asking," Alaida said, cautiously, "but have you never seen a Raven-Slave before?"

"I'm not really from around here."

"Are you lost?"

"I...I guess I am."

The girl glanced about and then leaned in a little closer before speaking. "I have heard that Theiridoon does not allow any of the Slave Races within its borders. It that where you are from?"

Jamie leaned in as well, careful to measure his movement in response to hers. He would have liked to get even closer. "I, um, no," Jamie said. "At least I don't think so. Where are we anyway?"

Alaida tipped her head in the other direction. "We...are at Gavrin's Inn."

"No, I don't mean the inn, I mean everything. This village is called Tavnic, right? Where is Tavnic?"

"Tavnic is in the Costal Providence?" she replied, making it a suggestion more than an answer. "In the nation of Finttiranos?"

"Finttiranos," Jamie said with a sigh. That did confirm what those soldiers had been saying earlier but it didn't make it any easier for him to figure out where that was. "Do you know where Finttiranos is by any chance?"

Slowly, Alaida shook her head.

"Are we still on Earth?"

"Earth?" Alaida said with a timid shrug and an uncertain laugh. "Like...dirt? The earth is beneath our feet..."

Slave or no, she couldn't be so ignorant about something that had to be common knowledge. Jamie gripped the edge of the porch as he leaned in. He knew he wasn't going to like this answer, but he had to know. "No, not earth as in dirt, Earth as in the planet. It has a moon, but it's whole, all in one piece. Are you sure there wasn't some disaster that might have smashed it, maybe a long time ago?"

"The moon has always been like that," Alaida said. "And this world, it is called Terrarhea."

"Terrarhea?" Jamie's fingers left splintered marks in the wood under his hands. If he hadn't already been seated, his knees probably would have buckled. But at least he now had his answer. On some level he'd known this couldn't be Earth but to confirm it suddenly made everything feel so much more alien and dangerous -- and infinitely farther from home. "Are you sure you've never heard of a planet -- of a world called Earth before?"

Again, Alaida shook her head.

Jamie dropped his face into his hands. There had to be a way to reason this out. If he had gotten here somehow, there had to be a way to get back. "Do people ever leave Terrarhea?"

Alaida once again took in their surroundings before speaking in a voice only Jamie could hear. "Terrarhea is closed to the stars. It has been for a thousand years. Or so I have heard. Raven-Slaves are not supposed to concern ourselves with such matters, but I do know that such talk is dangerous."

"Dangerous?" Jamie rolled his head in his hands to face her. "Why?"

"Travel beyond Terrarhea is against the law. One would likely be arrested for even attempting such a thing. If it were discovered that someone had come from beyond..." Alaida bit her lip and looked directly at Jamie with those big amber eyes of hers, "I would not want to imagine what the punishment might be."

Jamie felt his skin grow cold. Is that why those robot-piloting maniacs had been after him? "Um, I never said I wasn't from...Terrarhea," Jamie said, the strange name fumbling from his lips.

"I did not mean to imply you were not." Alaida smiled and cast down her eyes.

This time, it was Jamie who glanced around to make sure no one was listening. "Why is it illegal? Have you ever heard of someone breaking that law?"

"No, I do not believe so. The people of Terrarhea do not want their world polluted by outside influences." It sounded like she was reciting something she'd once heard.

"But that would have to mean there are other people out there, wouldn't it? People who can travel beyond Terrarhea?" After everything else Jamie had seen today, the idea of space travel and people living amongst the stars no longer seemed quite as farfetched as it might have been just a few hours earlier. However, even if he could find a way to contact such people, would any of them really want to risk the trouble involved with simply helping him? Even if they would, would they be able to get him back home?

"As I understand it, humans came to this world long ago in order to escape the death of their homeworld, but most of them left soon thereafter. Those living here now are the descendants of those few who chose to remain behind and make Terrarhea their new home. I suppose there would almost certainly have to be others still out there, though I doubt anyone has any way of contacting them."

So Terrarhea was some kind of colony world then? But humans came from Earth. Unless these people on Terrarhea weren't really human after all. That seemed unlikely since they all looked and acted so terribly human. Or was Earth just another such outpost world colonized by the same primogenitors? Jamie had heard about crackpot scientists with such theories but that was the stuff of science fiction, wasn't it? "Do you know where the people living here came from originally?"

Once again, Alaida shook her head in the negative, sending fine strands of jet-black hair drifting across her face. Jamie almost reached out to brush them aside but only stopped himself at the last moment. He didn't want to press his luck.

"What about Raven-Slaves? Did they come from somewhere else too?"

Alaida shrugged. "I am sorry, but I do not know. To teach a Raven-Slave scholarly matters with intent is a crime. Most of what I have told you I merely overheard from the lessons that my former masters gave their children."

"You've got to be kidding me." What kind of barbaric world was this? "They keep you uneducated on purpose?"

"The Slave-Races exist only to serve, and our duties do not require us to know such things." Alaida paused and looked into the blackness beyond the porch. "Which I suppose that would make it unlikely that we could exist anywhere humans do not."

That sounded awfully insightful for someone who was thought of as little better than an animal. "Are you trying to tell me there is no such thing as a free Raven-Slave?"

Alaida laughed. "A free Raven-Slave? That would be like...making a Human into a Slave!"

"You don't have those here?"

She jerked back as if slapped. "Do you have them where *you* come from?"

"Well...no, not really...not any more...not for the most part any way."

Alaida's brow wrinkled as she tried to comprehend the things Jamie was saying. "The enslavement of Humans? *That* is terrible. Is your home really that barbaric?"   .

So Terrarhea had found a way to eliminate Human slavery, but only through the enslavement of an entirely different race, one that didn't even realize they were being exploited? It didn't seem like a fair trade. However, hearing Alaida's words so closely echoing his own thoughts, Jamie couldn't help but laugh. Alaida's expression grew puzzled as she considered Jamie.

"Why are you laughing?"

"I was just thinking the same thing about your world. It's all kind of ridiculous, isn't it?"

Alaida thought about that for a moment, then smiled as well. "Perhaps it is."

For a time, the two of them sat in silence, looking out into the darkness beyond the porch with the sounds of the tavern a distant hum. Jamie had experienced silence when talking to girls in the past; long, painfully awkward silences that seemed to stretch on forever without end, both parties only growing more tongue-tied with each antagonizing second that crept by. This, however, felt comfortable, soothing, as if even this stillness carried more meaning than most conversations he'd had with other people. He suspected the two of them could have sat like that all night without speaking another word and been perfectly happy.

Unfortunately, without anything more concrete to occupy his thoughts, that nagging sensation from before once again intruded into his conscious mind, this time far more insistent than ever before, as if the rubber band had been pulled so tight it was moments away from breaking. Jamie tried to push it aside, thinking that he might very much like to try holding Alaida's hand, but heavy steps on the wooden deck behind him drove any such notions from his mind.

He and Alaida both turned, Alaida springing to her feet with something of a pained yelp, Jamie merely looking up questioningly at the three large men glaring down at them. He started to ask what they wanted when one of them, a rotund man with a dirty mustache hanging from his upper lip and a stained apron stretched across his sizable midsection, cut him off.

"What the hell do you think you are doing!" he snapped, seizing Alaida by the wrist and pulling her back onto the porch. Her eyes wide in terror, she tripped on the steps and nearly fell but the fat man only dragged her across the boards and pushed her roughly into one of the empty chairs at a nearby table.

Jamie shot to his feet, not really knowing what he intended to do, but possibly moments away from punching this man who was mistreating Alaida. The other two men stepped between them and Jamie hesitated, realizing he didn't know what the customs of this place were, or how much trouble he might cause by doing something so rash.

"You know you are not allowed outside of the kitchens!" the fat man said to Alaida.

Alaida quailed in her seat, turning her face away from him and trying to make herself as small as possible. "My apologies, master. Nadia said they needed more drink on the porch and I thought that I -- "

"You also know you're not supposed to be doing any thinking!" the fat man said. Seeing him draw his hand back in preparation to slap her, Jamie stepped forward, ready to push the other two men out of his way if need be.

"Leave her alone!"

The fat man paused and swung his gaze in Jamie's direction. Letting go of Alaida's wrist and lowering his hand, he said, "The girls here are not free!"

"Master, he is just another customer," Alaida said in a small voice.

"You be quiet!" the aproned man said. The two men stepped aside so that he could wave a menacing finger under Jamie's nose. "I've seen your type before, traveler," he said, the harsh spices on his breath washing across Jamie's face. "You come into my tavern and try to use my services without paying. Alaida is only one of my kitchen slaves but I might be willing to let you have her for the night if you have the coin. She would be very cheap, but I suspect you do not even have enough money for that! Show me otherwise and she's all yours."

Jamie gritted his teeth. That tension pulling at his brain had grown so intense that it now took an effort just to keep focused on what was happening right in front of him.

"We were just talking," Jamie said. "I didn't even drink anything."

"Talk or a room, the girls are the same price! Get this beggar out of here, boys."

Jamie started to protest; but it was more of a fight with himself than with the bouncers as he tried to retain some coherence against the overwhelming pressure threatening to tear his mind to pieces. One of the two men shoved his palm into Jamie's chest. Jamie stumbled backward, his heel dropping over the edge of the porch. He fell but he never reached the ground. As the image of Alaida sitting huddled in her chair spun through his vision, that imaginary rubber band in his head finally broke, and his surroundings vanished, replaced by darkness.

CHAPTER 7

Something soft and warm tugged at Jamie's hand, pulling him along as he ricocheted off some unseen obstacle in the blackness, its sharp edge yielding with a hollow thud of crumpling cardboard.

"Come on! Hurry up," a strangely familiar feminine voice said. The tugging at his hand became more insistent. The girl urging him on giggled and then, with a crash, sunshine streamed in around them. Blindly, Jamie stumbled though a portal of light and came skidding to a halt as his senses adjusted to the new surroundings.

The mingled smells of cooking foods wafted through the air as a ceaseless chattering of voices echoed all around him. High above, warm afternoon sunlight streamed in through a pyramidal skylight of glass. Wall panels of dingy brushed metal and stained concrete columns made Jamie wonder if he had now found himself in some new dystopian world.

However, the tiny handful of people milling about in the vast sea of tables and chairs stretching out before him made him think otherwise. Some were waiting in line at the food stalls around the perimeter, carrying brightly colored shopping bags, while others were seated at the tables with their friends as they munched on nachos and corndogs and the like. Most were dressed in clothes that didn't even seem all that strange to Jamie's eye.

It actually looked like Earth. And not only that, but a dying shopping mall not far from his school that he'd only ever visited once or twice before. It was only now that Jamie noticed his clothes were the same ones he'd been wearing that morning, right down to the rumbled tee-shirt. Behind him, a large metal fire door marked "Employees Only" closed with a heavy mechanical clunk.

"Sit down, act natural!"

The identity of his companion, her voice still so eerily familiar, only now began to dawn on Jamie. Slowly, he turned to one of the nearby tables where April, breathing heavily and giggling, had hastily taken a seat and was motioning Jamie to do the same.

Arms limp at his sides, he merely stared back.

The doors through which they had just came, burst open to disgorge a man wearing a security uniform. He looked about, eyed Jamie critically for a few moments, and then rushed off into the food court.

"Oh my god, that was so close!" April laughed, no longer able to pretend as if she hadn't been concerned by the security guard's close presence. "And he was staring right at you!"

Maybe this wasn't Earth after all. "Where am I?" Jamie said, more to himself than to April.

"Third floor food court by the look of it," April said, leaning back in her chair and gazing through the glass guard rail that was all that separated them from a three story drop into the atrium below. A sudden sense of vertigo seized Jamie and he stumbled, just barely landing on the edge of the chair across from April. "Are you okay?" she asked. Her face contorted into an expression Jamie had never seen on it before. Was she worried? About him?

This had to be some kind of trick. Had he been sleep walking? Lorrie and April must have found some way to lure him here after he'd passed out in Mister Fisher's class just so they could make a fool of him in public. However, apart from April, he didn't recognize a single face in the sparse assortment of late afternoon shoppers. Nor were any of them the least bit interested in what he and April were doing together.

"How did we get here?"

April smiled with relief. "I know, right? Who would have thought the two of us would end up here after Mister Fisher kicked us out of class this morning. When you said we should go somewhere and I suggested the mall, I was mostly just joking. I can't believe you actually wanted to come here. I mean, honestly, why does anyone still come to this dump? But I'm actually having a lot of fun. Sure beats the principal's office, that's for sure." Kicked out of class? Principal's office? She leaned forward and surveyed the food vendors along the far wall. "That place over there does make some good fried soba noodles though. Are you hungry?"

Jamie shook his head even though his stomach rumbled at the thought of food. The huge clock in the main courtyard read almost five o'clock. Had he eaten anything at all today?

"What's going on?" Jamie finally managed.

Her brow wrinkling, April sat back in her seat and considered Jamie critically. "Hanging out at a crappy mall like our Neanderthal ancestors used to?"

"But...how, why?"

"What do you mean?" April said, shaking her head and throwing out her hands.

"Me? With you? Just hanging out? Then what the hell were we doing back there?" Jamie jerked his thumb toward the fire door. Had that security guard been after them just because they'd been in a restricted area or was it something else? He checked his pockets, but they were empty, not even his wallet or cellphone.

April's eyes narrowed. "Oh my god. Did you really think that just because of that little stunt in Pre-Calc, I'd throw myself at you? I'll admit you're more interesting than I gave you credit for, but a little sweet talk and a romantic afternoon doesn't mean I'm just gonna let you have your way with me!"

"I didn't mean...wait, what?" Jamie felt his stomach roll. What did she mean by a romantic afternoon? Maybe -- just maybe -- Terrarhea had all been some crazy dream world conjured up by his imagination, but the notion that his body had been seducing girls while his subconscious had been otherwise engaged was just too much to be believed. "What did we do? Am I going to have to get shots now?"

April slammed her palms down on the table as she stood. "You really are just like all the other guys aren't you! You thought that just because of my reputation, I'm easy? Well, screw you!"

"Hey, wait!" Jamie called after her as she stormed off. She didn't stop, which was probably for the best. He didn't even know why he'd tried to stop her. What could have possessed him to make a pass at someone like her? What would possibly have even made her agreeable to such a thing?

Terrarhea had been bad enough, but now this? Jamie sat back in his chair and ran his fingers through his hair, flinching when he brushed against the lump on the back of his head. There could be no doubt he was back in his own life, but what had happened in his absence?

Hopefully, his wallet and cell phone were still safe in his locker where he'd left them...right next to all the homework from last night that likely hadn't gotten turned in. And if he really had left school that morning after Mister Fisher's class as April had said, he'd also missed out on all the assignments for today as well. Not that he liked homework, but he liked making it up even less. Getting back to the school was going to take a while -- unless he and April had also stolen a car in addition to playing hooky. After everything else that had so far happened today, it wouldn't have come as much of a surprise.

Across the food court, the security guard from before was making his way back in Jamie's general direction, scrutinizing everyone in the area. Jamie stood and hurried for the nearest exit, trying his best not to look like he was hurrying. His feet moved so slowly in comparison to the way he'd been able to run on Terrarhea. In fact, his every sense felt muted and dull. Had his entire life always been this drab?

By the time he made it back to the school, his legs were beginning to ache from all the walking. Only a few months ago, that same walk wouldn't have phased him in the least. He was getting out of shape. It would have been nice to have a little of that infinite Terrarhean stamina now. Going straight to Heather's might have saved him a few blocks of travel, but he didn't like the idea of leaving his things at school overnight. Unfortunately, the last of the athletics staff was just pulling out of the parking lot after evening practice. The entire school would be locked up tight now. The sun was also slipping quite low in the western sky and the air had taken on something of a chill. At this rate, he wasn't going to make it back to Heather's before dark. With one last look at the silent school building, Jamie turned and headed on his way.

As he walked, he kept turning over the events of the day in his head but, no matter how many times he tried to reason things out, nothing became any more clear. If he really had run off with April in the middle of school, he couldn't remember it. His memories of Terrarhea, however, were still just as clear in his mind as when he'd experienced them. Whatever that place had been, it still didn't feel like any dream, even now that he'd woken from it. The only positive thing about being back in his right mind was that that persistent nagging sensation was gone.

He had heard that people with brain tumors sometimes suffered from hallucinations and had difficultly remembering things. After all the troubles he'd recently had to endure, it certainly didn't seem too far removed from the realm of possibility that something like that would be the next inevitable obstacle in his path. On the other hand, maybe his mind had simply reacted to all those stresses by retreating in on itself to escape reality for a few hours. That definitely sounded better than dying slowly of some malignant growth in his head.

Coming to that conclusion, Jamie couldn't help but laugh out loud right there on the sidewalk. Only his life could have fallen to such a point where insanity was the best outcome he had to look forward to.

It was about then that Jamie realized he'd stopped at the alley behind Walter's Cafe. Apart from a few more bags of trash having been added to the dumpster, it didn't look much changed from that morning. With everything else that had happened in the meantime, Jamie had completely forgotten about that old man. Could his strange black box have been coated with some sort of drug that Jamie had absorbed through the skin? Or perhaps it had emitted an exotic energy wave that induced hallucinations.

Or maybe Jamie was just grasping at straws. That homeless man had simply been a troubled old soul who was hanging onto an ancient PDA he'd found in the trash. Why not blame the crow that had scratched his hand? Or the bump he'd taken on the head. Or even Lorrie's slipshod hypnosis technique? He definitely wasn't about to entertain *that* as a cause for the day's events, so why would he consider any of those other ludicrous notions?

Jamie continued on his way at a more leisurely pace. Hopefully, Heather would still be at work. As Jamie's guardian, she probably had a right to know about what had happened to him. But she already had enough things to worry about without her little brother going insane too. It was probably just stress anyway, nothing at all worth losing sleep over. Besides, after the way they'd parted company that morning and everything that had happened since, Jamie had no desire at all to face her right now. All he wanted was to seal himself away in his room. His heart sank, however, when he saw her car parked in the driveway. Maybe if he slipped in the side door he could make it to his room without being seen. Unfortunately, he found Heather in the kitchen, directly in his path.

"Where the hell have you been!" she said the moment he stepped through the door, sounding honestly authoritarian for a change. So much for avoiding even a little of the fallout his daydream had caused. "I've been trying to call you for hours now!"

"You know they don't let us have our cell phones turned on in school," Jamie said.

"From what your vice-principal told me on the phone, you haven't been at school since first period."

"Like you're one to talk!"

"Jamie, I'm trying really hard not to be the bad guy here but you're not making it easy."

Just a few short hours ago, hadn't he been lamenting the fact he'd never get to talk to her again? He closed his eyes and took a deep breath. "I'm sorry. I didn't mean that."

"It's okay," Heather said with a sigh. "I know I sound like a bit of a hypocrite. I wasn't exactly a model student back in the day. And I got into a lot of trouble for it. But not you. You're supposed to be the good kid. What happened? Where were you?"

As if the death of his parents and his forced relocation weren't cause enough for a little teenage rebellion? "On an alien planet fighting giant robots?"

"Jamie!"

Yeah, that's about how he thought the truth might play out. Maybe a different version of it might work better, something a bit more vague. "I don't really know. Everything is just kind of a blur. I may have skipped a few classes...or, all of them."

"Jamie," Heather said, rubbing the bridge of her nose. "I know things are tough right now but, please, you can't be doing this. You know those social service bastards were against letting you stay with me from the beginning. If you start doing stuff like this, they're not going to let it slide."

"It's not something I planned. It just sort of happened. And I wasn't doing it for fun. I was miserable all day long." Another not-quite-lie.

Heather stepped forward and grabbed Jamie by the shoulders. "I know you don't like it here, so maybe it's a bit selfish of me to ask, but I really need you to keep it together right now. If it wasn't for you, I don't know what I would have done after Mom and Dad died."

"What are you talking about?" During that terrible time, Jamie had been numb to the world, hardly able to remember what day it was. He certainly hadn't done much of anything to help Heather. It was she who put her entire life on hold for nearly a month dealing with the chaos of settling their parent's estate. "All I did was get in the way. I made things harder for everyone."

"Do you really think that? I didn't want to deal with any of that stuff. If it was only me, I probably wouldn't have. Knowing you were counting on me was the only reason I was able to keep going."

"But that doesn't mean you want me here now. You had your own life before this. Now all your plans are ruined because of me."

"Come on, Jamie, don't be stupid." Heather gave him a shake. "Yes, things are a little tough right now but that doesn't mean I don't want you here. You're my little brother! I'm not going to abandon you just so I can flip this house for a few bucks. You and I are the only family the two of us have left. We have to watch out for each other."

Jamie dropped his gaze to the floor as tears began creeping into the corners of his eyes. These last few months he'd been trying to keep out of Heather's way as much as possible so that she wouldn't have to deal with him any more than necessary. But maybe she was right. All he'd done by keeping his distance was isolate both of them from the best means of support either of them had.

"It's okay," Heather said, embracing him in a hug.

"I'm sorry," he said, throwing his arms around her as well. "I'm so sorry for everything."

"You don't have anything to be sorry for. It's okay, it really is. We'll get through this. Things have to start getting better sooner or later."

Without prompting, memories of Terrarhea flashed through Jamie's mind. "What if they just keep getting worse?" he said.

Heather held him out at arms length and looked him in the eyes. "We're not the first ones in the world who've had bad things happen to them. If we let this defeat us, we don't have anyone to blame but ourselves."

Again, she was probably right, but the words made the hairs on the back of Jamie's neck stand on end. "That sounds like something Dad would have said."

She laughed. "It does a little bit, doesn't it? Sorry, I wasn't trying."

"No, it's good. I really miss them, but it almost makes me think they're not completely gone."

"Now who's trying to sound like Dad?"

This time, it was Jamie who laughed. Heather gave him another gentle shake and looked at him critically. "So, are you going to be okay?"

With a sniffle, Jamie nodded.

"Well, if you're good, I'm good." Heather retrieved a note pad from the counter. "So, I'm gonna give you a note for tomorrow. We'll say you were having trouble dealing with everything that's happened recently and you needed some time alone. The school knows what happened to Mom and Dad, so they should cut you some slack."

"A note? I think they do that online now," Jamie said, watching as Heather scribbled furiously.

"Anyone can hack into those school accounts. It takes a real professional to hand-write a note like this."

"As you would well know."

"Who knew I'd ever have an opportunity to put those forgery skills to legitimate use?" Heather ripped the page off with a flourish and handed it to Jamie. "Just don't go making a habit of this, okay?"

"Scout's honor," Jamie said, drawing a cross over his heart.

"That might mean more if you had ever been a scout," Heather said, eyeing him skeptically.

Perhaps it was a bit premature to make any kind of promises without even knowing what had caused today's adventure, but if Jamie had any say in it, Terrarhea was a one-time incident that was never going to be repeated. From this point on, he'd do his very best to avoid dirty old street people and their questionable personal effects, or diseased birds and their hypnosis techniques.

"I don't know about you, but I'm starving," Heather said. "What do you say we sit down for a change and have ourselves a real supper together, like we're actually family?"

"An actual supper?" Jamie couldn't help but smirk. "Does that mean you'll be ordering pizza or Chinese?"

"Hey! I can cook!" Heather said, and then added: "when I have too!"

"Instant ramen noodles do not count."

"Smart-ass." Heather slapped him playfully on the side of the head, causing the bump he'd received earlier to throb. "But just for your information, I was thinking of getting a little crazy tonight and ordering Thai instead."

"Really?" Jamie's stomach growled.

"What? I know for a fact that you like Thai food so don't give me that look!"

"It's not that," Jamie said. "I just wouldn't have thought you knew."

"Jamie, Jamie, Jamie. You're my kid brother. Unfortunately, I know far more about you than I'd care to."

CHAPTER 8

As it turned out, they never managed to sit down at the dinner table. While chatting and waiting for their order to arrive, Jamie decided to see just how difficult it would be to remove the kitchen cabinets when they finally got around to remodeling the kitchen. Heather helped loosen the screws holding on the doors and once they got started, they didn't stop until they'd actually pulled down all the cabinets hanging above the peninsula that separated the kitchen from the dining room.

The cabinets' absence left ugly brown splotches of plaster that hadn't seen paint since the house was brand new, but it did open up the space and began to hint at the possibilities a remodel would bring about. Jamie and Heather might very well have kept going until all the cabinets in the entire kitchen had been removed if the doorbell hadn't rung, signaling the arrival of their supper.

They ended up eating directly from the takeout cartons while standing at the debris-strewn countertop, joking back and forth and reminiscing about the old days. It was one of the few times in months since either of them had laughed -- not just a courteous chuckle or a fatalistic response to the absurdities fate kept throwing their way, but real, genuine laughter.

Heather also agreed to Jamie's proposal that he might as well continue with the kitchen demolition after school each night. After all, they seldom used more than the refrigerator and microwave, both of which could easily be relocated to just about any room in the house. The stove they could do without for the time being, and the laundry sink would work just fine for cleaning up until they eventually started putting things back together. The mismatched collection of dinnerware and the odd assortment of ramen noodles that Heather had been storing in the cabinets easily fit into three rather small cardboard boxes.

Jamie turned in early that night. Even though he'd apparently been sleepwalking most of the day, he still dropped off to sleep the moment his head touched the pillow. His dreams were surreal and muddled, just like every real dream he'd ever had in his life. Elements of his old life back home and his new one here with Heather all jumbled together with what he'd seen of Terrarhea to create seething, incoherent scenes of lunacy where giant robots stalked him through a myriad of familiar settings where he could do nothing but watch helplessly as Heather and Alaida were killed by them in a variety of ways, over and over again.

He awoke the next morning gasping for breath as his alarm clock blared from the nightstand. Sweat soaked his bed sheets and he felt no more rested than he had the evening before. He wasn't entirely sure how he got ready that morning and made it to school. Each passing car on the street brought back the memory of giant metal fists speeding toward him. No matter how many times he told himself there was no reason to fear, he still cringed involuntarily at every single one, painfully aware that he was now completely powerless to defend himself if one of them did mean him harm.

The school accepted Heather's note with no more than three or four accusations that it must have been a forgery. However, Jamie's skipping of class had apparently been far overshadowed by some mysterious incident involving Mister Fisher. April had mentioned something about that as well, and though the Vice-Principal chastised Jamie about it for nearly ten minutes straight, he never offered up any solid clues about what had actually happened. With no memory of it himself, and not being given any chance to defend himself or even ask questions, Jamie could do little but sit quietly and wait for the man's tirade to end. Eventually, he escaped with little more than a slap on the wrist, the vice-principal citing Jamie's newness to the school as his primary reason for lenience, but not without issuing a number of dire warnings and outright threats before sending him on his way.

Jamie stepped out of the Vice-Principal's office, his ears still ringing. Other students standing nearby eyed him curiously. Apparently, everyone in school had heard about the incident in Mister Fisher's class and were now curious to find out more about who had perpetrated such chaos. Jamie just felt numb. Before he could make it out of the office waiting room, the school's guidance counselor, Mister Clark, caught Jamie's attention and waved him over to his office.

"I really have to get to class," Jamie said. From the sound of things, he was already in enough trouble without adding a tardy to his record as well.

"This will only take a minute," Mister Clark said around his telephone's receiver. "And if you're late, I'll have a word with Mister Fisher about it. Have a seat."

Jamie lowered himself stiffly into one of the two chairs across the desk from where Mister Clark sat talking on the phone about an upcoming school fundraiser. As he waited, Jamie looked around at the various adornments hanging on the walls. Absent, in stark contrast to all the other guidance offices Jamie had seen in his life, were any of the tacky motivational posters that teachers seemed to think kids actually found motivational. A single abstract painting done in stark black and white with just a few splashes of red and yellow hung on one wall, while a cluttered bulletin board occupied another. Behind Mister Clark's desk hung an assortment of framed diplomas and honors along with a suit coat neatly on a hanger. When his call finally came to an end, Mister Clark rose out of his seat just enough to swing the office door closed.

"Something grab your interest?" he said with a smile that looked honestly friendly.

Jamie nodded toward the diploma he'd been examining. "Are you a real psychiatrist?"

Mister Clark chuckled. "I was, once upon a time."

Mister Clark practically looked fresh out of college. He certainly didn't look old enough to have a 'once upon a time' in his past. Maybe it was just the sharp, skinny-fit suits he always wore that made him seem younger than he really was.

"So, anything you'd like to tell me about yesterday?" he prompted.

Jamie shrugged. What was there to tell? "I skipped class. Kids do it all the time. Why do I get the fifth degree when I do it?"

"Well, I was more referring to what happened in Mister Fisher's class."

Jamie was about to shrug again but stopped himself. He didn't need it becoming a habit. "I don't remember much about that."

"From the sound of it, that would make you the only one in this whole school who doesn't know what happened."

Only 24 hours ago, barely anyone even knew who he was; now the whole school was talking about him? Jamie forced his body not to tense. If Mister Clark really was a psychiatrist, he'd probably be able to read more from Jamie's mannerisms than from anything he might actually say. In reply to Mister Clark's incredulous gaze, Jamie said, "Honestly, I don't remember much of anything from yesterday. I just kind of zoned out."

"Like a daydream?" Mister Clark didn't sound overly disbelieving. Was it possible Jamie might actually be able to tell him what really happened? He was a psychiatrist after all. But he was also a member of the school faculty. He could just as easily have Jamie committed as laugh him out of his office.

"Sure, a really intense daydream," Jamie replied in a measured tone.

"Well, everyone spaces out from time to time. Sometimes, back when I was still seeing patients, I'd finish an entire session without having heard a single word they said."

Maybe Jamie had been a bit premature to give any credit to this man's abilities. "That doesn't sound like the best way to help people."

"Probably not, but then, my heart wasn't really in it. Most of my patients were the children of rich parents who just wanted me to prescribe them drugs to keep them under control. They didn't like it much when I actually tried to help them with the underlying problems. It was pretty stressful. That's how I ended up here. I needed a change of pace."

And a drastic cut in pay, Jamie thought.

"Look, Jamie," Mister Clark continued, "I'm familiar with the circumstances that brought you to our school, so I know you've been through quite a lot these last few months. That's enough to make anyone what to avoid dealing with reality. Acting out in class isn't good for anyone though, least of all you. I've seen your test scores. You're a solid A-minus student and you're not even trying. If you need more of a challenge, we can help you find more constructive ways to express yourself."

How could he possibly make school any more of a challenge for Jamie, put in walls and a moat? "I get by in class but that doesn't mean I'm smart. Mister Fisher's class is tough enough without making it even harder."

"There's a difference between difficult and engaging. We do have programs here that you might find suit your particular talents better than what you've so far experienced."

He wanted to put Jamie in Special Ed classes? That would certainly make school more challenging, especially once his classmates found out about it. "Yeah, I don't really think so."

"I know what you're thinking. But these are not remedial classes or anything like that. They teach advanced material but in a format that individuals with a more intuitive sense of learning, such as yourself, may find more engaging."

"I'll...think about it."

Mister Clark's smile was friendly enough, but Jamie knew this former shrink had seen right through his noncommittal reply. "Let me know what you come up with."

"Yeah, okay."

Mister Clark sat back in his chair and peered at Jamie across the desk. "I know things might not be easy for you right now but believe me when I tell you that I've seen kids in situations like yours before. Maybe our advanced programs aren't your cup of tea, but you do need to find some constructive way to deal with the things that are troubling you. Otherwise they are just going to eat you up from the inside."

"That's pretty much the same thing my sister keeps telling me."

"She sounds like a smart woman."

Jamie couldn't help but snicker. Mister Clark and Heather would probably make quite the couple.

"What is it?" Mister Clark said, only half smiling, not sure what the joke was actually about.

"Nothing. It's just that my sister's always had a thing for doctors."

"Oh, is she seeing anyone?" Mister Clark said, his expression suddenly very serious.

Jamie eyed the guidance counselor warily. Heather could certainly do worse than the young, former psychiatrist. In fact, Jamie had seen enough of her boyfriends in high school to know that she already had. But just because Mister Clark was the only member of the school faculty who had so far shown Jamie even a small modicum of respect didn't mean they were suddenly friends. Or that he wanted the man dating his sister.

"I'm just kidding." Mister Clark laughed. "But seriously, is she cute?"

Jamie merely shook his head. "She's on Facebook. Look her up if you want."

"I might have to do that," Mister Clark said, still laughing. "But in all seriousness, think about what I said, okay? Maybe talk it over with that smart sister of yours?"

Despite himself, Jamie shrugged. "Okay."

"You might as well get going. You should still have plenty of time to get to Mister Fisher's Class."

"Um, thanks," Jamie said, shaking his head once again, as he slid out of his seat and stepped into the lobby. He didn't know if he should trust the man's easy-going nature or be suspicious of it.

That early in the morning, bodies crowded the lobby outside the school offices as other students sought to accomplish various administrative tasks. Both they and the faculty took notice of Jamie the moment he stepped into their midst, many whispering amongst themselves after stealing a glance in his direction. Apparently, they really did know more about what he'd been up to yesterday than he himself did. He did his best to ignore them but was forced to linger while waiting for the steady flow of people to clear. When he finally managed to make his move, he found himself coming face-to-face with April as she stepped out of one of the other offices.

She stared at him a moment, her expression grave. Jamie was probably the last person she wanted to see this morning, but then, the feeling was mutual.

"Hi," she said at last, her tone frosty but not altogether adversarial.

"Um, hi," Jamie said, looking for an escape route as the crowds once again boxed him in.

"So what'd you get?"

"A week's detention," Jamie ventured.

"Yeah, me too. They're getting soft. But even they have to admit all you did besides playing hooky was be a smart-ass."

Why was she talking to him? Hopeful this wasn't merely a prelude to some sinister revenge. When a hole finally opened in the crowd, Jamie leapt for it.

"Yeah, I guess. I've really got to get to class."

"Yeah, I know. I have the same one, remember?" April fell in right alongside him. "But after yesterday, I was kind of wondering if you were ever gonna bother showing up again."

Jamie felt his skin grow cold. Mister Fisher wasn't the nicest of teachers on his best days, but if Jamie had done something to warrant this kind of interest from the entire school, maybe finding a way to avoid his class for a few more days wasn't such a bad idea. If Terrarhea was going to swallow him up again, he wished it would just hurry up already.

"No," he said. He couldn't allow himself to think like that. He didn't want to go back there ever again.

"No?" April said. "No what?"

"Nothing." Jamie shook his head as he pushed through the lobby doors and into the hallway beyond. He hadn't even realized he'd spoken out loud. If he kept this up, he'd start looking like the crazy person he could only hope he wasn't.

"Jamie, hold up one second!" April grabbed him by the arm. Jamie suddenly felt like he'd been locked in a cage with a dangerous animal. "I have to ask you something and I don't really care what your answer is -- I really don't. I just want you to be honest with me about this. If you lie to me, I will destroy you, do you understand?"

From that determined glint in her eye, Jamie had no doubt she would do exactly as she threatened. Swallowing hard, he nodded, only hoping that he would even be able to answer her question.

"I gave this a lot of thought last night and I still can't figure it out. I mean, I can't believe that everything you said yesterday was just an act."

That wasn't really a question; not that he knew what she was even talking about. "I…"

April sighed. "Did you only say those things to me just because you were trying to get in my pants?"

"What!" Jamie said, heat flashing up from his collar as he glanced around at the nearby students. Every last one of them had suddenly given up all pretense of pretending as if they weren't trying to listen in on the two of them. April didn't seem to care in the least and merely stared Jamie down. "No, of course not!" Jamie said in a whispered hiss as he turned his back to the onlookers. "Some of the details from yesterday might be a little vague, but I can guarantee you that I definitely wasn't trying to…um, do that."

"Then what were you trying to do? Why did you ask me to come with you?"

He'd actually asked her that? This just kept getting more and more confusing. But it did raise an interesting question. "Well, why did you *agree* to come with me?"

This time, April quailed. "I…don't really know. I guess, after what you did in Mister Fisher's class and then when we started talking on the way to the principal's office, I realized there must be more to you than I'd given you credit for. I mean, I've never had a conversation like that with anyone in my entire life. It was like you knew more about me than I did. When you said we should ditch this place, it sounded like a good idea at the time."

What could he have possibly said to April that could have had such a profound effect on her in less time than it took them to walk from Mister Fisher's classroom to the principal's office? Jamie was barely able to talk to girls normally; there was no way he could have been that debonair in his sleep. If only he could tap into a small bit of that charm now.

"Look, I'm sorry, but I don't really remember much about yesterday. Most of it's still a blur." He was getting sick of explaining it that way but it had so far worked fairly well for him.

"I don't doubt it. My head was kind of spinning too. I can still hardly believe half of what you said to Mister Fisher." She paused and laughed. Then, deepening her voice as if in parody of someone, she said, "*Are you supposed to be a mathematics instructor?*"

"Is that supposed to be me? Did I say that?"

April laughed again. "He looked like he was gonna start throwing things! It was hilarious! I couldn't stop laughing, even when he said he was gonna send me to the principal's office too if I didn't." She took a deep breath and shook her head. "I suppose it's too much to ask for a repeat performance?"

This was just too much. That couldn't have really happened. Jamie tensed suddenly at the nearby sound of metal clashing against metal. Eyes wide and a cold sweat on his forehead, he spun to identify the source of the noise, his instincts already rushing to the conclusion that it had to be one of those metal giants long before the more rational parts of his brain could tell him that it was just a locker being slammed shut.

"Jamie?"

He turned to see April standing close, her hand on his arm. He hadn't even felt her touch. Pinching his eyes closed, he jerked away and took several long breaths, trying to calm himself. The first bell rang, and Jamie slumped back against the wall as the sharp siren blared in his skull like the reverberations of an explosion.

"What is wrong with you?" April said. "Don't tell me you're having a panic attack. I mean, you did bring this on yourself. Now come on."

She started down the hallway, but Jamie lingered, leaning against the wall. "I did not bring this on myself," he whispered under his breath. "I didn't."

When April realized Jamie hadn't followed her, she paused and turned back. "Come on, we're gonna be late."

Jaw clenched, Jamie staggered into the crowds and followed after April, trying his best to ignore the noise and bodies pressing in from all sides.

CHAPTER 9

The glare Mister Fisher sent Jamie's way when he entered the classroom instantly had him rethinking his decision not to skip pre-calc. The look Lorrie flashed April was almost as poisonous. This couldn't really be the same life he'd been living yesterday, could it? Jamie dropped heavily into his desk, the stares of his classmates pressing him low in his seat. Once the second bell rang, Mister Fisher stood silent at the podium for several long moments while the rest of the class sat holding their breath, alternating their attention between Jamie and their teacher.

"Alright, class, let's begin," Mister Fisher said at last. Jamie tensed in his seat, half-expecting the world to disappear around him once again. "Unless, of course, Jamie would like to take over again today."

When Terrarhea didn't sprint him away, Jamie almost found himself hoping that it would. Whatever happened yesterday had clearly offended Mister Fisher on a deeply personal level and the teacher wasn't about to let such a humiliation go unanswered. He spent the majority of the period ranting about respect and courtesy, clearly trying to taunt Jamie into some new punishable offence.

Apparently, while Jamie's mind had been daydreaming of Terrarhea, his sleepwalking body had begun openly questioning Mister Fisher's abilities as an educator and then went on to demonstrate several mathematical techniques which had completely dumbfounded the teacher. Without any of that mysterious knowledge to draw on now, all Jamie could do when Mister Fisher asked him to elaborate on some of those formulas today, was slump down in his seat and endure the mocking laughter of both teacher and classmates.

Even when that torment finally came to an end, Jamie could not find respite in any of his other classes. All of his teachers had seemingly joined forces in support of Mister Fisher. Before yesterday, Jamie had merely been a name on their attendance rosters. Now, he'd become a troublemaker and an anarchist, only one step removed from a murderer or a rapist in their eyes. From the way they hounded him at every turn with their overt taunts and jeers, it was a wonder they even let him in school at all.

And if all that weren't bad enough, he also found it almost impossible to keep his mind focused on the mundane academic pursuits of the day. He quickly lost count of how many times he missed a teacher's mocking question because his thoughts were otherwise occupied by what he'd experienced on Terrarhea. Explanations didn't even enter into it today. Those events just kept replaying themselves over and over again in his mind, still as real and visceral as if he'd truly lived through them.

The slightest sight, sound, or smell would instantly set him on edge and have him looking over his shoulder in expectation of some otherworldly threat. Other memories needed no provocation at all to monopolize his thoughts. Alaida, for instance, still seemed too perfect to have simply been the creation of his subconscious. Despite his desire never to return to Terrarhea, he still found himself wishing that he could see her again.

At lunch, Jamie found a secluded corner of the school grounds seldom frequented by any of the faculty and few of the students. He'd had enough of their stares and whispered remarks to last him a lifetime. A few moments of solitude were all he wanted. He suspected Derek and Alex would show up eventually, as they usually did, but most days they were content to eat their lunches in silence while reading their comic books. Not today, however.

"I'm telling you, man," Alex said, "you've got balls of steel for going after April like that."

"It's true," Derek added, barely able to pull his face out of the graphic novel he'd just opened. "Even though April is a complete slut, you're risking serious reprisals from Seth."

So far today, Jamie hadn't crossed paths with Seth or any of his friends. Unfortunately, from the rumors that were circulating through school, there were already a number of completely false reasons why Seth might seek retaliation against Jamie.

"I wasn't going after April," Jamie said, resolved to the futility of trying to set the record straight, especially with these two, but feeling the need to do so regardless. "I don't even like her."

"Apart from her utter disdain for persons of our social standing, what's not to like?" Alex said. "She's hot and she sleeps around with almost anyone!"

"Really?" Jamie said. April did have a tendency to skirt the legalities of the school's dress code, but Lorrie's morals seemed far more flexible than her friend's and no one ever talked about her the way they did April. "Like who?"

"Seth for one," Alex said. "She's got to have really low standards to go out with someone like that."

"And...?" A moment of silence followed.

"Jayce Hawkins," Derek said with a sudden air of victory.

"Oh yeah, Jayce Hawkins!" Alex agreed, nodding vigorously.

"Who is Jayce Hawkins?" Jamie still didn't know most of his classmates by name, but he was almost certain he'd never heard that one before.

"He was in junior high with us," Alex said. "Him and April were only dating for about a week when they started getting it on big time. And then, completely out of the blue, she just dumped him."

"Most of her boyfriends don't last much longer than that," Derek said over the top of his book. "I think Seth must be the current record holder."

"Yeah, she's a real love 'em and leave 'em type," Alex said. "It's only a matter of time before she rips your heart out through your chest, *khali-mah* style." He thrust his hand forward and then withdrew it, palm up, his spread fingers twitching as if holding a still beating heart.

"You should be careful," Derek said. "Things always get ugly with her."

"I already told you guys: I'm not interested in her," Jamie said. "And I'm pretty sure she's not interested in me either."

"If it was me," Alex said, tossing the imaginary heart to the ground, "I'd break it off right now."

"No you wouldn't," Derek said. "You'd hang on to the bitter end and then beg for a little more because she'd be the first girlfriend you've ever had."

"Like you're one to talk!" Alex shot back. "All I'm saying is now that Jamie's got what he wants from her, it would be best to cut her loose before things *can* get ugly."

"But we didn't do anything," Jamie said.

"Then you better hurry up," Alex said. "She's not gonna give you a whole lot of time."

"That is, if Seth doesn't get you first," Derek said.

Alex nodded enthusiastically.

Jamie merely rolled his eyes. This was like arguing with a brick wall. "Why do you guys even keep track of this stuff?"

"Living vicariously through the rest of the student body is about as close as the two of us can come to getting any action around here," Derek said.

Alex sighed and shrugged in agreement.

Were these really the only friends Jamie could hope for? "Haven't you read that one already?" he asked Derek, the heat rising in him, desperate to lash out at anything which might wound.

"I have. Three times, in fact." Derek held up three fingers to emphasize the point but still not looking up from the page. "I just got to the best part."

The afternoon passed more quickly than the morning had, though without much substantial difference in the attitude of his peers. All he wanted was to go home and hide in his room. However, even once the final bell rang and the school began to empty, he still couldn't be done with the place.

Detention was held in the study hall next to the library. He'd never had to attend one before and had been hoping to grab one of the seats in the back of the room where he could sit unobtrusively. Sadly, he found that the detention regulars had already claimed all those seats by the time he arrived. He made his way down the rows of wide, two-person desks and selected one off to the side of the room, as far removed from everyone else as he could manage. Hoping the room wouldn't receive many more than its current handful of detainees, Jamie got to work on his homework from the last two days. With luck, giving his mind something to focus on would help to keep at bay all the other thoughts that kept crowding in.

At the sound of heels on the tile floor, Jamie absently looked up to see who else would be joining them. Standing in the doorway, April spotted him looking and promptly made her way in his direction.

"I suppose we're gonna be doing our time together," she said, dropping her books on the desktop next to Jamie, "At least it's only one week right?"

"I was just thinking the same thing," Jamie said, eyeing her out of the corner of his eye. As April slung her book bag and purse over the back of a chair and then flopped down in another on the other side of the desk, Jamie considered relocating. Unfortunately, at this rate, she'd probably just follow him.

The teacher who would apparently be supervising detention that day, an older woman wearing a beige skirt and sweater, entered the room and took a seat at the front desk. With hardly more than a glance at the gathered students and a quick survey of the roster, she put on her glasses and began reading a paperback novel which she pulled from her bag. Hopefully, her presence would at least keep April quiet.

"Looks like we got Mrs. Hawthorn," April said. "I think she wants to be here even less than we do; doesn't care what we do as long as we don't disturb her latest romance novel."

With April's reputation, it shouldn't have come as much of a surprise that she had such an intimate knowledge of these things. Jamie wanted to scream. Instead, he said, "So, do you come here often then?"

April shot him a wry smile across the desk. "I really hope that wasn't a pick-up line."

"What? No!" Jamie threw up his hand in defense. "I didn't mean it like that! That was an accident!"

"Good," April said with a chuckle, "because if it was, it would have been really lame. What are you working on?" Without asking permission, she pulled his notebook over to her side of the desk "Pre-Calc? After yesterday, I thought you'd have every problem in the book done by now."

"Reports of my genius have been completely fabricated," Jamie muttered.

April laughed. "So, how'd you do it then? Study up on YouTube videos?"

"I must have."

"And here I was hoping you'd be able to help me knock out tonight's assignment.

"Sorry, I'm still trying to figure out last night's."

"Yeah, these were tough." April grabbed Jamie's pencil and began scribbling over his work. "I think I still remember how to solve most of them though."

"Hey, what are you..." Jamie made a half-hearted attempt to snatch away the pencil, or the notebook, but couldn't bring himself to do something that might result in a physical confrontation -- not while half the kids in the back of the room were watching the two of them so intently.

"So," she said as she worked through the first of the math problems, "Arthur or Lancelot?"

Jamie looked around, thinking that she must have been addressing someone else. He was the only one in earshot, however. "Um, excuse me?"

"Remember? From yesterday. Knights of the Round Table? Arthur or Lancelot? You never answered before that rent-a-cop found us."

Which meant he wasn't likely to have any idea of what she was talking about. Nonetheless, he racked his brain trying to think of some way to answer her riddle. All that came to mind, however, were images of ridiculous knights prancing around on imaginary horses and followed by squires clapping coconut halves together.

"Um, Lancelot?" Jamie said.

"Really?" April said, looking up at him through her bangs. "You really think Guinevere should have run off with the young, handsome knight, just because her husband was busy fighting wars to keep their kingdom in one piece -- even knowing that doing so would probably mean the end of the kingdom?"

Clearly, they hadn't been talking about old movies. And she'd also given this topic quite a lot more thought than Jamie ever had. Yesterday, the very idea that someone like April would have given any thought at all to Arthurian legend would have seemed strange. Now it didn't seem any more out of place than all the other things he'd experienced in the last twenty-four hours. "Well, Arthur then."

"You mean you'd want Guinevere to stay in a loveless marriage with a man who's more concerned with politics than his own wife?"

Jamie sat for a moment, wondering if he should, in fact, argue for one of Guinevere's suitors over the other, or if this was all just some kind of trap. "I'm sorry," he said. "What's the right answer?"

April laughed and shook her head. "There is no right answer, I just wanted to know what you thought. No one else has ever wanted to listen to anything I ever had to say about it." She paused in her writing, then sighed and set the pencil down. "I told Lorrie what you said to me yesterday, about how I should go to college and study medieval literature after high school, and she just laughed at me. I don't know why, but it really pissed me off. We got into a fight and now we're not talking to each other."

"Oh." If Jamie didn't have to put up with both Lorrie and April, maybe some little good had come of his time spent on Terrarhea after all. Now all he needed to do was find a way to get rid of April too.

"Not that I really care," April said. "Lorrie would be happy living the rest of her life in a tiny apartment with the first guy to knock her up and working at some dead-end, part-time job earning minimum wage. Not me. You were right. I should do something with my life."

Not knowing what to say, Jamie merely nodded. Maybe not everything from yesterday was quite so difficult to figure out after all. April wasn't nearly as stupid as everyone thought her to be and when Jamie had somehow noticed as much, she was simply grateful to have someone to talk to with whom she could carry on a somewhat intelligent conversation with. Jamie might not have been an expert in any of the things she went on about during the rest of their time in detention, but he had always been a good listener and April needed little encouragement to prattle on about the likes of King Arthur, Chrétien de Troyes, and her theories concerning courtly love and chivalry, while also throwing in a fair amount of ordinary school gossip here and there.

By the end of their first day's detention, Jamie's pre-calc homework from yesterday had been completed and they'd also managed to work through a handful of the problems they'd been given for tomorrow. The assignment did seem a little easier when they tackled it together, though neither April nor Jamie were particularly better at the subject than the other, so they had to muddle through as best they were able, each filling in certain areas of weakness in the other's ability.

When they were finally allowed to leave, April trailed along at Jamie's side. He hoped that this had less to do with any desire she had to continue hanging out with him than it did with the fact only one exit from the school remained unlocked at that hour. Outside the doors, they found a six-foot-two wall of muscle wearing a letterman's jacket standing in their path.

"Hi, Seth!" April said, going to his side. He offered no greeting in reply and instead glared at Jamie.

"What's this crap I hear about you and April?" he demanded of Jamie.

After having been on edge most of the day, jumping at shadows, Jamie now found himself strangely calm. As big as Seth was, he wasn't nearly as menacing as a Terrarhean war-bot. Meeting Seth's gaze, Jamie shrugged. "We were in detention?"

"That's not what I meant, moron!" Seth lunged forward and pushed Jamie back against the unyielding brick wall of the school. Maybe levity wasn't the best way to approach this. "I'm talking about yesterday. The two of you skipped class together and now you're acting like best friends."

"Seth! Cut it out!" April said, tugging at his arm. He didn't seem to notice. "We just talked."

"Oh yeah?" Seth grabbed Jamie by the shirtfront and rapped him off the wall, knocking the wind out of his lungs. Leaning in close, Seth bared his teeth. "What'd you talk about then?"

Gasping for breath as Seth's knuckles dug into his chest, Jamie managed to say, "Medieval Literature." Under the circumstances, something as close to the truth seemed like the best defense.

"Medieval literature?" Seth's nostril's flared and he slammed Jamie into the wall yet again, this time hard enough that the bump on the back of his head, which had just started to fade, collided with the brick. As pain lanced across his skull, Jamie hissed through his teeth and his eyes began to water. If Seth hadn't still been holding onto him, he might very well have fallen to his knees.

"Seth!" April said, again pulling at his arm. This time, he absently brushed her away, like a mosquito.

"What the hell would April know anything about goddamn medieval literature for!" Seth demanded of Jamie.

He didn't even know something like that about his own girlfriend? April's standards were quite low indeed.

"Come on, Seth!" April said. "Jamie was just helping me with my homework! You know how hard Mister Fisher's classes are. Would *you* be able to help me with that?"

Jamie *had* heard Seth was still in remedial math. Seth's lip curled back and his attention shifted to April. She stared back, hands on hips. For a moment, Jamie thought Seth might now hit her instead. However, after glaring at her for what seemed like a very long time, Seth threw Jamie against the wall one final time and then let him tumble to the ground. Maybe Seth did possess some small shred of civility after all.

"Freak," Seth said to Jamie, "If I hear you try anything with April again, you're a dead man."

"I'm sorry, Jamie," April said. "Are you okay?" She started to move toward him, but Seth grabbed her by the arm and pulled her back. Jamie also held out his own hand to keep her at bay. The last thing he wanted was to give Seth's jealousy any more ammunition to use against him.

"I'm fine," he said, sitting up and leaning back against the wall, "Just go."

"Sorry," she said once more over her shoulder, mouthing the word more than speaking it as she allowed Seth to pull her toward his car. What a girl like her saw in someone like Seth, Jamie could not even begin to understand.

CHAPTER 10

As was typically the case, Heather hadn't yet gotten home by the time Jamie got there himself. Setting his book bag down on the dining room table, he stood for a long time staring at the small portion of blank wall the two of them had exposed last night with their demolition efforts. It really did change the entire character of both the kitchen and the dining room. Wondering what it would look like once they'd removed all the cabinets, he took up an electric screwdriver.

He'd only intended to take off a few more doors before finding something to eat, but once the doors were off, it proved easy enough to unscrew the remaining upper cabinets and stack them in the garage with the others. The countertop was already loose in more than one place so when Jamie tested it with a crowbar just to see how much effort that would take to remove, the whole thing popped free in several large yet manageable pieces.

It seemed pointless to leave it like that, so he carried them out as well, only leaving behind the segment surrounding the sink. He then proceeded to empty out the remaining cabinets and place their meager contents in the plentiful moving boxes Heather had saved just for this purpose. The lower cabinets were a little more difficult to knock loose but once he figured out the first one, the rest came free without much effort.

The work wasn't so difficult that he'd rather be doing something else, but it still required just enough concentration to keep his mind from wandering. As the time ticked by, thoughts of Terrarhea barely even popped into his head more than once or twice. When Heather finally got home about four hours after Jamie had first started, she found him exploring the plumbing fittings under the sink.

"What the hell, Jamie!" she said. "When I said you could work on this after school, I didn't mean you had to do the whole thing in one night."

"It wasn't that tough," he replied, his head still under the sink. "I'm just trying to figure out how to unhook these pipes down here. They look pretty old and I'm afraid they might break if I force them too hard."

"Well, let's not flood the basement. Not tonight at least. We can always get a plumber to deal with the sink if we need to." Standing back, she smiled and shook her head. "Wow, this isn't bad at all."

Jamie stood and for the first time took in the whole room. The dust and debris littering the cracked vinyl flooring crunched underfoot and the exposed walls which had been hidden behind the cabinets looked even more dingy than the areas they'd already seen, but what had been a dark, cramped, little room now looked wide and open. It really was quite a transformation.

"Next, the plaster comes down?" Jamie said, still staring at the work he'd accomplished.

"Next, I'm gonna eat something," Heather said. "Assuming you haven't cleaned out the frig yet."

"I didn't mean right now. And no, I haven't touched the frig."

"Good," she said, popping open the door. "And as far as this place goes, the next step is renting a dumpster. At this rate, you're gonna fill up the garage before the weekend. Tomorrow, you can start taking the trim off the windows and doors in the living and dining room if you want. Have you eaten yet?"

Jamie shook his head.

"Got any ideas? I don't know what I'm hungry for."

"I saw a box of spaghetti when I was cleaning out the cabinets," Jamie suggested. Heather brightened at the prospect. "But I didn't see any sauce anywhere."

Heather's shoulders stooped for a moment but then she shot up straight and threw open the freezer door. "Ah-ha!" She seized a container and slammed it down on the countertop. "We're in luck! I knew it was a good idea to freeze the last half of that jar. We even have parmesan in the frig."

As they both helped prepare supper, they started to talk about where to put the remaining furniture during the demolition. After eating, they began to experimentally move a few things around. Though Heather had at first declared work was to stop for the evening, they'd soon gone ahead and squeezed her meager collection of living room furniture, along with the refrigerator, into the third bedroom. Heather had previously set-up the room as a home office, but had only ever used it rarely, so the change didn't come as much of a loss.

"It looks like my first apartment in college," she commented once they had finished.

It might have been cramped but was by no means unusable. This arrangement would allow them to complete their demolition of the living room, dining room, and kitchen without requiring them to evacuate the house entirely for the duration. Once those areas became livable again,

70

they'd then abandon the bedrooms so work could begin on them. It would require a bit of patience and coordination, but with how smoothly things had so far gone, neither one of them felt the least bit discouraged. Now that they had gotten started, it seemed there would be no stopping this little project of theirs. Jamie turned-in for the evening actually looking forward to something for the first time in quite a while.

The next day did little to dampen his eagerness, even though he did have to muddle through a day of school before he could get started. He did his best to avoid April and Seth, but even with her boyfriend's warnings, April insisted on sitting next to Jamie once again during detention. This time she didn't even let him start his homework before sidetracking him with more of her pointless trivia. Fortunately, after having gotten caught up after his day off, he'd already been able to complete the majority of his homework during various breaks throughout the day, leaving only pre-calc. This, the two of them dabbled with as they talked.

The more Jamie listened to her, though, the more he felt as if Derek and Alex's lurid opinion of her didn't quite fit with the reality. Several times he tried to steer the conversation toward the reasons behind her reputation, but it was only when he mentioned Jayce Hawkins in passing did he get anywhere.

"Oh please!" April said with a snort. "That loser barely got to second base but then he started telling everyone that he scored a homerun. *That's* why I dumped him."

"That's not what everyone seems to think."

"Some rumors just never die," she said, gripping her pencil like a knife and glaring into the distance. "That was nearly three years ago and even though him and his family moved away, people still believe his version of things over mine. Because of him, every boyfriend I've ever had thinks I'm easy. When they start getting too grabby, I cut them loose. I may have a reputation, but I'm not a slut."

On a certain level, Jamie could certainly sympathize. No one was ever going to believe that he hadn't consciously been aware of what had happened in Mister Fisher's class, or that he and April hadn't been up to anything more than merely chatting about medieval literature afterward.

"You and Seth have been together for a while, though, right?"

"Not really," April said, absently doodling in the margin of her textbook. "Just since the end of summer. He's kind of a moron but at least he knows where all the best parties are. Plus, he's way more interested in football than in anything else. And I do mean *anything*."

From the way the two of them had been together since the start of the school year, Jamie had assumed they'd been an item for a long time. "Sounds like true love to me." Jamie said with a roll of his eyes as he went back to his own textbook.

April pushed it out of his hands. "This isn't the middle ages," she said. "We don't have knights riding around slaying dragons; we have to make do with what we have. I can't be like Guinevere and just ask Lancelot to lose a duel to prove his love for me."

Jamie cast April a sidelong glance. "I though you said Guinevere only asked Lancelot to ride in a wagon to prove his love."

"The duels come later."

Friday came and went, marking the fourth day of their detention together. Even though they were finally able to finish the entirety of Mister Fisher's homework in a single sitting, Jamie still felt reasonably certain that what little help he got from April was not offset by the continued physical threat posed by her psychotically jealous boyfriend. As they parted ways, well away from where Seth would be waiting, April turned to Jamie and said, "I'll see you on Monday."

"Yeah..." Maybe she'd lose interest over the weekend and Jamie would finally be free of her.

When Jamie got home, he found a giant metal cube, nearly as high as his shoulder, filling over half the driveway. It appeared the dumpster that Heather ordered had finally arrived. Jamie didn't think they'd be able to fill it even half full with everything they would eventually tear out of the house, but after hauling the accumulated debris from the week's demolition activities out of the garage and carefully breaking everything down as flat as possible, he began to consider that they might actually need something even bigger. The wooden trim Jamie had been able to remove the night before, he set aside: Heather was going to try stripping off the accumulated years of paint and varnish so that they might be able to reuse it.

With room in the garage once more, Jamie set his sights on tearing out the matted carpeting in the living room. Underneath, he found wide wooden floorboards which had once been a rich golden brown but had since become dinged and stained by countless years of wear. When Heather saw them, she got down on her hands and knees with a block sander before even changing out of her good clothes. The small patch of bare wood she exposed with her efforts gave them both a better idea of how beautiful it would look once they refinished the whole floor, which further exploration revealed continued into the dining room and down the hallway to the bedrooms.

Saturday morning, he and Heather worked together to break loose the plaster and lath hanging from the walls and ceilings, getting showered with nearly a century's worth of dust and dirt and dislodging countless long-abandoned mouse nests, along with a few that were still in various states of occupancy. That afternoon, they spent hauling wheelbarrow loads of debris out to the dumpster and vacuuming up piles of dust.

Now, with only bare studs for walls, the rooms felt very dark, but strangely, much bigger than they had before. Being able to look into the opened walls was like seeing a museum exhibit of historical building components from the last hundred years. After a dutiful inspection of their handiwork, Heather happily confirmed that her suspicions about the building's structure not requiring any major repairs where, in fact, true. Some of her plans to add new windows would require a few small modifications based on what they'd unearthed, but overall, the house had good bones.

"A true monument to deconstruction architecture," Heather commented as the two of them stood in the center of the gutted living room, drinking sodas. The dislodged light fixtures hanging canted from bare joists overhead cast harsh shadows across the room and turned the windows into dark mirrors as darkness fell outside. "I hope you're staying on top of your homework with all the work you're been putting in on this little project."

"If it weren't for April bugging me during detention, I'd have too much time to work on my homework," Jamie said, pulling the dust mask off from around his neck and shaking plaster dust out of his hair.

"April? That bitch you told me about from your pre-calc class?" Heather looked puzzled but then smiled mischievously. "Why's she bugging you during detention? I knew you'd been acting weird all week, but I never would have thought that it was because you and her got together."

Jamie's heart sank. He'd been so careful not to mention April's involvement in what had happened, knowing full well that this is exactly how Heather would react when she found out.

"There is no me and her," Jamie said. "We've just been working on our pre-calc homework together since we both got stuck in detention on the same day."

"What's she in for?"

"Um...she ticked off Mister Fisher."

"Same as you? On the same day?" It had been impossible to keep everything about that day from Heather, so she *had* learned that an altercation in Mister Fisher's class had been the catalyst for Jamie leaving school on Monday, but he'd so far been able to keep her in the dark about most of the details.

"Honestly, it wasn't very hard. That guy's a complete jerk. He was gunning for somebody and he just happened to pick us."

"What were you two doing? Did he catch you passing love notes?"

"I told you, we're not even friends." It was bad enough Jamie had to put up with this at school, but now he had to deal with it at home too? "He thought I was giving him attitude and April just thought it was a little too funny."

"I do have to admit, from what you told me about her, she never really seemed like your type."

"Like you would have any idea what my *type* is," Jamie said with a rueful chuckle and took a drink from his soda.

"Yeah, here I was thinking it was some girl named Elita."

Jamie nearly chocked on his drink. "Alaida?" he sputtered and coughed as the soda burned up into his sinuses. "Where did you hear about her?"

"Oh, so she is real? You've only been mentioning her in your sleep all week long."

"I've been talking in my sleep?" Ice water suddenly surged through Jamie's veins. He knew his dreams had been troubled, but he never suspected that he'd been speaking out loud as well. "And you've been listening in?"

"Not on purpose," Heather said, picking at the tab of her soda can. "It's not so much that you've been talking as...screaming?"

"Screaming?"

"Yeah. Loud enough that I can hear you in my room with the doors closed. I've tried waking you up a few times but you're so out of it that you just roll over and go back to sleep. At first, I just thought it was a nightmare, but it's happened nearly every night this week. I've been meaning to ask you about it because, honestly, I'm starting to get a little worried."

Jamie stared at the distant wall. "It's just…some bad dreams. That's all."

Both of them remained silent for several moments as the house settled around them. The headlights of a car pulling out the neighbor's driveway flashed across the room through the open windows.

"So, who is she?" Heather said at last.

"Who?"

"Elita?" Heather said. "Alaida?"

"*Alaida* is just a…a waitress I met at a…restaurant," Jamie said, these half-truths becoming easier and easier each time he told one. "It was on Monday. I'd been having a really rough day and she was just nice to me, okay?"

"Have you asked her out yet?" Heather said.

Jamie sighed and glared back at her. "I met her once. We talked, briefly. I do not have any idea why I'd be dreaming about her." Heather snickered. "I didn't mean that I've been dreaming *about* her, she's just *in* my dreams." That didn't really sound any better.

"Well, I hope you at least gave her a decent tip," Heather said. From that mischievous glint in her eye, Jamie knew that all he'd done was dig his grave even deeper. "Is April going to be jealous?"

"Why would April be jealous?" Jamie threw up his hands. This was just like when they were kids. "There is no me and April! And why am I even arguing about any of this with you?"

"Because I think you are in desperate need of some sisterly advice," Heather said, putting her arm around his shoulder and giving him a shake. "I do happen to know a thing or two about girls after all."

"No," Jamie said flatly. "Advice about girls in the last thing I would ever want from you."

"Ouch," Heather placed her hand over her heart, "that hurts. But how would you even know if my advice is any good or not if you've never given it a try?"

Jamie's eyes grew wide and he stepped out from under Heather's embrace. "Remember when you came home for Memorial Day and suggested I should make a move on Kristie?"

"Yeah," Heather said, nodding and smiling at the memory. "You two were perfect for each other! I know you'd been friends since kindergarten and everything, but she was *definitely* your type. You would have made the cutest couple."

"You know what?" Jamie said. "I *did* follow your advice, and that was the worst idea ever! After we…afterward, things just got weird between us. We actually stopped talking to each other completely."

"What?" Heather drew back as if slapped. "I never heard about that! The last time I saw you together, I thought you were still good."

That would have been at their parent's funeral. Though Kristie had indeed been sympathetic, there had been a distance between them which Heather apparently hadn't noticed. "That was the first time we'd spoken in a week."

"Oh. Sorry…"

"It doesn't matter anymore. We probably could have worked it out but what's the point? I'm here now and she's still there…"

"I am sorry, Jamie. When I brought you here to live with me, I never really thought about everything you were leaving behind. There was just so much going on and then they started talking about taking you away. I never really gave you a choice, did I?"

"What other choice did I have? Besides, it's not really all that bad now that I'm starting to get used to it here. Starting over fresh was probably just what I needed."

"I hope you're not just saying that to make me feel better."

"Would I really have any reason to make you feel better after the way you were just teasing me?" Jamie said, punching her on the shoulder.

"Do you want to talk about April some more?" Heather said with a mischievous smile.

"No."

"Then how about Alaida?"

Before Jamie could say anything, Heather's phone pinged with the arrival of a text message. She dug it out of her pocket, took one look at the screen, and groaned. "Crap. I told some friends I'd go out with them for drinks tonight, but I completely forgot." She looked around at the scattered tools and last remaining piles of debris. "Looks like I'll have to cancel."

"You should go. I can finish up here."

"Come on, we started this together, we might as well finish it together," Heather said, trying to put on a bold front.

"Don't worry about it. I got this. Go: have fun."

"You sure?"

"Positive."

"Well...okay. I'm gonna take a shower and get ready," she said heading for the back hallway. "No wild parties while I'm out."

Jamie looked around at the rusty nails hanging from the walls and the thick layer of plaster dust covering the floors. "Yeah, party at the 'Fight Club' house. That would be great."

"Compared to some of the parties I went to in college, this place could be the Ritz," Heather said as she disappeared around the corner.

Monday marked Jamie's last day of detention, during which April once again insisted on talking to him the whole time. Afterward, he was simply grateful their paths would never have reason to cross again. However, a few days later, she once again sought him out under the pretense of working on their pre-calc together. It didn't take Jamie long to realize all she really wanted was someone to talk to. Things with Lorrie hadn't improved, and Seth was just as dense as always. This, she apparently thought, meant Jamie was her only other option.

Most of the rumors about the two of them had simmered down considerably, though none had gone away entirely. Seth for one, was not about to let the matter rest and he remained aggressively possessive of April, forcing Jamie to maintain a wary vigilance every moment of the school day. More than once, Jamie toyed with strategies that might drive April away, but most of them seemed likely to result in Seth seeking some kind of vengeance on her behalf.

Although, maybe a few temporary bruises would be worth the long term freedom he'd enjoy afterward.

In the weeks which followed, Terrarhea was never far from Jamie's thoughts. While he was able to get through a day every once in a while without thinking about it too much, when it did intrude on his thoughts, it left him in a distant state of mind which even Heather was not oblivious to. Most of the time, he was able to deflect her inquires, merely citing his lack of restful sleep as the reason for his behavior.

Work on the remodeling project progressed at a steady pace, though not nearly as quickly as it had that first week. They needed to reinforce some of the floor joists which had been turned to Swiss cheese by past plumbers and electricians, patch holes in the sheathing where air was leaking through, run new wiring for all of the electrical, completely redo the kitchen plumbing to match the new layout Heather had come up with, and prepare the openings for the new windows. At the same time, they had to keep an eye toward the second phase of their renovations so that any of the current changes wouldn't complicate what they next had to do.

There were also inspections that needed to be cleared at every step of the way. Jamie spent a great deal of time researching not only the building techniques themselves but also the building ordinances, so that between himself and Heather, they only ran into a few minor hold-ups along the way. Heather did hire professionals to upgrade the ancient fuse box and water heater in the basement, as well as to install the new windows and doors. That cut into her budget further than anything else so far but having a dependable water supply and a front door that actually latched without having to slam it shut was worth it.

Besides, with the amount of effort Jamie put in on the project, he was already saving her quite a bit on labor alone. It was hard, dirty work, and he spent nearly all his free time at it, but it gave him something to do that had a purpose. So much of his life had seemed completely beyond his control lately, it was nice to look back after completing a task and see real, tangible results. For a time, Heather tried to match his dedication to the project but her real job took up much more of her time than his schooling did. Jamie also insisted that she not completely abandon her own life. Whether it was just a night out with friends for drinks or a date with her latest mystery guy, he always made it clear that Heather should not feel guilty about taking time off for herself.

Though he did need her help from time to time, he much preferred working alone whenever he could. It allowed him to get lost in the job at hand, focusing all his energy on that one task alone so that he wouldn't have any time left to think about the other things in his life. Throwing himself so completely into the work also left him totally exhausted at the end of each day. Sometimes, it even allowed him to sleep through an entire night without waking up in a cold sweat. Though his dreams remained troubled, they were only dreams and he seldom remembered them, not at all like his memories of Terrarhea, which remained just as clear as the day he'd first experienced them.

Looking back on that morning he'd gone to Terrarhea, Jamie slowly came to the conclusion that if there had been an outside cause for what had happened, it could only have been that homeless man's black box he'd picked up off the street. Of all the things that had happened that morning, it alone was the only one unexplainable enough to assign any special significance to at all.

Urged on by some lingering hope of enlightenment, Jamie did go wandering through the neighborhood once or twice in hopes of finding that wizened, old street man. If he and his black box were really the cause of anything at all, had he assaulted Jamie on purpose or was he as much a victim as Jamie was, his mind scattered by whatever it had done to him long ago? One day when feeling especially bold, Jamie even stopped at Walter's Café to ask if any of the employees had ever seen the old man going through their trash. They were all nice enough to humor him but not a one could remember seeing anyone who fit Jamie's description of the old man.

Whatever the truth, the effects of his time on Terrarhea still lingered in nearly every aspect of his life. Heather remained in the dark about Jamie's temporary break with sanity, as did Mister Clark, who continued badgering Jamie to give him a definitive answer regarding his interest in the school's advanced learning program. Mister Fisher and the other teachers still carried a grudge and April still seemed determined to drive Seth into a jealous rampage by lurking about with Jamie every opportunity she got. Rumors about Jamie still circulated at school and occasionally classmates he'd never met before would approach him and leave disappointed once they found out he was much less of a rebel than they'd led themselves to believe. Others now went out of their way to stay away from him. Derek and Alex were the only ones in the entire school who seemed interested in cultivating a genuine friendship, but Jamie assumed even their reasons for doing so were suspect. If they couldn't have a popular friend, an infamous one would be the next best thing.

"Doing anything tonight?" Derek asked him one Friday afternoon as Jamie tossed his books into his locker at the end of the day.

"We were going to run the circuit and thought we'd ask if you wanted to come along," Alex said. 'Running the circuit' was their term for visiting every single comic shop within an hour's drive, searching through musty long-boxes in the hope of finding buried treasures only their encyclopedic knowledge of comic books would ever find interesting.

Jamie shrugged. With Heather's remodeling project halted until the electrical inspector stopped by on Monday, he actually had nothing to do. "Why not? It's not like there's anything else to do around here on a Friday night, right?"

"Except maybe go to Seth's party," Alex said.

"Unless you're not invited," Derek added. "Which I know for a fact none of us were."

"I was just saying." Alex grew defensive. "It's not like I want to go. We'd be ripped to shreds if we set foot anywhere near his place."

"How *does* he manage to throw a kegger every other weekend without getting into trouble?" Derek said.

Jamie picked up his backpack and swung his locker shut. "His parents are always going out of town and his brother hooks him up with the beer." When the other two flashed him questioning looks, Jamie added, "April told me."

Assuming a terrible German accent, Derek said, "Und just how are zee two of you getting on?"

"There is no two of us, Doctor Freud," Jamie said. "April's going to be at the party with Seth. I think that should tell you everything you need to know."

"I see, go on."

"Maybe we should call the cops on them," Alex said distantly.

"On Jamie und April? I do not sink zee police vould be interested in a cheating girlfriend."

"No, on Seth's party! Everyone there is underage, and they have beer. We could ruin their night so easy!"

"Yeah, about that," Jamie said, setting a hand on Alex's shoulder as they walked down the hallway, "You know Seth's older brother, the one who gets him the beer? He *is* a cop."

"Oh. Well, on to the comic shops then."

"Lead the way," Jamie said.

Unfortunately, Jamie never made it. One instant he was walking along the street with the two of them, rolling his eyes at Alex's latest stupid joke, and the next, his world was replaced by another.

CHAPTER 11

Jamie's leg crumpled as if missing the last step of a staircase. He staggered, trying to regain his balance but the stiff clay underfoot pulled at his heavy boots and a fluttery red piece of tattered fabric entangled his neck and flailing arms. An incomprehensible jumble of noises assailed his ears and a searing heat so intense he could feel it through his leathern garments beat across the right side of his body. His every sense reeled from the sheer intensity of it. It was all too loud, too bright, too textured -- simply too much all at once.

And above him loomed a gigantic metallic form, vaguely humanoid in shape. He lurched away with an inarticulate yelp and crashed to the ground. There could be little doubt he had once again found himself on the world of Terrarhea. But how could this have happened? The first time had simply been brought on by stress. He was certain of it. He was doing so much better now, and he certainly hadn't been associating with any dirty, old street people or their strange black boxes. He was making friends, starting to fit in, his life was starting to have purpose again! This couldn't be happening!

In the several moments it took Jamie to reign in the chaos battering his senses, he came to realize the robotic machine sat strangely still and quiet. A pair of hatches on the underside of the angled prow were even hanging open to expose the empty pilot's seat, if one could even call it a seat. It consisted of numerous articulated segments suspended from a pair of telescoping rails which were currently extended downward out of the belly of the machine. Had he fallen while stepping out of that? Was this machine supposed to belong to him?

Not far away, the timbers of a small building stood out like a blackened skeleton against the roaring fire which had engulfed the rest of the structure. Both it and Jamie were situated on the flat top of a low ridge covered in grass and a mottled assortment of scraggly trees. The ridge reached out across several concentric fields of plowed earth and crudely trimmed hedgerows. In the very center stood a round, earthen berm that sheltered a small cluster of squat, timber buildings. Past the fields, a heavy forest of grotesquely large trees dominated, their massive boughs, full of bright green leaves, sagged as if pulled low by some brutally unrelenting weight.

From the buildings, Jamie could hear the sporadic gunfire of energy weapons, and from the forest, something like the howls of wolves. He could almost make out vaguely humanoid shapes moving through the foliage at ground level, but a raspy grating noise from the direction of the burning building drew his attention with a start. To call it a voice would not have been wholly accurate but when the same sound was repeated, and with greater insistence, there could be no doubt it was indeed meant to be words.

"Why you stop, Reaver?"

Frantically, Jamie scuttled away from the trio of creatures which had just spoken. Much like their words, they may have passed for human under less than ideal conditions but not here in the morning light. Backs hunched and shoulders stooped, they wore no clothes, but every inch of their sinewy bodies were covered with a coarse grayish-brown fur. Their fingers and toes sported hooked claws while their prominent, narrow jaws, canine noses, golden eyes, and pointed, articulate ears lent their faces a distinct bestial quality.

With no weapons close at hand, Jamie stumbled back to his feet and balled his fists, again feeling the strange way his body reacted more quickly on this world. Hopefully, if these things, whatever they were, decided to attack, he wouldn't need anything more to deal with them. The three creatures followed him with their amber eyes but otherwise didn't appear the least bit intimidated by his display.

The one nearest to Jamie stepped forward. "Work yet to do," it said. The words were guttural and rough, as if the mouth speaking them was more accustomed to growling than proper human speech. The other two looked on, their expressions quizzical.

Why were they looking at him? Why were they even talking to him? Up until a moment ago, he hadn't even been here.

An especially loud energy discharge from the buildings sent Jamie skittering in the opposite direction as he ducked his head, remembering well the lightning guns he'd faced the last time he'd been on Terrarhea. The three creatures turned toward the noise with indifference since the shot hadn't even been directed at them but instead at one of the dark shapes moving through the woods. It dropped to the ground at the edge of the fields like a puppet whose strings had been cut. Jamie could now see it looked just like these three creatures standing in front of him.

"Get out of here!" Jamie yelled, swiping his arm through the air. Though they could obviously talk, reasoning with them still made him feel like he was merely talking to a wild animal. With luck, Derek and Alex would notice something wrong with Jamie back in the real world and wake him up before this latest dream could get any worse. "Go on! Leave me alone!"

"We had deal." the creature said. The other two bared fangs and offered throaty growls of agreement. Jamie took a step back as it took one forward. Around its neck, the first creature wore a rough leather cord tied off to a small sack. It took hold of the sack and ripped it from the cord, holding it out before Jamie in one of its clawed hands. "We helped you, now you help us!"

Why were these things addressing their concerns to Jamie? "You...you must have me confused with someone else."

"Trick," one of the other creatures said in a voice even less understandable than the first.

"Betray," said the third.

"We know your scent, Reaver!" the first creature said, its dirty talons digging into the small sack before throwing it to the ground. It landed at Jamie's feet and spilled a large handful of shiny gold coins into the mud.

About that same moment, more of the creatures began pouring out of the forest and bounding across the open fields toward the cluster of distant buildings. Sporadic bursts of energy streaked out to meet the advancing hoard but managed to drop only a few of the howling creatures. As they closed on their target, a woman's pitched scream sounded over the noise of battle.

"What are you doing?" Jamie said. "Are there people in there?"

"You promised help be rid of those kill us!"

After returning from his last time on Terrarhea, Jamie might have allowed the rational parts of his brain to explain away all of that as nothing more than a stress-induced hallucination. Now he could not deny what he knew to be true. Terrarhea wasn't an illusion and it wasn't a dream. It was just as real as Earth. Maybe he was going mad, but at that moment, the greater insanity would have been to ignore what was happening right in front of him.

"I didn't promise you anything!" Jamie said, his voice threatening to crack. "And I'm not going to let you hurt anyone!"

"You break deal?" the leader said, stepping forward and baring glistening fangs.

"I told you I didn't make any deals!" Jamie replied, but he was unable to plead his case any further.

Unleashing a savage cry, the first creature bounded forward, followed close behind by the other two.

"Betrayer!"

"Kill you!"

If it weren't for Jamie's heightened reflexes, he would not have been able to sidestep the slashing claws of the first creature as easily as he did. As the other two came at him in a furious storm of snarls and barks, Jamie pushed one of them aside. It stumbled into its comrade and both of them went down in a heap just as their leader again threw itself at Jamie.

Whatever these things were, they were much faster than mere humans. It was all Jamie could do just to avoid their attacks. Again and again they came at him, never slowing, jaws snapping close enough that he could smell their carrion-scented breath and feel warm spittle on his face. Maybe running them off wouldn't be so easy after all.

One of the creatures launched itself at Jamie, its arm extended skyward for a wicked downward slash. Jamie dropped back and drove his arm forward in order to hold his opponent at a distance. However, his outstretched palm collided with the creature's gapping maw. That, combined with the downward motion of the creature, resulted in a sickly cracking sound and a pronounced yelp.

Jamie cringed away as the creature dropped to its knees and clutched a now misshapen jaw, whimpering and sputtering blood. Jamie hadn't meant to do that. No matter what these things were, he didn't want to hurt them. They, however, had no such qualms regarding Jamie. If he didn't start fighting back he'd never be able to bring this fight to an end.

In that brief moment of indecision, the two remaining creatures charged Jamie without offering their fallen comrade even a glance. Jamie let fly with a wild swing of his arm, but the leader ducked around it and used the momentum to spring right back. It was so fast Jamie had to retreat hastily but that only left him open to the other creature.

It fell upon him from behind, clawing at his back and shoulders, trying to pull him down. Stumbling, Jamie threw up his hands to protect his face as the creature's claws raked across his skin. It wouldn't let go. It wasn't going to stop until its prey was dead. Jamie spun violently, almost losing his balance, and threw the creature off his back with a determined heave.

The inhuman bark it unleashed as it crashed through the wall of the burning building caused Jamie to wince yet again. In a frantic thrashing of limbs, the creature shot out of the flames trailing a fountain of embers. As the air filled with the smell of burnt hair, the creature writhed about on the ground, shrieking and convulsing, large patches of its skin blistered scarlet.

Jamie tore himself away from the sight and spun just in time to avoid the leader's latest assault. It now seemed faster than ever, a berserker wrath burning in its golden eyes. Jamie dodged as best he could but a pair of swipes from his foe added several additional tears to his poncho. An inch closer and they would have found his throat. With a snarl of his own, Jamie threw himself at the creature. Its claws made contact more than once, but Jamie ignored them and drove his fist down with all the strength he could muster. This close, the creature could not evade, its best effort merely turning Jamie's strike into a glancing blow. Still, with all Jamie's strength behind it, his attack drove the creature to the ground.

It quickly scuttled out of Jamie's range and remained at a low crouch, eyeing him hatefully and grasping its shoulder. Its lips curled back to reveal its fangs and Jamie braced himself for another attack.

Before it could, however, a rustling from the direction of the burning building distracted them both. Emerging from the bushes there, a young woman stumbled into the open, coughing and using her hands to shield herself from the heat of the fire. Her face was smeared with black streaks and her dusky blonde hair had been pulled back into a loose ponytail from which several strands had come free. She took one look at the scene before her and skidded to a halt, her gray eyes growing wide. "Oh crap," she muttered, fumbling for something under the long leather apron she wore.

The creature was in motion a split second before Jamie, launching itself at this newcomer. She managed to draw a small knife, but it would have done little to protect her. The creature was furious, rendered blind by rage. Just as it was about to fall upon the girl, Jamie grabbed it by the shoulders and wrenched it away, pulling it right off its feet. They fell to the ground, Jamie driving his arm across the thing's chest. That knocked the wind out of it, but only for a moment. After a brief fit of coughing, it resumed its struggles, Jamie's weight pressing down on it the only thing keeping it from doing much more than slash at him with the claws on its hands and feet.

"Hold it down!" the girl said.

She came into Jamie's line of sight the same moment her knife flashed in front of his face. Preoccupied with the creature under him, Jamie didn't even comprehend what was happening until the blade sliced through its throat. In a flood of crimson, the creature instantly lost its strength, its hands feebly clutching at clumps of muddy grass as blood bubbled from its mouth.

Jamie leapt to his feet and backed away from both the dying creature and the girl who had just killed it. She had no interest in Jamie, however. Her contemptuous gaze fixed first on the dying creature and then, raising her knife, on its fellows. Burned or broken, neither of them looked like they had any interest in continuing this fight.

The one with the misshapen jaw glared at Jamie.

"You will pay!" it said, spittle and blood flying from its mouth. "Away!"

It threw back its head to the sky and that last word became a mournful howl. Jamie shivered as it was answered by a chorus of similar cries from within the forest. The two injured creatures went loping for the trees even as the ones in the distance who had just made it to the buildings now turned and fled as well, leaving the ground around the berm littered with their dead. The moment they reached the forest, they almost seemed to disappear, as if Jamie had simply imagined them. The only one left was the one laying at Jamie's feet, its chest heaving one last time before it released its last breath with a long heavy sigh.

"Oh my god," the girl said, spinning through a slow circle to confirm that the creatures had really fled. "You saved my life. I think you might have saved everyone."

Jamie had to rip his eyes away from the body of the dead creature. The girl standing before him was tall and willowy and about the same age as he was. Looking closer, he could also see that most of the black marks on her face were not soot, but actually grease. She had a cunning glint in her eyes as she stared at Jamie with a furtive smile on her lips. He looked away and cleared his throat. "What happened here? What are these things?"

"They're Wolf-Slaves," the girl said, as if that were explanation enough. After wiping the knife blade clean on the grass, she tucked it back into the sheath on the inside of her apron. "Ciante has been having problems with them ever since he opened this mine two seasons ago. They come around sometimes and take a goat or two, once in a while a chicken, but always in the night so no one sees them. This is the first time they've ever tried anything like this."

Jamie had to let all the words sink into his brain for a few moments before he muddled out their meaning. He'd forgotten that even Humans on Terrarhea were difficult for him to understand at times. When he next spoke, he tried to put a little of her accent into his own words.

"Wolf-Slaves..." Jamie whispered, only now realizing why the fallen creature's golden eyes had looked so familiar to him. It must have been another of the slave races that Alaida had mentioned. But she'd said that all slaves existed only to serve their masters, not kill them.

Suddenly he found it very difficult to continue thinking of the fallen creature as an 'it' instead of a 'he'.

"Why were they doing this?" Jamie said, the creatures' accusations still ringing in his ears.

"They're only animals," the girl said, a little perplexed. "Who can figure them out. They were trying to kill us so we killed them. I wouldn't be surprised if they try again."

"But..."

With a prolonged creak, the frame of the burning building began to list drunkenly and then toppled over completely. With a crash that sent a swirling cloud of embers into the sky, what little remained of the building's walls fell into the bed of red-hot coals within the stone foundation.

"It's a good thing you happened to be passing by when you did," the girl said. "Did you hear the fighting all the way from the road?"

For some reason, Jamie couldn't stop staring at the dead Wolf-Slave. The girl had confirmed his own rationalization that they were little more than creatures, wild animals. Back home, where hunting had been a major aspect of almost everyone's lives each fall, Jamie had seen plenty of dead animals before, but none of them had been like this one. Was it just because it looked somewhat human and was almost able to speak, or was there something else, like the way they'd been talking to him as if he and they had had some kind of agreement?

"My name's Onorah, by the way," the girl said, holding out her hand to Jamie. He looked at it for a moment before reaching out and shaking it in reply.

"I'm Jamie," he said, distantly.

Her cheeks dimpled but at least she didn't giggle openly as Alaida had done. "Hey, cheer up," the girl, Onorah, said, nudging him in the shoulder. "You did good work here. When I saw your titan come out of the woods I just knew the cavalry had arrived. If it was me, I wouldn't have gotten out, but then, you obviously know how to handle yourself in a fight."

"My titan?"

"Yeah, your titan-Mech," Onorah said, nodding toward the giant metal robot. She walked over to it, gazing up at it like one might admire a classic hotrod. "I've never seen one like it before. Clearly a custom job, am I right? Is it Thieradoonian?"

It seemed there could be little doubt it was supposed to belong to him, and since Onorah wasn't taking offence to him having it, it must not have been against the law for him to own a walking war machine. But how was he to answer questions about something he knew less than nothing about? He shrugged. "I don't really know."

Her brow furrowed. "You don't know?"

"I...I just got it," Jamie said. That seemed like a logical enough explanation, but it would only justify a certain degree of ignorance. "I...won it in a card game."

Onorah's eyes grew large and she laughed. "Really? You must have the devil's own luck! I bet the other guy was pissed. Can I take a look?"

"Um, I guess so, sure."

Smiling broadly, Onorah ran over to the open cockpit and began examining the controls. "Pretty basic setup. Nothing at all like the military ones, huh?"

Compared to the arrays of crystal switches and brass knobs Jamie remembered from his one encounter with a military 'titan-mecha,' this one did indeed have a much more simplified panel with only a single control handle on each of the seat's armrests.

As Jamie walked closer, the boxy toe of his boot tapped something metallic on the ground. He'd all but forgotten about the bag the Wolf-Slave had thrown at him. He stooped down and picked up one of the gold coins. One side bore the image of a stern-faced woman, or possibly a man, surrounded by words written in that mysterious alphabet Jamie couldn't quite read. The opposite side had been stamped with what looked exactly like a large Arabic numeral "five."

"I've never heard of Wolf-Slaves carrying money before," Onorah said, having crawled halfway over the back of the pilot's seat to get a better look inside.

The small pile of coins didn't look like much, but then Jamie had no idea what kind of value this Terrarhean currency might hold. Scooping up the coins, he filled the sack and retied the cord. "What should we do with it?"

"After everything you did here, you might as well keep it," Onorah said. "Spoils of war, right?"

She hopped out of the machine, still more interested in it than the coins. It must have been mere pocket change. Absently, Jamie tucked the sack into his belt and turned back to the titan.

The body was long and it tapered to a point in the front. The machine had no head to speak of, just a curved roll cage across the top that appeared to be the only protection for the open-air cockpit situated toward the front of its sloped prow. The legs, currently folded neatly underneath so that the bottom of the main hull was nearly resting on the ground, were jointed like the hind legs of a dog or a cat. When it walked, it must have done so on its toes alone. The arms lay on either side with hands big enough to pick up a grown man with ease. The whole thing was heavily armored with overlapping plates of pale gray steel over an inch thick, all of which were covered with numerous gouges, burns, and scattered patches of rust. Individually, none of the parts looked particularly sleek or refined. In fact, Jamie could see numerous places where crude repairs had been performed with little concern for appearances, but as a whole, the machine screamed of power and speed.

Taking advantage of the many knobby projections, Onorah climbed one of the arms, quickly scrambling up onto the machine's back.

"Is this a rumble seat?" she said, releasing a latch which allowed the flat portion of the hull directly behind the cockpit to rotate backward on rear-mounted hinges. The hatch itself had to be at least a foot thick.

"Hold on a second," Jamie said, clamoring up after her. He still had no idea what this thing was or who it was really supposed to belong to. Who could tell what secrets might be hidden away inside.

Onorah, however, had already figured out that the hatch could be locked into place in an almost vertical orientation and that it contained several compartments of its own, one of which she folded open into a bench seat wide enough to accommodate three.

"How did you know that was there?" Jamie asked, finally having climbed high enough to peer over the top of the hull.

"A lot of civilian titans have them," Onorah said, stomping on the corrugated bottom of the cavity left by the raised hatch. "It looks like you have a pretty good-sized hold under here too."

She pulled on a latch which allowed the floor to retract rearward, rolling up something like a garage door into the compartment below.

Jamie had absolutely no idea what the titan's hold might contain but with the way those Finttiranos soldiers had spoken of him, his thoughts instantly turned to images of dead bodies stuffed into a trunk. The reality proved to be a bit more mundane: just a lumpy pile of heavy canvas tarps with a shovel and pick laying on top. Clearly unimpressed, Onorah rolled the compartment shut. Before Jamie could tell her not to, she next popped open one of the compartments directly above the rumble seat. When she saw what it contained, she gasped in surprise. Cursing his luck, Jamie climbed over the top of the roll cage and hurried to see what she had discovered.

"Is that a Type 1a Blaster Rifle?" Onorah said in awe.

There had to be at least ten firearms slotted into the rack inside, along with at least one sword and several knives, all of them sporting those faintly glowing symbols Jamie remembered from his last time on Terrarhea. Most of the guns had polished wood fittings, much like the hunting rifles Jamie was familiar with back home. However, the one which had captured Onorah's attention was something else entirely. If the distinct green and black color scheme hadn't betrayed its military origin, the short, bulky frame would have. It looked like it could have been designed by the same people who'd built those military titan-mechas. Reverently, Onorah pulled it out of the rack and extended the telescoping stock.

"I've always wanted to see one of these up close," she said. "I didn't know civilians could get them."

"Then maybe we shouldn't be messing with it," Jamie said. This is exactly what he'd feared.

"It's fine," Onorah said, still focused on the gun. Turning it over, she flipped a catch which allowed the foregrip to rotate down and release a long, cylindrical magazine. The moment it slid out, the symbols on the body of the gun, which had been glowing a dim shade of yellow, faded away completely.

"This is a high-capacity power cell," she laughed as she examined the magazine. "Look at it. It's gotta have quadruple the output of the old S2's!"

Rather than a spring-loaded box of shells, this magazine looked more like a battery, but with a row of glowing crystal contacts down the top instead of metal ones. Onorah slapped it back into the weapon and rotated the switch above the grip. "Six fire settings," she said. "Three wide-dispersion for crowd control, knocking down doors, and close-quarters combat, and three tight beam settings for long range firing. It's supposed to be effective out to almost five hundred and fifty meters."

Lifting it to her shoulder, she pointed it into the distant woods and sighted through the iron sights on top of the barrel; a barrel which wasn't hollow at all but instead looked like a capped cylinder of black metal. Onorah tapped the side of the grip above the trigger and a disk-shaped projection appeared in front of her eye. "It's even got a telescopic array. I've never seen one this clear." Before Jamie was forced to pull the weapon out of her hands to prevent her from test firing it, she lowered it of her own accord.

"Now that is a real work of art," she said.

"Onorah!" a stranger's voice called out from somewhere down below. "Are you okay? Onorah!"

Looking over the side of the titan, Jamie could see a small group of men and women, with two young boys as well, approaching from the direction of the buildings. Three of them were armed with rifles and the rest carried axes, shovels, or stout wooden clubs. Though dressed much like the citizens of Tavnic had been, their clothes were more soiled, and their expressions considerably more grim. Jamie could imagine that's exactly what a Terrarhean lynch mob looked like. And without any Wolf-Slaves left for them to take out their aggressions on, would they now turn on the only other outsider in their midst?

CHAPTER 12

"Onorah?" the man at the head of the mob called again.

After giving the gun a last, long, wistful look, Onorah returned it to the rack and closed the hatch over it. Then, over the side of the passenger compartment, she said, "I'm fine. Is everyone else okay?"

"Just a little scared is all," came the reply from below. "When we saw the shed here go up, we tried coming for you, but those critters had us boxed in good. We just hoped you'd be able to hunker down and make it through alright."

"I found a low spot in that ditch over there under some brush until it caught on fire too," Onorah said, leaning over the side and carrying on in a casual tone. Carefully, Jamie peeked over as well, mindful that he could find himself looking down the barrel of one of those guns they carried. Apart from the few who were examining the titan-mecha or had gone to check on the fire, all eyes turned on Jamie.

"And who's this then?" the man who had been speaking said. He was a bear of a man, well into his middle years and with several days of beard stubble on his face.

"This is Jamie," Onorah said. "You should be grateful he was passing by when he was. If he hadn't stopped to help, things would have been a lot worse."

With everyone now looking at Jamie, he had to fight the urge to slink back out of view. The two boys who had come with the crowd snickered loudly at the sound of Jamie's name. Meanwhile, the man who had been speaking narrowed his eyes.

"Just happened to be passing by?" he said. "That's damned convenient."

"Damned fortunate is more like it!" Onorah shot back. Climbing over the roll cage and down the side of the titan, she paused only long enough to gesture for Jamie to join her. After taking a moment to weigh his options, he followed. As little as he wanted to get involved with whoever these people were, he didn't think that hiding on top of the titan-mecha would have been a very dignified way to handle them.

"We all know there's only one reason for anyone to be out here and that's the same reason we are: this mine," the man said. "More than likely he was planning to rob us and those Wolf-Slaves just happened to beat him to the punch."

"Give it a rest, Ciante," Onorah said, hopping the last few feet down to the ground. "Not everyone who takes that road is trying to jump your claim."

The burning shed, having been reduced to nothing more than a smoldering bed of coals, no longer seemed to be in danger of setting anything else on fire so those of the group who'd been investigating, abandoned it as a complete loss and rejoined the others at the parked titan-mecha.

"Is he the Red Rogue?" one of the boys said, tugging at the hand of a woman. One of the men, a rifle propped across his shoulder, spat. Finally reaching the ground, Jamie began to regret his decision to do so.

"Hush now," the woman said, ushering the boy behind her as she tried surreptitiously to move a little farther away from Jamie herself. Jamie swept his gaze across the gathered people. While they were trying to look as if the boy's question had not unnerved them, it clearly had. Jamie wasn't even sure he could blame them. Those soldiers he'd fought had made the same assumption of him. Did Jamie and this "Red Rogue" look that similar? Or was the Red Rogue the role he was supposed to be portraying in this little fantasy production? Too bad he couldn't ask the Wolf-Slaves. They'd spoken as if they'd known him, but they'd called him Reaver. Had they meant it as a name or just a description?

"Who's the Red Rogue?" Jamie whispered to Onorah while trying to keep his eyes on the crowd.

She laughed and spoke loudly enough that everyone could hear her. "He's just some campfire story people tell to scare each other. Even though no one's ever seen him, he gets blamed for every unsolved crime from here to Carkalium."

"That's because he kills everyone who sees him," the other boy said.

"I bet he's the one who killed all them soldiers in that convoy," the first boy added enthusiastically.

"What?" Jamie said. Myth or not, the Red Rogue was apparently a bandit of some kind, but wasn't that basically the same thing as a reaver? An uneasy wave of murmurs rippled through the group as people shifted their feet. It was turning out just like last time: he showed up out of nowhere and suddenly everyone started accusing him of crimes he couldn't have possibly committed. Unless these boys were very mistaken, there was no way they could have been referring to those two military titan-mechas Jamie had accidentally destroyed; they weren't a convoy and the soldiers piloting them had both lived.

However, this world of Terrarhea clearly kept moving forward even without him in it. That had to mean it wasn't a dream. But whose life had Jamie stepped into and what became of him once Jamie took his place here? Was he now back on Earth with Derek and Alex? Had he been the same one who'd caused all Jamie's problems at school last time? Was it even possible that he really was this Red Rogue character everyone kept accusing Jamie of being?

The only upside to this current situation was that a mob of angry miners would be easier to deal with than a couple of Military titan-mechas. If he had any say in it, however, it wouldn't come to that. "What are you talking about?" Jamie said.

"The convoy robbery!" one of the men in the back said, as if that were somehow explanation enough. Jamie shrugged and looked to Onorah for help.

She sighed and shook her head, again addressing the crowd. "Come on, he hasn't even heard about the robbery. Clearly he hasn't been around here in the last couple of weeks because that's all anyone's been able to talk about since it happened." Sighing again, she paused before going on, speaking to Jamie as much as the crowd. "A couple of weeks ago, some bandits attacked a military convoy heading out from Fort Yarzak with a load of old files. They killed all the soldiers, took their gear, and then torched everything they couldn't take with them. The official inquiry said they probably mistook it for a payroll transport. Does that really sound like the sort of thing a master criminal like the Red Rogue would do? I'm telling you, he's a myth."

"He is not," the young man with a rifle propped on his shoulder said. Again, he spat. "My grandpa saw him once when he was working the Seaward Caravan route. Said it still gives him nightmares; the way that fellah moved, killing everyone in the entire convoy like he was just out for a afternoon stroll."

"Be quiet, Rorrin" the first man said. "Apparently he didn't kill everyone in that convoy if your grandpa lived to tell about it." The younger man suddenly felt the need to examine a clod of mud near his boot. "You know your grandpa likes his tall tales. Besides, he hasn't worked the Caravans in over fifty years. Unless this boy ages really well, there's no way he was around back then."

This man Onorah had called Ciante was the last one Jamie thought would speak on his behalf. Maybe he wasn't in for a fight after all.

The man continued, "I bet he's just some wannabe noble boy out on the Grand Tour who thought it would be fun to loot our mine after watching us all get killed by those filthy varmints."

"He's the one who chased the Wolf-Slaves away," Onorah said. "He fought off their leaders. I saw him do it. He saved your lives."

The man grumbled under his breath and his face contorted as if he had just smelled something bad. "No doubt looking for a reward."

"Look," Jamie said "I don't want any trouble, or a reward. I'm just passing through."

"Where're you headed?" the man said, his eyes narrowing.

That was a very good question. The last time Jamie had been on Terrarhea, the experience had only lasted part of a day. However, it seemed to have been marked by that strange nagging sensation in the back of his head. Now that he took the time to think about it, that same tension was back, only slightly less intense and not quite as noticeable, as if it were the same song being played but at a lower volume and a slower speed. He could only speculate, but if it did somehow coincide with the length of time he had to spend on this alien world, it seemed as if this trip was going to last even longer than his first. With that much time to kill, he could think of only one thing to do with it.

"I'm going to Tavnic."

"Tavnic?" the man said.

Jamie knew this place had to be Terrarhea, but he hadn't stopped to consider that he could very well be miles and miles from where he'd been last time. Tavnic could be on the other side of the planet and these people might never have even heard of it.

"It's a town on a ridge with a big wall around it and this huge tavern with lots of, um, Raven-Slaves...?"

"Raven-Slaves..." one of the other young men holding a rifle said. He sported an intricate tattoo of interlocking feathers and claws drawn in black ink that circled one of his bare forearms from elbow all the way to wrist. "Not much better than Wolf-Slaves if you ask me."

"They might clean up a little prettier, but all them damn slave races are still just animals," the man Ciante had called Rorrin said. He had a similar tattoo of a single feather and fang on the inside of his wrist, each one followed by a number of tally marks. "They sure as hell ain't human, no sir."

Ciante chuckled and shook his head. "So, what's the matter boy, can't find a willing girl who'll do it for free?" Others in the crowd chuckled as well. "I suppose your parents bought you that fancy titan-mecha there, gave you a bag of money, and just set you loose in the world to seek every manner of debauchery you can find."

"Debauchery?" Jamie said, waving his hands. "I'm not looking for any debauchery. I'm just trying to get to Tavnic."

More laughter rippled through the crowd, though Jamie wasn't entirely sure why. Staring back at them, he again had to resist the urge not to flee into the woods just as the Wolf-Slaves had done. At least it didn't look like they would be trying to lynch him anymore.

"We all know where Tavnic is," Onorah said, stepping between Jamie and the others. "I live there."

"Oh. Well. Then..."

"The road runs pretty much due north, right to Tavnic." Onorah said. Before she even began to point in that direction, Jamie looked across the fields. On the other side, through a narrow row of recently thinned trees, he could see a ribbon of light-colored gravel. "I could actually use a lift if you're headed that way."

"A lift?" Jamie said, the first thing to enter his mind being an image of him carrying her on his back as he ran down the road. Then he glanced over his shoulder at the titan-mecha and realized she expected him to be able to pilot it. She had all but seen him arrive in it after all.

"Onorah, are you sure that's a good idea?" one of the women said, casting a wary gaze at Jamie.

"With everything that's been going on lately," another woman put in, "we took a vote and decided it's just too dangerous to stay here. We're going down to Blue-Rock Outpost until things calm down." Ciante's expression soured ever further. Apparently, he'd been on the loosing side of that vote. "Why don't you come with us? It'll be safer there and we can figure out a better way to get you home."

"That's probably not a bad idea," Jamie said. He had no ill intentions toward Onorah, or anyone else, but even he had to question the sense of asking a complete stranger for a ride just so she could get home a little sooner. Besides, if she insisted on coming with him, he'd then have to explain that he didn't know the first thing about operating a titan-mecha, which would only look like some lame excuse to get out of helping her. Better if she simply gave up the idea all on her own.

"Blue-Rock is in the wrong direction," Onorah said. "And who knows when the next convoy will come through that I can book passage with. I need to get home as soon as possible, or my dad is gonna kill me. With a titan like this, Tavnic can't be more than an hour away, right?"

Jamie's mouth opened but no words came out. He didn't have any better idea of how fast the machine was than how to operate it.

"It's all a moot point unless we can get the RB-8 up and running again," Ciante said. "Without that, we won't be able to pull all the wagons. Did the Wolf-Slaves get it?"

"I don't think so," Onorah said. "And I was almost done with the repairs when they attacked so I should be able to finish up pretty quick."

"Just enough time for us to get all our essentials packed," Ciante said, turning to one of the women. "We better get started right away, Martia. We'll leave Rorrin and Darvey out here to keep an eye on things."

"Yes, that's a good idea," the woman said. She looked Jamie up and down. "In case any of those things come back."

"I wanna stay too!" one of the two boys yelled, pulling at Martia's dress.

"Yeah, me too!" the other added.

"Come on kids," Ciante said, "Back to the house. Let Onorah work."

"But I'm gonna be Onorah's apprentice when I get older!" the first boy replied. "I can give her a hand!"

Onorah kneeled next to the boy and ruffled his hair. "Don't get ahead of yourself there, Glonny. I'm just an apprentice myself. I still have to pass the licensing exams."

"Oh, you shouldn't have any problems with those stupid tests," the boy said, his expression revealing his own loathing of such things.

"But I can't take on an apprentice until I'm a real magesmith, so you better run along with your parents now."

"Okay..." he said, his whole body twisting sullenly as only the very young can do.

The group began moving off, back toward the buildings behind the berm. Though the two boys continued complaining, they too departed with the rest. Soon, only Onorah, Jamie, and the two young men with rifles remained on top of the green ridgeline.

"This shouldn't take too long," Onorah said, heading back the way she'd originally come from. "We'll be able to hit the road in no time. Do you want to give me a hand?"

Jamie glanced first at the parked titan-mecha and then at the two young men. They had apparently lost all interest in keeping an eye on anyone and had gone over to the fallen Wolf-Slave instead. If Onorah really insisted on coming with Jamie to Tavnic, he had hoped he might have an opportunity to try the machine out first before making a fool of himself in front of her, or anyone else. "I don't really know anything about...what do you need help with?"

"Some of the hatches are a little easier to remove with two people," she said.

Rorrin, the one who'd spoken earlier about the Red Rogue, kicked the Wolf-Slave in the ribs. The body quivered and rolled halfway over and then flopped back lifelessly.

"That's a big one, alright," he said to his companion.

"Definitely going in our collection," the other young man said, drawing a long knife and stooping down next to the body. He took a handful of the Wolf-Slave's matted hair and drew the blade across its forehead, slicing off a large patch of skin and hair. Maybe they had a right to blow off some steam after having nearly been killed by the Wolf-Slaves, but this was taking things too far. Jamie wanted to throw-up but found the notion in his brain completely unsupported by the sensations in his body. Was he really so cold that these sorts of things didn't affect him the way they should have any normal human being?

"Maybe I will give you a hand," Jamie said, following after Onorah. The two young men remained behind, repeatedly sticking their knives into the dead Wolf-Slave and hooting with joy each time.

CHAPTER 13

Behind the remains of the burned shed, the land dropped down to the level of the fields. A narrow foot path had been cut into the side of the short incline and was lined on either side by wild shrubs and weedy trees which grew continually thicker the lower Onorah and Jamie went.

"Sorry about that," Onorah said once they were out of earshot. "The people out here don't always take too kindly to strangers. A lot of time you can't blame them. This is a big territory and not very populated. The military can't be everywhere all the time. And now all this bandit nonsense has gotten everyone on edge too."

"They seem to like you well enough."

"When your wardcaster breaks down out here, we're the only magesmiths around for miles," Onorah said, her voice swelling with pride. "Well, except for the army magesmiths stationed at Jarzak, of course, but they don't make house calls for civilians."

"And you're a magesmith...apprentice?" Jamie said as he pushed a thorned branch out of his way. Without revealing his own ignorance, he could only speculate that a magesmith was a mechanic of some kind. Onorah couldn't have been much older than Jamie himself, but here on Terrarhea, people apparently grew up quickly. "Did you come out here on your own?"

"Yeah, this was a pretty simple job. And with luck, I'll only be an apprentice for another six months."

"Is that when you take those exams you mentioned?"

"Yeah, I've been studying like crazy for nearly a year now. Coming out on field calls like this is about the only free time I have anymore." She smiled at Jamie over her shoulder. "Fortunately, Ciante is pretty rough with his equipment so I always have plenty of opportunities."

Near the bottom of the incline, they came to a small gully which cut into the side of the ridge. There, the brush had mostly burned, but much like the shed above, only a few stray licks of flame remained.

"That's where I was hiding," Onorah said as they walked past. "It was nothing but bramble bushes so I figured even those Wolf-Slaves might not want to take too close a look at it. But then one of the walls of the shed collapsed into the head of the ravine and everything caught fire."

At the very bottom of the path, they continued along the edge of the field, which Jamie could now see wasn't plowed at all, but instead had been churned up as if by some gigantic machine, leaving nothing behind but an uneven landscape of mud clods and small boulders interspersed with muddy pits half-filled with water. With the addition of a little barbed wire, it wouldn't look much different from pictures Jamie had seen of World War One battlefields.

"You said this is a mine?"

"They're looking for resonator crystals," Onorah said. "Ciante's been scrounging together cash for operations like this for years. Every time he starts a new one, he's certain he's going to hit it rich but only ever ends up making enough money to finance his next attempt. This time he decided to go farther out into the wilderness. I guess the Wolf-Slaves didn't like that. Things had actually been looking up for him before all this happened."

Behind them, at the top of the ridge, Jamie could still hear the two young men cackling sadistically. If Ciante and his people had been treating the Wolf-Slaves like that from the beginning, maybe the creatures weren't completely unjustified in trying to drive the miners out.

Ahead stood an open-fronted lean-to which had been dug out of the side of the ridge. The roof was built of heavy timbers and the three rear walls consisted of tightly stacked field stone. A couple of shelves heaped with random pieces of junk lined the back wall and in the very center of the shed, taking up the majority of the space, stood a hunched-over, robotic machine not all that different from those small ones Jamie had seen wrestling outside of Tavnic.

"Well, time to get started," Onorah said, going over to a large, wooden toolbox near the machine's feet. It stood taller than it was deep and had a stack of various sized drawers down the side. She went through these, pulling out a diverse range of tools which she set aside in a neat pile. An assortment of hammers, pry bars, and pliers were easy enough to identify but most of the others remained a mystery to Jamie. The sheer variety alone was baffling, and all appeared to have been handmade. Some looked heavy enough to work iron in a forge while others were so delicate they would not have been out of place on the work bench of a jeweler or watch smith.

The last tool Onorah selected looked like nothing more than a tiny glass orb about the size of a shooter marble, but when she shook it back and forth a few times, it began to glow with a brilliant white light. That's when Jamie realized it was just like the streetlights he'd seen in Tavnic, complete with a shard of floating crystal in the very center, only much smaller.

Onorah proceeded to make a pinching motion with her fingers behind the sphere which caused the light to focus itself into a fine beam. After shaking it again, this time up and down, she touched it to the side of her forehead, moved it a few inches away, and then let go. Instead of falling, it remained floating in midair right where she'd left it, moving in response to her motions as if connected to the side of her head by some invisible rod.

"What?" Onorah said, catching sight of Jamie's puzzled expression. When she turned to address him, the beam followed her gaze and flashed across his eyes. "Sorry about that." She tapped the top of the sphere which dimmed the beam.

"What does...how does it do that?" Jamie said and pointed at the tiny sphere before even realizing that to question something that was clearly commonplace here would only reveal him as even more of an outsider than he was already.

"Yeah, it is pretty neat for a mini gloworb, isn't it?" Onorah said, missing, or perhaps choosing to ignore, the actual point of Jamie's question. "It took me a long time to figure out how to squeeze this many wards into one this small, but it was worth it."

"You mean, you built it yourself?"

"Yeah, designing my own wardcasters is way more fun than repairing other people's half-assed designs, but you gotta pay the bills, right?" Onorah gestured to the mecha. "Take this one, for example. Whoever built it was barely a magesmith if you ask me. I've lost track of how many times I've had to get it up and running again. One little thing gets out of balance and the whole thing goes offline. I keep telling Ciante he needs to buy a real harvester instead of trying to make do with this old vulcan-mecha but clearly, it was the cheapest thing he could get his hands on. I think I've narrowed down the current problem to a power imbalance in the secondary ward matrix. If it's anything more than that, I'll have to get it shipped back to Tavnic so I can work on it in the shop. We'll need to get the lower access panel off before I can know for sure though, and to do that, we'll have to remove the power cell and hook up a set of relays. Are you ready?"

"Uh, sure." Jamie could only hope he'd learn something about what Onorah was doing here, because so far, he had no idea what she was talking about.

The power cell she'd mentioned proved to be a metal box about the size of a large fish tank, secured to the back of the machine by a series of heavy steel latches. It was a good thing Jamie was along to help because he couldn't imagine Onorah being able to lower something that heavy to the ground all by herself. The inside surface of the power cell had two rows of crystal contact points which aligned with a corresponding set built into the machine. In principle, it didn't look all that different from the magazine Onorah had taken out of the gun they'd found in the titan-mecha.

Once they'd gotten the power cell out of the way and removed a square plate of metal from the back of its mounting bracket, Onorah took a matched pair of crystal-studded devices out of her toolbox and placed one over the crystals on the power cell and the other over the ones in the machine. She hadn't done anything to fix either one in place that Jamie could see, but after giving them a tug which proved they were both locked on quite securely, she tapped several smaller crystals on top in a seemingly random sequence. Though nothing connected the two devices, their crystals began to glow and pulse soothingly in perfect synchronization. The many symbols and shapes that covered both the robotic machine and the power cell, which had looked like nothing more than etched patterns in the metal up to this point, now began to glow with a faint orange light as well.

Simultaneously, the robot lurched slightly. Jamie could see right away what had caused it. While sitting idle, the loose-fitting disks of interlocking steel which comprised the majority of its joints had been hanging slackly from each other, but as soon as Onorah applied power, the opposite halves of each joint separated from the other, leaving nothing but a few millimeters of empty space between them, as if held equidistant by magnets. Jamie took a step back, his eyes wide as he tried to make sense of it all.

Nonplused, Onorah reached through the pilot's roll cage and wiggled the joystick on the left armrest. The low whine emanating from deep inside the machine's inner workings rose in pitch slightly but then returned to its previous level when she released the controller. Frowning, she tapped her gloworb again, cycling through a number of different brightness until finally settling on one in particular. "Now the fun part begins," she said and climbed through the access port they'd opened. She got in no farther than her waist and then had to twist around before working her way inside by inches until she was finally sitting on the lower edge of the port with her legs dangling outside.

Where Jamie might have expected the interior of the machine to contain engines, gears, and pistons, it had instead been built from a clockwork assemblage of glowing crystals, metal rods, and other unidentifiable pieces, none of which seemed to have any bearing on the operation of the machine at all. With all that nonsense cluttering the inside, there wasn't much room left for Onorah to move around, but she'd positioned herself so that her arms were overhead and she could just barely reach some intricate arrangement of brass hoops which held what looked like small pieces of red quartz.

After watching her work for a while and handing her tools as she asked for them by description rather than name, Jamie only grew more confused. Often muttering and cursing to herself, Onorah wriggled and twisted from one area to the next, seemingly at random; waving her hands over glowing crystals or using the various tools in her kit to bend and tweak their encompassing metal frames by degrees, first one way and then back the other. Occasionally, something she would do caused the glowing symbols to shudder or fade, but another quick adjustment would bring them back to full intensity. Eventually, Jamie began to wonder if she really knew what she was doing at all.

"No that's not it either!" Onorah eventually said, pounding on a glowing crystal with her fist. "Damn piece of Wind-Hammer junk!"

When Jamie took the time to examine the vulcan-mecha, he quickly realized how little sense any part of it made to him. For instance, how could instructions from the controls in the pilot's compartment be relayed to a point as distant as the machine's hands with all those weird, floating hinges interrupting the path at every joint? There wasn't a wire, tube, or hose that he could see which bridged across a single one of those gaps. Stranger still, there weren't any gears, cables, or pistons to make any of those joints move, either.

"What exactly are you doing?" Jamie said.

"I'm trying to adjust the matrix of this ward array," Onorah said, her voice muffled from inside the machine as she strained to reach some distant component. "There's something in here that's throwing off the alignment of all the other arrays that connect to it, creating a catastrophic imbalance in the overall distribution ward."

"I don't get it," Jamie said. He'd had enough of trying to bluff his way through this. If he was forced to watch Onorah much longer, he thought he might end up going just as crazy as she was starting to seem.

Onorah slumped down as much as her confines would allow and sighed. Craning her neck so that she could look at Jamie through the hatch, she said, "Sorry. Being around this stuff all the time, I forget that most people use wardcasters everyday without stopping to think about how they actually work."

"That's okay." Jamie looked up at the machine and then back to Onorah. If he was going to be stuck on Terrarhea for any length of time, he might as well figure out how this technology of theirs worked. And here, right in front of him, was an energetic young apprentice magesmith who had just given him an opening to be as ignorant about the topic as he wished to be. "Actually, I wouldn't mind hearing more about it."

"Really?" With a renewed sense of calm, Onorah began looking around at all the intricate assemblies surrounding her. "First, we have to start with the flows of magic."

"Magic?" Jamie said. Onorah seemed too intelligent to be so naïve about something like that. Maybe Jamie should have given more serious thought to the state of her sanity from the beginning.

"EEPs if you want to get technical, but it's still magic no matter what you call it." Her voice became distant as she traced something along the inside of the machine with the tip of her finger. "Esoteric Energy Particles are a universal power source that permeate all of existence and defy all physical laws. At background levels, they aren't concentrated enough to do much with, but they're stronger in some places than in others. Certain types of objects can also interact with them. Living things are a good one but resonators are even better. Their unique crystalline structures are especially sensitive to ambient magical energies."

As she continued speaking, she twisted in order to follow whatever it was she was examining. "By configuring multiple resonators into a matrix, we can trap that energy, which is how we make power cells. When we direct that energy into another object, we can focus and realign it by using strategically placed resonators and regulating spells that we bind to the object. These are known as wards, or magescript, and we can use them to make the magic do just about anything we want, so long as we know the right ways to manipulate it. If we do everything right, the power flows through the wards and casts the desired effect when it's activated. Thus: a wardcaster."

Jamie wasn't sure he was ready to buy all this talk of resonator crystals and magescript, but Onorah sure seemed to believe it. And after everything he'd seen, maybe magic was the only way to explain all these strange Terrarhean devices.

"Okay, maybe that makes sense for a...a blaster rifle, but why use it for everything else too? Wouldn't regular machines that use gears and springs and batteries be a lot less complicated?"

"Basic engineering principles have their place but they're not very efficient. All they do is take stored energy and redirect it through some overly complicated series of moving parts to do work. You waste more energy collecting it than you get out of it and then you waste even more energy converting it into something else. Wards skip all those middle steps and directly alter the physical relationships and forms of both matter and energy at a near one-hundred-percent efficiency."

Onorah stopped at one of the glowing symbols and tapped it thoughtfully with her finger. "However, that is just theoretical. No matter how pure your materials are and how exact you are with the construction, each piece is always going to be unique and will need to be individually tuned so that it will work in tandem with all the other binding materials and resonators. Even if you have two identical wardcasters that do the exact same thing, the magescript will always be unique to each one. The more time you spend tuning a wardcaster, the more efficient it will be, but also more expensive, or course."

"That almost sounds like something you read in a book."

"Sorry. With my exams coming up, it seems like I've been doing nothing but reading books," Onorah admitted with a laugh.

"It must take a lot of studying to become a magesmith."

"That, and hands-on experience. But if you don't have the gift, neither of those will do you any good. Could you hand me those big brass tongs and the little pry bar with a handle and a split end?"

Jamie scanned over the collection of tools and selected the two which most closely matched Onorah's description. After another seemingly random series of adjustments, Onorah sat back and eyed her handiwork. "Could you try the stick again?"

"Um...oh, right." Jamie went around to the front of the machine and gingerly moved the same control Onorah had tried earlier. Again, the whine from inside the machine increased, but this time the vulcan-mecha's left arm shot forward, passing close enough to Jamie that the breeze created by its speeding fist ruffled his hair.

"Careful!" Onorah called out. "We just needed to see if it worked."

"I think it does," Jamie said, very slowly returning the controller to its original position and keeping a close eye on the arm as it lowered back into place accordingly. By the time he returned to the back of the machine, Onorah had already extracted herself from the interior and was starting to fit the access panel back into place.

"Thanks for the help," she said. "That went a lot faster with an extra pair of hands." After the two of them had gathered up all the tools, Onorah paused and looked at Jamie with a serious expression. "Just out of curiosity, were you ever tested?"

"For what?"

"For the gift."

"The what?"

"I'll take that as a 'no'," Onorah said with a chuckle as she stood and went back to the toolbox. Before placing each tool back into its proper drawer, she was very careful to wipe away any grease or other dirt with a rag. Since she seemed to be very particular about where each one went, Jamie merely handed them to her one-by-one so that she could put them away herself. As they worked at this, Onorah continued with her explanation, "Wardcasters can only be created through an intuitive understanding of how the energy will flow through the different materials and how it will be influenced by the wards. It's literally something you're either born with or you're not. If you don't have the gift, there aren't any diagrams or instruments that you could ever use to build, or even repair, a wardcaster."

Much like Terrarhea's casual acceptance of slavery, this aspect of their society also came as something of a shock to Jamie. When nearly everyone on Terrarhea was reliant on wardcasters for their livelihoods, and potentially their very survival, it seemed almost underhanded to force them to use the elite services of magesmiths in this way.

"Only about one person in a thousand has the gift," Onorah continued, "and about half of those only have enough potential to sort resonator crystals. The other half need to be trained from a young age to ever have any chance of becoming a magesmith. If you're never tested, you can go through your entire life without realizing you have the gift. That's why most countries have some kind of procedure to test as many of their kids as possible in order to find the best candidates. Unfortunately, it's a lot more common for people to slip through the cracks than you might think."

"Yeah, that's probably what happened to me then," Jamie said, desperate to seize any thread that would allow him to explain away his ignorance.

"Were you ever curious?" Onorah said, her eyes narrowing. "If you wanted to, we could do an unofficial little test right here."

With government agencies searching for magesmith candidates, the last thing Jamie wanted was to find himself on anyone's radar for anything more than he already was. He held up his hands and tried voicing his objection but Onorah had already grabbed a large, rusty can from one of the shelves in the back of the lean-to and begun to pick up small pieces of gravel from the ground and put them into it.

"What if someone doesn't want to become a magesmith?"

"No one's obligated to do anything with the gift if they don't want to. This is still a free country after all. Besides, you don't have anything to worry about, even if you do have the gift. You're already too old to start training. Little Glonny out there *has* the gift and he's probably already too old. Unless you're raised with the training, you'll likely never be able to do much with it at all."

"Oh, good," Jamie said. "I mean, that's good to know."

Onorah now had the entire bottom of the can filled with small stones, all roughly the same size and shape. "These are all ordinary stones." She then held up another which didn't look any different from the rest. "This one is a resonator, low grade, yes, but still a resonator. It would need to be cut and polished to be of any use in a wardcaster, but even like this, someone with the gift should be able to tell it apart." She tossed it in with the others and gave the can several good shakes before holding it out in front of Jamie. "Now, without looking, reach in and pick out the resonator."

Jamie laughed and shook his head. Despite Onorah's apparent sincerity, something in the back of his mind insisted she was only leading him along so she could have a good laugh at his expense. He began to reach for the can but stopped short. "What's it supposed to feel like?"

"You'll know it when you feel it." Onorah gave the can another shake and smiled. "Don't worry, it doesn't hurt."

"I didn't think it would," Jamie said, putting his hand into the can. At least, he hadn't until Onorah had mentioned it. Casting his eyes toward the ceiling, Jamie ran his fingers through the stones in the bottom of the can. Some were rough, others smooth, but he was pretty sure that was not what Onorah meant by being able to feel a difference. Back and forth he went, and then stirred them all several times. Apparently, he didn't have the gift because they all just felt like rocks, nothing more and nothing less. He was just about to tell this to Onorah when the tip of his finger brushed against one of the stones and he froze. It had to have been his imagination. That particular stone still felt slightly rough and gritty against his fingertip but what he'd felt hadn't been a physical sensation at all.

The corner of Onorah's lip twitched with an expectant smile. Jamie forced his own expression as flat as possible, regardless of how quickly his thoughts were suddenly rushing. It had to be some kind of trick. Slowly, he raked his fingertips through the stones once more only to find his hand stopping in the same place, resting against what he somehow knew was the same stone as before.

Without removing it from the can, he picked it up and rolled it between his fingers. He couldn't even begin to wrap his mind around the sensation of it. Unbidden, the idea of a sixth sense flashed into his mind and once there, could not be pushed aside. This really was like having a completely new sense, entirely different from the other five. And how could one even begin to explain sight to the blind or sound to the deaf?

"Anything?" Onorah asked, clearly suspecting she already knew.

Jamie dropped the stone back in with the others and ran his fingers through them again, feeling that one unique stone brush past the edge of his fingers for the last time. At random, he grabbed another stone and pulled it out of the can. Onorah's smile disappeared the moment she saw it and then turned into a frown when Jamie set it in her outstretched hand.

"How'd I do?" Jamie didn't have any difficulty faking a look of chagrin.

Onorah pursed her lips and then poured the stones back onto the ground. "Oh well," she said, dusting off her hands. "You might not have the gift but at least you still make a pretty decent shop hand. I guess you can't be good at everything."

Jamie laughed. "What do you mean by that? I'm not good at much of anything."

"You can obviously handle yourself in a fight."

"That was luck."

"Well then, between that and winning a titan-mecha in a card game, you're damn lucky. And you're not that bad looking either."

Having just started to refute Onorah's belief in Jamie's luck, he choked on his own words when she made her second claim. Back on Earth, girls never said things like that to him. The fight with the Wolf-Slaves had clearly given her an idealized impression of him, one far removed from reality. Either that or she really was completely crazy.

Footsteps from outside the lean-to saved Jamie from having to respond.

"Hey, Onorah," Rorrin said, his friend, Darvey, a short distance behind with a bloody chunk of fur and skin tied to the end of his rifle. "How much longer?"

"We're all wrapped up here," she said. "Should be ready to go."

"Great!" Darvey said, rushing forward and tossing his rifle to Rorrin. "I'll take it over to the compound."

Rorrin, who hadn't been expecting the rifle, nearly dropped both his own and Darvey's. "You always get to pilot. Let me have a go!"

"I already called it," Darvey said as he raised the roll cage out of the way. "You shoulda been faster."

"We better put the power-cell back in first," Onorah said. "You wouldn't get very far only connected with my relays."

Rorrin and Darvey both shared a suspicious look with the other, as if unwilling to help for fear that one or the other might lose his chance to operate the machine. Grudgingly, they both set their rifles aside and helped lift the power cell into the back of the vulcan-mecha. Jamie could have done it himself but made a good show of looking just as weak as the others. Once finished, Onorah came alongside Jamie, wiping her hands on a soiled rag.

"I have to run over to the compound and check on their other vulcan," she said. "Could you take my tools up to your titan?"

"Are you really sure you don't want to go with them?" Jamie said. In front of the vulcan-mecha, the two young men had begun arguing once more over who should have the right to pilot the newly repaired machine. "You know, I haven't had a lot of practice with that titan yet." Or any at all.

"I just want to get home. I don't care if the ride is a little rough. Can't you help me out here?"

"Okay, I guess if you really don't mind."

"Great! I'll meet you up there in a little bit." With that, she turned and jogged off toward the buildings in the distance. As she passed Rorrin and Darvey, she called out, "Would you two cut it out already and just get it done?"

"Yeah, okay, fine," Darvey admitted sullenly. After some more back-and-forth between the two young men, they began a spirited game of rock-paper-scissors to settle their argument. Now all Jamie needed to do was figure out how to pilot his own machine. Although, if these two knew how to operate one, how hard could it be?

CHAPTER 14

Onorah's toolbox was outfitted with a handle on top and a pair of large wheels on the bottom which handled the rough terrain well, though anyone with less strength than Jamie might have had trouble pulling it up that narrow path. The grassy meadow atop the ridge, torn and matted from machinery and foot traffic showed few signs of the fight which had taken place there just a short time ago. A few stray specks of blood where the Wolf-Slave had fallen were all that remained. Darvey and Rorrin must have disposed of its body after having had their fun with it. A shifting breeze brought the smell of burning hair and roasting meat to Jamie's nose and he suddenly realized what they'd done with the body. He hurried past the burnt-out building without looking into the bed of coals inside the foundation and made his way to the titan-mecha which everyone insisted belonged to him.

He stopped several paces back and stared up at it. It was a lot bigger than that vulcan-mecha. An accident in this thing could easily kill someone, not the least of which being himself or his passenger. Would it be too late to come clean and tell Onorah that he didn't know how to pilot it? Maybe he could just let her drive. She'd probably enjoy that. But then what was Jamie to do if he had to leave Tavnic with it later? Better to try his hand at it here without anyone around to see him fail.

Jamie rolled the tool box a little farther away and then walked up to the open pilot's compartment. With the way the various segments of the seat were currently arranged, it looked something like an overly complicated bear trap. When he stepped into it, he wouldn't quite be sitting but rather standing nearly upright. Jamie took a final deep breath and backed into the chair, placing his feet into the metal waldos at the base. They fit his boots perfectly, and as he leaned back into the worn leather cushions that covered the rest of the seat, his body fell into each depression and contour as if it had been made specifically for him and no one else.

Apart from the puck-like joysticks at the end of each armrest, he could see no controls, switches or monitors, either of the sort he was familiar with back home or of the style he'd seen in similar Terrarhean machines. If he couldn't even find an 'on' switch, this whole experiment was going to be short-lived. His hands fell over the control pucks easily and his fingers slipped right into the molded recesses, discovering an intricate, multi-part switch under each finger. He didn't even have a chance to test any of them because at the very moment he gripped the pucks, a low whine began to emanate from deep within the body of the machine. It built quickly to a steady hum and Jamie could feel the machine come to life around him. On some intuitive level he couldn't even begin to understand, he knew that this entire contraption was now awaiting his commands.

"Whoa." He jerked his hands away from the pucks and the noise instantly dropped away and stopped, leaving the machine inert once more. That had felt nearly as strange as being able to sense a resonator stone, as if the machine had become a giant extension of his own body while he'd been in contact with the controls.

Haltingly, he placed his hands over the pucks once more and again the machine powered up, eager to carry out his wishes. Now, if he could just get the seat into the machine, he might actually have a chance of figuring out the rest. Rocking the pucks first one way and then the other did nothing until he pulled them both rearward at the same time. That caused the seat to retract smoothly on its rails and Jamie tensed as he passed through the open hatch, looking about expectantly to ensure he wasn't crushed against the inside of the cockpit during his ascent.

As it lifted him into the machine, the segments of the seat began to readjust themselves and padded clamps snapped snuggly into place over his legs and torso, keeping him well-restrained but not trapped. The moment his feet cleared the front hatch, a pair of thick metal plates slid shut with a clang. The feeling of claustrophobia would have been overpowering if not for the open roll cage above. When the seat finally came to a stop, Jamie found himself sitting in a comfortable recline with his head and shoulders just barely sticking out above the top of the machine's hull.

Once the rails latched firmly into place, the various segments of the seat unlocked, each one floating freely of the others and giving Jamie the impression that he was floating. The joints of the machine also unlocked and the entire titan-mecha began to sway lightly. A sense of vertigo shot through him, and bound into the machine as he was, Jamie quickly realized that the seat was using his movements to direct those of the titan-mecha.

He let out a surprised chuckle. Maybe this wouldn't be so hard after all. In fact, surrounded by several tons of compliant steel, he felt invulnerable. Now he wanted to try this thing out more than ever.

Gingerly, Jamie straightened his legs in a manner he hoped would cause the titan-mecha to rise out of its current crouched stance. The drone from the power plant grew louder and the sound of whining joints filled the cabin as the entire machine lurched upright, its torso rotating backward until Jamie could see nothing but blue sky through the roll cage. He jerked his legs to counterbalance the titan-mecha's movement and to keep it from going over onto its back, but that only sent him falling forward. The ground plummeted back into sight and rushed forward to meet him.

Muttering incoherently through clenched teeth, Jamie mashed at the control pucks. Without any other controls to be seen, they had to manipulate the machine's hands and arms. Both limbs did, indeed, shoot forward, proving his theory correct, but he still had no clear understanding of how the controls manipulated them. Stiffly, the arms wedged themselves between the falling machine and the unyielding ground with a bone-jarring crash. If Jamie hadn't been secured within his seat, he would have been thrown right through the front roll cage. As it was, he nearly bit off his tongue.

Maybe this wasn't going to be so easy after all. At least the machine didn't power down when Jamie peeled his hands off the control pucks. And as disastrous as that had been, his first attempt to pilot the machine had proven quite enlightening. He was almost certain that if he was just a bit more gentle with the controls, he would have better luck.

Through tiny, incremental motions of both his legs and the pucks, Jamie worked the machine back until it was balanced on its feet once more. Before going any further, he paused and took several deep breaths.

Again, he eased the machine upward. Rather than panicking when the cockpit rotated forward, he merely gave the controls a subtle nudge and the machine righted itself. Still, he only allowed himself to breathe again once the machine had finally risen to its full standing height of nearly twenty-five feet, with him at the very top. The segments of the seat now moved in time to the swaying of the machine, subtly providing Jamie with feedback to keep everything balanced.

It was with only a little trepidation that Jaime took his first step. The machine's weight shifted to the left and he felt like he was falling for a brief moment before the right foot swung forward to catch the entire machine with a soft yielding of joints that turned what could have been a crash into nothing more than a shudder. Now in motion, Jamie quickly brought the left foot forward.

This time, he laughed at the top of his lungs. Piloting the titan-mecha was less like driving a car and more like riding a horse. His movements only provided the initial nudge to get things started. After that, the machine interpolated exactly what he wanted to do and took care of the finer points itself. Trying to use it like a giant puppet only confused the system. It actually couldn't have been any easier. And when Jamie considered just how difficult so many aspects of his life had recently become, he couldn't help but laugh.

The machine stumbled when Jamie stopped its forward advance, but he managed to keep it from falling completely. Rotating the titan-mecha's feet, Jamie turned to the left and next set off down the length of the grassy ridge. He experimented with making the machine turn while in motion and different ways of getting it to stop and start. Several of the small trees lost branches when he misjudged distances but for the most part, piloting the machine felt like second nature to him. Getting the arms and hands to work with any degree of finesse took a bit more effort, but it wasn't long before he was picking up fallen tree trunks and snapping them in half with a simple twist of the controls. It was actually kind of fun.

So engrossed with the machine, Jamie didn't even realize Onorah had returned until she called out to him. "Not bad! Are you sure you just got that thing?"

Jamie turned the machine and took a few steps in her direction. "Thanks, but this thing makes it look easy."

"You'll have to let me give it a try sometime," Onorah called back. "The others are starting to head out. We can go whenever you're ready."

No matter how confident Jamie had become with the titan-mecha, he remained extra cautious when lowering the machine's palm to the ground for Onorah to climb onto with her tool box, and even more so when he lifted her up to the passenger's compartment. When she finally hopped down into the depression on the machine's back, he breathed a small sigh of relief. Onorah secured the toolbox to the side of the compartment with a few straps and then stood leaning against the front roll cage directly behind Jamie.

"All good to go back here," she said, the excitement thick in her voice.

"Okay, here we go," Jamie whispered as he eased the machine forward. Having just learned how to operate it and never having had a passenger before, he sure hoped this was safe. Of course, whoever put that seat back there must have know what they were doing.

Regardless of what he tried to tell himself, Jamie felt his composure evaporate as the titan approached the edge of the ridge and he lost sight of the ground in front of him. Onorah let out an expectant cry like one might at the peek of a roller coaster. It quickly turned into an ear-splitting sheik of joy as they dropped over the edge and began barreling down the side of the ridge. Teeth bared and eyes wide,

Jamie didn't share her enthusiasm, though he did add his own cry to hers. So far, all his practice had been on level ground. Now he suddenly needed to learn all the nuances of keeping the machine balanced on a downward slope while dodging the trees which kept jumping into his path. The titan also gained speed quickly with so much mass behind it. By the time they neared the bottom, it felt like they had to be moving as quickly as any speeding automobile.

Jamie jerked at the controls to avoid a final tree that stood alone at the edge of the fields where the ground leveled off once more. The titan shifted violently to the left but its right arm still glanced off the tree's trunk, sending the machine pirouetting around it and forcing Jamie to frantically compensate. Several steps into the barren field, he brought the machine to a plodding walk and looked back at the ridge. From down here, it didn't look nearly as steep or as tall as it had just felt. Onorah laughed loudly and slapped her open palm against the titan's hull.

"That was great!" she said. "Don't stop now!"

If only she knew how close she'd just come to dying, she probably would have been begging him to leave her with Ciante and his fellow miners rather than urging him on. Jamie could see the small caravan of vulcan-mechas and wagons leaving the berm and so he angled in their direction, hoping that Onorah might still change her mind and save him from the guilt of accidentally maiming her.

The uneven mud and boulders of the fields were little hindrance to the titan-mecha as Jamie piloted it toward the distant road Onorah had pointed out earlier. They arrived just as the last of the miners had assembled there as well. Their two vulcan-mechas each pulled a large wagon laden with supplies and the miners themselves. Apparently none of them would be walking but it would still be a slow trip. Everyone was stationed at the edges of the wagons, keeping a close eye on the surrounding woods. If those Wolf-Slaves decided to attack them while they were still on the road, Jamie doubted it would end well for any of the miners.

"Before we head to Tavnic," Jamie said, "should we maybe go with them, just to make sure they make it okay?"

"We'll be just fine on our own," Ciante called out from the nearest wagon. "But if anything happens to Onorah, we'll have your head!"

"Why don't you just make sure Emlee doesn't redline that old T-72 again," Onorah replied good-naturedly. "But I'm sure I'll be seeing you all soon enough. Be careful out there. My dad'll send you the bill."

"I should send this young fool a bill for that mess his titan-mecha made of my fields," Ciante muttered in a voice Jamie was obviously not meant to hear. Even though he failed to see how a few footprints, albeit giant ones, could have done much damage to what was essentially a torn up patch of dirt, Jamie chose not to make an issue of it and merely watched as the caravan of miners got underway, heading south.

In the other direction, the road wound its way through the forest roughly due north. The thick vegetation had been cut back far on each side, leaving that beige ribbon of gravel open to the hazy blue sky above. The road surface was relatively level and wide enough to accommodate at least two machines the size of Jamie's titan-mecha side-by-side.

"Now let's see what this titan of yours can really do," Onorah said, leaning down through the roll cage so her face was near Jamie's. "I bet this thing can make Tavnic in under an hour."

Jamie started slowly, walking at a comfortable pace and gradually increasing the speed until he had to shift the machine's cadence to one more suitable for running. His first few steps like that shook the machine, not all that badly, but certainly with enough force that an entire journey undertaken in that manner would have been incredibly uncomfortable. Without the benefit of being strapped-in and isolated from the jarring by an articulated seat as Jamie was, Onorah had to hold on tight to keep from being rattled right out the back. Fortunately, she didn't question his skill as a pilot before he figured out that the trick was to establish a gliding sort of stride that smoothed out the footfalls into little more than a profound rocking motion. Clearly finding that much more tolerable, Onorah threw both her hands skyward and cried out as her long sandy hair streamed out behind her.

They were moving quickly now, maybe not quite as fast as a car on a highway, but certainly faster than any ordinary car could have handled this particular road, and certainly more smoothly. The titan easily stepped right over potholes and washouts without needing to break its stride. Even on those few occasions when Jamie misjudged his step and did hit such an obstacle, the titan's legs compensated by absorbing the majority of the shock in the length of their travel.

The road slowly began veering to the west and eventually ended at an intersection with a nearly identical road running north-south once more. Onorah indicated a right turn and Jamie set off again. From that point on, the unbroken walls of green forest on either side of the road would sporadically break open to reveal tiny homesteads that had been carved out of the wilderness. However, all signs of human

1 1 5

habitation, including the road on which they traveled, looked tentative at best, as if the trees had only been beaten back temporarily and would rush in to reclaim what had been taken from them the moment someone stopped maintaining these token vestiges of civilization. Most of the farmers working the land at these farms took notice of Jamie only incidentally, looking up as the titan passed and then returning to their labors.

The morning mists had burned off by then, leaving behind a thick haze which turned the sun into an indistinct orb as it climbed behind the clouds. The temperature was also rising, and the only breezes were those created by the forward motion of the titan-mecha. It wasn't long until Onorah grew complacent with the simple exhilaration of speed and sat down on the floor of the passenger compartment so that she could lean forward and talk without needing to shout too loudly over the rush of the wind.

"So, are you on the Grand Tour?" she said.

Did she mean like back in old days when rich young people went touring around Europe on extended holiday? It might be a good cover, but he didn't know exactly what it might entail. "Not really," Jamie said. "Just kind of…traveling, I guess."

"No, I didn't really take you for the type. Their kind usually come through with a bit more…flamboyance: fancy clothes, lots of money, big talk, you know?"

"Sorry to disappoint."

Onorah laughed and slapped Jamie on the shoulder. "I personally think a custom titan-mecha is way more impressive than all that; even if it is a little beat up. You know, I could tune it up for you if you'd like; buff out all those scratches, maybe even figure out a way to incorporate some anti-corrosion wards to keep it from rusting. It's weird that it doesn't have any. They're usually standard on most mechas."

"Really," Jamie said, content to simply let her ramble rather than having to come up with new ways to evade her questions.

"In fact, I don't see any external magescript. That's really weird."

"Weird? Why's that weird?"

"Keeping it all internal is expensive as hell. Usually only elite military units bother with that. Most military doctrines actually consider the magescript to be an intimidation tactic. If they really need stealth, they just cover it with a cloak."

Jamie supposed it wasn't much different than the bright colored uniforms worn by soldiers back in the eighteen-hundreds. In fact, he could well imagine how unnerving it would be to have a whole team of soldiers with their faintly glowing equipment steadily advancing on his position in the dead of night.

"I suppose whoever built this one must have been a rich, trophy hunter," Onorah said. "I've heard some of them do that. Most people don't use titan-mechas for hunting though."

Unless it was commissioned by a notorious bandit, someone like the Red Rogue, who wanted to be able to sneak up on his own prey without being seen.

"Although even just a new paintjob would certainly spruce things up," Onorah said. "I'm thinking completely black except for a red stripe down each side and some silver gilding here around the cockpit."

"That would...certainly make it stand out in a crowd." Which was probably the last thing Jamie needed at the moment.

"Come on, you can't go wrong with a little gilding!" Onorah said, sharing a laugh with Jamie. "Finttiranos has the best magesmiths anywhere but all the new designs we're putting out these days just don't have the same flare as the classics. Sceotia's stuff might be absolute crap, but at least their designs still have some style. I'd love to be able to build a titan of my own design someday. "

"Not a lot of demand for titan-mechas in Tavnic?"

"Not these days," Onorah said, "but did you know Tavnic used to be a magesmith town? Back then, it was known as Golonque and it was one of Badooria's main military manufacturing centers: five hundred magesmith families all living in those walls, building wardcasters for the Badoorian army. They turned out a lot of titan-mechas during the war against Finttiranos."

She sounded wistful about it, as if it were less like a slave labor camp and more like some romanticized version of those factory towns from back during the industrial revolution. "What happened to them?"

"After Badooria was annexed, all the magesmiths were reassigned to Finttiranos magesmith towns and Tavnic was repurposed as a wilderness outpost." When Onorah said 'annexed' and 'reassigned', Jamie was pretty sure she actually meant 'conquered', and 'forcibly relocated'. "The walls and the sewer system are about the only things left from back in those days."

If magesmiths were really as rare as Onorah said, it made sense that a government would want to protect them, especially the ones building their weapons. That was probably also the reason a whole town full of them would be located in the middle of nowhere. Jamie had always thought the walls to be a bit oversized for a small village with the limited strategic importance of Tavnic. However, with bandits in the countryside and every building he saw looking like it was on the verge of being absorbed by the wilderness, Jamie couldn't shake the feeling that these were also signs of a once grand society now on the decline.

"A while back someone published a guidebook that mentioned Tavnic in a footnote about the Badoorian War," Onorah said. "Every year since then, a few people on the Grand Tour stop by Tavnic long enough to have some drinks before moving on to spend their parents' money on something more interesting. Not that I can blame them. If I had the opportunity to get out of Tavnic, I'd jump at it."

"You don't like it there much?"

"It's so boring. I'd love to be living out on the road like you are, seeing the world. You've probably seen more than I ever will. Where's the best place you've been on your travels so far?"

Jamie remained silent for a moment as he considered this. The only answer he could come up with wasn't even the least bit false. "Home," he said.

"Really?" Onorah sounded disappointed. "Is it nice there?"

"Some of it," Jamie said, remembering his tiny hometown. "Other places, not so much."

"I suppose I know what you mean. Me and my dad aren't originally from Tavnic. I actually grew up in a magesmith town called Iron Spur. Have you ever heard of it?"

Jamie shook his head. Onorah reached into her pocket and pulled out a small brass pin. She held it out so Jamie could see the enameled symbol of a sword over an anvil surrounded by laurel branches. "This is their maker's mark. If you ever see it on a wardcaster, you'll know its one of the best."

"I'll have to remember that," Jamie said. Taking a stab at translating the symbols, he added, "Victory through superior weapons?"

"More or less," Onorah said, looking wistfully at the pin before putting it away again. "Sometimes I really miss that place."

"Could you ever go back? Maybe after you pass your exams?"

"Maybe," Onorah said, though she didn't make it sound like much of a possibility. "Iron Spur manufactures most of the high-end military equipment for the army. It's unlikely they'd take on a newly licensed magesmith who doesn't have any experience with weapons design."

"That's too bad."

Onorah shrugged. "You can never really go home, right?"

"Yeah," Jamie agreed somberly. What would there be for him back in his old home? His new life with Heather was all he had left and he wasn't even sure what was becoming of that at the moment.

A melancholy silence descended on them, and though they continued chatting from time to time, there were also plenty of opportunities for Jamie to continue taking in the scenery. A few times during a particularly long stretch of silence from his passenger, Jamie would look back to see Onorah nodding off or yawning. Between the heat, the humidity, and the rocking motion of the titan-mecha, Jamie could see why. However, despite all that, and even with his heavy clothing, Jamie wasn't even sweating.

The farther they went, the more locals they saw traveling along the road, typically manning vulcan-mecha propelled wagons piled high with logs, or towing field implements pulled by shaggy, bison-like animals that stood at least ten feet high and sported multiple sets of thin, gracefully curving horns atop their massive heads. Some bleated long, low cries and shuffled their hoofed feet at the titan's approach while others didn't even spare it a glace.

Using his status as little more than a tourist, Jamie learned from Onorah that the beasts of burden were called noxard and that the local farmers' primarily cash crop was something called gromak. Most of the agriculture in the region, however, was geared toward logging. Something about the climate made the types of trees that grew there some of the most highly prized species on the entire continent. In addition to these exotics, which offered the highest profit margins, the numerous mills in the area also produced the majority of the lumber used in Finttiranos for such mundane needs as building houses and furniture.

If the position of the sun was any indication, it must have been slightly before midday when Jamie stopped on the crest of a small hill. The land had been rising gradually for some time and rolling hills were becoming common. Ahead, the mists were less thick and the sun seemed brighter, rendering the sea of treetops below in painfully vibrant shades of green. About a mile or two farther on, the road curved around a palisade wall of thick timbers encircling a rather sizable assortment of buildings. It was by no means a metropolis, but it certainly seemed larger than what he remembered of Tavnic.

Yawning and stretching, Onorah stood up. "Are we there?"

From their vantage point atop that hill, Jamie could see all the large industrial buildings with their plumes of white smoke within the north end of the wall while the majority of the smaller, more human-scaled buildings were mostly clustered along the inside of the western wall. Under closer examination, he could see that the land dropped away east of town, creating the ridge which the wall followed along that side. Also, within the eastern quadrant, he could make out one large building in particular whose cascading roofs seemed almost to glow green in the sunlight from all the moss growing on the roof tiles. It had been night the last time he'd been here and he'd only seen a small portion of Tavnic, but he knew he recognized that building.

Onorah yawned again and tapped a leather band strapped to her wrist. An array of floating figures appeared in the air above it. "Wow," she said, "not quite as fast as I'd thought but we did make good time." A second tap caused the projected clock face to vanish.

Jamie hesitated before starting the titan into motion again. Alaida was down there, maybe in that big building at this very moment. He'd spent weeks thinking about her, hoping for just one more opportunity to speak with her. Now he had his chance and he wasn't actually sure he had the nerve to go through with it. She probably wouldn't even remember him, just one more traveler among the hundreds she'd likely crossed paths with since then. However, if he didn't at least try, he'd never know. Just being able to see her again would be worth it. Smiling nervously, Jamie nudged the controls and started the titan down the road toward the distant village.

CHAPTER 15

As Jamie approached the city wall, he felt dwarfed. It was just as tall and stout as he remembered, twice as high as his titan, and the tress growing right up to the edge stood even higher yet. The road angled directly toward the city but then took a sharp, ninety-degree turn at the base of the wall as it skirted the perimeter on its way north. At the bend in the road stood a huge gate that would have been big enough to accommodate Jamie's titan-mecha with room to spare if it had not been sealed shut at the moment. Above the gate hung a large wooden sign engraved with a single word. Even with all the odd characters that Jamie couldn't quite make out, he was still pretty sure it read simply 'Tavnic.'

"That's weird," Onorah said, leaning against the front roll cage. "Why are the gates closed?" Yelling up at the hoardings above the gate, she said, "Hey, what gives? Open up already!"

"Onorah, is that you?" a sleepy voice called down from above. Momentarily, a young man wearing the green jacket and steel helmet of a town guardsman poked his head out through one of the loopholes, rubbing his eyes. "Whoa, nice titan!"

"Never mind the titan, Renny," she called back. "Just open the gates!"

"Uh," he said, scratching his jaw. "I can't really do that at the moment. The village just went on alert. No unauthorized titans are allowed inside right now."

"What the hell kind of rubbish is that?" Onorah said.

"Sorry. Major Addinez's orders. You'll have to talk to him if you want to bring it inside. You can still park in the Annex Yard though."

"Bloody soldiers." Onorah kicked the bulkhead in front of her. "Fine, we'll park in the Annex Yard."

"What's going on?" Jamie said, eyeing the yawning guardsman as he disappeared inside the hoardings once again.

"Nothing new." Onorah crossed her arms and dropped onto the rumble seat. "Just hang a left here and head along the wall. The Annex Yard is right on the other side of this bend."

Warily, Jamie directed the titan along the route indicated. He'd enjoyed traveling with Onorah, but this talk of alerts and soldiers had put him on edge. It had apparently soured Onorah's mood as well because she said nothing as she sat there in the passenger's compartment, glaring ahead at nothing in particular.

As the titan rounded the curve in the wall, a second, slightly shorter wall came into view bulging out from the main fortification and forcing the road to once again divert around it. This barrier was elevated atop a rocky outcropping which placed it higher than the road but it wasn't nearly as elaborate as the main wall. A single gravel path led up to a keyway gate in the side. From the way it was situated, one wouldn't be able to see inside until they were already through the gate. Jamie glanced back at Onorah and she motioned for him to go on through, looking no more pleased than she had since receiving news of the alert.

With no guards to challenge him, Jamie advanced up the path and through the gate. The side and overhead timbers left plenty of room to maneuver but he still kept the titan on a tight leash. It would only take a single careless swing of the titan's arm to pulverize any one of those heavy timbers and potentially pull the whole gate down on top of them.

Rounding the last corner, Jamie brought the titan to a lurching halt and very nearly fled right back the way he'd just come. The perfectly flat yard of dark gravel that spread out ahead of him stretched from the base of the higher village wall on his right, all the way to the inside of the Annex Yard's lower wall on his left. And at the far end of that oval-shaped enclosure stood two Finttiranos military titan-mechas.

"Don't tell me they came this morning!" Onorah cried, jumping out of her seat. "This is just my luck! Quick, park over there!" She pointed to an open corner of the yard.

Giving the machines a second look, Jamie could now see that their cockpits hung open and the men inside were not even the least bit interested in him. Lacking any military spit-and-polish whatsoever, they weren't even dressed in military uniforms, just dirty coveralls. In fact, the only one present wearing one of those long green tunics was a man on the ground trying to direct the two machines into a pair of vertical hangers built into the side of the village wall. At the moment, however, he was far more concerned with avoiding their footfalls than anything else. Another two of the same machines lay silent and motionless on a pair of huge flatbed-like trailers in the middle of the yard.

"Come on," Onorah urged. "Hurry!"

"Um, right..." If this was a trap, Jamie couldn't quite figure out how it was supposed to work.

He eased the titan into the corner of the yard Onorah had pointed out, thankful that it was just about as far away from those other machines as possible. Very carefully, he backed it up to the wall so as to keep it as unobtrusive as possible and hoping all the while that he didn't hit anything. In addition to all the lean-tos built against the inside perimeter of the yard, which sheltered milling equipment and battered vulcan-mechas, crates and barrels had been stacked up high in between until very little of the walls themselves could any longer be seen.

As Jamie began dropping the titan down into its parking crouch, an older guardsman with coat hanging open across his belly, came strolling in their direction and called up to Jamie's passenger.

"Hey, Onorah, Valerian was looking for you!"

"Thanks, Drigaldo!"

Before the machine had even completely stopped moving, Onorah scrambled down one of the arms and dashed across the gravel lot toward the other titan-mechas. Jamie's own machine held him in restraint for a few moments longer as his seat dropped out of its belly. The guardsman stood a short distance away with a friendly smile stretched across his wrinkled face, leaning on his blunt-headed spear and waiting for Jamie to disembark. Hopefully he didn't want to see some kind of identification; Jamie was relatively certain he didn't have a titan-mecha license.

The clamps didn't snap open until the seat was fully extended, and by that time, Onorah had already reached the flatbeds. Though the four titan-mechas at the far end of the yard did share a certain design aesthetic with the robots Jamie had fought previously, they didn't look nearly as sleek, as if older models of a similar type. They were also quite weathered and marred by what looked like years of hard use.

Jamie didn't want to get any closer to them than he had to but figured he should at least make an effort to say goodbye to Onorah before heading into Tavnic. The moment his hands left the control pucks, however, the titan grew silent once more and those other titans suddenly looked much bigger and more dangerous than they had just a few seconds ago.

As Jamie stepped out of the waldos, the bag of coins he'd earlier tucked into his belt fell to the ground at the feet of the guardsman. Jamie froze, certain that no matter how little money was in that small sack, it would place him under scrutiny. He made a hasty grab for it but the guard got to it first. He tossed it in his hand a few times, listening to the jingle of coins. Jamie felt his blood run cold.

"Hear ya go," the guardsman said, his smile never faltering as he handed the bag back.

Jamie accepted stiffly, swallowing hard as he tucked it back into his belt and muttered his thanks.

"No problem at all," the guardsman said, tipping back his steel helmet and wiping the beaded sweat away from his brow. "We 'o the town guard are always happy to help. My name's Drigaldo. You a friend of Onorah?"

"Yeah, I guess," Jamie said, stealing a sideways glance in her direction. Practically laughing, she had climbed onto one of the trailers and begun examining its titan-mecha cargo. "I ran into her out at the... at Ciante's... mine? She needed a lift so I helped her out."

"That was awfully considerate of you. It's not safe for anyone to be traveling out there alone these days."

"So I've heard," Jamie said absently, having lost sight of Onorah.

"It's a damn shame, really. I never thought I'd live to see the day when we actually needed titan-mechas stationed in a place like Tavnic." The guard motioned to the far end of the yard with end of his staff. "The government's been telling us for years that they'd be assigning us village guard units the old Mark-4s once they finished transitioning the military over to the new Mark-5s but I never wanted to get bumped to the top of that list for something like bandit trouble and Wolf-Slaves."

Jamie eyed the war machines the guard had indicated. How much of the village's worry was Jamie's own fault? After all, his destruction of those two military titan-mechas was likely being categorized as just another of these bandit attacks that had gotten everyone so on edge. Those MK-4s might have been older, but they were still bigger than Jamie's titan and they looked more heavily armored as well, not to mention the weapons they undoubtedly had access to. If it came to a fight in Tavnic, he wouldn't want to put any money on his chances. At least no one here had yet accused him of being a criminal.

"I should probably get going," Jamie told the guard. "I've got business in town."

The guard pointed toward a large timber structure protruding from the main village wall on the other end of the Annex Yard. "There's a set o' stairs in there that will take you up to the village. Enjoy your stay. We'll keep an eye on your titan in the meantime."

"Ah...thanks," Jamie said, moving off in search of Onorah.

Crossing the yard, he made sure to keep the flatbeds between himself and the two titans that had already been unloaded. The soldier on the ground was growing furious with the snickering pilots who were now purposely mishearing his every instruction. Like so many things on Terrarhea, the trailers at first looked commonplace but, upon closer inspection, their otherworldly nature became clear. Both of them floated about a foot off the ground without any apparent means of thrust. Instead of wheels, each one had eight crystalline globes projecting from the underside of their frames that could be seen to glow faintly wherever they were in shadow.

In addition to the titan-mechas the flatbeds had transported, they were also loaded with a fair number of wooden crates which a mixed group of uniformed military personnel and civilians were busy unloading. Until Jamie had rounded the front of the nearest flatbed, they had been hidden from his view. Seeing those soldiers so close, Jamie probably would have abandoned his search for Onorah if she hadn't been standing right there.

"Oh, hi, Jamie," she said, glancing up for only a moment from the sheaf of papers she was reading. "Can you believe this, not only did we get four Mk-4's but they also sent two replacement energy cells for each one and a complete basic armament package!"

"Um," Jamie said, his interest elsewhere at the moment. The soldier directing the two standing machines now seemed to be scrambling for his life as the laughing pilots nearly smashed him underfoot time and time again in what they no doubt intended to look like a series of accidental blunders. "Is he okay? That looks kind of dangerous."

"What?"

It took Onorah a moment before she realized what Jamie was talking about. Then she simply dismissed it with a wave. The man standing on the ground finally threw down his clipboard, howling at the pilots until one of the two machines brought its foot down right behind him.

He jumped nearly three feet into the air, spinning and launching into an unbroken string of obscenities as the pilots nearly doubled over in laughter.

"He's fine," Onorah said. "These military types are too high strung. They need to loosen up and learn how to take a joke."

"Is that so?" a stern voice said from nearby. "Hey there! Stop that horseplay! All four of these titans should already be in their hangers by now!"

Instantly, the two pilots of the machines ceased their dangerous joke and slouched down in their seats. Onorah and Jamie both turned to see a pair of men standing behind them. The difference in their heights would have been comical if the shorter of the two wasn't wearing a military uniform as he glared at Jamie and tapped the end of his swagger stick into his open palm. With three gold bars on each shoulder board, he looked important. Jamie swallowed hard.

"Onorah, you remember Major Addinez, don't you?" the tall man said. He, at least, was dressed in civilian attire, and working garb by the look of it. With his neatly trimmed beard and easy smile, he should have been the less authoritarian of the two, but something about his stance made Jamie feel like he was facing down his school's vice-principal all over again.

"How could I forget," Onorah replied, hiding her chagrin by turning away and placing the clipboard on top of a crate. "How are you doing today, Major? File any exciting reports lately?"

"I might have one shortly," he replied, peeling his gaze away from Jamie. "One about a young magesmith apprentice nearly getting herself eaten by Wolf-Slaves."

"Wow, word sure travels fast." Onorah rolled her eyes. "I haven't even been back five minutes yet."

"Ciante just called it in from Blue-Rock Outpost," the tall man said, his voice firm.

"Is that why the gates are closed? Because of a few Wolf-Slaves?"

"I've been assigned to keep this village safe and that's what I intend to do," Major Addinez said. "I have no reason to justify my actions to you or anyone else."

"How could you have been that reckless?" the tall man said to Onorah, his voice rising. "Why did you even go down there the way things are right now?"

"I've been to that mine a dozen times before," Onorah said. "How was I supposed to know something like that was going to happen?"

"You should have checked with us first," the major said, his voice level but carrying a threatening edge. "Magesmiths are valuable personnel: even impulsive young apprentices. It's my job to determine which risks are validated."

"You could have been killed!" the tall man said.

"It wasn't all that bad. They just burned down a few sheds and made some noise. No one was even hurt."

Except for the Wolf-Slaves, Jamie thought.

The tall man frowned and shook his head. "It's bad enough you went down there on your own but afterward you hitched a ride back with a complete stranger? Sometimes I wonder if you have any sense at all."

"Dad, it was fine!" Onorah said, her voice rising just a fraction.

Jamie, however, was suddenly very much on edge. Now that he looked closer, he could see the familial resemblance between father and daughter. Not only were they both respectably tall and shared the same shade of sandy brown hair, but they also had the same determined glint in their eyes as they stared each other down.

"Besides, even if things had gotten worse, Jamie here could have handled it. As it was, he drove the whole pack off all by himself."

Jamie quailed as two sets of scrutinizing eyes turned on him. He could probably still make it to his titan-mecha before they knew what was happening.

"*This* is the one who drove off the Wolf-Slaves?" Major Addinez said. Apparently, he'd been expecting someone more heroic.

"Is that true?" Onorah's father added, his own disbelief tinged with a healthy dose of wonder.

"I didn't really do anything," Jamie said, laughing nervously. "I just stood up to them and they pretty much ran away."

"He's being modest," Onorah said, stepping close. Jamie tensed. "You should have seen him. He took on three of them at once with his bare hands."

"With his bare hands?" Major Addinez said, one eyebrow rising.

Why did Onorah need to bring Jamie into this? Major Addinez was already suspicious enough.

"She's exaggerating," Jamie said. "I'm sure Onorah could have handled things all by herself. Once she got out that knife -- "

"Yeah, like Jamie said, it wasn't that dangerous," Onorah said, cutting him off mid-sentence, no doubt to prevent her father from hearing just how involved she'd gotten in the fight.

"I should really get going," Jamie said. Saying his goodbyes to Onorah wasn't worth the risk of being recognized and having a bunch of Finttiranos soldiers try to arrest him again.

"He's got a business meeting at Gavrin's," Onorah volunteered.

"Will you be staying in Tavnic long?" Major Addinez said.

"I'm not really sure." That mounting sense of irritation in the back of Jamie's mind definitely felt stronger than when he'd first arrived, but still closer to the beginning than to the end. "We'll see how things go...at my meeting."

"If you're still in town this evening, please stop by our shop," Onorah's father said. "We'll treat you to a home-cooked meal. It's the least I can do after you saved my daughter's life."

Onorah cast her eyes skyward and her shoulders drooped. "Dad..."

"That's awfully kind." Jamie began to back away as he spoke. "But you don't really need to do anything like that. I was just happy to help."

"If you change your mind, stop by anyway," Onorah's father said.

"I'll remember that. It was nice meeting you all."

Frowning, Major Addinez kept a wary eye on him as Jamie backed into one of the piled crates and nearly lost his balance. With a scoff, the Major finally turned to Onorah's father. "Valerian, I want these titans running at full combat efficiency as soon as possible."

"Great!" Onorah said. "I can start on these two while you get to work on the ones they're putting in the hanger."

"No, I need you back at the shop," her father said. "I'm going to be here a while and we need someone there in case anyone stops by."

"But if we work together, we can have this done in no time."

"Onorah, you don't have any experience working on military equipment and I don't have the time to teach you right now."

"How am I supposed to get any experience if you won't let me work on them with you? Besides, if you just let me watch you do the first one, you know I can figure it out from there."

Major Addinez gripped his baton hard enough that the leather creaked. "Valerian, we don't have time for this."

"Yes, Major, in a moment." Then to Onorah, he said, "This is not a discussion. Go back to the shop, now."

Onorah threw out her hands. "My exams are coming up fast! Without hands-on experience, there's no way I'm gonna be able to pass the sections on military arms and armor!"

"Doing well on those sections is only important if you're trying to get into the Army Magesmith Corps," her father replied.

"At this rate, joining the AMC is the only way I'll ever get out of this stinking little backwater!"

If this was any indication of what dinner with the two of them would look like, Jamie was glad he'd not committed himself to going. Onorah stood glaring at her father for a moment, but before he could reply, she turned on her heel and stormed across the yard, seizing Jamie by the elbow as she passed.

"Come on, I'll show you around."

"Onorah, we'll talk about this later!" her father called after them.

Thankfully, Onorah did not say anything in reply.

CHAPTER 16

Walking at a steady clip, Onorah led Jamie to the stairs which the guardsman had earlier mentioned. They climbed up through a darkened tunnel with a raised portcullis at each end. The top emptied onto a wide, neatly paved street, lined on one side by timbered buildings and on the other by the city's curving wall.

At the head of the stairs stood a pair of soldiers, though instead of being dressed in those unmistakable dark green uniforms, these two were encased in suits of hulking body armor of the same color. With the glowing magescript, large shoulders, and v-shaped visors, they almost looked like smaller, slightly more human-proportioned versions of their titan-mechas. If their faceplates hadn't currently been raised, no part of their bodies would have been visible at all. Jamie wouldn't have even been able to tell that one of them was a woman. Military-looking crests and markings had been stenciled on their arms and chests, and slung over their shoulders were rifles identical to the one Onorah had discovered in Jamie's titan-mecha. Both of them had been leaning casually again the wall, chatting, but catching sight of Jamie and Onorah, they stopped and eyed them closely as they passed.

Why did this keep feeling more and more like a trap? Unintentionally staring back, Jamie's toe caught on the edge of a cobblestone and he stumbled into the street, almost colliding with a man carrying a sack over his shoulder who didn't even notice. The woman soldier whispered something to her comrade and both of them broke out laughing. Casting one last look in their direction, Jamie hurried to catch up with Onorah.

By daylight, Tavnic didn't feel much different than it had at night. The air still smelled like wood smoke and sawdust and every surface in sight seemed to be slightly damp, with every nook and cranny host to one or more layers of vibrant green moss. Echoing along the inside curve of the city's wall, the high-pitched whine of saws could be heard almost constantly.

"Are all those soldiers just here for the titan delivery?" Jamie asked once he and Onorah moved a little further on, heading down one of the side streets that opened off the main thoroughfare at regular intervals. "I don't remember seeing this many the first time I was here."

There were plenty of villagers out and about as well, sometimes filling the streets shoulder-to-shoulder where they had to share it with huge wagons pulled by vulcan-mechas or noxards. Many of the pedestrians tipped their hats or offered friendly greetings to Onorah as they passed, but their expressions turned somber when they caught sight of Jamie. He'd seen those same looks back in his old hometown and had probably given them a few times himself. In a small rural community like Tavnic, Jamie was just another outsider, one the residents didn't want lingering about any longer than necessary.

Onorah, still fuming from the argument with her father, finally came to a stop, as if having completely forgotten about Jamie until he'd spoken. "After the convoy robbery, the army's been on high alert thinking the bandits might strike again. Yarzak even sent each of the villages in the area a squad of soldiers just in case anything happened. We got Addinez."

"You don't like him much?" Jamie ventured as the two of them began walking again, this time at a more sedate pace.

"Remember what I said about those soldiers needing to relax? That goes double for Addinez. He's a bureaucrat, not a soldier. It's like he thinks that just by following all those military rules and regulations, it makes him some kind of tactical expert. All the security restrictions and curfews he's already put in place are just pissing everyone off. And now he's jumping at shadows like a spooked bocksnard just because of a couple of Wolf-Slaves? They never come anywhere near towns, especially ones as big as Tavnic. Even if they did, they'd never get over the wall."

As much as Jamie hadn't liked the way Addinez looked at him, the man hadn't actually seemed like a tyrant. "He's just trying to keep everyone safe, right?"

"As if his polished boots are going to make any difference if someone does attack. I think this is the first time he's actually been allowed to be in command of anyone and the power's going to his head. I mean, in addition to the soldiers he brought with him, now he's got the town guard dancing to his orders too. They might answer to the military in an emergency but this hardly qualifies as one in my book."

She gestured down one of the streets they were crossing. "That is the heart and soul of Tavnic: the lumber mills." In the distance, Jamie could see a number of large buildings and warehouses behind which a continual white cloud of what could have been either smoke, dust, steam, or a combination of all three, rose into the misty air.

As they kept walking, the buildings passed out of sight a moment later. "That would explain all the sawdust." Here in the light of day, it seemed more vibrantly yellow wherever it clung to the damp buildings and settled on the ground.

"It gets into everything," Onorah said. "Me and my dad spend most of our time repairing the dust seals on houses. It gets so boring. That's why I go on field calls whenever I can."

"Even with bandits out there?"

"No one kills magesmiths on purpose. Like Addinez said, we're too valuable. Bandits might take me prisoner, force me to fix all their gear, but the worst that could happen is that I get ransomed. The *government* would probably even pay it."

"What about the Wolf-Slaves? You said they didn't have any use for money."

Onorah looked at him thoughtfully. "Yeah, and they don't use wardcasters either, so they probably would have just killed me. But how was I supposed to know they were going to attack the mine? I've never heard of them doing anything like that before."

They walked another block over cobbled streets, Onorah pointing out a bakery which she claimed made the best cinnamon rolls she'd ever tasted and a clothing store which she seemed to think was the only one in town worth bothering with because she and her father had installed custom built fabricators for them, whatever those were.

"So what does your mom do?" Jamie said, having so far heard no mention of the woman.

Onorah shrugged. "She's been gone a while now."

Just like Jamie to put his foot in his mouth. "Oh, I'm sorry. I didn't mean to..."

"No, she's not dead," Onorah said, dispassionately. "At least I don't think so. She left years ago. That's how we ended up here in Tavnic. My dad used to be one of the top researchers at Iron Spur but when Mom ran off, he went after her and dragged me along, even though we both knew she didn't want us to find her. My dad doesn't talk about it anymore, but I know he'd still rather be out there looking for her."

"That's...too bad. I'm sorry."

"I'm not. If I ever saw her again, I'd probably try to kill her."

"Seriously?" Jamie practically would have sold his soul to be able to see his own mother again. He knew he shouldn't pry, but after Onorah's last statement, he had to know more. "Did something happen?"

"Yeah: I was tested for the gift," Onorah said with a snort. "I was only four or maybe five at the time. Before that, she'd been a great mom but afterward she started getting distant and cold with both me and my dad. You see, she was a technician and she barely had enough talent for even that. My dad, on the other hand, was one of the best magesmiths Iron Spur had ever seen and they were saying I had more potential than even him. My mom always resented that."

"Are you really sure that's why she left?"

"It doesn't matter. She knew that my dad would go after her and that we'd lose everything if she did leave. So, either she was just being incredibly selfish, or she was purposely trying to get revenge. Either way, I'm glad my dad never found her before giving up and settling down here. I don't think I ever want to see her again."

"That really is too bad," Jamie said. He didn't know what was worse, losing one's mother completely or knowing she was still out there but wanted nothing at all to do with you.

"Sometimes, I think my dad just wants me to suffer as bad as he did by making sure I never have a chance of getting out of this town."

"Let me guess, being able to work on those military titans back there would have helped your chances of getting a job at Iron Spur?"

"Maybe," Onorah said with a sly smile, "but mostly I just like titans. It certainly wouldn't have hurt my chances though."

They continued on, passing a shop selling fine clothes and another, second-hand fashions. The smell of baking bread wafted out of a bakery, while accountants hunched over their ledgers next door. There were hardware stores, cafes, homes, groceries and many more; all of it looking decidedly archaic to Jamie's eyes. The use of simple manpower was certainly more prevalent here, but once he looked past the differences, none of it was really all *that* dissimilar from what he would have expected to see in a similarly sized town on Earth. Apparently the people living here used wardcasters for everything they needed, but the end results -- the products they produced and the services they preformed -- were little different from the technological counterparts Jamie would have been more familiar with. Eventually, Onorah stopped in front of a solid, three-story building of white stone and stucco with several large windows facing the street.

"Well, this is our shop," she said, making it sound like the low point of the entire tour. Through the two windows just slightly above street-level, Jamie could see a showroom inside filled with cabinets and display cases containing all manner of devices he couldn't even begin to identify.

"Tavnic's kind of nice," Jamie said. "In a way, it reminds me a little of my hometown."

Onorah thought about that for a moment and then laughed. "The only part of Tavnic that reminds me of home is the sewers." Checking the time, she said, "Wow, it's almost noon. Do you want to get something to eat? I know a place that makes pretty good mirdrax pies. Even though they don't actually use mirdrax around these parts, they're still really good. It'd be my treat."

Dueling priorities suddenly welled up within Jamie. On the one hand, he still wanted to see Alaida, without even knowing if she wanted to see him. On the other, here was another intelligent young woman who actually did want to spend time with him.

"I should probably get going," Jamie said. He was so close to the one thing -- the one person -- that he would have willingly returned to Terrarhea for, he couldn't allow himself to be pulled off track without at least first trying to see her. "It's been an interesting morning though. I'm glad I was there to help out."

"Me too. I'm glad we met. If you have time this evening, I hope you do stop by. Sometimes me and my dad can get on each other's nerves but its not usually that bad. Plus, he is a really good cook."

"I'll see how things go."

Onorah pointed down the length of the street in the opposite direction they had just come. "Gavrin's is that way. Go all the way to the end of the street and hang a left, you can't miss it."

Now that Onorah mentioned it, things were starting to look a bit more familiar. Jamie even thought he might have recognized a few of the houses. "Thanks. I'll, um, maybe see you around."

"I hope so," Onorah said, offering him her hand. "Take care, Jamie."

"You too, Onorah." He took her hand, releasing it after a few halting shakes, and smiled, feeling his collar grow warm. After the morning they had just shared, something about the gesture just seemed far too impersonal. Unfortunately, he could think of nothing else that would have been better suited under the circumstances and so he simply offered a brief wave as he turned and headed down the street. He glanced back after passing several houses and just caught sight of Onorah's back as she stepped through the door to her father's shop.

Within minutes, he'd crossed the remainder of the village and found himself standing once again in front of the tavern. Without the sound of revelers echoing from inside, the place looked lifeless and brooding. Hopefully, it was open for business at this early hour. Condensation dripped lazily from the mossy eaves as a bare-footed Raven-Slave meticulously swept the front porch. With her pale skin, iridescent black hair, and yellow eyes, there was no mistaking what she was, but even as beautiful as she was, she wasn't Alaida.

Jamie paused and glanced back the way he had just come. Maybe he had been too quick to brush Onorah off. After all, he didn't even know if Alaida would want to see him again. They'd only spoken for a few minutes the last time Jamie had been here. His stomach twisted as he considered that in the weeks since their paths had crossed, he might not have occupied her thoughts as she had his.

As Jamie considered his next move, a small group of sweaty men and women, peppered with sawdust from the mills, strode laughing onto the porch and through the front doors of the tavern. Taking a deep breath, Jamie followed after them, crossing the porch in a few long strides.

The doors opened easily on well-oiled hinges. Inside, the great room that had been filled to capacity when last he saw it, now sat almost empty. The group which had entered ahead of him took seats at one of the tables, joining a handful of similar groups scattered about the room as Raven-Slaves swept in to take their lunch orders. Elsewhere, lone men hunched over drinks which they had possibly been nursing since the night before. One of the Raven-Slaves who was busy wiping down an empty table looked up at Jamie with her amber eyes but quickly returned to her work. Alaida didn't appear to be among any of the staff working the front room either.

Jamie made his way toward the bar in the back of the room, intent on asking the Raven-Slave there for help in his quest, but she turned and disappeared just as he got close. An arched doorway in the stone wall behind the bar opened onto a hallway. From the sounds of rattling pans and sizzling oils, Alaida might have been back there somewhere, helping in the kitchens to prepare for the lunch hour.

Jamie was just about to try flagging down another Raven-Slave when the same fat proprietor he remembered from last time stopped on the other side of the doorway. Breathing heavily and face flushed red, he issued some hasty orders to a pair of Raven-Slaves who bowed obediently before gliding off. He was just about to go on his own way when he caught sight of Jamie. Instantly, he turned an even brighter shade of red and pointed toward the door.

"Out!" he said as he waddled around the bar. "I told you before: no coin, no service!"

Garvin reached for Jamie with thick, greasy hands; no doubt intending to push him right out of the tavern. Jamie could have manhandled him with ease but instead brought him to an abrupt stop simply by jingling the bag of coins he'd taken from the Wolf-Slave in

Gavrin's face. Licking his lips, the man looked at the bag, then Jamie, and finally the bag again.

"What'll you have then?" he said feebly.

Jamie smiled. Finally, a real victory. "I want to talk to Alaida."

"Alaida?" Gavrin's brow rose and then, eyeing the bag of coins once more, he frowned.

Jamie felt his heart sink. He hadn't stopped to consider that maybe Raven-Slaves changed hands more frequently than even Alaida had led him to believe. "Is she still here?"

"Alaida's busy right now, but maybe I have something else you might enjoy. Girls, get over here!" He clapped his hands and all the nearby Raven-Slaves instantly came drifting in his direction.

"No, I want Alaida." Jamie tossed the bag of coins to Gavrin. After having made it this far, he wasn't about to give up now.

Gavrin caught the bag against his chest and fumbled with it for a moment before he was able to get a firm grasp. Then, clutching it in his chubby fingers, he waved it in Jamie's face. "Now you listen here! I don't care how much money you throw around; I'm not going to bend over backwards just to satisfy your every whim! After what you did to my bouncers, I should have you arrested!"

As Jamie remembered things, it was the bouncers who'd attacked him. "I want Alaida," Jamie repeated, even more firmly than before.

Gavrin shook the bag of coins again, but the words he had started to speak died on his lips as he reconsidered what it was he was holding. Face twitching with irritation, he pulled loose the strings and fingered through the coins inside. He was only at it a moment before he clamped his fingers around the purse and waved the other Raven-Slaves away with a growl. "Go on, the lot 'o ya! Back to work, ya lazy bitches!"

Gavrin walked back behind the bar and stormed away through the doorway, disappearing from sight.

"Hey, wait a second!" Jamie took several halting steps in pursuit but ultimately stopped at the edge of the bar. Had Gavrin wanted him to follow or was he just supposed to wait here? Many of the growing lunch crowd had taken an interest in Jamie's conversation with the innkeeper and were now talking amongst themselves as they kept a curious eye on him. As the minutes ticked by, Jamie started to wonder if Gavrin might have simply run off with all his money. How long could it really take to track down Alaida anyway? Her duties couldn't have been *that* important.

Jamie was just starting to think about setting off in search of him when Gavrin returned, dragging a half-dressed Raven-Slave behind him. Jerking her by the arm, Gavrin shoved her at Jamie. She let out a startled cry as she stumbled and fell against his chest. She felt so fragile and vulnerable. Tossing disheveled hair out of her face, she looked around with a pair of bewildered, amber-colored eyes. Even disarrayed as she was, there was no mistaking Alaida. Torn between welcoming her with a smile and bearing down on Gavrin for treating her so roughly, Jamie never got a chance to do either.

"There, she's all yours!" Gavrin tossed Jamie a small leather binder and again pointed at the door. "I'd never be able to turn a profit with one that plain anyway!"

"Wait, what's all this?" Jamie said, steadying Alaida with one hand and holding up the binder in the other. At the same time, two large men emerged from the back rooms, cracking their knuckles and angling toward them.

"Go on now!" Gavrin cried with a wave of his arm. "Get out of here before you go giving the rest of my stock ideas!"

Jamie could do nothing but sputter incoherently as the two men ushered him and Alaida past the tables of gawking diners and out through a side door at the end of the bar. It slammed shut behind them and bolts could be heard promptly locking it closed.

CHAPTER 17

The small porch on which Jamie and Alaida now stood faced one of the city streets that ran alongside the tavern. After making sure Alaida was steady on her feet once more, Jamie bent down so he could look into her downcast eyes. "Are you okay?"

She nodded but said nothing, her expression unreadable. Unnaturally graceful as ever, she began straightening her clothes and smoothing her hair, keeping her eyes fixed on the deck boards in front of her bare toes the whole time. Running his fingers though his own hair and groaning, Jamie backed away so she could have her space. All the times he'd imagined a second meeting with Alaida, he'd never once considered it happening anything like this.

Inside the leather binder Gavrin had given him were a number of dog-eared papers with an official look to them and a single brass disk slightly smaller than the palm of his hand. One side bore an elaborate seal surrounded by writing and the other an image of a bird in flight, not all that different from the sign hanging in front of the tavern. Below this was more writing but this looked like it had been stamped into the metal rather than being minted as part of the coin like all the rest. Is this what authorized him to be with a Raven-Slave? It didn't seem like it should have been that complicated.

Now that Alaida had finished as best she could with her ministrations, she lowered her hands to her sides and stood perfectly still. It must have been a sign of deference, but she somehow made it look as if she was simply being demure.

"Alaida, do you know what just happened in there?" Jamie said. He held out the leather binder and the metal disk. "Do you know what this is?"

Alaida lifted her face just enough that Jamie caught a glimpse of her amber-colored eyes peering though her long, black hair. "Those are my papers and seal of ownership," she said, her voice perfectly level. She must have missed the meaning of Jamie's question and thought he was testing her. "Now that you have purchased me from Master Gavrin, they show that I am your property."

"Property? What! You mean, like, permanently?"

Alaida nodded and Jamie felt his chest tighten. The very notion that slavery existed here on Terrarhea was unsettling enough, but to unexpectedly become a slave owner himself made him feel as if he'd just committed a most unforgivable sin. It didn't matter that Alaida was a Raven-Slave (whatever that meant exactly), it didn't make her any less of a person.

"No, no, no," Jamie said, prancing in a small circle. "This is all wrong. Just like that, you're supposed to belong to me? I can't own you!"

Alaida went rigid as she looked directly at Jamie, her face taut with worry.

"Alaida, I'm sorry, but this was an accident. I wasn't trying to buy you."

"You--you do not want me? Does that mean you will be returning me to Master Gavrin?"

Jamie shuddered at the thought of turning Alaida back over to that disgusting little man now that she was free of him, even if it was by accident. He wouldn't wish that fate on anyone, least of all the captivating girl standing before him. "I do want you -- I mean, I'd never give you back to him."

Collapsing in on herself as her eyes grew wide, she said, "Then you plan to sell me at auction?"

"What? No!" Jamie said, more forcefully than he had intended.

Alaida clasped her hands in front of her and snapped to a rigid position of attention, again lowering her eyes.

"Please don't do that," Jamie said, fitfully clutching his hands into fists. Hopefully that one brief moment they'd talked hadn't just been a fluke. He was certain they'd had a connection and he was certain she'd felt it too. "I'm not going to sell you at auction or anywhere else." Jamie sighed and shook his head. He feared he would regret the answer to his next question, but he also knew he had to ask it. "Do you remember me?"

Alaida remained silent for a moment before looking at Jamie once more. "Y-yes, of course I remember you, master," she said. "You are Jamie, from the faraway land of Dirt."

Her expression betrayed no emotion, but her voice carried the slightest hint of amusement. Was she making a joke?

"That's Earth," Jamie said.

"Yes, of course, master. Earth."

That time she was definitely being blithe. Her voice would have sounded like music if she hadn't addressed him the way she had. "Don't call me that."

"I do not understand."

"I don't want to be your...master," Jamie said. Under the circumstances, the word felt absolutely repugnant on his lips. "Just call me 'Jamie'."

She tipped her head to the side and her face contorted into that charming look of confusion he remembered so well from their first meeting. "If you did not wish to purchase me, why did you pay master Gavrin so much?"

"What do you mean?"

"When he took me from my duties, he said that I had been purchased for ten times my worth."

"Ten times?" Apparently, there had been far more money in that sack than Jamie had figured. No wonder Garvin had been so determined to get the transaction done with as quickly as possible. Not that Jamie would have haggled if he had known. He still couldn't comprehend the idea of putting a price on another person.

He took Alaida by the shoulders and looked into her big, amber-colored eyes. "I don't really know how things work around here and I wasn't trying to buy you but I'd never send you back to Gavrin or anyone else who just thought of you as a thing to be bought and sold. All I wanted was another chance to see you and maybe talk with you some more."

Alaida tipped her head the other way as if to say, "That's all?" Though still plainly confused, she smiled. All the troubles and pain Jamie had endured up to that point suddenly seemed like nothing more than minor nuisances. It had all been worth it just to see that smile.

From the street, someone loudly cleared his throat. Jamie and Alaida both turned to see a lanky man watching them from not too far away, dressed in a clean set of clothes with a finer cut than the laborers constituting the majority of the foot traffic out today. Alaida instantly dropped her gaze and collapsed in on herself.

"Little early in the day for that sort of thing, ain't it, chief?" the lanky man said as he pulled a long, thin cigar from his coat pocket.

"What's he talking about?" Jamie whispered to Alaida.

Without looking up, she said, "It is considered inappropriate to consort with a Raven-Slave in public like this."

Jamie dropped his hands to his sides. "Sorry, I didn't mean to...um..." Why was he apologizing? They hadn't done anything wrong. "We were just talking."

The lanky man had strolled over to their side of the street as he slid a ring-shaped wardcaster around the end of the cigar which simultaneously sliced off the end and lit it.

"Just talking?" he said. "Your hands were all over her. I saw it clear. There are good and decent folk out who don't need to be seeing that sort of thing this time o' day."

Something about this man's smug superiority made Jamie want to punch him right in the face. Jamie took a step in his direction and said, "What sort of thing? Being nice to someone? Treating them with a little bit of respect? Would there be some time of day when that sort of thing *would* be considered appropriate?"

The man took a long drag from his cigar and then slowly blew out the smoke. "It's you're funeral, chief." He gave Jamie one last look and then turned and strolled away down the street. Jamie watched him leave but as he did, he noticed others who had taken an interest in their conversation.

"I think we're drawing some attention. And none of it good."

"If you would like to talk, I think I may know of a place that we could do so more privately," Alaida said, eyes still downcast.

"Well, just so long as no one else accuses us of 'consorting' again."

Alaida looked up at him and she laughed. "No, we would not want that. This way." As she went to step off the porch, down onto the dusty street in her bare feet, Jamie caught her by the arm, heedless of the additional looks it garnered.

"Wait, don't you have any things?" Jamie said. "Like maybe a pair of shoes or something?"

She smiled. "Raven-Slaves don't wear shoes."

"What about a change of clothes or personal effects? Don't you have anything?"

"Raven-Slaves *are* property, we do not own property."

"Oh, of course," Jamie said, rolling his eyes as he followed Alaida off the porch and into the streets of Tavnic. Being midday, there were more people about than Jamie had yet seen in the village but he and Alaida stayed to the outer most streets as they made their way south, saving themselves from the majority of the attention they would have attracted if they'd ventured any further toward the interior.

The undeveloped land within the eastern portion of the village walls extended part way along the southern edge as well. Though it wasn't as wide here, tapering away to nothing near the southwest gate, the trees had been allowed to grow freely, creating something of a wooded lot at the base of the southern wall. Alaida left the dirt path they had been following and led Jamie through the weeds and shrubs into the very center where the trees overhead had choked out the majority of the underbrush. What Jamie first took to be a narrow pile of moss-covered stones stretching along the top of a short berm, proved to be the remains of an old foundation once they got closer.

"It is very quiet," Alaida said. "Almost no one ever comes here."

At its highest point, the crumbling old wall barely reached Jamie's shoulder. Much of it, however, had collapsed completely, leaving nothing but a few base courses of cut stone surrounded by piles of rubble on each side. Even where the wall still stood, the mortar had mostly crumbled away, leaving the stones loose and wobbly. The large slabs that had been used to pave the interior had heaved considerably, giving many woody little shrubs a foothold, but still left ample room to walk without having to contend with the weeds.

Jamie ran his hand along one of the dressed stones sitting askew at the base of the building's wall. "Are these ruins of the old magesmith town?"

"I would not know," Alaida said. No doubt more of that forbidden knowledge Raven-Slaves weren't supposed to have. "Years ago, I used to play here with my first masters' children."

The two of them wandered around the collection of fallen stones for a time, Alaida telling Jamie about herself and her life. It seemed that she had been shipped to Tavnic quite young and had first served as companion to a pair of children. She spoke about those times with a fond remembrance but to Jamie it sounded like she had been little more than a family pet. As she grew older, she had been trained to help with the housework but was eventually sold to a second family. There, she kept their household by performing all the cooking and cleaning duties. She had also handled most of the shopping, a task which required her to be taught how to count and handle money, two skills which she was still quite proud to have learned. Though she seemed not the least bit distressed by the fact she had never been taught how to read. When that couple's finances begun to suffer, they were forced to sell Alaida to Gavrin in order to finance their move to a distant city in search of work.

Though the innkeeper might not have seemed like the sort, the Finttiranos government had given him a license which made him a quasi-official government agent and also the only slave broker in the area. As such, he was required to oversee all transactions involving any slaves. Without his stamp on a slave's papers of ownership, a sale conducted in Tavnic would not be considered legal. He earned a respectable income from the fees associated with this requirement, but the tavern was his primary source of profit. In addition to the entertainment services it provided the village, it also acted as the local slavery clearing house. Though most of the slaves living there were directly owned by Gavrin and were used for the running of the tavern, many were only there temporarily, either on hold-over while in transit from one city to another, or individuals he purchased from the local populous with the intent of reselling to someone else at a profit. Apparently, Gavrin had been intent on keeping Alaida until he could determine if she would make a good addition to the tavern staff but Jamie's offer proved too good for him to pass up.

Jamie listened to it all with rapt interest. Not only did he not want to miss any detail which would help him better understand this society, but the way that these people bought and sold a race of beings like used cars proved difficult for him to even comprehend. Even more confusing was the way Alaida could discuss it all without showing the slightest bit of rage or distress.

"That sounds horrible," Jamie said. After hearing all of that, he was practically ready to march back across town and convince Gavrin the error of his ways, one fist at a time.

"Most Raven-Slaves end up in places like that far younger than me. I was actually quite fortunate to have avoided such a fate for as long as I did."

Jamie closed his eyes and took a deep breath. If he didn't calm down, Gavrin was going to end up in a hospital, or whatever the Terrarhean equivalent was. "If you don't mind me asking," Jamie said, trying to redirect his thoughts, "how old are you?"

"I will turn eighteen in four months."

"You're only seventeen?"

"Were you looking for someone older?" Alaida said, frowning playfully.

"No, I just thought...I mean, from the way you behave...you don't seem like most seventeen-year-olds I know." After having heard about all the things she'd lived through in her life and yet remain so serine about it all, Jamie would have guessed her to either be much older or much younger.

"Oh, and how old are you?"

Jamie smiled nervously. Maybe he was old enough to own a titan-mecha but surely Terrarhean law would frown upon a minor owning a slave. "I just turned...I...I'm sixteen?"

"There is no need to tease me," Alaida laughed. "Surely you must be twenty, at least."

"Well, okay, sure, let's go with that."

Alaida laughed again and lightly stepped across one of the fallen piles of stone and up onto the top of the block wall. The loose stones wobbled underfoot, but she glided along as if walking on flat ground. Reaching the end of the wall, she hopped across a gap at the corner of the foundation and landed with ease on top of an even more precariously situated stone.

"You're pretty good at that," Jamie said.

Still balanced on the stone, she turned on the tips of her toes so that she faced Jamie and bent at the waist with hands on her knees. "It is not exactly a useful skill. Or a terribly difficult one to master."

"You think so?" Jamie said, climbing the same pile of stones Alaida had. The soles of his boots twisted off every angled face they came down on and nearly sent him falling to the ground more than once. With some small degree of effort, he reached the top of the wall, but those loose stones didn't make it any easier for him to find his balance. Maybe if he were barefooted like Alaida it wouldn't have been quite so much of a challenge. "Yeah, easy," Jamie said, arms extended wide. He wasn't all that high, but the jumbled stones below didn't look like the softest place to land either.

Alaida continued farther along her section of wall, hopping over several other gaps with the same incredible grace she had already displayed. Jamie followed, growing more confident as he went. His own inhuman speed and dexterity helped but even those didn't allow him to match Alaida's skill. Soon, their antics evolved into an impromptu game that had the both of them hopping between boulders and laughing so hard it sometimes became difficult to do much else.

Even once they grew tired of that, they continued talking about everything and nothing at all. Sometimes one of them would sit and listen to the other. At other times, they would carry on in lively conversation as they strolled aimlessly between the fallen stones. It didn't matter what they were doing or what was said. Almost no topic seemed forbidden and the two of them laughed together like old friends who had known each other all their lives.

144

The only hesitancy Jamie had when he talked about his past was because Alaida had no point of reference to understand a place like Earth. Details only confused things so he kept it as simple as possible, which Alaida didn't seem to mind. Otherwise, the half-truth that Jamie was a traveler from a faraway land, which he had earlier stumbled upon while talking with Onorah and which Alaida now seemed to have presumed, seemed as good a way as any to explain his current situation without getting too specific about things like his mysterious connection to the Red Rogue or the madness potentially taking over his mind.

While sitting side by side on one of the large stones and joking back and forth about nothing of any real importance, Alaida leaned over and knocked her shoulder against Jamie's. Not expecting the gesture, Jamie had to make a hasty grab for the edge of the stone in order to keep from falling off the end. Even though he laughed as he recovered, Alaida's expression fell and she recoiled from him as if he had just yelled at her.

"Are you okay?"

"I am sorry." Alaida folded her hands in her lap. "It is just a little disconcerting when I realize what I am doing here with you. I have never carried on like this with a Human before. When I talk with you, it feels more like the way me and my sister Raven-Slaves speak with each other when no one else is around."

"A sister?"

"Well, a brother, I suppose," Alaida said with a quiet laugh. That really wasn't much better. In Jamie's mind, neither option came even remotely close to describing the connection the two of them seemed to share. "Not that I would know if I even had a brother. Or a true sister for that matter."

"How would you not know something like that?"

Alaida tipped her head curiously. "At the farms where slaves are born, we never even know our parents. We are cared for by the overseers and when we are old enough to perform our duties, we are sold at market. It is likely that I have at least some brothers and sisters, or possibly many, but no slave would ever have any way of knowing for certain."

"You're born and raised on farms?" Jamie suddenly felt a new urge to go have words with Gavrin. As incredible and wondrous as Terrarhea sometimes was, at other times it was down right barbaric. "I can't believe anyone would ever allow something like that to exist."

Alaida shrugged. "That is simply the way things are. Do you have any family where you are from?"

"An older sister," Jamie said. "Her name is Heather. I live with her..." He trailed off, trying to think how best to continue. "My parents...they died a few months ago."

"Oh!" Alaida cried, sitting up straight. "I am so sorry."

Jamie took a deep breath and slowly let it out. "It was an accident -- they got hit by a drunk driver on their way back from dinner one night."

"That is terrible." Alaida placed her hand over Jamie's.

"I try not to think about it too much. I know I'd never be able to forgive the person who did it but I don't know what I might try to do if I let myself hate him." Jamie paused and shook his head. "Afterwards, everything was so crazy I didn't really have a lot of time to think about anything. There was so much legal stuff to take care of and then social services started talking about putting me in foster care because I didn't have any other family besides Heather and they didn't think she would be able to take care of me. She really fought for me though. It's been tough but she's real supportive."

"I am glad you have someone like that," Alaida said. "What of this place where you live with your sister? What is it like?

"Well, it's a...a huge city, completely on the other side of the state from my hometown. Most of the time, I can't even wrap my head around how big it is. There are people everywhere. There's no place you can go where you can get away from the noise. Even at night, there's this...hum in the air. And the school I have to go to is just torture."

"You are attending a school?" Alaida said with genuine interest. "That is a rare privilege. I've never known a scholar before."

"A scholar?" Jamie nearly laughed. "A public-school education doesn't make anyone a scholar."

Alaida sank back slightly. "It still sounds exciting."

"Not quite the word I would use for it but I suppose it does keep me on my toes." Jamie tossed a stone out into the tall grass. "If you had to live through it, you'd understand. I don't really know anyone there. I don't fit in. The teachers don't like me."

"Don't you have any friends at all?" Alaida said.

Jamie thought back over the last few weeks and his increasingly muddled social life. "Well, kind of, I mean, I know some guys I hang out with sometimes and there's this girl who won't leave me alone."

Alaida leaned in mischievously. "A girl?"

"Not like that," Jamie said. At least he didn't think it was. "She's...it's complicated."

"How complicated? Have you kissed her?"

"What?" Jamie stammered. "She's got a boyfriend. I think she just likes bothering me."

Alaida's eyes narrowed as she scrutinized Jamie, "Have you ever kissed a girl?"

"What?," Jamie said, feeling his collar growing warm. "What kind of question is that? Of course I have!"

"Oh?" Alaida didn't look as if she believed him. "Then tell me about your first kiss."

Jamie laughed, shaking his head. From Alaida's stern expression, however, she wasn't going to take 'no' for an answer. "Fine," he said at last. "Fine. It was a girl named Kristie."

Alaida, still watching him intently, raised her eyebrows, prodding him to continue.

Sighing, Jamie shook his head yet again. "Okay, fine," he said. "Me and Kristie had been hanging out on a Saturday afternoon with another friend of ours named Jack. The three of us had been best friends since kindergarten and we always did everything together. I don't even remember what we'd been doing that day, but afterward, Jack got a ride home since his parents own a farm outside of town. Me and Kristie only lived a few houses apart, so we were walking home together when we stopped at a park and just started goofing around on the playground equipment. There was no one else around and Kristie started talking about comic books, which she does all the time. Even though I never got into that stuff the way she does, she was just so passionate about it as she was standing there on one of the swings that I just couldn't stop thinking how cute she looked."

No longer looking quite so mischievous, Alaida had leaned forward, listening closely to Jamie's every word. He'd never actually spoken about this with anyone before.

"I'd never really thought about her like that before. Earlier that summer, when Heather had been home to visit, she'd tried to convince me that Kristie and I would make a good couple. At the time, I thought she was just trying to get under my skin, the way she always does, but when I was there in that park with Kristie, there was this moment and...I just kissed her. I don't really know what I was thinking, but I know for a fact that she kissed me back. It was..." Jamie fumbled for words, waving his hands as if trying to conjure one out of thin air.

"Awkward?" Alaida said in a small voice.

"No," Jamie said. "It was...perfect. Like the way you can only ever dream of getting it right. Neither of us said much after that. I walked her home, and then the next day, *that's* when things got awkward. It was like the two of us didn't know how to talk to each other anymore. For a long time, we could barely even look at each other."

"Were you ever able to come to terms with her?" Alaida whispered.

"Sort of," Jamie said. "Not really. It was a couple of weeks later that my...parents died." Alaida whimpered suddenly. He knew she would understand if he didn't go on, but now that he'd started this story, he had to finish it. "Kristie came over to my house after the funeral to offer her condolences. She hugged me and I was sobbing the whole time. We talked for a while, but I could tell it wasn't like before. That one perfect kiss had cost me my best friend. We haven't spoken to each other since I moved away."

"Jamie, I am sorry." Alaida squeezed his hand. "I did not mean to upset you. I was only teasing."

Jamie laughed around the lump in his throat and gripped her hand. "It's okay. I'm fine."

Alaida put her arm around him and rested her head against his shoulder. "You should talk to her," she said, her whispered statement cutting through the chirping of insects which filled the air. "It is not good to leave something like that unresolved between friends."

"I know. I really should. It just never seemed like the right time. I don't even know what I'm supposed to tell her."

"You do not need to *tell* her anything, you just need to talk to her. Even if she does not feel the same way about you, true friends are hard to find. One small moment of embarrassment should not be allowed to end a friendship that strong."

But if it had been ruined so easily, maybe it had never been all that strong to begin with. And as much as he'd always liked Kristie, the connection they shared was nothing at all like the one Jamie had discovered here with Alaida.

Maybe Alaida only thought of Jamie as a brother, but he'd known from the first time they met that they shared some intangible bond; a bond that went far beyond any typical relationship. Speaking that afternoon, he'd only become more convinced of that fact, as well as realizing just how deep and thoroughly unexplainable that connection was.

"Alaida," Jamie said, staring out into the trees, "I know we haven't known each other all that long, but we're friends too, right? And I don't mean just because I'm, I mean, because I...because Gavrin gave me those papers and that seal. I mean, not because you feel obligated, right?"

"Of course we are friends." He felt her body shift alongside his as she looked up and squeezed his hand once more. "I have been a member of several households and even though most have always been kind to me, I do not believe that I ever would have called any Human a friend before you. I have seldom enough been able to call other Raven-Slaves friend."

"I've never really had a lot of friends myself."

Alaida looked away, laying her head on Jamie's shoulder once more. "When I was younger, there was an elderly Raven-Slave that I would often meet when shopping at the market. She was very wise, and I always enjoyed talking with her. When she became too old to perform her duties, she was sold to a distant slave-farm and her masters replaced her with a young girl who saw me as only a rival, not a friend. That is the way most of the others behave at the inn. They are always pandering for Master Gavrin's favor while undermining any who might challenge their position. Being as common as I am, the only interest they had in me was as a target for their jests. Even the others who did not hold such high favor were little different. They might not have been as blatant in their methods, pretending to sympathize in order to gain my trust so that they could then betray me and advance themselves, but I think that only made them more cruel."

Jamie knew exactly what she meant. He'd seen that same thing over and over again in school. He had never been particularly popular himself but at least he'd seldom found himself that far down in the social pecking order. "Friends have always been a quality-over-quantity kind of thing for me."

"Then I feel particularly fortunate to have your friendship."

CHAPTER 18

For a time, the two of them sat in silence, leaning against the other and watching the shadows lengthen through the trees. Slowly, the steady whine of the sawmills in the distance became less constant, gradually replaced by the incessant chattering of people flowing out into the village streets. It was still some time later when Alaida finally sat up and tipped her head to the side with that questioning gesture she had.

"Mast -- I mean, Jam..." As comfortable as the two of them were talking to each other, breaking years of conditioning would not be easy for her. "May I ask you a question that has been on my mind for some time now?"

Jamie turned toward her. "You can ask me anything you want."

Alaida stood and walked to the far side of the foundation, wringing her hands. After having had her laying against him for so long, it now felt like something was missing. "I understand that you did not intentionally purchase me," she said, picking her words carefully, "but...why did you choose me?"

"And not one of the other Raven-Slaves?" Jamie said. Alaida nodded. "I don't really know the answer to that myself. You just seemed...special, I guess."

"But I am not special," Alaida said, almost pleading. "I am quite plain for a Raven-Slave and my skills are limited only to matters of keeping a household. Surely your money would have been better spent on someone else."

"Alaida, don't ever say that." Jamie jumped to his feet and crossed the distance between them. Placing his hand on her cheek, he said, "You are special. I've never met anyone like you before."

Forcing a smile, Alaida stepped out from under his touch as if simply shifting her weight. "And being a traveler, I suppose you have met many?"

"A few, I suppose. And I can honestly say that you are, by far, the most interesting one I've ever met."

"My own experiences are somewhat more limited than yours, I am sure, but I suppose I thought the same of you after our first meeting." Alaida paused and looked down at her hands. "Although, after the way it ended, I was afraid I might have never had a chance to see you again."

The hairs on the back of Jamie's neck suddenly stood on end. "And just how did our last meeting end?"

"You don't remember?"

"The whole thing is kind of a blur. I remember Gavrin and his bouncers came over and pushed me off the porch, but after that..." Of all the topics they'd covered that afternoon, this one had yet to come up. Now that it had, Jamie suddenly found something he would choose to be evasive about. "I'd like to hear how you remember it."

"After you got back up, you stared at them for a time. Your eyes were so cold, I thought I might be looking at a completely different person. Boric tried to send you on your way again but you broke his arm."

"I...I did?" Jamie looked down at his hands. Here on Terrarhea, he certainly had the capability to break a man's arm with ease, but could he have really done that without even realizing it? Or had it instead been the work of the Red Rogue? Was there even a difference? After the way Gavrin had treated Alaida, Jamie had certainly *wanted* to do something like that to the innkeeper and his men. If given another moment at their first meeting, he very well might have. Heavily, he put out a hand to steady himself against one of the nearby stone walls.

"Are you alright?"

"I think so, maybe." Was he? Or was he going mad? "What else?"

"After that, you glared at Master Gavrin once more and then simply walked away. It happened so quickly; I did not even know what I was seeing at first. I do not think Master Gavrin did either. One moment Boric reached for you and the next he was on the ground with his arm bent in the wrong direction and you were headed for the gates." She paused. "It...scared me."

"You don't have anything to be afraid of. I'd never do anything to hurt you." Could he say the same for the Red Rogue? Hastily, he pushed the thought from his mind. He couldn't really be sharing bodies with a man like that. That was crazy. "I'll make sure nothing bad ever happens to you. I'll protect you."

"No, I was not scared of you." Alaida took a seat on one of the fallen stones and folded her hands in her lap. She stared at them for some time before going on. "I was scared of myself because I wanted to see you hurt all of them. And that is not something that a slave should ever think."

"Alaida, I may have bought you, but as far as I'm concerned, you're free now. You don't have to think like a slave anymore."

"Your home must be very far away indeed. I was born a slave and I will die a slave. This is the way it is for every slave; for every member of all seven slave races."

"Even the Wolf-Slaves?" Jamie said. "They're one of your seven slave-races, right?"

Alaida nodded, though plainly confused by Jamie's line of questioning.

"Well, I ran into a pack of them this morning and they didn't have any masters."

"You did? It is a wonder you were not hurt. Most Wolf-Slaves have all gone feral. They are little more than mindless beasts that attack anything they can kill. Hardly anyone keeps them anymore."

Apparently, prejudice wasn't confined only to the human population of Terrarhea. "I suppose 'feral' is a good enough description for them as anything, but they weren't mindless or beasts. They may have been a little rough around the edges, but they were at least as smart as some humans I've met." Seth and Gavrin came to the forefront of his thoughts. "The point is, living out in the wild like that, without any owners, they're not slaves anymore. They're free."

"Wolf-Slaves may be free, but even they are still slaves. It does not matter where or how one lives; we are all of us forever slaves. It is not something that can be taken away or given. It is an inborn part of what we are. Just as you are Human, we are Slaves."

Jamie threw out his hands. "Are you telling me that just because your eyes are yellow and 'slave' is part of what they call you, that that's all you'll ever be?"

"There is more that separates a human from slave than the color of our eyes," Alaida said.

"Okay, sure, the Wolf-Slaves I met were definitely...unique, but they were still basically the same as everyone else. Do you and me really look all that different from each other?"

"Do you have talons?" Alaida said, brushing her hair to the side and turning so that Jamie could see a tiny black claw laying flat against her skin near the top of each shoulder blade. They were the same shade of pearlescent black as her finger and toenails. Before now, he'd simply assumed her nails had been painted, but now he realized this was their natural coloration. Forgetting his manners, Jamie kept staring at the talons right up until Alaida let her hair fall back into place, again hiding them from view. "All Raven-Slaves have them. Our eyesight and hearing are also much sharper than any human's.

Bear-Slaves are incredibly strong. Stoat-Slaves are exceptional diggers who can see in near total blackness. Panther-Slaves can leap extraordinary distances and climb almost anything. You have seen Wolf-Slaves for yourself. All of the slave races have the same yellow eyes and none of us can bare children with humans. So, you see, we are actually quite different from humans."

As she spoke, Jamie began taking a closer look at Alaida than he had in the past. When all the unique characteristics which she shared with no human were taken as a whole, they did indeed add up to a being that wasn't quite human. Even a revelation like that would never change the way Jamie thought of her, but it did raise a flurry of questions in his mind. Apparently, on Terrarhea, a slave wasn't someone forced into a life of servitude, it was one of seven specific races who were expected to serve.

"You mean you're like...a completely different species?" Jamie really wished he would have paid more attention in biology class. "From the sounds of it, you're better than humans. Why do any of you serve them?"

"Because that is the way things are. Regardless of what you may wish, I could no more choose to stop being a slave than I could choose to fly. As long as someone holds my seal, the law demands that I must serve them."

Was it really possible to brainwash someone that completely? Jamie couldn't imagine that there was any living thing in the entire universe that didn't want its freedom, no matter what it may have been told all its life. He picked up the leather binder which held Alaida's seal and tapped it against his open palm.

"What if we destroyed it?" Jamie said, "or...just threw it away?"

He made as if to throw it out into the tall plants beyond the ruined foundation but Alaida shot forward like a bolt, holding up her hands to stop him. "No, please! If the authorities asked for proof of my ownership and it could not be provided, I would be taken away. When the status of a slave can not be determined, they are classified as contraband and returned to a slave farm."

Jamie shook his head. That was not a fate he would ever wish on anyone. There had to be some way to make this right. "Here," he said and tossed the binder to Alaida. "I'm giving it to you. Now you own yourself."

Alaida caught it out of reflex, with more dexterity than most humans would have been able to manage under similar circumstances. The moment she realized what she had done, however, she dropped it as if it were a red-hot coal. It fell open as it hit the ground and landed with the glistening gold seal on top. "No! You can't do that. A slave isn't allowed to touch their own seal."

"Why? Because someone's afraid they might steal it and run away?"

Alaida opened her mouth to reply but could not. By her own words, such a thing would not be possible. If slaves existed only to serve, the idea of running away should not be something they would even be able to consider. Of course, she'd also told Jamie that a slave could not own property. Did that include even herself?

"If you really think that I'm your master and that you have to obey me, then I'm ordering you to take that seal as your own and never take another order from anyone ever again. One way or another, I'm setting you free."

As if running out of energy, Alaida dropped to her knees. She reached for the binder but couldn't quite bring herself to actually touch it. She looked up at Jamie, her eyes wide and watery. "Why?" she said. Jamie couldn't tell if she was demanding an explanation or accusing him of something horrible. She should have been celebrating, not getting upset.

"Because it's the right thing to do. No one deserves to be a slave, no matter what they call you. I can't help everyone, but I can help you. Maybe it's selfish…but if I left you as a slave, I'd never be able to live with myself knowing that I could have done something and didn't."

"But…" Alaida looked at the seal once more and then up at Jamie. "What am I to do? Do you wish me to live in the wilds as the Wolf-Slaves do, hunting wild game with my bare hands and eating its raw flesh?"

"No, of course not," Jamie said. Unfortunately, if the idea of a free Raven-Slave were so alien to this world, how many other choices would she have? Jamie kneeled down in front of her. "I'm sure we can figure something out."

Alaida bit her lip as she considered this. "Could I…come with you…on your travels?"

Jamie felt his heart jump up into his throat. He could hardly believe he'd heard that right. A girl as beautiful and charming and lovely as Alaida wanted to be with *him*? Maybe Terrarhea was only a dream after all. He felt like laughing and cowering in fear at the same time.

"Remember, Alaida, I'm not your master. I'll try to help you do whatever you want, but you don't have to come with me." Those were possibly some of the hardest words he'd ever uttered.

"But I would *like* to," Alaida said slowly. "I would very much like to go traveling, not with my master, but with my friend." Finally, she reached out and picked up the leather binder, careful not to touch the actual seal, but definitely resolute in her movements. As she stood, Jamie did so as well.

"If you're really sure you want to," Jamie said.

"I am. Besides, there is little, if anything, a Raven-Slave can do on her own. If I was with you, everyone would assume you were my master, and it would save both of us from having to answer what I am sure would be many difficult questions."

Pretending to be her master wasn't much better than actually being one, but she did make a very good point. There was also the matter of what would happen to her if Jamie were whisked back to Earth like last time. Up until now he hadn't even allowed himself to think that far ahead. As Alaida had just made clear, there was no way to even pass her off as human in the short term. Perhaps they could find someone to take care of her until Jamie returned. Or maybe he could outfit her with a camp in the wilds somewhere where she could live comfortably and not at all like the savage Wolf-Slaves. Or maybe setting Alaida free was the one good deed he'd needed to perform in order to also set himself free from this cycle of shared worlds. Unlikely as it might have been, he would have hoped for it more strongly if it didn't mean he'd never get to see Alaida again.

Or maybe the Red Rogue would know what to do. Jamie shuddered at the thought. Even if someone else was in control of this life on Terrarhea when he was back on Earth, Jamie was almost certain he wasn't going to trust Alaida's safety to a possibility that insubstantial. No matter what happened, he would do whatever necessary to protect her.

That nagging sensation had grown progressively more assertive all afternoon, but even if it did mark how much time he had left on this world, it felt like hours away from breaking. They still had time to come up with a plan.

"Are you hungry?" Alaida said.

Jamie hadn't thought about food all day long. In fact, he wasn't even a little bit hungry, even after all he'd been through. Alaida, on the other hand, must have been famished. Her life as a slave, however, had probably trained her to never say anything so self-important. Getting her to leave all that conditioning behind was going to take some work.

"Yeah, I could probably eat," Jamie said. It was doubtlessly true, even if he didn't feel like it. Unfortunately, he had overlooked one thing.

"Is something the matter?"

"I think I might have given all my money to Gavrin."

He really should have thought this through. Even though he'd set Alaida free, she was still just as much his responsibility as if she were still his property. Until he could find a way to make sure she would be alright on her own, it would be up to him to take care of her. Jamie patted himself down as if checking his pockets. He was a little surprised when he discovered his clothes actually had pockets; he'd never thought to check before. In one, he found a yellowish-gold coin marked with a large number "two" and three smaller coins which bore a number "five" on one of their silvery faces.

"Sorry," he said, holding them out in the palm of his hand. "I think that's all I've got."

Alaida, however, was not disappointed. "Fifteen taleks or two duxts," she said with measured precision and then picked up two of the silver coins. "Five taleks apiece would likely be more than enough for a meal."

"Really?" Jamie tossed the two remaining coins in his hand. This monetary system was going to take some getting used to. "So how much does a Raven-Slave cost then?"

"That would be difficult to say since there are many factors that go into the price. I suppose my own worth might be about ten sorin." Seeing Jamie's expression, she quickly elaborated. "A sorin is worth ten cron, a cron is worth ten duxt, a duxt is worth ten taleks, a talek is worth ten deiren, and a deiran is worth ten shellig."

"So, one duxt for two meals..." Jamie mused. If he assumed a talek was roughly equivalent to a dollar and he'd paid Gavrin ten times what Alaida was worth... His eyes grew wide as he did the math. That small sack of coins had been roughly comparable to one hundred thousand dollars! No wonder Garvin had been so nervous. He probably wasn't the type who'd be willing to grant a refund either.

"I...could go without if you have more important uses for the money," Alaida said, passing the coins back to Jamie.

"No, I don't have anything more important. Even if I did, I wouldn't let you starve." Jamie paused and smiled. "Not after I paid so much for you."

Alaida tilted her head and looked at him quizzically. Slowly, her expression melted into a bewildered smile and soon they were both laughing.

"Where should we go?" Jamie said. "Any good restaurants in town? We have enough money for a little bit of a celebration, don't we?"

"I do not believe there are any restaurants that would allow a Raven-Slave to eat there," Alaida said. "Besides, with your...limited coin, I think the market would be a better option. I have heard the food served at several booths is very good."

Jamie again considered the four coins in his hand. If that really was all they had, he'd have to make it last as long as possible. Onorah had offered him the hospitality of her father's house, but it probably wouldn't be good manners to show up on her doorstep with a newly purchased Raven-Slave in tow.

"Okay," he said. "Let's check out this market."

"This way," Alaida said, setting off through the underbrush.

CHAPTER 19

As they made their way back toward the streets of the village, their surroundings were cast into murky shades of gray. Jamie hadn't noticed until now that the sun had all but disappeared from the sky, though not because it had set, but because a bank of dark clouds had begun moving in from the south. It was brighter once they emerged from under the canopy of the trees, but the sky remained a uniform blanket of gray clouds sliding by just overhead. Alaida guided Jamie through a narrow gap between two houses, and as they emerged on the other side, a sudden movement sent Jamie jumping back with a startled cry.

On the other side of a simple wooden fence stood a strange creature about as tall as Jamie's waist. From out of the dark, leathery skin covering its head, a pair of keen eyes stared back at him. The rest of its body sported a coat of small feathers that shimmered red and green. Its back legs were thick and ended in clawed feet with splayed toes, but it kept its small front arms tucked up under its chin as it walked with a purposeful, bobbing gait. If it weren't for the gaping mouth filled with rows of sharp teeth, it almost could have been some kind of giant, flightless bird.

Having heard Jamie's cry, Alaida looked back. "Is everything well?"

Jamie shuffled along the edge of the pen, keeping a wary eye on the creature who continued watching him just as closely. He then noticed another one on the other side of the fenced yard who let out a shrill chirp. Whatever they were, the fence didn't look high enough to keep them in if they decided they wanted to get out.

"What are those things?"

It took Alaida a moment to realize what Jamie was referring to. "They are chickens," she said, still perplexed and now on the verge of laughing. "Do they not have chickens where you come from?"

"Chickens? Of course we have chickens. They're just a little smaller." Jamie held his hands apart to indicate the rough dimensions of a Earth chicken. "And they don't have so many teeth."

Alaida's face contorted as she tried to imagine something so outlandish. "A chicken that small would hardly have any meat on it at all."

"Less, maybe," Jamie said, still eyeing the 'chickens' as he and Alaida edged beyond the fence, "but I never had to worry that they were going to disembowel me."

Alaida laughed. "They are harmless. Now come, the market will be closing before too long."

All afternoon, Jamie had seen the featureless back of a long, single-story building from their vantage point at the ruined foundation. He had also heard the indistinct bustle of activity coming from the other side, but he didn't realize this was the market Alaida had spoken of until they arrived. Shaped something like a question mark, the whole building consisted of individual stalls facing the street where vendors could set up to sell their wares. The straight portion of the building opened directly onto the street for quite some distance and the booths there predominantly sold things like dry goods, herbs, fruits, vegetables, and meats. Many of these vendors were beginning to close up for the night, but further on, where the building curved away from the street, around the edge of a semi-circular plaza with a handsome stand of mature trees in the center, several of the booths were still doing brisk business. Laborers crusted with sweat and sawdust got in line right behind office workers in rumpled clothes for the many varieties of ready-to-eat foods being offered at the stalls. Even though he still wasn't very hungry, all the rich smells filling the air made Jamie curious about all the different options.

"Which one would you recommend?" Jamie said as a Raven-Slave hurried past in the opposite direction, carrying a bag of flour in her arms while keeping her eyes on the ground.

Alaida watched her pass and seemed to shrink in on herself a little, surreptitiously slipping the leather binder that held her seal of ownership into the end of her dangling sleeve. "It is a shame we do not have a kitchen to make use of," she said in a small voice. "We could stretch your money much further if I could prepare the meal myself."

"I'm sure you're a great cook but we can afford to splurge a little." Besides, the last thing he wanted after setting her free was to put her to work in a kitchen. Motioning towards the nearest stall, where the customers were walking away with large, steaming turnovers, he said, "What's this one selling? Are those meat pies?"

"Yes," Alaida said, barely lifting her eyes, "I have never eaten them, but I believe they come in two varieties, mirdrax and jackelope."

"Jackelope? Really? I've got to try that. Although I've heard good things about mirdrax too. What do you think? We can get one of each so both of us can try them?"

"If you wish."

Alaida's eyes flittered toward the stall and then back to the ground. Jamie could see several customers waiting in line who were eyeing the two of them, but it was no worse than the looks Jamie had been getting all day from almost everyone in town. Setting a hand on her shoulder, Jamie said, "Alaida, are you okay?"

"Yes. Fine. I will wait for you over there, by the trees."

"Wait, what?" Jamie started to say, but she had already moved off, headed toward the trees in the center of the plaza. Jamie threw out his hands. He couldn't see any Raven-Slaves among the lines of people waiting for food. Apparently, this was another of those things that a Raven-Slave wasn't supposed to concern herself with. Hopefully, he wouldn't need any help ordering. Stealing one last look at Alaida, who had taken up position near an assortment of unused tables and chairs, Jamie got in line.

It moved fast enough but Jamie still had plenty of opportunities to hear the way the other customers ordered their food so that he felt confident he'd be able to manage the same when it came his turn. He kept a watchful eye on Alaida who remained in the same spot the whole time, trying to make herself look as unobtrusive as possible. As much as Jamie didn't want to see her act like a slave, he had to admit it probably wasn't a good idea to antagonize the townsfolk any more than necessary, not when they outnumbered him so drastically.

"One mirdrax and one jackelope with an order of chips," Jamie said when he reached the head of the line, mimicking the way the others had ordered before him.

In all the transactions he'd so far watched, the tall woman behind the counter would instantly ramble off a total, the customer would hand her some coins, and she'd promptly give them their change along with the order. This time, she put both her hands down flat on the counter and leaned forward as she glared at Jamie. The sweeping line of her blouse revealed a row of black tattoos along the edge of the left collarbone in the shapes of a feather, a claw, a fang, and several others. Though they had been done in a different style than the markings Jamie had seen on those two young men at the mining camp, these tattoos had clearly been created to express a similar meaning, whatever that was.

"Two pies?" she said, her gaze shooting across the plaza to where Jamie knew Alaida stood. They even had rules against Raven-Slaves eating their food?

"Yeah, I'm very hungry," Jamie said, his voice taking on a sardonic edge. "Two pies, and an order of chips. Eleven taleks, if I'm not mistaken."

He dropped the three five-talek coins on the counter in front of the woman. If there was one thing he'd learned about Terrarhea, it was that money still spoke just as loudly here as on any world. The corner of the woman's lip twitched but she snatched up the coins just as willingly as Gavrin had done. She then stormed away to the back of the booth where another woman had, up until now, diligently assembled each order. This time however, the first woman shared a few harsh words with her, and she looked back at Jamie over her shoulder. More words, becoming increasingly heated, were spoken between the two. The second woman finally seized the coins from the first and hastily grabbed two foil-wrapped pies and a large paper sleeve filled with what looked like potato wedges from the back counter. The food she tossed down in front of Jamie as she went to the cash box and then threw several silvery coins down on the counter as well.

"There!" she said. "Now bugger off!"

Jamie gave the woman a long level gaze which she returned with a glare, her nostrils flaring with each breath she took. Taking his time, Jamie scooped the chips back into their wrapper and then gathered everything up. The crust on one of the pies had split open in the transaction but still appeared to be perfectly edible so he decided not to make an issue of it. A few of the other customers either offered Jamie jibes of their own as he walked away or they gave encouragement to the woman behind the counter for what she had just done. Most, however, looked the other way, pretending not to have seen a thing. Jamie ignored them all. He crossed the plaza to where Alaida had all but disappeared behind one of the flowering shrubs growing at the base of the trees.

"Well, that was fun," Jamie said, setting their hard-won goods down on one of the nearby tables which was similarly hidden from view.

Silently, Alaida carefully counted up the coins which Jamie had also set on the table. "Two taleks and three deiren," she said when complete and offered them to Jamie.

He slipped them back into his pocket with the others and they both sat down at the square table, Alaida with her back to the trees and Jamie on the corner next to her. "I'm pretty sure we got overcharged for this," he said. "Maybe they just thought that with service that friendly they deserved a big tip. At least they didn't spit on anything."

The two pies were big half-circles nearly a foot long and plump with fillings. Jamie took the broken corner from the damaged one. It contained pale chunks of meat in a thick gravy with chopped vegetables and a spattering of spices. Whatever was in it, it sure smelled good. He blew at the rising steam and said, "Which one is this?"

"Mirdrax," Alaida said, nibbling at one of the chips.

Jamie took a small bite; almost certain he was going to burn his tongue but unwilling to wait any longer. Though it did prove to be quite hot indeed, his mouth must have been just as tough as the rest of him. He couldn't identify any of the spices or the vegetables in the pie, but their flavors were all perfectly balanced with the meat. The crust, meanwhile, was light and buttery with just the right amount of salt. "Wow, that's good!" Only half joking he added, "It tastes kind of like chicken."

"It is chicken," Alaida said, her voice and expression flat. Jamie frowned. Maybe that wasn't a joke on Terrarhea. "Mirdrax are not easily farmed and they can be dangerous to hunt in the wild. Since chicken tastes similar, most people use it to make mirdrax pies instead."

"So why do they still call them mirdrax pies?" Jamie said, popping the rest of the portion into his mouth.

Alaida shrugged without looking at him.

"And what is a mirdrax anyway?"

"A large, scaled creature that walks on four legs with its belly on the ground. They have huge mouths with long teeth and are known to attack people in the wild."

"Another dinosaur?" Jamie said.

"What is a...diner-sore?" Alaida said looking up at him.

"Giant lizard-like creatures that died out millions of years ago. Some of them evolved into birds." Alaida's expression contorted into one of complete puzzlement. "Never mind. It's not important." Jamie broke the other pie in two and handed the larger half to Alaida. This one looked like it contained the same assortment of vegetables, but the meat was much darker and had been shredded instead of cubed. Both from the look of the gravy and from the smell, it had also been flavored more strongly with spices. After just one bite, Jamie could tell that it had been done to mask the distinct taste of wild game. It certainly wasn't unpleasant, but Jamie definitely preferred the mirdrax.

Alaida started with a small bite of her own and quickly followed it with a larger one, and then an even larger one after that. Watching her attack the pie with growing enthusiasm, Jamie couldn't help but wonder if her thinness was a natural trait shared by all Raven-Slaves or if Gavrin starved the ones he owned in some misguided attempt to make them more appealing to his customers. Or maybe to save money. Or just out of simple cruelty.

"What do you usually eat?" Jamie said.

Alaida suddenly stopped and looked up at Jamie, swallowing awkwardly. "My apologies," she said, her cheeks reddening. "I have all but forgotten my manners."

"Don't apologize. You're obviously hungry; a lot more than I am. I was just curious since you said you'd never had these before."

"Porridge or gruel usually. Most owners allow us to eat their leftovers if they will not keep. At the tavern, I was one of the newest Raven-Slaves so most of the others had first pick of such things, however."

Jamie shook his head and absently bit into one of the chips. The crisp outside had been heavily seasoned while the inside was a delicately textured swirl of red and purple. It easily put to shame the best french-fry Jamie had ever tasted. "They don't even need ketchup."

"Ketchup? On chips?"

"You guys don't do that here?"

Alaida shook her head slowly, as if reconsidering her opinion of Jamie's sanity.

"Well, at least you *have* ketchup. Or do you? It's like a red sauce, right?"

"Blue," Alaida said.

"Blue ketchup? That's just too weird." As Alaida began to snicker, Jamie haltingly said, "What?"

"No, our ketchup is red as well."

"Blue ketchup!" Jamie laughed and tossed the end of his chip at Alaida. She let out a shriek as she shielded herself.

"If you do not want them..." Alaida reached out and pulled the package of chips over to her side of the table.

"Hey! I didn't say that." Jamie made a grab for the chips. "Those are actually really good. And I think you still owe me some more of that mirdrax pie."

"I am not so certain of that," Alaida said with mock sincerity as she held back the remaining portion of the pie protectively.

"Oh, so that's the way it's gonna be, is it?"

Having just forgotten about all the eyes on them, Jamie and Alaida both jumped back in their seats when a man suddenly rushed over from beyond the edge of the plaza and slammed his palms down on the tabletop.

"What the bloody hell do you think you're doing!" he said, his voice a barely contained shriek.

Tall and lanky, he was clean-shaven, and his shoulder-length blond hair had been pulled back into a neat ponytail at the base of his neck. The long black coat he wore had been buttoned up tight to his neck and the matching, wide-brimmed hat on his head had been pulled low over the round glasses on his face. Though tinted, the lenses did little to hide the wide, furtive eyes staring out from beneath.

Even if he wanted to start a fight, he didn't look like much of a threat. Jamie, however, had had just about enough of all these Terrarhean prejudices to last him a lifetime.

"Hey!" Jamie said. "What's the big idea! We're trying to eat here!"

"Oh, I can see that." The man nodded frantically. "I can see that quite plain." He paused and looked back over his shoulder and then said in a harsh whisper, "The whole bleedin' city can!"

Taking the seat across the table from Jamie, the bottom of the man's coat fell open to reveal the dark green tunic and trousers he wore underneath. Jamie didn't even need to see the military insignias on his collar to now know what this man was. However, Jamie still had no idea what his interest in him was. Rather than reach for a gun or try to arrest him, the man rubbed his hand across his face. Jamie merely tensed in his seat, preparing himself for anything at all that might come next.

CHAPTER 20

"What the hell?" the man said. He looked at Alaida and shook his head tiredly. "What the bloody hell? I sincerely hope you did not throw all that hard work out the window just so you could spend a little time with a Raven-Slave, especially one this ordinary. Even more especially when it puts my head on the chopping block right alongside yours."

This wasn't making any sense at all. How could anything Jamie have done with Alaida possibly endanger some random soldier he'd never met before? With things the way they were, all Jamie could manage was, "Huh?"

"Under normal circumstances, I wouldn't care a wit about your personal proclivities, but can you just imagine my surprise when I got to this dump and saw that titan of yours parked out there in the Annex Yard? 'No,' I think to myself, 'he couldn't really be crazy enough to bring that incredibly conspicuous thing to what is supposed to be a clandestine meeting. This has all got to be part of his big master plan and he's just trying to put me off my guard.' But then it seems like everyone is talking about the owner who's strolling around town with a Raven-Slave on his arm like he's on bloody holiday!"

Looking to Alaida for help, Jamie saw she had become so startled, she sat frozen in place with the uneaten portion of her pie still in hand. Sitting very stiffly in his own chair, Jamie said, "D-do you know me?"

"What?" The stranger glanced around the plaza, unconsciously causing Jamie to do the same. "Of course I don't know you! We've never met, spoken, or communicated in any way, shape, or form -- and don't forget it!"

"Hold on a second. What are you talking about?"

"Right, down to business then, is it?" As the man reached into his coat, Jamie half rose out of his seat, expecting a gun. Instead, the man drew out a thick sheaf of dog-eared and yellowed papers all haphazardly shoved into an equally aged manila folder. He threw them down on the table in front of Jamie with a slap. "There, it's all yours. Please take it out of my life forever. If I never see that bleedin' file again, it'll be too soon."

Jamie looked at the folder, then at the man. Nothing he'd said was helping to clarify things in the least.

"So, are we even now?" the man said. "No more clandestine attempts to blackmail me into getting myself killed for you? Because I've gotta tell you: I'm done; out; finished."

"Out?" Jamie said. "What do you think you're getting out of?"

"Oh my god! Is that the way you're gonna be about this? I did what you wanted! Can't we just both go our separate ways? You don't need to kill me too! I'll keep my mouth shut! No one else has to die, alright?"

"Okay, that's enough!" Jamie said. The man snapped his mouth shut and sat up very straight and rigid in his chair. Did he really think that Jamie was going to kill him? Did he actually think that Jamie was capable of such a thing? "Now who are you, what is this file, and just what the heck is going on here?"

The man's eye grew even more wide as he shook his head. "Is this some kind of test? Do you really think I've forgotten how serious all this is? I'm a dead man if they find out what I've been up to. I probably won't even get a trial, just disappear in the middle of the night."

Jamie's voice took on a razor's edge as he leaned forward in his chair, "Tell me." The man threw up his hands to shield his face. "Who are you and what's this file?"

"Fine," the man said. "Fine. I'm Lieutenant Del Mamdon, junior files expeditor at Yarzak Depository. Several weeks ago you approached me with detailed information concerning my...distribution of controlled recreational substances to certain members of the personnel there. You also expressed interest in a very specific file we had at the Depository and you made it clear that if I did not help you get it, the truth about my entrepreneurial activities would become known to my superiors. So, yes, I am well aware of the situation I find myself in. You have been the one holding the headsman's axe over my neck since the first time we met."

Alaida, sitting absolutely still and staring with blank eyes, let out a tiny whimper.

"I'm not going to kill anyone," Jamie said, frowning as he glanced hastily from Alaida to the man.

"Well, that's good to know," the man said, straightening his coat a little. "But there it is, exactly what you wanted, fully decoded." He jabbed his finger down on top of the file. Jamie stared at it but could see no reason for all the melodrama. The man, Lieutenant Mamdon apparently, or Del (Jamie had a hard time thinking of him as a military officer for some reason) seemed to believe that Jamie should have been more impressed. "Do you even have any idea how much trouble it was, sneaking that entire file into the decoder room, one page at a time, so that no one would notice? Any other decoder in the entire country would have worked just as well, but of course

Yarzak is the one place in possibly the whole world that would know what the file was."

"And what is it?" Jamie gingerly rotated the file to face him as if it might be poisoned.

Del's mouth dropped open. "Really? We've been over this before. It's old research notes by some magesmith named Major Ommto that got misfiled with his duty record when he retired. Yarzak doesn't handle those types of files, we only deal with archived personnel records. All magesmith related documentation is housed in the capital. So, when that file suddenly fell off a shelf a couple weeks ago and someone realized what it was, it was scheduled to be shipped there. Of course, you somehow found out about it and were so interested in it that you tried to break in and steal it. But that didn't go so well for you, did it? That's when you came and recruited me to do your dirty work for you. Is that good enough for you or should I keep going?"

As he'd listened to the man's rant, Jamie's skin had grown increasingly cold. With the tip of his finger, he flipped back the cover of the folder. It was a thick brownish cardboard, almost as stiff as wood which creaked as it fell open. The document on top of the stack was a form of some kind, partly hand-written, but all of it in that Terrarhean script. He flipped over a few more, each one equally unintelligible, but some of the letterhead bore a crest depicting a sword, an anvil, and a wreath. Then he noticed something else had been inserted between two of the pages further down, a bulky object which had caused all the papers above and below it to become deformed. Jamie flipped ahead and froze, letting the pages he'd been turning slide out of his fingers.

In the middle of the page sat a small scrap of metal, not quite as big as his hand and barely as thick as tin foil, but permanently domed in the center and edged with jagged burn marks, like a piece of shrapnel recovered from an explosion. The most interesting aspect, however, was the black finish which seemed to shift and waver in the light like the multi-colored sheen of oil floating on water. He couldn't believe what he was seeing. Staring at it, he'd even stopped breathing. It looked exactly like that old homeless man's black box that he'd picked up off the street all those weeks ago, right before his first excursion to Terrarhea.

Del had grabbed several chips from the forgotten wrapper and had been absently popping them into his mouth one at a time. Swallowing, he said, "Yeah, I know you didn't want to part with it, but it was just like I said. Whoever encoded those pages originally used that piece of scrap metal as the decoder resonator key. But there it is, all safe and sound. I didn't lose it."

Jamie's eyes remained fixed on the strange little object as he slowly reached for it. Maybe that old man's black box had been the source of his troubles all along. If touching it had been the start of everything, would touching this shard now be the end of it? His fingers stopped just short of picking it up, however. Even if such a fleeting hope could be true, he couldn't take the risk that it might leave Alaida abandoned here alone. Del might also still have answers as to what was going on in the first place.

"W-what is it?"

"Hell if I know," Del said, taking another handful of chips. "Even decoded, I can't make heads or tails of that magesmith gobbledygook. Near as I can tell, that little piece of metal is what he was researching."

"Wait, you said I tried to break in? When was that? When did they find that it had been misfiled?"

"I don't remember. It was a couple of weeks ago, almost two months maybe? It was found a couple of weeks before that. No one cared much about it until you tried to steal it, though. I remember the whole base was on alert for nearly a week afterward because of those two titan-mechas we lost. By the time they started letting us have passes again, I was meeting my supplier here in Tavnic when you approached me with your little proposal. If only they hadn't decided to beef up security when they shipped that file out, we could have been saved a lot of trouble. Honestly, when I told you about that armed convoy, I was really hoping that you'd realize how stupid this was and just give up. I never thought that you'd actually rob them, with the help of those Wolf-Slaves, no less."

Jamie fell back in his chair as if he had just been punched in the gut. It was all tied together. All of it. The Red Rogue, Reaver, whatever he called himself, had somehow found out about this file and/or the scrap of metal and then tried to break into Yarzak Depository in order to steal it -- at almost the exact same moment that Jamie had first encountered that strange black box on Earth. When the Red Rogue had been forced to run without acquiring his prize, Jamie interrupted and made things worse by destroying those two titan-mechas. Having failed to steal the file from Yarzak, the Red Rogue recruited Lieutenant Del Mamdon to get it for him, only to discover that the military, now on alert, was planning to ship out the file under heavy guard. Jamie's doppelganger might be tough but even he must have realized he needed help to take on an entire armed convoy. Somehow, he convinced a pack of Wolf-Slaves to help him and then made the whole thing look like a botched robbery by petty bandits. The Wolf-Slaves, in turn, had likely gotten his agreement to help them wipe out a pesky mining camp which had been killing members of their pack. The robbery allowed him to get the shard of strange metal, but the file that went with it had been encoded. To solve that problem, he'd gone back to his inside man. But, because as far as everyone at Yarzak was concerned, the file had been destroyed in the robbery, Del had needed to be extremely careful in decoding it. If Jamie hadn't once again come along, the mining camp likely would have been wiped out and made to look like it had been destroyed by the same bandits who'd attacked the convoy, Del would have passed the decoded file over to him at their meeting, and then the Red Rogue could have gone on his way without anyone the wiser.

But why had he been trying so hard to get this strange piece of information? Did he know what the shard of metal was? He and Jamie were obviously connected in some way, if for no other reason than their shared appearance, but it seemed inconceivable that the shard didn't have at least something to do with what was happening as well. Even if the Red Rogue did know what it was, he had been just as unprepared for any of this as Jamie had been. Was it supposed to have been some great prize that ended up being a curse instead? Or had this been the intended outcome all along and it had just happened too soon? Jamie couldn't see how that latter option could be possible. Why would anyone ever want to trade places with him? Besides, this was all just speculation. All he'd really learned here was how all the pieces of his time away from Terrarhea fit together. If he wanted to know more, he'd have to start looking for answers himself.

"So who's Major Ommto?" Jamie said, finding it hard to pull his eyes from the shard of metal. If that file contained his notes, then he must know more. "You said he retired? Where is he now?"

Del sighed and shook his head. "Do I have to repeat everything we've already been over?"

Jamie met his look with a steady stare. "Just humor me," he said, more firmly this time.

"Fine. Yarzak is the national records depository for all military service records so we do have him on file. Apparently, he was some big shot in R&D at Iron Spur. He retired with a whisper over twenty years ago and there's nothing else in his file after that. In all likelihood, he's dead by now. Maybe you could go break into the taxation bureau next. I'm sure they'd know where he ended up." Del reached for another chip and muttered under his breath, "And they're in Karakalum so you'd have to find someone else to harass."

In the emerging twilight, hastened on by the darkening clouds, a nearby streetlight flickered and then sprang to life. Del looked over his shoulder as if it had been a weapon's flash. "So are we square?" he ventured. "You're not gonna kill me now, to tie up loose ends, are you? I'll admit I'm a criminal, maybe not on the same level as you, but a criminal nonetheless so I do have to assume a certain degree of risk when undertaking these sorts of activities. And I realize your reputation is...somewhat unsavory, but you never struck me as being a terribly dishonorable person -- a little scary yes, but despite that, I thought we had an admirable working relationship. I still don't like the way you dragged me into this and I don't like the way everything went down with the convoy but I do appreciate the kickbacks and I have completed my end of the bargain so I'm hoping we can at least part company on amicable terms. Killing me won't help your situation at all, especially right here in the middle of town."

"Please, for the last time, I'm not gonna kill you!"

"Well, good, it's nice to know that we can still be civil about this, even under the circumstances, but I really need to get the hell out of here. If I could make a suggestion, you might want to think about doing so as well." As he rose out of his seat, he grabbed the last chip out of the wrapper and tossed it into his mouth. "I'd say it's been fun, but it was nothing of the sort. Nothing personal, but I hope I never see you again." With a tip of his hat, he turned and hurried out of the plaza.

CHAPTER 21

Sitting in his chair, Jamie's eyes darted about as his thoughts raced. He wasn't entirely sure he followed all the implications of what Del had said but he was pretty sure that man had been right about one thing: they needed to get out of town. Maybe it was simple paranoia, but those soldiers had taken far too much interest in Jamie when he'd first arrived in Tavnic.

Unfortunately, they couldn't just run, they still needed supplies. As much as Jamie didn't want to leave Alaida to her own devices, he simply didn't have enough time to help her with anything else. They'd have to buy a tent and some food at the very least. There had to be shops in town that would sell such things. Or would it be more dangerous to stay here even long enough to do that? Why had he wasted so much time? He'd been certain they'd have more than enough to sort Alaida's situation out. Now it felt like he was running late to school after having forgotten to study for that big final exam.

A single raindrop landed on the papers laid out before him, darkening the yellowed page with a starburst of minuscule droplets which seeped into the paper irregularly where aged fingerprints and smudges had long ago left their marks. Alaida leaned across the table and touched Jamie's arm, her fingers trembling.

"J-Jamie?" she whispered. "What is going on? Who was that?"

Jamie barely knew more than she did but it wouldn't take much effort to figure out that Del had essentially called Jamie a criminal and given eyewitness testimony to that fact. Alaida had already known Jamie was not a fan of the Finttiranos authorities, but he hadn't mentioned that they might also suspect him of being a bandit as well. What must she be thinking now? Unfortunately, they didn't have time to deal with that right now either.

"Alaida, where's the nearest town to Tavnic?"

"S-Sornam lies to the north of Tavnic about an hour's ride by barque, I believe."

"And how fast is a barque?"

"Perhaps as fast as a man running."

That meant his titan could cover the same amount of ground considerably quicker, and certainly with time enough left over to take care of their supply needs without having to worry about being arrested in Tavnic.

"Come on," Jamie said, standing. "We've got to get out of here."

Reacting without really thinking, Alaida began gathering up the uneaten portions of their meal.

"Leave it," Jamie said. "No, bring it. I don't know." He had no idea what he was doing. "We've just got to get moving."

Having already scooped everything up along with the file Del had left them, Alaida appeared more ready than Jamie felt as she stood there expectantly with the bundle clutched to her chest. Jamie took her by the free hand and headed out of the plaza and into the street at a fast walk. They weren't too far from the Annex Yard. With luck they could get to his titan and be out of the city in just a few short minutes.

Rounding the corner of the market plaza, Jamie skidded to a halt as he saw a whole group of soldiers wearing those armored suits coming in his direction with rifles at the ready. Pedestrians got out of their way, most hurrying off the street entirely. Turning a gasping Alaida to follow him, Jamie started to set off in the opposite direction only to see a mixed group of armored soldiers and village guardsmen armed with those blunt-headed spears coming from that direction. Hastily, he altered his course to take them to the cross street which angled away from the plaza into the heart of Tavnic only to discover yet another group of armed soldiers and guardsmen, this one led by none other than Major Addinez himself.

Scrambling out of the line of fire, the people gathered in the plaza ran to safety past the guards while the merchants either dropped the shutters over their booths or simply abandoned their businesses completely. Further down the street, a handful of citizens gathered to watch at what they must have figured was a safe distance.

Trying to keep Alaida behind him the whole time, Jamie turned in a wide circle, his eyes darting about for an opening that would allow for their own escape. However, in a clattering of equipment and armor, the soldiers and guardsmen had already encircled the open end of the plaza, creating a continuous, semi-circular barrier with Jamie at the very center. If it weren't for the stiff breeze blowing the dark clouds overhead, the once lively market would have been completely still.

Jamie shuffled sideways several steps only to find the head of every guard and soldier, along with the muzzle of every weapon, following his movements exactly. There could be no doubt they were here for him. He'd already waited too long. He should have fled the moment Del told them to. He shouldn't have spent all afternoon talking with Alaida. He never should have come back to Tavnic in the first place.

As the guards and soldiers slowly advanced, tightening their perimeter, Major Addinez stepped to the front, his swagger stick gone and his hand now resting on the hilt of a pistol hanging from his belt. The magescript-covered armor he wore looked like a lighter version of the soldiers' own, covering only major portions of his torso, arms, and legs. The helmet left his face exposed, save for the clear, slanted visor which covered his eyes.

"Place your hands on top of your head and get down on your knees," he said in a loud, clear voice that carried throughout the plaza. "We are here to place you under arrest."

Jamie's first through was that Del had set them up. His second was that Del would be in just as much trouble as Jamie if anyone got caught. There also wouldn't have been need for that whole rambling conversation; he could have simply pointed Jamie out at a distance. Even if he'd just been captured after their meeting, Major Addinez wouldn't have had time to organize all this so quickly. No, this was just bad luck, incredibly bad luck mixed with bad timing and bad planning as well.

"Arrest me?" Jamie said, his voice wavering. This couldn't really be happening. As bad as it looked, there still had to be a way out of it. "I'm not a criminal."

"You are wanted for your suspected involvement in the attempted break-in of Fort Yarzak, the destruction of two Finttiranos Mark-5 titan-mechas, assault of their pilots, the robbery and destruction of Convoy 1-1-3-8, and the murder of eight military personnel."

"Jamie?" Alaida said in a barely audible whisper which only Jamie's sensitive ears could have heard. That one plaintive question, however, said far more than Jamie wanted to hear: she was starting to wonder if he really wasn't the criminal everyone thought he was.

Staying in front of Alaida, Jamie raised his hands in a gesture of calm. The soldiers tensed and fixed their weapons on him all the more firmly. A few of the guards flipped switches on their spears that caused the blunt metal heads to become charged with hissing arcs of pale blue electricity.

"Just hold up a second," Jamie said. "This is a mistake. I'm not who you think I am."

"You match the description we have of the one responsible for the destruction of our titans," Major Addinez said, his frown deepening. "You may have been able to take them out with that fancy titan of yours but this time I think we have the upper hand. You even paid for that Raven-Slave with money identified as having been issued to the convoy. If you can prove your innocence, then come quietly and explain it to us."

Except Jamie had no way to prove his innocence. Even if the Major was so inclined to believe his outlandish tale of sharing bodies with the real culprit (something Jamie still didn't quite believe himself), Jamie had still been the one responsible for the destruction of those titan-mechas. It probably wouldn't have been a good idea to correct Major Addinez that he'd actually done that with his bare hands either.

Jamie swept his gaze across the gathered soldiers and guardsmen. There were too many of them to fight. Even if he tried, Alaida would almost certainly get caught in the crossfire. If he simply tried to run, would she even come with him, or would she now prefer whatever fate awaited her as a prisoner rather than as the companion of a wanted criminal? But he'd gotten her into this. Now he had to find a way to keep her safe, no matter what.

"Okay," Jamie said, motioning once again for everyone to remain calm. "Okay, I'll come with you. Just don't hurt Alaida. She's got nothing to do with any of this."

"That's not something you need to worry about at the moment."

"I'm not gonna do anything unless you can tell me Alaida will be okay."

"We're not here to hurt anyone," Major Addinez said, his hand twisting around the grip of his sidearm, "unless you try to resist." He turned to two of the armored soldiers and motioned them forward to take Jamie into custody.

"Excellent work boys," a voice Jamie remembered well called out from the rear of the gathering. His blood boiled when he saw Gavrin, the fat innkeeper, pushing his way past the outer most layer of guards. They weren't trying all that hard to stop him as he made his way toward Major Addinez. "I'm take the gash off your hands, Major."

"Keep him back!" Major Addinez barked. "He's not to have any involvement in this!"

"What are you goin' on about?" Gavrin shot back, struggling against the two guards who'd only half-heartedly stepped forward to restrain him. "Get your bloody hands off me Bohdi! You've still got a tab to pay off, you know!" The guard he'd spoken to cast a sideways glance at the ground and let him go.

Splitting his attention between their exchange and the two advancing soldiers, Jamie felt his skin burn hot. Why Gavrin of all people? If there was one person Jamie would never let anywhere near Alaida, it was him.

"You stay away from her!" Jamie said, putting out a hand between Gavrin and Alaida.

Raising his voice, Gavrin again addressed Major Addinez, "As the property of a criminal, that makes her contraband. She's bound for a farm and as the only licensed SAA representative in the village --"

"You should be grateful I haven't had you arrested already!" Major Addinez said. That brought Gavrin to a sputtering halt. "You knowingly accepted *stolen* money for the purchase of that slave but you only admitted to such after we questioned you about it. You should have come to us right away if you suspected something."

"I am an upright and honest representative of the Slavery Affairs Agency," Gavrin said with indignation. "I hadn't yet had time to --"

"You also transferred ownership without performing any of the required background checks," Major Addinez continued, "And you neglected to file the proper paperwork for the sale. The only reason you would have for doing that is to hide the source of the funding. If I turned her over to you, she'd likely disappear from the records entirely."

"But you can't just --"

"She *will* be confiscated as evidence and processed as contraband, but you'll have no part in any of that. After the investigation here is complete, you'll be lucky if you keep your license, let alone your freedom."

All his bravado evaporating in an instant, Gavrin seemed to collapse in on himself and began whimpering like a child. Jamie would have enjoyed it more if not for Major Addinez's next words. Pointing at Jamie and Alaida, he said, "After the way you handled things here, she's contraband even if this man isn't a criminal."

Alaida let out a low whine and her grip on Jamie's arm tightened to the point that it was likely going to leave marks in his skin. From their talk that afternoon, Jamie knew exactly what she feared.

"No!" Jamie said. "I won't let you send her to one of those filthy slave-farms!"

The nearest solider must have taken Jamie's outburst as a sign of resistance because he sprang forward. Up close, those big, armored suits were even more intimidating, making the soldiers who wore them appear less human. As the solider raised the butt of his rifle in preparation to smash it into the side of Jamie's face, Jamie reacted without thinking, leaping forward and grabbing for the weapon.

He might have been willing to submit to these people, but he had no interest in being beaten as well. His past experiences with hand-to-hand combat told him that he should be able to tear the gun away from his attacker with relative ease, but on this occasion, the soldier not only kept his grip but actually fought back against Jamie. The magescript etched into his armor burned a little brighter as he actually pushed Jamie back a step. Of course this wardcaster armor wouldn't just protect the wearers, it also heightened their abilities.

Baring his teeth, Jamie threw his full strength against the soldier, finally twisting the rifle out of his hands. He didn't bother taking it for himself but instead let it go spinning through the air. He didn't want to fight any of these people and the moment he picked up a firearm, even if it was in self-defense, the others would no doubt open fire with impunity.

Stunned by the way Jamie had just disarmed him, the soldier was further shocked when Jamie slammed both hands against his armored chest. The soldier stumbled backward two or three steps before finally crashing down on the hard cobblestone plaza. The second guard tackled Jamie from the side, using the armor's considerable mass and power to drive his shoulder into Jamie's ribs. As Jamie's feet left the ground, he caught sight of several more soldiers breaking formation to come and help their comrades.

"No!" Major Addinez shouted over the sudden chaos of the moment. "Hold your positions! Guardsmen forward! Close to melee distance and engage with stun-spears!"

His words, however, fell on deaf ears as the nearest soldiers charged forward en-masse. At the same moment, Jamie crashed to the ground with the full weight of the armored soldier on top of him. He was aware of the impact and the pressure on his ribs from both the ground below and the guard above, but it didn't so much as knock the wind out of him.

The fall seemed to have hindered the soldier more than Jamie, his grip slipping as they landed. Jamie fought back instantly, kicking and pushing his attacker away. The soldier obviously hadn't been prepared for that because Jamie managed to claw his way back to his feet before the other soldiers were quite on top of him.

In the confusion, Alaida had scuttled to the edge of the plaza, her head low. At the soldier's perimeter, the village guardsmen in their plain steel helmets and green overcoats advanced as an uneven and halting mob, every one of their blunt spear heads now crackling with arcs of electricity.

Jamie cursed under his breath as he sidestepped another soldier who tried to tackle him and then punched another so hard his helmet went flying and knocked one of the approaching guardsmen off his feet. The first of the guards to come within range thrust his spear at Jamie between two of the soldiers. The head glanced off Jamie's shoulder as electricity raced into his skin. He jerked away with a hiss. It felt like getting struck in the funny bone, numbness cascading down his arm and into his shoulder.

"Hit him again!" and variations of the same, were shouted from multiple mouths as more spear heads came jabbing in Jamie's direction. He jumped back, barreling over a soldier who had been trying to outflank him, and ran to Alaida's side, grabbing her around the waist and throwing both of them over the counter of the nearest market stall.

They landed in a heap on the floor just as a section of the wall not too far above their heads exploded in a cloud of heat and splintered wood. Jamie could hear Major Addinez shouting outside but his words were lost amidst the frantic cries of the soldiers and guardsmen who had all given chase. Alaida lay on the floor next to Jamie, breathing in short raspy gasps.

"Are you okay?" Jamie asked.

She nodded, though the bewildered look in her eyes suggested she hadn't even understood the question.

"Come on, we have to run." Jamie pulled Alaida to her feet and pushed her toward a door in the back of the stall. At a crouch, she hurried past sacks of grains and dried beans and threw open the latch. Jamie was only a moment behind her, but it was enough of a delay that he had to dodge a bristling salvo of spear heads being thrust at him over the countertop. One of them caught him in the small of his back, nearly dropping him to his knees.

With a growl on his lips, he took hold of the spearhead and wrenched the weapon away from the guardsman holding it. Again, numbness lanced up the length of his arm, but he ignored it, using the captured spear to knock the others aside and then throwing it back at the ones attacking him. He heard a strained cry and saw one of the guards drop to the ground, quivering and convulsing as if shot by a stun gun, but Jamie had already left them behind, crashing through the back door and slamming it shut behind him.

Alaida stood waiting for him on the other side, trying to look in all directions at once while still holding her bundle tightly. They'd found themselves in a yard of trampled grass and dirt. A building to their right blocked the way back to the street while also hindering the soldiers who were no doubt already circling around the end of the market in search of their prey.

Without having really given much thought to the village's layout since first entering, Jamie knew that the street in front of the market would lead them to the barred gate which had turned him away that morning. From there, it would be a simple matter of following the street which ran just inside the western wall to find their way to the Annex Yard. However, with all those soldiers out there, it might be far better to cut through the heart of the village so that they could try losing their pursuers on one of the many smaller streets.

Back inside the market, Jamie could already hear them scrambling into the stall. He took Alaida by the hand and hurried in the opposite direction, paralleling the street by cutting through the backyards of the homes and business which fronted it. He wasn't even sure she wanted to come with him any longer, but he certainly wasn't about to leave her behind.

CHAPTER 22

As Jamie and Alaida hurried away from the market, the towering village wall to their left steadily grew closer as the land behind the buildings began to rise into a narrow berm of earth that looked as though it might actually abut the back side of the wall near the distant gate. If they didn't attempt to break across the street and move deeper into the village soon, they would find themselves pinned between the backs of the buildings and the wall.

However, most of the shops and houses were built tight to each other without even a narrow alley that would provide a way back to the street. Whenever a passage did present itself, Jamie always thought he heard the heavy footfalls of armored boots on cobblestones just around the corner and thus kept moving.

The next building they came to, a three-story rectangular box clad in wooden clapboards, had a wide alley separating it from its neighbor. With few remaining options open to them, Jamie changed direction and led Alaida back toward the street at a hurried skulk.

Nearing the end of the alley, he motioned for her to stay back as he eased around the corner to make sure the way was clear. What he saw, however, were three soldiers about half a block away who spotted him almost instantly. Jamie jumped back just as a barrage of energy pulses streaked across the end of the alley, ripping into the building behind him.

"Back!" he cried, chasing after Alaida who was already in motion as smoldering bits of dry clapboard rained down on their heads. Before they even reached the rear of the building, a torrent of rifle fire began walking down the side of the building right on their heels. Amid the resultant explosions, Jamie tackled Alaida around the back corner of the building and pressed her to the ground, shielding her with his own body as flaming bits of wood torn loose by the weapon's fire still pelting the side of the building fell around them.

Looking back toward the market, Jamie could see a group of guardsmen closing from that direction as well. They needed a different route. The berm didn't go quite to the top of the wall, but maybe it would get them high enough that Jamie could jump the rest of the way carrying Alaida. They might even be able to use the battlements at the top of the wall to make their way to the Annex Yard. If worse came to worse, they could always jump down the other side and simply hope for the best. At the moment, it was all he could think of.

"We've got to get to the top," Jamie said, again in motion. Pulling Alaida along behind him, he powered up the grassy side of the berm. She was gasping for breath and barely able to stay on her feet, let alone keep up, but they couldn't afford to dawdle now.

"Jamie..."

Alaida's hand suddenly became an anchor dragging Jamie to a stop. He turned to see her looking back at the building they had just passed. From their new vantage point two-thirds of the way up the side of the berm, the soldiers were nowhere to be seen. If they kept running, they could get away. However, it was impossible for Jamie to not see the cause for Alaida's concern.

The far side of the building was ablaze, likely caused by all the gunfire the soldiers had unleashed. Black smoke billowed out through the back door while a whole extended family hurried out as well. All were coughing fitfully but several were crying hysterically and trying to go back in, held back only by their more level-headed peers. In the brief moment Jamie and Alaida stood there watching, the flames grew to such an intensity that the house already looked like a lost cause. The guardsmen who had been following in pursuit of Jamie now stopped to hastily assemble a fire brigade. Jamie could only guess that the flames were forcing the soldiers in the street to find an alternate way around.

Haltingly, Alaida pointed toward the gable of the building where the small face of a child could just be seen behind a window. The evacuees had apparently noticed as well. One burley man who'd wrapped his head with sodden towels made it no more than a few steps into the building before he'd been forced to retreat, his clothes already smoldering. Hacking uncontrollably, he fell to his knees and shook his head ominously in response to the shrill cries of a woman who the others were trying their best to comfort.

Jamie took a single step back toward the building. As much as he'd like to blame this on the soldiers alone, it was just as much his fault as theirs. If he hadn't come to Tavnic, if he hadn't been so careless in the things he'd done, these people would still have their home and that child wouldn't be trapped.

But he and Alaida had evaded their pursuers for the moment and the Annex Yard was just a short distance away. They were home free. He couldn't turn back now.

"Go," Alaida said. "If you think you can help her, you should try."

That was all Jamie needed to hear. Already charging down the hill, he called back to Alaida, "Keep going! Find a place to hide! I'll catch up!"

He didn't wait for a reply. The people gathered at the back of the house, just beyond the heat of the flames, jumped in shock as Jamie flew past them and bounded through the open back door, running face first into the unrelenting wall of heat on the other side. The hands he threw up to shield his face did nothing to lessen its intensity. His lungs felt like they were filled with fire. Flames were everywhere, slithering across the floors, curling up the walls, and rolling across the ceilings amid dark plumes of smoke. An arrangement of low tables and easy chairs still looked oddly domestic despite the flames lapping around their charred wooden edges and engulfing the upholstery.

It was a wonder Jamie could even see any of it, but apart from the sensation of heat all over his body, it didn't actually hurt. Though after nearly being blown to pieces by an exploding titan-mecha, that didn't really come as much of a surprise.

In the hallway beyond, he could just make out a flight of stairs going up. Despite the fact it too was nearly engulfed in flames, he dashed up the steps three or four at a time, leaping over the most damaged sections. At the second floor, his route became less clear. The child had to be at the very top of the building, but his way to the next flight of stairs was blocked by a solid wall of flame which had eaten away most of the floorboards in the hallway and was quickly doing the same to the underlying structure.

Jamie was just about to try jumping around it when a loud creak sounded from above and the second flight of stairs collapsed entirely. In a cloud of embers, it crashed into the flight below, destroying them both. Over the roar of the flames that rushed in to fill the gapping hole left by the stairs, Jamie heard the pitched scream of a girl from above. He didn't have time to waste on a clever plan.

With a running start, he jumped toward the third floor, bypassing the need for stairs entirely. He would have cleared the distance with ease had the floor beneath his feet not given way just as he launched himself over the howling column of rippling flame below. With most of his momentum now gone, he thrashed for a handhold as the upper landing drew near. He wouldn't allow himself to fail. He had to get to that girl before the flames did. He had to make it back to Alaida before the soldiers.

The tips of his fingers latched onto the edge of a smoldering timber. The wood groaned under his weight as Jamie swung himself up, caught a second hold with his other hand, and then pulled himself over the edge onto his belly, clear of the flames licking at his feet. Rugged as his garments were, they were starting to smolder. If he didn't get out of there soon, they would ignite just like everything around him.

The structure on the third floor was a little more sound but tongues of flame were already starting to work their way between the floor boards. Levering himself to his feet, Jamie could see only one way to go, a sealed doorway at the end of the hallway. He ran between walls covered with slinking flames that curled into the ceiling rafters overhead and reached out for him as he passed. When he arrived at the door, he didn't even bother trying the latch. Instead, he hit it with his shoulder, ripping the hinges right out of the frame. There was no point in being careful. If things were worse on the other side, he'd already failed.

Wispy gray smoke filled the room beyond and pieces of burning thatch were dropping down from the peaked roof. The window Jamie had seen from the ground was in the wall opposite and a young girl dressed in a night gown and coughing from the smoke turned in shock at his entrance. Though tears had made long black streaks of the soot on his face, her eyes lit up the moment she saw Jamie. He crossed the room in two steps, and she needed no encouragement whatsoever to climb into his arms.

That room might have been the last safe refuge in the entire building, but it wouldn't stay that way much longer. They needed to get out now. Though, with the stairs destroyed, there would be no going back the way Jamie had just come. The young girl wouldn't have even survived that the first time. Now things would be even worse. Backing away to the far side of the room as he eyed the window, Jamie threw his poncho over the girl.

"Keep your head down and hold on tight, okay?"

The girl said nothing, but she gripped his neck like a steel vise and nodded her head against his shoulder. He really hoped he wouldn't end up regretting this.

With a running leap, Jamie threw himself at the window. Smoke rising from the lower floors clouded his vision as he smashed through the glass into the air outside, frigid against his skin after the inferno inside the house. Hastily, he braced himself for a landing as the ground loomed into his blurry vision all too quickly.

He hit what must have been the steep slope of the berm. Despite his best efforts to stay upright, he fell over onto his back and slid several feet down the damp grass. Frantic shouts came from all around. As he blinked the soot out of his eyes, numerous hands came at him and hauled him roughly off the ground. The girl was torn away, and Jamie prepared himself for yet another fight.

However, to his utter disbelief, the villagers surrounding him as he staggered to and fro weren't attacking, they were patting him down with blankets and slapping him on the back, offering hearty praise for a job well done. The woman he'd seen crying on his way into the building was kneeling nearby, holding the rescued girl tight and crying so hard Jamie couldn't understand a word she was saying to him. From the grateful look in her eyes though, the meaning was clear enough.

The building Jamie had just jumped from was now completely engulfed in flames that reached high above the village and made the deepening twilight seem even darker. Villagers and guardsmen alike swarmed around it like ants, fighting the flames as best they could. The house was clearly a lost cause, but at least their frantic actions had prevented the blaze from spreading to any of the neighboring buildings.

With the situation no longer quite so dire, Jamie didn't have any further need to waste time playing hero. Pushing his way out the of crowd as respectfully as he could, his heart sank when he looked up the berm and saw Alaida kneeling in the grass, surrounded by three armored soldiers. Their weapons weren't quite pointed at her, but the menace in their stances made their intentions clear enough. With back hunched and hands trembling, Alaida looked at Jamie through the fine strands of her hair, her eyes vacant. Backlit by the fire, Major Addinez strode up the side of the berm with several more soldiers flanking him on either side. A fat raindrop hit Jamie right in the face just as he prepared himself once more for the worst.

"Stand down," Major Addinez said to Jamie. "It's over."

"Like hell he is!" one of the villagers standing over Jamie's shoulder said. "Ain't ya seen what he just did?"

Jamie was so startled by the outburst that he wasn't able to do much else but stand there stupidly and listen to the muttered agreement from the other villagers.

"One act of benevolence does not counteract all the crimes he's committed," Major Addinez said. "He's a murderer!"

"Allegedly!" one of the other villagers shot back. "He hasn't even had a trial yet!"

"A criminal investigations unit will be dispatched to look into things," Major Addinez said. "But after only a cursory look inside his titan's hold, I doubt they'll arrive at any other conclusion."

"Your men have done more harm to this village than this young man ever has!" a third villager added.

"My men had been instructed to hold their fire unless their lives were in danger," Major Addinez said. When he cast a harsh glance over his soldiers, several of them dropped their gazes and looked away. "Clearly some of them were unable to follow those orders and they will be disciplined appropriately. However, the fact remains that this young man is wanted in connection with multiple crimes. If he doesn't surrender now, we will be forced to use more drastic means to subdue him."

Jamie looked around at the soldiers, at Major Addinez, at the villagers, the guardsmen, and the fire. He couldn't keep fighting, not with Alaida in danger -- not with the whole village in danger. With a tightness all through his body, Jamie slowly lifted his hands into the air. His knees hadn't even touched the ground before two soldiers rushed in to wrench his arms around behind his back and snap heavy shackles over his wrists. He'd find a time to escape once they let their guard down. Then he and Alaida would break free and leave this place behind them forever. He just needed to wait for the right moment.

Villagers watched agape as the soldiers pulled Jamie back to his feet. The family he had just helped huddled together for support and stared in bewilderment. The few guardsmen present who hadn't stopped to help with the fire now held their spears limply in their dangling arms. Jamie could do little but watch as Alaida was nudged into motion by the butt of a soldier's rifle.

Despite the wind, the roar of the fire, and the increasingly frequent raindrops, an uneasy stillness had fallen over this area of the village. And through that stillness, carried on the wind, came a chorus of mournful howls from beyond the village wall.

Grasping the side of his helmet, Major Addinez half turned away from the gathering, his face pained with concentration. "Say again?" he said. Baring his teeth, he turned back around and took in the small cluster of guardsmen with a swipe of his hand. "You guards, take the prisoner to the gaol. Soldiers, I want on the wall now! I'm also activating every auxiliary militia member in the village."

The soldiers sprang into motion after only a momentary hesitation while a roll of confused looks passed between the guards.

"Stupid time for a drill," one of them muttered.

"This isn't a drill!" Major Addinez shot back. "I want every able body who can use a weapon stationed on that wall within five minutes!" The howls had become more intense, some of them sounding like they were coming from right on the other side of the wall. To Jamie, it also sounded like a sort of rhythmic chanting had been mixed in with all the other more bestial noises. It was probably just his imagination, but it still made the hairs on the back of his neck stand on end.

Pointing into the blackness beyond the wall, Major Addinez said, "Do you hear that racket? I've just been informed by the perimeter guard that there's a pack of Wolf-Slaves out there so big its got the entire village surrounded! We don't have enough bodies to keep them out if they're as determined to get in here as they seem."

The mumbled statements of disbelief from everyone present didn't offer any reassurance against the howls growing louder and more frenzied with each passing minute. As Major Addinez and his soldiers hurried off toward the wall, a gaggle of six guardsmen took possession of Jamie and Alaida. Jamie's mind was a conflicting swirl of emotion as one of the guards nudged him into motion with a small tap on the shoulder.

Wolf-Slaves at Ciante's mine, now here in Tavnic, despite what Onorah had said about them never coming near cities. They weren't supposed to attack mines either, but both cases shared one undeniable connection: that's where Jamie was, the person they now thought had betrayed them this morning.

CHAPTER 23

The guardsmen formed a circle around Jamie and Alaida as they led them through the streets of the village. Major Addinez had issued orders for everyone to stay indoors until the situation with the Wolf-Slaves was resolved and, for the most part, it looked as though he had been obeyed. The streets, still brightly lit by the gloworb streetlights, stood nearly empty, save for an occasional pedestrian hurrying toward the wall carrying an aged hunting rifle or back to his home to be with his family. The rain had also started falling now in a fitful spattering of cold drops which were already starting to soak through everyone's clothes. The guards moved at a moderate pace as they made their way towards the center of town, mostly talking amongst themselves in subdued tones.

"Do you think Yarzak will send someone down to deal with those Wolf-Slaves?" one of them whispered to his comrades.

"One of the soldiers said the relay points had gone down," another said. "There's no way we'll even get a message to Yarzok."

"You mean no one's coming to help?"

"Why the hell would the relay points go down now of all times?" said another, his voice betraying a growing sense of fear. "You don't suppose the Wolf-Slaves did it, do you?"

One of the other guards scoffed loudly, perhaps a bit too loudly. "Those filthy creatures aren't smart enough for anything like that." Though he'd started sounding firm and confident, he trailed off at the end as if he couldn't quite believe his own words.

"This is nuts," the first guard said. "We shouldn't be wasting our time here when the village is in trouble."

As their talk continued, the guards seemed to lose interest in their prisoners, often throwing up their hands in frustration or shaking their heads somberly.

Alaida walked beside Jamie with shoulders stooped and head bowed low as rain dripped from her hair. In her unshackled hands, she still carried the file Del had given them. Apparently, a lowly Raven-Slave wasn't worth the trouble to restrain, or even search. She kept her eyes fixed only on the ground in front of her and said not a single word. Casting a sideways glance at the guards, Jamie whispered her name as loudly as he thought might go unnoticed. She did not reply or even look in his direction. So engaged in their own discussion, the guards hadn't seemed to notice either.

"Alaida," he said again. This time, her face swung in his direction, though her eyes were vacant and barely seemed to register his presence. His chest tightened to see her like that. This was all his fault. "Alaida, you've got to believe me, this is all a big misunderstanding."

"Are you the Red Rogue?" she suddenly demanded, cutting him off.

"No!" Jamie said, still whispering. "Of course not!"

"But you are a criminal." It wasn't a question.

Jamie sighed in frustration and shook his head. He needed to make her see reason. He needed to convince her that he wasn't the murdering bandit everyone thought he was. He didn't even know why it mattered anymore. He simply couldn't let her go on thinking of him like that. "They have me confused with someone else."

"But all the things that soldier, Lieutenant Mamdon, said. He knew you. And the money?"

"I...I found it," Jamie said, knowing just how pitiful that sounded as an excuse, even if it wasn't entirely false. "I was just in the wrong place at the wrong time."

Alaida's frown deepened and her head lolled from one side to the other. "That does not sound as if it would make a terribly compelling argument in the courts."

"I don't care about convincing them. That doesn't matter. Right now, I just want *you* to believe me."

"Why?" Alaida shook her head and turning her attention back to the ground. "Why do you care about the opinion of a slave? If you are found guilty of even half the things you have been charged with, you will likely be executed." Jamie cringed, realizing that he was probably guilty of at least half the things Major Addinez had accused him of. Not that Alaida's fate would be much better. Though a dutiful slave would never think to bring that up directly. What she was really saying was: "Haven't you done enough to me already?"

At the darkened corner of two streets where the light from the nearby gloworbs didn't quite reach, one of the guards held up his hand and said, "Alright, stop."

There didn't appear to be anything special about the spot. There weren't even any doorways or windows opening onto that particular intersection. It certainly didn't look like any jail. Jamie felt a sinking sensation in the pit of his stomach as the guards stood shuffling their feet and sharing guilty looks with their fellows. Had they grown tired of the distraction Jamie had caused them, and instead of taking him into custody, were they going to execute him on the spot?

Jamie tested the restraints on his wrists. He had figured that he'd have to escape at some point after he'd surrendered himself, he just hadn't figured it would be so soon. Unfortunately, as he strained against the manacles, they held fast, the magescript etched into the bands only glowing more brightly. Maybe his plan hadn't been such a good one after all.

"Are we all in agreement?" the lead guardsmen asked his comrades. Gravely, they all nodded or muttered their taciturn agreement.

With growing urgency, Jamie twisted his hands in the manacles. He couldn't break free. They were going to kill him and Alaida on this lonely street corner and there was nothing he could do about it. One of the guards behind Jamie stepped forward.

In a breathy rush, Jamie addressed the whole group. "Please, whatever you do, just don't hurt Alaida! It's my fault she's in trouble! She's got nothing to do with any of this!"

"Steady boy," the guardsman behind him said, placing a hand on his shoulder as he tapped the manacles with a small metal ring connected to his belt by a thin chain. "We don't want to hurt you."

To Jamie's utter surprise, the restraints on his wrists fell away.

"We all know what that starched shirt from Yarzok says you're supposed to have done," the guardsman said. "Hell, some are even calling you the Red Rogue himself. Frankly, we don't care if you are. You saved those miners from the Wolf-Slaves this morning and then you rescued that girl after it was those soldiers who nearly got her killed. You shouldn't be locked up. You should be getting a reward. Unfortunately, the most we can offer you is a chance to get away."

Solemn faced, all of the guardsmen nodded. Warily, Jamie kept an eye on them all as he backed away to Alaida's side. "Are you going to get into trouble for this?" Jamie said, still half expecting them to use his freedom as an excuse to gun down an escaped prisoner.

"You seem like a pretty capable young man. I don't think that the great and powerful Major Addinez would find it too hard to believe that you got away from us simple Guardsmen."

Slowly, the guardsmen parted around Jamie and Alaida as they gathered at the edge of the street, their spears propped lightly on their shoulders.

"I really don't know how to thank you guys."

"Just get going. We won't be able to wait very long before we'll have to call in that you escaped."

"I understand. Thank you." Taking Alaida by the wrist, Jamie set off toward an alley on the opposite side of the street. "Come on, Alaida, we have to go."

Alaida, however, did not follow, leaving Jamie merely tugging at her arm. Looking back, the expression of fear on her face nearly crushed him.

"Alaida, please, we don't have time for this." Jamie gave her hand another tug, but her feet remained anchored firmly in place. Shaking her head, she moved her mouth in wordless recrimination. She now thought he was a bandit, if not the Red Rogue, then certainly just as bad.

"Alaida," Jamie said in a soft voice which the watching guards would not be able to hear. He could have forced her to come with him, she couldn't have resisted, but that would only further tarnish his image in her eyes. "I know this is my fault you're in this situation and I'm sorry, but we have to go. After I get you out of here, you don't have to stay with me if you don't want, but if you stay here, they're going to lock you up. Please just come with me."

Alaida clenched her teeth and let out a low moan from deep in her throat. Jamie felt much the same. After their lengthy conversation that afternoon, he'd thought the two of them would always understand each other. Now, after just a few accusations by those soldiers, she saw him as nothing more than the lesser of two evils. As if forcing her whole body to move against her better judgment, Alaida at last relented and haltingly stepped forward. Jamie did not have time to question her motives, he merely set off toward the alley once again, this time with Alaida hurrying along at his heels.

By the time they arrived at the end of a cross street which gave them a view of the entrance to the Annex Yard, the rain was coming down in thick sheets as bursts of lightning flashed through the sky directly overhead. Between the weather and Major Addinez's curfew, the streets had remained empty and they'd been able to make good time. Unfortunately, the rain had apparently done little to discourage the Wolf-Slaves. Their frenzied howls could still be heard drifting across the village.

Quietly, Alaida slumped in the leeward side of a building's stoop as Jamie leaned out to get a better look at the passage that led through the wall to the Annex Yard. Unlike when he'd come through it that morning with Onorah, a portcullis gate of thick metal bars now barred the end. Despite the shadows and the rain, Jamie could just make out a pair of armored soldiers standing guard inside. He fell back behind cover with a heavy sigh. Even if he could find a way to open the portcullis, or simply tried to rip through it, the soldiers inside would gun him down before he finished. Another flash of lightning, followed almost instantly by a ground-rattling crack of thunder, briefly illuminated the top of the village wall. It looked even higher than it had the last time Jamie had seen it. Even if he could find a way over, the moment he and Alaida got out, they would be set upon by the entire hoard of Wolf-Slaves. They needed that titan, if not to outrun the Wolf-Slaves, then simply to overpower them.

"Do you know of another way into the Annex Yard?" Jamie said.

Eyes downcast, Alaida merely shook her head.

Jamie pounded his fist against the side of the concrete stoop. How much longer did they have before the guardsmen would be forced to report Jamie's 'escape'? They couldn't just stay there, crouched in the shadows like the criminals everyone thought they were.

"We need to get off the streets until we can figure something out," Jamie said. In the moment, he could only think of one option. Its suitability was questionable at best, but it was all they had. "Come on, I might know where we can lay low for a while."

Shivering, Alaida rose stiffly, her long skirt sticking to her legs and her straight black hair matted around her face. Jamie was grateful she didn't resist. He hadn't stopped to consider just how cold the rain felt. If he couldn't get her warmed up, evading the soldiers might be the least of his worries.

Again, Jamie led the way through the deserted streets. Once, they stopped hastily and retreated into the shadows of an alley as a door swung open on the street just ahead and a young man hurried out carrying a gun. He hadn't seen them, however, and rushed off in the other direction, likely going to offer his support to the village's defense.

After another couple of blocks, slinking along in silence, Jamie and Alaida arrived at their destination without any further delays. The windows of the building before them were dark and the front door was locked. As Alaida waited at the bottom of the stoop, staring down the length of the street with a faintly bewildered expression, Jamie knocked at the door.

"Wh-why did you come here?" Alaida whispered.

"She's a friend," Jamie said, looking back over his shoulder. "I think she might help us." He hoped she would.

Footsteps only Jamie was likely able to hear approached from the other side of the door. A latch was thrown, and the door swung open.

Inside stood Onorah, illuminated by a small gloworb in her hand. Alaida shied away from the light.

"It's you," Onorah said. "I've been listening to the soldiers over the relay net. They say you're the Red Rogue."

Alaida cringed even more.

"I may have gotten into some trouble with the military a while back," Jamie said, "but I'm not who they think I am."

When Onorah looked past Jamie at Alaida, her frown deepened. "So that's the business you had to take care of at Gavrin's."

"She's a friend. She got caught up in this by accident. I'm just trying to keep her safe."

Onorah stood silent, her narrowed eyes boring into Jamie. She was probably going to turn them in. After all, she had no reason to believe a word he said. He hadn't even been able to convince Alaida of the truth, why would Onorah believe him?

After several long moments, she sighed and stepped out of the doorway. "Come on, we need to get you two off the street before someone sees you. I just heard a report that you'd escaped from the guards. They might have their hands full with the Wolf-Slaves at the moment but it's best not to take any chances."

"Thank you." Jamie stepped inside with Alaida close behind. Onorah leaned out through the door and looked both ways down the street before closing it behind them.

They found themselves in what must have been the main showroom for the magesmiths' shop. Precise rows of display cases marched across the room and lined the back wall behind a glass-topped counter. The soft glow illuminating the wares inside the cases provided the only light. With dark beams on the walls and ceilings interspaced with panels of smooth white plaster, and an elegantly tiled floor underfoot, the whole room looked particularly modern by Terrarhean standards.

"Come on in back," Onorah said. "My dad's helping Major Addinez's men get their equipment sorted out so you should be safe here for a little while."

She lead them through a door behind the counter which passed down a short hallway lined on either side by several offices and a storage room before emptying into a cavernous room that looked more like the inside of a barn than the front of the building might have suggested. The heavy timbers flanking the doorway had been worn smooth and stained black from the countless grease-smeared hands that must have touched them over the years. Acrid smells of hot steel and old oil hung heavily in the dry air as they stepped inside. Gloworbs suspended from the ceiling activated upon their entrance, filling the space with warm light. However, the numerous pieces of equipment scattered about in various states of disassembly, cast dark shadows in many of the corners. Work benches covered with tools, parts, and smaller pieces of equipment seemed to fill the remainder of the space, leaving little room to walk but Onorah made her way through the maze without once checking her stride.

In the center of all that organized chaos, a sizable patch of floor, surrounding an arrangement of anvils and vises, had been left clear. From a cabinet above a wash basin, Onorah pulled out a pair of warm towels which she handed to Jamie and Alaida. On a nearby worktable sat a round box covered with glowing crystals and brass switches that squawked out periodically with the voices of soldiers and guardsmen reporting on the movements of the Wolf-Slaves. From the sounds of it, the besiegers had not yet tried to breach the walls, but the voices in the broadcasts were starting to sound panicked.

"Are they here for you?" Onorah said with a nod toward the box. "I mean, after what you did to them at the mine?"

"Yeah, I think they are," Jamie said, running the towel over his face.

Alaida was likewise doing her best to wring the worst of the rain from her hair and dangling garments. A shiny kettle sitting cold on one of the benches instantly grew warm when Onorah touched the handle, causing the magescript that covered its surface to glow. She poured a steaming cup of what looked like tea and passed it to Jamie. Her level gaze bored into Alaida for a moment before she poured another and offered it to the Raven-Slave. Hands shivering, Alaida accepted with a contrite nod and whispered thanks before taking a seat on the edge of a metal shop stool.

"I'm really grateful for this, Onorah," Jamie said. "I don't want you to get into any trouble, though. As soon as I figure out what we're doing, we're gone."

"After you saved my life this morning, it's the least I can do."

Jamie attempted a smile. "I think I'm gonna owe *you* after this."

Onorah shrugged, her expression flat. "Now we just need to figure a way to get you out of the city." She paused for a moment as she gazed into the rafters. "That alone wouldn't be too difficult if it weren't for the Wolf-Slaves. With so many of them out there, they'd tear you to shreds if you tried to sneak past." Again, she looked at Alaida, no doubt wondering if that might not be such a bad thing. "We need to get to your titan."

"I was thinking the same thing, but the soldiers have the Annex Yard completely sealed off."

"That's standard procedure in an emergency. I'm sure you noticed that the Annex Yard doesn't have gates on the outside walls. Without being able to secure the stairway, the rest of the village would be completely open to any attacker who got into the Annex Yard. However..." As she again stared off into space, the corner of her lip curled upward in the hint of a smile, "That might actually work to our advantage."

"It will?" Jamie said.

Onorah suddenly set off in a flurry of motion. From a cabinet near the doorway she pulled out an armful of long black coats which she brought over and tossed down on one of the work benches. They looked like they had been oiled to make them water resistant.

"These will keep us dry," she said and then began shrugging into one of the coats.

Jamie handed one to Alaida and took the last one for himself. Dutifully setting aside her cup and towel, Alaida stood and quickly donned the garment, either due to her conditioning to follow orders without question or because she was still too dazed to think for herself at the moment. Jamie hoped that tonight's events hadn't traumatized her permanently. Once into the coat, she picked up the sheaf of papers Del had given them and held it close to her body. Jamie had almost completely forgotten about the file. Motioning to Alaida, he took the documents, leaving her with only her own papers and seal of ownership. Those she furtively slipped into one of the coat's large pockets. Jamie meanwhile flipped through the file. The edges looked a little damp but the heavy cover and Alaida's careful handling had saved them from complete destruction.

"Onorah, do you think you might be able to take a look at this for me?"

"Not to be a bad host, but we should probably get moving as soon as possible," Onorah said as she pulled her ponytail out from under the collar of her coat and left it hanging forward over her shoulder. Siding up alongside Jamie, she craned her head to get a look at the papers. Then her brow furrowed and she snatched the whole bundle out of his hands. "What the hell? These are magesmith research notes, and old ones at that. They should be locked away in a vault somewhere. Where did you get them?"

Far from sounding accusatory, she was actually excited -- even more so than when she'd found that gun in Jamie's titan-mecha. Setting the folder down on the nearest bench, she began scanning each page with interest before flipping ahead to the next. "Are these all by Major Ommto?"

"Y-yeah." Jamie looked over her shoulder. "Have you heard of him?"

Without taking her eyes from the papers, she laughed and said, "Everyone from Iron Spur has heard of Crazy Old Man Ommto."

"Crazy?" That didn't sound very promising. "What do you know about him?"

"He was some genius designer in the Army Magesmith Corps from back in the old days. When my dad was just a kid, he actually met Ommto once. Supposedly, he was responsible for coming up with most of the cutting-edge technology in the military's newest generation equipment." Onorah trailed off as she focused on one of the pages. "Holy crap, these are his original notes for the armor wards that are used on everything from the military's personal body armor all the way up to the Mark-5 titan-mechas." She turned to the next page and froze, much as Jamie had done upon first seeing the metal shard sandwiched between the pages. "Whoa...what is that?"

"I was kind of hoping you might know."

Onorah picked it up and turned it over, her eyes narrowing as she examined it from every possible angle. "It doesn't have any wards, but it feels weird. I wonder if it's some kind of prototype or failed experiment." Setting it down, she went back to scanning the pages, looking for an answer to her question.

"Do you know whatever happened to Major Ommto?"

"As the story goes, he went crazy on the eve of his retirement and got himself kicked out of the army. They say he ended up out near the Heigelries border on his family estate raising goats for the rest of his days."

"Is he still alive?"

"Could be, I suppose. He'd be downright ancient though if he is." Onorah paused and looked at Jamie, her expression stern but curious. "Why do you have these? Where did you get them? Is that why the soldiers arrested you?"

"As far as I know, they don't even know I have them. Someone gave them to me, I'm not really sure why, though. I think they might be important."

Onorah went back to the document and began scanning the pages more thoughtfully. "They *would* be important, but only to a magesmith. You're not some spy are you, working for Secotia or Theiridoon?"

"I don't even know where those places are."

"Ja -- Mas --" Alaida touched Jamie's arm and pointed to the box on the counter which had continued relaying the soldier's transmissions this whole time. The constant voices coming from it had long ago become little more than background noise which Jamie hadn't been paying much attention to.

"Acknowledged," a modulated voice, which sounded very much like Major Addinez, said from the box, "Magesmith Alpha en route to HQ."

"Onorah?" Jamie said. "Who's 'Magesmith Alpha' and where's 'HQ'."

"Huh?" Onorah looked up from the papers. Finally registering what she had already heard, she shot up straight. "That would mean my dad is coming back here!" she said, grabbing a leather satchel off of a hook and dumping the assorted tools it contained onto the bench. She stuffed Major Ommto's research notes inside, folded the top flap closed, and tossed it to Alaida, who had begun looking about the room as if expecting an armed assault to come barging in at any moment. "Don't lose that!" Onorah said, setting off toward the far end of the shop. "Come on, we gotta hurry."

Alaida jerked the satchel's strap over her shoulder and gripped it with both hands in a white-knuckled grip as she and Jamie both hurried after the young magesmith. In one back corner of the shop, Onorah rolled back a timber barn door just enough so that she could stick her head out and take a look around. The sound of rain crashing down on the cobblestones outside came surging through the opening. It was falling so hard now that they wouldn't be able to see someone coming from five feet away. Of course, that also meant no one else would be able to see them either.

"Looks clear," Onorah said, pushing the door back a little farther. She had to raise her voice against the sheet of rain which beat against her the moment she stepped outside. "Let's go!"

CHAPTER 24

One step through the door and the rain instantly soaked their hair and began running down the back of their necks. The coats had wide collars which could be turned up to make something of a partial hood, which helped, but in the face of that unrelenting storm, nothing would be able to keep the rain out completely. As Onorah moved along at a jog, a flash of lightning lit up the sky and briefly washed away the fuzzy spheres of illuminated raindrops surrounding the streetlights. The accompanying crack of thunder came a second later, still loud enough to rattle windows, but sounding far removed after the earlier and much closer strikes.

Periodically, Onorah would look back to make sure Jamie and Alaida were still following. None of them said a word as she led them down one narrow street after another. The final thoroughfare they turned onto was nothing more than an alley that came to a dead end after about a hundred feet. At least the tall buildings on either side helped to shield them from the worst of the wind-driven rain. Near the back end of the alley stood a large metal dome about six feet across. Onorah went up to it and gripped the crank handle mounted on top. She had to lean into it to get it to turn but once it broke loose, it spun without effort and she only had to give it a nudge to keep it spinning. When it came to a stop, she easily lifted back the domed lid on its counterweighted hinges to reveal a metal ladder beneath that disappeared down a round shaft of pitch black.

Jamie eased up to the edge of the shaft and cautiously peered down into the darkness. He could just make out the bottom some fifteen or twenty feet below, a smooth floor of what had been dry concrete up until the hatch had been opened.

"Go on," Onorah whispered even though the sound of the rain would have been more that enough to drown out their words if spoken at a more casual volume.

Alaida stood with her back to Jamie, her head in constant motion as she scanned the rooftops and windows around them. He had to tug her sleeve to get her attention and then she responded almost too readily, waiting only long enough for Jamie to go down the first few rungs of the ladder before descending the shaft right above him. Onorah followed last, pulling the hatch closed and spinning the handle on the inside to seal it once more.

When Jamie reached the bottom of the ladder and stepped off onto solid ground, a series of recessed slots in the walls came to life with a soft glow. The whole domed room they had found themselves in had been cast from some gritty, yellowish concrete with rounded corners that made it look more like weathered sandstone than some industrial product. In stark contrast to the streets above, everything down there was eerily quiet, save for the distant sounds of flowing water coming from the two passages that opened off of the room. Alaida accepted Jamie's help down the last few rungs of the ladder without complaint or thanks. Onorah jumped down last and shook out her coat.

"Are these the sewers you told me about?" Jamie said.

"Yeap. Back when Tavnic was still a magesmith town, it had a whole system of sewers and tunnels under it to run the factories. All magesmith towns are built like that. Growing up in Iron Spur, it was one of the chores for all the kids living there to help clean the sluiceways. Me and my friends used to spend so much time playing down in those tunnels. Most of the ones here don't get used any more but I still like coming down here once in a while because it reminds me of home."

She pulled one of her small gloworbs from the pocket of her coat and activated it with a quick side-to-side shake before first pointing it down one of the passages and then the other. "Before Tavnic was repurposed, the Annex Yard used to be an evaporating pool where they dumped the wastewater from all the different manufacturing processes. At some point, it got filled in and they put up the wall around it but some of these pipes still lead out there."

"That almost sounds too easy."

"With all the rain, our feet are going to get a bit wet." Onorah finally selected the passage directly ahead of them. "And probably a bit more as well."

The passage sloped down steeply and did not possess any of the built-in illumination of the first room, leaving Onorah's gloworb as the only source of light. She went first, holding it up so that Alaida, who followed directly behind her, could see where she was going. Jamie took up the rear, his eyes rendering their surroundings, even in total darkness, in dim shades of gray and black.

The floor and walls were bone dry at first, but the lower they went, the more damp they grew, eventually turning slick underfoot. Onorah must have been prepared for this because her stance had shifted even before they reached that section of the tunnel. Alaida's bare feet handled the change in surface much better than Jamie's heavy boots. He quickly began dragging his fingers along the roof and sides of the pipe in order to keep from falling flat on his back every other step he took.

They eventually reached a smaller, rounded pipe into which the first passage terminated. Onorah ducked as she stepped into the small trickle of cold, murky water running through the very bottom. They could just barely stand up straight in the very center of the pipe, but walking would require them all to keep their heads down. Again, Onorah looked both ways down the length of the pipe before heading off to the left.

"How well do you know these tunnels?" Jamie said, trying very hard not to make it sound like an accusation.

"Don't worry, I know where we're going. The thing is, I'm not actually supposed to come down into the tunnels without permission. One time when I snuck in, I accidently ran into a maintenance crew. When my Dad found out, he grounded me for a month. Now I just get a little paranoid whenever I come down here."

Under the circumstances, a little paranoia probably wasn't a bad thing. Jamie's keen ears could detect no sounds in the tunnels other than those of flowing water and the splashing of their own footsteps but he still had to constantly hold himself in check not to keep asking how much longer they still had to go. That relentless tension he felt in the back of his mind had escalated to such a point that it now seemed certain he wasn't going to have enough time to outfit Alaida with the gear she would need to survive on her own. Not that the Wolf-Slaves would likely make that possible. Even if he were able to outrun them, he wouldn't be able to leave Alaida out in the wilderness with those savages. Unless an alternative presented itself quickly, Jamie might be left with no other option but to gamble on the Red Rogue to watch over her in his absence.

The tiny stream in the bottom of the pipe they traversed grew deeper the further they went, fed by randomly spaced outlets in the sides which sometimes only trickled and sometimes gushed.

"This is only rainwater, right?" Jamie said at one point.

Onorah's laugh echoed through the pipe. "Don't worry, the sanitary sewers are a completely different system." After a pause, she turned and looked back at him. "Unless they've overflowed."

His face twisting, Jamie glanced about underfoot and Onorah laughed even harder.

"Watch your step here," Onorah said. Up ahead she stepped down into a much larger pipe, this one filled almost to waist level with a brisk stream. Jamie held Alaida's hand as she lowered herself into the water and braced herself against the current tugging at her long skirts.

"Maybe we should have brought a boat," Jamie said as he stepped down as well and instantly felt the cold water fill his boots and turn his leathern garments slick against his skin.

"That would have been a lot of rowing," Onorah said. "We're going upstream. Not very far though."

It was still quite a distance, made to seem even farther because of the constant struggle against the flowing water. Alaida suffered the worst. If not for Jamie walking behind her, her clothes would have dragged her down into the water more than once. Eventually, he put his arm around her waist to help her keep her balance. By the time Onorah led them out into another cross tunnel of similar proportions to the previous one, Alaida was already winded and sweating. After all she'd already been through this evening, she must have been completely exhausted, both physically and mentally, but she never once complained or allowed herself to slow their progress.

"How much further?" Jamie asked as they paused to let some of the water drip from their clothes. The pipe they currently found themselves in was mostly dry and had barely a trickle of water flowing through the bottom.

"We're almost there." Onorah pointed the beam of her gloworb ahead of them. At the farthest extents of the light, Jamie could just make out a section of the tunnel where a crudely constructed transition turned it from round to square and then back to round again. "That's near the base of the village walls. There used to be a gate valve there to release overflow, but it got ripped out when it stopped working a couple of years ago. I remember they had to dig up the whole street just to get to it. Come on."

Beyond the repaired section of pipe, the way curved gradually to the left until it eventually dropped into a dusty chamber with square edges and plenty of room for all three of them to stand up straight again. To their right, five pipes barely big enough to crawl through protruded from one wall. On the opposite, a single oval-shaped pipe sloped gradually away in a straight line. At the very end, they could just barely make out a faint light.

"That would be from the spotlights on the wall," Onorah said. "They have them all turned on, hoping to scare away the Wolf-Slaves."

"It's obviously not working," Jamie said. The faint howls of the Wolf-Slaves could still be heard echoing through the pipe from beyond. That, along with the thought of finally being exposed after being underground for so long, made everything suddenly seem more dangerous once again. "Alaida, why don't you wait here for a little bit while we check things out."

She nodded and slumped back against the side of the chamber. With her wet hair and clothes and still gripping tightly to the strap of the satchel, she merely stared at the floor of the chamber. It didn't even seem possible that just a few hours ago she and Jamie had been laughing together in that ruined foundation of stone. How could he have so completely ruined her life that quickly?

"Let's go," Onorah said. She paused then, considering the gloworb in her hand, and then passed it to Alaida. "Here. We don't need to make it any easier for someone to spot us."

This last run of pipe stood shorter than the previous ones so they both had to squat as they walked, the distant square of light growing larger and more harsh the farther they went. The howls of the Wolf-Slaves also became louder until, by the time they arrived at the end of the pipe, there was little else that could be heard. The outlet had been a rectangular box set at an angle into the base of the village wall with a grate of heavy steel bars across the end. One of the lean-tos, clearly a later addition, covered the end of the pipe and a stack of barrels partly blocked the view out into the rest of the Annex Yard.

Through a gap between one of the posts supporting the roof of the lean-to and a pile of crates, Jamie could see his titan, still sitting in the back corner of the yard just where he'd left it. He could also see armored soldiers walking along the top of the wall, their gazes fixed on the forest beyond as they carried their rifles at the ready. Jamie pulled off the black coat Onorah had given him and handed it to her. It would only get in the way of piloting the titan.

"What a racket," Onorah said. "And it's supposed to be like this all around the village." She listened to the rhythmic chorus of the howls for a moment. "Do you hear that? It's almost like they're chanting something. Like 'river,' almost?"

Jamie had heard it too and it made his blood run cold. "No," he whispered, his mouth dry, "Reaver."

"What's that?"

"Nothing."

Jamie couldn't even imagine how many Wolf-Slaves it would take to make that much noise. There had to be thousands of them out there. And every last one of them had come for him. If he went out there, they were going to kill him. If he stayed in the village, however, not only would he be putting everyone there at risk from those same Wolf-

Slaves once they grew tired of waiting for Jamie to come out, but as an escaped fugitive in the eyes of the law, the soldiers would likely gun him down on sight once they found him.

"Onorah, I know things are a little crazy right now but I was wondering if I might be able to ask a huge favor of you," Jamie said. Onorah's eyes brightened intently. "Is there any way you might be able to hide Alaida for a while -- maybe even down here in these tunnels? I mean, just for a little while, until I can come back for her."

As Onorah's expression turned critical, Jamie instantly regretted asking the question. "Jamie, I'd help if I could but there's no way I could keep her hidden, down here or anywhere else. The moment you power up your titan, they're gonna know right away that you used these tunnels to get past the guards. They're not gonna let anyone down here until after they're done with their investigation. Besides, do you seriously think you'll even be able to come back here? After all that's happened, there's no way you'll ever be able to show your face in Tavnic again."

Jamie ran his fingers through his hair. Unfortunately, Onorah was probably right. For all he knew, if he returned to Terrarhea again, the Red Rogue could already have taken him half-way to Heigelries, wherever that was. Jamie shook his head. How could he have been so stupid as to get Alaida involved in all this madness? "Maybe, I don't know, if I sold her to you? I mean, if I wasn't her owner anymore, maybe the authorities wouldn't have any..."

"Magesmith's aren't allowed to own slaves," Onorah said, gravely shaking her head. "It's against the law. Slaves aren't even allowed inside magesmith towns."

"I'm sorry. That was stupid of me to even ask." Jamie felt like throwing up. The very idea of selling Alaida remained so repugnant that for him to have even considered such a thing must have meant he wasn't thinking straight. The only chance he had of protecting Alaida was to bring her with him and hope for the best. "You've already helped us more than we deserve."

"Don't mention it." Onorah's cheeks took on a rosy glow as she looked away. "Although, I was thinking that maybe...I could come with you too?"

"What? Are you crazy? I'm wanted by the Finttiranos Military and there is a whole army of Wolf-Slaves out there that is probably going to try and kill me the moment I leave! I don't even know what I'm doing or where I'm going."

"Exactly, you need my help," Onorah said, attempting a smile.

"You hardly even know me."

"I know you're a good person, if for no other reason than you care so much about the fate of a single Raven-Slave. And if you're a criminal, you're one of the most inept I've ever heard of."

"Um, thanks...I guess. But that still doesn't make you coming with me a good idea."

Onorah blew out her breath. "Maybe, maybe not. But I'm starting to feel that if I don't get out of this place soon, I'm gonna be stuck here for the rest of my life, running that repair shop someday and never being able to do anything meaningful with my life, just like my dad. I'm afraid that if I let this chance go, I might never get another."

"Don't be so quick to leave your family behind. Once you pass your exams, you can do anything you want -- you'll certainly have a lot more options than if you run away in the middle of the night with a fugitive. Until then, you've got to appreciate the time you have with your father. Trust me on this. I'd do just about anything to have a little more time with my parents."

Onorah rubbed her shoulders as she looked out through the gate. "Maybe it was kind of a stupid idea..."

Staring at the pieces of gravel in the bottom of the pipe, Jamie said, "It certainly has been a good day for them."

"Well, in that case..."

Jamie looked up just in time to see Onorah place one hand on either side of his face as she leaned across the pipe and kissed him. Squatting there stiffly with eyes wide, Jamie's mind barely even had time to comprehend the lingering soft warmth of her lips on his before she parted.

"Sorry," she said, her face reddening through her smile. "I wasn't sure if I'd ever get another chance to do that either."

Jamie muttered something incoherent. Usually girls never even wanted to talk to him unless it was to make fun of him. They certainly never had any interest in kissing him completely out of the blue like that.

"Just consider it for luck," Onorah said.

"Well, um, thanks."

Onorah laughed and shook her head as she turned back to the grate. "You're gonna need all you can get." Reaching through the bars as far as she could, she strained to reach something out of sight before finally laying hands on it. With a tug and a metallic clank, the bottom edge of the grate popped loose, allowing the whole thing to swing open. Jamie turned back down the pipe and called out Alaida's name in a whisper. The faint light from the gloworb illuminating the square chamber at the other end went out and then a moment later he could make out Alaida's shadow against the blackness as she entered the tunnel. By the time she arrived, Jamie and Onorah had both clamored through the grate and were standing under the lean-to, hunched behind a stack of crates. There was no way to escape that feeling of being exposed now.

The rain had slackened somewhat while they'd been underground, though it still fell upon the metal roofs of the lean-tos circling the Annex Yard loudly enough that it would help to mask any noise of the escape being orchestrated. Jamie could also see that the titan wasn't quite as untouched as he'd first assumed. What looked like a tarp hung over the side, dangling from the passenger compartment. Nearby, another tarp had been spread on the ground with an assortment of Finttiranos military weapons arranged on top. From the puddles that had formed around them in the folds of the tarp, they'd apparently been left out in the rain. Whatever had been going on here must have been abandoned quickly for no one to have even bothered to cover them.

"Were they searching my titan?" Jamie said.

"I think so," Onorah said. "I heard some of it over the relay net, but I only started listening after they started looking for you. I think they found some guns in the hold with serial numbers that matched the ones issued to Convoy 1-1-3-8."

The Red Rogue had likely been planning to use those guns at the attack on the mine to make it look like the same people had been responsible for both attacks. Even though the titan and the things inside it weren't really his, Jamie still burned red thinking that someone had started rummaging around inside the moment he let it out of his sight. If they hadn't, he and Alaida would have been safely on their way by now.

"You didn't really win that titan in a card game, did you?" Onorah said. Alaida looked on keenly as well, suddenly very interested to hear Jamie's answer.

"I...just sort of, found it..."

"You found it? A custom rig like that? Are you sure the previous owner didn't let you take it just to frame you and keep the authorities off his own trail?"

"No, I don't think any of this was part of his plan."

"Do you have any idea who he might be?"

"Sure," Jamie said, "the Red Rogue, right? That's what's everyone is saying, isn't it?"

"You know how I feel about that. But whoever it is, he's gonna be pissed when he finds out about this: either because you taking his titan wasn't part of his plan, or because you didn't let yourself get arrested."

Just what would the Red Rogue think of all this when he found out about it? Jamie couldn't imagine he'd be very happy. "All the more reason not to put this off any longer."

Jamie held out his hand to Alaida who promptly took it. She was shaking and her fingers were cold, but at least her grip was strong. Thankfully, Jamie wouldn't have to convince her to come with him all over again, especially in front of Onorah. Turning to Onorah, Alaida held out her hand, the darkened gloworb laying in her open palm. Frowning, Onorah stared at it for a moment.

"Keep it," she finally said. "The coat too. I think you're going to need them more than I will."

Alaida cradled the tiny wardcaster in her hand and nodded solemnly. "Thank you," she whispered.

"Good luck," Onorah said to Jamie. "Once you get out of here, just keep running as fast as you can and don't stop until you leave all this so far behind it'll never be able to catch up to you again."

"Thanks again," Jamie said. "For everything."

He glanced around the edge of the lean-to's roof. The bright lights shining down from the top of the main wall washed out all sight of any guards, soldiers, or just common citizens who might be standing watch up there.

"Just don't get yourself killed," Onorah said.

"That's not part of the plan."

Onorah chuckled. "Oh, so there's a plan now?"

"Sure, 'staying alive' is the plan. I'm just making up the rest as I go."

Taking a deep breath, Jamie tightened his grip on Alaida's hand and dashed out into the open space that separated them from the titan. All but certain the alarm would be raised the moment they showed themselves, Jamie kept his eyes focused on the titan and nothing else. He could hear the sound of his boots splashing in the puddles, of Alaida's hurried breath, of the rain ringing off the metal roofs, of the Wolf-Slaves howling beyond the walls. The titan wasn't very far away but it seemed to take forever to reach it. Jamie threw himself into the harsh shadows created under one of its arms and pulled Alaida in behind him. For a moment, Jamie looked up at the walls of the village and listened for a shout or an alarm. All he heard were the Wolf-Slaves and their hateful chant, calling for the blood of their sworn enemy.

With most of the spotlights directed out into the trees beyond the walls, the Annex Yard wasn't actually as brightly lit as it had first seemed. The long shadows cast by the search lights only made the contrast so much more apparent. Unless someone decided to turn them off, it wasn't going to get any better. Again, taking a moment to prepare himself, Jamie whispered for Alaida to stay put and then left the shadows to climb up the side of the titan.

Looking over the side of the passenger compartment, he could see that the roll-away floor had indeed been opened. Inside the gaping hold were several satchels that had been opened to reveal the hand tools they contained. Meanwhile, a shovel, an axe, and several other long-handled tools remained in their rack at the front of the compartment. More heavy tarps and a handful of wooden crates filled with scrap metal and broken wardcasters took up the remainder of the space. None of it looked nearly as incriminating as the row of weapons laid out down on the ground. Jamie could see at a glance that the soldiers had so far missed the compartment above the seat which contained even more guns. At the moment, he didn't know if that was a good thing or not.

Calling down for Alaida to join him, Jamie was happy to see her scramble up the side of the titan just as nimbly as she had been able to balance on top of the rocks in the ruined foundation.

"Get inside," he said, helping her over the side and down into the hold. "Stay down as low as you can and don't put your head up until we are out of here, okay?"

Crouching down amidst the damp tarps, she nodded, feeling around the edges of the compartment in search of a handhold. The rumble seat certainly would have been more comfortable for her, but it would also make her an easier target if anyone started shooting at them. Even down in the hold as she was now, there still wasn't any guarantee that a lucky shot from the top of the wall wouldn't find its way inside.

Pushing these thoughts out of his mind, Jamie tossed the dangling end of the tarp hanging over the side of the compartment to the ground and then dropped down after it. He all but threw himself into the pilot's seat, and just like before, the moment he placed his hands over the control pucks, the machine came to life around him. It both filled him with a sense of power, knowing what he could do with it, and also an equal sense of dread as the dull hum of its engines seemed to cut through all the other noises filling the cool night air. The seat retracted and the machine's joints unlocked, once more giving Jamie control. He turned and saw Onorah smiling encouragement from the lean-to where they'd parted ways. He raised his hand in a wave of goodbye and then brought the titan-mecha to its feet.

CHAPTER 25

Jamie swore he could feel the eyes of the guards atop the brightly illuminated wall boring into him as he eased the titan into a moderate walk and set off toward the north gate. He wanted to go running for it with all possible haste but knew that would not only be more conspicuous, but it would also make navigating the keyway gate nearly impossible. Regardless, after only three steps, he nudged the titan to go a bit faster.

He'd only gone four more steps beyond that when he heard the first cry of alarm. A moment later one of the search lights swept across the Annex Yard and Jamie kicked the titan into a dead sprint. From behind, he heard a soft thump and a muffled cry as Alaida rocked against the side of the cargo hold.

"Sorry!" he called out while keeping his eyes fixed on the rapidly approaching gate. As the searchlight finally locked onto him, Jamie gritted his teeth and launched the titan into the gateway, finessing the controls so as to shift the titan's massive bulk first one way and then the other. As if by some miracle, the huge machine seemed almost to glide through the zigzagging gate and then emerged on the other side without marring a single timber.

Jamie's elation at the successful execution, however, was short-lived. The ground inside the gateway had been dry but the downward ramp on the other side was slick with rain. Rounding the first turn, one of the titan's feet slipped in the gravel and the other splayed wide to compensate. For the briefest of moments, Jamie felt the whole machine lurch forward and the inevitable thought of crashing right over the edge, nose first, compelled him to jerk at the controls in a frantic display which somehow righted the machine and sent it off in the correct direction once more. The titan's whole body sank and then rose up again with a sense of weightlessness as it reached the bottom of the ramp and then sprinted north along the gravel road at the base of the village wall.

The suddenness of his departure must have caught the guards unaware, but it wasn't long before searchlights began to swing around to meet him. A single angry streak of bright yellow from a blaster rifle flashed across the bow. Jamie didn't turn around to see if there were any more like it. The wall of the village slowly began to arc away from the road and then, suddenly, the titan was swallowed up in trees on both sides and Tavnic vanished behind them.

"Alaida! We made it!" Jamie cried over the howl of cold wind blasting him in the face. Even though they'd cleared this latest hurdle in their path, he wasn't about to slow down until the Wolf-Slaves were far behind them as well. "Alaida?"

The titan's stride faltered as Jamie twisted in his seat to look back into the passenger compartment, certain that all he would see was a lifeless corpse. Instead, he nearly crashed the titan all over again when he found himself looking right into Alaida's face as she peered over the front edge of the hold.

"Are you okay?" Jamie said, turning back to the darkened road ahead.

"Yes..." was Alaida's tiny reply. Several long moments of silence followed. "How can you see where we are going? There is barely even enough light this night for a Raven-Slave to see by."

Jamie just shook his head. Now probably wasn't the best time to try and explain all these strange abilities he possessed, especially when he didn't even understand them himself. "It's fine," he said.

The landscape and the road itself looked little different from the track Jamie had traveled south of Tavnic, even in the crisp shades of gray his eyes rendered them in. The bigger hindrance to his navigation was the damp hair which kept finding its way in front of his eyes. Having already been soaked to the skin back in Tavnic, it looked unlikely that either Jamie or Alaida would be able to dry out any time soon. Sporadic bouts of rain continued to fall from the starless sky. Even when they did not, any gust of wind would blow even more rain out of the treetops.

Huddled behind the compartment's forward bulkhead to stay out of the wind as much as possible, Alaida was only marginally better off than Jamie. Even with the oiled coat buttoned all the way up to her chin and the collar held closed with one hand, the rain still found its way inside and left her a miserable-looking heap.

They continued in silence for quite some time, Alaida no doubt cursing her luck and Jamie pondering what options they still had available to them. With the strain on his consciousness still building, he was running out of time to come up with something. The only howls they'd heard for quite a while had been far off to the south. Unfortunately, the Wolf-Slaves had already followed Jamie all the way to Tavnic from the mine and they also knew his titan-mecha so they would almost certainly be in pursuit.

Sornam, the village that Alaida had mentioned, probably wasn't going to be of much help to them at all. If it was as small as Alaida seemed to think it was, it wasn't likely to offer any better defense against the Wolf-Slaves than Tavnic had. And from the looks of the supplies already in the titan's hold, they wouldn't be able to buy anything better to help Alaida survive on her own that they didn't already have. That meant all they could do was keep moving and hope that they made it far enough before Jamie's time ran out. But just how far would they have to go to leave the Wolf-Slaves behind them forever?

Even with the urgency created by that dire threat, the unrelenting monotony of the road started to lull Jamie into a dreary sense of complacency. All the trees had long ago started to look the same and each sweeping curve of the road blurred together until it felt like they weren't getting anywhere at all. Jamie had already pushed the titan to its maximum, but he still wished it could go just a little faster. If they could just put a little more road between them and their pursuers, maybe then they would have gone far enough.

As they rounded one particular turn which proved to be slightly sharper than all the previous ones, Jamie nearly cried out to see that the road ahead appeared to dead end into a thick stand of trees and shrubs. They were going so fast, it would be impossible to avoid a crash. It would be just his luck to escape death at both the hands of the Wolf-Slaves and the Finttiranos Military, only to kill himself by wrapping the titan-mecha around a tree in the middle of an abandoned road.

Then, at the last possible second, he noticed that the road took a sharp, ninety-degree turn to the right. With branches snapping against the side of the roll cage, Jamie wheeled the titan around just in time. Behind him, he heard Alaida thump against the side of the cargo hold with a pained whimper.

"Sorry," Jamie started to say, but he didn't get much further than the first syllable. Just beyond the turn, the road dropped away under an arching canopy of tree branches. For a brief moment, the titan's leading foot did not contact ground and instead just kept falling. Jamie tensed at the controls, fearing he had just driven them off a ledge. The foot finally crashed down only a few feet lower than Jamie had been expecting, but it landed in a gully of loose gravel that shifted violently underfoot and sent the whole machine lurching wildly to the side.

Jamie was vaguely aware of Alaida sliding to the other side of the cargo hold, but if he wanted to keep the titan upright, he could not spare any of his focus. He flailed about with the machine's arms as its other foot came down in more of the same shifting gravel. Now they really were falling, the entire machine hurtling nose-first into the blackness ahead. More frantically than ever before, Jamie manipulated the controls, hoping to save them from what now seemed inevitable.

Unfortunately, the left foot snagged on something, probably an exposed tree root. There was nothing Jamie could do now. He didn't even have time to react before the titan came to a sudden, jarring stop. His body was thrown against the restraints which held him in his seat and a wave of icy water washed over the prow and spilled across his legs. In that same moment, Alaida's cry of surprise and shock pierced his chest like an arrow. He dimly sensed a flash of movement pass overhead as the force of the crash threw something from the back of the titan.

Jamie's world slowed to a crawl as he focused on a spot at the edge of a shallow stream lined with the same rounded pebbles that had caused the crash. Alaida lay there, face down and unmoving, one bare leg laying in the cold water.

"No, no, no." Jamie said, trying to crawl through the front of the roll cage and lashing out against the restraints which still bound him to the seat. With the underside of its hull laying flat on the bottom of the stream, the machine groaned and rocked around him as it tried to translate his struggles into movement. He couldn't even lower the seat until he got the titan back on its feet.

"Alaida!" he called out, leaning as far forward as the restraints would allow. She still wasn't moving. She looked... No, she couldn't be. "Alaida!"

The titan's gigantic hands splashed up waves as Jamie dragged them through the water with all the urgency he could summon. Planting them against the heaps of river rock they mounded ahead of them, Jamie levered the machine up to its knees.

A lone howl from back the way they had just come split through the night, causing the hairs on the back of his neck to stand on end. After all the distance they'd covered, it sounded far too close.

"Alaida!" he tried again. "Please, wake up!"

Grabbing her limp form with the titan might have been the fastest course of action under the circumstances, but even if he could manage a maneuver that delicate, he might just end up hurting her even worse. Why had he ever thought it was a good idea to go back to Tavnic and see her again? Even life as a slave had to be better than the hell she'd had to live through since meeting Jamie.

He nearly lost his breath when Alaida stirred, dragging one of her arms through the smooth river rocks. Haltingly, she sat up, clutching her head. After looking about with glazed eyes for several moments, she pulled her legs out of the running water and tucked them underneath her, seemingly baffled by how they had come to be there.

"Alaida!" Jamie said.

Groggily, she looked up as if only now realizing he was even there. But her eyes quickly lost focus and drifted off to stare into the blackness all around them. If all she'd received from the fall was a concussion, she'd been lucky. There shouldn't be anything preventing him from moving her…as long as he could get her to concentrate.

Jamie levered one of the titan's arms out from under the machine and extended it towards Alaida with the palm up. "Alaida, come on!" he said. "We have to go, now!"

This time, she managed to meet his gaze, though her brow furrowed, and she kept blinking hard as if to keep her attention from wandering.

"Come on, just climb on," Jamie urged. They didn't have time for this.

Squeezing her eyes shut and placing her hands over her face, she shook her head. When she looked again her eyes seemed to have regained a bit of their normal shine. However, they quickly grew wide and her mouth dropped open as she scrambled to her feet, stumbling backward.

She looked terrified. Of Jamie? How could he possibly get her to safety if she refused to even come near him?

A thump sounded from the back of the titan and Jamie twisted in his seat to see the true source of Alaida's fear. A Wolf-Slave had jumped onboard and now lunged at him, leading with its clawed hands and snarling through long strands of dripping saliva. Jamie pushed at the controls, causing the titan to lurch backward as it stood, bringing the back of the pilot's roll cage right up into the Wolf-Slave's ribs with a crunch and a gasp of lost breath.

Several more thumps followed before the titan reached its feet. A clawed hand slashed through the top of the open cockpit and sharp claws buried themselves in Jamie's shoulder. They did not break his skin, of course, but Jamie bit out a curse and wrenched his shoulder as far forward as the seat's restraints would allow. He felt the Wolf-Slave pulled off its tenuous perch atop the roll cage, its wrist twisting at a very unnatural angle when the claws remained stuck tight and the rest of its body went over the edge. As the falling Wolf-Slave's weight tugged Jamie sideways in his seat, the titan bucked in that direction as well.

A second set of claws would have found his face if not for the sudden movement. Instead, the would-be attacker's foot slipped and practically fell right into Jamie's outstretched hand. His fingers closed around the ankle and he pulled it away hard enough that it made a loud popping noise. The Wolf-Slave it belonged to let out a high-pitched yowl and tumbled over backward, fruitlessly lashing out for a handhold as it disappeared over the edge.

Jamie hadn't intended to be so rough. He didn't want to hurt any of them, but he wasn't about to let them hurt Alaida either. After getting her into this, he had to protect her, no matter the cost.

The clawed hand snagged in Jamie's shoulder suddenly gave way just as another Wolf-Slave heaved itself through the bars of the roll cage in a fury of gnashing teeth and swinging claws. Jamie did his best to shield his face from the attack, but he had no leverage to fight back.

Frantically, he twisted his legs within the control seat and the titan spun, one of its feet crashing down in the stream with such force that it knocked Alaida back down to the ground. It also forced the Wolf-Slave to hold on tight to keep from loosing its balance. This gave Jamie the opportunity to drive his elbow into the thing's face. As the Wolf-Slave jerked backward out of the cockpit, a fountain of blood blossomed forth, red even in the darkness. Jamie threw the titan's nose toward the sky and the Wolf-Slave fell against the back of the rumble seat, its hip glancing off the edge. For a moment it looked as if it might have found a grip, but an instant later, it rolled over the side to join its fellows on the ground below.

Now facing back the way he had just come, Jamie's heart sank. Appearing black on that moonless night, the tree branches overarching the stream made the pebbled shores look like a domed crypt. Wolf-Slaves began emerging from seemingly every shadow; hunch-backed, sopping wet, and snarling with murder in their eyes. There had to be hundreds, if not thousands of them, lining the banks of the river, well beyond the reach of the titan.

"Reaver!"

That single word, spoken with such force and venom, cut through the night despite the howls and cries of the advancing Wolf-Slaves. The voice sounded like gravel rolling around in a metal barrel, and when Jamie turned toward its source, he saw that it matched its owner well. A gnarled old Wolf-Slave stood back within the wood-line, perched atop a large rock and leaning heavily on a twisted staff nearly as bent as he was. His wiry gray fur had been braided in places and knotted with beads and colored feathers in others. His teeth flashed black as he glared at Jamie across the chaos spilling down the stream bank.

On either side of the rock stood two Wolf-Slaves who each looked on with a bloodlust of nearly lunatic intensity. One of them was missing large patches of fur where it had been burned away and the other's jaw seemed to hang at a strange angle. If there had been any lingering doubt that all this was the result of what had happened at the resonator mine that morning, this removed all trace.

"Reaver!" the old one said, pointing with a bony finger, "You die now!"

Taking that as their cue, the gathered Wolf-Slaves swarmed down the banks of the stream like a living tide, every last one of them intent on only one thing: Jamie.

Even with the titan-mecha surrounding him, the sight made Jamie's blood run cold. He'd never seen anything like that before in his life. He wouldn't have even been able to imagine it before now. Though some of them were armed with crude wooden clubs or jagged pieces of scrap metal, they had to realize it was suicide to face a titan-mecha like that.

Unfortunately, it wasn't hard to believe that there really were enough of them to simply overwhelm the titan and tear him out of the cockpit. Alaida, still stranded on the ground, wouldn't last more than a few moments under that assault. There were so many Wolf-Slaves now and more just kept coming, from the woods and splashing down the length of the river.

CHAPTER 26

Alaida had been forced to retreat beyond the titan's reach, all the way to the edge of the stone-lined banks where she pressed her back against one of the massive trees growing there. More Wolf-Slaves had begun emerging from the forest on that side of the stream as well, some of them passing within several feet of her, but focused so totally on Jamie that they failed to notice her.

Retreat no longer seemed to be an option. Jamie had to find a way to drive them back before what little luck he and Alaida still had left ran out completely. Forcing himself to loosen his grip on the control pucks, Jamie brought one of the titan's massive feet crashing to the ground just ahead of the advancing Wolf-Slaves. The impact created a small crater and sent up a spray of river stones and water in all directions. They may have wanted him dead, but they didn't deserve to die in return over what was essentially a huge misunderstanding. If Jamie was careful, a display of the titan's power would force them to realize just how futile their attack was and they would simply retreat. He took a swing in front of their leading ranks with one of the giant metal hands. Coming face-to-face with several tons of fast-moving steel, their inborn desire for self-preservation would surely force them to reconsider this hopeless course of action.

Jamie cringed as several of their number charged right into the titan's arm, only to be knocked aside like ragdolls. Were they really that ignorant of what they were doing? Or had bloodlust simply overridden their common sense? Retreating a step, Jamie tried again, this time to hold them back. However, what was meant as a nudge became a collision when the solid wall of moving bodies met the unyielding metal of the titan's hands.

Those who hadn't been left mangled on the ground by Jamie's attempt at lenience sprang onto the titan's arms and scrambled toward the cockpit. One of them leapt onto the nose of the titan and thrust itself between the roll bars, snapping at Jamie like a mad dog for a brief moment before loosing its grip and falling off. It had been so close Jamie could smell its putrid breath. Images flashed through his mind of being ripped piece-by-piece from his seat, leaving Alaida below completely defenseless.

Jamie retreated another step and reared the titan back, thrashing its arms through the air. With each violent snap, some of the Wolf-Slaves slipped off and went sailing into the forest beyond. Those that had already clawed their way onto the titan's back cried out with startled yelps to suddenly find their level footing turn vertical. Multiple thumps sounded off the armor plates as they went plummeting into the endless ranks of their comrades swarming about the titan's feet.

Jamie tried to tell himself the cracking sounds he heard when he stepped backward into the stream were river stones shifting under the titan's feet and not the snapping of bones. He didn't even want to think about what he might yet have to do if he didn't find a way to keep the hoard back.

Nearby, a hefty log lay half-buried in the dark river-stones. Jamie pulled it free, the other end still attached to nearly an entire tree's worth of dripping branches and half-rotten leaves. In that same motion, he swept it though the advancing Wolf-Slaves like a giant broom.

"Get back!" he cried.

It knocked scores of Wolf-Slaves to the ground in a single swipe but the ones behind the fallen kept coming, undaunted, howling like mad and throwing themselves at the machine which would surely mean their deaths.

"Please, just stay back!" Jamie pleaded as he swung the log again and again, the smaller branches snapping off with each impact. He was now surrounded on all sides, so that no matter where he lashed out, it was impossible to miss. Some of the Wolf-Slaves stayed down and lay motionless after being struck. Most got right back up, limping or bleeding, and again continued forward.

Couldn't they see how hopeless this was? Revenge couldn't be worth all their lives.

Unfortunately, there was little Jamie could do for Alaida except try to keep an eye on her and hope the Wolf-Slaves continued to overlook her presence. He was reluctant to get too near her with the branch because a single miscalculated swing would do just as much harm to her as to his attackers. However, this same caution also had the unintentional result of concentrating the Wolf-Slaves near Alaida's position; and it wasn't long before one of them finally noticed the stranger in their midst.

They had all been driven into such a frenzy that they would have killed anything that wasn't a Wolf-Slave like them, but they still retained enough sense to advance on her warily, unsure if she might be just as dangerous as the true target of their rage. Alaida had somewhere laid hands on a stout branch which she now brandished in both fists like a club. However, from her wide-legged stance and the jerky way she pointed the weapon first at one of them and then the next, it wasn't hard for them to figure out that she would be easy prey.

Taking advantage of Jamie's lost focus, the Wolf-Slaves again charged the titan, many of them swarming over the outside of the machine in an effort to get at the pilot. The first one to reach the cockpit howled wildly as it thrust an improvised blade of rusty scrap metal through the bars of the roll cage. One eye still on Alaida's situation, Jamie pressed himself as far back in the seat as he could, feeling the rush of air from the blade against his face. Bucking the titan first one way and then the other, Jamie knocked that Wolf-Slave loose but more of them crowded forward to take its place almost instantly. The entire view from the cockpit became shrouded by more attackers, swinging weapons so recklessly they either glanced off the roll cage without finding their intended target or they missed entirely and ended up wounding their comrades instead.

Jamie groaned through his clenched teeth. He had all this power at his fingertips and he still couldn't do anything. Even if he could get to Alaida now, the Wolf-Slaves who'd boarded the titan wouldn't make it any safer than the ground.

With a scream on his lips, Jamie thrashed the titan back and forth as he swung one of its arms above the cockpit, sweeping away most of the attacking Wolf-Slaves in a single motion. Their bodies bent sharply where the titan crashed into them.

One Wolf-Slave managed to duck under the attack but lost its footing in the process. It would have fallen entirely if the jagged edge of its blade hadn't gotten caught between the bars of the roll cage. Clinging desperately to the handle as it dangled over the edge, its eyes met Jamie's with a look of worry and fear that reminded him just how human all of them were under their animalistic façades. Before now, he hadn't stopped to consider -- or perhaps he hadn't allowed himself to consider -- exactly who these Wolf-Slaves attacking him might have been. Seeing this one with all the fury and bloodlust stripped away, Jamie only now realized it was just a scared kid, and a girl at that. A moment later, she lost her grip and disappeared from sight.

Down on the ground, Alaida let fly with a wild swing at the first of the Wolf-Slaves who'd decided to come at her. Either through luck on Alaida's part, or overconfidence on her attacker's, she succeeded in cracking him in the side of the head. He fell with a howl, clutching the spot of impact, but the others now charged forward as one.

Still forced to fight against the Wolf-Slaves who had already managed to get onto the titan, and those on the ground trying to do the same, Jamie could do little but watch in horror as Alaida's plight grew more dire. She managed to land a few more strikes against her foes but her skill with the club was far too feeble to do any real damage. Within moments, the Wolf-Slaves were pulling her to the ground as she tried her best to push them back with nothing more than her own bare hands.

Hearing her shrill cry of absolute terror, Jamie simply reacted, heedless of the Wolf-Slaves currently endangering his own safety. If he didn't at least try to save Alaida now, she'd be dead for certain, one way or another. The titan surged out of the river, knocking the last of the stowaways off its back from the sheer violence of the maneuver, and dropped the log it had been using as a club. Several Wolf-Slaves who had climbed the overarching trees had the unfortunate luck of choosing that moment to try and make a jump onto the titan. Instead of alighting on the machine's back, they landed in the shallow water below with several pained splashes.

"Alaida, get down!" Jamie cried as he crossed the titan's arms above the cockpit and launched the machine into a jump. The Wolf-Slaves who had been attacking Alaida looked back in surprise. Teeth clenched to the point of breaking, Jamie brought the titan's hands down as hard as he could, sweeping them outward away from Alaida. There would be no room for error. He couldn't even let himself think what would happen if he misjudged by even an inch.

One moment, some twelve Wolf-Slaves had been standing at the base of a tree, surrounding a huddled black shape on the ground. The next they were gone, their shattered bodies either having been flattened into the ground or turned into deadly projectiles that cut down their fellow attackers beyond. Alaida was all that remained, the stark white skin of her face standing out beneath wet bangs that had been blown across her eyes by the force of Jamie's attack. Though visibly shocked, she was still alive.

Jamie's whole world contracted down into an imaginary bubble of space with Alaida at the very center. He wouldn't let any of the Wolf-Slaves get any closer than that, even if he had to smash each and every one of them beneath the titan's fists to do it.

He'd tried to show them the folly of going through with this madness. They'd had plenty of opportunities to leave. At this point, they were the only ones who carried any blame for what was to come next. Would one more fallen Wolf-Slave really make a difference anyway? Would a hundred? Or a thousand?

A scream on his lips, Jamie lashed out with such fury that it made his earlier attacks seem sedate by comparison. A backhanded strike brushed the front ranks away. A blow from the reclaimed log crushed another group flat. A kick at the dark pebbles underfoot created a cloud of fast-moving shrapnel which tore into a wide swath of the attackers, dropping them instantly to the ground. He kept in constant motion to prevent them from getting onboard once again.

Occasionally, he would hear a metallic clang that meant one of the Wolf-Slaves had gotten close enough to strike the titan. However, their crude weapons couldn't hurt its thick armor and a single quick step solved the problem with nothing more to mark its passing than the slight resistance of a body falling beneath a metal foot. Jamie had no shortage of foes. The howls of pain from the dying were overshadowed by the omnipresent war cries of the living who continually pressed forward to replace the fallen.

If they wanted a fight, he'd make sure they would soon realize this was one they could not win.

Jamie raged against that never-ending surge of foes for longer than he could remember, or maybe it just seemed that way because of how each bone-jarring impact played out in slow-motion detail before his eyes. If he could have looked away or closed his eyes, he would have, but he couldn't allow his focus to waver for even a moment. There was simply too much at stake.

The old Wolf-Slave, still perched upon its rock and well beyond the violence of the fighting, let out a guttural howl that seemed intended to encourage his forces onward.

It was only once Jamie broadened his view of the battlefield beyond the immediate conflict surrounding him that he realized the Wolf-Slaves further back no longer looked quite so eager to throw their lives away. Still flanking the old one, the Wolf-Slave with the singed fur and other one with the broken jaw were busy badgering those nearest them to continue the attack through the use of punches, kicks, and even bites.

Something about that scene, more than all he had so far witnessed, made Jamie's pulse quicken and his hands clench into fists. This wasn't some act of collective bloodlust brought on by a desire for revenge, it was being forced upon these people by a select few who had made a bad deal with a dubious partner and were now making their pack-mates pay for that mistake with their lives.

With a cry and a snarl on his lips more befitting the Wolf-Slaves, Jamie drew back the log he still held in the titan's hand and launched it at those three gathered around the boulder. It sailed across the stream and crashed into the ground somewhat short of his intended target but the trunk snapped in half and the lower portion flipped high into the air.

Seeing it coming straight toward them, Broken-Jaw and Singed-Fur each leapt out of the way, leaving the old one staring down the log as it tumbled across the top of his boulder perch, sweeping all trace of him away in the blink of an eye.

Save for the trickling of the stream and the raindrops dripping from the leaves, the night suddenly grew absolutely still. The Wolf-Slaves closest to Jamie crouched expectantly just beyond the reach of the titan as if awaiting further orders and unsure what to do without them. Those near where the log had come to rest bent down over what must have been the body of the old one. One-by-one, they threw back their heads and let out a long, mournful howl which instantly seemed to sap any remaining fight out of the whole pack.

Broken-Jaw and Singed-Fur looked just as dumbstruck as the rest, staring first at the log and then each other. Singed-Fur made one futile attempt to reignite the frenzy of a few short moments ago, shoving several Wolf-Slaves in Jamie's direction and howling, but his battle-cry sounded forced. Most of the others stood about listlessly, muttering to their comrades while keeping a wary eye on Jamie.

Slowly, they began to vanish, one-by-one backing away into the darkness of the forest. Singed-Fur let out another howl and snapped at them as they passed, but none seemed interested in continuing this hopeless operation any longer. Trying to look in all directions at once, Broken-Jaw watched with visible frustration as the hoard they had assembled abandoned them.

Alaida had gotten back to her feet and regained her club, though it didn't look like she would be needing it. The only Wolf-Slaves left on the battlefield didn't look like they would ever be able to hurt anyone ever again. Jamie tried not to think about how many bodies there were, floating in the water at the edge of the stream, laying on the pebbled banks, and wrapped around the trees in the forest. He picked the titan up and turned it to face the two ringleaders who still stood in the forest, now all alone.

Singed-Fur crouched down and bared his teeth, readying himself for a fight, but Broken-Jaw's stance wavered and then he turned and ran into the forest after the others. Singed-Fur barked something unintelligible after him, considered Jamie one last time, and then followed his comrade.

Jamie kept his eyes on the forest for what felt like several minutes after they left, the raindrops falling from the leaves sounding far too much like someone moving through the woods. However, he could see no further trace of them, and on some instinctual level, he knew that they had really gone. Alaida was likewise on the alert, so much so that she turned with a start when Jamie called her name. He'd dropped the titan down and jumped out of the seat as soon as the restraints released, running across the loose stones.

"Alaida, are you okay?"

She considered the club in her hands as if having completely forgotten that she still held it and then tossed it aside. Jamie reached her just as she fell to her knees, catching her in his arms and going down with her.

"Are you okay?" he said again, his voice cracking as he held her by the shoulders so that he could look into her eyes.

She nodded somewhat haltingly. Her clothes were torn in several places, her hands were skinned, and at least one set of claws had left three bloody marks across her neck and down to her shoulder, but miraculously, none of her injuries appeared to be life-threatening.

"Jamie, are *you* okay?" she said, reaching out and running her thumb across his cheek to wipe away the tears streaming from his eyes.

"Wha-what?" he said, wiping his palm across the other cheek and only now realizing that he was even crying. "Alaida, what did I do? I...I killed them."

"They are just Wolf-Slaves. They will not be missed."

He turned and could see at least three bodies laying not far away. He was the one who'd taken their lives and he didn't even know how he'd done it. There had been so many, how could he have kept track? Did they have families that they'd left behind? How many mourning children and widows had he created this night? Looking more closely, he was almost certain that the bodies of the women nearly equaled the bodies of the men. What had this world forced him to become?

Before Jamie could start counting the rest of the fallen, Alaida grabbed him and turned his face back to look at her. "Jamie, they were trying to kill you. If you had not acted, they would have killed us both."

"But..." Alaida pulled him back when his gaze again began to turn. "But how can I justify any of this? I keep telling you I'm not the Red Rogue, but if I'm capable of something like this, does it really matter? I'm just as bad. Maybe even worse!"

"Jamie, I know you are not the Red Rogue. If he were here, he would have slaughtered them all without any regret."

Jamie's eyes' shot open wide. In the heat of battle, he'd been able to completely overlook the nagging sensation in the back of his mind.

Now, he realized it had been stretched almost to the breaking point. Very soon, the Red Rogue *was* going to be there.

"No, no, no!" Jamie shot to his feet, pulling away from Alaida and clutching the sides of his head. What was that maniac going to think of this mess Jamie had made of things? What was he going to do with Alaida? They didn't have enough time left to find a place for her to hide. Jamie grabbed Alaida by the shoulders and pulled her to her feet.

"Alaida you've got to listen to me! Remember that time when we first met at Gavrin's Inn and you said it was like I changed into a completely different person? I think that might happen again, soon! I think I might have to leave you here!"

"I don't understand," Alaida said, her face growing long. "The Wolf-Slaves are gone. Why must you leave now?"

Jamie didn't even understand it himself. That's why he'd been hoping to find a better opportunity to bring this up. Or find a way to avoid telling her entirely, as vain a hope as that might have been.

"I don't have any control over it," Jamie replied. "Sometimes -- most of the time here on Terrarhea, I'm not me, I'm somebody else...I'm...I think maybe I'm supposed to be the Red Rogue."

Her brow wrinkling, Alaida shook her head as she tried to make sense of what Jamie was telling her. Her voice trembled when she said, "I have heard of people who think they are really two different people in the same body. Is that what you mean?"

"Multiple personality disorder? No, nothing like that. Well, maybe a little... I don't really know what's happening, but I know for a fact that I have a life back there on Earth. It's more like we're switching bodies with each other. And right now I don't have much time left here so you've got to convince him to help you."

"I don't..."

"Alaida, please!"

"I will try," she said, though it seemed all too clear she didn't really understand what he was asking of her. Jamie didn't even know what he was asking himself. For all he knew, he'd just saved her from the Wolf-Slaves only to face an even greater danger all by herself.

"I'm so sorry," he said.

And then, Jamie was gone.

CHAPTER 27

People were screaming all around Jamie yet the noise still sounded dull to his ears after the hyper-clarity of Terrarhea. The air felt damp and the thin strip of sky visible between the red brick walls of an alley glowed with the soft light of those minutes right before sunrise. Standing lightly on his toes with hands raised in front of him, palms facing down and slightly bent, knuckles bruised, Jamie fumbled on his own feet.

"Wha--?" he began to say but didn't get much further than that.

Not far away, Seth stood snarling around a foundation of dark red blood running from his nose and mouth. His own hands were balled into fists, one of which was coming right at Jamie. He saw it coming and had just enough time to realize that he should try to get out of the way, but his body wasn't able to react as quickly as his mind. The fist collided with the side of Jamie's face and Seth followed the blow through with the full strength of his heavily muscled body, barreling Jamie over as if he had just been hit by a truck. Jamie knew that it had to hurt, but at the moment, all he felt was a strange numbness that came from a total sense of disbelief.

A collective gasp rose up from the crowd surrounding them. Up until now, Jamie hadn't even realized they were the source of the screaming. As he fell, his body twirling limply, he caught glimpses of faces he recognized from school. He even thought he might have seen Alex and Derek among them. But that couldn't be right. The rest of these people were more likely to be friends with Seth than those two. Like April, standing there in a pink mini skirt and looking like someone had just told her that her favorite brand of nail polish had been discontinued. And honestly, did she always need to wear something pink? It wasn't as if anyone would ever mistake the anorexic body squeezed into those clothes as anything other than a girl's.

Jamie hit the ground hard. This time he definitely felt the impact. The rough asphalt stung his palm and elbow where it tore away the skin, and stars filled his vision as his skull rebounded off the pavement. If the pain wasn't proof enough that he had returned to Earth, the near loss of consciousness definitely was. A sharp follow-up kick to the ribs sent him rolling onto his side with a moan. Somehow it seemed appropriate that after everything he had survived on Terrarhea, he was now going to be beaten to death by a dumb jock in an alley.

Prancing back and forth on the tips of his toes like a prize fighter, Seth laughed down at Jamie. "Where's all that kung fu crap now, you pathetic little freak?"

Kung fu? Maybe this wasn't Jamie's Earth. Unless the Red Rogue had once again been doing with Jamie's life as he pleased. Maybe Jamie was asleep, and this was just another dream. Something like that would have been easier to believe if the pain hadn't felt so real.

"Seth, cut it out!" April cried over the crowd. She tried to intervene, but a cackling boy with reddish-blonde hair, pale freckled skin, and a letterman's jacket, held her back. Struggling to break free, she said, "You're gonna hurt him!"

"Yeah, that's kind of the point, you two-timing slut!" Seth said, a bloodthirsty grin on his face. Jamie had managed to pick himself up onto one elbow and was looking for some gap in the crowd that he might be able to slip through and escape, when Seth punched him again, sending him right back to the ground.

What could possibly have happened this time? It clearly wasn't just about Jamie and April working on their homework together.

Addressing April once more, Seth stalked in a ring around Jamie, "Every time I turn around, you're hanging out with this asshole, even at my own party, which he wasn't even invited to!"

"Oh grow up, Seth," April said, rolling her eyes. "I'm not your damn property! I can do whatever I want!"

"But you're supposed to be with me!" Seth howled, spittle flying from his lips like a rabid dog. "And then I find you in a back room last night making out with this piece of crap!"

"We weren't making out!" April said. "And what did you want me to do all night, just sit around and watch you play X-Box? I mean, when was the last time you even took me anywhere other than football practice?"

Seth's lip curled back, and his nostrils flared. "Screw you. Screw the both of you!"

Taking a knee alongside Jamie, he pulled him off the ground by the shirtfront. Jamie tried his best to ward off Seth's renewed attack, but more blows followed in quick succession, each one falling like a sledgehammer and accompanied by some new jibe or insult. At least Jamie thought that's what Seth was saying. After the first couple of punches made it through to his face, Jamie wasn't able to comprehend much of anything. With head lolling drunkenly, he merely hoped to pass out quickly so as to spare himself any more of the immediate pain.

Just as Seth drew back for one more, April finally managed to slip free of her captor and threw herself between Jamie and Seth. "Stop it already!" she said. "You've won, okay?"

Seth tensed his fist, as if to strike Jamie right through April, and bared his teeth, viscous blood pooling in the crevices. After several long moments, he shoved Jamie back down to the ground. Jamie remained just conscious enough to remember hoping in vain that the pained whimper he heard had not been his own.

"I should have known better than to hook up with a slut like you," Seth said as he stood, glaring down at April and wiping the blood away from his nose with the back of his hand. He turned and delivered one more swift kick to Jamie's side which curled him into a ball. "You want him so bad? There, he's all yours."

Watching Seth leave, April bent over Jamie protectively, heedless of the blood as she cradled his head in her lap. Several of Seth's teammates fell in beside him, pushing their way through the now silent crowd and disappearing into the street beyond. Now that the show was over, the majority of those who'd gathered to watch began to quietly slip away too, whispering amongst themselves. Soon, all who remained with Jamie were April, Derek, and Alex.

The two boys stepped near, staring at Jamie with a look of either disbelief or awe. April, meanwhile, had pulled a tissue from her purse and was trying to dab the blood away from a cut above Jamie's eye. Oddly, the fierce way April watched Seth leave appeared just as genuine as the concern and sympathy in her eyes as she now looked at Jamie. No wonder everyone had been whispering, this was a scandal to be sure.

"Dude! You are freakin' awesome!" Derek said. Or maybe it was Alex.

"What are you talking about?" Jamie managed to say, his whole face feeling swollen and stiff. Savoring the cool pavement under him and staring up at the pale sky overhead, he felt as if he could have lain there all day, if only he weren't also gagging on April's flowery perfume. "I just got the crap kicked out of me -- in front of half the school."

"Yeah, but when you challenged Seth last night at his own party, no one thought you were actually going to go through with it." That time, Jamie was almost certain it was Alex who'd spoken. "What you did took serious guts."

"And not only were you the first one to show up, which made him look like a chicken," Derek said, "but you also got in the first couple of punches without him even laying a hand on you. For a while there, I actually thought you were going to win."

"Yeah, where did you learn to fight like that? You've gotta teach me some of those moves!" Then, with no small amount of mirth, Alex added. "It's things like this that give us little guys hope. You may just be my new hero."

All this reverence made Jamie want to scream. None of it made any sense. Why would Jamie have ever ended up at Seth's party? Why had April abandoned Seth in favor of Jamie? How had he ended up involved in some pre-arranged fight with Seth? Maybe he could still make a run for it.

Jamie sat up, pain lancing through his ribs where Seth had kicked him. As black flecks began to drift across his vision, he lowered his head and took several deep breaths. It helped but it also made his ribs hurt even worse than before.

"Should we call an ambulance?" Alex said, his earlier amusement with the situation turning grave. "Are you alright?"

Of course he wasn't alright. But only partly due to the physical injuries.

"I'm fine," Jamie said. Taken individually, none of the wounds he'd suffered were worse than anything he'd ever endured before, like that time he'd cracked his head falling out of Jack's hayloft or when he'd torn up his leg and arm when he crashed his bike on that gravel road down near the quarry outside his hometown. He couldn't have even guessed at how many times he'd gotten cut while playing in the woods near his old home. If anything, the worst part now was how tired he felt. He could have curled up and gone to sleep right there at the end of the alley.

"Are you *sure* you're okay?" Derek said. "I mean, you really don't look so good. After the beating you just took, you might have a concussion or something."

"Yeah," Alex agreed. He held up his right hand with three fingers extended. "How many fingers am I holding up? Can you tell me what day it is?"

Head still down, Jamie glanced up at them. "What day *is* it?"

By this time, the sun had started to rise, painting the tops of the buildings around them with a bright glow. On the sidewalk outside the alley, a pair of spandex-clad joggers cast the four of them a sideways glance and then quickened their pace.

"We were going to those comic book shops," Jamie said. "Was that just last night?" It seemed like a lifetime ago.

"Yeah, it's Saturday morning," April said, her voice taking on an edge as she glared at Derek and Alex. "Why don't you two losers beat it? I can handle this."

And now April wanted to play nurse? Jamie had had enough of this. Pushing her away, he forced himself to his feet. Swaying with shoulders stooped, he only managed to remain upright for a few seconds before he started to totter. April leapt up to catch his arm and Derek sprang forward to grab his opposite shoulder. Jamie hissed when their support put pressure on his injured ribs.

"Whoa there, Reaver!" Alex said. "Maybe you should take it easy for a little while."

Jamie pulled away from Derek and wheeled on Alex, despite the fact his head again began to swim. "What did you just call me?"

Alex quailed. "I was just joking."

"No, why did you call me that? Where did you hear it!"

Alex lifted his left eyebrow. "Um, last night you said that's what they used to call you back home, or something like that."

Derek again caught him by the shoulder, but this time Jamie's loss of balance had nothing to do with the injuries. Reaver really had been the one in control of things on Earth while Jamie had been on Terrarhea. Which meant it was Reaver who'd picked the fight with Seth. If not for Jamie's interference, he might even have won. It also meant Reaver was back on Terrarhea, this time with Alaida. Jamie wouldn't even have a chance of knowing what was happening there at this very moment until (or if) they switched places again. And that might not be for weeks, by which time it would be far too late to do anything to protect Alaida.

Jamie pinched his eyes shut and clenched his hands into fists, his fingernails digging into his palms. Why couldn't he get anything right? Why did this madness have to be his life? He moaned around the lump forming in his throat.

"Jamie?" April said.

"Look," he said, "I appreciate the...concern, but I'm just gonna go home." Jamie turned and took a few tentative steps toward the end of the alley. As much as he hated the way April walked alongside him, holding his arm, he might very well have ended up on the ground again if she hadn't been there to lean on. All he wanted was to lock himself away in a dark room by himself so he could cry himself to sleep.

"I'll take you home," she said. "Where do you live?"

"Over on Skaalen," Jamie said. If he'd been thinking clearly, he might have been more hesitant to let April know such privileged information, but at the moment, all he wanted was to get home as quickly as possible by any means necessary, even if that meant having to rely on April. Derek and Alex trailed a short distance behind, looking uncertain about what they should be doing.

"That's like twelve blocks from here," Alex said.

"Yeah," Derek added, "and I have a car." He pulled a set of keys from his pocket and pressed a button on the fob. A minivan parked on the other side of the street from the alley flashed its lights and chirped its horn.

April's gaze could have killed. "That's a *minivan*."

What likely would have escalated into another argument, Jamie ended before it began by hobbling toward the parked vehicle. "I don't really feel much like walking this morning."

While April helped Jamie into the back, Derek climbed behind the steering wheel and Alex called shotgun. Jamie reclined his own seat back as far as it would go, sinking into the upholstery and leaning his head back. In the adjacent seat, April leaned over and again dabbed at one of the cuts on Jamie's face. So far unsuccessful in getting her to stop, Jamie tried once again. Having her touch him like that made his skin crawl, reminding him that when she looked at him, she wasn't seeing Jamie, she was seeing Reaver.

"I can't believe I'm riding in a minivan," April said, undeterred from her ministrations.

"Yeah, my *Mom's* minivan," Derek said, looking at her in the rearview mirror as they pulled away from the curb. "So please try not to get any blood on the upholstery." A split second later, everyone slid forward in their seats and tires screeched when he mashed the breaks in order to narrowly avoid hitting a passing car.

"Are you trying to get us killed!" April cried. "Do you even have a learner's permit?"

"No!" Derek said, "so why don't you stop distracting me!"

Alex turned around in his seat, "Yeah, why don't you just keep your slut mouth shut!"

"Would everyone just shut up!" Jamie said, cutting off April's response.

Staring down Alex with a look of abject hate, April considered Jamie's request for a good, long time. Alex, meanwhile, continued glaring at her from the front. As Derek finally got underway again, they both sat back in their seats.

"Dickhead," April muttered.

"Trollop," Alex said.

Jamie had been forced to leave Alaida behind on Terrarhea just to deal with this? It had to be the worst kind of joke in the entire universe. At least Alex and April didn't renew their hostilities. Jamie closed his eyes and again leaned his head back, taking the tissue from April so that he could hold it to the cut himself.

Jamie kept telling himself that Alaida would be alright. After all, while Reaver did seem capable of great violence at times, he wasn't a complete maniac. He almost seemed to have some twisted code of honor. Yes, the last time they'd switched back to their proper worlds, Reaver had broken the arm of one of Gavrin's men but he hadn't actually done anything to Alaida herself. Maybe he'd do so again.

Of course, that could also mean, while he wouldn't hurt her, he might not bother to save her either. Leaving her stranded there in the middle of that stream with a hoard of Wolf-Slaves still lurking in the forest would be just as bad as if he killed her himself. On the other hand, he'd already shown a soft spot for April on two different occasions now. Maybe he'd feel similarly about Alaida and take pity on her. Or maybe he'd consider her competition and do away with her.

Groaning, Jamie thumped the back of his head off the headrest, which inadvertently made him feel as if the entire car was swimming around him. He had to seize the armrests to keep from falling out of his seat.

About the same time, Derek's grip on the steering wheel turned his knuckles white as he pulled up to a red light with overly deliberate care. "Oh crap, there's a cop over there," he said, staring at a police cruiser stopped on the opposite side of the intersection. "Everyone act calm. Don't draw any attention. I really don't have time to get arrested this morning. I have to get this car back before my Mom gets home from work."

"Oh yeah, which street corner is she on these days?" Alex said.

"Ha ha," Derek said, not taking his eyes off the police car even to blink. "You know she works third shift down at the McMillan Factory."

"If it's her minivan, why didn't she take it to work?" April said, her tone only slightly adversarial.

"Ironically, it's safer to take the bus," Alex volunteered. "Down in that part of town, it's almost impossible to find parking, and if you can, your car probably won't be there at the end of your shift."

"If he pulls us over," Derek said, still focused on the cop, "we just have to tell them that we're trying to get Jamie to a hospital because he hurt himself practicing parkour and we couldn't wait for any adults to drive us so we did it ourselves."

Alex snickered. "Everyone got that?"

"Parkour?" April hissed.

"Sure," Derek said, looking at her in the rearview mirror like she had just insulted his manhood. "You know, like free-running?"

"I know what parkour is," April said. "But I don't think anyone would end up looking like this practicing parkour unless he had a death wish. I mean, what would he have been doing, jumping off buildings face-first?"

"So what's your idea?" Alex said.

The light turned green and the police car started forward. Meanwhile, Derek kept the minivan at a dead stop.

"How about: don't get pulled over?" April said, as if it were blatantly obvious.

Suddenly, Derek's eyes bulging, the minivan screeched out into the intersection, sprinting past the police car in the other lane. What could have ever lead Jamie to believe that it was a good idea to trust any of these three to get him home safely or quickly? What did the police do with minors caught driving without a license? What about the passengers? He hoped they wouldn't actually be arrested. He couldn't count on a sympathetic cabal of village guardsmen to set him free this time. However, the officer behind the wheel didn't even look over at them.

Watching the police car disappear in the rear window, April called out, "When I said, 'don't get pulled over,' I didn't mean you should try and outrun him!"

"Maybe we should just stick to side streets," Alex said, gripping his armrests tightly.

"Right," Derek said, still staring straight ahead.

Somehow, they actually made it to Heather's house without jumping an curbs or running over a single pedestrian, though there may have been a few close calls once or twice.

"You okay from here?" Alex called out the window as April and Jamie climbed out onto the sidewalk in front of the house. Jamie's whole body had begun to ache while riding in the minivan, but at least his head felt more clear now, which made walking a little less of a chore.

"Yeah, I can manage," April said.

"I wasn't talking to you," Alex said. "Take it easy, Jamie."

"Yeah, and don't do anything else stupid," Derek said, leaning around his passenger.

"At least not without calling us first so we can watch."

"Thanks for the ride, guys," Jamie said. After they drove off, that now left Jamie with only April to get rid of. Unfortunately, he didn't have much time left to do it in. "Thanks for everything, but, you know, I really can manage by myself from here."

"I've gotten you this far," April said, walking at his side, "I might as well make sure you get to your front door at least."

"Really, you don't have to," Jamie said as they climbed the front stoop. He made a show of fumbling in his pocket for the key, hoping that if he took too long to find it, she might lose interest and leave. Unfortunately, the front door opened of its own accord and Heather burst into the opening.

"Jamie, where the hell have you been! And what the hell happened to you!"

"Um..." Somehow, Jamie had completely forgotten that Heather was probably going to be a little upset that he hadn't come home last night. The truth was certainly one way he could have answered her question, but that wasn't exactly something he wanted to retread at the moment, especially when it wasn't even clear to him what had happened himself. "Would you believe some guys were showing me a couple of parkour moves and I fell face-first into a dumpster?"

"That has got to be the stupidest excuse I've ever heard!" Heather said, throwing up her hands. After her time in high school, she would certainly be an expert at spotting stupid excuses. "I know what someone looks like when they've been in a fight."

"Yeah, but you should see the other guy," Jamie said. "Not a scratch on him."

"Jokes? Really? Jamie, your face is covered in blood!"

"Don't worry, most of it's mine." After months of barely being able to carry on conversation with Heather, the quips were suddenly coming to him just like when they were kids. Not only did they allow him to sidestep the truth, it just felt good to reclaim some of the normality from the old days, even in these most abnormal of times. Jamie stepped around Heather and through the door. Much to his disappointment, April stayed at his side the whole way.

"It's nothing really," April volunteered. "Just a few scrapes."

"And who the hell are you?" Heather said, staring aghast as the three of them stepped inside.

"Who the hell are *you*?" April shot back.

"Heather this is April," Jamie said. "April: Heather."

Heather jerked back as if slapped. "*You're* April?"

"Yeah," April said. "And just who is *Heather*?"

"I'm Jamie's big sister. You know: his legal guardian?"

"Oh." April didn't sound as if that really meant anything to her. Still holding onto Jamie's arm, she looked around at the bare stud walls and open ceiling rafters. "You live here?"

"It's a work in progress," Heather said, her eyes narrowing. "Now, Jaime, would you tell me where the hell you've been all night? I understand that you might want to go out once in a while -- I can't really try to convince you not to -- but at least answer your phone when I call so I know you're okay. Don't just send me a text that says, 'busy now'."

"Did I really send that?" Jamie said. April smirked as if remembering something funny, which earned her another scowl from Heather. Jamie dug his cell phone out of his pocket and reviewed the sent messages. The only text that had been sent from his phone last night went out at 12:18 and was worded exactly as Heather had said. He also discovered four ignored calls and about fifteen texts, all from Heather.

"How much did you have to drink?" Heather said.

"I couldn't really say," Jamie said edging toward the back hallway. He certainly didn't feel drunk and the aching in his head probably had more to do with the beating Seth had given him than a hangover.

"All he had was water," April said. "I really wouldn't have thought things would have ended up the way they did with him being completely sober."

"You were out all night at a party, and you weren't even drinking?"

Jamie's face went slack. "Are you mad at me because I was out partying all night or because I *wasn't* drinking?"

"I'm not mad at you! I just wish you hadn't blown me off."

"I'm sorry," Jamie said. "It was a crazy night."

"Are you gonna tell me what happened to your face?"

"No?"

Heather sighed and shook her head. "Are you really okay?"

Jamie traced the edges of the room with his eyes. "I'm just really tired. I don't think I got any sleep last night. Can we talk about this later?"

"Fine!" Heather said, throwing up her hands. "Just clean yourself up before you go to bed."

Eyes half-veiled, Jamie gave her a thumbs-up and headed toward the back hallway.

April took a step after him. "Can I talk to him alone for a minute?" she said to Heather, her manner softening only marginally.

Heather eyed them both critically. "Okay," she finally said, "But no funny business."

"I don't think I'm even physically capable at the moment," Jamie said.

Casting her eyes skyward, Heather said, "Why me?"

CHAPTER 28

With April following close behind, Jamie pushed the hanging sheet of clear plastic aside and trudged down the hallway to the first door on the left. Once inside his room, he dropped wearily onto the edge of his bed and waited for April to say her piece. She paced back and forth in front of him twice before eventually sighing and turning to face him.

"I'm gonna be honest with you, Jamie. I didn't think you were really paying attention all those times I talked about Lancelot and Guinevere."

Jamie's brow furrowed. "What do you...?" He trailed off as realization began to dawn. In the stories, Lancelot couldn't profess his love to Guinevere because she was married to King Arthur. So instead, he had agreed to a progressively humiliating series of requests from the Queen in order to prove that he would do anything for her. The final proof of his love had been losing a duel on purpose.

"Wait, that's crazy! You think I picked that fight with Seth just so I could lose to him?"

"Don't take this the wrong way, but a fight between you and Seth could only really end one way, intentionally or not."

"But that's not -- "

"It was still the most romantic thing anyone's ever done for me." Staring into his eyes, April touched Jamie's cheek. He felt his heart beat up into his throat. After a moment, she smiled and stood up straight once more. Maybe it was just his imagination, but Jamie could have sworn she had almost kissed him. Maybe if not for all the blood she would have. "I should probably let you get some rest. It's been a long night. I'll call you later, okay?"

"Um, yeah, sure, whatever," Jamie said, fumbling over even those simple words. As if getting beaten up in front of an audience hadn't been bad enough all on its own, it had also turned Jamie into the perfect symbol of chivalry and courtly love in April's eyes. What was even worse, he couldn't even completely blame this on his doppelganger. Reaver might have started the fight, but losing it was all Jamie's doing.

April stepped into the hallway and then turned back to address Jamie one last time. "But just so we're clear, this doesn't mean the two of us are together now. I might be willing to give you a chance and see where things go, but don't go getting any ideas, okay?"

Jamie fell onto his back and covered his face with his arm as be began laughing bitterly. "No worries."

Someone was clearly having a joke at his expense, he might as well laugh about it, even if it did make his ribs ache. By the time he got himself under control again, he heard the front door being opened. With nothing separating him from the living room but a single layer of plaster and lathe, the voices of the two girls on the other side of the wall were only slightly muffled.

"Thanks for making sure Jamie got home," Heather said in all sincerity.

After a pause, April said, "Don't mention it."

"Can *you* tell me what happened last night?"

There was another pause. "I don't really think it's my place." Jamie heard heels on the concrete stoop.

"Are you okay getting home by yourself?" Heather said.

"I can manage."

Jamie continued laying there, staring at the ceiling, his legs hanging over the side of the bed. He knew that if he only closed his eyes, he'd be asleep. But he wasn't about to pass out without first washing the blood off his face. Trying to sit up made his ribs hurt so he instead rolled back to his feet with a pained gasp. As he did so, he caught a glimpse of the mirror hanging on the wall and had to stop to take a second look. No wonder Heather had been so concerned. All the blood and swelling had turned his face into that of a stranger. If he'd expected something about himself to look different just because his circumstances had changed, now it certainly had.

A quick shower washed away the grime, but it did little to lessen the pains in his body, or the memories in his mind. His thoughts kept going back to Alaida and wondering what had become of her. He knew he should have also felt continued remorse for the lives of the Wolf-Slaves he'd taken, but even when he forced himself to dwell on what he'd done to them, he couldn't make himself feel more than a mild sense of regret.

And that only made him wonder all over again just how different he and Reaver really were. While Reaver would let nothing stop him from getting his hands on that shard of metal, at the end of the day, Jamie had been just as intent on acquiring and keeping his shiny new Raven-Slave. Reaver broke the law, stole, and killed to get what he wanted, and Jamie had done exactly the same. The only difference was that Reaver was better at getting away with it.

After applying some ointment and bandaging his cuts, his face looked a little better, even if the swelling and bruises still left it somewhat unrecognizable. After Jamie returned to his room, Heather knocked at the door bearing some aspirin, a glass of water, and an ice pack.

"I thought you might need these," she said.

"Thanks." He tossed back the pills and downed the water in a single gulp. He hadn't realized until now that he probably could have knocked back a few more just like it. The ice pack he pressed to the side of his face as he collapsed onto his bed.

"So that was April, huh? Cuter than I was expecting. *Definitely* not your type."

"Maybe you do know something about me after all," Jamie mumbled around his swollen lip. The ice made it feel even bigger than it already was.

Heather chuckled dryly. "I can't believe you never told her about me."

"It never really came up." Jamie yawned. "Usually, she does most of the talking. I just have to listen."

"That doesn't sound very romantic."

"Why should it be romantic?"

"Because she's your girlfriend," Heather said from somewhere on the edge of Jamie's awareness.

"She's not my girlfriend," Jamie muttered. That, at least, was one thing he and April agreed on.

Heather said something else, but Jamie was already fast asleep.

He awoke some time later, still laying in the exact same spot he'd fallen asleep, only with a blanket pulled over him and golden rays of light slanting sharply across his room. He began to think that he'd only been asleep for an hour or two when he glanced at the clock and realized it was actually late in the afternoon. The slightest movement seemed to cause his entire body to cry out in pain so he remained laying there, motionless, alternating between staring at the cracks in the ceiling and drifting off into periods of half-consciousness.

His thoughts shifted at random, always returning eventually to those topics he'd already completely exhausted. Was Alaida still okay? What did Reaver think of what Jamie had made of his plans? Was Jamie now going to be hounded by Seth at every turn? Just who and what was Reaver and how were he and Jamie connected?

Jamie finally managed to roll over onto his side and retrieve a pencil and notebook from his desk. Just that simple movement proved to be more of a challenge than he would have thought. Still laying on the bed, he flipped the notebook open to a blank page and began making a list of all the things about his trips to Terrarhea. He included facts about the place he'd learned from Alaida and Onorah, the dates and times of the changeovers, what he was doing at the time, and what Reaver had been doing as well. He also listed questions about the situation to which he did not yet have any answers for, biggest along them: why was this happening in the first place. Unfortunately, the questions quickly became just as numerous as the facts. As he scribbled sketches of things he'd seen, places he'd been, and people he'd met, the whole exercise became a single rambling narrative of his experiences, not only with Terrarhea, but also the ways in which Terrarhea had influenced his life on Earth. He let no detail, no matter how small, escape his scrutiny. None of it offered any insight or clarity to the situation but it did begin to create an illusion of order over something that was probably just impossibly chaotic.

"Knock, knock," Heather said from the other side of Jamie's door as she tapped lightly on the frame. Slowly, she peaked around the edge. "I heard you moving around. How're you feeling?"

"Like crap." Jamie sat up with a groan and flipped his notebook closed.

"Glad to hear it." Heather crossed her arms and leaned against the door frame. "Hopefully that'll teach you not to go around picking fights. Clearly, you're not very good at it."

"I didn't start it."

Heather lifted an eyebrow. "Was she worth it at least?"

"I don't know if we were actually fighting over April," Jamie said and then met Heather's level stare. "No, seriously, I really have no idea what we were fighting about."

"So, who was it?" Heather took a seat on the bed alongside Jamie. "That Seth kid?"

"Why?" Jamie's shoulders suddenly felt very tight. "You're not thinking of getting involved, are you?"

"I'd be lying if I said I wasn't pissed the hell off right now," Heather said, clenching her fists. "Part of me wants to find out where this guy lives and go over there right now to pay him a visit with the business end of a baseball bat."

"Having my big sister fight for me isn't going to make things any better. You know how these things work. I've got to deal with it myself. If you get involved, it'll never go away."

"Would you have said that to Mom and Dad? I'm supposed to be taking care of you, the same as they would have."

"If Mom and Dad were here, I wouldn't be in this situation. I'm not trying to blame anyone. I'm just saying that's the way things are. We can't change it."

"I don't know," Heather said, shaking her head. "I still want to cave that bastard's head in."

"It's over. He won and I got the girl, apparently."

Heather leaned back on her elbows and looked up at the ceiling. "Wow, don't sound so excited about it. You're not still crushing on that Alaida girl, are you?"

For a little while there, Jamie had managed to put Alaida out of his mind. Now he crumpled as the uncertainty of her fate washed over him yet again.

"What is it?" Heather said, sitting up and placing a hand on Jamie's shoulder.

"I...I saw her again yesterday, last night, whatever."

"Alaida? Was she at the party?"

"Sure." That might have been a lie but the rest wasn't and he really needed to talk to someone about this, even if it was only in half-truths. "We talked again but she had to leave town. And she's with this real creep of a guy and I have no way of getting in contact with her to know if she's okay. I'm just really worried about her."

"Should we call somebody? I mean, how old is she?"

"She's not a minor if that's what you mean." Jamie couldn't very well tell Heather the truth about that particular fact, or she might take it upon herself to try and help Alaida, something that was completely impossible for either of them. "I don't even know where they went. It's just so frustrating."

"I'm sorry. You really like her, don't you?"

Jamie paused to consider if he really wanted to go any further with this conversation. Heather, however, looked genuinely concerned for a change. He sighed, not really knowing how to reply. Alaida had definitely been a friend, at least until she discovered that Jamie might be the Red Rogue, but did the potential exist for her to become something more? At the moment, all Jamie really wanted was for her to be safe. "I've never met anyone like her before. It's like we're..."

"Soul mates?"

Jamie shook his head. "That sounds kind of hokey but, yeah, kind of."

"There was a time I would have said that same thing about you and Kristie but apparently I was completely wrong about that one. I'm sure she'll be okay."

"Yeah." Jamie's head drooped.

Heather gave his shoulder a squeeze and a shake. "Are you hungry?"

"Starving," Jamie said around a sniffle.

"I'll order us a pizza," Heather said, climbing to her feet. "What do you want on it?"

"Anything's fine." Not only would Jamie have eaten anything that she put in front of him at the moment, but the idea of picking pizza toppings right now just seemed so meaningless.

Once Heather left his room, closing the door behind her with a soft click, Jamie bent over to retrieve the cell phone from the pocket of his jeans laying in a heap on the floor. His ribs cried out as he stretched to reach it but the more he moved, the easier it was to deal with the pain. With phone in hand, he laid back on his bed and flipped through his contact list, eventually arriving at one with a picture of a freckle-faced, redhead whose hair had been done-up in pigtails. Jamie couldn't help but smile. No one should have been able to pull off looking that stereotypically cute, but Kristie always made it look easy. His finger hesitated over the "call" button for only a second before he pressed it. After Alaida had urged Jamie to try and repair this damaged friendship, he owed it to her not to keep putting this off.

The phone rang four times in a row without anyone picking up. Kristie had to see that it was Jamie who was calling. Maybe she didn't even want to talk to him anymore. It was just about to ring for a sixth time, and Jamie's had thumb drifted over to the "end call" button, when someone picked up.

"Jamie?" Kristie said from the other end of the line. The sound of that voice alone sent images of Jamie's hometown crashing through his mind. He really should have done this a long time ago.

"Yeah," Jamie said, fumbling with his phone as he brought it back to his ear. "Hi, Kristie. I know it's been a while, but I was hoping we might be able to talk a little."

"Um." Her voice shifted as she moved the phone away for a moment. "Sure, I've got a few minutes. I've actually been meaning to call you. It just..."

"Never seemed like the right time?" Jamie suggested.

"Exactly. I mean, after everything that happened with your parents and you moving away and...and that time in the park, I just didn't know what to say."

"I know exactly what you mean." Jamie suddenly felt light. She had just said the exact same thing he'd been thinking for months. Maybe Alaida wasn't the only one on the same wavelength with him after all. "I kept putting this off thinking that I'd eventually figure it out, but it just never happened. Someone recently convinced me that I shouldn't keep avoiding it though."

"I'm glad. It's good to hear your voice again."

"Yeah, yours too."

Suddenly, a third voice called out from Kristie's end of the conversation. "Hey, Kristie, do you see my tie anywhere?" Distant and barely audible, Jamie still recognized it.

"Is that Jack?" he said.

"Um, yeah," Kristie said, crunching noises coming over the line as she shifted the phone in her hands. "It's not in here," she called out to Jack. "Did you look in the basement?" Jamie didn't hear the reply, but Kristie's voice returned to his ear more clearly. "Sorry about that. Miguel called in sick, so Jack had to help his parents milk the cows and now we're just a little behind schedule."

"Oh," Jamie said. What could the two of them be running late for that required a tie? "If I caught you at a bad time I can call back later."

"No, it's fine. I don't have anything else to do while I wait for Jack."

"So...what are you guys up to?"

The pause which followed stretched on until Jamie began to wonder if their call might have been dropped. When Kristie did eventually reply, she was almost whispering. "Um, we're going to the school's fall formal..."

Jamie felt his heart sink into the pit of his stomach. "Together?" His voice was nearly as soft as Kristie's had been.

Another pause. "Yeah."

"Um, wow, I mean, I didn't think you liked those kinds of things." In all the time Jamie had known her, Kristie had never once had anything good to say about school functions of any kind. In fact, the two of them had once considered it a badge of honor that they'd never attended a single school sporting event or dance or even a pep rally.

He could practically see her shrugging. "I've never been to one before. How would I know if I liked it or not?"

"Yeah, okay. I guess that makes sense," Jamie said, his reply coming on auto-pilot. "And with Jack too, huh?"

Jamie could hear Kristie cover her face as she sighed. "Jamie, me and Jack have been going out for a while now."

The hand holding the phone dropped away from Jamie's ear. From a rational point of view, it made sense, he supposed. Jack, Kristie, and Jamie had all been friends since long before any of them had ever harbored a romantic feeling toward anyone. They always got along well together, and they shared more than a few interests. That's why Heather had encouraged Jamie to pursue Kristie. With Jamie out of the picture, of course Jack would step in to fill the role he'd vacated. It all made perfect sense.

"Jamie?" Kristie said, "Me and Jack...I mean, it's part of the reason I didn't know what to say to you."

Yes, it was all perfectly logical. So why did Jamie feel like he'd just been stabbed in the back? "But you stopped talking to me *before* I moved away."

"*You* weren't talking to me either, remember?" Kristie's voice had now taken on the same defensive edge Jamie had just used. "And the first time Jack asked me out was a few days before you went and kissed me. That's what I was trying to tell you in the park that day. But after that kiss, I didn't know what to say. I mean, my two best friends were practically fighting over me all of a sudden! And then your parents died and you moved away and...and..."

Jamie chuckled bitterly. Jack had beaten him after all, and only by a few days. At least it was actually starting to make more sense now.

"Jamie?" Kristie said, the concern thick in her voice.

"Is that Jamie?" Jack said from a distance. "Let me talk to him!"

"Hey! Hold on!" Kristie's voice grew distant as Jack sputtered in the background about putting Jamie on speakerphone. "I don't think that's a good idea right now." Her voice again becoming clear, Kristie said, "Jamie, are you okay?"

"I...I should probably let you guys get going," he said, his throat suddenly very tight. "I'm...glad you two...um..."

"Jamie you know if you ever want to talk, you can call us anytime, right?"

"Yeah, I know." And why was that his responsibility? Kristie could have let him know what was going on long ago rather than let him keep thinking that kiss in the park had actually meant something. "I miss you guys, both of you. Take care."

"Yeah, you too, Jamie. Bye."

"Hey Jamie!" Jack's urgent voice cut in. "We still -- "

Jamie hit the "end call" button and dropped the phone onto his bed.

So that was that. Kristie, the girl he'd actually pursued, didn't want anything to do with him. Of course, that's not exactly what she had said, but thinking about it in those terms made the whole thing easier to swallow. Alaida, the girl he shared more in common with than anyone he'd ever met, only thought of him as a sibling at best and a criminal at worst. He didn't even know if she was still alive. April, the girl who Jamie could barely even stand, was the only one who was actually interested in him. April *was* way more attractive than Kristie was cute, but that didn't really make up for all her less-appealing characteristics.

When the pizza came, Heather ate a few pieces and Jamie devoured the rest. Regardless of how meaningless it might have seemed, he was still famished. Unlike Reaver, he still got hungry. Returning to his room afterward, he only intended to lay down for a little while so as to let his wounds rest.

He awoke the next morning, still stiff and sore. He spent the majority of the day adding to his journal of Terrarhea. At some point in the afternoon, April called, as she'd promised she would. She apparently just wanted to chat but Jamie didn't know what to say to her, didn't want to say anything to her, and so it ended only a few minutes after it began, with April sounding rather dissatisfied. Derek and Alex called as well, ostensibly to see how Jamie was doing, but mostly to reminisce about the adventures of Friday night. Through careful prodding, Jamie managed to discover much about what Reaver had been up to while in his body.

Apparently, he had accompanied Derek and Alex to the comic shops as Jamie had been planning to do. Though the two boys noted that he had been somewhat less talkative than usual, he had also displayed a curious interest in the comic books they were shopping for, as well as any other cultural references that might have come up during their travels. Once that had run its course, the three of them had gone back to Derek's house to play video games, something else that Reaver demonstrated considerable skill with after only a brief learning period. According to Derek, the decision to investigate Seth's party had only come to the forefront because Alex kept bringing it up. Alex, however, claimed that he had only mentioned it once or twice. Regardless, even though they had been nearly ready to call it a night, Reaver ended up dragging them to the party. It was shortly after they snuck in that they crossed paths with April, and Reaver abandoned them to spend time with her. That period of Reaver's activities was something which Derek and Alex could only speculate about.

Now alone, the two boys managed to avoid causing any trouble by sticking to the shadows. With their interest in gossip, they knew everyone at the party. Unfortunately, everyone also knew them. Derek did apparently talk to a girl named Nikki for quite some time, ranting to her about the dismal state of modern comic book publishing. Alex claimed she only listened for as long as she did because she had been too polite to excuse herself, and had only been saved in the end when her boyfriend came looking for her.

The next they saw Reaver, he and Seth were arguing about something which quickly descended into threats of violence. April tried to play peacemaker, but her best efforts only resulted in a temporary postponing of what had become an inevitable fight. Reaver selected the time, dawn, and Seth the location, the alley holding significance to everyone involved except Jamie. Reaver left with Derek and Alex, and the party broke up shortly thereafter, well past midnight. The two of them spent several hours camped out in Derek's Mom's minivan after driving around to random locations that had struck Reaver's interest and letting him go off to wander on his own for a time. When he grew tired of that, the three of them visited an all-night dinner to wait for dawn. The rest Jamie had already learned from firsthand experience.

Their narrative provided Jamie with enough additional information to continue his journaling well into the evening. Unfortunately, it still didn't provide any enlightenment. Jamie couldn't even figure out who or what Reaver was supposed to be. He could sweet talk a high school girl from Earth just as easily as he could blackmail a Finttiranos military officer into risking his life for him. He was even able to make a tenuous alliance with the Wolf-Slaves, a race that notoriously distrusted and avoided humans. Maybe he wasn't even human, but rather some being more closely related to one of the Slave-Races. After all, he could bend plate steel with his hands, survive fiery explosions without a scratch, and run faster than the world's greatest athlete. He didn't get hungry, tired, or even sweat.

And then there was the very real possibility that he might have been a magesmith too. Onorah had said Ommto's notes would only be of interest to one and the hold of his titan-mecha had also contained various tools and wardcaster parts. Most importantly of all, he also seemed to have the 'gift,' as Onorah had called it. Or did he? Was that something contained within an individual's physical form, or was it a more ethereal trait, one that might travel with a mind to a distant world? Jamie had, of course, never sensed a resonator stone in his life until Onorah had made him aware of them, but that could also have simply meant that Earth didn't have any.

The easiest explanation for everything was also the one Jamie least wanted to consider: that Reaver was just a fractured piece of Jamie's own psyche. His extensive television education continually filled his mind with hopeless tales of multiple personality disorder—killers and rapists and villains, all hidden under layers of competing and contradictory personalities, all sharing the same body. There were also certain parallels between Jamie's activities on Terrarhea and Reaver's on Earth. Though, following that train of thought, the comparisons quickly grew increasingly tenuous, and sometimes, ridiculous. At its core, that line of reasoning just didn't make sense.

Besides, Jamie couldn't bring himself to think that Alaida was just some fragmentary element of the real-life experiences he was having with April. Reaver hadn't even known about Jamie's troubles with Seth until Alex had brought it up. And from the sounds of it, he hadn't gotten involved in that fight out of any sense of revenge on Jamie's behalf, but simply because Reaver didn't take flack from anyone. Reaver might have been on the trail for answers, tracking down that black shard of metal, but he still seemed to have barely more idea of what was happening than Jamie.

CHAPTER 29

"Jamie, do you have a minute?" Mister Clark said, singling Jamie out of the crowds making their way past the school offices that Monday morning. Two day's worth of rest had helped Jamie recover considerably from his injuries, and though he still ached all over, his face was no longer quite so swollen as to make him unrecognizable. Reluctantly, Jamie joined the guidance counselor in the relative calm of the office lobby. "What happened to you?" Mister Clark said, waving his hand over his own face.

With a level gaze, Jamie stared at the man for several moments. "Why do I think you already know the answer to that?"

"Because you're a very intuitive young man."

"Look, I got into a fight. No big deal. And since it happened on a weekend and nowhere near the school, I don't think you have any jurisdiction."

"Jamie, I'm not a cop," Mister Clark said, almost laughing, "And I'm not trying to get anyone in trouble either. But I am trying to look out for you. You're a smart kid and I'd hate to see you throw away all these opportunities you have going for you right now by getting involved in this kind of dangerous behavior."

As if Jamie had any control over what kept happening to him. It was Reaver and Seth who were engaging in that kind of behavior. Jamie was just along for the ride.

"I hope you at least managed to settle whatever it was about."

"Who knows." Jamie glanced through the glass doors of the lobby into the hallway filled with all his fellow students. "You'd have to ask the other guy."

"I thought you didn't want me getting involved," Mister Clark said, which drew a critical gaze from Jamie. "Jamie, your sister is worried about you."

Jamie's eyes narrowed. "You talked to my sister about this?" If she'd told him about the fight, what else might she have mentioned? He thought he could trust her. Maybe he'd been wrong.

"It's not like that," Mister Clark said, waving a hand. He paused to clear his throat. "She...reached out to me because she wanted to know how you were doing. I have to admit, she was a little surprised when I mentioned those advanced classes I wanted you to think about. I mean, you completely ignored me after we spoke, but you never even talked to her about them either?"

"I didn't ignore you," Jamie said. "I said I'd think about it, and I still am."

"Well, you missed your chance because now it's too late to get you in this semester."

Good, that should table this discussion, Jamie thought. "That's too bad," he said.

"There's always next semester. And before you say you'll 'think about it,' let me point something out that you might not have realized yet: every math class after pre-calc is taught by Mister Fisher. And when you ace pre-calc this semester, they're not going to let you go back to something easier."

"The semester isn't over yet. Still plenty of time to earn an F."

"I don't think even you'd be audacious enough to sabotage your own grade like that."

"At the rate we're going, Mister Fisher will probably do it for me."

"The point I'm trying to make here is that Mister Fisher doesn't teach any of the advanced classes."

The chance to get out of Mister Fisher's classes did sound intriguing. Not only would it save him from having to put up with that bastard, it would also mean he wouldn't be in the same class with April anymore. Then she'd have no reason whatsoever to keep insisting on doing their homework together. Granted, next semester was still a ways off, but he couldn't deny Mister Clark made a very good point.

"Why don't you mull it over," Mister Clark said, "for real this time, and let me know when it comes time to sign up for next semester's classes, okay?"

"I'll do that," Jamie said. And this time, he actually might.

As Jamie stepped out of the office, three of his fellow classmates who had been going down the hall in the opposite direction, bumped into him. Rather than the attack Seth had perpetrated all those weeks ago, this was just a friendly jostling.

"Hey, Jamie," one of them said as he passed, "I hear you're into parkour."

Jamie stood dumbfounded as the three of them passed around him.

"You should come hang out with us sometime," one of the others said.

"Yeah, we've worked out a couple of awesome courses," the third said over her shoulder as they all three moved on. "You'd love it!"

Jamie stood rooted in place, staring at their backs. He'd never spoken to any of them before. He'd certainly never spoken to anyone about being interested in parkour. With a sigh, he shook his head. This sounded too much like the work of Alex and Derek.

As Jamie rounded the corner to the hallway with his locker, he saw a textbook go skittering across the floor. It hadn't been kicked maliciously, merely caught on someone's toes as they'd been walking, but no one in the hall seemed particularly interested in retrieving it. Jamie recognized it as the book used in his history class, but it was only when he saw another book from one of his other classes did a sickening sensation begin welling up in his stomach. With pulse quickening, Jamie pushed through the last few people separating him from his locker only to find his fears confirmed.

The door to his locker hung open wide and the contents had been dumped onto the floor and scattered about the hall. A few of his fellow students looked on, snickering, but most didn't seem to care in the least, either stepping around Jamie's scattered belongings or tripping over them when they didn't even realize they were there. It wasn't hard to figure out who was responsible. One of the onlookers, a tall, thin boy with pale, reddish hair and thickly freckled skin stood on the other side of the hall with arms crossed and a toothy grin stretched across his bony face. Of all Seth's comrades, this freckled skeleton was definitely one of the easiest to pick out of a crowd, even if Jamie had never caught his name.

Sighing, Jamie stooped and began picking up his things.

"Hey, freak, was that slut worth it?" the freckled boy called out.

Very carefully, Jamie set the books he'd gathered into the bottom of his locker and stood to face his heckler. Much to Jamie's surprise, the other boy's stance suddenly turned defensive, as if expecting an attack. All Jamie did, however, was take a step in his direction, which resulted in the other boy taking one back.

"Stop calling her that," Jamie said. He might not have wanted anything to do with April, but he was getting a little sick of the way everyone talked about her. "You don't know anything about her."

"I know she's a slut," the freckled boy said, trying to rally his nerve. The jeer, however, fell flat.

"Wow, that's original. How'd you ever come up with that one?"

The other boy bared his teeth. "How'd you like another beat-down, you loser?"

246

Jamie threw out his arms and took another step forward. "What are you waiting for? I'm right here!" The other boy's face twitched and instead of coming at Jamie, he actually drew back. "Yeah, that's what I thought. Seth might be able to get away with stuff like that because he's the star of the team. But you? You're just another name on the roster. Nobody cares about you." Jamie turned and took in the other students who'd stopped to watch the exchange. "Right now, I think most of the school is more interested in April than you. And what's she ever done except have some rumors told about her? So really, which one of us is the loser here?"

"You're dead, you know that!"

"Take a number," Jamie said, shaking his head as he went back to collecting his things. The other boy looked about as if searching for further support. Finding none, he disappeared into the crowds with a curse on his lips.

Jamie had heard rumors that most of the lockers could be broken into if one wanted. Supposedly, there was a way to jimmy the frame with a crowbar, but the easiest way was simply to find out which senior had had that locker before graduating and convince them to supply the combination.

By the time the first bell rang Jamie still hadn't finished gathering all of his belongings. As he made a hasty stack of his loose papers, a pair of shapely legs ending in pink tennis shoes stepped up alongside him.

"Here, I think this is the last of it," April said, handing him two textbooks and a random assortment of papers.

Jamie considered the source of this kindness for a moment before accepting. He'd really been hoping she'd have come to her senses by now and discarded him like all her previous boyfriends. "Thanks," he said, stuffing them into the locker and rising to his feet. "But you didn't have to do that."

"You didn't have to stand up for me just now either," she said.

Jamie slung his backpack into his locker and retrieved his pre-calc textbook from the disorganized pile in the bottom. "You saw that?"

"Most of it," April said, her voice cracking.

Jamie turned and really looked at her for the first time this morning. All the makeup she wore didn't do anything to hide the red in her eyes. "Are you okay?"

Sniffling as she drew the back of her hand across her nose, she turned away from Jamie, nodding. "It hasn't been the best morning."

"Have they been coming after you too?"

"Not like this," she said. "But I don't think I have any friends left. All the ones who didn't side with Lorrie when we had our falling out are now siding with Seth. No one will even talk to me anymore."

"If they're picking sides just because of what happened over the weekend, I don't think they were ever really your friends."

April scoffed and shook her head. "Where'd you get that from, a self-help book?"

Jamie shrugged and offered a weary smile. It was probably something his dad had once told him. The second bell rang, echoing through the now empty halls. "I guess we're gonna be late."

"Great. Now we'll have to put up with Mister Fisher's BS too. Wanna go hang out at the mall again?"

Jamie opened his mouth to reject the idea but found he couldn't. Her suggestion was actually really appealing at the moment. "We probably shouldn't," he said with some effort.

"Yeah, you're probably right." April took a step toward Mister Fisher's classroom. "You coming?"

"We might as well get it over with," Jamie said, falling in alongside her. Apparently, their luck wasn't all bad that morning because it turned out that Mister Fisher had called in sick and the substitute that the school had found to monitor the class in his absence hadn't even managed to start taking roll by the time Jamie and April slipped into their seats.

They didn't end up covering any new material all period and the second half turned into nothing more than a study hall during which the students were given the opportunity to get a head start on tomorrow's homework. Twice during the class, April glanced back at Jamie with a hollow look in her eyes, and for the first time since he'd met her, he thought he might have actually known what she was feeling -- mainly because he felt exactly the same.

They'd both become strangers to this world. No one looked at them as they really were but rather as fabrications of what everyone thought they were. Jamie had been living that existence for weeks, ever since his first brush with Terrarhea and Reaver. He only now realized that April had been living with it for much longer and it was only now that the reality of it had finally caught up to her.

They parted ways, of course, after that first period, but April promised to track Jamie down later so they could spend lunch together. From the way she looked at him with that dejected expression when she said it, Jamie couldn't bring himself to say anything other than, "Okay."

The rest of the morning was spent in a dream-like state as Jamie drifted from one class to the next. The jarring mix of reactions he got from the school bewildered him. Most of the students liked Seth, they wanted to be Seth, so they couldn't understand why anyone would ever want to pick a fight with such a beloved personality, especially over a trashy slut like April. That was just downright unpatriotic.

The teachers were especially critical of the situation and each class would start with a repeat of the same drama, wherein the teacher would ask Jamie in the most condescending manner possible what had happened to his face. Since it was clear they already knew perfectly well what had happened to his face, Jamie chose not to respond with anything more than silence. More than once, and regardless of what the day's subject matter actually was, he and his fellow students got to sit through a lecture warning about the dangers of what would happen if one of the school's star athletes was injured and unable to compete in any sporting events. No one ever came right out and named names but the implications were clear enough: what Jamie had done was not just an assault against Seth, it was also a direct attack against the entire school, designed to destroy its reputation. Of course, the school's reputation was something that Jamie cared absolutely nothing about.

Occasionally, some of the students who had witnessed the fight first-hand would lean in expectantly, hoping for Jamie to respond with some new nugget of gossip. Each time they were let down, left with nothing to do but whisper amongst themselves and quickly turn away whenever Jamie noticed them. Fortunately, none of them had come forward to offer themselves as a witness so there was really nothing anyone could do to him.

There was also a small minority of students who had been picked on and beat-up by Seth, as well as those who saw themselves as Seth's rivals. All Jamie got from any of them was envy and bitterness. None of them had ever stood up to Seth the way Jamie had. None of them had ever gone toe-to-toe with Seth in a street fight. None of them had ever managed to bloody Seth's nose. But Jamie had (at least with Reaver's help). Even though he'd lost, it was far more than any of them had ever found the nerve to do and now they resented him for it; a newcomer who had shown them just how uncommitted they actually were.

Others just looked at him with fear in their eyes, as if he were some kind of rabid beast, liable to fly into a violent rampage at the drop of a hat. As with all the rest, he simply tried his best to ignore them.

As promised, April found Jamie at the beginning of their lunch period when he stopped to fill his water bottle from a drinking fountain. She followed him in relative silence to his secluded retreat. Derek and Alex, of course, had beaten them there and where already settled in. Despite the cloudy skies and the cool breeze, that corner of the school offered enough shelter for them to enjoy those last few pleasant days of the season.

"So this is where all the rejects hang out," April said, frowning.

"Yeah," Alex said around the straw of a juice box. "From what I hear, you should feel right at home."

April's frown deepened but she didn't retaliate as she typically would have. Instead, she took a seat on the edge of a concrete abutment flanking a nearby emergency exit.

"Could you guys just tone it down a bit?" Jamie said.

Alex flashed him a look that said, "What?"

Jamie sat down in the grass at the base of the abutment and opened his own lunch, a sandwich of luncheon meat and American cheese on white bread. Seeing as how April hadn't brought a lunch of her own, Jamie felt a little guilty eating his in front of her. Figuring it was only courteous of him to do so, he offered her some of his potato chips.

"No thanks," she said. "I never eat lunch."

"So that's how she stays so skinny," Alex said. "And here I just thought she was bulimic."

Jamie cast an incredulous glare in his direction which went right over the other boy's head. Clearly, he'd never be able to get through to them. "Hey, I've got a question for you two," Jamie said instead. "You guys haven't been telling people that crazy story about me getting hurt practicing parkour, have you?"

April, who up until this point had been satisfied watching the passing cars on the distant street, now sat forward.

Derek laughed, perhaps a bit too loudly. "No. Of course not."

"Not exactly, anyways," Alex added. "But after the way you climbed Seth's fence at the party, we may have mentioned to a few people that you do have some killer moves."

"You climbed Seth's fence?" April said. "The one in his backyard? That thing's, like, twenty feet high."

"Probably closer to twelve, but I'll concede, it was still pretty cool," Derek said. "He went right over like nothing and then popped the latch from the other side to let us two in."

"Why didn't you just come in the front?" April said as she took one of Jamie's potato chips.

"Yeah, why didn't we?" Jamie said.

"We were entering enemy territory," Alex said. "We weren't about to stage a frontal assault."

Jamie couldn't help but wonder if the military analogy had been their choice of words or Reaver's. Scoffing under her breath as she shook her head, April sat back and returned to watching the passing traffic.

"Hey, I have a comic book question for you guys," Jamie said. Now that he had their attention, it seemed like a good opportunity to field something he'd been wondering about. Disguising it as something related to comic books was the only way he could think of to not come across sounding too crazy when asking it. "Say, if a supervillain swapped Batman's mind with some regular guy on the street, do you think he'd still be able to do all his martial arts stuff?"

"Oh, you mean like that one issue of Detective Comics?" Derek said.

"Don't you mean Justice Society?" Alex said.

"No, you're thinking of that other one, with that guy and the thing."

"Oh, yeah, you're right," Alex agreed. Jamie could hardly believe that someone had already explored this idea, not once, but twice.

"And of course, Batman would be able to use all his martial arts," Derek said. "I mean, he'd be limited by the physical abilities of whoever it was that he got himself stuck inside, but half of that fighting stuff in just mental anyway."

"What I want to know is: Why?" Alex asked of Jamie, his voice dripping with contempt.

"Huh?" Jamie had thought these two would have dove right into a comic book themed debate without asking about the reasons for it. Did Alex even suspect why Jamie had asked in the first place? He probably shouldn't have brought it up so soon after that parkour talk. "It's just a hypothetical question," Jamie said, hastily trying to divert from the truth.

"No, I mean why would the supervillain swap out Batman's mind?" Alex said, nonplused. "Just think about it: he's got Batman strapped down to the operating table, completely at his mercy, and instead of just killing him or looking under his mask, he goes through all the trouble of switching his mind out with some regular schmoe? It doesn't make any sense."

"What if it was all part of his master plan to impersonate Batman?" Derek volunteered.

"So why not kill him after taking his body?"

"Because he wants his own body back afterward and he wants Batman to live with the soul crushing sense of despair that will come from all the terrible crimes the villain commits in Batman's name."

"Sounds like a lot of work just to frame the guy," Alex said.

"Well, then, if it was just some regular guy off the street, maybe it was an accident."

"How do you accidentally swap your mind with a complete stranger?"

"Simple: Batman's fighting some psychic villain and they're doing battle on the astral plan. When Batman finally lays the bad guy out, the psychic backlash knocks him into the body of some guy who just happens to be walking past. But when this innocent civilian realizes that he's now Batman, he goes on a tear through Gotham city, using Batman's celebrity status to get into all kinds of trouble. All the while, Batman, in the other guy's body, has to track him down and defeat him without any of his special gear or physical training, just his mind."

"That actually sounds kind of cool," Alex said.

"Yeah, I know," Derek said, polishing his fingernails on the front of his shirt, "I'm sure DC will be contacting me any day now to start writing for them."

"You wish!"

Quickly thereafter, Derek and Alex reverted to their old topics of discussion, leaving Jamie's "hypothetical" scenario by the wayside. It had probably been too much to hope for much enlightenment from the likes of them anyway. With April still uninterested in their conversation, Jamie merely sat and ate his lunch, occasionally listening in or simply dwelling on his own thoughts. He certainly had enough of them to keep himself occupied for far more than just the length of any one lunch period.

When the bell rang, Derek and Alex disappeared in short order. Jamie took his time, hoping that April would likewise choose to head back inside with all due haste. Instead, she lingered, almost lethargically.

"Jamie," she said as she gathered up her purse and stood at the same time Jamie did, "I was wondering if I could walk home with you after school today?"

"Um, why?" The farther April stayed from his house, the better.

Looking at the grass along the sidewalk, she said, "I wanted to apologize to your sister. I wasn't exactly all that friendly the last time we talked."

And just how was he supposed to turn her down for something like that? Just because he didn't want to be her boyfriend didn't mean he had to be rude to her. "Um, I'm sure she understands. Things were pretty crazy that morning."

"Still, I'd like to tell her in person."

Jamie was never going to get rid of her, was he? "Well, I guess, if you really want to. Although she doesn't usually get home from work right away so maybe you could just stop by later?"

April shrugged, "I don't mind waiting. We can work on our Pre-Calc."

"I, um, okay, I guess."

"I'll meet you at the north exit?" April said as she turned to leave.

"Sure," Jamie said, shaking his head.

CHAPTER 30

Jamie had brought everything with him that he'd need for his next class, so after disposing of the remains of his lunch, he cut across one of the service drives that ran between the school building and the bowl-shaped athletic field behind. Seldom used during the school day except by students looking for a secluded spot to sneak a cigarette between classes, it also made an excellent shortcut between Jamie's lunch spot and his next class.

If April insisted on staying so close to him from now on, moments like this might end up being Jamie's only opportunities for privacy. He wouldn't have minded the attention so much if it had been from Alaida, but that would have meant he was trapped on Terrarhea again and likely being hunted by the Finttiranos military, Wolf-Slaves, and who knew what else.

With his thoughts on other topics, Jamie didn't notice he wasn't quite as alone as he'd thought until someone stepped into his path from behind a dumpster. Heart suddenly racing so quickly it felt as if it might burst through his chest, Jamie began backing away the moment he saw Seth. Two more boys, both even bigger than Seth, stepped around the corner of the building behind Jamie. Another two came into view behind Seth.

There could be little doubt this was a trap. Frantically, Jamie looked for a way out. The school building formed a hard edge along Jamie's right without any unlocked doors that he might be able to use to get back inside. No windows at ground level looked onto the driveway either. Anyone on the floors above would have to be looking straight down to see anything going on in the alley. To Jamie's left, a tall, chain-link fence separated him from the grassy slope that formed the perimeter of the empty athletic field, allowing him a clear view of freedom without letting him actually get there.

Seth cracked his knuckles as he stepped forward, a sinister grin stretched across his face. His lip bore a trace of discoloration and swelling but he didn't look nearly as injured from their fight as Jamie still did. Jamie backed away, trying to keep an equal distance between Seth and the two boys behind him.

"Look, I don't want any trouble," Jamie said. "You won. I'm fine with that."

"But I wasn't done yet," Seth said. "I wanna finish what I started before that bitch of an ex-girlfriend got in the way."

How much more was there to do? He'd nearly reduced Jamie to unconsciousness before April had interfered. A shiver ran down Jamie's spine imagining what it would feel like to be struck by those fists in his current condition.

The fence was too high to jump in a single leap but there was a dumpster not too far away which might provide a steppingstone for him to get into the bleachers on the other side. Unfortunately, it would also do the same for his attackers.

"Look, you won, I accept that."

"Really?" Seth said, strutting over and leaning against the dumpster Jamie had just been eyeing. "Did I really win? Or did you let me win? Because the way you started that fight, was nothing like the way you ended it."

"Why the hell would I *let* you win?"

"Rumor has it that you threw our fight just to make April feel sorry for you."

How had Seth found out about that? As far as Jamie knew, April had never discussed the story of Lancelot and Guinevere with Seth. And with her current ranking in the school's social standings, she wouldn't have been overly inclined to tell anyone else about it either.

Seth chuckled grimly, obviously reading something in Jamie's expression. "Yeah, Lorrie told me about it. April did always like her stupid romances. Although if you ask me, loosing a fight ain't no way to impress a girl. I prefer to win."

Of all the things that Lorrie could have actually remembered from her friendship with April, why did that have to be one of them?

"I wanna see what you really got," Seth said, stepping forward. "Ain't no one around to impress this time except me."

The two guys blocking Jamie's escape to the rear were big but not quite big enough to cover the entire lane. Maybe Jamie could draw them to one side with a feint and then break through the gap on the other. Being football players, they were probably better at things like that than Jamie was, however.

Nervously, he bounced on his toes once or twice to see if could draw on any of those special skills Reaver seemed to display. If that maniac really was just another aspect of Jamie's own mind, they both should have had same abilities. Unfortunately, the fact Jamie couldn't even imagine how he might be able to fight his way out of this situation only seemed to reinforce the likelihood that he and Reaver were, in fact, two separate entities.

Seth noticed Jamie's change in stance and his smile broadened as he continued to advance. Striking a mock crane-stance, Seth said, "Ya gonna get all medieval on my ass again?"

In that moment, Jamie saw his opening: a small dip in the ground at the bottom of the chain link fence created a tiny gap, mostly covered by tall grass which the groundskeepers hadn't bothered to cut. With Seth currently off balance from his own antics, Jamie broke into a run, sprinting right past him. Seth and his cronies sprang into motion almost instantly, scrambling to catch their prey. Jamie didn't bother to look back. He had eyes only for that gap in the fence.

As he got close, he threw himself into a feet-first slide across the pebbly asphalt. If he misjudged this by even a little, he'd end up with cuts all over his body from the rusty ends of the fencing. Although, if he didn't try, Seth would very likely put him in the hospital regardless.

He shot into the gap amidst a spray of gravel, a sharp pain slicing across the bottom of his left forearm and a rattling of fence behind him. His face passed within an inch or two of the frayed wire ends above and then he burst out onto the grassy slope beyond, already pushing himself up to his feet and breaking into a run.

At the bottom of the slope, he hopped over the short fence there and onto the running track. Somehow in all that, he'd actually managed to keep a grip on the books he'd been carrying. His left arm now hurt and he caught a glimpse of blood as he looked up toward the service drive, but he didn't have time to worry about injuries right now.

His five would-be attackers were gathered at the fence, Seth frantically spurring the others to take up the chase. One of them noticed the dumpster and began to climb it, the others quickly following suit. That would give them access to the adjacent bleachers, but they would still have to circle around the tunnel that led back into the locker rooms. That gave Jamie a very small head start which he wasn't about to squander.

Unlikely to outrun them over open ground, Jamie instead fled down the length of the locker room tunnel as fast as he was could. He knew there would be gym classes this afternoon so the doors to the locker rooms had to be unlocked. At least he hoped so. If they weren't, this chase would come to a short end and his attackers would have him cornered in the perfect secluded spot to carry out their assault without any interruptions whatsoever.

The natural sunlight didn't reach very far into the tunnel and the single light fixture overhead provided only a sickly yellow glow that was barely enough to see the pair of solid metal doors at the end. Jamie went to the one on his left first. The handle wouldn't move, and the door didn't even rattle in its frame when he pulled on it. With mounting urgency as he hurried to the other door, he glanced down the tunnel. He could see no one yet, but they couldn't have been far behind by now. The second door's handle didn't turn either. Jamie nearly began to curse his own ill-conceived plan but then the door swung open easily when he merely gave it a tug.

Without sparing a moment, he dashed inside, thinking that he might have heard the sound of multiple hurried footsteps echoing down the tunnel behind him. The bright lights on the other side of the door momentarily blinded him, but he didn't stop, rounding the dimly perceived bends in the hallway and then breaking into a much larger room. The high-pitched shrieks of several girls in various states of undress assaulted his ears as he sprinted down an aisle between two rows of lockers, holding up his clutch of books to shield his face from any witnesses who might try to identify him.

Jamie urged as much speed from his legs as he was able and kept his gaze focused straight ahead, trying not to see anything other than the large yellow sign indicating the way to the gym. He cleared the locker room in a matter of seconds and sprinted through the keyway passage beyond. A commotion had erupted behind him, probably from Seth and the others following Jamie into the girl's locker room, but he didn't stop or even slow to find out more. The gymnasium was empty and so was the hallway outside. He kept running past several classrooms and around two corners before he finally slowed to a fast walk, breathing hard as he looked over his shoulder.

He didn't hear any sounds of continued pursuit. Hopefully, the girl's gym teacher had intervened and detained Seth after Jamie's own entrance had placed everyone on alert. Even if she hadn't, and Seth forced his way through, it should still have slowed him down a little. With his way clear for the moment, Jamie just had to figure out what to do next.

Abandoning school entirely and heading straight home was definitely a seductive notion. Less appealing would be to make his way to the school offices and notify someone about what had just happened. Maybe Mister Clark would be able to help. Unfortunately, Jamie knew that even if the guidance counselor was willing, the rest of the school administration would just sweep the incident under the rug. And once Seth found out Jamie had tried to turn him in, he'd only make things even worse for him.

No, his best course of action was simply to continue his routine as normal, or at least as normal as possible under the circumstances. At a fast clip, Jamie headed for the nurse's office. One of the loose wires from the fence had put a long gash down the entire length of his forearm and the blood had run in a trickle all the way to his fingertips. It wasn't anything life-threatening, but it would likely earn him a trip to the nurse's office anyway if he went straight to class. Besides, the nurse was the closer of the two destinations, and if Seth's crew hadn't given up or been stopped, they would likely still be looking for him. No sense to stay out in the open any longer than necessary.

The nurse didn't believe Jamie when he told her that he'd merely scraped his arm on a loose section of chain-link fence while walking past, but then she didn't appear to be the type of person who would have believed him even if he'd told the truth. She also seemed reluctant to offer any medical aid whatsoever.

As Jamie sat there on the edge of an examination table, listening to her complain, he watched through the office window in silence as Seth, the freckled boy, and one of his other goons passed by in the hall outside. Their jeering voices carried through the halls right up until a teacher intervened and sent them on their way. In the end, the nurse grudgingly disinfected and bandaged Jamie's scraped arm, acting the whole time as if she were breaking all kinds of rules just by doing that. Jamie also managed to get a tardy slip from her, but only after insisting on it.

More whispered remarks followed Jamie throughout the rest of the day. Between classes, he moved cautiously through the halls, trying to keep one eye pointed in every direction at once. The afternoon seemed to stretch on forever. Jamie could barely concentrate on anything being said in any of his classes. In the very likely event that Seth continued to hold a grudge, Jamie would now have to be constantly vigilant every moment he was at school, and probably a considerable amount of time outside of it as well.

When the last bell of the day finally rang, Jamie headed for his locker but stopped at the end of the hallway and surveyed the crowds of students before going any farther. This would be one of the few places and times anyone would know where to find him. It was only after he'd been standing there for nearly three full minutes that he realized Seth and all his cronies would be at practice right now, the one school activity they couldn't afford to miss, even with their elite status. Still, Jamie gathered his things and left through a different exit than the one he typically used. He even decided to take a different route home. Even though it would add several blocks to his walk, it didn't seem like such a bad idea to be a little cautious at the moment.

CHAPTER 31

On his way home, Jamie cut across a small park, one he'd often seen from the outside while passing by but had never actually visited before. The north edge and part of the east were lined with a tall hedge row while the south and west sides had a fine assortment of mature shade trees whose leaves were starting to turn a vibrant red. Together, they made the trimmed lawns and crisscrossing paths through the center of the park feel more private, even though the whole place was so small one was never completely out of sight from the streets beyond. When Jamie's cellphone rang, he came to an abrupt halt and sighed. He didn't even need to see the name of the caller to know who it was.

"Hi, April," he said, answering the phone and pinching his eyes shut.

"Where are you?" April demanded. "I've been waiting here forever!"

"Um." With phone pressed to his ear, Jamie looked up at the dark clouds that were starting to move across the otherwise pale blue sky. "Short version: I forgot."

"You…?" April held the phone away and muttered a curse. Bringing it back with a sigh, and trying very hard to keep her composure, she said, "Where are you now?"

"Serrano Park?"

"What? Did you say Serrano Park? That's not even on your way home."

"It's kind of a long story."

April groaned. "Don't go anywhere. I'll meet you there in, like, five minutes."

Jamie wanted to ask her why they didn't just meet at his house, but instead, he said, "Okay. I'll be here."

"You better be," she said and then hung up.

Jamie dropped the phone from his ear. He almost screamed into the sky at the top of his lungs but restrained himself out of courtesy to the mothers whose children were amusing themselves on the nearby playground equipment. Instead, he trudged over to the edge of the park and dropped onto one of the park benches near the hedgerow. There were certainly worse people than April who could have been stalking him, but if this was any indication of how things were going to be between them going forward, Jamie would have preferred the solitude his life had been before all this began.

With head hanging low, Jamie absently reached down and ran his fingers through the chalky, beige gravel at his feet. Not surprisingly, none of the stones called out to him the way that resonator crystal on Terrarhea had. Maybe Jamie didn't have the gift like Reaver did. Or maybe he was just going crazy.

"Stop wasting your time," a man's voice said from over Jamie's shoulder. It sounded distant and remote, like the person speaking had other things on his mind. "The magic has moved on from this earth."

Jamie turned and very nearly fell off the park bench when he saw who had spoken. That same old man from the first morning he had disappeared to Terrarhea was standing not more than two paces away. Looking every bit as ragged and grimy as the first time Jamie had seen him, his eyes still had the glazed quality of someone who wasn't quite aware of his surroundings.

This time, however, his appearance struck Jamie differently. He couldn't quite put his finger on it exactly, but the man's features didn't quite seem entirely Caucasian and his darkened skin, which Jamie had first assumed to be the result of a life lived outdoors, could just as easily have been its innate color. Even that beat-up coat he wore, with the leather accents and tarnished buttons, almost looked like the sort of thing someone from Terrarhea might have worn.

After reigning in his initial shock, Jamie almost leapt off the bench and grabbed the man by the front of his coat, shaking him violently and demanding answers. However, without taking his eyes from the man even to blink, Jamie slowly rose to his feet and said, "It's you."

The old man looked at Jamie, though his expression didn't convey any sense of recognition. He might not have even realized that Jamie was a person and not some tree or shrub.

"Why did you say that?" Jamie said. He made his way around the park bench with overly deliberate caution, as if any sudden movements on his part might cause the old man to vanish like the illusion Jamie feared he might be. "What do you know about magic?"

"Magic?" The old man said, almost frantically, looking around him as if expecting to see a bird swooping past his head.

"You just said it: that the magic is gone! What did you mean?"

The old man snapped his head around to look at Jamie, his eyes wide. "All the magic *is* gone. You must be able to see that! No one dances or sings anymore. It's all just digital streaming downloads!"

Jamie paused no more than two steps away from the old man. Maybe he was just a crazy homeless person after all.

There was one thing, however, that Jamie knew he had to have an answer for, even if he might have been confused about the rest. "Hey!" Jamie said, snapping his fingers to draw the man's attention which had once again wandered. It worked only to a degree. "Hey, I've got a question for you. Do you remember that black box of yours that I found? What did you do with it?"

The old man's brow grew even more wrinkled than it already was.

"Please," Jamie said. "I just need to see it again. It's important."

"The key..." the old man said knowingly. "The key is knowing what's important."

Jamie growled. "Focus. I gave it to you: a little black box about this big. Do you know what it is?"

"A black box? It didn't come from a plane crash!" The old man threw back his head and laughed. "*That* is key!"

This time, Jamie really did grab the old man by the front of his coat. Nearly snarling as he bore down on him, Jamie said, "You have to remember something!"

Even though the old man was taller and broader than Jamie, he whimpered and quailed like a child facing a fuming adult.

"Do you still have it!" Jamie said as he began rummaging through the old man's gapping coat pockets. He felt a screwdriver and a small pad of paper and several candy bar wrappers, but nothing that could possibly have been the black box. The old man started moaning miserably and waving his arms in a pitiable attempt to fend Jamie off. At that, Jamie released him and stepped back. He didn't hurt people to get what he wanted.

"No," Jamie whispered to himself, "I'm not Reaver."

Hunched over, the old man backed away, shaking his head vehemently from side-to-side. "But you are a lot alike. I never shoulda' trusted him. You shouldn't either."

Just as Jamie was about to write this old man off as a lost cause, he had to go and say something like that. Maybe his disturbed mind was just remembering someone in his life that had once betrayed him, but the coincidence of him mentioning it now was just too much.

"Who shouldn't I trust? Reaver? Do you know him? Why shouldn't I trust him?"

"You can't trust anyone these days," the old man said, nearly laughing once again, though nervously this time. "There's always someone out there trying to steal something from you. They'll even steal your identity now, that's what they say."

"Is that what Reaver's doing?" Jamie said. Reaver certainly had been running roughshod over Jamie's life as if he felt he owned it. But as Jamie considered that, an even deeper sense of dread settled over him. Was it possible this old man had been the victim of the same thing Jamie was now going through and this demented state of existence was the fate awaiting him at the end? "Is that what happened to you?"

"There was never anything to steal," the old man said in a despondent whisper.

"Hey, Jamie!" April called out from across the park. "Are you *trying* to piss me off?"

Jamie turned to see her stalking across the grassy yard, headed in his direction with her lips pressed into a thin line.

"The key box will no longer change anything," the old man said. "This cycle which has been set in motion can not be stopped. And you yet have your part to play."

His words sounded so lucid that Jamie spun around, half-expecting to see that the two of them had been joined by someone new. Instead, he merely caught sight of the old man's back as he disappeared through what must have been a hidden gap in the tangled hedge. Jamie didn't know what to make of that last statement, but he wasn't about to let the old man leave without explaining it. He lunged at the hedge, trying to push through as the old man had done, but the stiff branches were so intertwined they didn't make it easy. Regardless, he forced his way through, the prickly branches jabbing and scratching his skin.

Behind him, April broke into a run. "Jamie! Where are you going!"

Jamie ignored her, stumbling out onto the sidewalk on the other side of the hedge. He looked both ways for some trace of the old man and saw what might have been his coattails disappearing around the corner of the hedge at the end of the block. He sprinted after him, but when he reached the corner, there was no longer any sign of the old man. He might have doubled back into the park or crossed the street and fled into one of the businesses there.

Jamie dashed down the sidewalk, splitting his attention between every possible hiding place he passed. He made it to the other end of the park without seeing anything. Moaning through clenched teeth, he turned in a circle. The old man couldn't have gone any further than this. He had to have slipped away before getting this far.

At a slower clip, Jamie jogged back the way he'd just come, this time being especially careful with his observations. Reaching the other corner of the park, it seemed all too clear he'd completely lost his quarry.

Momentarily, April came jogging down the sidewalk, her heels clicking loudly on the concrete. "Jamie, wait up!" When April finally caught up to him, Jamie was still trying to decide if he should go looking through the alleys on the other side of the street or just give up. "What's going on?" she said, breathing hard. "Is something wrong?"

"Did you see where he went?" Jamie said, still scanning the street.

"Who?"

"The old man I was talking to. He ran through the bushes and disappeared. Didn't you see him?"

April slunk back, eyeing Jamie as if he might have just come down with leprosy. "I might have seen you talking to somebody, but I didn't get a good look at who it was or where they went. Who was he?"

Jamie ran his fingers through his hair as he once again swept his gaze across their surroundings. "I...don't know."

"Oh my god, what happened to your arm?" April said, taking hold of his bandaged forearm. He must have rubbed it against a branch while going through the bushes because it had started bleeding again, the blood already soaking through the bandage.

Jamie pulled it free and dismissed April's concern with a wave of his hand. "It was just Seth."

"What! Did he come at you with a knife?"

"What? No," Jamie said, finally pulling his attention away from the street. Even with April's help, it would take forever just to search everywhere the old man could have gotten to. Unless they were very lucky, he'd be long gone by the time they finished. "I scraped it on a fence when I was running away from him."

"God damn it. What is with him?" April said. Jamie hoped she didn't want an answer to that because he didn't have one. "I hope we're done running for now, though. These shoes aren't really made for it."

Jamie took in the pink-fringed sandals on her feet with a glance. "Weren't you wearing tennis shoes this morning?"

"I usually take them home on the weekend and then wear them back to school on Monday because I have gym second period." Now that Jamie thought about it, he actually didn't care. "I'm just glad I wasn't in the afternoon class. I heard some pervert went running through the girl's locker room when everyone was changing."

"Really?" Jamie said, trying to feign ignorance. "Do they know who it was?"

"Nah, no one got a good look at him, everyone was too busy trying to cover themselves up. As if any of those freshmen have anything anyone would want to look at."

"He must have been a total creep," Jamie said, stealing one final glance at the street and then the park as the two of them got underway. The old man might have disappeared, and this meeting might have left Jamie with more questions than answers, but if nothing else, it did prove to Jamie that he hadn't simply imagined him. He'd actually laid his hands of him. April had seen him too, sort of. But did his ramblings actually mean anything, or where they just a string of complete nonsense fitted together from the things Jamie himself had said? Some of it had almost seemed to make sense but was that just Jamie creating meaning where there was none to find?

The unvoiced brooding that April had been cultivating all day continued for another block before she finally spoke without warning, "Lorrie's going out with Seth now."

"Um," Jamie said, pulling himself from his own musings. "That was a quick rebound."

"Not as quick as you might think. They were actually running around behind my back for the last month or so."

"How do you know that?" Jamie said, knowing all too well it probably came across sounding like he was accusing her of being paranoid.

"Lorrie tracked me down this morning 'cause she wanted to rub my face in it. Afterward, everything started to make a lot more sense. Like all those times Seth'd bail on the plans we'd made without any explanation. Or those last-minute team practices that would come up out of the blue. I don't know why I'm still so pissed at him. I mean, I should be happy he's gone but part of me is still jealous that he chose Lorrie over me."

"You gotta admit, they are perfect for each other. Both of them are complete jerks." Unlike April, who was only partially a jerk.

"I think half the school knew about it before I did. No wonder none of them want anything to do with me anymore. They were all laughing at me behind my back this whole time. I feel like such an idiot."

"Well, you were dating Seth. That's not exactly something a smart person would do."

The look that April shot Jamie could have curdled milk. He only replied with a shrug and a lopsided smile. After a moment of trying to maintain her rancor, April smirked as well and shook her head. "Maybe you do have a point."

"I mean, seriously, Seth? Really?"

"Okay, I get it. It was a bad idea from the beginning. Why didn't you warn me before I went ahead and made a fool of myself for so long?"

"I'm pretty sure you *hated* me up until just recently."

"That's no excuse."

"Don't worry, the feeling was mutual," Jamie said. "In fact, I still hate you for the most part."

April chuckled and took hold of Jamie's arm, giving him a shove as she leaned into him. "You know, you're different than you were at the party."

Just as Jamie was starting to loosen up, he suddenly tensed. "Different how?"

"More suave. Not such a jerk."

Knowing Reaver, it was probably just an act he put on to gather information. "Almost like I was a completely different person?" Jamie ventured.

"No, you weren't *that* different," April said with a laugh. "You were still you, just better at it."

Jamie missed a step. So Reaver was a better version of him? Jamie did have to admit he did seem to have a better handle on Jamie's life than Jamie himself did.

"You okay?" April said as Jamie staggered to catch up again.

"Fine," he whispered.

"You also didn't smile as much," April said, still leaning on his arm, "and you weren't nearly as funny."

Too bad that wouldn't help him win any fights, or deal with his teachers, or better understand his homework, or get Heather out of her financial slump. It also didn't help him figure out how to contend with any of the girls in his life, and it certainly wasn't helping him get to the bottom of his mysterious connection to the world of Terrarhea. Jamie sighed and shook his head. With the way things had been going recently, it seemed somehow appropriate that one of the few traits he didn't share with Reaver was also completely useless when it came to solving any of his problems.

CHAPTER 32

Neither Jamie nor April spoke much the rest of the way back to Heather's house. As was to be expected that time of day, it sat empty when they entered through the side door.

"This place is a real dump," April said, taking in their surroundings as she walked through what had been the kitchen, always careful to stay as far away from the bare stud walls and random protruding pipes as possible. "Are you sure you and your sister aren't just squatting?"

"I've never actually seen the paperwork, so I suppose it is possible." Jamie strolled though the wreckage of the room with an indifference cultivated from long familiarity with the state of the place.

Frowning dubiously as she looked up into the rafters, April didn't seem to realize Jamie was only joking. "Why do you even live with your sister? Where are your parents?"

"They died a couple of months ago in a car accident." The loss of his parents still hurt no less, but he had explained it this same way so many times that he could now recite the words without having to think about the meaning behind them anymore. "Heather's the only family I have left."

"Oh, sorry. I didn't know. You don't have any other family at all? No grandparents or anything."

"I think I might have some distant aunts and uncles but me and Heather have never even met them."

In what had been the dining room, but was now just an extension of the larger kitchen and living room space, stood a wooden table surrounded by four matching chairs. Every surface, from the oval top to the turned legs, had been chipped, dinged, or gouged. It was another of Heather's projects, one which she'd discovered at some secondhand store and intended to refinish and use in the completed remodel. For the moment, she and Jamie had instead set it up there. Not only did it provide them with a place to stack their tools while working, but it also made for a whimsical exhibit of domestic life in the middle of all that destruction. Sitting on top, a handwritten note from Heather simply said, "Passed electrical inspection!"

Jamie had completely forgotten about that. The nights hadn't yet gotten cold enough to make the lack of insulation in the walls a major issue, but now that they could move ahead with that next step, it should make the house a little more snug.

"There's less dust in back," Jamie said, leading April through the plastic sheeting.

"Does your TV have internet?" April stepped into the makeshift living room and picked up the remote off the couch. "I saw the funniest video online last night."

She turned on the TV and sat down on the couch, navigating to a video of an amateur parkour enthusiast running through a series of raised concrete planting beds in the plaza outside of some large business tower. Jamie dropped his backpack to the floor and took a seat on the arm of the couch. The way the young man on the screen seemed almost to glide over the obstacles in his path looked hypnotic in their execution. It made Jamie think of the way he was able to run when he was in Reaver's body, floating mere inches above the ground between each of those gigantic steps he took.

The performance on screen continued right up until the athlete vaulted himself over one of the planting beds and then missed his landing on the next, sending him into a face-first slide across the edge of the rough concrete. April nearly doubled over in laughter and Jamie cringed. The video ended with an image of the bloody scrapes running diagonally across the young man's face and a deep cut that had sliced right through his lip.

"See, I was wrong," April said, still laughing, "Your face *could* have ended up looking like that from practicing parkour. Oh wait, this is another good one." Again, taking up the remote, she selected one of the recommended videos that had popped up onscreen. Together the two of them spent the rest of the afternoon alternatively watching parkour videos on the TV and occasionally working on their homework.

It could have been worse. After all, April was easily one of the most attractive girls in the whole school and here she was, hanging out with Jamie at his house, sitting right next to him on his own couch. But as soon as he started thinking like that, his thoughts would turn to Alaida and what had become of her. Images of her lying dead in a ditch somewhere would instantly fill his mind and he could no longer laugh at the latest video of someone failing in spectacular brilliance.

The dark clouds Jamie had earlier seen grew thick overhead until the landscape outside was cast into a premature twilight. The rain started shortly thereafter, falling in sporadic showers that never seemed to last more than a few minutes at a time.

"Do you have anything to eat?" April asked at one point.

"Um." Jamie considered the question thoroughly. "Probably not. My sister's not really a fan of grocery shopping. She gives me enough money to buy stuff for my lunches and at night we usually just get takeout. I think we might have had a bag of potato chips around here a couple nights ago." Jamie dug into one of the boxes containing random foods stuffs they'd liberated from the kitchen and extracted a half-empty bag of chips, neatly folded shut at the end.

"I don't think I'm that desperate," April said.

About an hour later, she suggested they give the chips a try after all, but before she could break them open, the sound of a door slamming shut echoed through the empty front of the house.

"Jamie, I've got some really bad news," Heather called out from somewhere in the vicinity of the dining room. "They were all out of cavatappi, so I had to get radiatore instead." There was a rustling of shopping bags and then her footsteps came into the back hallway. Arriving at the door to the makeshift living room, Heather stopped short the moment she laid eyes on April. "You again."

"Yeah. Me," April said, staring back up at Heather, "Again."

"I hope you two aren't getting into any trouble," Heather said. Leave it to her to go leaping to conclusions like that.

"Just doing our homework." Jamie held up his notebook for emphasis.

Heather looked at the TV which was currently showing a video of a parkour athlete falling off a wharf into a raging surf. "Yeah, I can see that."

"We can do both," April said.

Even sinking lower into the sofa cushions didn't make Jamie feel any more comfortable being trapped between these two. He cleared his throat, catching April's attention, but it took her a moment to realize his intent. When she did, she sat back with a sigh and threw out her arms. "The reason I came over today was to apologize for the way I acted the last time we met, so…. I'm sorry."

Heather stood in silence for several moments, her face slack. Finally, she shrugged. "Well, in that case, apology accepted. We were all a little on edge that morning."

Jamie's eyes shifted from one to the other, looking for some sign the apologies had really been accepted. The way they kept glaring at each other seemed to suggest they hadn't. Jamie hopped to his feet and grabbed the remote, turning off the TV. "Sounds like you could use a hand out there."

April and Heather both followed Jamie into the dining room. The rain had started falling constantly now, sounding loudly off the exposed roof above. On the dining room table sat two plastic grocery bags containing a box of pasta, several onions and bell peppers, fresh mushrooms, a package of Italian sausage, a jar of pasta sauce, and some shredded mozzarella cheese.

"What's with the pasta?" April asked. "I thought you said you didn't go grocery shopping?"

"It's sort of a thing we started doing a little while ago," Jamie said. "Once a week, we sit down and have a meal together. Pasta's about the only thing we're any good at making though."

"We had been sticking with plain spaghetti, but Jamie here wanted to expand our horizons, so we've started trying out some new things. Nothing too fancy yet but tonight it was going to be baked cavatappi with sautéed vegetables and Italian sausage."

"We have to keep things simple because my sister's the only person I know who can burn water."

"Hey, that only happened once!"

April smirked. "Well, it sounds like you guys have plans so I should probably be getting home."

"It's raining pretty hard out there," Heather said. "Do you want a ride?"

"Nah, if you're doing something special, I wouldn't want to get in the way."

"The forecast said it probably won't last too long," Heather said. "Why don't you just stay and have supper with us and then we can drive you home afterwards?"

Over April's shoulder, Jamie waved his hands and shook his head in the negative as he mouthed, "No." He must have misread the situation: Heather must not have disliked April as much as he thought. Or maybe her desire to torment Jamie simply outweighed her dislike of the other girl.

Heather saw him but she smiled warmly to April. "We'd love to have the company."

"Well..." As April looked back at Jamie, he quickly dropped his hands and forced a smile onto his face. "If it's really not any trouble."

"No. None at all," Jamie said through clenched teeth.

"Let me call my mom and let her know." April pulled out her cell phone and stepped into the demolished living room for some privacy.

"What are you doing?" Jamie hissed under his breath as soon as she was out of earshot.

"Do you really want to send her out in that rain?" Heather almost would have sounded sincere if it weren't for that devious smile she wore.

Jamie's eyes narrowed. "I know what you're up to."

"Oh, and what's that?" Heather said with overblown innocence.

Jamie merely glared at her and shook his head, which earned him a mischievous laugh from Heather as she headed into what remained of the kitchen.

"Mom!" April said into her phone, her voice suddenly carrying quite clearly from the other room. "Mom, calm down!" She glanced over her shoulder at Jamie and Heather who both quickly turned away and tried to look as if they hadn't been listening in -- not that it would have been possible for them not to.

The ancient stove which had come with the house had the distinction of being the only thing left from the original kitchen, now standing alone and isolated amidst the bare stud walls and exposed floorboards. Since they wouldn't actually need to get rid of it until they started putting things back together, they had left it where it was so they could still use it for their single, weekly, home cooked meal. Jamie gathered some pots, cutting boards, and knives from the back room while Heather washed the vegetables in the laundry sink. Turning them over to Jamie, she said, "This was your idea, so you get to do the hard part. I'll brown the sausage and get the water boiling."

Even busying themselves with preparations for the meal couldn't have prevented Jamie and Heather from catching snips of April's conversation in the other room. "Did you take your medication?" she said in a softer voice than her earlier cries. "Okay, do you need me to come home? Are you sure? Okay, I'll see you later. Yeah, you too. Bye."

"Everything okay?" Heather said once April joined them.

"Oh, yeah, just parents, you know?"

Jamie glanced at Heather, finding her looking back at him. "Yeah, parents..." he said.

"Here, give me one of those," April said after watching Jamie fumble with one of the bell peppers for a moment or two. She quickly deseeded it with a deftness Jamie couldn't come close to matching. But when it came to chopping it up, her technique left a chaotic pile of dissimilarly sized pieces while Jamie's were all neat and uniform. She left the onion for Jamie while she took care of the last pepper.

"Do you want something to drink?" Heather said as she popped the cork out of a bottle of red wine.

"Sure," April said, "I love wine."

"I meant we have sodas in the fridge," Heather said in a deliberate, overly stilted affectation, setting the bottle down well out of April's reach. "After all, you are still minors and I am a responsible adult."

"Don't let her fool you," Jamie whispered. "It's all an act."

April snickered and shook her head but retrieved a soda for herself and one for Jamie as well without argument.

Between the three of them, they were able to sauté the vegetables without burning anything too badly. None of them were quite sure how best to gauge the doneness of the pasta for this particular recipe so they simply took a guess and hoped for the best. Once everything was put in the oven, they stood around the kitchen while it baked, Heather asking a plethora of questions about their lives, which started innocently enough, but with the more wine she had to drink, seemed to become increasingly designed simply to embarrass Jamie. Surprisingly, April took it all in stride, the two girls quickly joking back and forth with none of the earlier malice Jamie feared would tarnish their every meeting. When the oven timer sounded, all three of them agreed that the bubbly, golden-brown texture of the cheese on top looked absolutely perfect.

"This is really good," April said after they'd taken seats at the table and started eating.

"You sound surprised," Heather said. "After all, you helped, so if it didn't turn out, you'd have no one to blame but yourself."

"Or Jamie," April said.

"True," Heather agreed. "Our natural talent can only overcome so much incompetence."

And now they were teaming up on him. Jamie liked it better when they were at each other's throats. "So, Heather, what's this I hear about you and Mister Clark going around behind my back?"

Heather nearly choked on a mouthful of pasta. It took several gulps of wine and a fit of coughing before she was able to say, "What are you talking about?"

"He talked to me today about the fight. He said that you'd reached out to him."

"Oh, yeah, well. Did you really expect me not to do *anything*? I had to see if someone at your school might be able to help. Or at the very least, keep an eye out for you."

"Why Mister Clark?" April said, shoveling a loaded forkful of pasta into her mouth.

"What's with the third degree?" Heather took a long drink of wine. "Jamie mentioned once that he didn't seem like such a bad guy so I figured he might be worth a try." Turning to Jamie, she said, "So, what did he say?"

"Not much really," Jamie said, painfully aware of April's eyes on him. "He just asked me about the fight and those classes."

"Why doesn't the school care about this at all? I'm gonna call him back tomorrow."

"He's only the school guidance counselor," Jamie said. "There's not really anything he *can* do. But don't worry, I'm handling it."

"How?"

Jamie speared several pieces of pasta and vegetables with his fork. "One day at a time."

Heather just shook her head and took a very long drink from her glass. For several minutes afterward, the only sounds to be heard were the scrapping of forks on plates and the rain falling on the roof. April was the first to break the silence, asking of Heather, "So are you in college?"

Heather laughed. "No, I've been out of college for a couple of years now. I'm an architectural designer at a little firm downtown."

"Is that something like an interior designer?"

"It's an architect who doesn't have their license yet," Jamie said.

"Oh. Why don't you have a license?"

Heather swirled the remaining wine around the bottom of her glass and then drained it in a single gulp. "Short answer? It costs a lot of money."

"But you must be doing okay to be able to afford a house though, right?"

Heather paused as she poured herself another glass of wine.

"April, do you have any brothers or sisters?" Jamie said. "You've never mentioned anything about your family."

April pushed a piece of bell pepper around her plate with the end of her fork. "I have a step-brother and a step-sister. They're both in college, studying engineering."

"What about your parents?" Heather said with genuine interest.

"Um, my step-dad travels all over the country doing maintenance on some special kind of factory equipment. I don't really understand it, but he's almost never around. My mom, she..." April paused, glanced at Jamie, "she can't work, so she stays at home."

"Oh," Heather said, sharing a look with Jamie over the rim of her glass, both of them no doubt wondering how that fiery telephone conversation fit into this rather nebulous description.

April must have realized it as well because she hastily added, "I mean, she's a great mom. Sometimes it just gets a bit...tough, I guess, without anyone else around most of the time. The two of us get by pretty well though."

"And all I get is *this*," Jamie said, motioning to Heather.

She tossed a crumpled napkin at him across the table.

By the time they finished eating, the rain had completely ended and the clouds had even broken up enough to let a little of the setting sun through. April thanked them both for the meal and insisted Heather did not have to drive her home. Jamie saw her out the front door and she'd already made it to the bottom of the front steps by the time he followed after.

"Heather seems to think that I should walk you home," he said, hooking his thumb back toward the house.

They both caught a glimpse of Heather's silhouette moving away from the living room window.

"You know, I kind of like your sister but I could do without all the matchmaking."

With hands in his pockets, Jamie walked side-by-side with April across the wet front lawn. "You and me both."

Near the sidewalk, April stopped and turned to face him. "Jamie, can I tell you something? I wasn't trying to keep secrets earlier when you asked about my mom. It's just that, well, she's...got issues, I mean, like, mental issues, you know? Sometimes it can get pretty bad. No one at school knows about it though and I'd prefer to keep it that way."

"Not even Lorrie?" From what April had told Jamie, the two girls had been friends for years. "How did you keep something like that from your best friend?"

"It wasn't always easy, but I knew that Lorrie would have made a big deal out of it if she'd known. I mean, my mom's on medication and most of the time she's perfectly normal, but sometimes...she's not. I shouldn't care, but if this got around school..."

"You don't even have to ask. We all have a secret or two we don't want anyone to know about. I'd never do anything like that to you or anyone else."

"I know you wouldn't. I guess I've been rethinking my opinions of lots of people recently." April looked down at the grass. "So what's yours? Your secret, that is?"

Her expression was completely flat. Jamie couldn't tell if she was joking or if she actually wanted an equally intimate secret in payment for the one she'd given him. He threw out his hands. "I actually moonlight as a notorious criminal on an alien planet."

April smiled and hugged Jamie warmly. "I had fun tonight," she said, backing away across the yard, "even though you are a complete dork. I'll see you at school tomorrow, okay?"

"Where else would I be?" Jamie said with a thin smile and a wave.

He watched until she disappeared from view. Heather was clearing the table when Jamie drifted back into the house. Upon seeing him, she sighed with overblown theatricality. "You just let her leave on her own? You really are hopeless, little brother."

"You do realize that she's just using me until she gets over her break-up with Seth, right? It wouldn't surprise me if they're back together in a week."

"That's why you have to be more assertive. You have to let her know what you want."

"But I don't even like her that much."

Heather set down the stack of dirty plates she'd just picked up. "Is this about that Alaida girl again, because in all honesty, I don't think you should be pinning all your hopes on a girl like that. I mean, she's with someone else, and you said yourself that you've only talked to her twice. Plus, she's how much older than you? April's a nice -- well, a nice enough girl who's the same age as you. The two of you seem to get along pretty well and she's right here, not running out of town at the drop of a hat with some jerk."

"Alaida's not even two years older than me and I know for a fact that you've dated guys who were at least that much older than you. And if you're saying that I should stay away because she's with someone else, April was with Seth when she started hanging with me."

"You don't even know if you'll ever see her again."

"I will," Jamie said, almost more to himself than to Heather. He had to. He couldn't let himself think for even a moment that he wouldn't, regardless of what that meant for him.

"I'm not trying to be mean," Heather said. "I just don't want to see you make a mistake that you might end up regretting later. Do you really want to let the first real girlfriend you've ever had slip through your fingers just because of some pipedream?"

"April's still not my girlfriend. Even she'll tell you that." Unfortunately, he couldn't deny that Alaida's affections might indeed have been out of reach. Jamie crossed the room and reached for the dirty dishes. "I'll take care of those."

Heather snatched them away before he could lay a hand on them. "No, I've got it. Why don't you finish your homework? And maybe no more parkour videos until you're done?"

When Mister Fisher returned to class the next day, he did not fail to notice Jamie's bruised face or miss the opportunity to poke fun at it. This time, however, no one else in class laughed at any of his jokes, as if they feared Jamie might lash out with physical violence. In the end, Mister Fisher eventually retreated to the topic of the day like a comedian whose performance had just fallen flat.

Each morning, Jamie left for school early, though not so he could get to class on time, but rather so that he could wander the streets and alleyways of the neighborhood in a vain hope of finding that crazy old man once again. He never saw so much of a trace of him, however.

At school, Jamie's locker was again broken into between classes. This time, if he hadn't been lucky enough to catch the culprit in the act, his things would have been thrown in the trash and he would have lost them completely. After that, he decided it was time to call on a favor from Mister Clark who was able to convince the school administration to replace Jamie's lock. That, however, only resolved one of the issues plaguing him.

Avoiding Seth and his acolytes became a new routine for Jamie. Most of them kept to habitual schedules so it wasn't hard to choose routes and places that they seldom frequented. The caution did mean that Jamie had to hurry from one class to the next, but even when rushed, he never let his guard down. For the most part, it worked, even if it did keep him on edge almost constantly. Only once or twice did he have a close call, but even then he was able to evade his potential aggressors before they spotted him in kind.

April proved to be a more persistent nuisance. The more that Jamie tried to distance himself from her, the more determined she seemed on spending as much of her free time with him as possible. Daily, she would find Jamie between classes, sit with him at lunch, and usually wanted to walk home with him too, outwardly so they could work on their homework together, but mostly just so she could talk about whatever was on her mind that day. Even though it wasn't all bad, Jamie knew that if it weren't for Reaver's interference in his life, she wouldn't have been interested in him at all. At the best of times, it felt like he was leading her along, lying to her about who he really was, just like all her supposed friends had been doing to her for so long.

CHAPTER 33

"Have you asked April out to the big Halloween party yet?" Derek said as he and Jamie were leaving school one afternoon. With Halloween quickly approaching, preparations for the various parties being thrown seemed to have monopolized everyone's interest.

"Nope," Jamie said. "She's all yours."

"No, I didn't mean I wanted to ask her," Derek said, laughing. Then his expression turned thoughtful. "You think I'd have a chance?"

This time Jamie laughed before saying simply, "No." If it would have been that simple to get rid of her, he would have done it already. Unfortunately, it had been over a week since Jamie had pulled his "Lancelot" and April still hadn't gone back to Seth. In fact, she didn't even seem to miss him or Lorrie all that much anymore.

"You really shouldn't get a guy's hopes up like that," Derek said. "I was just starting to imagine what kind of slutty Halloween costume she'll be wearing."

"Hey, speaking of costumes," Alex said as he came upon the other two boys, "have you got yours picked out yet?"

"Nah, I'm not really a costume kind of guy." Jamie had already had more than enough of being someone else to last him a lifetime. Besides, Seth and his friends were probably going to be at this big party as well.

"No, come on!" Derek said. "You've gotta go. Every year they do a theme and this time it's the Roaring Twenties! Me and Alex are going as gangsters! It's gonna be awesome."

Jamie started to voice his disinterest when Alex broke in. "You don't have to dress up as someone from the 1920's if you don't want to. Lots of people don't. The main reason they do a theme is to try and keep all the girls from dressing like sluts."

"Of course, most of them will just dress as slutty flappers this year," Derek said. "Not that I'm complaining."

"We've already hit up a bunch of vintage clothing stores and we've found some really cool stuff," Alex added. "In fact, we bought just about anything we thought might work so we've actually got way more than we need. If you wanted, you could put together something with the extras."

"Just don't touch my violin case," Derek said. "That little beauty is my pièce de résistance."

"Yeah, whatever," Alex said, bristling. Clearly, he didn't like the idea of being outdone by his friend. "You want to come with us tonight? Most of the shops have already been pretty well picked over but there are a few more that we were gonna check out."

"You're finally ready to get yourself a costume?" April said as she unexpectedly came up behind Jamie, causing him to jump. Wearing a white tee-shirt and a black pleated skirt, of course the ensemble would not have been complete without that pink bomber jacket she had on as well. "I'll help you pick something out."

"Like anyone should ever trust your sense of fashion," Alex said, "especially for a Halloween costume. What do you even know about the roaring twenties anyway?"

"More than you two, I'll bet," she said, taking in both of them with the same sort of expression one might make when finding a loaf of bread covered in mold. Seeing that Derek, who had remained strangely silent this whole time, was staring at her oddly, she placed her hands on her hips and fixed him with a sharp gaze. "What are you looking at?"

Pushing his glasses up, he turned away hastily. "N-nothing."

"Come on, Jamie, why don't you ditch these two losers and come with me," April said. "I still need a few things to finish off my costume anyway. We can find something for you too."

"Hey, we asked him first!" Alex said.

"Where are you going, that cheesy party store downtown?"

Alex laughed loudly. "That sounds more like your type of place. We have some real vintage clothing stores we're going to."

"Like where?"

"If you don't know about them already, then you don't deserve to be told."

"Look guys," Jamie cut in over them, "I don't even want to go to any Halloween party, in costume or not."

"Come on! Don't be such a wet blanket!" Alex said. "Just come with us. I'm sure once you get into the spirit, you'll change your mind."

"No," April said, taking hold of Jamie's arm, "you're coming with me. Because even if you don't want a costume, I need a second set of eyes to help me with mine."

"Why don't we all go together?" Derek said, his voice nearly cracking from nervousness. Both Alex and April turned on him as if ready to tear him apart with their bare hands. He cringed but continued. "I mean, April might know about some places we haven't been to yet and she might not know about some of the places we've been. They carry mostly women's clothes anyway so I'm sure she could find all kinds of dresses there."

April crossed her arms and let out a huff. "I already have a dress."

"I hope it's not one of those cheap costumes from eBay," Derek said. "It'll probably fall apart before you even get to the party."

"I'm kinda hoping it does," Alex said.

Derek's eyes grew wide at the prospect. "Oh, good point!"

"I always knew you guys were nothing but perverts," April said, shaking her head.

"What? No, I'm not a pervert!" Derek said. "I'm just trying to be helpful."

"Whatever," April said. "But for your information, my mom's making my dress for me."

"Your mom?" Alex said. "What are you, Amish?"

"My mom makes awesome clothes!" April jabbed a finger in Alex's face. "She studied fashion design in college! She even made this jacket for me."

"Really?" Jamie said. If she hadn't said anything, he never would have suspected. Even now that she had, he still couldn't pick out anything in particular that would have betrayed its origins. Is that how she always found so many things to wear in pink?

"Pretty nice, huh?" She smugly flipped the collar. "Which is why I only need some accessories to finish off my costume. And maybe a new pair of boots."

"Boots?" Alex said. "I thought you were going as Jamie's moll, not a Goth-chick."

"Not for my costume! And I'm not going as anyone's moll!"

"You know what?" Jamie said. "I think Derek's got the right idea. Let's just all go."

"You're really gonna make me hang out with these two all night?" April said.

"No one's asking you to stick around," Alex said.

An hour later, things had not markedly improved. One of Derek and Alex's favorite comics shops was on the way to their first destination and since it was having an "under new management" sale, the two had insisted on stopping in to check things out. Jamie had initially thought it would be a short stop, so he'd been able to convince April to humor them, but even his patience was starting to grow thin.

"I thought we were going shopping for costumes, not all this geek stuff," April said, glowering over the rows of dusty shelves and tables laden with boxes of plastic-sealed comic books.

"It's just their process," Jamie said. "I'm sure we'll get there eventually, right guys?"

Derek was busy showing off his most recent find to Alex and didn't even seem to have noticed Jamie's question.

"Why does everyone keep staring at me?" April said out of the side of her mouth as she glanced over the tops of the shelves at several disheveled young men gathered near the checkout. Now she knew how Jamie felt at school.

"This kind of place doesn't get many customers like you."

"What do you mean, 'like me?'"

"Girls," Alex said without bothering to look up from the long box he was currently flipping through.

"Pretty girls, in any case," Derek said, just as engrossed in a shelf of trade paperbacks as his friend.

"Especially one dressed like a slut," Alex added. Maybe they were paying closer attention then Jamie had thought.

"Come on," Jamie said, ushering April out of the way before she exploded at them. "Just ignore them. Besides, it is kind of a compliment." After all, if she didn't want people to stare, maybe she shouldn't have worn such a short skirt. "Hey, look: 'Pride and Prejudice,'" he said, pulling a hardcover graphic novel off a nearby shelf. While April's true passion was medieval literature, Jamie also knew she had a soft spot for all the classic romances.

She took the book from him as if he had just fished it out of a toilet and flipped through the pages without any real interest. "Oh, just what I always wanted, a picture book of one of the greatest romance novels of all time. You don't suppose they have a coloring book version too, do you?"

Jamie rolled his eyes and suppressed a smirk. Not for the first time that evening, he wondered why he was even bothering to try and get April and the others to get along. In the end, it didn't even really matter if he succeeded or not. Even if this whole experiment went down in flames, he wouldn't be out anything.

"I'll see if I can get them to hurry up," Jamie said, leaving April alone in the aisle just as one of the young men who'd been looking at her from across the store slunk in from the opposite direction wearing a lopsided smile. She rolled her eyes and sighed, shaking her head, which quickly sent him scurrying away in fear.

Somehow, Jamie did manage to hurry them along. As Derek and Alex were headed for the check out, Derek stopped on his way past April and offered her a thin book with large pages. "Here, I found this one for you."

He held it in such a way that she could only see the blank back cover. She glared at it for a time and then at Derek. "What is it?" she said, clearly expecting a trick.

"I think you'll like it," he said.

With a sigh, she took it from him and turned it over so that she could see the cover of a Pride and Prejudice coloring book for adults. Alex started laughing. April shoved the book back into Derek's chest, turned, and walked away. "I'll be waiting outside."

"Hey, what's your problem?" Alex cried after her, smiling broadly, "That's one of the greatest romance novels of all time!"

As she headed for the exit, April raised her middle finger over her shoulder, which only made Alex laugh even harder. Derek, looking dumbfounded, merely stood there clutching the coloring book to his chest. Jamie put a hand on his shoulder, pointing him toward the checkout and taking the book out of his hands.

"Come on," he said. "Fun's over, okay? Can you guys try not to antagonize her too much tonight?"

"I can make no guarantees!" Alex said.

"I wasn't trying to be mean," Derek whispered. "I just thought it was kind of funny, you know, after what she said?"

Jamie patted him on the back. "Don't worry about it. You know how she can be."

Shortly, he joined her outside where she stood on the sidewalk, stepping back and forth from one foot and the other. "You okay?" Jamie said, his breath forming white clouds in the chilly air.

"Why do you hang out with those two?"

"Why do you hang out with me?" This earned him a questioning look from April. "I mean, it's not like either of us have a whole lot of choices when it comes to friends."

"You really think that's why I hang out with you, because I don't have any other choices?"

"Well, yeah. Why else would you?"

April turned and started walking down the sidewalk, leaving Jamie wondering if he had said something to upset her. After all, if Reaver hadn't instigated that fight in the alley, April would have still been with Seth and best friends with Lorrie. A moment later Derek and Alex stepped out of the comic shop with their purchases. "Come on," April said over her shoulder. "I thought we were looking for Halloween costumes. Let's get going already."

The first two stops on Alex and Derek's list proved to be places that April had already visited, but at least these stores did have a large selection of women's clothing so she had something to keep her occupied while the other two browsed. Jamie did his best to poke through the racks as well but didn't find anything of real interest.

April chose their third stop. At first, it looked like it was going to be as big a dud as the first two, but then Alex found a battered old violin case that was priced at only a couple of dollars, making it an even better deal than the one Derek had earlier found. Derek meanwhile unearthed what looked like a brand-new pair of wingtip shoes in his size. April even found a tweed flat cap which she briefly considered for herself, but after putting it on Jamie, decided that it looked perfect on him. He actually thought it looked kind of ridiculous but he kept that opinion to himself. With all the good luck they were having, Jamie's entourage was starting to forget that they actually hated each other. He wasn't about to do anything which might disrupt that unprecedented achievement.

Everyone was actually starting to enjoy themselves by the time they got to the next store. April's mood only improved even further when she discovered the perfect pair of boots that she'd been hoping to find. Derek and Alex also managed to locate a few more items to round out their costumes. In fact, the more stores they visited, the better luck they had. April even found the last pieces she needed to complete her own outfit. Of course, none of it was actually from the nineteen-twenties but most was at least old enough to look like it could have been.

By the time they'd exhausted most of the potential stores they had to visit, it was getting late enough that the remainder probably wouldn't still be open by the time they got to them so they decided to head home. Before they all went their separate ways, however, someone suggested they stop for some food. Even Jamie had to admit that didn't sound like such a bad idea. Apart from the few snacks they'd had while shopping, none of them had eaten in quite a while. As it turned out, Walter's Café was the nearest restaurant still open at that hour. Even though it wasn't too far from where any of them lived, none of them had ever actually eaten there before. And on a night when all of them were in high spirits, that made it the perfect choice.

The inside was full of character, with heavy dark timbers and atmospheric lighting. The yellowed decorations hanging on the walls suggested a Germanic sort of theme, but this wasn't carried through to the menu which appeared to be largely American.

"Oh! They do have schnitzel!" Derek said, looking at the menu as April and Jamie slid into the other side of the booth from him and Alex.

"And quesadillas and pizza and gyros," Jamie said, giving his own menu a quick scan. "I think they have all their bases covered."

"I'm getting the schnitzel," Derek declared. "I don't even know what that is, but I'm getting it. It even comes with spätzle!"

"What's spätzle?" April said.

"No clue," Derek said, still scanning his menu.

"Oh look, they even have a crossword puzzle on the back of the place mats," Alex said.

"All I got is a stupid connect-the-dots," Derek said, doing an admirable job of feigning disappointment. "However, even on that bombshell, I think we still did pretty well tonight."

Alex promptly muttered, "Despite some of the company we had to keep."

"Too bad we couldn't get Jamie interested in anything," April said, completely ignoring the jibe.

Jamie bristled slightly at her comment but didn't say anything. He wasn't about to start an argument after April and Derek had actually gotten to the point where they weren't insulting each other every time they spoke; even if that ceasefire had been formed around their shared desire to ensure Jamie ended up with a costume for the party. He'd managed to prevent them from doing so all night, and now that the shopping was over, there was little they could do to push him any further on the matter.

"Are you really not gonna do anything for Halloween?" Derek said.

"Look, I just don't feel like it this year, that's all."

"Don't worry, you might not have picked anything out but I've still got you covered," April said, reaching into one of her shopping bags and pulling out the flat cap they'd tried on at one of the shops. Without waiting for approval, she pulled it down on top of Jamie's head.

"I didn't know you were actually going to buy this thing," Jamie said. He'd only just started to take it off when April spoke up, causing him to pause.

"Come on, it looks good on you!" Even though she was laughing when she said it, she did sound sincere.

"Yeah," Derek said, agreeing with April. "Very hipster."

"The only thing missing is a pair of horn-rim glasses and a handlebar moustache!" Alex added, cackling uproariously.

"Then it's definitely going in the trash!" Again, Jamie reached for the cap. He probably wouldn't have actually followed through on the threat even if April hadn't grabbed his arm.

"Oh, come on," she said. "I'm being serious, it really does look good. Besides, it's a gift. You can't just throw it out."

"Well, in that case, it only seems appropriate that I give you this." Leaving the cap on his head, even though it did make him feel a little foolish, Jamie reached into his only shopping bag, the lightest by far of any of them, and emptied it completely with the removal of a "Pride and Prejudice" coloring book which he placed on the table in front of April. Derek and Alex instantly broke out laughing. April just stared. Jamie was relatively certain she wouldn't get mad at him for this, but thought it best to be careful nonetheless. "Remember, it's a gift," he said, smiling, "you can't just throw it out."

"You actually bought it?" She looked more dumbfounded than offended. "For me?"

"Well, sure," Jamie said. "It's like Derek told me: after what you said at the comic shop, it was just too good to pass up. Plus, I know how much you like the classics."

"It's true, I did say that," Derek said.

April flipped through the book. "Now if we only had some crayons," she said, the sarcasm thick in her voice.

"Don't worry, I got this one!" Alex leaned across to the next booth. It currently sat empty of patrons but had a cup full of crayons in the center of the table for use with the activities on the backs of the paper place mats.

As the four of them sat waiting for their food, they passed the coloring book back and forth between them, offering snide comments about each others' skills with a crayon and generally laughing at everything said. April, clearly having inherited her mother's artistic talent, proved to be the best of them by far, providing subtle shading and gradation to the pictures even with the crude tools available to her. In order to not come out looking like the worst among them, Alex in turn played the fool by coloring like a four-year-old might, using colors at random and barely staying inside the lines. Jamie tried his best to achieve something passable, but his flat coloring stood out just as crudely next to April's work as Alex's did. Derek, meanwhile, struggled so hard to match April's skill that he spent nearly twice as long as she did to achieve only half the quality, all the while being ribbed by the others to hurry up. Even after their food arrived, the coloring book kept making the rounds as they ate, along with far too many jokes about finding a man with good prospects.

As the other few patrons still in the restaurant eventually went on their ways, the wait staff kept a close eye on the table of laughing teenagers. However, apart from a number of too loud jokes, no one got so far out of line that the staff needed to interfere. When they were eventually asked to leave, it was only because the restaurant was getting ready to close for the night. All four of them settled their bills and prepared to leave without trouble, except for Alex, who had become increasingly intent on completing at least one of the pictures in the coloring book with as much skill as he was actually able.

"Come on, just another minute," he said, still hunched over the book as everyone else stood and gathered their belongings. "I'm almost done with Mister Rochester here."

"You mean Mister Darcy," April said, taking the book away from him and putting it into one of the four plastic shopping bags she'd acquired throughout the evening. "Mister Rochester is from 'Jane Eyre,' not 'Pride and Prejudice.'"

"All the same to me," Alex said, tossing down his crayon and sliding out of the booth.

Derek, meanwhile, cast his friend a suspicious look. "How would you even know any of the characters from either of those books?"

"Hey man, I've got three sisters! You think I don't pick up some of this stuff just through osmosis?"

"Well, I guess I'll see you guys later," Derek said, waving his goodbyes. "I've really gotta get home. My mom doesn't like me staying out this late."

"Mine either, but what's she gonna say?" Alex said, tossing on his coat. "Come on, Derek, let's bounce. See you losers tomorrow."

"Later," Jamie said.

As Alex started ushering his friend toward the exit, Derek waved again and said, "Um, good night, April."

"'Night," she said with her back to him as she pulled on her own coat. "Here, hold these," she then said to Jamie, passing her shopping bags to him, "I gotta use the bathroom."

He waited for her in the vestibule and the manager locked the door behind them when April finally joined him and they stepped back outside together.

CHAPTER 34

"You know, Jamie, I had a real good time tonight," April said as she took back her shopping bags, "even if your stupid friends had to come along."

"Yeah, well, you know how they can be." Jamie had never set out to get them all to accept each other, but it looked like things had worked out okay after all. Maybe if Alex wasn't always at April's throat from this point on, and vise versa, Jamie might actually be able to find a few moments of peace once in a while at school.

"Well, I guess," she said, hooking her hair behind her ear. "I should probably say goodnight, too."

"Yeah," Jamie agreed. From here, they each lived in opposite directions. All Jamie really wanted was to get home and go to bed. They had school tomorrow and none of the teachers had gotten any easier to deal with. Still, Heather's advice to Jamie from the evening the three of them shared a meal together kept ringing in his mind. It was late and he really should ask if she'd like him to walk her home. Of course, if he didn't say anything soon, he'd be too late. He'd just started to open his mouth when a group of people came around the corner of the building, all laughing and roughhousing amongst themselves. The moment they caught sight of Jamie and April, a stillness fell over them and they stopped dead in their tracks. Jamie and April likewise tensed and grew silent.

Seth stepped forward from the group as his friends spread out across the sidewalk. "Well, if it isn't April and her new faggot boyfriend," he said with a sneer. "Funny running into you here."

"Yeah, real funny," April muttered. Jamie held his tongue, knowing well that anything he said would only antagonize Seth. "But we were just leaving so..."

"What's the hurry?" Seth took up position directly in front of April, making himself like a brick wall. Though Seth's friends looked plenty threatening, they hadn't quite boxed Jamie and April in completely yet. If April could defuse the situation, they might still be able to get out of this without trouble. "We hardly ever talk any more. We should catch up on things."

"Seth, we really have to get going," April said as she started to walk away from him.

"You been doing some shopping?" Seth lunged forward, tearing one of the bags from April's hand. "Whacha got there?"

"Hey!" April went after the bag, but Seth held it out of her reach. When Jamie took a step forward, the Freckled Skeleton stepped into his path.

"Hey, look: feathers!" Seth said, pulling out a tuft of colored feathers which April had planned to use for her costume's headdress. He waved them in her face, jerking them away as she snatched for them. "You two planning on having a little fun in the bedroom tonight?"

"Just give them back, you jerk!" April snapped.

All of his friends laughed and Seth tossed the feathers to one of the boys before going back into the bag and coming out with the coloring book. "Oh, lookie here guys, April's got herself a coloring book. Did your mommy and daddy buy that for you?"

"Seth, why do you always have to be such a jerk?" Jamie finally said. The taunting smile dropped from Seth's face as he turned to Jamie. He looked like he was ready to kill something with his bare hands. "Why do you even care about April anymore? I mean, you've got Lorrie now, which is all you ever really wanted the whole time you were with April anyway, right? Are you really so insecure that you can't just let her go? Just leave her alone already."

Seth tossed April's things to the ground and closed with Jamie, throwing back his shoulders and tightening his hands into fists. Jamie stood his ground and met Seth's gaze.

"It's not so much April as you," Seth said, poking Jamie in the chest with one of his thick fingers hard enough that it actually sent Jamie stumbling back half a step. "The fact you even exist disgusts me. You're like a cockroach or a piece of dog shit. Every time someone looks at you, they just want to throw up. I'd be doing a community service by getting rid of you."

Jamie couldn't even comprehend where this kind of hatred had come from. Even taking into account Reaver's interference in Jamie's life, it didn't seem to warrant this level of animosity. Maybe Reaver had realized, after only one glance, that violence was the only way to deal with someone like this.

Suddenly, a nearby door swung open with a crash and four middle-aged men and women stumbled out into the midst of Seth's friends, laughing drunkenly before they even realized what they were interrupting. As Seth and his friends all looked over their shoulders to see what the commotion was, Jamie grabbed April by the wrist. "Come on!"

She hesitated only a moment, already in the process of trying to gather up the things Seth had thrown to the ground. Jamie couldn't help but notice she grabbed the coloring book first and the bag with the rest of her things, second. The feathers she had no choice but to abandon completely, being far beyond her reach.

Seth and his friends turned the moment Jamie and April were in motion and a chorus of heavy footsteps on concrete could be heard pounding after them. He and April dashed around the corner at the end of the building and down the length of the alley beyond. At the back end, it turned and then branched off between all the buildings on the block. Temporarily out of the sight, they ducked down one of these other passages at random and kept running as fast as they could until they broke out onto the sidewalk at the other end.

After getting turned around in that maze of alleys, Jamie only had a vague idea of which way they were headed but he was almost certain it was away from Heather's house. April took the lead at that point, sprinting across the street just ahead of several passing cars and into another alley on the other side.

Just before losing sight of the street behind, Jamie stole a look over his shoulder only to see Seth and the Freckled Skeleton emerge from the alley he and April had just left behind. Jamie's heart sank when they caught sight of their quarry in that same moment, yelling loudly to their scattered friends and charging out into traffic amid a cacophony of screeching tires, blaring horns, and shouted curses.

The next street Jamie and April found themselves on was mostly houses with small front lawns. She ran down the length of the sidewalk with Jamie close behind. They turned at the end of the block, the sounds of Seth and his fellow athletes growing closer. There was no way Jamie and April were going to outrun them, especially on these nearly deserted streets.

To stand and fight would be even more hopeless. Jamie would likely face a similar beating to the last one, if not worse, but it might at least save April from a similar fate. Unless, of course, Seth was no longer feeling quite as chivalrous as he had on previous occasions. With him and his friends in their current state, who knew what else they might try to do to her. No, they had to keep running, no matter what.

"Quick! Over here!" April said as she ducked into one of the yards. The shadows were deep there thanks to the tall plantings that blocked the bright lights of the neighbor's garish Halloween decorations. Head low, April ran along the back side of a hedge which paralleled the sidewalk and then crouched down alongside the owner's garage, pulling Jamie into the shadows right behind her.

Jamie's heart was beating so loudly in his ears that he could hear little else besides his and April's gasping breath.

"Did you -- ?" Jamie whispered, but April silenced him with a sharp hiss.

Momentarily, they heard footsteps rush past on the sidewalk. Several more sets followed and then someone stopped just a short distance away.

Jamie could feel April recoiling away from the light. From their vantage point, they couldn't see anything of the street beyond without giving away their position. All they could do now was sit quietly and hopefully wait them out.

"What the hell!" Seth said. His voice sounded like it had come from right on the other side of the hedge. April whispered a curse and pinched her eyes closed.

"Where did they go?" Seth said, his footsteps carrying him away from Jamie and April. A few noncommittal replies came from farther down the street and then Seth turned and started back the way he had just come. "You bunch of idiots. No wonder we never win any games."

Without warning, Jamie felt April slip her hand into his and grasp it tightly. Involuntarily, he squeezed hers just as strongly. Seth kept pacing back and forth, sometimes cursing, sometimes shouting insults at his friends to motivate them, but never more than a few feet from where Jamie and April crouched silently in the darkness.

After what seemed like hours, but could not have been more than a minute or two at the most, the shouted cry of an adult from somewhere in the distance caused Seth to stop and turn in that direction. Another cry followed the first and this time Jamie could make out something about "calling the cops." One of Seth's friends replied with a colorful request for someone to mind their own business, but that only earned another sharp warning from another adult voice. A few more taunts and insults were thrown back and forth between the two sides before Seth's friends eventually came scrambling back to him and they all retreated in a disorganized mob.

Finally allowing herself to breath again, April used that first gulp of air to swear profanely. "If I knew you were gonna cause me this much trouble, I never would have gone with you that first time to the mall." Despite her words, she squeezed Jamie's hand again.

"It certainly would have made my life a lot easier too," Jamie said.

In the darkness, he could see her eyes flash as she looked at him and started to say something. Before she could get it out, however, a man called out from right behind them, gruff and angry. "What do you think you're doing on my property! Get the hell out of here. Go make out in somebody else's yard, you punks!"

Jamie and April were on their feet and in motion before he even finished, running once more down the sidewalk, this time in the opposite direction Seth and his friends were headed. Even in the face of what they'd just been through, Jamie and April started giggling uncontrollably as they ran past the silhouetted faces of people standing on their front porches, watching to find out what all the commotion had been about. By the time they reached the next street over, still holding hands, they were both laughing so hard they had to slow down so that they could catch their breath.

"My place is just another couple of blocks," April said.

"This time," Jamie said, "I think I *better* walk you home."

"This time, I'm not gonna try to stop you. And I wouldn't even say 'no' if you wanted to carry some of these bags for a while, either."

Jamie took the offered shopping bags, leaving April with only her purse. "Did you lose anything?"

"I don't think so," she said. "Just the feathers. I'll have to go back tomorrow and buy some more."

They didn't say much else the rest of the way. April lived in a small apartment building on the second floor which she pointed out by the illuminated windows as they approached. "Looks like my mom is still up." She paused thoughtfully. "I don't know if... I'd invite you up but... You know, I told you that she's fine most of the time, but I don't..." She threw up her hands and sighed.

"Don't worry. I get it. Besides, I don't need to meet her, it's not like I'm actually your boyfriend."

"Hmm, maybe," April said. Before Jamie could ask what she meant by that, she stood up on her toes and kissed him. It was tender, less impassioned than Onorah's kiss had been, but it left Jamie just as wooden and unable to respond, his hands weighted down by the bags he still carried.

"I'll see you tomorrow," April said as she rocked back on her heels and took her shopping bags from Jamie.

"Um, yeah," Jamie muttered as she went on her way. He remained on the sidewalk, staring at the front door to her apartment building long after she had gone inside and disappeared from sight. It was only when he finally turned away and started for home that he finally took another breath.

He strolled along the residential streets without feeling any real urgency to be anywhere, but always with a watchful eye out for Seth or any of his friends. Heather had texted him while they'd been at Walter's Café, wondering how much longer he was going to be out, so after having replied to that, she shouldn't have started worrying about him yet.

It wasn't that Jamie didn't want to go home. He just needed some time to put some order to everything in his head. It had certainly been a strange night. He still wished he didn't have to deal with Seth and April and all the rest, but at least he now had friends and had even sort of found a way to fit in, even if it was with the other misfits. Maybe if his bouts with

Terrarhea had really just been caused by his own stress, he could yet find a way to beat it.

"Heather, I'm home," Jamie said, sticking his head into their makeshift living room.

Heather looked up from where she lounged on the couch. "Nice hat."

Having completely forgotten he was still wearing the flat cap, Jamie snatched it off. "Yeah, um, goodnight," he said, hastily going off to his room as Heather laughed.

Jamie closed his eyes and fell backward onto his bed with a sigh.

Landing, however, he suddenly felt hard stones pressing against his stomach and his eyes were no longer closed. Instead he found himself staring down a dark tunnel at some gigantic, long-eared, horned beast centered in a halo of light at the other end. With a yelp, Jamie drew back, his fingers tensing around whatever he held in his hand. A faint hum filled his ears and his whole world became awash in light.

Laying prone in a shallow gully of smooth white stones, Jamie appeared to be looking through a fringe of slender grasses at a shoreline covered in more of those same stones. In his hands, he held a rifle that had to be nearly as long as he was tall. Apart from the gurgling of water and the chirping of insects and birds all around him, everything was still and peaceful. He could see no sign of the creature that had startled him until he tentatively looked through the rifle's scope. Again, his vision closed down to a single tunnel of black, centered on a light brown lump laying some distance away in an open patch of stones.

He sat up and looked around. There was no one in sight. In fact, he couldn't see anything that would hint at any other human ever having set foot in that place. A bright sun shone down from a clear blue sky and glinted off the drifting waters of a nearby river. The other shore had to be at least a hundred yards away. Beyond the flat expanse of pale stones stretching away from the edge of the water, the bank rose up steeply and a solid line of trees stood along the top. The rocky shores harbored a few scraggly shrubs and stands of grasses between the bleached logs of driftwood and dried lengths of aquatic plants stranded ashore in the last flood.

As if in a dream, Jamie rose to his feet and tossed the corner of his tattered red poncho over the shoulder of his leathern garments. So he was back on Terrarhea again, and after barely a week in the real world. He'd been a fool to let himself think for even a minute that this was over.

Picking up the rifle by the handle on top and trudging across the shoreline with loose stones shifting under his feet, he made his way towards the furry shape he'd seen through the scope. Despite his senses having snapped back into hyper-sensitivity, he felt strangely numb. He came to a halt with the fallen body of the creature at his feet, staring down at it in silence for nearly a minute.

It didn't look as big up close as it had through the rifle scope, but it was still nearly the size of a medium dog. Covered head to toe with a soft, light brown fur, it looked something like a rabbit or a kangaroo, only with a tiny pair of branching horns rising from the top of its head. In its side, Jamie could just make out a small black circle of singed fur.

"Really?" Jamie muttered. "I just shot a jackelope?"

Back home, during hunting season, Jamie had seen plenty of dead animals, but this was the first one that he'd ever shot himself. At least, it was the first animal that he'd ever killed *on purpose*. With a slight chill creeping down his spine, Jamie swept his gaze across the trees lining the river. He couldn't see any Wolf-Slaves hiding in the shadows up there, but he suddenly found it very hard to shake the feeling of being watched.

Then, with a rising sense of urgency, he once again scanned the river shore.

"Alaida." Where was she? "Alaida!"

There was no rely. Had Reaver left her behind after all? Was she even still...?

As Jamie again took in his surroundings, this time more intently, he caught sight of something just beyond a large sweeping bend in the river, perhaps half a mile upstream. At that distance it was hard to make out clearly, but the sharp geometric lines stood out starkly against its organic surroundings. Jamie raised the rifle to his shoulder and sighted through the scope. It took him a moment to find the object once again, but when he did, there was no mistaking it as anything other than Reaver's titan-mecha, parked at the edge of the river.

In all haste, Jamie slung the rifle over his shoulder and picked up the jackelope by its front legs. Reaver wouldn't have left his titan behind and if Alaida was to be found anywhere, that would be the first place to look. Jamie tried his best to ignore the way the dead creature's head rolled sickeningly like some limp rag doll as he set off at a quick jog toward the distant titan. If Alaida was over there, this hunt would have been as much for her as Reaver.

He barely noticed the landscape around him as the titan grew ever closer. Occasionally he would lose sight of it as he had to navigate around a thick stand of shrubs or ford the gully of a stream emptying into the larger river, but he had only to keep the river to his right and he knew he would eventually reach his goal. When he finally crested a small ridge of river stones that had formed against a large log, the titan stood not more than a hundred yards away, looking very much as it had the first time he'd seen it. However, it also looked just as unoccupied as the rest of this place.

"Alaida!" Jamie called out, crossing that final distance at a sprint and dropping both the jackelope and the rifle halfway. "Alaida!"

He circled the titan, but she wasn't there. The storage pod that formed the cover over the top of the titan's hold and also acted as the back of the rumble seat had been rotated ever farther backwards and lowered on a pair of telescoping rails that formed a ladder from the ground up to the titan's back. He climbed the ladder and looked into the open hold but couldn't see any trace of Alaida there either. Returning to the ground, he gripped the sides of his head as he looked out across the river.

Where was she?

Where was *he*?

Was this anywhere near Tavnic, or even any of the other places on Terrarhea he'd visited? She could be anywhere. And unless Reaver had left Jamie a note and a map, he'd never have any way of finding her again. All the anxiety that had been building in him the past week as he had been forced to live with the constant frustration of not knowing Alaida's fate suddenly came boiling out of him with a howled scream across the water.

"Alaida!"

Chapter 35

As the echoes of Jamie's outburst died away in the distant hills, he felt his whole body lose all desire to keep going. He just wanted to collapse right there on the beach and give up. What was the point of all this anyway? He'd saved Alaida from both Finttiranos Soldiers and from Wolf-Slaves, and yet he'd still lost her. Even if he went looking for her, where was he to start? He had absolutely no idea where he was.

Couldn't he be allowed a single moment's peace without having to worry about his own or Alaida's safety? At least if Terrarhea refused to leave him alone, did it have to keep tormenting him like this?

Suddenly, the calm of the riverside shattered with a familiar voice from just upriver, spoken in hurried tones, "Yes master, I am here."

The first thought that flashed through Jamie's mind was that he had imagined those words. But as he turned and saw Alaida hastening toward the titan with a bundle of wood in her arms, his jaw fell open. He stood stark still, unable to do anything but stare. It was Alaida. It was really her.

Finally breaking free of his stunned stupor, Jamie set off to meet her, smiling like a fool. "Alaida, are you okay?"

Scuttling to a stop, Alaida frowned and her forehead wrinkled, her bare feet shifting in the loose stones as she nearly lost her grip on the twigs and branches she carried. "Y-yes, master, I am well..."

Jamie stopped short as well. She must have thought he was still Reaver. "Alaida, it's me: Jamie."

She took a step back, clutching the bundle of wood in her arms more tightly. "But master, you told me never to call you that."

"I'm not Reaver. It's Jamie, I'm back." He took a single step forward but went no farther. Alaida looked like she wanted to run back into the small stand of trees from which she had just emerged. What could have happened in his absence to bring on a reaction like this? He thought she would have been happy to see him again. Of course, he'd never actually explained things to her very well. She had to be pretty confused right now.

"Do you remember what I told you that night at the stream after the Wolf-Slaves attacked us?" Jamie said. It took an effort to keep his voice calm and soothing. He wanted to laugh and hug her tightly, but she didn't look as if she would appreciate any such thing at the moment. Why did even this have to be so difficult?

Alaida bit her lip, the conflict plain on her face. "You said many things that night..."

"No, the part about being two different people, do you remember that?"

Haltingly, Alaida nodded.

"I told you that it's like I'm switching bodies with someone else, with Reaver -- with the Red Rogue. Most of the time, I'm on a completely different planet. I have a life there. Everything I told you about myself is part of that world. I live there most of the time, but for some reason, it's like my mind started getting brought here and put inside this body. I don't know why it's happening, and I don't have any control over it. It's completely random and it never seems to last very long before I go back."

Some of the tension had dropped from Alaida's body but she still looked just as confused as before. "How is such a thing even possible?"

Jamie shook his head. "I don't know. It doesn't make any sense to me at all. But on my world, we don't have magic or magesmiths or wardcasters so who knows what's possible on *this* world."

"And you think this...*Reaver* is responsible for what is happening?"

"Maybe," Jamie said. "But I don't think so. He seems nearly as confused by it as I do." Or did he? "What happened after I left; after the fight?"

Alaida paused, eyeing Jamie questioningly. "You were crying, nearly hysterical. Then your expression changed, like the drawing of a curtain. You were confused...angry. You demanded to know who I was, where we were, and what had happened. You made me tell it many times. I did not know why. I was frightened."

"That wasn't me. That was Reaver."

Alaida still looked skeptical but at least she didn't voice her doubts. "After I told you everything I could think of, you had me get in the titan and we left that place." Seeing Jamie's grimace, Alaida quickly amended her statement, "*He* told me to get in the titan." She flinched as if expecting to be slapped for referring to her master in the third person, but Jamie merely beckoned her to continue. "We moved quickly; west, I believe. You, that is to say, he, never said much except to ask me more questions about how we had ended up where we were. I told him everything I knew, but I did not always know the answers to his questions."

Alaida paused again and looked down at the ground as she hugged the bundle of sticks to her chest. Jamie suddenly felt his skin grow hot and his insides cold. "Did he hurt you?"

Still looking at the ground, Alaida shook her head. "He was very interested in the papers that Lieutenant Del Mamdon gave to you and about the things that Mistress Onorah told you about them. The day after leaving the steam, we stopped for a time so that he could read through each page at least twice. Afterward, he went off on foot by himself for nearly a whole day. I was starting to think that I had been abandoned when he did finally return. Except for a few times when we stopped for supplies, we have been traveling almost constantly ever since."

"Did he tell you anything about what was in those papers or what he was doing?"

Alaida pursed her lips. "He tells me very little, but he did want me to know that no matter what happened, we had to continue following this river upstream. He had me repeat it many times until he was certain that I would remember."

Jamie stepped forward, gazing into the distance where the river disappeared from view around another large bend. The rolling hills of green beyond stood unmarred by buildings, roads, or even the smoke from a single lonely fire. Still clutching the firewood tightly, Alaida turned so that she remained facing Jamie, but at least she didn't back away. "He anticipated that you would return, did he not?"

"Yeah. He's looking for that Major Ommto guy. And he wants me to keep going even if he's not here to do it himself." Jamie chuckled ruefully. He'd been worried about Alaida all this time for nothing. It seemed Reaver had found his own reasons to keep her safe. "He's using you as a go-between for us. Do you know how much farther we still have to go?"

Alaida shook her head.

"Is anyone still following us?"

Alaida shrugged. "We have been moving quite quickly but I do not believe he has been overly concerned about staying out of sight. Early on, we passed through several villages without incident but the last few days I have not seen any settlements at all and not so much as another traveler. As far as I know, there has been no sign of Wolf-Slaves since that night you drove them off at the stream."

Jamie stood in silence for some time, still staring into the wilderness. Wherever they were, it seemed they were, indeed, totally alone. What had Reaver learned from those papers? Did he know what Major

Ommto's significance was to all this? Did he even know what awaited them ahead, or had his vague instructions to Alaida been as much from his own lack of knowledge on the matter as a desire for secrecy?

Standing no more than an arm's length away, Alaida shifted her feet in the smooth stones. After several failed attempts to speak, she finally said, "May I ask you a question?"

Jamie nodded.

"Why did you purchase me from Gavrin," she said in a very soft voice, "and not one of his other Raven-Slaves?"

Jamie turned to Alaida, shaking his head. "Um, it's like I told you last time. I don't really know. Because you're special, I guess?"

At that, the corner of Alaida's mouth twitched into the start of a faint smile. She'd asked Jamie almost that same thing the last time they'd been together, and Jamie had answered it in nearly the same words.

"You didn't tell him that, did you?" Jamie said.

"I did not mean to be secretive. It simply seemed too…presumptuous of me to say such a thing."

Jamie nearly laughed. "Well, that's got to prove I'm not him, right?"

"Not necessarily…" Alaida said slowly. "Though it does make it seem less likely."

"But the only way that would make sense is if I've always been him and I was just playing mind games with you back in Tavnic. Do you really think that I'm Reaver right now and that I'm just testing you to see if I can catch you in a lie?"

Alaida's head tipped sharply to the side as she examined Jamie. "No," she said at last. But her expression remained thoughtful. "Will he…be returning again?"

Jamie cast his thoughts inward to that relentless niggling that had always accompanied his excursions to Terrarhea. It was more faint than the last time, so much so that he wouldn't have noticed if Alaida hadn't mentioned it. It was also ticking along at an even slower pace. Jamie shrugged. "A couple of days maybe."

Alaida's golden eyes opened wide. "Days?"

"Yeah. I guess each time I come here, it's longer. And each time I go back there, it gets shorter…" Suddenly, Jamie felt a coldness well up inside him.

"What is it?"

"Reaver," Jamie said, rubbing his face with the palms of his gloved hands, "He's back there right now, in my home, with my sister."

Alaida stepped forward and, balancing the firewood in the crook of one arm, she placed a hand on Jamie's shoulder. "I am sure she will be well. He is too cautious to do anything rashly. And he has no reason to do her harm, does he?"

"No, I don't think so, but so far they've never crossed paths before either." Jamie shook his head and groaned. "What happens when she figures out that he's not me? Even if he keeps a low profile and tries to pass himself off as me, she's going to have plenty of time to see through him."

"I..." Alaida began to speak but then stopped herself.

"What is it?"

"I would not be so certain of that, myself. There are differences between the two of you, yes, but the similarities are far more numerous."

Jamie's shoulders stooped as he lifted his face skyward and closed his eyes. April had said almost the same thing to him. "Do you think that me and Reaver could really be the same person? That maybe I am just sick and all this is part of my imagination?"

"I do not think I am just a part of your imagination. And I *know* this world is real. Could it be *your* world that is not?"

Jamie took a very deep breath and opened his eyes. "No. This is really happening. I know that." Jamie had been over this too many times to start questioning it all over again. He knew Terrarhea was real. He knew Earth was real. And he knew that Major Ommto and that small shard of black metal had something to do with it all. "When can we leave?"

Alaida glanced toward the titan and then looked at the firewood she held in her arms. "We had stopped here because we had no food left. He seldom eats anything, so it is mostly only for my benefit that he ever goes hunting. But I suppose we could go a little farther yet..."

So focused on trying to convince Alaida that he wasn't Reaver, Jamie hadn't noticed until now that Alaida's clothes were the same ones she'd been wearing when they'd left Tavnic. They were also quite soiled, as was her once perfect skin. Her fine black hair had lost some of it's unique bluish sheen, as well, and wasn't nearly as neat and straight as the last time he'd seen her. It looked as though she'd been able to sew-up the damage to her dress where it had been torn by the Wolf-Slaves but the three scratches on her neck and shoulder still showed out red and scabbed on her skin.

"Did the Wolf-Slaves hurt you?"

Alaida's brow furrowed but then her expression turned to one of realization as she touched the marks on her shoulder. "Not badly. It has healed quickly."

"When's the last time you --" Jamie had been going to say, "were able to take a bath," but caught himself at the last moment, realizing how rude that might sound. Instead he cleared his throat. "I mean, I already shot a Jackelope so we might as well take care of that before we head out again." Alaida looked up at Jamie with eyes wide. Just how long had it been since they'd last stopped for food? "And you know what, as long as we're here now, maybe we could set up camp for the night and take a little break until tomorrow morning."

"Are you certain?" Alaida sounded like she couldn't quite believe her good fortune. "We usually only stop long enough to restock our supplies before moving on again; usually no more than an hour or two at the most."

"Since we're not in any danger at the moment, I don't see what harm it could do." After all, Jamie had actually just been hoping for an opportunity exactly like this. He'd be lying to himself if he claimed not to be concerned about Heather, but Alaida had to be correct. At worst, Reaver might disappear again, leaving Heather to wonder about what had become of him, but he wouldn't do anything to hurt her. Reaver had no reason to, and so far, he'd actually proven himself to be quite civilized with the women in Jamie's life. "Besides, we don't even know how much farther we still have to go. Even if we started right away, we might just spend the rest of my time here traveling. There's no sense in wearing ourselves out."

"It would be nice to sleep on stable ground again after having spent the last week only doing so in the back of a moving titan-mecha," Alaida admitted. "And I did find some mushrooms and potatoes while gathering wood. I could actually prepare them properly for a change."

"Unfortunately, I don't know much about butchering Jackelopes," Jamie said.

Alaida smiled and that was enough to lift Jamie's spirits considerably. "I can manage. He does not usually get involved with these things apart from the actual hunting. Where is it?"

Alaida dropped the wood off at the titan-mecha and then followed Jamie to the place where he'd left the jackelope.

"It is a very large one," Alaida said as she got down on her knees and rolled it over. "This will do nicely."

"Reaver did most of the work; I just showed up and accidentally pulled the trigger."

Jamie helped Alaida take the carcass to the edge of the riverbank. She had a small knife with her which she deftly used to gut and skin the animal in what seemed like only a few strokes. When Jamie asked where she'd learned how to do that, she explained that one of her former owners was something of a sport hunter and it had been her responsibility to prepare the game he would often bring home. Jamie had seldom seen this part of the hunting process himself but as he helped Alaida butcher the animal, he stopped thinking of it as a once living creature and now nothing more than meat. When they'd finished, Jamie took those few pieces of offal which Alaida had not saved and the skin and buried them far from camp.

Meanwhile, Alaida used a small metal cylinder, no bigger than her thumb and covered in glowing magescript, to start a fire with the wood she'd gathered. At her suggestion, Jamie set up a small iron pot filled with water over the fire and then took the potatoes she'd gathered down to the river and scrubbed them clean in the clear water. They were small, knobby things that looked more like artichokes than potatoes, but they smelled wonderful wherever the skin had been torn.

When Jamie returned to the fire, he found that Alaida had gotten several wooden cutting boards and knives from the titan's hold which she was using on the various cuts of meat. The organs and tougher cuts, along with some fresh herbs she'd found while collecting the firewood, she was currently mincing together with a pair of heavy knives. Though she offered no smile or other greeting, at least she no longer flinched away when he sat down next to her and watched he work.

"Alaida, ever since that night I had to go away, I've been worried about you," Jamie said. "I'm glad you're okay. I really missed you."

Alida paused in her vigorous chopping and wiped her brow with the back of her wrist. "Though I didn't realize it at the time," she said, "I suppose I missed you as well. If you would like, you can place those bones in the water now that is boiling."

"What's he like?" Jamie said, doing with the small pile of broken jackelope bones as Alaida had asked.

Going back to her mincing, she didn't reply right away. "He does not say much of anything. He is also very serious all of the time. I do not think that I have ever seen him smile."

"Is he..." Jamie stirred the pot, watching the frothy brown marrow float to the surface. "Do you think he's as bad as everyone seems to think he is?"

Again, Alaida paused, this time wiping her knives clean against each other. "I do not have any reason to doubt that he was responsible for that robbery and the murder of those soldiers near Tavnic," she said. "He seems driven to achieve his goals but cares little if he has to break the law to do so. He has no doubt done many other terrible things that I do not know about, but I do not think that he is truly evil."

"Just a little sociopathic?" Jamie said. Alaida tipped her head to the side. "He thinks that that the rules of society don't apply to him."

"That might be a very apt description."

"Not that it makes things much better."

"No, I suppose not," Alaida said, going back to chopping.

CHAPTER 36

Once finished with the minced meat and herbs, Alaida began rolling it into balls while Jamie watched the pot and strained out the bones. Afterward, he added the potatoes and continued stirring occasionally. Alaida next moved onto the larger cuts of meat, slicing them into very thin strips and setting them aside in a pile. When Jamie again asked if there was anything he could do to help, Alaida sent him off to find small sticks which they could use to skewer the strips of meat in preparation for drying them. Both these steps didn't take long and soon they had almost all of the meat arranged around the fire.

The very last of the meat, a few of the nicest looking cuts, Alaida placed inside a small glass-topped box she retrieved from the hold of the titan. About the size of a shoe box, the four sides were made of metal and covered with magescript. The top and bottom panels felt like glass, but when she activated the wards, they became flexible, pressing in tightly against the meat from both sides like a vacuumed-sealed bag. Alaida explained that it would keep the meat fresh almost indefinitely, but it was unlikely that they'd have to wait that long before using it.

Now that the potatoes had been given some time to boil, Alaida dropped the meat balls into the water and moved the pot a little farther from the fire so as to let them cook more slowly. She washed the utensils in the river with Jamie's help and then the two of them put everything away in the appropriate crates in the titan's hold.

"It will still be a little while yet until the soup is ready," Alaida said as they finished. "If you do not have any objections, I would like to…clean up a bit beforehand."

"No, go right ahead. I mean, that's why we're here, right, to relax a little?"

"Thank you. Would you like me to wash your clothes as well? I know that they have not been washed at least as long as mine have."

"No, that's okay." Jamie's tough leather garments were worn and weathered, but they didn't really feel all that dirty. Since Reaver didn't actually seem to sweat, it probably made sense. The poncho, however, had clearly come into contact with more than its fair share of mud and grease.

"Are you certain?" Alaida said.

Jamie laughed nervously. From what he'd seen while rummaging through the supplies in the titan's hold, it looked as though he wouldn't have anything to change into if he let Alaida take the clothes he was wearing. Besides, he wasn't about to make her do his laundry for him. "If you really think they need to be washed, I can do it myself."

"It really would not be any trouble at all. Here, you can use this," she said with a long sigh as she handed him a towel. "I promise not to peek."

Jamie shook his head and opened his mouth to speak but Alaida met his gaze with a stern expression and offered him the towel yet again.

"Fine," he said at last, taking off the poncho and tossing it over her arm as he took the towel.

She flashed him a self-satisfied smile as she gathered up a satchel of toiletries and another towel before walking down to the river's edge. Completely forgetting his own concerns about Alaida seeing him naked, Jamie stood and stared at her back as she began taking off her own clothes. Flushing a bright shade of red, Jamie turned his back just as Alaida's dress slipped down over her pale shoulders. She hadn't tried to be subtle about it, hadn't told him not to look, hadn't even tried to cover herself. Was she intentionally toying with him, or was this another one of those things that people did differently on this world?

Jamie quickly stripped out of his clothes and wrapped the towel around his midsection before turning back around. True to her word, Alaida hadn't peeked. However, crouched down in the water with her back to Jamie as she began scrubbing out her clothes against a large flat stone with a brush and a bar of soap, she was now clothed in nothing more than a towel as well, though hers was much more revealing than Jamie's.

Jamie took a deep breath and averted his eyes as he began walking down to the river. Terrarhean girls were no easier for him to figure out than those of his homeworld. Looking the other way and blushing even more fiercely, he handed his things to Alaida. He could tell from the tone of her voice that she had looked his way as she took them and thanked him, but he didn't want to risk further embarrassment by looking at her in return. Instead, he crouched down next to her, still facing the other way as he heard the water splashing around their dirty clothes.

"If you would like," Alaida said, "you could wring these out and spread them on those large rocks there to dry."

"Um, sure, no problem," Jamie said, his voice crackling. He chanced a glance in her direction and saw the clothes to which she was referring. He also saw the briefest glimpse of her pale thigh. Turning quickly away, Jamie gathered up the clothes without looking and took them a few paces upstream.

In order to keep his thoughts from wandering, he busied himself with wringing as much water from each piece of clothing as he could before laying them out on the sun-warmed stones. He only had reason to pause when Alaida passed him several pairs of her undergarments. Did she really place so much trust in him that she didn't mind him handling them? He was still trying to figure out how best to deal with it when he heard a loud splash from behind him.

Jamie turned to see Alaida's towel laying abandoned on the shore and her swimming out into the calm waters created by a crude jetty of boulders. Having already scrubbed herself down after finishing with the last of the laundry, she left a trail of soap bubbles in her wake. The afternoon sun glinted off the rippling waters, preventing Jamie from seeing much of her from the neck down, but that didn't make the reality any less startling.

With a deep breath, she dropped below the water for a moment to rinse out her hair and then resurfaced with a gasp and a laugh. "It feels wonderful to be clean again," she said, treading water at the edge of the river's current. Even at that distance, she had to be able to see just how red Jamie's face was. "And I don't remember the last time I went for a swim. You could join me if you would like. The water is cold but not entirely unpleasant."

At that, Jamie finally turned away, waving his hands. "No, I'm fine right here."

"Do you not know how to swim?" Alaida paddled a little closer to shore.

"Yes, I know how to swim. I just...don't feel like it right now."

"Humph," Alaida said.

At the moment, Jamie cared less about disappointing her than appearing like a complete boor. The next thing he heard, though, was a loud splash, followed quickly by a wave of cold water crashing down over his head. He whirled on Alaida who had covered her mouth to stifle a laugh.

Pushing matted hair out of his eyes and sputtering, Jamie said, "What was that for?" Alaida drew back, her expression darkening. Jamie pitched his eyes shut. Alaida had only been trying to have some fun and Jamie had probably made her think that Reaver had returned. "I'm sorry. I'm not mad at you. You just caught me by surprise, that's all."

Alaida bit her lip. "Then you would not be surprised by this?" She quickly brought her hands around and threw another splash of water in Jamie's direction.

He scuttled out of the way but was only partly successful in avoiding it. "Hey! What's the big idea?"

"Did you not say that the reason for us to spend a little time here was to relax and enjoy ourselves?"

"That doesn't mean you have to keep splashing me."

"Perhaps," Alaida said, putting on a look of mock hurt as she shrugged, "perhaps not."

Again, she splashed Jamie, and this time he didn't even try to dodge. Blowing water from his lips, he cast a stern gaze in Alaida's direction. She had now taken on a look of complete innocence as she pushed herself out a little farther from shore.

"Okay, you win," Jamie said. "But this means war."

Charging out along the jetty of boulders, Jamie only cast his towel aside at the last moment before leaping high into the air and crashing down in the water with a cannonball splash that left Alaida retreating with a shrill cry of laughter. The water swirled and bubbled around Jamie, pulling him under. It was much colder than Alaida had made it out to be, and if he'd been in his own body, he likely would have been gasping for breath from the shock of it. When he rose back to the surface, he found Alaida sputtering and blinking water out of her eyes.

Jamie laughed. "Are we having fun *now*?"

"Nearly."

Smiling wickedly, she splashed Jamie yet again and he promptly retaliated in kind. What followed was a water fight as ferocious as it was meaningless, since they were both already as soaked as they could possibly be. Jamie's earlier hesitation all but vanished, no longer concerned about preserving his modesty, just in having some plain, simple fun. Both of them needed it. Unabashedly, their laughter echoed from the distant hills, neither of them caring in the least if they were really as alone as it seemed they were.

Their confrontation only came to an end when Alaida rose up behind Jamie with a loud burst of laughter and put her hands on his shoulders, forcing him underwater. Once below the surface, she no longer had any leverage on him and Jamie slipped free, quickly turning the tide by taking hold of Alaida by the arms. As they both surfaced once again, now facing each other, their laughter was no longer quite so energetic as it had been just a moment before.

It would take more than a simple game for Reaver's body to become winded, but staring into Alaida's eyes, Jamie now found it hard to breathe at all. Alaida appeared likewise short of breath, her chest rising and falling with each deep breath she took.

"Alaida," Jamie said, the feel of her skin warm and slippery in the cold water, "I'd really like to kiss you right now."

Almost imperceptibly, Alaida's smile wavered and she drew back, no more than a fraction of an inch, but it was enough that Jamie noticed. As that tiny gap opened between them, he could feel their moment of shared frivolity all but evaporate.

Alaida hesitated before replying, "You...can certainly do so if you wish."

Releasing Alaida, this time it was Jamie who backed away, and much more than just a few inches. The way she'd said that hadn't been an invitation or even consent. "Alaida, I'm not trying to force you to do anything. It's like I said before, you're not a slave, you don't have to do anything if you don't want to. I just thought that, I don't know, that you might have felt the same way..."

"I..." she cast down her eyes. "I... should check on the soup."

With that, she swam around Jamie and headed back to shore. He watched her leave but turned around before she stepped out of the water, letting himself sink below the surface. He shouldn't have asked; he should have just kissed her. Of course, that probably would have ended even worse. Maybe Heather had been right about Alaida. It was kind of pointless pining after a girl who might never think of him as anything more than a friend. He remained below the water for several minutes, not even growing short of breath before he eventually resurfaced.

On shore, Alaida had wrapped the towel around herself once more and was tending to the soup just as she said she would, paying no mind at all to Jamie or the river. Jamie emerged from the water and quickly snatched up his own towel. His clothes were still wet and looked like they would be for quite some time yet. At this rate, they might not even be ready to wear before nightfall. Not quite willing to face Alaida just yet, Jamie sat on one of the rocks and looked out at the river gliding past.

Not for the first time, he considered this strange body of Reaver's. If it weren't for the incredible things it was capable of, Jamie would have been hard pressed to know that it wasn't his. The scar on his arm where he'd wiped out on his bike that one summer wasn't there, as were a few more recent and less permanent marks, but otherwise, nearly every crease and bump and hair looked nearly identical to his own body. Apart from the two different lives they must have lived, they were perfect copies of the other. But which one was the original? Or were they both duplicates of someone else entirely? The old man Jamie had now seen twice on Earth, and who might have possibly had some connection to all this, didn't look a thing like Reaver or Jamie, even taking into account his age and the rough life he had obviously lived. As Jamie had often concluded in the past, it was pointless to speculate too much about his condition without more information to go on.

The sun had dropped quite close to the tops of the distance hills when Jamie finally rose and returned to the fire and Alaida.

"Are you okay?" he said.

"Yes," Alaida replied. "The soup is ready if you would like some."

"Alaida, I'm sorry if I did anything to upset you earlier. I just thought..." Jamie sighed and sat down on a log of driftwood that they had earlier dragged near the fire. "I don't know what I was thinking. I'm just sorry, okay?"

"You do not have anything to apologize for," Alaida said, stirring the pot. Into a small, earthenware bowl, she ladled out a portion of soup, complete with two of the meatballs and several potatoes. The mushrooms were floating on the surface and the broth gave off an earthy aroma that made Jamie's mouth water. When she passed the bowl to him, along with a metal spoon, Jamie held up his hands, unable to accept.

"I'm not very hungry. I don't think I need to eat any more than Reaver does. Besides, I wouldn't want to take any away from you."

"There is plenty here. I doubt I will be able to finish it all by myself before we leave in the morning anyway. And you did help make it."

"I don't know how much I really contributed, but I am kind of curious to see what it tastes like," Jamie said, finally taking the bowl from her.

Alaida portioned out another bowl for herself and took a seat at the other end of the log. He waited for her to begin eating before he tried the soup himself. After just one sip of the broth, he quickly went back for one of the meatballs and his eyes grew wide when he popped it into his mouth.

"Is it not to your liking?"

Jamie hastily swallowed and laughed. "No, this is incredible! After seeing what you put into these meatballs, I didn't think they could taste this good! I mean, just a couple of hours ago, that was a jackelope and you turned it into a whole meal right here in the middle of nowhere with hardly anything at all to work with. You weren't kidding back in Tavnic when you said you were a good cook. This is awesome!" With vigor, Jamie went back to his bowl for another taste.

"Thank you," Alaida said with a smile as she blew on her own soup. "One never knows how wild game will turn out until it is finished."

"Reaver doesn't know what he's missing."

"I think I would rather share this with you than with him," Alaida whispered and then took another sip of broth.

Alaida went back for several more servings before she had eaten her fill. Jamie could have eaten just as much but he held himself in check. He certainly wasn't full, but then he wasn't really hungry either. A part of him wanted to simply enjoy the meal without analyzing everything, but there were other matters here that needed to be considered. Reaver didn't need to eat, and by extension, Jamie probably didn't either. Alaida did, however, and every bit of food he took for himself meant less for her. Ideally, this shared situation between Jamie and Reaver would come to a swift end, but in the meantime, Jamie needed to look out for Alaida, as well as himself, and he couldn't do that if he didn't identify the limits of Reaver's endurance. Better to do so now, rather than in the heat of some conflict that risked both their lives.

The sun disappeared behind the tops of the hills quite early. It would still be several hours yet before night fell completely, but the temperature quickly began to drop. After shaking her clothes out near the fire, Alaida decided they were dry enough to get dressed once again. While she busied herself with that, Jamie checked on his leathers. They had not dried nearly as quickly, but he slid back into them despite the slick, clammy feel against his skin; if not to speed their drying with his own body heat, than just so that he wasn't the only one left wearing nothing more than a towel.

As twilight overtook their little camp, a slight breeze began blowing off the river, bringing with it a damp chill to the air. Alaida spread out a thick woven rug before the fire and wrapped a blanket around herself as she took a seat on the ground with her back against the log they had earlier been sitting on. After Jamie stoked the fire back to life, he joined her. Neither of them said a word but it wasn't like back in Tavnic when they'd spent the whole afternoon together. Here, they sat close, not quite touching, both of them staring at the crackling logs in the fire with an almost palpable barrier running between them.

Just like with Kristie, Jamie began to worry that he had now ruined this friendship as well. Though Alaida remained friendly enough, Jamie could tell she was keeping herself guarded. He just didn't know if this was because of the unwelcome advances he'd made while swimming or if she simply remained uncertain about her own situation, knowing that Reaver would eventually return to throw her life into chaos once more.

What he did know was that he didn't need to try and persuade her to feel the same way about him as he did about her. Just being with her in this place was enough. What he really wanted more than anything was to find a way to protect her, so she wouldn't have to keep living in fear and anxiety. But what could he possibly say or do to convince her of that?

When Jamie reached out to take her hand, to offer what friendly reassurance he could under the circumstances, Alaida stood before he was able and went to the pile of firewood the two of them had collected that afternoon. It could have been bad timing or simple coincidence, but Jamie suspected otherwise.

"Alaida, I'm..." he trailed off, not really knowing what to say. "I'm really sorry I got you into all this," he said at last.

Alaida looked at him across the flames as she placed a few more pieces of wood into the fire. "If given a choice between your old life and this one," Alaida said, her smile melancholy, "which would you rather have?"

Jamie opened his mouth to speak but hesitated. He missed his life on Earth when he wasn't there, but he also missed his time with Alaida when she wasn't near. "I'm not sure I can answer that."

"Neither can I," Alaida said. Jamie had to admit it would be difficult to choose between a safe life as a slave or a dangerous one on the run with a fugitive from justice. She cast her gaze skyward, toward the star-filled sky above. "Your home is out there somewhere, yes?"

"I guess," Jamie said, looking up at the stars as well, "but I don't really know for sure." After all, he hadn't traveled to Terrarhea in a spaceship, or anything of the sort. He definitely found it difficult, if not impossible, to think about Earth being one of those distant points of light.

Since moving in with Heather, where the lights of the city hid most of the stars from view, Jamie had started getting used to not seeing them anymore. Even back in the old days, when his family had gone camping in the middle of nowhere, he couldn't remember ever having seen this many stars all at once. Reaver's sharp eyes made them appear as if stacked deep in layers, almost like he could actually see the distances between each one and himself.

With the fire crackling happily in the background, Terrarhea's shattered moon began to rise in the eastern sky. It filled Jamie with the same sense of both unease and wonder as it had the first time he'd seen it.

This time, however, he noticed a strange, ghostly shadow drifting slowly across the more tightly packed fragments surrounding the center of the formation. Jamie climbed to his feet, as if that extra elevation would help him better see what was happening hundreds of thousands of miles away.

"Do you see that?" he said, pointing, even though he knew it was a meaningless gesture when dealing with such vast distances.

Alaida squinted at the moon. "What?"

Jamie came along side her and explained what he was seeing until Alaida gasped and said, "Oh yes, I see it now! That is one of the Little Sisters! Your eyes must be very sharp indeed to have seen it."

"Little Sisters? Do you mean, like, small moons?"

"Something like that, I believe," Alaida said, unable to take her eyes away from the sight. "Scholars say there are seven of them in total but they can never all be seen at once. When I was very young, I remember all of Tavnic turning out into the streets and extinguishing all the lights in the village just to catch a glimpse of three of the Sisters at once. They said that it was an event which would likely not be repeated in our lifetimes."

"Seven tiny moons," Jamie mused. The shadowy form continued drifting along its path. It wasn't spherical but it wasn't jagged like the fragments of the scattered moon either. Instead, it was somewhat oblong, its edges marred and lumpy. To Jamie it looked something like a sprouted potato floating through space. "So, what do you call all the little pieces of the big moon?"

"All of them together are just called Luna. The scholars have names for the larger ones, but most people do not bother with them. You told me once that your world only has a single large moon? That would be so very strange -- Oh, look! She's spreading her wings!"

Jamie didn't need Alaida to point out what she had seen. On either side of the Little Sister, a tiny point of light sprang into existence, shimmering at first but then blazing forth brightly. He stared, unable to wrap his head around what he was seeing. After a moment, he ran over to the titan-mecha and took up the long rifle from where he'd propped it up against one of the machine's arms. He brought the scope to his eye and located the Little Sister before twisting the magnification dial all the way to its maximum.

"Quickly, make a wish, before her wings disappear," Alaida said. "If you do so, it will surely come true."

Making a wish, however, was the last thing on Jamie's mind. That 'Little Sister' wasn't a moon at all, at least not a natural one. It was a man-made satellite, and its wings were a pair of solar arrays reflecting the sun back down to Terrarhea's night side. To be visible to the naked eye at such a distance, it had to be huge.

"Alaida, here, take a look." Jamie offered her the rifle. "It's some kind of space station."

Her eyes grew wide and she put up both of her hands with a gasp. "It is against the law for a Slave to touch a wardcaster that could be used as a weapon."

Jamie glanced around at the darkened hills. "I don't think anyone's going to turn you in."

But then, it was such a heavy weapon, even if she did take it, she probably wouldn't be able to hold it up. Instead, Jamie set it on the ground and released the catch which held the scope in place. Even that one piece was as long as his forearm, but it was still much more manageable than the whole rifle. Alaida looked at it skeptically for a moment before finally taking it in hand and raising it to her eye. She made a curious sort of noise but didn't seem overly impressed by the revelation that one of her Little Sisters wasn't actually a supernatural deity.

The light of its "wings" grew more intense until it reached its peak and then began to dim, just like its appearance, only in reverse. This time, Jamie could understand that the fading was caused by the rotation of the satellite on its axis. When they blinked out completely, the Little Sister became nothing more that a dark shadow drifting in front of Luna once more. Only the faintest reflection of light along its sunward side betrayed its existence at all. Without Jamie's incredible vision or a telescope, most people probably wouldn't be able to see even that.

Was it magesmith in design, like everything else on Terrarhea, or had it been placed there by those others who Terrarhea had closed themselves to long ago? Or maybe it hadn't been made by human hands at all but by some other intelligence entirely. Unfortunately, Jamie could only come to the conclusion that none of that mattered. The solar panels should have been facing the sun at all times, not spinning erratically. It must have been abandoned, maybe for hundreds, if not thousands of years.

Alaida dropped the rifle scope from her eye, still gazing up into the sky. "Did you make a wish?"

"Yeah," Jamie said, just as absorbed in the shadowy form of the Little Sister as Alaida was. At the very last moment before the wings had vanished, Jamie had indeed been able to formulate a hasty appeal to whatever power it was that typically ignored such requests, despite what the more logical parts of his brain told him. "I wished I could go back home for good and bring you with me."

"You...?" Alaida handed the scope back to Jamie and retrieved her blanket from the rug where she left it. "You are not supposed to tell anyone what you wished for," Alaida said in a small voice, wrapping the blanket around herself tightly. "Otherwise, it will never come true."

"Alaida, do you know what a space colony is?"

Alaida shook her head.

"It's like...a whole country with farms and cities and factories, all sealed up inside a giant metal can, floating in space. That's what we saw; not a moon, a space station!"

"I did not know that made a difference."

"But --" Jamie cut himself off. Did it really matter if it was a derelict space colony instead of a naturally occurring rock? He already knew that there were people out there beyond this world, or at least there had been at one time, so this revelation didn't really provide him with any new information. Without a rocket ship, either a moon or a space station were as equally far out of reach as Earth was. "Okay, you're right. It doesn't make a difference." Jamie sat down on the log once more. After a moment, Alaida joined him. "Have you ever had any of your wishes come true?" he said.

"No..." Alaida said, but then with a smile, added, "Not yet."

CHAPTER 37

Alaida spent the night laid out on the rug before the fire, bundled in several blankets and sleeping soundly. Not feeling the least bit tired himself, Jamie kept watch while making sure the fire never got too low and also tending to the drying strips of meat. For a time, he considered retrieving the satchel of papers from the titan-mecha to look at them and the strange scrap of metal once more. Alaida had pointed it out to him earlier so he knew right where they were. The more he thought about it, however, the more he began to wonder if touching the shard might somehow hasten his departure from Terrarhea, and at the moment, that was the last thing he wanted.

Thus left with nothing to occupy his thoughts but second guessing his decision to waste time by camping at the river, he'd figured it would be a long wait for dawn, but the time actually flew by. In fact, when the sky first began to brighten in the east, he actually wondered if he'd somehow drifted off to sleep even with Reaver's superhuman constitution.

However, he could trace his thoughts back in an almost unbroken line to the time Alaida first fell asleep. He'd still been perfectly aware of what was happening around him all night, but on another level, it was like his thoughts had down-shifted into an almost dream-like state. Maybe that was all the sleep Reaver's body needed. It would explain how he could pilot a titan-mecha for days on end without stop. And it certainly left Jamie feeling refreshed, rather like a good night's sleep, but without any of the grogginess upon awakening.

Alaida first stirred when the sky had taken on a uniform shade of deep blue but before the sun had climbed high enough to be seen above the hills. She sat up in her blankets, stretching and yawning, her eyes still veiled with sleep.

"Good morning," Jamie said.

At the sound of his voice, Alaida's whole body tensed and her eyes shot open wide as her head whipped around in Jamie's direction.

"Whoa, don't worry," he said, holding up his hands. "It's still me."

She let out her breath, relaxing beneath her blankets. "My apologies. For a moment, I completely forgot where I was. I have not slept that well in a long time."

"Then I guess it was a good thing we stopped for the night. You obviously needed it."

"I do appreciate your thoughtfulness." Alaida climbed to her feet, and keeping the blankets wrapped around her shoulders, she held her hands in front of the fire. "Do we have time for breakfast, or shall I start breaking camp?"

"I do want to get moving again, but I think we have time for breakfast first. So, what's on the menu?" Jamie said, already knowing the answer. "Eggs? Toast? Sausage?"

"Stew," Alaida said with a smile. She uncovered the soup pot and gave it a stir. They'd left it at the edge of the fire all night to keep it warm, and in that time, the meatballs and potatoes had all but broken apart, turning the leftovers into a thick porridge. It still smelled good, and Jamie had no doubt it would probably taste even better than it had the night before now the flavors had been given time to mix, but the look of it alone was enough to make him glad he didn't need to eat any of it.

Alaida excused herself to tend to her morning needs in the seclusion of a nearby thicket while Jamie began packing up everything they would no longer need before departing. The river drifted by their campsite glassy smooth that morning and birds had started chirping excitedly in the trees beyond the riverbanks. However, those same trees harbored deep shadows in the predawn light and Jamie was once again overcome by the feeling of being exposed and vulnerable, as if someone was watching him from those same shadows.

When Alaida returned, now wide awake, Jamie handed her a bowl of stew while he began packing away the strips of dried meat in a waterproof, canvas sack under Alaida's instruction. Rising several times from her seat, she clearly would have preferred to do it herself, either out of a desire for perfection, or a simple continued sense of servitude. In either case, Jamie wouldn't let her.

"It doesn't look like much now, does it?" Jamie said as he snapped one of the twigs in order to get the meat off. As it had dried, it had shrunken considerably, making it almost impossible to remove without breaking the twigs.

"With care, it will still be enough to last a few days." Seeing Jamie suddenly glance into the trees, Alaida froze and followed his gaze. "What is it?"

"I thought I heard something," Jamie said, focusing entirely on the dense vegetation growing at the top of the steep riverbanks. He wasn't sure what it had been, or even if it had been a sound at all. Maybe it had just his own imagination getting the better of him. He certainly couldn't see anything. "Probably just an animal."

Alaida stood, half-finished bowl of stew in hand, and watched the trees as well. "I do not see --"

But then they both saw it: Wolf-Slaves. They burst through the underbrush and leapt straight down the high embankment to the pebble-strewn beach. Snarling and barking, there had to be at least a dozen of them, all charging toward Jamie and Alaida. And out in front of the others ran one who's jaw hung crooked and another whose body was covered with bright red splotches of exposed skin where his fur had been burned away not too long ago. Jamie knew them. He was the one who'd given them those distinctive features and he had hoped never to see them again, yet here they were, miles and miles away from where he'd last encountered them.

"Alaida, get back!" Jamie cried, pushing her behind him and spilling her bowl of stew to the ground as they scuttled away, putting their backs to the titan. There was no way he'd be able to bring that machine online in time to deal with this threat. He'd have to use his own two hands, just like the first time. Except he now had Alaida to defend as well.

This is why Reaver had never allowed any time for idle breaks like the one Jamie and Alaida had foolishly enjoyed here; not out of a maliciousness for Alaida's comfort or even an obsessive desire to reach his destination, but because he knew the Wolf-Slaves were still following him. Jamie cursed himself. Why did he keep making these mistakes? Why couldn't he be more like Reaver?

As the Wolf-Slaves closed with their prey, Singed-Fur and Broken-Jaw drew up short, letting their comrades go on ahead. Jamie bared his teeth at the sight of it. This was just like that night at the stream, those two making the others do their dirty work for them while they stayed well out of harm's way.

"Alaida, keep back," Jamie said as he advanced to meet the first of the Wolf-Slaves. No different than before, they threw themselves at him like wild animals, snapping with glistening teeth and raking the air with their claws. Without Reaver's senses or his reflexes, Jamie would have been torn apart before being able to throw a single punch, but he dodged their best opening attacks with ease and retaliated before they even knew what was happening. He pushed one aside and it rebounded off the titan's giant metal foot with a loud clang and a pained howl. Another he shoved in the opposite direction where it tripped in the loose shore pebbles and fell across the campfire, avoiding the flames but knocking aside the stew pot and all the dried meat.

Another step forward brought Jamie face-to-face with his second wave of foes. The first he caught with a fist to the stomach which sent it crumpling to the ground. But that is where his luck ended. One of the other Wolf-Slaves managed to hook its claws into Jamie's poncho and pull him off balance, turning his latest punch into nothing more than a glancing blow. More of the Wolf-Slaves swarmed over him, biting and clawing at any part of him they could find. As soon as he threw one off, another would instantly take its place.

Jamie growled and pushed himself backward with all his strength. At least two of the Wolf-Slaves were slammed between his body and the side of the titan-mecha. Their grips went slack, and Jamie used the opening to twist away from the others. He would have turned on them again if not for Alaida's shrill cry. She cringed not far away in one of the gaps between the titan's massive arms, a Wolf-Slave having seized her by the arm and trying to pull her into the open.

Jamie lunged forward and grabbed her attacker from behind, lifting it off the ground and throwing it bodily at its comrades who where already nipping at Jamie's heels. They went down in a heap as Jamie put himself once more between them and Alaida. This was hopeless. He'd been trying not to hurt them too badly, but unless he started putting them down hard, they would just keep coming. As much as he might have benefited from being more like Reaver, he couldn't let himself become that much like him. He'd already gone much too far down that road and he wished to go no farther.

As the Wolf-Slaves regrouped for what might very well be their last assault, Jamie readied himself for the worst. They couldn't hurt him, but they could do terrible things to Alaida. If it came to that, he'd just have to take her in his arms and run for it, completely abandoning the titan where it stood, along with all their supplies. But these Wolf-Slaves were fast, and they could cover as much ground as a swiftly moving titan-mecha. Would Jamie even be able to outrun them?

Just as the Wolf-Slaves began to move en masse, a streak of orange flashed through the corner of Jamie's eye and a shape dropped from the top of the titan into the gap between him and the Wolf-Slaves. Anticipating some new threat, Jamie tensed as Alaida's grip tightened on his arm.

However, this wasn't another Wolf-Slave, it was a slender young man -- a boy really -- with a head of unruly reddish hair, a bright orange bandana tied around his neck, and pair of dark goggles over his eyes. He wore a pair of weathered hiking boots on his feet, padded suspenders over a dingy beige shirt, and baggy cargo pants that had been cut off below the knees. From his back hung a leather satchel, brightly decorated with beads and dangling bits of knotted thread and feathers. The folded stock of a carbine protruded from one side and the handle of a machete from the other. His gloved hands remained empty, however, as he faced off against the enraged Wolf-Slaves.

"Beat it," he said to them, his stance relaxed but firm as he pointed with his thumb downriver. "You're not supposed to be here."

Strangely, the Wolf-Slaves froze in their tracks. Some of them looked to their comrades for support and a few even took a step back. At that, the two leaders finally stepped forward, Broken-Jaw pushing his way to the front. His fangs were bared and his eyes mad with rage as he pointed a hooked claw at Jamie. "Betrayer!"

"Seriously?" The young man shook his head, causing his shaggy hair to sway back and forth as he again addressed the Wolf-Slaves. "You guys just don't know how to take 'no' for an answer, do you?"

"He dies now!"

Broken-Jaw lunged past the young man, heading straight for his nemesis. Jamie barely had time to flinch before the Wolf-Slave fell to the ground alongside its own severed head. Tearing his eyes away from the body laying at his feet, Jamie looked up to see that the young man had drawn his machete, a long, heavy thing with a kukri blade that now dripped with blood. Jamie had barely even seen him move, let alone dispatch the Wolf-Slave.

The young man stepped toward the Wolf-Slaves, arms spread and machete held in one hand with a casual flair. "Anyone else?"

The Wolf-Slaves practically fell over themselves retreating off the beach, scrambling up the steep bank in clouds of dust, and disappearing into the trees beyond. The young man watched them go and then let out a self-satisfied chuckle before flicking the blood from his blade and wiping it clean on the body of the fallen Wolf-Slave. Sheathing it in a fluid motion, he rose up and smiled with a toothy grin as he offered his hand to Jamie.

"Hi there, name's Medraut," he said. Though his eyes were obscured by the tinted lens of his goggles, they still sparkled cheerfully beneath.

Alaida remained behind Jamie, her fingernails digging into his arm as Jamie stared at this strange newcomer. He had to be around Jamie's age, but he was nearly a full head shorter and his relaxed stance seemed completely at odds with what they had just seen him do.

Finally withdrawing his hand when he realized Jamie wasn't going to shake it, Medraut said in no less jovial tones, "So what are you doing out here? This is a long way from civilization. It's awfully lucky I happened upon you when I did."

"Um, we're traveling," Jamie said, struggling to even say that. mechanically, he pointed upriver. "How did you...?"

"Oh, I heard the commotion from out on the road. Looks like I got here just in time."

"There's a road?" Jamie glanced back to Alaida, but she looked nearly as puzzled as he felt.

"Yeah, the Cavadanian Road. It's just over that ridge there. Not much of a road in these parts, more like a trail, but it's the best way through the wilds out here. I saw tracks from your titan a ways back. I'm actually really glad I caught up with you. I was hoping I might be able to bum a ride."

"You...huh?"

"I thought you might be able to give me a lift?" Medraut clarified. "It looks like we're headed in the same direction. I don't usually like riding on titans, but with all those Wolf-Slaves out there, I figured it would be easier than traveling on foot."

"Are there a lot of Wolf-Slaves out there?" Jamie said.

"Oh yeah!" Medraut said with a laugh. "I nearly walked right into a whole pack of them just this morning."

"You did?" Finally regaining some small degree of his composure, Jamie scanned the hills for more signs of the creatures. "What are you even doing out here? And how did you scare off those Wolf-Slaves like you did?"

"Ah, they're not so tough if you know how to stand up to them," Medraut said, wandering over to the remains of the ruined campfire. Only now remembering that the dismembered body of the Wolf-Slave still lay at his feet, Jamie inched away from the titan. Alaida remained close behind every step he took. Medraut had stooped down near the overturned pot and dipped his gloved fingertips into the spilled stew. "That's not bad," he said after licking his fingers clean. "My compliments to the chef."

"Th-thank you," Alaida whispered reflexively.

"As to why I'm out here, I'm just passing through, same as you," Medraut said. Spying one of the dried strips of meat laying on the ground, he snatched it up and popped that into his mouth as well. "Oh, I love Jackelope jerky! You see, I'm heading to a job out west. No rest for the wicked, am I right?"

"A job?" Jamie said, no longer surprised that a Terrarhean this young would already have a career. "What do you do?"

"I'm a tracker and wilderness scout by trade but me and some friends of mine are headed for Ikourria to sign-up for the war. I just needed to take care of a few things down south before I headed out so... What do you say, can I get a ride? I'll help pull my weight. I can hunt, I'm a great cook, and I can even sing."

"I don't think we...I mean, we appreciate what you did, but we usually travel alone. Besides, it would probably be safer for you on your own."

"Are you talking about the Wolf-Slaves? Yeah, they seem to have it in for you good. What did you do to piss them off so bad?"

"Well, um, I don't really know. They've been following us for a while now. I think they kind of have me confused with someone else. So, you see --"

"Don't worry, I can help you out with that too," Medraut said. "I know how they think, and I have more than a few tricks we can use to lose them. Plus, with this titan-mecha, it'll make things a hundred times easier. So how about it?"

He certainly seemed confident, and if what they'd seen of his abilities so far was any indication, he was also quite capable, if not a little dangerous as well. Jamie turned to Alaida with a questioning expression. She said nothing in reply but did shake her head in objection, so faintly it was barely a movement at all. Jamie understood how she felt, but this might have been too good an opportunity to pass up.

"Do you know much about this area?" Jamie said, turning back to Medraut. "We're kind of looking for someone who lives upriver from here. Someone named...Ommto?"

Medraut shrugged and waggled his head back and forth. "I've passed through a few times, but I mostly stick to the Cavadanian road. It follows the river pretty close through this area, but they go their separate ways near where the river comes out of the mountains. I think there might be an old estate out there somewhere north of the road. I've never been there, though, and I wouldn't know who lives there either. But then, unless this fellow you're looking for is a hermit, there aren't many people at all living out in these parts."

Jamie had to fight down a giddy smile. Onorah had said something about Major Ommto having retired to his family estate. It all sounded too perfect. "How far away is it?"

Medraut pursed his lips and looked into the sky as he considered the question. "Two days? Eh, we could probably be there by noon tomorrow."

That strange sense of something pulling at Jamie's subconscious was far from an exact gauge, but if he wanted to see with his own eyes what it was Reaver was searching for, this would be cutting it close.

"Okay. We'll give you a lift, at least as far as that estate."

"Excellent!" Medraut again offered Jamie his hand. This time, Jamie promptly shook it. Alaida meanwhile clutched Jamie's arm even more tightly. "You won't regret this! I can tell already, we're gonna be good friends."

"If you can lose these Wolf-Slaves and get us to that estate, I wouldn't doubt it. My name's Jamie. This is Alaida."

"Nice to meet you. Now, let me help you clean up this mess!" Medraut sprang into action, picking up the dried pieces of meat and stuffing them into the sack as Jamie had started.

"Jamie, a word?" Alaida whispered, gently easing Jamie away from the young tracker. Once they were out of earshot, she said, "I do not think this is a good idea. Something about him unsettles me."

"He is a little...energetic." Jamie stole a glance at Medraut as the young man continued picking up the scattered remains of their camp. "And I don't know how far we can really trust him, but he did just save our lives and he seems to know what he's talking about. If he can help us, would that really be such a bad thing?"

"Perhaps not..." Alaida leaned over to look around Jamie just as Medraut glanced in their direction. He flashed her a wide grin and Alaida quickly drew back out of sight. She frowned.

"At most, it's only two days," Jamie said.

Alaida took a deep breath and set her shoulders firmly. "Let us hope it is less."

CHAPTER 38

Now in cautious agreement of their new companion, Jamie and Alaida rejoined Medraut at the remains of their campfire. He had already extinguished the flames and salvaged what little of the stew hadn't spilled out of the pot during the fight. Alaida tried her best to not keep skulking into Jamie's protective shadow but was only partly successful.

"This looks like everything," Medraut said, retrieving Alaida's dropped bowl as well. "It seems a shame to waste the last of that stew, but we probably shouldn't stick around here any longer than we already have."

"There is not much left," Alaida said, her voice submissive and her eyes fixed on the ground, "Perhaps we can bring it with us and clean the pot and bowls later." Jamie clenched his jaw. Back in Tavnic, they had talked about the need for Alaida to play the part of being Jamie's slave in the presence of others but he'd never given much thought to what that would actually look like until now.

"An excellent idea, *Lady Raven-Slave!*" Medraut said.

Jamie couldn't quite tell if his words had been meant in jest or in mockery. Regardless, to hear Alaida addressed in such an impersonal and dismissive manner suddenly gave him a little more empathy for Alaida's concerns about this young man.

"Her name's Alaida," Jamie said, perhaps a bit more sharply than he had intended. Alaida glanced in Jamie's direction but then quickly averted her eyes again.

"Huh? Yeah, of course," Medraut said, apparently having missed Jamie's tone. "Having a titan to carry all our gear is going to be quite a change for me. I'm used to carrying everything I need on my back. Shall we load up?"

"Yeah..." Jamie said. He still hoped this was a good idea. "Alaida, you know where to put everything?"

She nodded. "Yes, but..." she fumbled over her words, likely unsure if she should have tacked a 'master' onto that statement. In the end, she sidestepped it entirely, saying, "Your rifle..."

"Oh, um, right," Jamie said. The weapon was still propped against the side of the titan-mecha. Apart from their cooking supplies, that was the last piece of gear that still needed to be stowed away. However, it was clearly too long to fit into the titan's hold the way it was right now. It had to be able to be broken down for storage, but Jamie had no idea how to do that. Even if Alaida knew how from having seen Reaver do it, a mindful slave wouldn't be able to touch it herself with Medraut around. Maybe pretending that Alaida was still Jamie's slave wouldn't be so easy to pull off after all.

As Alaida went to raise the storage pod and reconfigure it from a ladder into a rumble seat once more, she paused briefly by Jamie's side and whispered, "There are brackets in the cockpit to hold it. The barrel will stick out the top."

"Thanks," Jamie whispered back.

He did find the brackets Alaida had mentioned but his first try to fit the rifle into them resulted in the weapon falling right back out again when he gave it a tug. Medraut looked down from above, his outstretched arms hanging from the roll cage as his head and shoulders dangled limply. "Need a hand with that?"

His tone had been friendly enough, but it raised Jamie's hackles, nonetheless. "No, I've got it. Sometimes, it's just a little tricky."

"Okay." Medraut shrugged and kept watching.

Jamie tried to keep his groan as quiet as possible. His next attempt to fit the rifle into place didn't work either but at least he finally realized what he was doing wrong.

"The latch isn't -- " Medraut began to say but Jamie cut him off short.

"Yes, I see it," he said, just as he snapped the rifle into place with a satisfying click. This time, giving it a solid tug didn't cause it to so much as wiggle within the restraints. At least that was taken care of. "Are we ready?"

"Yes, I believe so," Alaida said from above, her voice remaining guarded.

Jamie took one last look across the pebbly beach. It suddenly looked rather barren without their meager little camp. Yesterday, when he'd first seen the titan parked on that very spot, it had seemed like an act of colonization. Now, the exact same sight looked bleak and desolate. The sense of foreboding wasn't helped by the body of the dead Wolf-Slave still laying where it had fallen.

"Shouldn't we bury him?" Jamie said.

"Nah," Medraut called down from above, "they always come back for their own. Then, with a laugh he pointed to the trees beyond the riverbank. "Now let's hit the road!"

"Okay, hold on tight," Jamie said. He climbed into the pilot's seat, the contours of the multi-segmented seat fitting his body just as well as he remembered. The machine also came to life just as easily as it had the last time. In hardly any time at all, the hatches had closed below him and he was looking out through the roll cage at the shadows of the eastern hills quickly retreating across the landscape toward the rising sun. While Alaida braced herself in the corner of the rumble seat as Jamie brought the titan-mecha to its feet, Medraut stood and held on tight to the roll cage.

The steep riverbank at the edge of the beach proved to be nearly as tall as the titan-mecha but Medraut pointed out a low spot that wasn't too difficult for the machine to climb. The trees above, however, were tightly spaced and Jamie had no choice but to knock down a path through them to make any progress.

As he did so, branches snapped back against the roll cage, causing Alaida to recoil first one way and then quickly the other. Medraut remained standing the whole time, dodging when needed but largely un-phased by the chaos surrounding them. Jamie began to fear their progress might be slowed to a standstill, but as the ground rose away from the river, the trees became larger and less tightly packed. Once they crested the ridge which paralleled the river, Medraut pointed straight ahead.

"That's the road there," he said.

Jamie had to look twice before he saw what Medraut was talking about. It really was little more than a trail, just a dirt path winding its way through the trees. If they'd been in a hurry, they probably would have passed it by without even noticing. As things were, it was barely even wide enough to accommodate the titan-mecha. However, the number of large branches that had been purposefully snapped off high above the ground did suggest that others with titan-mechas had made this same trip before.

"Just hang a right and follow the road," Medraut said. "We should be able to make pretty good time from here but if you find yourself in Heigelries, you'll know you've gone too far." Yawning, he tossed his pack to the floor of the passenger compartment and flopped back on the rumble seat. Alaida shifted all the way over to the far side, looking like she might have kept going farther if she hadn't run into the side bulkhead.

"What about the Wolf-Slaves?" Jamie said.

Stretching out his legs and crossing his arms, Medraut closed his eyes and settled back into the seat. "Give it an hour or two, then I'll work my magic."

The main reason Jamie had agreed to let Medraut come with them was to help avoid the Wolf-Slaves. So far all he'd done was point them in the same direction they would have been heading anyway. And now it looked like he was going to take a nap.

Seeing that Alaida was still holding on tight to the side of the passenger compartment, Jamie set the titan-mecha into motion again with a particularly violent first step which threw Medraut right out of his seat. Before sliding down onto the floor, the young tracker managed to grab hold of the edge just in time.

"Sorry about that," Jamie said over his shoulder. "Sometimes it's a little rough getting started."

Now looking wide awake, Medraut laughed with genuine mirth. "No worries! That's why I usually prefer my own two feet."

Once they did get underway, Medraut quickly fell asleep, despite Jamie's initial attempt to prevent him from doing so. The more Jamie thought about it, the more he regretted having done so. From the sounds of it, Medraut had been traveling through the night, dodging Wolf-Slaves the whole time. Jamie would have been remiss if he'd forced anyone to continue facing that by themselves, even if they didn't have any services to offer in exchange for a ride. If Medraut was tired, let him sleep. Alaida kept a wary eye on him, though, still holding tight to her side of the passenger compartment.

The terrain they crossed that morning was much more rugged than the land around Tavnic had been. The Cavadanian Road snaked down hillsides and crossed through wide valleys. In some places, it was just a lightly trampled path through a field of wild grasses. In others, it climbed switchbacks cut into the sides of rocky hills. After only an hour on the road, Jamie had all but stopped being impressed by each new vista that presented itself with the cresting of a ridge or the opening of a clearing.

Even if they'd wanted to stop and appreciate any of those natural wonders, they couldn't afford to. There were still Wolf-Slaves on their trail and so Jamie kept their pace brisk. At times, he would hear Alaida make some startled gasp when they rounded a bend in the trail on their way down a steep incline, but she never spoke, either to question Jamie's skill or to make small talk. Jamie himself wasn't in much of a mood for conversation anyway. The hills looked deserted, but then they had right before the Wolf-Slaves had attacked too.

True to his word, about two hours into their journey, Medraut sat up in his seat, stretching and yawning loudly.

"Yeah, this doesn't look too bad," he said, standing at the side of the roll cage. "I'm gonna take a look around on foot. Just keep following the trail and I'll meet up with you in a couple of miles."

Jamie turned in his seat to ask what Medraut was talking about just in time to see him vault over the side of the still-moving titan-mecha. Images raced through Jamie's mind of the young tracker being swept out of the air by one of the titan's arms or pulverized beneath its feet. The machine skidded to an abrupt stop and twisted away from what seemed certain to be Medraut's mangled body. Instead, Medraut stood unscathed on the ground several paces removed from the titan's path, laughing.

"Hey, how about a warning next time. You almost took my head off stopping like that!" He ducked and made a comical chopping motion through the air just above his head. Waving and smiling, he dashed up the side of a rocky slope sparsely covered with thorny shrubs. "See ya in a bit!"

Jamie watched him vanish from sight and then turned to Alaida. "Did you see that? He could have killed himself."

Alaida was staring, as well, with mouth agape. "No rational human would ever act in such a manner," she said. "Clearly, he must be insane. Do you still think it was a good idea to trust him?"

Hearing Alaida's reaction suddenly made Jamie's own concern seem tame by comparison. "I don't think he's crazy. I think he's just really good at what he does. Haven't you ever seen acrobats or stuntmen who could do things like that?"

Alaida did not look convinced. Spying the satchel which Medraut had left behind, she shot out of her seat and kneeled down in front of it, hastily pulling open the straps.

"Alaida, what are you doing?" Clearly, in some things, she was more assertive than in others. "You can't just go through his things like that!"

"We do not know anything about him," Alaida replied as she tore back the top flap. Inside were just a few camping supplies, some spare magazines for his weapon, and a small sack of dried meat. "It...it could have been a bomb," Alida said, going through the bag's contents a second time, as if disappointed that it didn't contain anything more sinister.

"Are you satisfied now?"

Alaida gave Medraut's possessions one last look and then shoved them back into the satchel and cinched the straps down with all her strength. Thinking better of it, she then loosened them slightly and arranged the pack once more in the corner of the passenger compartment just as Medraut had left it.

"Now that you've got that out of the way, can we get moving again?"

Alaida dropped heavily into the rumble seat and crossed her arms. "I will not apologize for what I did."

"I didn't say you should." Shaking his head, Jamie turned back to the road ahead. "You were concerned, I get it. But now you can see he's got nothing to hide, right?"

"I would not go so far as to say, 'nothing'."

Apparently, it wasn't just the humans on Terrarhea who were intolerant of others. Jamie sighed as he put the titan-mecha in motion once more. If they didn't get moving soon, Medraut would be left wondering what had become of them. "I'll admit he's a little strange, but is he really *that* bad?"

Alaida sat silently, staring straight ahead. Finally, she shook her head. "It is not something that I can put into words. He simply...unnerves me."

"Can you at least try not to act so weird around him all the time? I don't want him intentionally getting us lost just because he thinks we're a couple of jerks."

"How can you know he has not already led us astray?"

"This road does have a lot of twists and turns but we're still headed west," Jamie said. How exactly he knew that, he wasn't sure, but something inside him told him with unerring certainty that they were still on course. If only they could tune that sense of direction to point them toward their destination. "Besides, the river is still over there to our right. I've seen it a couple of times already so we can always go back if we really want to."

Alaida looked out through the thick forest that had once again enveloped the trail. The river was out of sight at the moment, but it wasn't long until Jamie caught a glint of sunlight sparkling off of water through the foliage and pointed it out to Alaida. A moment later, as the titan powered up the side of a hill, the trees opened around them, providing a panoramic view of the valley beyond. They could now see the river quite clearly in the distance, as well as the hundred-foot waterfall where it crashed over the top of a sheer cliff.

"Would you really want to be trying to find a way around that?" Jamie said.

Alaida sat back in her seat with a simple, "Humph."

CHAPTER 39

The land leveled off for some time as they crossed the top of a large hill, but the trail eventually dropped back into another valley. The path down had been cut back into the steep hillside, creating a vertical wall of dirt on their right as high as the titan's shoulder and a sharp drop-off on their left. Things were made even more precarious by several rocky gullies which angled across the path. At the larger ones, the trail had been sculpted down into and back out of them, but the smaller ones looked like little more than washed out sections of the trail.

When Jamie carefully jumped the titan across these nuisances, sometimes the loose dirt underfoot would shift unpredictably and send the machine stumbling. He always managed to recover without serious incident, but by the time they neared the bottom of the hill, his shoulders were tight from the constant care needed to keep the titan on its feet.

He was just about to breath a sigh of relief when he heard a loud thump on the back of the titan and Alaida's sharp cry. He'd heard that before, exactly the same as when the Wolf-Slaves had boarded the titan during their fight at the stream outside of Tavnic.

Jamie turned his head as far as he was able, but instead of a Wolf-Slave, it was only Medraut clinging to the side of the titan's roll cage. Panting and sweating profusely, he laughed as he swung through the bars with the skill of a gymnast and landed on the floor of the passenger compartment. Alaida once more cringed back in her seat, pulling her feet in tight. Since the titan was still in motion and Medraut didn't seem to mind, Jamie didn't bother to stop or even slow down.

"Wow! That was fun!" Medraut said, drawing the end of his neckerchief across his face. "We're really making good time."

The titan had finally reached the bottom of the hill and began following the trail through a stygian glade of dark trees growing in close on either side. In places, the worn earth of the path turned into a rippling washboard where large roots swelled out of the ground and brackish water pooled between. Elsewhere, large boulders and ancient trees stubbornly stood their ground and demanded the travelers go around them.

"So, did you see anything?" Jamie said.

"Oh yeah, you bet I did," Medraut said. "There was a whole pack of Wolf-Slaves out there."

"That close?" Jamie swept his gaze over their surroundings. Alaida let out something of a muffled yelp.

"Don't worry," Medraut said. "They weren't following us. But I left a few surprises for them in case they come this direction."

"What kind of surprises?" Jamie said. "Traps?"

"No, nothing like that," Medraut said with a chuckle. "They hunt mostly by smell, so you'd be surprised how much it throws them off just to spread around a little goplisam blood and some ground pepper root. If we keep moving as fast as we have been, I'll bet they'll be so far off our trail by noon it will take them days to find you again."

"Really?" Jamie said. Maybe Reaver wasn't as skilled as Jamie had thought if he hadn't been able to do in weeks what this young man had just accomplished in a few hours. "It's that easy? They'll really be gone?"

"Well, I wouldn't say it was easy." Medraut dropped into the rumble seat once more, much to Alaida's chagrin. "Not just anyone can do it, but if you know what you're doing, then it's not all *that* difficult."

"How did you learn?"

Medraut laughed. "You know, growing up, I wasn't all that different from those Wolf-Slaves out there. I've been on my own for as long as I can remember, fending for myself, living off the land. I picked up things here and there from the people I met who didn't run me off or try to kill me on sight. But that's civilization for you. Me? I'd rather spend my time out here with those Wolf-Slaves. Them, I can at least understand."

"If they weren't trying to kill me, I could agree with that." Jamie knew their situations weren't the same, but, in some small way, he could definitely relate to Medraut's point of view. "But then it seems like someone's always trying to take a swing at me. I just wish they'd leave us alone."

"Really? I'd'a thought you to be the type who loves a good fight."

Jamie suddenly felt very cold, like when both April and Alaida had compared him to Reaver. "Why would you think that?"

Medraut's smile turned cruel as he considered Jamie for a moment. "The way you handled those Wolf-Slaves back there. A guy like you must be pretty tough."

"Doesn't mean I like to fight," Jamie said in a small voice.

Medraut laughed loudly. "Come on! For a guy who just wants to be left alone, you're packing some pretty heavy firepower here! I bet you could make some serious money out in Ikourria with this titan-mecha of yours. Those little nations are always hurting for armored units. And Ikourria's more desperate that most. You could probably write your own paycheck!"

"Is that why you're going there, just to make some money?" Jamie said, his voice taking on an edge. "If you really like being out here on your own, why get involved in something like that?"

"Do you know anything about Heigelries?"

Only remembering that Onorah had mentioned it being near the Ommto Estate and that Medraut had said something about it being up ahead of them, Jamie shook his head.

"You really have no idea what you're doing, do you!" Medraut's laugh sounded almost spiteful, though his manner still seemed friendly enough. Climbing back to his feet, he swept his arm out to their right. "You see those mountains way out there on the horizon? They run pretty much southwest to northeast along the entire border between Finttiranos and Secotia."

Jamie looked but could barely see anything of the mountains Medraut had pointed to besides the serrated line of the horizon.

"Up ahead and to the south is Heigelries," Medraut continued. "Something like fifty years ago, it used to be an independent kingdom that built some of the best wardcasters in the entire world." He pulled the carbine from his pack and extended the stock. "This is one of theirs. I picked it up out in Meirithan about a year ago. It's nearly seventy-five years old and it can still shoot the wings off a juzza at a hundred yards. That's why Finttiranos decided to invade. The Heigelriesians put up a good fight, but in the end, the Fintties still took it all for themselves, killing anyone who opposed them and forcefully relocating hundreds of thousands."

"That's pretty harsh," Jamie said. Though, from what he had seen of Finttiranos, it wasn't hard to imagine something like that happening. In fact, it sounded a lot like the history of Tavnic.

"These days, they call it the Heigelries Control Zone. I spent some time there as a young lad. There's a lot of good people there, but the whole place is still under martial law and the Fintties keep them all under their thumb. It's pretty grim. And now Secotia is gearing up to do the same thing to Ikourria."

"So, you want to help stop it from happening there."

"Not exactly," Medraut said. "Secotia's been flexing their muscles for years now, trying to get Ikourria to join them willingly, but everyone knows that ain't gonna happen. Ikourria's putting up a brave front and telling their people that if Secotia does invade they're gonna turn it into another Clattemo, but I ain't holding my breath for that either. They're gonna fight to the last man and they're still gonna lose. I mean, Secotia's weapons are a hundred times better than when they invaded Clattemo and that was barely nine years. And even though Clattemo managed to draw their war out for years and years, even they still lost in the end. At the very least, everyone thought Secotia might slow down their plans a bit, but at the moment, people are saying the invasion is gonna happen before autumn."

"So why fight if it's already a lost cause?"

"Me and my friends will cut out before Ikourria falls -- wouldn't want to stick around and be charged with any trumped-up war crimes -- but if this latest war gives me a chance to bloody Secotia's nose before it's all said and done, I'll take it."

"You must really hate them," Jamie said.

"I hate all the Biregeth Alliance Nations!" Medraut twisted his hands around the rifle he still held. "Secotia, Thieradoon, Finttiranos: they're always throwing their weight around; stepping on the little guys and taking whatever they want. I wouldn't even be here in Finttiranos right now if I didn't have to be."

That, Jamie could *definitely* relate to. The titan had finally broken out from under the dark canopy of trees into a wide expanse of marshy ground populated by cattails and a few solitary trees. The titan's feet did not sink it very far, though they still sent up gigantic splashes of water and mud with each step. The sun, which had been brightly shining all morning, had now become muted by a line of dark clouds drifting in from the south.

"Sooner or later, one of the Biregeth Nations is going to gobble up every last one of the little kingdoms and nations still out there." Medraut paused and laughed. "It would have been so much better if they'd just wiped each other out three-hundred years ago rather than signing that stupid non-aggression treaty." Again, he laughed, this time shaking his head before kneeling and returning his weapon to his pack. "Sorry about that, sometimes I can get a little worked up about these things. Hope I didn't offend you at all."

"Um, no," Jamie said. Apparently, this cycle of conquest was a common thing on Terrarhea, the larger nations constantly growing larger and more powerful by forcibly annexing the smaller ones. And why? Just to control everything? "I can't say I feel all that much different, actually."

"I knew there was a reason I liked you guys," Medraut said, clapping Jamie on the back hard enough that it nearly threw off the titan's stride. "So where are you from? You have a really weird accent. Half the time, you sound like a four-year-old."

"You--? What--?" Jamie stammered. Most of the time, he could still understand the things these Terrarheans said, despite the many extra words and odd pronunciations, but he'd never given much thought to what he sounded like to them.

"Oh yeah!" Medraut laughed. "I've heard some Thieradoonian who had such a thick accent they were hard to understand, but at least they didn't sound retarded."

If Medraut hadn't been trying to offend him before, he'd done a pretty good job of it now. Though from that easy-going smile he still wore, it didn't look as if he'd even realized it. "Is it really that bad?" Jamie glanced back to Alaida for some support, but she withered under his gaze and then quickly looked out at the passing scenery.

"Looks like it's gonna rain," Medraut said, lifting his nose to the sky and suddenly quite serious once more. "Probably won't last long but if you have a raincoat, you might want to get it out."

Strapped into the open-air pilot's seat as he was, Jamie didn't think a raincoat would do him much good. After their experience fleeing from Tavnic, it was doubtful how much benefit one would be for Alaida either, but it had to be better than nothing.

"There is a tarp in the hold I can put over the top," Alaida said, tripping over her own words as she watched Medraut out of the corner of her eye.

"Great!" Medraut said. "Let me give you a hand."

Together, the two of them rolled back the cover on the titan's hold and pulled out the tarp which Alaida had mentioned. It had been fitted to perfectly stretch across the top of the roll cage and even had attached straps so that it could be cinched down tight. Jamie brought the titan to a stop at the top of the next hill so that Alaida and Medraut could spread it out and secure it in place without having to contend with the wind. Alaida left the side flaps tied up for the time being so as to not completely close in the back. Once they got underway again, the tarp did flutter a little in the breeze but for the most part remained quite rigid.

Medraut kicked back in the rumble seat once more and laughed. "Wow, I'm gonna get spoiled traveling like this. Usually when it rains, I just get wet."

Though the sky continued to darken the rest of the morning, it did not actually rain. When he wasn't napping, Medraut was almost always talking, going on about all manner of topics, most of which Jamie knew nothing about and could offer little in return except for an occasional nod or noncommittal reply. Alaida remained disturbingly quiet, never once voicing her own opinion on anything. Jamie couldn't quite tell if it was because Medraut seldom addressed her directly, as if it was improper for a slave to take part in a conversation between two freemen, or if she was still that unnerved by the tracker's presence. But then Medraut didn't seem to care whether either of them said much of anything. After being out in the wilderness for so long on his own, he was apparently just happy to have someone besides himself to talk to for a change.

When Jamie did occasionally ask a question about something that sounded interesting, Medraut was always happy to elaborate -- perhaps a bit too happy, since his tone typically took on a scornful edge when explaining something which he probably thought should have been common knowledge. Regardless, Jamie listened intently to everything the young tracker said, filing away every scrap of information just in case it might help him better understand this world or help prevent him from getting into some new trouble in the future.

Medraut also liked to tell jokes but he quickly discovered that without any context, most of them went right over Jamie's head. He seemed to take that as a challenge, always tossing in a joke or two between his other topics of conversation just to see if he could find one that would make Jamie laugh.

Not long before noon, Medraut set out on another scouting mission, racing through the trees to rejoin the titan some miles farther on. The sky had become so dark by then, with the rumblings of thunder echoing through the hills, it seemed as though Medraut might get caught in the middle of a full-fledged storm. However, he returned before any raindrops had fallen and reported that it did indeed look as if the Wolf-Slaves had lost their trail.

The rain began shortly thereafter, just a few drops at first, but then quickly building to a downpour that instantly turned the dirt trail into a slick ribbon of mud, and slowed their progress considerably. The tarp did a reasonable job of keeping the passengers dry, especially after they pulled down the side flaps, but Medraut still took a moment before they had finished to lean out into the rain and laugh in defiance of nature. Since the tarp didn't keep out all the rain, Alaida disappeared within the folds of the black coat Onorah had given her back in Tavnic. Jamie had it worse than the rest since the tarp stopped just above his head and didn't offer any protection at all when the titan moved at even a restrained pace.

The bulk of the thunder passed far to the south, though they did spy an occasional flash of lighting in the distance when cresting a hill. The heaviest of the rain didn't last long, but even once it passed, they were left to muddle through a constant dribbling shower which helped to dampen things ever further while preventing the trail conditions from improving in the least. Regardless, Medraut continued voicing surprise at how much ground they had already covered and thought that he might need to reconsider his original estimate.

For lunch, Medraut declined any of the leftover stew, leaving that for Alaida alone while he instead munched on more of their jerky. After all the trouble they had gone through to get that, Jamie was a little disappointed to see so much of it go to their guest.

Afterward, he treated his hosts to a song. Jamie cringed at first, unused to normal people singing for entertainment. Medraut's voice wasn't anything all that impressive either, but it was well-suited to the rowdy little song he belted out, and by the second verse, Jamie actually started to laugh at the off-color humor of the lyrics. He even caught Alaida snickering once or twice. This encouraged the tracker to sing a few more songs as well. He only stopped when the rain finally ended, though he didn't seem to be in any danger of running out of material.

They continued traveling the Cavadanian road for the better part of the afternoon. The hills grew ever steeper, with large slabs of bedrock reaching skyward between the trees which grew from the precarious slopes. They crossed wide flood plains where the rivers had scoured clear all large vegetation, leaving only vast fields of wildflowers and waist-high grasses. If they'd been traveling on foot, the numerous rivers they had to ford would have presented a considerable challenge, but as it was, none of the rushing waters even reached higher than the titan's knees. The mountains Medraut had earlier pointed out became more prominent throughout the day but always out of reach, white-capped peaks resolving out of the hazy shapes before slipping away to the north as the titan kept ever westward. A new vista seemed to come into view around every other turn but they never more than paused to take a look, the urgency of the situation driving them onward.

Sightings of the river became less frequent, though Jamie was no longer even sure it was the same one when he did see it. At times, traces of the road became so thin that Jamie was left to wonder for a few steps if he'd lost it entirely, only to see it suddenly become clear again a little farther on. Side trails were rare, but on those occasions when they did present themselves, Medraut always told Jamie to keep following the main path. The sun peeked out between the lingering clouds from time to time, helping to dry Jamie and his passengers, but never with any great warmth. They still rolled back part of the tarp to let in as much light as possible.

When Medraut next left to go scouting, he first had to gently move Alaida's head away from where it had unintentionally come to rest on his shoulder as she dozed. As he leapt from the side of the titan, Alaida sat up and looked around groggily. Jamie felt it best not to point out what had just happened and kept moving forward without a word spoken. The monotony of the journey was starting to wear on them all. Even Medraut hadn't so much as told a single joke for the last hour or so.

At some point while Medraut was away, Jamie started tapping his fingers against the switches on the control pucks, producing a tiny click as he touched each one in turn. He hadn't even been aware of what he was doing until Alaida unexpectedly barked at him to stop, please. The two of them rode on in an even deeper silence after that. Being well into summer, the sun wouldn't be setting for quite some time yet but it still felt like they were running out of time. No one had ever claimed this would be a quick journey, but it was starting to become rather boring.

Just as Jamie began to wonder if they'd missed their latest rendezvous with Medraut, the young tracker dropped out of a tree and landed on the side of the titan's cockpit with a thump. Jamie didn't even have time for alarm before Medraut began speaking in a flurry. "Hey, you're not gonna believe this, but we've been making really good time! The trail to that estate you're looking for is just up ahead! If we keep going at this rate, we might even make it there before dark!"

"Are you serious?" Completely forgetting his earlier shock, Jamie sat up a little higher in his seat.

Even Alaida climbed to her feet and took a step forward so she could hear better. "Already?"

It was still possible this might not be the estate they were looking for. It might yet take days to get there and by then Jamie would be back on Earth, dealing with the likes of April and Seth. "How much farther?" Jamie said, trying hard not to sound too excited.

"I don't really know," Medraut said, all trace of the afternoon's melancholy gone and again smiling just as broadly as when they'd first met that morning. "I've never been there before. Should we find out?"

"Definitely!" Jamie said, picking up the titan's pace. They were now flying down a gallery of thin-trunked trees lining each side of the path where it ran along the top of a ridge. "So, where's this turn?"

Still holding onto the outside of the roll cage alongside Jamie, Medraut pointed past the nose of the titan. "There!"

"I see it!" Jamie said, his smile growing wider. He took the turn a little faster than he had intended, the titan's feet slipping in the still wet dirt, but he recovered without losing more than a moment, redirecting the machine into a long series of bounds down the side trail. It didn't look any better maintained than the road they had just left but that still made it better than any of the side trails they'd seen all day long. The trees remained thick along the trail, but they were definitely smaller, as if someone had at least been trying to keep them in check. Each step they took made Jamie's nerves buzz ever more keenly. If there was anyone living out here who could give him some answers, he had to be at the end of this trail.

Alaida stood at the front of the passenger compartment, holding on tightly to the roll cage as her black hair streamed out behind her. Still she said nothing, but Jamie could tell from her stance that she too was excited to find out what awaited them. Medraut remained clinging to the outside of the titan, laughing like a maniac as he hung on for dear life through every shuddering step the titan took.

With the close growth of trees, they couldn't see much of what lay ahead as they dropped down the side of the ridge and crossed a narrow valley. The ridge on the other side rose sharply in a series of switchbacks which Jamie maneuvered through as fast as he could. At the top, the land leveled off considerably and the trees became even more thin. Just ahead, Jamie could see an open patch of afternoon sun. He coaxed the titan to its limit. They broke through the last few trees blocking their view and then skidded to a stop, all three of them staring at the sight ahead. Medraut stood up, holding onto the roll cage with just one hand while Alaida pressed as far forward as the passenger compartment would allow.

Off to their right, a spur of the distant mountain range had suddenly come very close indeed, still far off but looking at least close enough that one could reach out and touch its jagged slopes. Spilling out from these in ever decreasing elevations, came countless foothills which started just as jagged and imposing as the mountains behind them, but turning more soft and rounded until they blended almost seamlessly with the hills the titan had been traveling through all day. Directly in front of the travelers, the land turned into a vast rolling prairie that dipped down from their vantage point atop the ridgeline and then swelled higher some miles away where it crashed into the most striking feature of them all.

Sitting there in that prairie, jutting out from the foothills on their right, stood an enormous, solitary, flat-topped hill. Its sides where nearly vertical and made from many eroded layers of rock. The whole thing looked something like a erratically stacked pile of mismatched plates. The top of the hill was vast and covered with dark trees even bigger perhaps than the largest specimens Jamie had yet seen on Terrarhea. Toward the center of that jungle, rose a thin, rocky spire, which sported its own lush covering of clinging vegetation. Its pointed tip had to rise several hundred feet above the tops of the trees surrounding it. Off to the north, the side of the hill fell away even more suddenly than on the other three sides, dropping down into a steep-sided bowl with a crystal blue lake at the bottom, fed by a thin waterfall flowing out of the foothills beyond.

"Look," Alaida said, the first of them to break the silence. "There are buildings amongst the trees."

Jamie had been so overwhelmed by the overall sight of it all, he hadn't yet had time to consider the finer details. Now that he took a closer look, he could indeed see what Alaida was talking about. The straight outlines of manmade structures could be seen, randomly spaced around the top of the hill. Jamie thought he could even make out what might have been a building, or maybe just the remains of a building, on the side of the central spire. If the whole top of the hill hosted such buildings, there easily could have been a fair-sized city over there. However, something about it didn't seem quite right.

"Is this the place?" Jamie said, unable to take his eyes away.

"I think so," Medraut said, his own voice distant. "But I don't see any smoke. If anyone's living over there, there should at least be a few fires burning. I don't smell anything either."

The closer Jamie looked at the buildings, the more certain he became that they were all ruins, and long abandoned ones at that. "Is *anyone* still living here?"

Medraut shook his head.

"Let's take a closer look." Jamie set the titan into motion once again. They crossed the prairie at a more restrained pace as the hill loomed taller and taller before them. The place really did feel deserted, but not haunted or cursed, just empty.

CHAPTER 40

"There's no way we'll be able to scale those cliffs in this thing," Medraut said as they closed within a mile or so of the hill.

Jamie couldn't disagree. The lowest of the cliffs which surrounded the hill stood at least a hundred feet high and they all stepped in and out so drastically that even if the titan could climb them, it would be a harrowing and slow assent which could easily kill everyone onboard if Jamie missed a single step.

"Head north towards that lake," Medraut said. "I have a hunch about something."

Jamie nodded and altered the titan's course. They arrived at the upper rim of the bowl-shaped depression shortly. From that vantage point, they could see that the surface of the lake in the bottom had to be about half as far below them as the top of the hill was above. Connecting those two points was a steep-faced cascade of pale gray slabs that looked like slate, some of which might have been as big as a car. A crescent-shaped beach made from smaller pieces of that same material stretched out to half-encircle the near side of the lake. The waterfall spilled into the opposite end, sounding only like a dull murmur at that distance and sheathing much of the surrounding water and cliffs with a pale veil of mist. To the east, the lake emptied through a large crack in the side of the bowl and flowed back in the direction they had been traveling all day. However, on the western side, zigzagging along the edge of the frozen landslide, they could plainly see a wide and elaborate set of stone stairs interspersed with small, ruined buildings and pavilions.

"Yeap, that's what I thought," Medraut said. "No one would have lived up there if they didn't have some way to get down to that lake. I think I see a way down over there."

Jamie followed his gaze and saw that the sides of the bowl were indeed less steep than the sides of the hill. They were also covered with moderately sized trees which would provide plenty of hand-holds for the titan. It might be a tricky climb down but nothing that the titan couldn't handle. The western side of the bowl looked even less steep, but to get over there, they'd first have to circle around the entire hill.

"What do you think?" Medraut said. "Good place to make camp tonight?"

The sun was starting to get low in the sky, but the last thing Jamie wanted to think about at the moment was turning in for the night. Now that they'd arrived, he wanted to take a look around and see if they could find anyone still living here.

"Hold on tight," Jamie said, as he picked out a place along the rim of the bowl and started the titan down.

Alaida threw herself back in the rumble seat and held on tight as the main body of the titan pitched sharply forward. Medraut even abandoned his perch on the side of the roll cage in favor of the passenger compartment -- though he did remain standing the whole way down. Jamie let gravity pull the titan toward the lake while carefully maneuvering around trees or using them to check his speed and make sudden changes in direction. The slope tapered off near the bottom and that's when they finally broke through the last of the trees and out onto the rocky beach at the foot of the lake.

Either through a natural process or some human contrivance, the smaller chunks of sharp-edged stone that comprised the beach lay relatively flat and flowed down to the water's edge at nearly the same level as the glassy surface of the lake. The vertical face of stone that reached up to the top of the hill stretched high above them, looking even more imposing from that low vantage point. Jamie took the titan into the middle of that stone landscape and dropped it down into its parking stance. By the time he stepped out of the pilot's seat, Medraut had already vaulted down to the ground and was slinging his pack across his shoulders.

"I'm sure glad I won't have to get back in that thing again for a while," Medraut said stretching and looking up at the cliffs which surrounded them. "I know we made really good time, but my back is killing me after sitting down all day!"

Alaida, who had just reached the ground herself and had been pressing her knuckles into her back, suddenly dropped her hands to her sides the moment Medraut had spoken.

"Should we go see if anyone's home?" Jamie said, already starting toward the stairs on the far side of the beach. Alaida hurried to catch up to him and fell in at his side, seemingly un-phased by the jagged stones under her bare feet.

"This place is so quiet, if anyone's still living up there, they should already know we're here," Medraut said, heading in the same direction, but arcing out along the water's edge. He caught a small piece of stone on the tip of his boot and flipped it up into his hand before testing its weight and then slinging it out across the lake. It skipped seven times before sinking.

At the opposite end of the crescent-shaped beach, a large formation of some harder type of stone jutted from the ground like a long, thin sliver that pointed out into the lake. The top had to be at least six feet above the ground, but its sides were stepped so it could easily be climbed. The trees growing on either side drooped above, turning the top of the stone formation into a narrow, cathedral-like space that inexorably drew one's gaze out to the lake. Medraut strode right out to the very end where the action of the water had undercut the formation and left a cantilevered portion suspended above the surface of the lake. The stone was so thin at the tip, it didn't look very strong. Medraut, however, jumped high into the air and landed heavily, just to test it. Jamie shuffled after him but stopped short of the end, unwilling to risk a swim at this time of day.

Crouching down and staring into the clear waters, Medraut said, "I'll have to come back out here tonight and see if any of those fish want to get caught."

After taking in the view as well, Alaida had made her way to the other end of the formation where the bottom of the stairs ended. As she stood looking up at them, Jamie joined her.

"It looks like quite a climb," she said in a soft voice.

"Then we better get started!" Medraut said, bursting past them and bounding up the stone stairs two or three at a time.

Jamie and Alaida started up the steps more slowly. The whole thing had been constructed from large pieces of stone. When new, they had likely been brilliant white, but now they were a dingy shade of pale gray streaked with mineral stains and pitted from long exposure to the weather. Long runs of stairs were interspersed with landings and terraces that offered places to stop and take in the gradually more impressive views of the valley below. Occasionally, portions of a roof or wall still stood complete enough to give an impression of what these intermediate structures might have looked like when new, but all were now in a state of ruin. Fallen pieces of carved stone laying about everywhere looked as if they might have once been an ornate railing. However, its presence wasn't missed until they had climbed higher and found an increasing number of steps which had heaved out of place. At first, these damages offered little hindrance, merely creating strange angles and uneven steps, but farther on, there were sections where multiple steps had been washed away entirely, leaving nothing but a precariously sloped gulley in their place. By then, Jamie and Alaida were already closer to the top than to the bottom, and Medraut was even farther ahead, so they kept going, careful to watch each step they took.

Down at the shore of the lake, the titan-mecha now looked like a little toy in the shadows of the surrounding cliffs. The twilight that had started to take hold down by the lake vanished when they reached the top of their climb and could once again see the sun off to the west, still resting above the horizon.

Jamie and Alaida caught up to Medraut in the remains of a wide plaza that had once stretched across the top of the cliff facing the lake. Its north edge had long ago collapsed to join the jumbled mass of stone below, leaving only a ragged, concave edge with a several-story drop on the other side. Farther back, the paving stones of the plaza had been turned rough and potholed by the infringing vegetation growing into any cracks it could find. It likely wouldn't be long until the dense trees growing at the perimeter took over the rest of the plaza as well.

"That's quite a view," Jamie said as he stared across at the outlying mountains. He'd never actually seen mountains before with his own eyes, but he suspected these might have been more impressive than most. "Whoever built this place sure knew what they were doing."

Drawn in by the vista as well, Alaida stepped to within a few feet of the edge. "You only say that because you have not seen what it is like in winter," she said distantly.

"What are you talking about?" Jamie said with a nervous laugh. He was still several steps away from the edge and that was already too near for him. Just seeing her standing as close as she was sent a nervous tingle racing up his legs.

"This place likely gets dreadful amounts of snow in the winter." Alaida turned away from the edge and came back to Jamie's side. "Can you imagine all the shoveling that would need to be done?"

"Okay, I'll admit, maybe it's not quite paradise," Jamie said, finally able to breath again. "But it is pretty nice at the moment."

"I will grant you that," Alaida said with a thin smile.

Medraut had wandered to the other end of the plaza where a collapsed pile of stones lay across what had likely been the main entrance to the plaza. As he walked back and forth, poking the stones with the tip of his boot and occasionally turning one over, Jamie and Alaida joined him. With a large base on either side of what had once been a street, it had probably been a huge gateway arch when it had still been standing.

"Hmm," Medraut said as he turned over a large, square-cut stone and stood back to examine it. "I think this is the right place after all."

Jamie could see four bold letters carven into the block, along with some additional writing below which had largely become unreadable from all the weathering. There was also a crest of some kind, showing a mountain with a sunburst behind it.

"What does it say?"

Medraut looked at Jamie and laughed. "Don't tell me you can't read either?"

"I…" Jamie quailed under Medraut's gaze. "Of course I can read… Just not that…"

Medraut rolled his eyes and shook his head. "It says 'OMMTO'. This has got to be the place, right? Looks like you're out of luck though."

"Maybe." Jamie stepped past the tracker, looking into the dark trees ahead. There were more buildings lining both sides of the street. All of them looked just as abandoned as the rest of this place, but some of them were partly intact. Maybe there could still be someone living here, deep within the dense interior. Even if not, they might be able to find something that had been left behind. Jamie cast his thoughts inward. The nagging sensation told him that he still had time left, maybe as much as a day yet. That would at least give them a decent amount of time to search the ruins tomorrow, but would it be enough to find anything?

"I'd like to take a quick look around while we still have some light," Jamie said, finding it difficult to pull his gaze away from the ruins.

"Knock yourself out," Medraut said, "I'm gonna head back down and see if I can't score us something for supper." He sounded disappointed. Apparently, he'd been hoping for more from this place as well.

Alaida took hold of Jamie's arm and looked first into the dark trees and then back toward the titan-mecha. "I will come with you," she said to Jamie.

"Then I'll see the two of you in a little while," Medraut said, heading back toward the stairs.

"We'll be back before it gets dark," Jamie said to him. Then to Alaida, "Let's get started."

The trail of age-pitted stones that led back into the trees was in even worse condition than the plaza. Where the thick roots hadn't been able to push the largest paving stones entirely out of the ground, they instead grew over them and swelled to such enormous proportions that it looked as if they might be trying to crack the stones with their sheer weight alone. The stillness below the trees seemed almost unnatural after having just been standing in the open air at the edge of the plaza.

They approached the first building with a silence that matched their surroundings and peered through one of the windowless openings in the stone façade. Inside, the roof and second floor had collapsed, filling the inside of the structure with a mix of damp, rotted wood and broken tiles. Small trees and shrubs had already taken root in the heap and had grown taller than the tops of the partly intact walls.

"I do hope that the entire estate is not like this," Alaida said.

Unfortunately, as they made their way deeper into the ruins, examining each building they came upon, it looked as though they would have no such luck. The street they followed eventually split and branched out into a seemingly random number of thoroughfares, all of which were in a similar state of disrepair.

Most were lined with more buildings, but not one of these once elegant structures remained intact. They did, however, give some impression of what the place must have looked like at its height. More than having been a simple family property, the Ommto Estate was more like an entire city; and a luxurious city at that. Everything had been made from stone, finely carved and intricately detailed. The mountain and sunburst pattern was a common motif on the many broken friezes and sculptures they saw, repeated over and over again nearly everywhere they looked.

Unfortunately, ruined beyond all recognition, it was impossible to tell what purpose any of the ruins had served. Many had trees growing right through the middle of them. Others were covered with layers of vines so thick that the rubble underneath was completely hidden from view. They didn't even see any sealed doors which might have at least offered the hope of hidden treasures. It was quickly looking as if the entire estate really was nothing but one gigantic ghost town.

In some of the spaces between the various blocks of buildings grew strange rows of trees which were smaller than all the others but had somehow managed to colonize a space around them with such dictatorial zeal that no other plants dared to encroach upon them. It was almost as if their very presence was somehow holding back the rest of the vegetation, allowing a few rays of sunshine to reach their leaves. Those that managed to receive the most light were covered with a fluffy layer of white blossoms that filled the air around them with a sweet, lilac-like scent.

"I wonder what happened to everything," Jamie said, his tone hushed as they finished circling a narrow, wedge-shaped block which had once held an open plaza and a large building surrounded by ornate columns. Now the trees filling the plaza were nearly as thick as the fallen columns and their branches met overhead, offering more of a roof than the building itself. "Onorah said Major Ommto must have moved back here about twenty or thirty years ago. This place looks like its been abandoned a lot longer than that."

"Trees do grow quickly," Alaida said, her eyes scanning the street ahead. "But I do agree that it does not look as if anyone has lived here in a very long time."

They kept going, speaking little. Unlike when they'd first started out, they now bypassed the majority of the collapsed buildings, giving each one only a cursory glance. It soon became apparent that all the streets radiated out from a central point, and curiosity over what might lie there drew them deeper into the ruins.

CHAPTER 41

Instead of some plaza, grand building, or other public place, the central hub for the estate proved to be the rocky spire they had seen from a distance when first laying eyes upon the hill. From what they could now see of it through the encroaching vegetation, it rose from the relatively flat ground atop the hill, its steep sides more of that harder, dark stone they'd seen down at the lake. Climbing it would have required mountaineering gear if not for the spiraling path that had been cut into the sides of the rock. It had been getting quite gloomy beneath the all-encompassing canopy but now they could see the orange rays of the setting sun angling across the path above.

"Want to take a look?" Jamie started to say, but Alaida stepped past him and hurried up the first section of ramp.

"It looks as if it might go all the way up," she said, bending back to be able to see up that high. "I will race you to the top!"

"Alaida, wait, we don't know if it's safe," Jamie said, but Alaida had already dashed on ahead.

Maybe he was being a little overly cautious. Having been carved directly from the spire, this path appeared to have weathered the test of time far better than the rest of this place. And Alaida was probably right about having a little fun again. The two of them had hardly had any chances to be alone all day, and now that they had one, they'd been wasting it with their solemn exploration of the estate. Jamie set off after her at a jog. He could have overtaken her with ease, but he didn't want this new wonder to pass him by without taking a little time to appreciate it.

The path alternated between runs of stairs and ramps as it climbed higher. At various points, it snaked its way though ruined structures that had been erected on the side of the spire but were now just rocky terraces. Elsewhere, they had to pass through tunnels burrowed right into the rock with openings cut into the side that turned what could have been dank caves into grand palisades of columns with light streaming through.

The path quickly carried them up into the trees. With the branches growing so close, it was often difficult to think of this path as being open on one side. When Jamie finally caught up to Alaida, she had stopped to stare out from one terrace that sat level with the tops of the trees. Their leaves formed a sea of green that rippled and flowed with the gentle breezes and then came abruptly to an end at the edges of the mesa, leaving only a pale blue sky beyond and the thin clouds tinted by the setting sun in the west.

"Whoa," Jamie said, coming up alongside her. "I bet this place would have been packed this time of day back when people were still living here."

"The view is probably even better from above!" Alaida again dashed on ahead. "Come!"

It was only now that they'd lost their protective shield of trees along the outer edge of the path that Jamie realized just how high they'd actually climbed. As they continued on, he found himself staying well to the inside edge of the path. Alaida, meanwhile, raced up each new leg of the path, laughing the whole time. Even this high, small patches of vegetation continued to find cracks and crevices in which to grow, climbing up the sheer faces of rock as if in blatant defiance of gravity.

The path finally ended at the remains of the building Jamie had earlier seen, though a round base of stones somehow hanging from the side of the rock was all that remained of it. The spire itself continued higher still, but as nothing more than a thin needle of stone which would not have been substantial enough to support any further stairs or paths. The ruined structure had probably been a tower at one time which might very well have reached even higher. Now, it was just a round patch of paving stones covered by rubble.

From that high vantage point, the sun was just touching the horizon. The wispy ribbons of clouds drifting through the sky had become illuminated in glowing shades of pink and orange and purple. Off to the south and the east, they could see the tall hills they'd been crossing throughout the day marching away into the distance. The further west their gaze wandered, the softer and more rolling the dark green hills became, eventually giving way to a gently undulating sea of light green prairie. In the north, the steep and barren mountains with their snow-capped peaks dominated. Jamie could understand why that natural formation had been chosen as the border between Finttiranos and Secotia. It didn't look as if anyone could possibly cross such a forbidding barricade.

Below them and all around, the top of the mesa looked like a single uniform blanket of green. If there were any buildings down there which might have held some special significance to this place, they were just as hidden beneath the canopy of trees as everything else. As Medraut had observed, there wasn't even any smoke from a fire.

"Is it not beautiful?" Alaida said, her eyes fixed on the view as she walked to the edge of the platform.

"And what about all that snow you were talking about earlier?" Jamie said as he continued scanning the forest below for some clue about where to begin their exploration. To search this entire place could take days, if not weeks.

"Snow?" Alaida laughed and threw out her arms, pirouetting right at the edge. As she turned, her toes scuffed in the dirt and sent several tiny pebbles tumbling over the side. "Up here, in this place, one would hardly have any cause for such concerns."

"Careful." Jamie slid as close as he dared. "That's a long way down."

"Oh, it is not dangerous." Loosely interlocking her arms behind her back, Alaida began walking at the very edge of the platform as if she were simply out for a casual stroll. "See, I am fine. Are you scared of heights?"

"I'm scared of falling," Jamie admitted. "Do you really want to press your luck?"

Alaida scoffed at the very idea. "I am not going to fall." When she reached the end, she turned again, displaying that impeccable grace Jamie remembered well from their first meeting, and began to retrace the steps she had just taken. "Sometimes, you complain like an old man."

"First Medraut and now you?" Jamie said, managing a nervous laugh. Just peeking over the edge made him feel dizzy. "Are you guys trying to gang up on me?"

Alaida laughed and turned to face the mountains once more, this time with her toes hanging over the edge and her arms raised at her sides. She closed her eyes and threw back her head. "Feel the wind? It feels like it could lift me aloft and just carry me away."

Jamie edged to within arm's reach of Alaida and held out his hand. "Come on, why don't you just give me your hand and step away from there?"

"Why are you so worried? It's not as if I'm in any danger!" As she threw down her arms with a huff and turned to face Jamie, one of her feet slipped in the loose grit and dropped over the edge, dragging the rest of her along with it. She gasped and flailed her arms as gravity pulled her toward the merciless void.

Jamie sprang forward, his feelings of vertigo completely overshadowed by a sudden bolt of sheer panic. His fingers slipped around one of her wrists. He grabbed on tightly with his other hand as well and for a brief moment, the two of them stood balanced there on the very edge of that deadly drop, Alaida hanging on by one foot alone and the rest of her suspended in space as Jamie strained to act as an anchor to keep her from going any farther. Despite his strength, he wasn't fixed to the ground and the slightest shift in weight the wrong way would send them both tumbling to the ground far below. Alaida, however, did not seem interested in offering any help, her body limb as she stared straight down the face of the cliff with a bemused smile on her lips.

Slowly, by inches, Jamie pulled her back until their center of gravity finally shifted in his favor and he was finally able to snatch her away from the edge, both of them falling in a heap on solid ground once more.

"Alaida! What the heck was that?"

"Wow, that was really close." Alaida climbed to her knees and brushed the hair out of her face. Her skin was flushed, and she was breathing as if she'd just run a marathon. Nearly giggling, she looked back at the edge as if she might try to throw herself off once again. Jamie pushed himself up and placed himself between her and the cliff.

"Are you okay?" he said. "You're acting kind of weird."

"Yes! Of course, I'm fine!" She let out a long, laughing sigh as she ran her fingers through her hair, pulling it severely back from her face. "I wasn't scared! Not for a moment!"

"You should have been! What if I didn't catch you?"

She suddenly looked very confused and the color drained from her face. "But...you did catch me." As her breathing turned into halting gulps, her body folded in on itself, making her looks very small as she huddled there on the ground.

"Alaida, are you sure you're okay?" Jamie placed a hand on her shoulder. The muscles in her back were spasming as if an electric current were flowing through them. If she got sick out here in the middle of nowhere, would they have any medicine to help her? How close would the nearest doctor even be? Suddenly tensing, she pressed her hands to her stomach and retched.

"Alaida..."

Jamie pulled the hair away from her face just as she convulsed again, this time emptying her stomach out on to the dry paving stones. Retching once more resulted in little more than a dry heave and she sat back on her heels, breathing hard and looking toward the sky.

After a moment, she swallowed and said, "I'm...I am feeling better now."

"What happened?"

She shook her head, strands of her hair damp with sweat. "I don't know. I must have let my excitement get the better of me. I am sorry I frightened you."

"You don't need to be sorry, just...be more careful next time." Jamie shook his head. He never thought he'd need to lecture Alaida about being more careful about anything.

Her eyes fixed on the ground, Alaida nodded. "Yes, I will do that." Jamie could almost hear the silent "master" tacked onto the end of her statement. Or maybe it was just the quiver in her voice which suggested it. Her body must have been flooded with adrenaline, completely unlike Reaver's. If not for that, Jamie suspected he would not have been nearly so calm.

"Can you walk?" Jamie said. "It's getting late, we should really get back to camp."

"Yes, I will be fine. I just need a minute."

Jamie helped steady Alaida as she climbed back to her feet on legs that trembled uncertainly. She sat down on one of the large building stones lying about the ruins and took a moment to quiet her breathing. Meanwhile, Jamie paced. The sun had nearly dropped below the horizon, leaving nothing more than a thin arch of light. Alaida took one more deep breath and then stood with renewed determination, despite the way she swayed slightly on her feet. If it really was just the excitement, it was probably best for her to walk off any lingering effects. As they started back down the spire, Jamie slipped an arm around her trembling shoulders. He almost expected her to shrug him off, but instead, she leaned into him, welcoming the support.

"So, do I really sound like a retarded five-year-old?" Jamie said. Alaida said nothing in reply and merely turned her head away to look out at the treetops. "Come on. Really?"

"Medraut said you sound like a four-year-old," Alaida said, correcting him.

Jamie sighed and shook his head. "I guess I'll take that as a yes."

"The sunset is really quite lovely from up here, is it not?"

"Yes, yes it is..."

CHAPTER 42

Once they dropped back into the trees, their surroundings grew as dark as night. Even once they came back into the open and went down to the titan-mecha, the last light of day was almost completely gone. Medraut was nowhere in sight and everything looked exactly how they'd left it. With Medraut being so skilled at everything else, Jamie would have thought he'd returned with a whole banquet by now. Alaida had become much more steady on her feet as they'd walked back to the titan and now professed to be feeling perfectly fine.

Together, she and Jamie gathered firewood from the surrounding woods and began to set-up what limited camping supplies they might need for the night. It was only as Alaida lit the fire and the first flames leapt up to dispel the growing darkness that they realized just how dark it had gotten. Medraut returned shortly thereafter, carrying the bodies of three rabbit-sized creatures.

"Whoo-hoo, what luck!" he said. "I came upon a whole group of them just as they were coming out of their den! I was able to bag these three all at once."

"Er, what are they?" Jamie said, eyeing the animals as Medraut set them down on the ground. They had short legs, a long head with tiny, round ears, and squat bodies covered all over with glossy, greenish-black scales.

"What? You've never seen a goplisam before?" Medraut said as he crouched over the kills and began skinning them with a long, thin knife. The blade flashed in the firelight, every motion precise and exact. "I know what most people say, but you haven't seen the way I roast them yet. It's one of my specialties."

"I can dress them for the fire if you would like," Alaida said, stepping forward.

"No!" Medraut suddenly sat up very straight and pointed the knife blade at Alaida. She froze in place and Jamie's whole body tensed as he prepared to wrest the knife from him if need be. "No, I'll handle this," Medraut said with a bit of a chuckle. "I told you that I'd carry my own weight and I intend to do just that, so why don't you just sit down and stay out of my way."

He returned to the animals, working quickly and efficiently with the knife as Alaida backed away. Between his easy smile and the nonchalant way he had held the knife even while pointing it at Alaida, Medraut probably hadn't meant any offense by his words or his actions. Having been on his own for so long had probably dulled him to some of the more polite aspects of society.

However, his manners were of secondary concern to both Jamie and Alaida at the moment. Medraut's goggles, which he'd been wearing since they'd first met, were now hanging loosely from his neck, giving his hosts the first clear look at his eyes they'd had all day long. The sight of them in the firelight had caused both Jamie and Alaida to stare in silent surprise. Except for the dark pupil in the center of each, his eyes were a single color throughout, devoid of any white at all surrounding the iris. They looked a lot like a slave's, except where theirs were golden, his were a deep shade of striated purple. Jamie glanced to Alaida for some sort of explanation, but looking just as confused as Jamie felt, she merely shook her head in reply to his unspoken question.

Medraut chattered on as he worked with the animals, seemingly unaware of the way Jamie and Alaida were now staring at him. Alaida had told Jamie that all of the slave races had the same gold-on-gold eyes so if Medraut was one of them, he must have been some kind of aberrant. Maybe that's how he could pass himself off as a human yet still do all those incredible feats.

"Um..." Jamie said, catching Medraut's attention. Glistening in the firelight, his eyes looked unhealthy, as if the whole of each were clouded with dark blood. Asking him outright about them seemed rude but Jamie could think of no other way to bring it up. He waved his hand in front of his own eyes to illustrate what he was trying to say and hoping that Medraut might catch on without him needing to say anything. "Your eyes...is that...are they...?"

"My eyes?" Medraut said. He stopped working with the meat and pulled his goggles up from around his neck so that he could look at himself in the reflection of the lens. Then, with a laugh he said, "Oh that. Sometimes I forget all about them. I can put these back on if you'd like. I know they make most people uncomfortable. "

"No, it's fine," Jamie said. "I've just never seen anything like that before."

"Let me guess: you're thinking I'm some weird mutation of one of the slave races."

Jamie shook his head. "What? No, of course not."

"Eh, that's what most people think," Medraut said as he returned to preparing the meat. For several long moments, the only sounds to be heard were the cracking of the fire and the river cascading over the distant waterfall. Again, Jamie looked to Alaida, but she again shook her head in bewilderment.

"So..." Jamie said at last.

"Naw, I'm human, same as anyone," Medraut said. "But I've had these eyes just about as long as I can remember. Maybe it's from all the wardcaster fallout that I was exposed to during my formative years down in Heigelries. Do you guys have any salt?"

"Um, yes, in the hold," Alaida said, already in motion. "I will get you some."

"Well thank you kindly, *Lady Raven-Slave*," Medraut said, flashing her a toothy grin.

Again, Jamie bristled at the way he addressed Alaida, but he held his tongue. As they were finding, Medraut clearly had plenty of rough edges despite his overall affability. Instead, Jamie said, "I didn't know wardcasters could do things like that."

"It's the resonator dust from all the wardcasters that were destroyed during the war. So much of it ended up in the ground and in the water that it's hard to avoid even now. I've heard it was really bad during the early days, but even today there are still kids being born with a lot worse than just weird eyes. As long as resonators stay outside the human body, they're completely safe, but inside? Not a good thing. Have you ever heard about magesmiths doing unsanctioned experiments to augment humans with wardcaster implants? Pretty gruesome stuff. Normally, I wouldn't put much stock in that kind of gossip, but after some of the things I've heard, it does make me wonder."

Alaida had returned and handed Medraut a small pouch filled with coarsely ground salt. Listening closely to the conversation, she sat down stiffly on one of the rugs they'd laid out around the fire.

"Human augmentation?" Jamie said, focused even more intently on Medraut's words than Alaida. "Is something like that really possible with wardcasters?"

Medraut shrugged as he began skewering each of the goplisams on a long, wooden stake. "Maybe they're just urban legends, but you always hear new stories cropping up about someone giving it a try. Rumor has it, that's what happened to Captain Redoni during the Clattemo War. The way the governments always try to cover this stuff up doesn't exactly help to disprove it either. They always tell us that the human body will violently reject even the simplest wardcaster implant, but then, I ain't no magesmith, so what do I know?"

Jamie flexed his hand, looking at the way the skin stretched and wrinkled. He couldn't feel anything inside him, but did this offer a possible explanation for what Reaver was? Could it even have been Major Ommto's work that was somehow responsible for turning him into this?

Now that Medraut had arranged the stakes around the fire, he took the knife that he had been using to prepare them, licked the blade clean, and then returned it to a sheath in his belt. Jamie began to ask if that was a very hygienic thing to do but stopped himself. Medraut had looked completely natural doing it, maybe this was just another of his quirks. Alaida, however, tensed and turned her head to the side with a tiny choking sound. Either Medraut didn't notice, or he simply didn't care.

"So what are you really doing out here?" Medraut said, flopping down cross-legged on one of the other rugs with hands on his knees. "You're looking for treasure, right?"

"No..." Jamie said, shaking his head. "We're really looking for someone named Major Ommto."

"But he's got treasure, right? Or he knows where some is?"

"We're just trying to get some information."

"You've come all the way out here and gone through all this trouble, just for information? It's got to be some really valuable information then."

"It is of a personal nature," Alaida said, "important to Jamie but unlikely to be of any interest to anyone else."

That had to be the most Alaida had ever said to Medraut before. Perhaps the most she'd ever said in his presence. Medraut considered her for a moment before returning his attention to Jamie.

"'Personal' doesn't necessarily mean it's *not* valuable."

"It's really nothing all that interesting," Jamie said. For Medraut's own safety, the less interest he took in Jamie and Reaver's shared condition, the better. Who knew what Reaver's reaction might be upon finding that this strange young man had somehow attached himself to their expedition? "And honestly, we really appreciate your help getting us here, but we can probably handle things from here."

"Oh, so now you're just gonna cut me out?" Medraut said. His dark eyes in the firelight gave him a certain maniac quality as he rubbed his hands together. "Then it must be really valuable after all."

"I'm serious, there's nothing to cut you out of."

"But I can help you look. That place is pretty big and I'm very good at finding things."

That was actually a compelling argument. With another set of eyes on their side, and one who was an expert tracker at that, their odds would have to improve considerably. But could he help them find anything with the small amount of time they still had left when they didn't even know what they were looking for themselves?

"Let me think about it," Jamie said.

Medraut clapped his hands together and grinned. "Yes!"

"I only said I'd *think* about it. And regardless of what we decide, we've got to be done with our search by tomorrow afternoon."

"Why the deadline?"

"Um...somebody's coming. He's...meeting us here and he doesn't like strangers."

"Oh come on, everybody loves me! So who is this guy: your boss or something?"

"No," Jamie said with conviction. "Definitely not."

"A buyer then? Maybe a financer?"

"No. He's more like...a business associate."

"Oh, a partner. I get it. He bought into this little endeavor of yours from the beginning and here I am just trying to sneak my way in at the very end. No need to explain any further. I'll help you look and then I'll make myself scarce. It's the least I can do to repay you for the ride and the company."

"We really do appreciate your help," Jamie said. "And I wish we had some better way to show it."

"Don't worry. I'll see if I can't track down a rallore or something like that for you guys tomorrow morning. That way you'll at least have some food for a while."

"That...would actually be very helpful," Jamie said. As much as Jamie didn't want to get any further into debt with Medraut, getting their food supplies restocked would probably be worth it. "Thank you."

"Like I said, don't mention it."

With those matters taken care of, Medraut returned to the same antics he'd been displaying on the journey to this place, singing and telling jokes and throwing in a bit of physical humor as well. No matter what he did, he never seemed to run out of energy, and the feral spirit which tainted everything he did only helped to make the performance livelier. By the time the goplisams had finished roasting over the fire, Jamie and Alaida were both having just as much fun as Medraut, their unabashed laughter echoing off the walls of the bowl-shaped depression in which they had camped.

"One for each of us," Medraut said, handing one of the spits to Jamie and the next to Alaida. "Dig in."

The outside of the meat had taken on a pleasant golden-brown color while a constant stream of fat dripped down the wooden spits. Medraut tore into his with relish, ripping off large chunks of the slippery meat with his teeth and chewing wolfishly. Jamie took only a small bite to start. It tasted a lot like pork, but the texture was spongy and soft. Alaida sampled her own demurely, pausing often to wipe the dripping fat from her lips.

"So, what do you think?" Medraut said, having nearly devoured all of his already.

"It's...not bad," Jamie said.

"Yes, this is...definitely the best goplisam I have ever tasted," Alaida said.

"See I told you!"

Nearly gagging after each bite he took, Jamie was only able to get through a small portion of his goplisam before he gave up. He wasn't at all hungry to begin with and probably didn't need any food besides. Alaida made a better showing of working though her own, but at a certain point, even her hunger wasn't enough to compel her to finish. Fortunately, Medraut didn't show any offence and actually seemed pleased to finish off their leftovers, stripping off every scrap of meat and even going so far to break some of the bones open to suck out the marrow. Watching him toss the remains into the fire, Jamie couldn't help but wonder what gourmet creation Alaida could have made from the goplisams if given the chance.

There wasn't much to clean up after the meal but Medraut insisted on helping. While he was down by the lake getting some water, Jamie leaned over to Alaida and whispered, "You didn't have to lie to him when he asked you how it tasted."

Alaida gasped and jerked away from Jamie, punching him lightly on the shoulder. "I did not lie. Once, when my former master had gone hunting, he returned with a pair of goplisams when he was unable to find anything better. Medraut's preparation was far superior to what the mistress and I were able to achieve."

Jamie chuckled even as he cringed.

"And now you know what most people say about goplisam," Alaida said.

Once Medraut returned, they all sat around the fire and listened to Medraut sing a few more songs. At one point, he pressed Jamie to join him in his current performance, a catchy reel with an infectious refrain that would likely be stuck in their heads for days to come.

"You do not want to hear me sing!" Jamie said in reply.

And after badgering him into trying the refrain, Medraut cut him off halfway through, laughing, "You're right, I don't want to hear you sing! What about you, *Lady Raven-Slave*?"

She at first tried to abstain, but Jamie even joined with Medraut in egging her on. Eventually relenting, she stood timidly and began to sing a much more somber song than most of the lively tunes which Medraut had been belting out. Her voice wavered on the first few lines but not nearly as badly as Jamie's attempt had been. The further she went, however, the more confident both her voice and her stance became. Medraut and Jamie's laughter quickly ceased and both of them simply listened, drawn in by the haunting way in which Alaida sang the words.

The lyrics told the story of two young lovers who were forever cursed to be apart, at first because of their families and then by a war, each of them always trying to return to the other only to be thwarted by fate at every turn. To Jamie, it sounded something like a poignant Irish folksong. The final verse explained how the two lovers, after years of being apart, were finally reunited when they were placed in their graves, which random chance had situated side-by-side in a distant cemetery far from their original homes.

As the echoes of her last words died away in the surrounding cliffs, Alaida's audience sat in silence for several long moments while she wrung her hands and glanced about at the ground before hastily retaking her seat at the fire.

"Wow, Alaida, that was great!" Jamie said.

"My apologies," she said, hiding her face. "I have never had any formal training in song but one of my former masters was always fond of that one, so I know it well."

Medraut began clapping slowly and deliberately. "No, I agree with Jamie. You nailed it perfectly, Lady Raven-Slave. Although I prefer the other ending."

He then went on to sing an alternate version of the final verse in which the two lovers did not die but instead simply gave up their hopeless quest to ever be together and decided to settle down in villages far from where their story had begun, only to discover that they had both chosen the exact same village. Beyond simply the words, the way Medraut sang them turned Alaida's somber tale into something playful and adventurous. Jamie couldn't quite tell if this was a version he'd actually heard before or if he was making it up on the spot. Regardless, it helped to dispel some of the shade which Alaida's telling, as lovely as it had been, had brought over the camp.

CHAPTER 43

Eventually, Alaida decided that it was time for her to turn in for the night. It had gotten quite late and all of them were eager to get an early start in the morning. When Jamie asked if Medraut would like to use any of the gear in the titan for his accommodations, he declined, instead preparing his own bed by chopping a few evergreen branches from a tree at the edge of the beach and arranging them into a small lean-to.

"Normally, I just sleep under the stars," Medraut said, "but it's gonna rain later."

Jamie looked up at the sky. The countless stars visible were only veiled by a few delicate ribbons of clouds. "Are you sure?"

"You might want to put up a tent if you have one," Medraut said as he used his machete to chop a long, thin branch from another tree. With his smaller knife, he began stripping off the leaves.

"I believe I will sleep in the titan tonight," Alaida said. The tarp they had stretched across the passenger compartment was still in place so all she would have to do is roll it back out to the edges to provide herself with plenty of protection from any rain. "Good night," she said as she climbed the side of the titan.

"Good night." Jamie wasn't any more tired tonight than he was yesterday. "I think I'll just hang out by the fire for a while."

"As for me," Medraut said, pulling a long piece of burning wood from the fire, "I'm gonna see if there are any fish in that lake before I turn in for the night."

Using a piece of string and a hook from his satchel, Medraut fashioned the branch he'd cut down into a fishing pole and then used the burning branch for a torch as he made his way to the end of the rock formation that reached out into the lake.

As Jamie sat at the fire, he kept glancing up at the top of the mesa. Since he wasn't going to be getting any sleep, he kept thinking that he might as well continue exploring the ruins tonight. However, he didn't want to leave Alaida by herself. Medraut had reassured them more than once as they made camp that there were no signs of Wolf-Slaves in the area but Jamie had let their situation fall apart more than once by allowing himself to grow too complacent. Medraut certainly appeared more than capable of keeping them out of harm's way but Jamie never would have forgiven himself if something happened to Alaida because he put too much trust in the young tracker after having known him for so short a time.

For a while, Jamie watched the fire, adding more wood to keep it high, but eventually grew bored with that and began pacing back and forth beside the titan. It was going to be a long night. When he heard Alaida rustling in the back of the titan and saw her sleepy face peak over the side, Jamie froze in his tracks. The shifting of the brittle stones under his heavy boots was not exactly quiet.

Smiling sheepishly, he whispered, "Sorry."

Alaida said nothing and dropped back out of sight behind the bulkhead.

Jamie considered his situation for a moment, now painfully aware of each sharp tinkling sound produced from even the slightest movement of the stones underfoot. Carefully, he tip-toed away from the titan and made his way to the rock formation that jutted into the lake. He could see Medraut sitting at the far end of the rock with his torch propped up over the water. Instead, Jamie went to the bottom of the stone stairs. On this moonless night, they only showed up as gray outlines in the starlight, winding their way up to the top of the mesa. It wouldn't be difficult at all to climb them and continue his search of the ruins.

However, even though he could see in the dark, that didn't mean his vision was as sharp as during the day. He could easily miss something important and then be left wondering if he should recheck everything in the morning once the sun was up. After several long minutes of contemplation, Jamie turned and walked out to the other end of the rock formation. Medraut looked up at Jamie's approach but didn't speak.

"Catch anything?" Jamie said as he sat down on the rock next to Medraut, his feet dangling over the edge.

"Nothing worth keeping," Medraut said with a shrug. "What are you still doing up?"

"Couldn't sleep. Part of me wants to go back up there tonight and look around some more."

"I wouldn't recommend it," Medraut said, gently dragging his line through the water. "I've seen ruins like this before. With all the collapsed buildings and hidden basements, in the dark it's way too easy to fall into a pit and get buried. Even if that doesn't kill you, there either won't be a way out or you'll end up pinned beneath the rubble and slowly suffocate to death."

"We didn't see anything like that before."

"That's what makes it so dangerous. You can do whatever you want, but if it were me, I'd just wait till morning. It's not so bad during the day when you can see everything."

Jamie glanced back toward the stairs. As much as he wanted to get started right away, Medraut did have a point. If he did find himself trapped in the bottom of an old basement, buried under a few tons of loose rocks, would Reaver's abilities be enough to get him out alive? And if not, would Alaida and Medraut even be able to find him afterward? Jamie crossed his legs under him and sat back. For a time, they just sat there, gazing out across the glassy surface of the lake in the starlight.

At last, Medraut broke the silence, "You must really want that information pretty bad. What happens after you find it?"

"I don't know," Jamie said, staring at the torchlight reflecting off the ripples created by Medraut's fishing line. "Maybe I can finally go home." He knew it was probably overly optimistic to hope for anything like that but he didn't know enough about what they were looking for to even speculate about any of the other possibilities.

"Home?" Medraut laughed scornfully. "What's so great about home?"

"Not much," Jamie had to admit.

"I can barely even remember mine anymore," Medraut said. "Probably means it wasn't worth remembering."

"Mine's changed so much, sometimes I can't even recognize it, but I'd go back in a heartbeat if it would end all this running around and fighting. I just wish there was a way I could bring Alaida back with me."

"So, what's with you and *Lady Raven-Slave* anyway? You from one of those countries that don't allow slaves? You're definitely not from Thieradoon. Meirithan?"

Jamie had never heard of that place but if they had outlawed slavery, maybe not every country on Terrarhea was completely backward after all. "No, my home's a lot farther away than that. But you're right, we don't keep slaves there."

Medraut looked at Jamie crossly. "I figured as much. You don't really treat her the way most people treat their slaves."

"Well, I don't really think of her as a slave. She's more of a friend."

"Yeah, a *friend*," Medraut chuckled, conjuring up a far more lurid connotation of the word. "I've heard of guys falling in love with their Ravens before, but those stories usually involve the SAA stepping in to fine one party and confiscate the other. Is that it? Are you two on the run from the authorities because they just didn't understand what the two of you have together?"

"No!" Jamie said.

"Come on, you can tell me. I'm not exactly a wanted man but there are more than a few places where I can't show my face anymore, if you know what I mean."

"That's not it at all," Jamie said. Although he did have to admit it was awfully close to the truth. "I accidentally got Alaida into some trouble a while back and they were going to send her to a slave farm. I didn't want *her* to be punished because *I* made a mistake. I didn't think it was fair so, yeah, we ran, but that's it. We're really just friends."

"So why not let her go?"

"What do you mean?"

Medraut sighed and shook his head. "The slave races don't have any problems living in the wild. Just let her go."

"I couldn't just toss her out to fend for herself!" Jamie said, even though that was exactly what he had once contemplated doing to her back in Tavnic when he'd been so desperate to actually entertain the juvenile fantasy of hiding her in the woods with a stockpile of camping gear. "How would she survive?"

"Come on, none of us really know what we're truly capable of until we go over that cliff. After all, instincts run pretty deep; maybe she's capable of more than you think she is."

"I know she is. But she's not just some animal that's guided by instinct. From what I've seen, none of the Slave Races are."

Medraut laughed as if he had just heard some fantastic inside joke.

"You don't think much of them, do you?" Jamie said. From the dismissive and distant way he always addressed Alaida to the nonchalant manner in which he dealt with the Wolf-Slaves, it was all too clear, and it was starting to get on Jamie's nerves.

Medraut laughed again, more fatalistically this time. "I like 'em fine. When they're free to live how they want." He pointed with his chin to the blackness beyond the glow of his torch. "When they're out there: in the wilds. Not when they're just pulled along by their masters and do whatever they're told. It's wrong that anyone thinks that they can own them but it's even worse that they allow themselves to be owned. It doesn't really matter if you think of them as slaves or not, if you're preventing one of them from finding out what she could be, then she's still just a slave and you're still her master."

A spattering of raindrops swept across the surface of the lake and pelted Medraut and Jamie. As they'd been talking, the stars had become blotted out by a thick layer of clouds and now the rain which Medraut had predicted had finally arrived. He stood up and wound his fishing line around his hand before untying it and tossing the pole and the torch into the water. As the flames went out with a sizzle beneath the surface of the lake, the world suddenly grew very dark.

Medraut pushed past Jamie and headed back to camp. "I'll see ya in the morning."

"Yeah..." Jamie said, his voice a soft croak. "Good night..."

More rain fell in big, cold drops straight down from the sky but Jamie didn't get up from where he sat. He'd wondered before if he was holding Alaida back from her true calling. Now Medraut had noticed as well. Was it really that obvious? Was he really being selfish by wanting to keep her safe? He didn't know, and he wasn't finding any answers sitting in the rain either.

It was some time later when Jamie returned to camp, his sodden poncho hanging heavily from his shoulders. Medraut had climbed under his branches and pulled them down on top of himself, turning his shelter into nothing more than a pile of brush. Not wishing to further disturb Alaida, Jamie leaned back in the titan's pilot seat and watched the coals left in the fire sputter and smolder in the rain.

In the small degree of protection offered by the machine above him, Jamie could watch the falling rain and listen to the cacophonous symphony it created without getting any more soaked than he already was. However, it was an infrequent drip on the back of his neck which quickly monopolized his attention. The tarp shielding the passenger compartment above had a small fold in the front where the rain would pool until it eventually overflowed and spilled down right on top of Jamie.

No matter how he shifted to avoid it, each time the stream of icy cold water fell, it always managed to hit the back of his neck with a ferocity that seemed almost malicious. His clothes were already soaked through to the skin and the cold had little affect on Reaver's body, but his jaw still grew tight and his shoulders stooped in anticipation of each new impact. He was starting to consider seeking shelter under the titan's body when he heard movement above and saw Alaida unfurl her long black coat across the top of the pilot's compartment, instantly stopping the drip.

"Thanks," Jamie whispered, though she had already disappeared back into the passenger compartment.

So much for not disturbing Alaida.

CHAPTER 44

The rain ended in the early hours of the morning and the clouds began to break-up shortly thereafter, leaving only a few lingering by the time the sky started to lighten. Jamie stoked back to life the few remaining embers in the fire which the rain hadn't completely extinguished and added dry fuel so that by the time Alaida and Medraut began to stir, they would be greeted by a blazing fire.

Morning arrived far colder than the evening that had preceded it. If Jamie had been in his own body, he probably would have had hypothermia by now. Most of the water had dripped from his clothes in the night but they were still damp and began to steam in the heat from the fire. Yawning, Medraut emerged from his shelter on all fours and stretched like a cat. Despite the makeshift nature of his accommodations and the complete lack of any bedding, he looked well rested and had hardly gotten wet at all. Alaida had faired just as well, though she kept a blanket wrapped tightly around her shoulders as the three of them gathered at the fire.

"I hope I didn't wake you guys up," Jamie said.

"No," Alaida said, shivering. "I have always found it difficult to sleep well in the titan, even when it is not moving."

Medraut kept yawning as he warmed himself by the fire, his head bobbing on a rubbery neck and his eyes drifting shut, even with his best efforts to hold them open. When he succeeded long enough for Jamie and Alaida to clearly see his eyes, they looked even stranger in the brightening light of dawn than they had last night around the campfire. Jamie had to keep reminding himself not to stare and Alaida couldn't quite bring herself to look directly at him. Medraut didn't seem to notice their behavior at all.

"Oh," he said, his voice thick with sleep as he reached into one of his pockets and pulled out a small pouch made of foil-faced paper. "I have some cariak here if you have a kettle to brew it in."

"Um, yes, of course," Alaida said and then promptly climbed up into the titan's hold and returned with a small, flame-scorched kettle and the bag of dried jackelope.

"I'll be right back," Medraut said, handing the pouch over to Jamie. "Just make sure to brew it stiff, Lady Raven-Slave. I like it strong."

Jamie folded back the edges of the paper to reveal a coarse blend of hard granules inside which looked something like dried orange peels. "Do you know what this stuff is?" Jamie said to Alaida as Medraut walked in the trees. Like a ghost, he vanished from sight after only a few steps.

"Yes," Alaida said. She placed the kettle, filled with water, in the fire and took the cariak from Jamie. "It is quite common as a morning beverage. Preparation is rather simple, but it can easily be ruined if one is not careful."

"Then I'll leave it up to you." Jamie checked the trees again and could see no sign of Medraut. "Hey, Alaida. Have you ever seen anyone with eyes like his before?"

Alaida looked out into the trees as well. "No, never. I have heard of birth defects caused by resonator dust as he said, but to my understanding, it typically results in stillbirths and abominable deformities."

"Do you think that he might -- I mean, not that it matters, but could he actually be a slave of some kind?"

"No. He is definitely not of the Slave-Races."

"You seem awfully certain of that."

"No two Slaves-Races are identical, but even besides their golden eyes, they each have physical characteristics that instantly set them apart from Humans. I will admit that I have never seen an Orca-Slave or a Panther-Slave, but I have heard enough about all the Slave-Races to know what each looks like. Medraut is Human."

"Or..." Jamie said, "could he be something else?" He paused to clear his throat and then crouched down next to the fire to poke it with a stick. "Like, I don't know, an alien?"

"You mean, a creature from another world?"

Jamie felt his cheeks growing warm for even having suggested it. He met Alaida's eyes for only a moment before looking away and nodding with a shrug. "Yeah."

Alaida again glanced into the trees. After a moment, she said, "Would he not then look less human?"

"I don't know. I've seen even less aliens than you have Orca-Slaves. But do you remember the first time we ever talked? You told me that humans weren't native to Terrarhea and that you didn't know where the Slave-Races had come from originally." Technically, that made of them all aliens, with the possible exception of the Slave-Races, depending on what their homeworld was. At the very least, Jamie was certainly an outsider to this world. "What would an alien look like here? I ended up here somehow. Someone, somewhere has to know something, and if we can't find Major Ommto, we're gonna have to start looking for alternatives."

Alaida mused that over for a few moments. Now that the water in the kettle began to boil, she sprinkled the cariak on the surface and then moved it out of the direct flames. "Perhaps, but I am still uncertain of him. You would need to find out much more about him before telling him any details about your situation."

"Tell who what?" Medraut said, stepping out of the trees with a sleepy smile on his face. Jamie and Alaida shared a curious glance. Medraut had been far enough away and they'd been speaking softly enough that it didn't seem possible for him to have overheard them. Was this another of Medraut's oddities, or had a wayward breeze simply brought their words to his ear?

"Nothing," Jamie said. "We were just talking about when we should head back up to the ruins."

Regardless of Alaida's caution, Jamie hadn't needed her warning about holding his tongue. Telling everyone they met that he was an alien sharing bodies with a wanted criminal would not help their situation in the least. Perhaps, if they could find some concrete information about what was going on and who was involved, then he might give serious thought to adding others besides Alaida to his list of confidantes, but for the moment, the less anyone else knew, the better.

"You two might as well get started right away," Medraut said, stifling a yawn. "Once I get some of that cariak in me, I'm gonna see about doing a little hunting but then I'll join you."

"Are you going to need any help?" Jamie said. With no desire to even taste the cariak, he could have started exploring right away. He'd already waited long enough and could now practically feel the ruins calling out to him.

"Nah," Medraut said, which brought a silent sigh of relief from Jamie. "I hunt better on my own."

Alaida lifted the lid on the kettle to peek inside and then closed it again. "I believe it is ready," she said.

"Ah, good." Medraut all but snatched the cup Alaida had poured for him out of her hands. Eyes closed, he held the steaming beverage to his nose and inhaled deeply with a smile on his lips. After letting it cool for only a few seconds he took a long sip. "That is good. My compliments. You can have some too, if you'd like." Medraut looked first to Jamie but then Alaida as well. "Both of you."

"Well, maybe just a little," Jamie said, trying not to keep looking toward the top of the hill. The cup Alaida poured for him was far more than he would have preferred. It had a citrusy smell but tasted more bitter than any coffee or tea he had ever sampled. Alaida, however, sat back in her blankets and savored each sip.

"Thank you," she said, her eyes downcast as she addressed Medraut. "I have seldom had opportunity to taste it fresh before."

Medraut drained his cup with a loud sigh and then quickly poured himself another. "Well, drink your fill, Lady Raven-Slave. It'll only end up dousing the fire otherwise."

As they stood around the fire, drinking their cariak, both Alaida and Medraut took pieces of jerky from the bag and chewed methodically at the tough meat.

"Too bad I couldn't catch anything last night," Medraut said as he chewed on one of the strips. With each cup of cariak he drank, his eyes became a little brighter and his back a little straighter. "As good as this is, a nice fried fish really would have hit the spot this morning."

Jamie remembered having had fresh fish on one of the camping trips he'd taken with his family. His dad had never cleaned fish before so there were still scales all over them, even after his mother had nearly burned them just this side of being edible. Needless to say, supper hadn't been all that appetizing, but Jamie couldn't remember ever having spent a better evening with his parents or his sister.

"After that jackelope stew the other night," Jamie said to Alaida, "I'd like to see what you could do with some fish."

"Fried," Medraut said, "that's the only way to cook fish fresh out of the water".

Alaida nodded while staring into the fire. "Breaded or battered, that would be quite good. Too bad we do not have any flour. Or butter."

"I should have rendered those goplisam's from last night," Medraut said with a laugh. "It wouldn't be quite the same, but then we would have had enough oil to deep fry just about anything!"

Alaida snickered behind her hand. "That is true."

"Those things were kind of greasy," Jamie agreed.

"That's what makes them so good!" Medraut said. "They just slide right down."

All three of them laughed, even as Jamie and Alaida both cringed a little at the thought of having to eat any more of that squishy meat dripping with oil. Once all the cariak had been drunk, the camping supplies put away, and the fire extinguished, Medraut took up his things and set off into the trees to do some more hunting while Alaida retrieved the satchel containing Major Ommto's papers and the shard of black metal from the titan.

When Jamie shot her a questioning glance, she said, "Just in case we do find something. Or someone. These may help convince him to assist us."

At the very least, they might help explain what it was they were looking for if they did find someone unfamiliar with Major Ommto. Alaida also brought with her the last of the dried meat and a canvas water skin. By the time they began climbing the stone stairs alongside the beach once more, the sky had lightened considerably, but the sun had yet to make an appearance. The shadows still lingered stubbornly in that depression surrounding the lake, keeping their world one of monotone black and gray.

"What did you think of the cariak?" Jamie asked, carefully picking his way across the undulating stone steps. "After the goplisam last night and now that stuff, I'm starting to think that maybe he's giving us the most disgusting things he can find, just to see if we'll eat them."

Alaida had been stepping across the uneven stones with a nimbleness that made her look as if she were merely walking over rough asphalt, but she paused to shoot Jamie an indignant look. "The cariak was not to your liking? I found it to be quite good."

"Really?"

"Yes," Alaida said as she got underway again. "Perhaps Medraut is not completely without his virtues after all."

Jamie chuckled and shook his head. If even Alaida could come around to accepting Medraut, then maybe there was hope after all.

The dark gloom of the morning, made even darker by the thick canopy of trees overhead, did not make the ruins look any more promising than the last time they'd seen them. In the slowly brightening sunlight, Jamie and Alaida began searching more methodically than they had the evening before, exploring each building on each block before moving on to the next.

They hadn't made it very far when a skittering of rocks from a nearby lot suddenly drew their attention. Not knowing whether to expect some new monster or the last remaining resident of this place, they hurried to the end of the building and slowly peaked around the corner. The yard beyond was covered with a carpet of bright green grass growing between and over the giant stone blocks of a neighboring building which had long ago collapsed.

And picking through that rubble was a small herd of shaggy, white, goat-like creatures. Despite their spiraling horns and the narrow fangs protruding from their upper jaws, they hardly looked like much of a threat with their spindly legs and bony flanks. The moment they caught sight of Jamie and Alaida, several of them let out a mournful bleating sound and the herd edged to the far side of the yard, hopping through the field of fallen blocks with an agility that seemed at odds with their thin frames.

"What do you call those?" Jamie said.

"Goats," Alaida said as if the answer was patently obvious.

"Of course they are." The one time Jamie asked, it had to be obvious. His mortification, however, was beat out by a sudden twinge of excitement. "Didn't Onorah say something about Ommto retiring to raise goats?"

"Possibly," Alaida said. "Though to be honest, I often find myself questioning much about what I remember from that night."

"Yeah, sometimes I feel the same way."

Too bad these goats all looked rather feral, as if no one had been taking care of them for quite some time. Maybe Major Ommto had indeed died as Onorah had warned. Or maybe he'd simply moved on to a more relaxing retirement elsewhere.

"Think Medraut might be interested in bagging one of them for us?" Jamie said as the creatures bounded over the fallen rubble and disappeared into the deeper ruins. "They look like they might be a little tough, but they'd still have to be better than goplisams, right?"

Alaida merely chuckled as they once more set out on their search. It wasn't long afterward that she suggested that they could cover more ground if they split up. With Medraut's warning of pitfalls, Jamie preferred they stay together in case any troubles did befall them, but as the sun grew higher, the perceived dangers seemed to retreat with the shadows and the two of them began ranging farther afield of each other as they worked in tandem to clear each block. It helped to speed up the search, but it didn't result in any finds more interesting than what they had already seen. By the time the sun was starting to shine down through the branches overhead, their separate explorations were carrying them both completely out of sight of the other for long stretches at a time.

The two of them would periodically link back up with the other to determine their next step, and it was during one of these times that Medraut finally rejoined them. He brought with him news that he had managed to bag a buck rallore and that he had already made the initial preparations needed to add it to their supplies of food. Alaida seemed pleased with this, describing a rallore to Jamie as a type of large stag whose meat was far more palatable than goplisam. When Jamie asked if they would need to break off the search in order to deal with that, Medraut assured them that further preparations could wait until later. He then proceeded to lay out a plan which he insisted would maximize their search efforts. Jamie saw no fault with his reasoning and so the three of them continued according to Medraut's suggestion.

They did make good time, eliminating a large swath of the ruins over the next few hours, but with each new section they cleared, they inevitably found two more that still needed to be searched. The earlier excitement they'd started out with was soon replaced with a monotone sense of dull repetition. With each new building that Jamie investigated, he tried his best to quash any thoughts of optimism. However, no matter how hard he tried, there was always a small flicker remaining that left him feeling even more disappointed when he didn't find anything. He knew it had been too much to hope that they would find something truly enlightening right away, but as the morning quickly disappeared, they had yet to find anything more interesting than rotting furniture and rusty old hand tools.

It just didn't seem possible that whoever had last lived here couldn't have left any more significant trace of their presence behind. If the grounds had shown the signs of looting, that would have been another story, but it didn't look as if anyone had set foot here in years. Its remote location had probably helped in that regard, but it was starting to look as if that wouldn't matter one way or the other.

Occasionally, they would meet with each other to discuss their progress and adjust their efforts accordingly, but each time, Jamie could see Alaida's disappointment in her mannerisms even before she spoke. She did a good job of not expressing those same feelings in words, but Jamie was finding it harder and harder not to let his own irritation color his every word and action. Alaida did her best to reassure him, but it only helped so much. Medraut, meanwhile, seemed to have taken on an attitude of pure business in order to hide his own feelings. He no longer sang or told jokes, he merely reported what he had found in simple, concise statements and then explained where he thought they should next deploy their efforts.

By the time the sun passed midday, Jamie had completely lost track of how many times he'd heard the same reports from his two companions of having found absolutely nothing of interest. Jamie himself had grown tired of telling them the same thing in return. And without anything even the least bit interesting to keep his thoughts focused on the task at hand, he found himself dwelling more than ever on the growing sense of urgency produced by the building pressure in the back of his mind. They were running out of time and there was still so much of the estate left to search. The place was simply too massive, sprawling out in all directions at once. Even if they had days to continue the search, there would be no guarantee they'd find anything.

And now it wouldn't be long before they'd have to find some magnanimous way to send Medraut away in order to protect him from Reaver. But that could wait a little while, at least. Surely it wouldn't make much of a difference if they did that now, or five minutes before Reaver's return. At the moment, they still needed his help.

Jamie and Alaida had once again circled back to their latest agreed upon rendezvous. Neither of them felt much like talking and so they sat down on a fallen wall and waited in silence for Medraut to join them. Jamie, perched on a large stone that stood nearly as high as his shoulder, kicked his feet idly. This whole endeavor had become hopeless. Maybe the best thing to do was to send Medraut on his way when he returned and then just wait for Reaver to come back so that he could figure everything out for them.

"I wonder what is keeping Medraut," Alaida said, her voice flat and emotionless. Usually he was the first one back to their meetings.

Jamie swept his gaze across the unrelenting sameness of the trees and ruins surrounding them. "Maybe he found whatever it is we're looking for."

Alaida let out a long sigh, her shoulders stooping. "Indeed."

By this point, the possibility that Medraut had actually found anything at all was so doubtful that Jamie couldn't manage even a faint twinge of false hope at the thought. But then Jamie found he couldn't even get worked up over the more likely possibility that Medraut had fallen prey to one of those pitfalls he'd mentioned last night. Of course they'd go looking for him if he didn't return, but at the moment, the most likely explanation was that the young tracker was simply running a little behind.

"Alaida," Jamie said, staring out into the forest. "I've still got a little time left before Reaver comes back, but I just wanted to say that I'm gonna miss you when I leave. I mean, I always miss you, but this time...it's gonna be worse."

Alaida lowered her eyes to the ground and interlocked her fingers. "Despite everything that has happened, the last few days have not been entirely unenjoyable, have they?"

"No, they have not," Jamie said, just as Medraut came into view. So used to the repeated statements of continued failure, it took both Jamie and Alaida a brief moment to notice the subtle change in Medraut's expression.

He jogged to a stop in front of them, face flushed, and took a few moments to quiet his heavy breathing. Regardless of the way Jamie had tried to deny it to himself, that fleeting sense of hope that had been tormenting him all day had suddenly returned.

When Medraut finally said, "I think I might'a found something," Jamie's whole body grew tense and he sat forward expectantly. "Come on, I'll show you."

CHAPTER 45

Medraut set off at a moderate pace, slow enough that Jamie and Alaida could easily keep up but fast enough that it helped to satisfy some of the urgency born from their long festering frustrations. They passed through more streets that looked exactly like all the others they'd already seen. The buildings and the trees didn't suggest anything out of the ordinary until they finally arrived at what had once been a small, irregular plaza.

Really, it was hardly more than a wide spot where three streets all met, but the buildings surrounding it didn't look quite as ruined as the rest. The vegetation also didn't appear to have quite as strong a grasp over the area as everywhere else. It all made this one small section of the estate look as though someone had still been living here long after the rest of the place had fallen into ruin. However, the lack of undergrowth made the surrounding trees seem even larger than they really were, especially with the way their branches met overhead, turning the plaza into a soaring cavern of green. Despite the wide-open feel, the air somehow seemed deathly still.

One of the buildings off to their right still had a two-story portico of columns and a wide balcony at the second floor running along the entire front façade. The stone with which it had been built had become stained with algae, and several vines now encircled the columns, but the building as a whole had somehow managed to retain a small degree of its original grandeur.

Its front door even appeared to have been intact up until very recently when Medraut must have forced it open. If nothing else, that one building in particular still had a roof, which completely set it apart from all the others. However, even in its current condition, things like a gravel ramp that eased the transition from the level of the street up the five or so steps to the front door, gave the impression that it had been repurposed by whoever had last called this place home.

"What's inside?" Jamie said.

"I think you should see for yourself," Medraut said, leading the way up the ramp and through the front door.

Inside, the air smelt musty and a little sweet. Most of the entire lower floor was a single room with high ceilings. Despite its size, it felt much smaller than suggested by the building's footprint because of the thick stone walls and tight grid of stout columns. When Jamie saw the makeshift stalls for livestock that had been haphazardly built throughout the space, he slowly began to realize that the thick, spongy dirt that covered the entire floor was actually a long decayed mix of manure and straw.

Medraut motioned to the stalls with his thumb. "From the smell of it, I'd say they used to keep their goats in here before they went feral."

"Pretty nice for a barn," Jamie said, looking up at the intricate carvings that covered the arched stonework. Elsewhere, he spied the skeletal remains of what might have been the ancestor to one of those goats they'd been seeing periodically all morning.

"Definitely a house originally," Medraut said. "There's a kitchen in back. Whoever was living here must have done some remodeling. Upstairs is more interesting."

In the very middle of the building, a rickety flight of wooden stairs led up to the second floor.

"How did you find this place?" Jamie said. By his reckoning, this building had to be far on the western side of the estate and much closer to the southern tip of the mesa than to the lake at the north end: well beyond Medraut's most recent search grid. They shouldn't yet have made it here for hours and hours, probably well after Jamie would have been forced to leave them.

"Had a hunch," Medraut said as he began to ascend the stairs, each tread creaking dubiously underfoot. "I saw some signs and they brought me here."

Alaida took hold of Jamie's arm as they followed Medraut up the stairs. At the top, they found another door, this one hanging askew in its frame where the hinges had torn loose from the rotting wood. A fairly large hole in the roof had stained the surrounding stone walls and created a few more holes in the floor as well. The moment they stepped through the doorway to the other side, they were assaulted by a rank smell that made Alaida recoil and cover her nose.

"What is that?" Jamie said.

"Through here." Medraut led the way across a large room that took up the majority of the back of the second floor. Light filtered in though the large, broken windows in the back of the room, illuminating the wooden crates and barrels, scattered hand tools, and work benches which cluttered the room. From the heaps of animal dung scattered about, some kind of small creatures had been making this their home for quite some time.

The simple wooden door which led back toward the front of the building looked like it had remained tightly sealed for many years and even still worked. The smell was even stronger on the other side.

This entire chamber had been built of stone, from the thick slabs below to the shallow barrel vaults above. Nearly every wall had been lined with shelving or cabinetry of one sort or another which in turn had all been filled to overflowing with all manner of papers, clothes, house wares, and just simple trinkets. In the very middle of the room stood a table and a couple of chairs, all of which were also covered with tall stacks of junk.

In fact, every horizontal surface in the room looked to be piled high with clutter. Even most of the floor was occupied by countless dingy cardboard boxes stacked all the way to the ceiling, many of which had slumped and collapsed into the ones below them and turned the room into one big maze

Dust or mildew covered everything and much of the furniture was marked by large cracks where the wood had dried incurably to a powdery texture. A few windows of clouded glass opened onto the balcony at the front of the building and let in a soupy light which did little to dispel the sense that they had just entered a tomb.

A wire hanger on each side of the door held a dusty gloworb. One was broken, its glass sphere cracked, but the other readily came to life when Alaida gave it a gentle shake. The light it cast on their surroundings only made them appear more dismal than they had in shadow. Medraut stepped aside and pointed toward a recessed niche in the side wall cordoned off from the rest of the room by the dangling remnants of a curtain. Jamie made his way between the piles of trash and gingerly eased the curtain back. As he did so, it fell loose from its rod and sent Jamie jumping back several feet, nearly screaming in fright at what he saw on the other side.

Within the niche, atop a bed covered in moldering sheets, lay the desiccated corpse of a man. He'd clearly been in that room for as long as it had been abandoned, time having reduced his body to little more than a skeleton draped in dried flesh and the tattered remains of his clothes. While Jamie remained far back, unable to look at the body directly, Alaida stepped forward, eyeing it intently.

"Do you think this is…" she whispered.

Jamie merely shook his head, retreating another step until he backed into a small table and sent the piles of paper stacked on top sliding to the floor.

Medraut retrieved an opened letter from one of the stacks near the door, holding it up to the light in order to read the address. "Rillek Ommto," he said and then looked at the body. "Looks like you've found your guy."

"Are we sure?" Jamie said. "I mean, there must have been hundreds of Ommto's living here. He could be anybody."

"Jamie, look," Alaida said. She pushed open a wardrobe near the bed whose door had been left askew. Inside hung a tunic much like those Jamie had seen worn by the Finttiranos military, the only difference being that this one was a dark crimson red instead of green. Alaida pulled it out of the cabinet and laid it across the back of an upholstered wing chair. The chest was covered with a number of metals and each of the black shoulder boards had three brass bars below an enameled pin of a sunburst behind a mountain.

"That's a magesmith uniform alright," Medraut said, "and with major's bars too."

Jamie looked at the body laying on the bed and then quickly away. This couldn't be how his quest ended. Major Ommto was supposed to have answers for him. He was supposed to provide Jamie with, if not a solution, then at least a path out of this cycle of shared worlds.

"No. There's got to be something else here." Jamie turned and began surveying the piles of junk filling the room. Most of it was just that: junk, the typical knickknacks and mundane things accumulated over the course of a very long life, and most of them now broken beyond any practical use. Someone as clever as Reaver might have been able to deduce a critical clue from it, but not Jamie. Just to sort through it all would take days. And he didn't have that long, maybe only an hour now at the most. Frantically, he scooped up some of the papers he'd knocked over and quickly flipped through them.

Each piece of correspondence had been written in the same exceedingly formal and precise hand as had been used on the papers Del had given them in Tavnic. Many even bore the Iron Spur crest on their letterhead. A large sheet of fine vellum that had been folded over on itself many times appeared to be the schematics for *something*, but they where drawn at a level of complexity that rendered the whole thing meaningless. And of course, Jamie couldn't read any of it other than those four characters he now knew spelled "Ommto," which he saw on nearly every piece of paper in front of him

Jamie held a random handful of papers out to Medraut. "What do these say?"

Medraut made no move to take them. He just stood there and gave Jamie something of a quizzical look. "You expect me to read all those to you? There must be thousands of them."

"But we've got to do something. There's got to be something here."

Medraut sighed and shook his head. "I think it's time you face facts. You went through all this trouble for absolutely nothing. There's no information here. There's no treasure! There's nothing of value whatsoever! Whatever led you to think that there was anything here to begin with!"

Jamie recoiled. He'd never heard Medraut yell before. It seemed completely out of character for the care-free tracker they'd come to know over the last day and a half. Jamie couldn't even fathom what he had to be upset about. Had he really been expecting to find treasure and riches here, despite what Jamie had told him to the contrary? Is that the only reason he'd been helping them from the beginning?

"If we just took a look around," Jamie said, "there might be a clue about his research or...or something. I've come too far to give up without even looking."

Medraut's eyes narrowed and he picked up a sheaf of papers from one of the nearby stacks. "Hmm," he said, scanning the cover, "Do you know what this is?"

Jamie didn't like that cold tone in Medraut's voice one bit. "What?"

"Kindling." Medraut pulled a small brass cylinder from his pocket, not unlike the wardcaster Alaida had used to light their campfire each night. Rubbing his thumb down the side caused a brief flare of magescript and then the papers burst into flame. With a flip of the wrist, he tossed them into a pile of similar documents in the middle of the room.

"Are you crazy!" Jamie said. He couldn't get to the flames without crawling over several boxes of junk and the fire was already starting to spread. Alaida let out a cry and dashed toward the fire, using the old tunic to try and smother the flames. Turning back to Medraut, Jamie cried, "What do you think you're doing?"

His expression having turned to stone, Medraut ignored Jamie as he began strolling toward the exit. Jamie lunged after him and grabbed him by the shoulder, wrenching him back around to face what he had just done.

"Why would you do that?" Jamie said, seizing Medraut by the collar.

Medraut just shrugged and threw out his hands.

"Jamie!" Alaida cried.

Still holding tight to Medraut's shirtfront, Jamie looked over his shoulder to see Alaida being driven back by the spreading flames, her best efforts doing nothing at all to hold them in check.

"You might want to do something about that," Medraut said, his voice annoyingly flippant.

Jamie growled through his teeth and let Medraut go with a shove. He leapt over a stack of boxes and through the quickly rising wall of flames. Already, the fire had spread across the room, leaping from one pile of dry wood and paper to the next, and turning the inside of the room into a smoke-filled oven. There would be no getting Alaida back to the door they'd entered through.

"Go! Get to the balcony!" Jamie cried, pushing her along ahead of him.

"But the papers," Alaida said, coughing even as she stooped down to retrieve random handfuls of scattered letters and sheaves of documents.

"Forget them!"

Apart from the smoke itself, who knew what else might have been in that room. The air already smelt downright toxic and if there was anything explosive hidden under all that junk, they wouldn't have to wait for a slow painful death from smoke inhalation. Jamie kicked the door leading out onto the balcony and the whole thing tore off along with the frame, rotating diagonally in the opening. He tried again to kick it out of the way, but his boot just went right through the rotten wood.

"Just go!" he said, nearly lifting Alaida through the opening. He followed a moment later, tripping over the fallen door and scuttling out into the open air right behind her. Coughing violently, Alaida doubled over as she leaned against one of the large stone columns.

"Come on, we gotta get down from here," Jamie said, scrambling to his feet. If the fire damaged the already compromised structure of the building, the whole thing would come down right on top of them. "Give me your hand."

In one hand, Alaida still held the singed remains of Major Ommto's tunic, and in the other, a sizable handful of papers. She tossed the uniform to the ground below and then took Jamie's hand. He swung her over the edge and dropped to his belly, lowering her as far as he could. It still left her feet dangling several feet above the uneven steps in front of the building.

"Okay," she said. "I can make it from here."

"Careful," Jamie said as he let go.

She dropped and landed on the edge of a step, her foot twisting out from under her. As she tumbled onto her back, she finally lost her grip on the papers which went fluttering into the air all around her. Jamie rolled over the edge and dropped down beside her.

"Are you okay?"

"Yes." On hands and knees, Alaida grabbed the scattered papers and shoved them into the satchel still slung across her shoulder. "Where's Medraut?"

"I don't see him," Jamie said, helping to shovel up the papers.

"Why did he do that?"

Pressing the last of the papers into her hands, Jamie shook his head. "I don't know. Maybe you were right about him from the beginning."

Accepting Jamie's offered hand, Alaida climbed back to her feet and coughed once more as she picked up Major Ommto's tunic. It looked as if that might be all they'd have to show for their efforts. Already, flames were starting to billow through the open doorway above and one of the windows shattered from the heat, sending shards of glass tinkling down into the street.

"I hope Reaver's not going to be too upset about this," Jamie said as they backed away to the far side of the plaza.

"How much longer?"

"Not long," Jamie started to say. But the words froze in his mouth when he heard a distant howl echoing through the forest to the south. Both he and Alaida looked into the trees, hoping that they might have misheard.

"Was that...?" Alaida said, even as the first howl was answered by another, closer and even more clear than the first...and then another, and another, and many more besides. Alaida gripped Jamie's arm hard enough that he could feel her fingernails digging into his skin. "Wolf-Slaves..."

There could be no doubt she was absolutely correct. But these howls echoing through the forest were not the maniac cries they'd heard that morning by the river. These were the calculated and purposeful howls of Wolf-Slaves on the hunt.

CHAPTER 46

"You have got to be kidding me!" Jamie said, gazing off to the south but seeing nothing through the thick vegetation. First Medraut had to go and destroy his one chance at finding answers, and now this, both right on the verge of Reaver's return.

Alaida gave Jamie's arm a tug. "Jamie..."

"Yeah, we should go." Again, she was right. Not only were those howls already too close to ignore, they were getting nearer.

"What about Medraut?"

After what that bastard had just done, it would serve him right to be left behind. Too bad his skills with handling Wolf-Slaves would have been invaluable right now. But since they'd escaped from Major Ommto's hovel, neither Jamie nor Alaida had seen any trace of him. Was he maybe regretting what he'd done and now couldn't bare to face them? Or was he simply brooding in the forest somewhere about having missed out on his big payday?

"He can take care of himself."

Just as Jamie took Alaida's hand and turned to leave, six figures strode out of the shadows at the south end of the plaza. Something about their straight-backed, purposeful stride gave Jamie pause. When he looked again, it took him a moment to realize they were actually Wolf-Slaves.

Their coarse, grayish-brown fur was well-groomed and their long hair was held neatly back with decorative clips or braided into tidy cords that fell past their ears. They were also fully clothed, wearing matching body suits of snug-fitting, gray leather that left their lower legs and arms bare. Engineered to provide ease of movement with molded plates of thickened leather protecting vital areas, their garments had the look of military uniforms. The impression was only strengthened by the swords and long knives hanging from scabbards strapped to their bodies and by the diamond-shaped insignia each of them wore on their left shoulder depicting a large number "11" over a stylized wolf's head gripping a sword in its mouth.

Even more distinct was the look of cool intent in their golden eyes, so unlike the feral restlessness Jamie had come to expect of their kind. Two of them took position in front, one male and one clearly female, flanked on either side by the others. They were all powerfully built but rangy, with an explosive grace in their every movement.

"What are they?" Alaida whispered. "I've never seen Wolf-Slaves like that before."

Jamie could only shake his head. He had actually been hoping Alaida might be able to shed some light on this new development. Howls could still be heard sounding through the trees all around them. Whoever, or whatever, these six were, their emergence did not seem to have changed the situation at all. Remembering how Medraut had driven off the Wolf-Slaves at the river, Jamie did his best to stand up as tall and straight as he could.

"What do you want?" he called out across the plaza.

Their expressions remaining cold, the male and female shared a glance but said nothing.

"Look, if you're here for trouble, I don't want to hurt you!"

"You won't," the female said flatly. Her words were perfectly pronounced, more so than some of the human villagers Jamie had spoken with in Tavnic. Something about that voice juxtaposed with her savage appearance turned Jamie's blood to ice.

The male lifted his right hand to the level of his shoulder and pointed at Jamie with two fingers. "Go," he said in a voice intended only to be heard by those near him, "as we discussed."

The other four Wolf-Slaves drew their blades and began advancing across the plaza with a methodical and lethal confidence in their steady march. In the shadows under the trees, their weapons glowed with magescript. So much for Alaida's belief that slaves never used wardcaster weapons. These wouldn't be like any of the other Wolf-Slaves Jamie had faced. With a great deal of luck, he might be able to deal with these six but if there were more of them lurking in the forest, he could imagine no outcome that would end well for him and Alaida.

"We gotta run," Jamie said. "Get back to the titan..."

And then what? Fight through them again like the last time, indiscriminately killing scores without regard for the fact that doing so would only make him more of a murderer than he already was?

Unfortunately, he couldn't see any other option.

Jamie grabbed Alaida's hand and together the two of them fled back toward the beach. He stole a glance over his shoulder to see the Wolf-Slaves set off at a sedate jog in pursuit. In made Jamie grit his teeth to see them undertake their endeavor in such an unhurried and dismissive manner, as if they were just playing with their prey.

More likely, they simply didn't think he and Alaida were worth the effort of taking seriously. They could very well have been entirely correct. Jamie had yet to have any lasting success against their kind. Even if he somehow found a way out of this, they'd likely become a constant threat that would dog his every moment on Terrarhea until he found a way to break free of this place or they finally finished what they had set out to do.

Running along the uneven cobblestones with ruins on both sides, Alaida's heavy breathing in his ears, and the soft padding of Wolf-Slaves behind, Jamie never once doubted the route they followed. Reaver's unerring sense of direction helped, but the radial orientation of the streets meant all they had to do was keep the spire ahead of them and then to their backs once they passed it. And as similar as every new portion of the estate had seemed that morning, Jamie now found he actually remembered most of the streets they traveled.

He knew that they would need to veer onto a side street ahead and just as they entered the intersection and began to turn onto the left-hand street, another two uniformed Wolf-Slaves stepped from the shadows on their right and joined in the pursuit with the others. Ahead, a long plaza lined on each side by a pair of tall, colonnaded buildings awaited them. It had the feeling of a narrow ravine that would leave them vulnerable to snipers from above.

Jamie cursed under his breath when he saw humanoid shapes moving within the ruins and the glow of magescript on their long blades. The Wolf-Slaves were already here. Jamie had heard of wolves on Earth using these same sorts of tactics. They weren't toying with their prey; they were herding them towards an ambush. But they already outnumbered Jamie and Alaida many times over and they were also far better armed. What could they possibly be waiting for?

Each new intersection and plaza they crossed added more Wolf-Slaves to the chase. To Jamie's ears, it sounded like a whole mob of them in pursuit, so many of their soft footfalls creating a dull roar in his wake.

If Jamie could just keep Alaida and himself alive a little longer, then Reaver would return. At this point it wouldn't be long. Yes, Jamie could just step out of the way and let Reaver do all the killing, as if that would somehow keep Jamie's hands clean. But would even Reaver be able to get them out of this one? If things got too dire, would he even bother to protect Alida, or would he just abandon her. He might have had use for her as a messenger, but from the sound of things, he had never been particularly warm to her. He likely perceived her as a grudging necessity, a disposable commodity that could easily be replaced if lost, not as the singular individual she truly was.

There had to be a solution to this problem. Jamie just had to figure out what it was. Maybe he had been too quick to abandon Medraut back there. Surely, he would have had some clever, and likely embarrassingly simple, answer to their current troubles.

Ahead, the tunnel of darkness cutting through the forest came to an abrupt halt where the street finally spilled back into the large plaza at the top of the cliff. The titan would be close now. If only they could bring the machine back online before the Wolf-Slaves completely overwhelmed them.

They broke into the light, Alaida throwing up her hand to shield her eyes from the blazing sun above. Jamie's own eyes adapted instantly, allowing him to quickly scan the edges of the plaza and confirm that it was free of Wolf-Slaves for the moment. At the very edge of the cliff, Medraut stood with his back to them, gazing down at the lake below. To have beaten them here, he must have come straight back after setting the fire. Jamie still wanted to cave his face in for that, but they could settle that later. Right now, they needed his help.

Pushing Alaida on ahead, Jamie turned to face the pursuing Wolf-Slaves. "Keep going, I'll try to slow them down." Thankfully, she didn't stop to question him but instead went running as fast as she could across the plaza. Jamie took a deep breath and then slowly let it out as he balled his hands into fists, watching the shapes of Wolf-Slaves resolve out of the forest's shadows. "Medraut!" he called over his shoulder, "Wolf-Slaves! Lots of them!"

"I know." Medraut turned and strolling away from the edge, his expression bored. "They're already here."

"We need your help!" Jamie said. The Wolf-Slaves began to emerge from the trees, and not just from the street Jamie had been following, but from along the entire perimeter of the plaza. Taking it all in with a sweep of his eyes, Jamie counted about fifteen of them -- no twenty. As they left the forest, their pace slowed to a steady walk, all of them advancing on Jamie with blades drawn. Without taking his eyes from them, Jamie backed toward the stairs. Why would they have brought him here? In the tight confines of the ruins, with plenty of opportunities for ambush, they would have had the clear advantage. Facing them here in the open didn't exactly help Jamie, but it didn't seem to offer them any benefit either. "Medraut, I think they're up to something!"

Medraut chuckled and shook his head. "So, you're not quite as stupid as you sound after all, huh?"

"What?" This was hardy a time for jokes. Regardless of what had inspired Medraut to start that fire, he was in just as much danger as Jamie and Alaida were -- unless he knew something Jamie didn't. Jamie glanced over his shoulder just in time to see three more Wolf-Slaves, attired like the others, ascend the stairs to the plaza.

Jamie cursed under his breath and Alaida let out a yelp as she went backpedaling in his direction. Medraut stepped in and caught her by the arm, inciting another cry, this one of both shock and pain as he forced her to her knees. She twisted in his grip, trying unsuccessfully to break free but Medraut seemed oblivious to her plight, instead glaring at Jamie.

"Stop it!" Jamie said, turning completely away from the encircling Wolf-Slaves. "You're hurting her!"

"Yeah," Medraut said, "and you're next."

Jamie stole a glance at the Wolf-Slaves. They had continued to close with him but then stopped, forming a solid perimeter around the narrow end of the plaza facing the cliff. Were they curious about how this dispute between Medraut and Jamie would play out, or did these uniformed Wolf-Slaves have some other agenda in mind besides Jamie's immediate execution?

"What is wrong with you?" Jamie said, addressing Medraut. "I thought you were our friend, but first that fire and now this? Whatever it is you've got against me; you'd better put it on hold for a little while. If you hadn't noticed, we're surrounded here! We've got to do something!"

"No!" Medraut's face contorted with absolute rage. It was an expression Jamie had seen many times before on the faces of those feral Wolf-Slaves he'd faced in the past. Medraut then laughed, as if at his own embarrassment, and ran a hand across his face. "I was never your friend."

"So, this was all just some kind of con from the very beginning, and you're pissed off because there was nothing here to steal from us?"

"Not quite," Medraut said with a chuckle. "I was just ensuring you lived just long enough to see everything you care about utterly destroyed."

Mouth agape, Jamie could do little but shake his head.

"The Wolf-Slaves..." Alaida whimpered, "you're working with them..."

"Listen here, Lady Raven-Slave, they're not working with me, they're working for me!"

Alaida's eyes grew wide and her face lengthened. "What are you?"

Medraut looked at Jamie, his eyes alight with rage. "I'm the Lord of the Wolves, you bastard!"

This couldn't be happening. Jamie had let a complete lunatic into their midst for nearly two whole days and hadn't even noticed just how unbalanced he really was. Of course it would be just like Jamie to make such a colossal mistake. He should have listened to Alaida's misgivings from the very beginning.

"You're crazy!" Jamie said, taking a step in their direction. "Wolf-Slaves don't have masters, none of them do! They're wild animals! You said so yourself!"

"He is our lord," one of the Wolf-Slaves said in a voice cold and level. It made Jamie's skin crawl.

"We are all his charges," another added.

Medraut smiled, baring his canines, and fixed Jamie with a piercing gaze. "That's right. I'm not their master, but all Wolves, everywhere, are under my protection! Even the ones that you killed, Reaver."

"What? How did..." Jamie suddenly felt like he'd been kicked in the gut. He had never mentioned Reaver to Medraut, had never given him any details about what had happened in Tavnic, and had certainly never told him about all those dead Wolf-Slaves.

"They told me about what you did," Medraut said, pointing with his chin into the distance, "the one with the burns and the other one with the jaw. It's my responsibility to look out for all the Wolves in this world: to guide them, to protect them...and to avenge them when necessary; even when they get themselves killed for doing something as stupid as making a deal with you!"

"I didn't make any deal with them. That was someone else!"

"You can't lie to me. They know your scent. Before I met you, I never thought it was possible for someone to smell as much like machine oil as you do. It's like you've spent so long in that titan, it's seeped all the way through your skin. There's no doubt you're the one responsible."

"I was just defending myself."

"And now you even admit your guilt."

"They were trying to kill me!"

"With good reason: you betrayed them."

"Just like you're doing to us now? How can you be such a hypocrite! You even killed that Wolf-Slave by the river."

"I told them all to leave you alone until I could get a better feel for who I was dealing with, but those two wouldn't listen. I killed him because he failed to follow my instructions. When you challenge a pack's leader, you either back down or you die. That's the way of the Wolves."

"And just who made you Lord of the Wolves!"

Jamie caught a glimpse of movement out of the corner of his eye as several of the gathered Wolf-Slaves shifted their feet. Medraut scowled at them, then chuckled.

"As much as I'd like to draw this out a little more, I don't really have time. Pressing matters require my presence elsewhere."

Jamie took a tentative step in Medraut's direction. Despite their apparent apprehension about something, the Wolf-Slaves were still just standing there, alert and watchful, but showing no signs of attacking. Alaida made another attempt to pull herself free, but Medraut's grip seemed unbreakable. No matter what the young tracker thought he was, there was no way he could possibly match Reaver's strength. If Jamie could just get Alaida away from Medraut, they might have a chance.

"Just let her go." Jamie took another step. "If you want to fight me, fine, but leave Alaida out of this."

"I don't want to fight you," Medraut said, "I want to kill you. But only after I make you suffer by taking away all your pretty little trinkets."

Jamie's whole body tensed. The one thing that Medraut had going for him in an all-out fight was his speed. If he did anything to Alaida, Jamie wouldn't even be able to get close before it was all over. "Please!" Jamie said. "Alaida's not a thing, she's a person! And she didn't do anything to you or those Wolf-Slaves. She doesn't deserve this just for being my friend."

Medraut scoffed. "You know those Wolves you killed? They were my friends. And they didn't deserve what you did to them either." Medraut wrenched Alaida upright and looked right into her face, bearing a toothy grin. "Goodbye, Lady Raven-Slave." He then pushed her away, right toward the edge of the cliff.

"No!" Jamie already knew he was too far away to do anything, but he shot forward on legs that uncoiled like springs. Alaida stumbled, fell, and rolled right to the edge, one leg going over the side. In a frantic clawing at the ground as gravity pulled her over, the tips of her fingers somehow latched onto a loose cobblestone, arresting her fall with a jerk, but leaving her in a precarious state.

Reaching out for her hand, Jamie made it to within an arm's length of her when he suddenly found himself sliding sideways across the rough ground after Medraut's boot heel collided with the side of his face.

"Ah! I've been waiting to do that a long time!" Medraut said as he hopped back and forth from one foot to the other with the nervous energy of a boxer just stepping into the ring. Looking down at Alaida, he shook his head. "You're not gonna make this easy, are you?" He then lifted his heavy boot and smashed it right down on top of her hand.

She let out a cry as she slipped a fraction of an inch farther over the edge. From where he lay on the ground, Jamie saw the expression of pain and fear flash across her face. It launched him back to his feet, propelling him directly at her attacker.

Medraut practically laughed as he stepped out of Jamie's way with a leisurely turn. Jamie stumbled to a stop with a snarl on his lips and spun on the young tracker. He wouldn't let things end this way, not for him or Alaida. Leading with his fist, Jamie charged once again, putting enough power behind this one punch to dent plate steel and shatter ancient trees. After all the things Medraut had done, he deserved no less.

However, Medraut shifted his weight ever so slightly and simply pushed Jamie's fist aside. Even as Jamie followed up by taking a wild swing at him with the other arm, Medraut ducked out of the way and kicked him in the ribs.

Jamie skidded right to the rim of the cliff, the heel of his boot slipping over the edge along in a cascade of tiny pebbles. Not far away, Alaida tried frantically to pull herself up, or at the very least secure her grip, but her every attempt only seemed to be making her situation worse. The bottom was a long way down, and even though the top of the cliff was a nearly vertical drop, the size of the stone slabs which comprised it offered plenty of ledges just big enough to support a person...if only she could get to one without falling all the way to the bottom.

"You're strong, I'll give you that," Medraut said, turning his back to Jamie as he walked in a wide circle and shook out the hand he'd used to push Jamie aside. "But you fight like a drunk borrang. If you weren't so tough, you'd a' been long dead by now."

Unfortunately, Jamie couldn't deny that. He shifted his eyes from Medraut, to Alaida, and then back. The moment Medraut turned back around, he came at Jamie, his hands and feet a whirlwind of punches and kicks. Jamie didn't even bother to meet him or counter any of it, instead diving out of the way and sliding on his belly to Alaida.

Hastily grabbing for her hand, Jamie accidentally knocked it loose. Her shrill cry cut off a split second later when Jamie seized her by the wrist with both hands, aborting her fall but leaving her with long, bloody scrapes where the sharp stones racked across the bottoms of her arms.

"Alaida! I'm going to let you go!" Jamie said, as he slid half his body over the edge, lowering Alaida as far as he could by one arm. Her already firm grip on his wrist tightened. "Trust me! There's a ledge right below you!"

"What the hell are you up to now?" Medraut said as he stalked toward Jamie, considering him like some amusing puzzle that needed to be solved.

Alaida looked down and then back at Jamie. From the fear in her wide eyes, she couldn't see what he had. Regardless, she nodded.

This would be close. The ledge was narrow and at least a full body length below. Plus, with Alaida blocking his view, Jamie could barely see it himself. He'd have to aim just right to ensure she reached it. After that, it would all be up to her.

Just as Jamie was about to let her go, Medraut struck him in the side with the toe of his boot. It didn't hurt any more than any of the other injuries he'd sustained here on this world, but it did jostle his whole body and send Alaida swinging erratically from the dangling end of his arm. It also unseated Jamie's precarious grip on one of the loose cobblestones he had been using to anchor himself. If he didn't get Alaida to safety right now, they'd both end up strewn across the stones below.

Again Medraut kicked Jamie. Feeling the cobblestone under his hand shift and start to pull out, it would no longer matter how tightly he dug his fingers in. Time slowed to a crawl as Jamie watched Alaida's body swing back and forth between breaths. Medraut's next kick and the taunt which accompanied it were distant in Jamie's mind. He knew where he needed to get Alaida to and that was all that mattered. He watched the arch of her next swing and then, at what he hoped was just the right moment, let go. His heart welled up into his throat as she fell, arms flailing and black hair fanning out around her pale face. She remained suspended there for so long, retreating, it didn't seem possible that she was on target. But then she stopped, crumbled from the impact, and threw herself against the side of the cliff. Even at that distance, Jamie could hear her gasping breath as she found a handhold in the rocks and pressed herself tight against them.

"You should have just let her fall." Medraut stooped down next to Jamie so he could look over the edge. "Now it'll only be worse --"

Medraut's words died with the sound of a crack as Jamie lunged off the ground, slamming the cobblestone in his hand into the side of Medraut's face. He saw a flash of blood as Medraut leapt back, a snarl on his lips. Once at a safe distance, Medraut drew his hand across his temple. He looked at the streak of blood in his palm for several moments, his purple eyes wide with disbelief. As he turned back to Jamie, his dark pupils grew tiny and the veins on the sides of his head and neck bulged. His hands tensed like claws.

"Enough playing around!" he howled. "Now you're gonna die!"

CHAPTER 47

Jamie knew Medraut was fast, but now he lashed out with a speed that even Jamie found difficult to follow. An attempt to block his first strike resulted in Jamie receiving three more before he even knew that Medraut had made contact. Try as he might, Jamie couldn't block even a fraction of what Medraut threw his way. It seemed as if just as many of his punches and kicks were feints as were actually intended to inflict damage. And for someone so small, he hit like a sledgehammer. It still wasn't enough to hurt Jamie, but it kept him off-balance, allowing Medraut to drive him back with each blow. All he could do was shield himself and try to stay on his feet.

In the middle of it all, Jamie caught a flash of magescript on the edge of his vision and instinctively jumped back. Somehow, without breaking the rhythm of his attack, Medraut had drawn the machete from his pack and turned what looked like just another punch into a slash with that deadly weapon. Jamie felt the hum of the blade slice through the air right in front of him. He also felt a distinct sting across the side of his raised arm.

"Finally!" Medraut said, laughing and throwing out his arms.

Jamie couldn't risk taking his eyes off Medraut for more than a moment, but with even just a quick glance at his arm, he saw a red stream of blood flowing from the long gash down the length of his forearm.

Jamie had experienced Reaver's body surviving explosions and claws, fists and stun spears without so much as a scratch. He'd begun to think himself invulnerable, but apparently a wardcaster blade in the hands of an expert could cut even him. Just how lucky had he been up to this point not to have gotten shot or stabbed by one of the many people he'd crossed paths with who wanted to do him harm? And now he was facing off against someone who not only had the skill to do him in but also a reason as well.

Running might have been the only option. Jamie glanced down to the beach. Along the face of the cliff, Alaida had slowly begun making her way toward the stairs. If Jamie could keep the Wolf-Slaves focused on him and Medraut, then it might give her at least a chance to get away. Unfortunately, there were more Wolf-Slaves below as well, milling around the titan-mecha. Neither Jamie nor Alaida had anywhere to run now.

Reaver would be coming soon but would Jamie be able to keep them alive even that long? Even if he could, he had no way of knowing if it would even guarantee Alaida's safety afterward. This whole situation was quickly becoming hopeless.

Regardless, Jamie planted his feet and raised his fists. If he didn't do anything, neither of them would be left with any chance at all of getting out of this. Fortunately, the cut on his arm didn't hurt. There was a sensation of something being wrong with it, but apart from that, everything still seemed to work just fine.

"How are you still standing?" Medraut said, twirling the machete in his hand as he circled Jamie. Jamie hadn't realized it before, but the braided leather cords worked with beads and feathers that hung from the back of the machete looked the same as the decorations the Wolf-Slaves worked into their hair. "Any one of those punches should have ruptured something for sure. But if you bleed, I guess I'll just have to take you apart piece by piece."

One moment, Medraut had been strolling along several paces away, looking completely relaxed, and the next, he lunged at Jamie, leading with the point of his blade. Being able to see the weapon this time, Jamie managed to dodge to the side, but only at the very last moment. He still felt the swirl of air it created in its wake and heard the snarl on Medraut's lips as he twisted his wrist and redirected the blade at Jamie's midsection.

This wasn't anything like facing off against those Finttiranos soldiers armed with guns or even the Wolf-Slaves he'd fought hand-to-hand. Here, he could not only see the hatred in his attacker's eyes, but a single misstep would surely result in more than just a few extra tears to his poncho. Leaping backward only bought Jamie the briefest of moments before Medraut slashed at him again.

With Jamie's strength, a single good punch might have turned the tables, but he didn't have time to even think about such things. The whole of his attention had narrowed to a razor's edge as he focused on Medraut's blade slicing through the air again and again, each time missing its intended target by only the thinnest of margins. Medraut was just too fast and skilled with that weapon for Jamie to counter him in any way. Eventually, he was going to find his mark and then that would be that.

As Jamie ducked away from Medraut's latest slash, his heel landed on a rounded stone which sent him stumbling awkwardly and left him certain that he had finally run out of luck. Medraut, however, didn't appear to have been expecting the move either and his follow-up attack was sloppy, nothing more than a wild swing in Jamie's general direction which left his whole side completely exposed. Jamie only had a split second to react, planting his rear foot and striking out at

Medraut with a balled fist. Medraut realized his mistake a moment too late, his eyes growing wide with panic as he tried twisting his body out of the way of Jamie's fist even as it made contact.

Medraut rolled with the punch and landed on a knee with the other leg kicked out wide for balance while keeping the machete raised in defense. Jamie, meanwhile, fell flat on his face, having overreached without first finding solid footing. He rolled away and pushed himself up on his hands as Medraut launched himself into the fight once more.

Jamie backpedaled wildly in order to stay beyond the reach of Medraut's flashing blade but if he wasn't careful he'd run out of ground. The cliff was already looming close and Medraut seemed to be driving Jamie right toward it. All he'd have to do is push him over the edge in order to finish this fight. And with Reaver still a minute or two away, Jamie was running out of time as well.

"Just stop moving!" Medraut cried, taking a particularly powerful thrust at Jamie with the tip of the machete. A weapon like that wasn't really designed for stabbing, but in the hands of someone like Medraut, that hardly made any difference.

Jamie threw himself out of the way. The blade passed under his outstretched arm but slashed across the side of his chest. His tough leather garments offered no resistance, parting against the edge of the blade like water. He tried to convince himself it hadn't actually cut his skin right up until he felt the rattling sensation of the blade scrapping across his ribs. At that, he reacted without thinking, kicking and flailing wildly. He had no plan; he simply knew he had to get Medraut away from him before he was chopped to pieces.

Somehow, one of Jamie's random blows caught Medraut's wrist. It knocked the young tracker's arm wide and the machete fell from his hand, clattering across the uneven ground. That might have been the opportunity Jamie needed, had Medraut not recovered almost instantly, leaping into the air and delivering a flying spin kick to the side of Jamie's head. It sent him to the ground hard and his head rebounded off a stone at the edge of the cliff, sending his vision lolling down into the void.

Chuckling grimly between breaths, Medraut tottered away to retrieve his weapon. At least Jamie had been able to wear him down a little bit before the end.

Below, Jamie could see that Alaida had made it safely to the stairs, but a pair of those uniformed Wolf-Slaves were ascending from the beach to intercept her. Jamie hissed through his teeth as he pressed a hand to the wound in his side. He couldn't quite bring himself to look at it for fear of what he'd see. The warm, slick blood had already soaked the side of his suit and was dripping between his fingers. At this rate, he wasn't even going to be able to save himself, let alone Alaida. Heather was going to be so mad if he went and got himself killed like this -- not that she'd likely ever know what had become of him.

"I'll tell you what," Medraut said as he bent down to recover the machete. The blade made a baleful shriek as it scraped across the cobblestones. "Why don't you stay right there, and I'll make it quick for you."

The ground was a long way down, Alaida was in dire trouble, and Jamie was now almost positive that he wouldn't last long enough against Medraut for even Reaver to be able to get them out of this. With one hand covering his side, he carefully picked himself off the ground.

"Screw you," Jamie said as he turned and jumped off the cliff as hard as he could, aiming for the distant stairs. He knew that even with Reaver's incredible strength to propel him, he wouldn't have been able to clear that distance over flat ground. But here, with the geometry of the cliff to assist him, the farther he fell, the longer he had to reach his target. He still didn't know if he would be able to make it, but he did know those sharp stones couldn't possibly cut him as badly as a magesmith blade.

As the ground opened up below, leaving him sailing through a vast emptiness, he heard Medraut gasp and a pair of heavy boots running to the edge. He felt the two halves of the wound in his side part as his arms pinwheeled in a frantic attempt to control his descent. Now that he was committed to this course, however, gravity had the greater say in such matters.

Even more quickly than the ground had initially receded, it now rushed up to greet him. Maybe he would make it to the stairs after all, but if so, only by the narrowest margin. He was also heading straight for Alaida and she had only now noticed Jamie's rapid descent.

Jamie began to cry out a warning but the words died on his lips as he hit the ground no more than an arm's length below her. His ankle twisted under him on the pitched stone tread and his knee buckled as the rest of his body came crashing down on top of it. He crumpled and rolled right into the pair of surprised Wolf-Slaves with such force they all three went crashing down the stairs, ricocheting off each step and fallen stone until finally coming to a stop at the next landing.

After watching in shocked disbelief for a brief moment, Alaida rushed down the stairs to join them. Jamie rolled back upright but his leg no longer seemed willing to take its share of his weight. One of the Wolves lay face down, moaning, while the other rose to its feet nearly as awkwardly as Jamie had. Balancing on his good leg, Jamie shoved the Wolf-Slave into a thorn bush alongside the stairs.

"Jamie!" Alaida ran to his side, reaching for his wound. "Are you --?"

"Come on!" he said, cutting her off and ushering her on ahead as he glanced back toward the plaza. The distance he had just covered looked ever farther than it had from above. It had been a miracle that he'd survived. He could see Medraut standing up there at the edge, staring on with mouth agape; right up until he saw Jamie looking back, and then he began yelling furiously for his gathered Wolf-Slaves to give chase.

Alaida took Jamie's arm as they hobbled down the next flight of stairs side by side. If they had been going up, he probably wouldn't have gotten very far. He'd likely broken something in that landing, his knee threatening to collapse under him each time he put too much weight on it, but at the moment he wasn't feeling any pain and he certainly didn't have time to stop and examine it. With the nagging sensation in his head having built nearly to its breaking point, it was difficult to concentrate on anything else.

"Reaver's almost here," he bit out as he leaned on Alaida far more than he would have liked.

"Will he...will he be able to help, do you think?"

Jamie shook his head. "I don't know." With all the punishment his body had taken, it seemed possible that even Reaver might cut his loses and simply run for it, abandoning Alaida to her own fate. He had to get her as far away as possible; give her as much of an advantage as he could before he ran out of time here.

From the previous trips they'd taken up and down the stairs, Jamie recognized the next landing which lay ahead of them. The path would cut sharply away from the cliff at that point and back into a thick stand of trees whose branches blocked out the sun and gave the impression of being under a pavilion like had originally stood there. There was also a game trail which snaked diagonally along the slope to the west. They'd never bothered to explore it, but if animals used it to get down to the lake, he and Alaida might be able to use it to get out.

Rounding the corner, however, they came skidding to a halt when they found their path blocked by the towering shape of a man. Their pursuers temporarily forgotten, both Jamie and Alaida stood rooted in place, unable to run or even look away. Whoever this newcomer was, he wasn't a Wolf-Slave, that much was clear. Draped in layers and layers of dark robes that entirely shrouded his body except for the pale skin of his head, he must have stood at least seven feet tall. The fact his face was that of an elderly man did nothing to offer any reassurance. His stark white hair, framed from behind by a wide, standing collar, had been combed straight back from this wrinkled brow like a fright wig. The way his head bobbed from side to side as he stared down at them with a furtive smile on his thin lips reminded Jamie of a venomous snake preparing to strike.

Just then, the first of the Wolf-Slaves that Medraut had sent in pursuit burst onto the landing. They too stopped short at the sight of this creature, but instead of being dumbstruck, they promptly dropped to a knee and bowed their heads. Their reverence seemed to please the creature and the wrinkles on its face grew deeper as its smile broadened.

The Wolf-Slaves' sudden entrance snapped Jamie out of his stupor and he turned to face them. Having forgotten his injuries, however, his leg crumbled and sent him crashing down to a knee as well. The impact caused the pressure building in his mind to yank at his consciousness, threatening to sweep him back to Earth. This couldn't be happening!

Tears welling up in her eyes, Alaida glanced at Jamie, silently pleading with him to save them.

He just couldn't leave, not now of all times!

He couldn't count on the Red Rogue or Reaver or whoever it was to solve all his problems for him. He himself was the only one who he knew would actually try to get Alaida out of this! Pinching his eyes shut against that mounting force pulling at his mind, he clenched his jaw so tightly it felt as if his teeth might break.

But it wouldn't go away. The tension just kept stretching itself tighter and tighter.

It was going to break.

No, he wouldn't allow this to happen, not this time!

But then it snapped, just like the other times before.

"No..." he said, tears leaking out around his closed eyes. "Alaida...I'm sorry."

CHAPTER 48

Slowly, Jamie opened his eyes, wondering where Reaver had brought him and what new danger he'd put him in this time. Instead, he saw the same stone landing where he'd been a moment ago and that same person -- that creature -- standing before him, a thin hand with claw-like nails extending from within its robes, reaching for Alaida.

A thousand questions all tore through Jamie's mind in a single instant, foremost among them, was he really seeing what he thought he saw? Had he somehow broken the link between his world and this one? The nagging sensation, which had been an ever-present companion on each previous trip to Terrarhea, had completely vanished from his mind. Was he now stuck here forever?

He didn't have time to consider answers. This was exactly what he'd wanted, a chance to save Alaida by his own hand.

A scream on his lips, Jamie launched himself into motion from his good leg. He charged to his feet with more speed than he'd ever before mustered from Reaver's body; like a bullet shot from a gun pointed directly at that grotesque parody of a man looming over Alaida. The creature lifted its bony arm in a slow, almost casual gesture, the hand dangling loosely from the wrist. Then, it brought it down in a lightning quick gesture, the hand snapping violently like the end of a flail. The motion had been slow and deliberate, seeming to take no effort at all on the part of this creature, yet it still intercepted Jamie, moving as fast as he was, and swatted him aside like a rag doll.

Jamie fell on his ruined knee and it twisted under him. He crumpled into a heap at the side of the trail in a pile of last falls leaves. He couldn't let things end this way, not after he'd been given another chance to get Alaida and himself out of this. He rolled, pushing himself back up almost instantly, but had no choice but to freeze halfway to his feet when he found three Wolf-Slaves standing over him with wardcaster blades pressed to his chest.

"You're quick," the creature said, its voice cool and methodical, with just an edge of elite sophistication, "and strong. But you don't have any leverage."

Its hand was on Alaida's shoulder now, Jamie all but forgotten. Standing rigidly, unable to back away no matter how much her bulging golden eyes said she wanted to, Alaida's whole body trembled as the creature took hold of her chin with its other hand.

"What a pretty little Raven," it said to no one in particular. Though its words were soft, they were anything but soothing.

Glaring at the creature and baring his teeth, Jamie slipped his good leg under him, ready to pull Alaida away from that thing, regardless of the Wolf-Slaves stranding over him, but one of them growled and kicked him in the chest with its bare foot, sending him right onto his back. Jamie might have been strong and fast, but it was just like that thing had said. If he tried to stand, the Wolf-Slaves would just knock him down again or run him through with their blades. Even if he could get to Alaida, that thing could easily snap her neck like a dry twig in an instant. He really did have no leverage of any kind here.

Ignoring Jamie entirely, the creature in the shape of a man bent close to Alaida with a knowing smile on its lips, twisting her face first one way and then the other, examining her like one might a rare butterfly. "Ah, yes. I know these features well," it said, still seemingly speaking only to itself. "Even after all these years, it never ceases to amaze me how so few genetic traits can be arranged into so many unique phenotypes. This combination is truly lovely, though: understated yet beautiful."

Suddenly, it looked straight into Alaida's eyes. "Do you fly, little Raven?"

Jaw quivering and tears streaming down her face, Alaida pushed back fitfully against its grasp, but to no avail.

"No?" The smile slipped from the creature's face. "Pity."

Next, the creature's face snapped in Jamie's direction. Instinctively, he found himself cringing away, wanting to scuttle into the bushes and hide from this bizarre creature.

"Do I know you?" the creature said.

Still holding Alaida tight in its grasp, the creature's head bobbled rhythmically between its shoulders like a slow pendulum as it now scrutinized Jamie with its yellow eyes. They weren't the golden-yellow of a slave's eyes, though, but a very human sort of jaundiced-yellow, the kind that came with advanced age. They remained sharp and alert, however, seemingly boring down into Jamie's very soul. He wanted nothing more than to get out from under that gaze, take

Alaida in his arms, and run; but he wasn't sure he even had enough nerve left to stand in the face of this thing. What good had staying on Terrarhea been if he wasn't even able to capitalize on it?

"Oh yes, that's it," the creature said at last with a self-satisfied smile that revealed a mouth of pristine white teeth, oddly perfect in shape. "You're one of Lareed's children, aren't you?"

All fear washed out of Jamie's mind in an instant. Did this creature actually know who he was, or perhaps more rightly, who Reaver was?

"What? Do you know me?" Jamie demanded in a voice that still shook, despite his newfound resolve. "Who's Lareed?"

"Hmm." The creature frowned and its head tilted sharply to the side, not unlike the way Alaida was prone to do when considering a question. "Such a disappointment. But then, it has been a day for disappointments, hasn't it Medraut?"

The creature now swung its gaze to the stairs which went back up to the plaza above. Just then, Medraut burst around the corner, murder in his eyes. The moment he caught sight of the creature, however, his face went slack and his feet nearly spilled out from under him as he abruptly came to a stop. Seeing Medraut, Jamie felt his skin flush as he pushed himself up on his hands. The only thing preventing Jamie from ripping into Medraut right there were the Wolf-Slaves holding him at bay.

"D-Doctor Calamestro," Medraut said, recognition in his eyes but his words quivering with both surprise and fear.

So they knew each other. Somehow, that didn't come as much of a surprise to Jamie. Or that this creature fancied itself a doctor.

"I told you to meet me at Fort Grassnar," the creature that was apparently named Doctor Calamestro said, his voice taking on a hissing sort of menace.

"I had something to take care of first," Medraut said, more in pleading than in defense.

"I told you to go to Fort Grassnar without delay," Doctor Calamestro said more insistently, his eyes narrowing.

Medraut braced himself as if expecting to be slapped but then took in Jaime and Alaida with a swipe of his hand. "But they killed my Wolves!"

"And now you intend to kill them?" His tone had grown calculating, as if he now considered allowing Medraut to do just that, simply so they could be on their way. Jamie and Alaida both shivered when his gaze fell on each of them in turn.

"Blood demands blood!" Medraut cried, his anger finally overcoming the tangible fear he felt toward this man.

Doctor Calamestro met Medraut's gaze, causing the young tracker to cringe. "Yes, disappointments all around today, it would seem." Releasing Alaida with an offhanded flick of the wrist which sent her tumbling to the ground alongside Jamie, Doctor Calamestro rose up to his full domineering height, his frame twisting fluidly under his robes as if somehow unconstrained by the geometry of his bones. He seemed almost to grow, towering over everyone present, his shoulders broadening and his eyes burning with an intensity so far unseen. Jamie could practically hear Medraut's pulse quicken as he took a step backward, this time stumbling on the edge of the stairs.

"Imagine my surprise when your Wolves informed me that you were not going to meet with me as you had been ordered."

Medraut shot an accusatory glance at the gathered Wolf-Slaves. More of them had continued to arrive as Doctor Calamestro held court and now they all lowered their eyes, unable to meet Medraut's gaze. Two of them, the male and female Jamie had spoken to in front of Major Ommto's burning hovel, looked away especially shamefaced.

Jamie took the opportunity to edge nearer Alaida and grasp her hand. Sniffling and trembling, she didn't return the gesture, instead grimacing and biting the inside of her lip as she gazed at him. "J-Jamie?" she whispered.

"Yeah," he replied in kind. "Something happened."

Finally, desperately, she squeezed his hand, thankful for anything reassuring to hold onto.

"Don't blame your Wolves, Medraut," Doctor Calamestro said, Jamie and Alaida completely beneath his notice. Raising his voice without actually yelling somehow made it even more chilling than if he had. "You're the one at fault here. I may have made you my Lord of the Wolves, but I'm still your lord! And that means you do as I say, when I say it, without question. If you choose to disobey me, you can be replaced. Is that understood?"

Medraut couldn't meet his eyes. His hands clenched and unclenched. "Yes Doctor," he said after a moment. His lip curled into a snarl which he forcibly smoothed. "But if you just let me kill this bastard, then I can go spring Zenushi's replacement for you. With my Wolves, we can --"

"Your Wolves?" Doctor Calamestro said. "Yes, they would have been quite useful if you had moved when I first told you. You could have recovered Saexon without any trouble whatsoever. By now, Finttiranos has already taken him into the fort. This complicates matters considerably. A single tame Wolf-Slave is a rare enough sight these days, so how do you plan to move an entire platoon of them through Grassnar's gates? No, that opportunity has passed."

Medraut slunk away without moving, as if a heavy weight were being pressed down on his shoulders. The Wolf-Slaves also quailed, even though they had specifically been excluded from Doctor Calamestro's scolding. Even Jamie felt some primal urge to burrow under the leaves and hide.

"So, I'll go in myself," Medraut said, glancing up for only a fraction of a second before dropping his gaze once more.

"Then you'll die, I'll need to find two replacements, and Finttiranos will have twice as many Lords of the Wild to examine." A snake-like hiss escaped Doctor Calamestro's lips.

Watching on, Jamie had started feeling like a complete outsider to this conversion. None of it had anything to do with him or Alaida, and if this Doctor Calamestro person had as much authority over Medraut as it seemed he did, then maybe sitting back and letting this all play out might be the fastest way out of this situation. At least that's what he had been thinking right up until Doctor Calamestro once more turned his attention to Jamie.

"That was quite an exit you made earlier. The landing alone would have killed any normal person, had they even been able to make such a jump. But then, I've heard you are not exactly normal, are you?"

Doctor Calamestro waved the Wolf-Slaves off as Jamie climbed to his feet. If his fate hinged on how well he presented himself here, it wouldn't do to face whatever was coming while laying in the dirt. With one hand covering his side, the other remained holding tight to Alaida's.

"Look, none of this has anything to do with us," Jamie said. Medraut snarled and took a step forward but stopped abruptly when Doctor Calamestro held up a single bony finger. Jamie had to force down his own desire to go after Medraut. "What happened with Medraut's...with the Wolf-Slaves was all a big misunderstanding. I was just defending myself and I'm sorry for what happened, I really am."

"And what about your injuries?" Doctor Calamestro said. Jamie shivered at the thought of having to ask this "doctor" for medical assistance. "Will you recover?"

None of the damages he'd sustained were hurting and the wound in his side seemed to have already stopped bleeding. His knee still felt a little uncertain but at least it didn't buckle any longer when he put weight on it. Maybe things hadn't been quite as bad as he'd first thought. Or maybe Reaver just healed extremely fast in addition to all his other abilities.

"I'm fine," Jamie said.

A sly smile creased Doctor Calamestro's thin lips. "Medraut, you are going to require assistance to recover Saexon...Human assistance."

Jamie shook his head, already not liking where this was going. Medraut wasn't the least bit pleased either.

"You want me to work with him!" Medraut cried, pointing his finger at Jamie like the tip of a sword. "He killed my Wolves!"

"You will do as I command," Doctor Calamestro said, only glancing at Medraut out of the corner of his eye. "Ryance is the only other lord in the area at the moment and he is still several days away. We must make do with the resources available to us."

Glaring at Jamie, Medraut said, "I don't need Ryance or his Panthers any more than I need him."

"And why would I ever help you with anything?" Jamie said. The thought of having to spend even another minute with Medraut made him burn hot with anger.

"Not that I am really giving you any choice in the matter, but I would make it worth your while." The way Doctor Calamestro bent his neck so as to bring his face to the same level as Jamie's made it look as if he had no spine. "Do this for me and I shall clear the slate between you and Medraut. All vendettas will be forgiven."

"You can't do that!" Medraut said, spittle flying from his lips as he charged toward Jamie, stopping only when Doctor Calamestro turned his gaze on him again.

Doctor Calamestro clearly had enough influence over Medraut to ensure his cooperation in this bargain -- Medraut wouldn't have become so agitated by the suggestion if that weren't the case -- but could Doctor Calamestro himself be trusted? As much as Jamie hated to even consider it, the only alternative was to spend the rest of his life looking over his shoulder in fear that Medraut and his Wolf-Slaves would come for him or Alaida.

"How do I know you'll keep your word?"

"Medraut has no choice. He will do as I say," Doctor Calamestro said. "As for myself, I am a man of honor."

"And what if I say 'no'?"

Doctor Calamestro's expression did not change in the least. "Then I will let Medraut kill you and your Raven-Slave right here."

Medraut pressed his lips into a thin line as he cracked his knuckles. It wasn't hard to imagine which option he hoped Jamie would choose.

"She's not my Raven-Slave." Jamie helped Alaida to her feet and placed himself between Doctor Calamestro and her. She held tight to his arm, her grip trembling. "And her name is Alaida."

"In that case," Doctor Calamestro said, his eyes flicking from Jamie to Alaida and then back, "if you refuse, I will then let Medraut kill you and Alaida. Is that clear enough?"

Jamie glanced back into Alaida's wide eyes. Her head twitched side to side in the smallest of motions, though if she meant to dissuade Jamie from agreeing to this bargain or if she simply no longer had any idea what to think, Jamie couldn't tell. He hardly knew what to think himself. If Doctor Calamestro could be trusted to honor his end of things, then it might be worth it. Besides, some form of penance was definitely in order for what Jamie had done to those Wolf-Slaves in Tavnic. As much as he would have liked to blame Reaver for setting all that in motion with his scheming, it was Jamie who had actually killed them. And it was his conscience that would never be clear of it.

Jamie met Doctor Calamestro's gaze. "So who's this Saexon person we're rescuing?"

Medraut kicked at the dirt and stalked away to the far side of the landing. Doctor Calamestro's pallid lips, meanwhile, parted into a parody of a smile. "A reasonable request," he said. "Like Medraut, whom you already know, Saexon is another of my associates. He was in the process of being initiated into my association when Finttiranos soldiers tracking down insurgents in the Heigelries Control Zone stumbled upon my laboratory and took him into custody as a suspected rebel."

"Suspected?" Jamie said.

Doctor Calamestro chuckled. It was a sound that sent chills down Jamie's spine. "We are not in the business of lending our aid to any such politically motivated activities." He spread his arms to encompass both Medraut and the Wolf-Slaves. "Our concerns are much further reaching than the petty affairs of any fleeting nation. I can guarantee you that Saexon has done nothing to warrant his arrest. However, his unique nature will undoubtedly make him forfeit to Finttiranos doctors for study."

If Doctor Calamestro had issues with the Finttiranos government, maybe he wasn't all bad. That didn't mean Jamie was ready to trust either him or Medraut, but from what he had seen of Finttiranos justice, Doctor Calamestro's story certainly sounded plausible enough. It just made Jamie wonder what this doctor was capable of doing to people that made them worthy of study. Jamie stole a glance at Medraut. Were his speed and strength Doctor Calamestro's doing? Could that even be something similar to what had created Reaver?

"Okay…" Jamie said. "If you keep up your end, and let me and Alaida go free afterward, I'll help you."

"Wonderful!" Doctor Calamestro leaned closer and put one of his arms around Jamie's shoulder. It was like being embraced by a corpse with the strength of a python. Bringing his mouth close to Jamie's ear, the old man said, "But if you fail to do as you have agreed here, then I will personally vivisect you in order to discover what it is you are. Do we understand each other?"

Jamie swallowed and nodded, a barely perceptible tip of the chin. "Yeah," he said, mouthing the word more than actually speaking it. Had this deal to regain his freedom just cost him his soul?

Doctor Calamestro straightened his back in a smooth, serpentine motion. "Excellent, now we are all friends."

Medraut growled under his breath and turned his back on them. The Wolf-Slaves all lowered their weapons and relaxed while somehow maintaining the appearance of being ready for action at a moment's notice. Medraut might have fancied himself the 'Lord of the Wolves' but they clearly answered to Doctor Calamestro first.

"I have been informed your name is 'Jamie'," Doctor Calamestro said. "Or would you prefer 'Reaver'?"

To hear Doctor Calamestro call him by name without having first supplied it was unnerving enough, but far worse was to be addressed by that second option.

"I'm not Reaver," Jamie said through clenched teeth. "My name is Jamie."

"As you wish. Now if you will excuse me for a moment, I must speak with Medraut." Doctor Calamestro glided away from them, barely any motion from within his robes to suggest the movement of legs.

Finally left to themselves, Alaida squeezed Jamie's arm as she watched Doctor Calamestro retreating from them.

"Jamie," she whispered. "How much time do you have left before...?"

"Reaver?" Eyes lowered, Jamie shook his head slowly. "Maybe a long time... Maybe never? I don't know. I think I might have broken something. The thing I feel that lets me know when he's coming, I pushed back and now its gone, completely gone."

"Truly? Does that mean he is gone forever?"

Jamie merely shook his head. Despite their situation, he still caught a hint of hope and excitement in her quivering voice. He couldn't blame her for that. Apart from never being able to see his sister again, and even with all these new developments surrounding Medraut and the Wolf-Slaves, Jamie wasn't so sure he really wanted to go back there either. Once they were free of the Wolf-Slaves, he might actually be able to find a way to truly enjoy this strange world and all of the wonders it still held.

CHAPTER 49

With Medraut and Doctor Calamestro speaking in hushed voices, and the Wolf-Slaves gathering near them, no one seemed to be keeping an eye on Jamie and Alaida any longer. If they ran for it now, they might be able to stay ahead of the Wolf-Slaves for a little while.

But only a little while. Eventually, they would be caught, and Jamie had no doubt whatsoever that Doctor Calamestro would follow through on his threat precisely as he'd spoken it. However, as long as Doctor Calamestro held up his end of the agreement, Jamie had no intention of going against his. Even if he wanted to try something that foolish, he wasn't even sure he'd be able to.

Being careful to turn away from Doctor Calamestro, Jamie surveyed his wounds as surreptitiously as possible. The cut on his arm had already sealed itself shut, leaving nothing to mark its passing but a thin red line across his skin surrounded by quickly coagulating blood. If nothing else, Medraut's blade was scalpel-sharp and had left him with a clean cut. Next, he delicately pulled his hand away from his side. Obscured by all the blood and the leather suit matted damply against his skin, the wound itself could barley be seen. When he hesitated going any further, Alaida reached out to help, but he waved her off. He wasn't such a coward that he couldn't face the injury Medraut had inflicted on him, no matter how bad he suspected it was. Biting down on his lip, he peeled back the cut edges of the garment. Underneath, the blood was much more moist than it had been on the surface, but it had definitely stopped flowing. In fact, when he gingerly pressed the edge of the cut, he found the two halves had largely reattached themselves except for a shallow bit right at the surface.

Alaida breathed in sharply. "I thought for sure that it had been much deeper."

"It was," Jamie said, shuddering at the memory of the blade skipping off his ribs. He put some weight on his knee and gave it a bit of a twist. Except for feeling a little stiff, it too was almost back to normal. Reaver, it seemed, was even tougher than Jamie had ever considered. The only reason Medraut had won that fight was because Jamie had panicked at the sight of a little blood.

Glancing across the landing, Jamie nearly jumped when he found Doctor Calamestro once again looming over him.

"Will you require any medical attention?" he said, his sly smile suggesting that he had already spied enough to know that Jamie did not.

"No. Like I said, I'm fine."

"And you, Alaida?"

Hastily, she folded her hands under the sleeves of her dress so to hide them from view. So focused on his own injuries, Jamie hadn't noticed until now just how badly her hands had been torn while trying to hold onto the edge of the cliff. In addition to the jagged and bloody fingernails she'd sustained from that, there were also the scrapes on her arms and the quickly coloring bruises where Medraut had seized her.

"Jeeze, Alaida, are you okay?"

"Yes, I will live," she whispered, ever conscious of Doctor Calamestro's menacing proximity.

"Very well. As I have said, time is of the essence and we have already dawdled here far too long as it is. We shall depart immediately." Doctor Calamestro held out his pale hand to Alaida, but she did not take it, instead shifting farther behind Jamie. The old man smirked and then indicated for both Jamie and Alaida to go on ahead of him, back down to the lake. They inched around him, eyes keenly on both him and the Wolf-Slaves. At the other end of the landing, Medraut scowled while issuing orders to his subordinates. They all nodded and offered close-fisted salutes over their hearts before dashing off to carry out his instructions. Catching sight of Jamie watching, he bared his canines and turned away.

Jamie took the stairs slowly at first, cautious of his injured leg. Alaida was there to help support him, and even though he quickly realized that he could manage just fine by himself, he found her closeness reassuring, especially with Doctor Calamestro following along right behind them. When Jamie began taking the stairs more quickly, it didn't come as much of a surprise to see Doctor Calamestro keep pace. With a face like an old man and a body that seemed barely human at all, Jamie couldn't begin to imagine what he really was.

Reaching the bottom of the stairs, Jamie helped Alaida down to the beach while Doctor Calamestro hopped down in a flutter of his dark robes. The titan, now only a short distance away, was under heavy guard by Medraut's' Wolf-Slaves, some of whom were actually armed with wardcaster blasters. It was hard to get an exact count, since they kept shifting positions, but combined with the others they'd already encountered, there now had to be more than thirty of them. In addition, a group of feral Wolf-Slaves had gathered along the water's edge, whispering to each other and stealing glances at Jamie and Doctor Calamestro. Though most of their kind looked so much alike, the one covered in burns Jamie recognized immediately.

A thin haze had settled in the depression around the lake, carrying with it the smoky tang of a bonfire. How long would Major Ommto's hovel burn before it went out? Or would it spread to consume the entire mesa and all the ruins on it? None of the Wolf-Slaves looked the least bit interested in such matters. With hands on their weapons, they seemed to have singled out Jamie as the sole cause for any concern here. He turned back to Doctor Calamestro as if to ask where they should go from here.

"We will be taking your titan." Doctor Calamestro made a gracious gesture, motioning Jamie onward.

Jamie considered the titan and then turned a raised eyebrow to the doctor. Once he had control of the titan, those Wolf-Slaves would become much less of a threat. Doctor Calamestro laughed.

"I trust you not to do anything stupid," he said, one hand reaching out and resting casually on Alaida's shoulder. She cringed, looking like she was about ready to crawl out of her own skin. "Now, if you would..."

"Fine," Jamie said. "Alaida?"

She nodded and slipped out from under the doctor's grasp, hurrying toward the titan and up the side.

Before Jamie could step into the pilot's chair, a commotion erupted from the feral Wolf-Slaves. Though the others tried to hold him back, Singed-Fur broke free and charged toward Jamie, howling like mad.

"What happens here?" he demanded. "Reaver must die!"

Jamie readied himself for another fight. Even if Medraut had made it back down to the beach, he probably wouldn't be inclined to run them off as he had done before. However, as Singed-Fur ran past Doctor Calamestro, intent only on Jamie, the doctor lashed out and grabbed hold of the Wolf-Slave. He came to a dead stop with a gargling chirp as one of Doctor Calamestro's talon-like hands completely encircled the Wolf-Slave's throat.

With a sigh and a slow shake of the head, Doctor Calamestro twisted Singed-Fur's neck, producing a audible crack. The feral Wolf-Slaves all cringed and cried out amongst themselves. "We don't have time for this," the doctor said to no one in particular, letting the limp body drop to the ground. To Jamie he said, "Time is of the essence."

Jamie took one last look at the dead Wolf-Slave and his friends, but none of them seemed interested in testing their own luck. The sight of Doctor Calamestro off-handedly dispatching one of them was almost enough to make Jamie rethink this agreement he'd entered into.

Unfortunately, it was his only chance at freedom. Nodding, Jamie threw himself into the pilot's seat with more force than usual. The titan obligingly came to life and pulled Jamie up into its belly. He had grown accustomed to how the machine operated, but he was especially pleased with the way he was able to convey a greater sense of menace as it rose upright. The Wolf-Slaves all backed a step away and fingered their weapons more tightly. Jamie smiled.

"Yes, very nicely done," Doctor Calamestro said, his voice coming from the passenger compartment. Jamie twisted in his seat, seeing Doctor Calamestro standing in the middle of the deck, one hand bracing himself against the roll cage. Jamie hadn't even realized he'd boarded. "Did you expect me to walk?" the doctor said, settling down in the rumble seat. His layered robes hoarded most of the bench, leaving Alaida with only a narrow sliver on one side. She stiffly cringed as far away from him as possible, looking more uncomfortable by far than she ever had sharing the seat with Medraut.

"How did you get here in the first place?" Jamie muttered through his teeth as he turned back around. In order to ensure Jamie's help, Doctor Calamestro couldn't do anything to harm Alaida, but that didn't mean Jamie had to enjoy giving him a ride.

"I have my means," Doctor Calamestro said.

"And what about them?" Jamie nodded to the gathered Wolf-Slaves. Even if the titan could carry that much weight, most of them would be left hanging off the sides.

Medraut had just descended the long flight of stairs and stood a short distance away, glaring up at Jamie. "We'll keep up," he said.

Doctor Calamestro then pointed past the sliver of stone that reached out into the lake. "We will be heading west. There is a trail up to the top of the ridge that I believe will accommodate your titan."

"Enide, Kaius," Medraut said to the same male and female Wolf-Slaves that Jamie had seen before, "Get the troop ready to move out. And tell the wild packs to hold position," Medraut glanced up at Jamie, murder in his eyes, "for the time being." Salutes were exchanged and two grey streaks shot off into the trees.

Jamie had to hold his impulse to swat Medraut aside with the titan as he passed. All they had to do was tough this out and then their troubles would be a thing of the past. He could certainly put up with both Medraut and Doctor Calamestro until then.

They found the trail Doctor Calamestro had mentioned without trouble. Though it was barely wide enough for the titan, it did provide an ample switchback path up and out of the depression surrounding the lake. When they reached the top, the scraggly trees behind them veiled any view of the lake and most of the mesa, but not of the dark column of smoke rising high into the air from the top of the plateau.

Ahead, the vegetation thinned, quickly giving way to a vast sea of swaying prairie grasses that rose and fell with the rolling hills as far as the eye could see. The sun hung closer to the horizon than its peak, turning it all into a contrasting interplay of darkly shadowed valleys and shining green crests. Farther north, the jagged mountains still loomed high and forbidding. Flanking the titan on either side, uniformed Wolf-Slaves spread out along the tree line like ghostly shadows.

"Fort Grassnar lies ahead, but even with the speed of this machine, it will still take us time to get there," Doctor Calamestro said. "We will have to travel through the night."

"Then let's get this over with." Jamie leaned into the controls and started the titan forward at a brisk sprint. The Wolf-Slaves set off as well, nothing more than grayish blurs, only occasionally seen gliding through the tall grass.

Once underway, there were no roads, or even paths, to follow, but the open grasslands offered few obstacles. Jamie kept heading due west, taking them over the low hills and through the shallow valleys, seldom needing to veer far from their course and always returning to it when he did. Doctor Calamestro said little, offering no commentary on their progress or even any additional directions. One of the few times he did speak was when Alaida reached out to brace herself against the side of the passenger compartment from a particularly jarring step the titan had just taken. Bumping one of her scrapes in the process, she quickly drew back with a pained hiss.

"Let me take a look at those hands, my dear," Doctor Calamestro said. Alaida did not reply and kept her hands tucked neatly in her lap but Doctor Calamestro gently lifted one by the wrist, between his bony thumb and forefinger.

Eyeing the two of them over his shoulder, Jamie called out, "Are you really a doctor?" If he did anything to Alaida, this deal of theirs would be over in a heartbeat.

"By that, you mean a physician? Not exactly, but I am more well-versed in the workings of the human body than anyone you will ever likely encounter." He took a moment to examine Alaida's hands from several different angles. "These will need to be cleaned." Without first asking for permission, he opened the water bottle which Alaida had brought with her while exploring the ruins and began scrubbing the dried blood from around her broken nails. Alaida grimaced but didn't appear to be in any more pain than might be expected under even the gentlest of aid. He worked methodically, and as he did, he said, "It's been a long time since I've heard someone assume that 'doctor' is synonymous with 'healer'. Here on Terrarhea, a doctor is simply a learned individual."

"I'm not exactly from around here," Jamie muttered, trying to stay focused on the route ahead and not his passenger.

"And where might that be, my boy?" Suddenly, Doctor Calamestro's words came out not in the jumbled and confusing manner of Terrarheans, but in a near perfect imitation of Jamie's own accent and phrasing. "Is that where you learned to speak this dialect?"

Jamie scowled and glanced over his shoulder. First Medraut and Alaida had made fun of the way he spoke and now even this strange creature was getting in on the game.

"Oh, I'm not mocking you, if that's what you think," Doctor Calamestro said, though Jamie swore he had spoken through a smirk. "English is your native tongue, is it not? I no longer thought it was spoken by anyone."

Hearing that, Jamie nearly missed a step. It took him a moment to regain the titan's rhythm as he replayed the doctor's words in his mind to make sure he'd heard them correctly. "Y-You know English?"

"I know a good many things," he said, a hint of irritation in his voice. "Now please, do try to keep the titan under control. You're only making it more difficult for me to assist Alaida."

"S-Sorry. But where? How?"

"It was another lifetime ago," Doctor Calamestro said as he wiped Alaida's hands dry with a rag. "Back before the world became so complicated."

"And what's that supposed to mean?"

From within his robes the doctor pulled a small ceramic jar. Removing the glossy metal lid, he handed both to Alaida. "Hold these," he told her. After sticking the tip of his finger into the jar, he withdrew a small amount of some oily paste which he began rubbing into Alaida's scrapes.

"Wait, what is that?" Jamie said. "Is it safe?"

"A healing ointment," Doctor Calamestro said. "Quite common."

Alaida glanced at the bulbous little jar and nodded in reply to Jamie's questioning gaze.

After several long moments of silence while the doctor continued working on Alaida's hands, Jamie sat restlessly in the pilot's compartment, waiting for further answer to his question. When it became clear that none would be forthcoming, he tried again.

"Can you at least tell me who Lareed is?" The name had been dancing around in Jamie's mind since he'd first heard it and he wanted to know why Doctor Calamestro would associate it with Jamie.

"Another man I once made a bargain with. Apart from the particulars of the deal -- which are of a strictly confidential nature -- I know next to nothing about him. Although in his case, the value of the exchange was far greater than a mere bit of assistance with a jail break."

"That's it?"

"Yes."

"But what's he got to do with me?" This was too good an opportunity for information: information Jamie hadn't even known he was missing until Doctor Calamestro hinted at it. Jamie had to keep pressing, even at the risk of offending him. "Did Lareed do something to you? Is he the one who gave you your...abilities?"

Doctor Calamestro laughed, a loud and raucous cry which made the hairs on the back of Jamie's neck stand straight on end. When he spoke, his voice had become a low hiss. "Don't think for a moment that possession of a small amount of ancient trivia puts you in a position of power over anyone, especially me. Lareed was just a man. I am much more."

From the way those Wolf-Slaves had bowed to him, he likely thought himself a god.

"You've got to tell me something," Jamie said.

"No, I don't," Doctor Calamestro said, his eyes narrowing. Alaida suddenly clenched her jaw in pain and her whole body went rigid as the doctor casually bent one of her fingers backward sharply, reminding Jamie that this wasn't a man or a god he was talking with, but a creature, just as he had initially thought of him at their first encounter. Before Jamie could do anything rash, however, the doctor released Alaida, as if he had simply been performing some diagnostic test. Carefully, he put the lid back on the ointment and folded Alaida's fingers gently around it. "Apply that several times a day until your injuries have healed."

Eyeing him warily, Alaida shied back as far to her side of the bench as the confines of the compartment would allow. Meanwhile, Doctor Calamestro once again settled in on his side. With at least a tiny bit of distance separating his two passengers, Jamie breathed a little easier. If another opportunity to pursue this line of questioning came in the future, he would take it, but for the moment, he had no choice but to let it rest.

It was some time after the sun set that Medraut temporarily boarded the titan, vaulting himself up onto the side of the roll cage in order to deliver a report of their progress in chilly tones to Doctor Calamestro. It seemed the grasslands would soon give way to forested foothills as their westerly course began to converge with the southwestern line of the mountains.

About half an hour after entering the densely forested terrain earlier identified by Medraut, Doctor Calamestro called for a short break and the young tracker quickly located a secluded clearing along their path just for the purpose. A vertical wall of moss-covered rock rising two stories high stood along one side, while boulders nearly as big as the titan-mecha and a wall of towering evergreen trees boxed in the other three. A thin trickle of water flowed over the top of the cliff and through a series of terraced pools before falling into a shallow pond at the very bottom.

Jamie felt no need for rest himself and would have liked to keep pushing on in order to bring this episode to an end as soon as possible, but he knew Alaida was probably in need of a brief rest stop. Had he and Alaida still been traveling blithely along with the Medraut they'd first met as their guide, it would have been a magical spot to make camp for the night; the three of them laughing and singing late into the night. Now, Jamie felt like he was walking on eggshells, constantly having to keep one eye on the Wolf-Slaves as he greeted Alaida at the foot of the titan.

About half of the Wolf-Slaves had taken up positions around the perimeter, their golden eyes ever watchful in the dark night. The rest refilled canteens in the pool and munched on field rations while a few others had scratched out a hasty latrine with their entrenching tools near a low stand of shrubs.

From their heavy breathing and the way their fur was matted with sweat, they'd all been pushing themselves hard, but not one of them looked even close to exhaustion. In fact, they were all in quite good spirits, talking and joking quietly amongst themselves. Jamie even recognized more than a few of them as having been at the Ommto Estate. Medraut had clearly not been exaggerating when he'd said they'd be able to keep up. They also kept watching Jamie and Alaida, their stern expressions inscrutable.

"You okay?" Jamie said to Alaida, keeping his voice low. These woods seemed just as uninhabited as the last they'd traveled through, but the tactical discipline of the Wolf-Slaves made him feel as if they were on the brink of being overrun by some previously unknown enemy force. "How are your hands?"

"Better," she said, tucking them back into her sleeves when Jamie tried to take a look. After having had Doctor Calamestro tend to them, she probably wanted nothing at all to remind her of that ever again. "How are your injuries?"

"Can't even tell they were ever there. Even the blood's dried up and flaked off."

"How is that possible?"

"I don't know. I'm just happy I'm not dead."

Alaida shook her head in disbelief. "I am sure we do not have much time here, but I would like to refill our supply of water while we have the opportunity."

"I'll get the water," Jamie said, taking the two leather bladders from her.

"Is Reaver still...?"

"Yeah, still no trace of him. But keep your eyes open around these guys. I still don't know how far we can trust them."

"You be careful as well," she said as she made her way toward the improvised latrine.

"Are you sure you do not need to go as well?" Doctor Calamestro said from directly over Jamie's shoulder. He jumped and turned to face the doctor. Jamie couldn't imagine how someone like that kept managing to sneak up on him.

"No," Jamie said, hefting the water bladders over his shoulder and heading for the pool. "I went before we left."

He had been on this world for days now and still didn't feel any more need to go to the bathroom than he did to eat or drink. It seemed Reaver existed in an even more unchanging state than Jamie had started to think of his own existence back on Earth.

Doctor Calamestro's concern, he was almost certain, stemmed purely from a desire to ascertain as much about Jamie as he possibly could. Between that, and how close-lipped the doctor had so far been about himself, it meant Jamie was not going to let him have any more information about his situation then was absolutely necessary.

The bladders each held several gallons of water and by the time Jamie had finished filling them both, the Wolf-Slaves were beginning to put their own supplies away as they made ready to move out once more. As Jamie took the water back to the titan, Medraut stepped forward to bar his path. So far, Jamie hadn't seen him at the clearing and had assumed he'd been out scouting ahead. He glared at Jamie as if Doctor Calamestro hadn't brokered any truce between them at all.

"Once this is all done," he said, his voice a low rumble, "I'm gonna find a way to make you pay for what you did to my Wolves."

"You might want to run that by your boss first," Jamie said, stepping around the young tracker.

"He said I can't kill either of you, but there are still lots of way I can make you suffer."

Jamie paused and met Medraut's gaze. "If you try anything, you'll regret it."

"My life's full'a regrets." Medraut said as Jamie continued on his way, "What's one more?"

Jamie met Alaida once more at the titan. "Definitely keep your eyes open around these guys."

While Jamie helped Alaida load the water into the titan's hold, Doctor Calamestro approached Medraut and the two began discussing further strategy. Even with the relative quiet of the forest around them, Jamie could only hear their hushed voices after he'd taken a few steps closer.

"We'll skirt the edge of this mountain spur for another couple'a hours," Medraut was saying. At least they weren't openly talking about any kind of betrayals. "When we come out on the other side, we're gonna be back in civilization again. There shouldn't be any military patrols this far from the Control Zone, but we'll have to be more careful."

"I trust the Wolves to lead us safety through," Doctor Calamestro said. "You, on the other hand, still have a way to go before regaining that same trust."

As Doctor Calamestro turned to rejoin the titan, Jamie could hear Medraut's low growl from all the way across the clearing.

"The Wolves will be guiding you from this point on," Doctor Calamestro said to Jamie as he walked past. "Follow their lead."

"Right..." Jamie said, dropping back into the pilot's chair.

CHAPTER 50

Once they got under way again, the trees that dominated the landscape were just as big as any Jamie had yet seen. The crests of the hills were no higher than those they had traversed to arrive at the Ommto Estate, but their sides grew ever more steep and far more rocky, turning the way forward into an overly complicated, three-dimensional maze. Without the Wolf-Slaves scouting ahead and picking the titan's path, they easily would have wasted hours and hours, if not days, backtracking over promising-looking trails that eventually dead-ended into insurmountable cliffs or angry rapids still swollen by spring melt. As it was, they zigged and zagged though the moss-covered forest, turning as indicated each time they came upon a Wolf-Slave stationed in their path. They never seemed to be headed west very much of the time, but they did maintain a steady pace.

Late that night, or perhaps early the next morning, when the fragmented remains of Terrarhea's moon rose above the horizon, the forest took on an ethereal quality as the diffused light from all those smaller rocks drifted through the treetops and illuminated the glistening moss with their mottled silver light. Alaida remained unwilling or unable to sleep. Every time Jamie glanced back to check on her, her eyes were open wide, either taking in their surroundings or keeping a furtive watch on her fellow passenger. Doctor Calamestro remained comfortably seated and quiet throughout, though his distant expression made Jamie wonder if he maybe slept with his eyes open, just like a snake.

The moon arcing through the night sky offered Jamie his only indication of the passage of time but, without any point of reference, it didn't provide any concrete gauge of how long they'd actually been traveling. To his mind, it sure seemed to be taking them a long time to get nowhere at all. But then the landscape began to change, so subtly at first that Jamie didn't notice until the changes were starkly obvious. The hills were still no less steep, but the valleys grew progressively wider and flatter. And between the increasingly frequent signs of logging and the trampled underbrush caused by large herds of cattle, the forest began to thin until they started to find large patches of it completely cleared and replaced instead with orderly rows of plowed fields. The sheer size of these fields was not at all like the tiny subsistence plots Jamie had seen in Tavnic, but something more akin to the large, industrial farms he was familiar with back home.

With the land opening around them, the Wolf-Slave guides were no longer needed quite so frequently and Jamie was able to start following established paths once more, at first, narrow little logging trails but quickly, well-maintained roads paved with crushed gravel. Jamie still caught sight of their Wolf-Slave escort from time to time, drifting along on either side of the titan-mecha in a wedge-shaped formation that grew wider and less tightly packed the more inhabited the land became.

Medraut returned at one point to report that the Cavadanian Road, the same one he'd led Jamie and Alaida on before betraying them, was just a short distance to the south. Instead of going straight through the foothills, as their little group had just done, it followed a path along the southern edge, which would have added a day or more to their travel time.

"If we really wanna make a good pace," Medraut said, "it'll take us right to Fort Grassnar in no time at all."

"No," Doctor Calamestro said with a flip of his hand. "Continue along this path for the time being. We have another destination before pressing on to the fort."

Medraut's brow wrinkled and he hung silent from the side of the roll cage for a moment before acknowledging the command and dropping back to the ground.

"Where are we headed?" Jamie ventured. They were starting to see more and more farmhouses and barns all the time now. It was still too early in the morning for most of the people who lived in them to be up, but it did make Jamie feel far more exposed than he had in days.

"I know the way well," Doctor Calamestro said. "Turn right at this next road."

Jamie followed his directions, taking the titan down a seemingly random series of back roads which looked like they served only the local farmers. He also saw more and more lights inside the farmhouses they passed. It was probably still too dark for anyone to see the strangeness of Jamie's one passenger with any degree of clarity, but the titan itself would definitely be noticed, if not identified.

"Um, how much farther?" Jamie said. "This titan's kind of unique and after what happened in Tavnic, I probably shouldn't be out in public with it more than I have to." Jamie probably shouldn't even be out in public himself; his face was probably on every wanted poster in the country by now.

Doctor Calamestro chuckled. "Oh, I wouldn't worry about that. Tavnic's practically on the other side of the country from here and the local authorities are seldom interested in the happenings outside of their territory. I doubt they've ever heard of the Red Rogue here."

Jamie certainly hoped so.

They'd been climbing a steep hill with a narrow gravel road cut into the side; but reaching the top, the road continued for only a short distance alongside a farm before passing between two large spires of worn rock and then dropping down the other side again. Ahead of them, framed between the two spires, lay a sight that brought Jamie plodding to a stop. The vast plane before them was far wider than any of the valleys they had yet encountered. It's green sides fell steeply away from the high terrain to the north, giving way to wide belts of fields interspersed with odd little bluffs of rock sticking up randomly throughout. Further south, the land tapered out into a dry, spreading prairie with rugged hills in the distance.

What drew the majority of Jamie's interest, however, was the large, oblong patch of ground at the base of the northern foothills that was covered with the lights of a sprawling city. It had to be at least twenty times larger than Tavnic. And that didn't even take into account the walled enclosure that spread out to the northwest, or the massive fortress built atop a ridge-like formation that ran diagonally along the southwestern edge of town. Even at that hour, Jamie's sharp eyes could make out the bustling activity of titan-mechas and wagons moving through its streets.

"Fort Grassnar," Doctor Calamestro said as if stifling a yawn. He stood and came to the front of the passenger compartment. "The city spread out there around the base of its walls is known as Tolfield and the compound to the north is the Boravion Slave Farm."

The walls of the fort had to be at least twice as tall as Tavnic's and they enclosed a space big enough to house tens of thousands of troops. Illuminated from within, the walls were filled with a wide range of buildings, some of which in the center almost had the look of modern high-rises. All vegetation had been stripped from the sides of the hill and replaced instead with rows of dragon's teeth, fences of barbed wire, and undoubtedly, many other hidden deterrents as well. The few gates to be seen where reached only by winding switchback roads that offered no cover whatsoever. The whole perimeter was well-guarded by numerous towers that intermittently flashed their powerful searchlights across the hillside and roads. To Jamie, it looked like a hornet's nest just moments away from erupting into an angry swarm of murderous death. When he'd agreed to come here, he'd never considered that he might have to go into an actual fort. Or that it would be so large.

Doctor Calamestro waved his arm toward the small farmstead directly to their right. "This, however, is our immediate destination."

The front driveway angled steeply up a rocky incline of some ten feet or so to arrive at a relatively flat yard with a white, clapboard house on the left, a large red barn directly ahead, and several smaller sheds to the right. If he hadn't been seated behind the controls of a titan-mecha, Jamie almost could have imagined himself back on Earth at one of the farms near his hometown. He shuddered to think what need a monster such as Doctor Calamestro would have with a farm as quaint and mundane as this, but was grateful all the same for any kind of delay that would prevent him from having to get any closer to Fort Grassnar now that he'd seen what awaited him there.

The Wolf-Slaves appeared from out of nowhere, sweeping through the outbuildings and securing the perimeter with military precision. The lights in the farmhouse were on and Jamie briefly saw a face in one of the windows before the curtain was thrown back into place. A moment later, the side door opened and a man stepped outside. Before the door swung closed again, Jamie thought he saw the shadow of a woman inside reaching after the man.

His head of white hair and wrinkled face marked him as being older than might have been suggested by the purposeful and confident way he carried his lean frame, even if there was the faintest suggestion of a limp in his stride. His clothes were the rugged sort one would expect of a farmer. Though worn, they were clean and trim. His expression remained stony as he approached them across the dirt yard.

Doctor Calamestro dropped from the side of the titan-mecha and slithered forward to meet him. Medraut stood at the doctor's side, several paces removed, while a handful of Wolf-Slaves, armed with rifles, created a semicircular perimeter facing the house. The old man stopped short of the doctor and took it all in with a dispassionate eye.

"It's been a while," he said. Something in the man's tone made Jamie think that he had been hoping it would have been even longer.

"It has indeed," Doctor Calamestro said. "I have need once more to impose myself upon your generous hospitality."

The old man looked up at Jamie in the titan-mecha and Alaida standing behind him. "You sure that's all?" he said.

"My associate *will* require the use of your barn in order to keep his titan-mecha out of sight for a day or so. And if we could make use of your dining room table and your expertise for a short while as well, it would be greatly appreciated."

Slowly the old man blew out his breath. "Alright then." He stepped past Doctor Calamestro and the titan-mecha, waving for Jamie to follow him. "You, come on."

Jamie glanced down at his captors but Doctor Calamestro was already making his way to the house while Medraut issued orders to the Wolf-Slaves with a quick series of hand gestures. Sighing, Jamie brought the titan around and followed the old man, ducking though the gaping barn doors after he rolled them back.

"You can put it down over there," the old man said, pointing to an empty corner of the barn that was otherwise filled with piles of hay and straw.

The roof beams above were high enough that Jamie didn't have to duck the titan down too low to get under them. He made it to the corner without so much as nicking one of them and then turned the titan so that it was facing the door. Frowning, the old man stood waiting below as the pilot's chair dropped Jamie out of the machine. Alaida climbed down as well and joined Jamie at his side. The old man didn't say anything, just looked at them.

"Um, hi. My name's Jamie. This is Alaida."

The old man considered Jamie's outstretched hand for a moment before finally giving it a firm shake. His grip was strong and his hands were covered with calluses. "Name's Len, Len Burke. This is my farm."

"Nice to meet you. I'm...sorry about all this."

"Not to worry," Len said, leading them back to the house. "I get the impression this isn't your fault."

Jamie opened his mouth to speak but held his tongue. Regardless of how rational this man might seem at the moment, Jamie still didn't know who he was. With Alaida holding tight to Jamie's arm, they followed him at a reasonable distance.

Just before they reached the barn door, Len stopped and turned back to face them. "Pardon me for asking, but how did you fall in with that one?" He pointed with his thumb back toward the farmhouse. There could be no doubt who he was referring to. "You don't seem like the sort he usually travels with."

"And what sort is that?" Jamie said.

"Slaves usually, though not like normal ones," Len looked at Alaida, "more like those Wolf-Slaves out there. Or one of those purple-eyed kids."

"Do you know who they are?"

Len blew out his breath and shook his head. "I don't even know *what* they are."

"Me either," Jamie said. Maybe this old man and him were in similar situations. "I kind of got stuck with them by accident. He says I have to help him with something. How do you know him?"

Len thought about the question for a moment. "He helped me with something a long time ago and I've been paying for it ever since." Again, Len shook his head and then led them out of the barn, rolling the door closed behind. "Come on, best not to keep the doctor waiting."

Doctor Calamestro and Medraut stood waiting at the side door to the house. The Wolf-Slaves had all dispersed. Jamie caught sight of one or two of them as they took up defensive positions around the farm buildings, but as soon as they were situated, they seemed to vanish completely from sight. As Jamie, Alaida, and Len joined the doctor and Medraut, the two of them broke off what had looked like a heated conversation, at least on Medraut's side -- probably still trying to convince the doctor to let him kill Jamie.

"Ah, our most gracious host," Doctor Calamestro said to Len. "Has everything been taken care of?"

"As long as you don't give anyone reason to come looking, it'll be just fine."

"Len, you know I've never done anything to harm you or your family. I have no intention of starting now, not after we've had such a productive relationship these many years."

Len remained silent, his mouth twisting as if he'd just tasted something bad. After a moment, he waved them through the door. "After you."

With a snarl on his lips, Medraut threw back the door and stomped inside. Doctor Calamestro followed a short distance behind and Len motioned Jamie and Alaida to go on ahead of him. Inside, they found themselves in a wide hallway, lined on one side with bulging coat hooks and an assortment of boots and shoes on the floor beneath. On the other, a doorway led into a large kitchen with a small wooden dining table and chairs in the middle. Ahead, the hallway emptied into what appeared to be a more formal dining room. In the doorway to the kitchen stood the woman that Jamie had seen earlier. She looked like a match for Len in age, spryness, and even the neutral manner in which she stood there, watching her home being invaded.

Medraut stalked past without barely sparing her a glance, his heavy boots thudding loudly on the wooden floors as he marched through the dining room and into the other rooms beyond, securing the building just as his Wolves had done to the farm.

"Emma. Always a pleasure," Doctor Calamestro said as he slid past her towards the dining room, pausing long enough to kiss the woman's hand.

She watched him with her eyes only, her mouth pressed into a thin line. "Of course."

"Emma," Len said. "This is Jamie and Alaida. This is my wife, Emma."

"Nice to meet you," Jamie said, shaking her hand.

"Likewise," she said. Her smile appeared warm enough, but Jamie wondered how much effort on her part that took. When she turned to Alaida, however, her expression changed completely, and she took hold of Alaida's injured hands. "My dear! Let me take a look at those!"

"No, it is fine, mistress," Alaida said, squirming. "My injures have already been tended to."

"It's okay," Len said, to both Alaida and Jamie. "Emma was a medic back during the war. She knows her stuff."

"At least let me put some bandages on them," Emma said, ushering Alaida into the kitchen. "Would you like something to eat? I was just about to put on breakfast."

"I-I can help, if you would like," Alaida said, but Emma pushed her down in one of the chairs and then went to the stove where several pans had hastily been set to the side.

"Nonsense, you just sit there. I'll take care of it."

Len put his hand on Jamie's shoulder and gave him a nudge toward the dining room. "Come on. No sense to worry them with whatever it is the doctor's got cooking."

CHAPTER 51

Jamie followed Len to the end of the hallway. The formality of the dining room, with its carven wainscoting, patterned wallpaper, and molded plaster ceiling contrasted somewhat sharply with the looming creature now dominating its center. Standing before the table, Doctor Calamestro had pushed several of the upholstered, high-backed chairs to the edges of the room and unfolded a somewhat dog-eared and weathered map on top of the lacy white tablecloth. Though his height and the volume of his robes appeared no less than they had before, the tighter quarters did not seem to confine him in the least as he glided about without ever coming close to bumping into a vase or scraping against a wall.

Medraut returned through one of the other two doors that led off of the room. "Building's secure," he said.

"Excellent," Doctor Calamestro said without looking up from his map. Watching from the far end of the table, Jamie thought it might have depicted the immediate areas surrounding Fort Grassnar. "Len, it is my understanding that Fort Grassnar houses its rebel prisoners at the northern end of the base?"

Len looked at the doctor critically. "Why the sudden interest in military matters?"

"Because they took one of my men without cause and I intend to get him back before they vivisect him. These two young men will be going in to retrieve him. With the proper information, no one will even realize he is missing until long after they are gone. I have no interest in making you betray any loyalties to your country or to the military which you served so well."

So Len had once been in the military. Did that mean both he and Emma had once been Finttiranos soldiers?

Len took a deep breath and shook his head. Pulling a pencil from his shirt pocket, he turned the map over and began drawing on the back. "Fort Grassnar is divided into three sectors." He sketched three oval shapes on the paper. Two of them just barely touched at their short ends while the third was squished in between and below them. "Each sector is compartmentalized from the others by interior walls. The Southeastern Sector is barracks, individual unit headquarters, and equipment: motor pools, armories, munitions, things like that. The Southern Sector," he pointed to the middle oval, "is all administrative: offices for brigade and up, fort operations, Control Zone management, and general military administration for the entire

Boravion Highlands. The Northwestern Sector is military intelligence and holding facilities for enemy combatants and military criminals."

"And where do they hold the rebels they take prisoner?"

"Things have probably changed since the last time I was in Grassnar, but they used to have a camp just inside the wall for the in-processing of any rebels they might have taken. All prisoners from the Control Zone were put in there for a couple of weeks while the boys from military intelligence sorted out the leaders from the followers from the innocent. They never found many of that last bunch, though."

"My worry exactly," Doctor Calamestro said. "Saexon would have been taken in a little over a day ago."

Len shook his head. "The last couple of months, they've really been cracking down on rebel activity in the Control Zone. They've been bringing in prisoners by the barque-load every other day. I've heard they've started rounding up whole villages, regardless of whether or not anyone has ties to the rebels. With that many prisoners, it will probably take them a couple of days to get to him."

"Yes, it was one of those raids which caught him up. He is clever enough not to bring notice to himself, but in his current state, he may not have much control over his own situation."

"What do you mean by that?" Jamie said.

"The process he was undergoing at the time of his capture will leave him weak and tired for several days yet. To an outside observer, he will look quite sick."

Medraut groaned. "Does this mean we're gonna have to carry him out of there?"

"If you find him alive, give him this." Doctor Calamestro reached into his robes and pulled out a syringe filled with some pale, greenish solution which he held out to Medraut.

"What is it?" Medraut said, making only a halting effort to take it.

"A serum which will make him well enough to travel under his own power for a short while. Inject the entire contents into one of his shoulders and the results should be almost instant."

"In-ject?" Medraut said, suddenly looking like he might throw-up all over the table. Even Len looked a little off put by the notion. "You mean, stick that in his skin and…and…?"

For someone who had no trouble cutting up animals and people alike with his blade, Medraut wouldn't have struck Jamie as the sort to be afraid of needles, especially when it wouldn't even be used on him.

Doctor Calamestro sighed and shook his head. "The non-invasive nature of most Terrarhean medicine has truly been a detriment to certain aspects of science."

"Just give it here," Jamie said. "I'll give it to him."

Doctor Calamestro glanced at Medraut, but the tracker still appeared to have no interest in taking the syringe. With no further word spoken on the matter, he passed it to Jamie instead. Made of metal and thick glass with a metal cap that screwed on over the needle, it was quite substantial. Hoping that they would not have to find out just how much punishment it could take, Jamie slipped it into his pocket.

"On the other hand," Doctor Calamestro said, "If they have taken mercy on him and rendered medical assistance, they may have already discovered his true nature. If they have made him completely unfit for travel, or if he is already deceased, you will have to destroy the body."

"That," Medraut said, "I can handle."

Len shook his head, giving expression to Jamie's own thoughts.

"However, don't think for a moment that you can simply abandon him, claiming he was already dead, or kill him yourselves and claim it was Finttiranos that did it. Trust me, I will know, and the consequences for such an action will be far worse than mere failure; for both of you. If he is still in any condition to recover, you will return him to me, without exception. I have no interest in replacing the Lord of the Stouts so soon after losing his predecessor."

Jamie gulped hard. Medraut scowled. They both however, nodded.

"As to the best way inside," Len said, "there's a breach in the northern wall from when Finttiranos took the town back during the war. They've refortified it since, but they've never repaired the wall. There's an intake facility there. Because of the terms of the armistice at the end of the war, Finttiranos can only stage full military operations in the Control Zone under specific conditions. Because of that, the officers who run Grassnar use mercenaries and bounty hunters to skirt the rules. That's what the intake facility is for; a place for their hired guns to turn over their prisoners and get paid. It's about as close as civilians can get to the fort without some kind of service pass." Len looked at Medraut and then Jamie. "And I don't think either of you'd be able to get one of those."

But they could pass themselves off as mercenaries? Jamie figured he'd just take that as a compliment and not think about it any further. There was something else however, which was bothering him enough that he figured it would be worth risking everyone's ridicule. "Why does

Finttiranos bother with mercenaries? Didn't they win the war? Can't they just do whatever they want?"

Medraut laughed scornfully. Len, however, spoke up more magnanimously. "It basically boils down to politics. After the war, rather than total martial law, Finttiranos decided to try a lighter touch in governing Heigelries. They allowed many of the existing government's administrative departments to continue with minimal interference, thinking that it would smooth the transition and make the people more willing to accept Finttiranos rule. Instead, the Heigelriesians used that limited freedom to establish an underground resistance movement and dug themselves in so deep, that by the time the politicians would let us do anything about it, it was already too late. Over the years, rather than fixing the underlying problems, they just keep putting more regulations on top of all the previous mistakes. It's been nearly fifty years and we're still spending more time containing Heigelries than governing it."

"Politics," Doctor Calamestro said with a sneer. "It is a bane on society. But, back to the matter at hand..."

"Unfortunately, I don't know much more about Intake. I was infantry. Even when I was stationed at Grassnar, I seldom had to deal with that side of things."

"How hard can it be?" Medraut said. "I'll figure it out."

"You *both* will," Doctor Calamestro said. "If only one of you returns, he will be left wishing neither of you had." He paused a moment to let his words sink in. "After you complete your mission, the Wolves and I will meet you in the no-man's-land south of the fort. I wouldn't want to bring any additional scrutiny to Len's farm. Here, I think, is a good location." He pointed with one of his bony fingers at a blob on the front side of the map which appeared to represent one of the bluffs scattered across the plane.

"And then what?" Jamie said.

"And then," Doctor Calamestro said, "provided everything has been resolved accordingly, you can go on your way." Medraut's lip twisted. "I'm sure Len will look after your property until you can retrieve it."

"Your titan will be fine here," Len said. "And we'll look after Alaida for you too, don't worry about that."

"...Thanks." With anyone else, Jamie might have been tempted to issue a warning or threat, but something about this man made such things seem unnecessary. He still knew next to nothing about him or Emma, but already he trusted them more than he did Medraut or Doctor Calamestro.

424

"Excellent," Doctor Calamestro said. "Now prepare yourselves. I do not wish to delay this any longer."

"Give me fifteen minutes to square away the pack," Medraut said. He stalked out of the room, bumping Jamie with his shoulder as he passed.

Jamie watched him leave but held his tongue. If Medraut kept behaving like this, it would only make what was already a vague plan even harder. "I should let Alaida know what's going on," Jamie said, leaving the room as well. After having spent the last several hours on Doctor Calamestro's leash, it came as a relief that no one tried to stop him.

Jamie found Alaida sitting in the kitchen, her hands and other wounds neatly bandaged and a glass of juice on the table in front of her. The way she sat there stiffly, watching Emma's every move at the stove, made Jamie certain that she was once again feeling uncomfortable about being relegated to the sidelines while someone else did work which she had been told all her life was her responsibility. The smells coming from the stove made Jamie wish he could have stayed a little longer to taste whatever it was Emma was busy preparing.

"How are you doing?" Jamie said.

Alaida nodded. "Mistress Emma has been quite generous."

"Oh please, none of that 'mistress' nonsense," Emma said. "Me and Len have never had any slaves, and this isn't an inn, so just 'Emma' is fine."

"I appreciate the help," Jamie said. "I hope it's not going to be any trouble if she stays here while I'm gone?"

"How long?" Alaida said.

"Not very. I hope." Although how long would it take to break into a fortified military base, locate an injured prisoner, and get him out without being noticed?

"She's welcome as long as need be," Emma said. "Me and Len have come to expect random requests from *that one*," she nodded toward the dining room. "This is probably less strange than most."

"Do you mind if I ask how you and Len know him?"

Emma considered Jamie's request for a moment. "I suppose there's no harm in it, especially since you seem to be in a similar fix at the moment. It was just after the war ended. Me and Len had gotten married and he was given this land for his service, like most veterans at the time. We built this farm, and we were going to start a family.

Only problem is, we weren't having much luck with that second part. All the physicians we talked to told us there wasn't much hope. We had just about given up when *he* showed up out of the blue, saying that one of the people we'd talked to had mentioned our situation to him and asking if we would let him help. Looking back, I know it was stupid to even consider help from someone who looks like him, but we were both young and pretty desperate."

"You mean he's always looked like that?" Jamie said, "Even fifty years ago?"

"Exactly the same," Emma said. That sent a chill down Jamie's spine, making him wonder if maybe the doctor really was some kind of god. "He gave us both an injection and then told us that he'd check in the next time he passed through. To be honest, I kind of thought that was the last we'd ever see of him. But when he showed up a few years later, me and Len already had two kids and another on the way. Whatever he did, it worked. We never would have had our family if it weren't for him and we've done what we can to repay him since. We've only ever seen him a handful of times, but he's never asked us to do anything illegal or dangerous and he's never put us in harm's way. Usually, all he wants is a place to spend the night."

Jamie shuddered at the thought of having to live with that kind of debt hanging over one's head for so long. He hoped Doctor Calamestro wouldn't try to extend the terms of his own bargain after it was concluded. "Can I ask you a question? Have you ever heard of someone named 'Lareed' before?"

Emma pursed her lips and shook her head. "Can't say that I have. Who is he?"

"I don't know; someone else that Calamestro made a deal with."

Emma chuckled darkly. "All these years, I thought me and Len were the only ones. Now I start to wonder what else he's been up to."

"I'm sorry about all this. We'll try to get out of here as soon as we can." Jamie took Alaida by the hand and pulled her to her feet. "Alaida, can I talk to you a second?"

They stepped back out into the darkened yard, but Jamie instantly felt the eyes of all those Wolf-Slaves, still hidden in their positions, boring into them. "Come on." He led her across the yard and through one of the man doors in the side of the barn. Inside, it was even darker than out, but at least it was quiet and they were alone.

"Alaida, I -- "

"Wait a moment," Alaida said, dashing off across the barn to the parked titan-mecha. She climbed the side, rolled back the hatch to the hold, and then reached inside to pull something out. Jamie had wandered over by the time she came back down to the ground and handed him the long, black coat that Onorah had given her back in Tavnic. "Here. Now just hold still." Lifting his arm and ducking under it, she pulled out a needle and thread, and even with the bandages on her hands, quickly placed a line of deft stitches across the cut in the side of Jamie's leather suit. "It is not perfect," she said with a frown. Jamie shivered at the feel of her fingers running over her rushed handiwork. "But it should keep you from looking completely destitute. And maybe you could wear the coat instead of your poncho? I know that Doctor Calamestro said no one would recognize you here, but why take the chance?"

She did have a good point, but Jamie had become so accustomed to the poncho that he'd feel naked without it.

"Here, let me help." Alaida folded the poncho back over Jamie's shoulders and then helped him into the coat. It certainly fit him better than it had her and the poncho now looked more like just a scarf instead of a giant flapping banner asking everyone who saw it to recall that story they had heard about a rogue dressed in red.

"Okay, you're right. This is probably a better idea."

Her smile was filled with self-satisfaction. "Just be careful."

"I will. Are you going to be okay here?"

Alaida nodded thoughtfully. "Len and Emma do not seem like bad people. I trust them."

"I do too, but I think you have better judgment for stuff like that than I do. Maybe if I'd listened to you before, we wouldn't be in this mess right now."

"Then Medraut and his Wolf-Slaves would have likely killed us at the river. We may yet be able to learn something new from the papers we saved from the fire. And you now know the name 'Lareed,' even if you do not know what it means. Reaver would have handled things differently, but I think you may have learned more than he would have under the same circumstances."

"Maybe..." In the back of his mind, Jamie kept thinking that Reaver would have had this whole situation resolved by now if he'd been the one in control. However, that didn't matter. None of it did. What was done, was done. They couldn't change things now. "Alaida, do you remember back at the river, when you asked me which world I would prefer if I had a choice, Terrarhea or Earth, and I said I didn't know?"

Alaida nodded.

"Well, I have an answer for you now: I'd choose this world, and not just because I might be stuck here now." He took a deep breath, already feeling his face grow red. From the very beginning, he'd avoided saying this, but now he couldn't leave it unspoken, not with the things he was expected to do in Fort Grassnar. "Even with how messed up things are right now; I'd choose it because you're here. I...care about you, a lot." Alaida cringed, no doubt embarrassed to hear Jamie spilling his guts to her like this. "And I know you don't feel the same way about me but that doesn't change anything. I just want to be here for you as long as I can, or until you tell me to leave."

Alaida stood there for several long moments in silence, her brow wrinkled and her jaw quivering. If he hadn't ruined things between them by his behavior while swimming, this probably had for certain. Later, he might regret having done so, but at the moment, he was just grateful to have it out in the open. What he'd said was the truth and he wouldn't be ashamed of that.

"I have to go." As Jamie backed towards the door, Alaida watched him go, still saying nothing. They could talk when he got back, if she still wanted to talk to him at all. He turned then and walked away. As he opened the door, Alaida finally called out after him.

"Jamie!" she said with a startled choke. "I-I *do* feel the same way about you! And that's what's scared me, not Reaver or any of the rest, but because a Slave is not supposed to feel this way about a Human!"

With his hand still grasping the door handle, Jamie's breath caught in his throat. Alaida had just... She really...

At the same moment, Medraut stepped into view on the other side of the door. "Nice disguise," he said with a chuckle and a roll of the eyes. "*No one's* gonna be able to recognize you now. Come on, let's go. Quit wasting time."

Jamie snarled at Medraut's back and then glanced hopelessly to Alaida. "I'll see you soon."

She nodded. "I will be waiting."

Jamie stalked across the barnyard, coming alongside Medraut just as he reached the head of the driveway where Doctor Calamestro stood looking out between the pillars of stone at the planes beyond. "Dawn will be upon us soon," he said. "Make haste. The longer Saexon is in custody, the greater the risk for you, as well as for him. I will meet you at the rendezvous." With that, the doctor slunk away down the driveway with an escort of Wolf-Slaves falling in around him as they headed in the opposite direction from the fort. None of the Wolves appeared to have remained behind. Alaida had returned to the house and now stood in the doorway, one foot on the stoop as she gazed after Jamie.

He offered her a smile and then sighed. "So, this is it then?" he said to no one in particular.

"Unless you'd rather back out," Medraut said, "in which case I'll happily kill you right here." He reflexively reached for his machete, but it looked like he'd entrusted his pack with one of the Wolves who'd just left. His scowl deepened.

Jamie blew out his breath. "That's quite the team spirit you've got there."

"The only reason I'm doing this with you is because I have to!" Medraut said, whirling on him. Jamie stood his ground, which actually seemed to take Medraut aback. Jamie smirked at the small victory. "Don't think for a second that we're friends. Once this is over, we're done!"

"My thoughts exactly."

Medraut's eyes narrowed as he sized up Jamie, probably wondering if he might yet be able to get away with killing him after all. Then he smiled, baring his teeth. "Hope you can keep up."

With that, he jumped down to the road and set off toward Fort Grassnar, quickly disappearing into the darkness. Jamie shook his head. If the soldiers didn't get him killed, Medraut probably would. After taking one final look back at Alaida, Jamie set off as well.

Chapter 52

It didn't take Jamie long to catch up with Medraut, which only seemed to make the tracker even more upset. Rather than continue exacerbating what was already a tenuous enough situation, Jamie decided to hold back a respectable distance, just to let Medraut feel like he was actually making things harder for Jamie.

With scarcely any large stands of trees on the plane surrounding the city and the fort, there weren't many options for staying out of sight. Even the outlying fields mostly ran from one to the next with hardly a hedgerow or fence separating them. And while it looked as if all the crops had been planted this season, none of them were yet high enough to offer any kind of concealment whatsoever.

Capitalizing on the little remaining darkness they still had left, Jamie and Medraut rushed along the roads. Occasionally, when presented with a shorter route, they would skirt across the edge of a field or down an access trail, but with the increasing numbers of people groggily setting out into the new day, the route Medraut chose to follow progressively became more indirect.

As the land leveled off below the foothills, Fort Grassnar loomed larger and taller the closer they got, its encircling walls towering high and menacing over the city of Tolfield. The edges of the city, which had appeared clearly marked by bright streetlights when viewed from above, now seemed indistinct as the outlying farm buildings began intermingling with those of the village.

Medraut's latest path had taken them down a drainage ditch filled ankle-deep with water. At least Jamie told himself it was only water. From the smell of the bordering cattle yard, he wasn't so sure. Ahead, Medraut had taken up position in a clump of weeds behind a low stone wall near a dirt road and a timber bridge that spanned the ditch.

Jamie charged up the side of the ditch, slipping more than once in the dewy grass, and threw himself down beside Medraut. One of the noxards in the yard on the side of the stone wall let out a startled bellow.

"Are you trying to get us killed?" Medraut hissed in a low whisper.

Jamie was no farmer, but he'd spent enough time on farms to know that the mewing of a few cattle in the night would not be cause for concern from even the most overprotective farmer.

Without waiting for an answer, Medraut snapped his gaze around to the road. There, a man and woman strolling away from Tolfield remained completely oblivious to the two onlookers crouched in the grass.

"Why are we even hiding anymore?" Jamie said. The people on the road just looked like farmers. "At this point, we're probably gonna draw more attention sneaking around like this than if we just walked in."

"Have you seen how big that place is?" Medraut pointed toward the city at the base of the fort. His voice had taken on an almost frantic edge.

"Yeah, which means more people. Which means it'll be less likely anyone even notices us."

"You're crazy if you think I'm just gonna walk in there!"

"Fine, do whatever you want." Jamie watched as the two people on the road crossed the bridge and then he stepped past Medraut, out onto the road. Medraut offered up several choice curses and tried pulling him back, but Jamie stood just beyond his reach, shaking out his coat. After a moment, during which no alarms or cries of surprise were heard, Jamie turned to Medraut and shrugged.

Medraut bared his canines. "Let's just see how far you get like that!" After a quick glance to confirm the road was still clear, Medraut dashed across to the other side and disappeared into the shadows created on the backside of a barn.

Jamie, meanwhile, set off at the quick but measured pace of a man who had places to be but wasn't yet running late. He passed two farmhouses, both brightly lit from within. As he knew would be the case, the people he saw moving about inside were far more interested in their own affairs than in some solitary traveler on the road. Jamie even offered friendly waves to some of the farmers he saw already at work. A few of them even returned the gesture.

Ahead, two wooden buildings, each three stories tall, stood on either side of the road with a single gloworb suspended on a line between. Beyond, there were more gloworbs and more buildings, many that looked like warehouses, but many more which could have been bars, retail shops, or apartments. There were more people about, as well, some of which were operating vulcan-mechas as they loaded barrels and sacks from the warehouses onto waiting wagons and various sized versions of those floating flatbed transports he'd seen in Tavnic. Most of the pedestrians out at that hour were clearly of a blue-collar sort but a small percentage were dressed more formerly for work behind a desk.

There were also more soldiers than Jamie would have liked, though none of them were armed or took the slightest interest in him. In fact, dressed in rumpled and half-donned uniforms, most looked like they were simply having a hard time seeing the ground in front of them. A lot couldn't have been much older than Jamie himself.

Passing around the corner of one building, Jamie was nearly barreled over by one young man pulling on his uniform's tunic as he ran off the end of a porch like he was being chased by a murderer.

Jamie peaked around the corner to see what could have caused such a reaction only to come face-to-face with a plump woman and two young, teenage girls, all giggling at something like it was the most terrific joke. Starkly backlit from above by the gloworbs hanging on the porch, it was hard to make them out in any detail apart from the long black dresses they wore.

"Hey there, soldier," the woman said upon seeing Jamie. As she stepped forward, the light on her face shifted and Jamie could see the gold-on-gold eyes of a slave. Having gotten so used to the surprise appearance of someone with eyes like that usually signaling an attack, he drew back with a gasp. His foot fell into one of the wheel ruts running through the street, twisting his ankle and sending him stumbling backwards.

"Whoa there, no need to get all excited!" the woman, a somewhat elder Raven-Slave, said. The two girls, who Jamie could now see were also Raven-Slaves, started giggling again. "Care to come in for a spell? I can show you a good time."

Regaining his balance, Jamie muttered some nonsensical reply before heading once more on his way.

"Well, come on back if you change your mind!" the woman said, waving after him with a towel. The girls merely giggled even louder.

Jamie didn't bother to look back. He just kept walking. In front of an empty lot, filled with nothing but grass and a few rocks, Jamie turned at the sound of a soft thump. There, Medraut stood in the shadows, flat against the side of a neighboring building and glaring back at Jamie.

"What is it with you and Raven-Slaves?" Medraut snapped.

"And how's all that sneaking around working out for you?"

"I've made it this far."

"Which is exactly as far as I've made it," Jamie said, "but without sneaking. Look, the streets are already packed and the sun's not even up yet. Do you really think you're gonna make decent time skulking around like that?"

"At least I won't end up in a cage!"

Jamie rolled his eyes. Under normal circumstances, Medraut and his Wolf-Slaves probably avoided cities at all cost. Even if this wasn't a new experience for him, he clearly wasn't coping well with all the people or the tight spaces. If only he'd thought about that before he'd ignored the first of Doctor Calamestro's orders to rescue Saexon, then he might have saved them both a lot of trouble.

"No one's gonna put you in a cage unless you give them some reason to," Jamie said. Medraut peeked out into the street and then quickly drew back into the shadows. "Don't tell me you're scared."

"No!" Medraut said with a loud, laughing sneer. "But why should I take any chances?"

Shaking his head, Jamie headed back into the street. "I thought you wanted to get this over with, not draw it out any longer than necessary."

He heard Medraut's distinctive growl and then the clomp of his boots on the cobblestones as he pushed past Jamie. "Come on, it's this way," he said, pulling on his goggles.

Jamie chose not to point out that he had already been heading in that direction. Medraut rushed ahead at a fast clip, his head in constant motion as he scanned every alleyway, cross street, and doorway. He spent so much time looking for danger that he had little left to watch out for his fellow pedestrians. Frequently, he had to jump out of the way of oncoming wagons or dodge groups of hung-over soldiers.

The lack of organization in the streets didn't help much in that regard. Without sidewalks to provide some segregation for foot traffic, or even painted stripes to separate directions of travel, pedestrians, mechas, and wagons all intermingled and weaved around each in a chaotic mess. In order not to lose sight of Medraut, Jamie had to hurry after him, often ending up in the same predicaments as Medraut himself.

They continued making their way generally toward the fort while skirting along each major street that looked like it would take them farther north. Slowly, those streets transitioned from dirt to cobblestone and the quality of the buildings became less rugged and a bit more refined. The structures farther away from the hill appeared to mostly be houses and apartments, but the closer they got, the more they changed to commercial ventures of one sort or another. Once into the thick of the Tolfield, Fort Grassnar remained ever-present on the hill above. The citizens going about their routines seldom looked up at it. Jamie tried his best to do the same so that he wouldn't end up looking like a tourist.

In addition to the green uniforms that Jamie had become more familiar with than he cared to be, there were also more and more soldiers dressed in uniforms of the exact same cut but with a crimson red replacing the dark green. Apart from the variety of patches and pins with which each was decorated, they all looked identical to the one found in Major Ommto's hovel. Medraut had mentioned it being a magesmith uniform at the time. Did that mean the red uniforms marked soldiers as belonging to the Army Magesmith Corps that Onorah had told him about? Their nicely pressed uniforms were about as far removed from Onorah's soiled aprons and oily shop as Jamie could imagine. Her desire to join their ranks now became a little more clear to Jamie, even if he would never share it.

At one point, as they waited for a line of laundry wagons to be pushed through traffic, Jamie and Medraut stood staring down one of the streets which radiated out from the fort. Most of the village buildings stopped abruptly where the path began climbing sharply up the side of the hill. To try and make it to one of the gates at the top, they would have to cover a lot of open ground.

It wasn't until they began arcing around the north side of the hill that they finally saw the breach in the wall which Len had mentioned. A portion of the otherwise dominating fortification sat open like a jagged 'V' reaching toward the sky. The slope of the hillside was less steep there and a terraced series of fortified buildings cascaded down from the base of the breach all the way to the bottom of the hill.

From Len's description, Jamie had assumed the breach would be some kind of permeable gate with little security. This looked like nothing of the sort. And with the sky starting to brighten with the first light of dawn, it would only make any attempts to sneak inside even more difficult.

"How are we supposed to get through that?" Jamie asked when they stopped for a moment to survey the route ahead. The streets had grown much wider in that part of the city, and though they were also much less busy, the majority of the foot traffic was now composed almost entirely of soldiers, very few of whom looked to be suffering from hangovers. Here, rather than feeling like just another anonymous face in the crowd, Jamie couldn't stop thinking that everyone who so much as glanced in his direction was planning to report him to the omnipresent authorities.

Medraut scowled as he set off once again but didn't bother with any more of a reply to Jamie's question than that. Jamie knew he shouldn't have worried about the soldiers. Medraut was far more likely to stab him in the back than any of them.

The farther they went around the north of the hill, and the nearer they got to the city's western edge, the more the buildings started to peter out. Farther north, the palisade walls of the Boravian Slave Farm were just starting to come into view. To the south, however, Medraut's interest had been caught by a large, rectangular plaza which opened off the side of the street and reached a considerable way up the side of the hill. Standing empty at that hour, it was lined on three sides by vertical, three-story buildings that continued the ubiquitous character of their neighbors while also achieving a greater degree of oppressive formality.

"Mercenary Yard," Medraut read from the signs posted at the entrance. "This is definitely the place. I've seen setups like this before. Just like that old guy said, we pass ourselves off as mercenaries to get in the front door. The army loves to make people wait so there's always a bunch of exams and background checks before they let you get registered as a merc. During all that, it shouldn't be hard to find an opportunity to slip away and sneak into the fort."

"Yeah, just that easy," Jamie said. Inside his head, he was yelling at himself to just turn around and take his chances with Calamestro's wrath. For the moment, Alaida was safe and unguarded. If he hurried, he might be able to get back to the farm and the two of them could flee before any of these self-proclaimed *Lords of the Wild* could find them. He knew it was a fantasy he shouldn't have even entertained. Now that he had, it kept rearing into his conscious mind every time he looked at what they yet had to accomplish.

"Just don't say anything," Medraut said. "Let me do the talking. Now come on -- whoa." He stopped short after only one step; his eyes fixed on something approaching from the west. Jamie had seen it too: a strange titan-mecha colored something like weathered brass in a matte shade of golden-brown, or possibly olive. It was hard to tell for sure since the color seemed to shift from one moment to the next depending on how the morning light struck it.

Hunched over like some angry insect, it dominated the street, walking with the casual yet haughty stride of a gunfighter. It had to be just as massive as any of the Finttiranos titan-mechas Jamie had seen, which made it even larger than his own. However, while those machines had a rounded and broad-shouldered silhouette, this one stood tall and thin with a profile made up of angular curves that swept from front to back in strong, bold lines. On its back hung a large cargo pod of some kind that shared the same design esthetic as the rest of the machine. Its feet were an array of splayed claws at the bottom of a foot articulated like a chicken's. Its long, whip-like arms swung fluidly from its shoulders thanks to all the extra joints they possessed. Those thin yet powerful arms ended into grossly elongated hands with blunt ends from which extended long fingers that tapered to delicate, needle-sharp points. The wedge-shaped head was adorned with glowing, red eyes in front and a long pair of segmented antennas in the rear that cantilevered over its back and swayed rhythmically with each step it took.

"What the hell?" Medraut said, staring at the mecha as it turned and entered the mercenary yard. "That looks Thieradoonian...but that would mean..."

"That would mean what?"

"Don't worry about it, come on," Medraut hurried around the corner and into the yard behind the titan.

The machine advanced to the far end of the plaza and then backed into one of the corners before dropping suddenly to its knees with a crash. The segments of its waist and hips rotated, lowering its chest closer to the ground. With a hiss of steam, the armor plates along the front split open and slid to the sides as the neat lines of golden magescript that covered the entire machine faded. Jamie could now see why Onorah had assumed Reaver's titan to be Thieradoonian. Though it was of a completely different design from this machine, they still shared a number of similar features.

From inside the opened hatch dropped a rig of some kind connected to an impossibly chaotic tangle of crystalline relay cords and venting hoses. Angled forward, the pilot hung from the apparatus like a marionette, his head lowered, a harness strapped around his chest, and his arms above fitted into a pair of controls on either side. As Medraut and Jamie approached, he looked up with a toothy grin. Jamie had intended to ignore him entirely, but now found himself staring.

The man who deftly extracted himself from the harness and dropped lightly to the ground moved with the same cocky, predatory grace he had displayed in the piloting of his mecha. He was tall, with a thin, sinewy frame and long arms that reached nearly to his knees. He carried himself hunched over at the shoulders and wore a long, sleeveless coat of black leather that left his arms and chest bare. His skin had a yellowish sort of olive cast to it and his pale, red hair had been shaved from the sides of his head but tied up down the center into five knotted queues that fell over his shoulder. His face was a series of intersecting planes that made his hollow cheeks and flattened nose look even more stark, especially with the way he smiled through his thin lips, revealing rows of teeth which Jamie was almost certain had been purposely filed to points.

Speaking in a lilting sort of sing-song accent that seemed to blur his whole statement into a single, long word, he said, "Hey dere, boyos, care ta make a lil' coin?"

Jamie's mind fumbled over the man's words far longer than was typical, as he tried to reason out the meaning of this strange new dialect. The pilot punched a large crystal on the side of his cockpit and a hatch on the bottom of the titan's cargo pod opened, dropping out the bloodied bodies of two men. From the way they fell to the ground in a limb heap without sound, they were almost certainly dead.

"Ah could use some 'elp luggin' dese bastards inside."

"We're kinda busy at the moment," Medraut said without stopping.

Though still smiling, the man yelled after them, shaking a fist in the air. "Ya' bleedin' ingrates! Ma money not good 'nough fer ya?"

Jamie tried his best to ignore the man as Medraut had done, scrambling after the young tracker to catch up. Under a prominent canopy at the head of the plaza, a pair of large wooden doors bore several directional signs which Medraut quickly scanned before heading through.

CHAPTER 53

A high atrium with a wide staircase that led up to the second and third floors awaited them on the inside. Overhead, the ceilings were exposed timber beams and simple decorative mouldings with plaster infill between. The walls were paneled with a repetitive pattern of smooth plaster and wooden panels. Hallways branched off in all directions with polished stone tile on the floors that extended unrelentingly throughout every visible corner of the building. Windows opening off those passages offered glimpses into offices, each arranged differently but all utilizing a nearly identical assortment of wooden desks, chairs, and shelves. While the design choices did lend a certain official air to the building, something about the monotonous uniformity of it all suggested that it had not been done to impress, but simply because this was the cheapest option available to the builders.

Jamie had expected some kind of security, but no one was even around to question them about their business. Apart from a few soldiers making their way through the halls, the footfalls of their boots ringing loudly off the hard flooring underfoot, the place looked mostly empty.

"Registration is on the second floor," Medraut said, reading from one of the many placards hung around the atrium.

"Do you really think they're not gonna have any security at all?" Jamie said as he followed Medraut up the stairs while looking over his shoulder.

"Of course they're gonna have security. But just look at this place. They haven't had any excitement here in a very long time. I doubt they even follow half of their security procedures anymore."

"And what about the other half?"

"Quit your whining."

Jamie thought it had been a legitimate question, which probably meant Medraut had absolutely no idea what he was doing and was just making this up as he went. At the top of the stairs, a hallway led off to the left and to the right. Only a few of the offices had soldiers inside, and typically only one or two at that, prepping for the day's work as they sipped from steaming mugs of cariak.

Directly ahead, a pair of double doors hung open, leading into a large, well-lit room filled with circular, standing-height tables like one might find in a bar. Counters lined three sides of the room while the fourth had a huge bulletin board on either side of the entry doors. These were covered with a miss-matched assortment of notices and wanted posers. Some looked brand new, others were yellowed and dog-eared to the point they were barely readable. Two soldiers in neatly pressed uniforms stood behind the counter and looked up from their work at the sound of Jamie and Medraut's entrance. The one to their left had a head of stark white hair and three black stripes on the cuff of his sleeve while the one in front of them looked considerably younger and had only two stripes.

"Can I help you with something?" the younger of the two said, sounding like it was possibly the least interesting thing he could do at the moment.

"Um, yeah," Medraut said, glancing over his shoulder. He had better not be thinking about running. This is why Jamie had wanted some kind of plan rather than just storming in completely unprepared. "Yeah, we're here to register as mercenaries," Medraut said, putting on a smile and walking up to the counter. Jamie meanwhile turned away, trying to make it look as if he were just examining the wanted posters.

The clerk tapped a stack of papers straight on top of the counter and then set them aside. "You'll need to fill these out." He pulled two papers out from below the counter and placed them in front of Medraut. "After we confirm your information, you'll be cleared to collect bounties on any posted individuals in the Control Zone."

"That's it?" Medraut said, scanning the papers. Even from across the room, Jamie could see at a glance that they were two copies of the same form, one for each of them, and that each was only printed on one side. "No examinations? No security checks?"

"Have you done this kind of work before?"

"A few times."

"Well, we don't mess with any of that stuff here," the clerk said. "Frankly, it's a waste of our time since most people who sign up don't last long enough to collect their first bounty anyways. We can't process any registrations until six, though, so if you want to wait," he gestured to the tables arrayed around the room, "feel free."

"Sounds great. Thanks." Medraut drummed the countertop with his fingertips and the moment he turned his back to the soldier, the smile dropped from his face. Jamie joined him at one of the nearby tables.

"So, what now?" Jamie said, careful to keep his voice low. With only the two of them in the room, he couldn't help but think those soldiers were intentionally eavesdropping on everything they said. "Do we wait?"

Jamie could practically hear the grinding of Medraut's teeth as he leaned heavily on the table and stared into the distance. "I thought that if we registered, we could get in further than this."

"Well, there's got to be another way, right?" Jamie said, forcing himself to remember the consequences if he and Medraut were unable to complete the task they had been given.

"Shut up!" Medraut said under his breath. "I'm thinking!"

"Fine..." Blowing out his breath and taking a step back, Jamie again cast his gaze across all the bounties posted on the wall. He didn't see his face on any of the posters so at least it did indeed appear that Doctor Calamestro had been right about no one in this region being interested in the Red Rogue. However, even after Jamie had reviewed every notice on both of the bulletin boards for a second time, Medraut still didn't look any closer to a solution.

As Jamie debated whether to risk Medraut's further ire by asking him how his plan was coming or simply pretend to peruse the wanted posters for a third time, a lanky fellow with long, greasy black hair wandered into the room. Wearing the simple clothes of a laborer, he didn't look much like a bounty hunter. As the newcomer stood for a moment in the doorway with his hands thrust deep into his pockets, Jamie couldn't help but notice the black tattoo of a feather on one side of his neck surrounded by several stacks of tally marks. On the other side was a matching tattoo of a fang, but with only three marks next to it. They reminded Jamie of similar tattoos he'd seen on some of the people he'd crossed paths with around Tavnic. The moment Medraut caught sight of him, he clenched his fists tight and snarled under his breath.

"Whoa, what's up?" Jamie whispered. "Do you know him?"

"No." Medraut glared at the man's back as he walked up to the counter. "But he's Enlightened Path."

"What's that mean?"

Tearing his eyes away from the man, Medraut turned to Jamie. "Are you serious? You don't even know what the Enlightened Path is? They're a bunch of anti-slave fanatics."

Jamie had never imagined that any such movements even existed on Terrarhea. Medraut had mentioned in the past that certain nations had outlawed slavery. Could it be possible that such sentiments were more widespread than he'd realized? "That doesn't sound so bad. What have you got against them?"

"Not Anti-*Slavery*!" Medraut hissed, keeping his voice low, "Anti-*Slave*! They believe that the Slave Races are an abomination and that every last one of them needs to be exterminated. Those tattoos on his neck show how many he's killed. The fang is for Wolves. That's three dead Wolves by his hand."

Jamie felt his stomach lurch. He himself had likely killed more Wolves than that, but that had been in self-defense, not cold-blooded murder in the pursuit of some twisted ideology. "And the feather?" he said, counting at least twenty-four tally marks next to it.

"Ravens."

Of course Medraut would find them of secondary consequence to his own charges, but to Jamie they were all of equal importance. That man was a murderer who had killed nearly thirty people and he was blatantly displaying the fact for everyone to see. Did those people in Tavnic belong to this Enlightened Path organization as well? It would certainly help to explain the reactions he and Alaida had gotten from some of them. Jamie thought he'd come to terms with all the repulsive things that Slavery entailed here on Terrarhea, but this came as a whole new shock. "How does anyone get away with that? Isn't it illegal?"

"Only if they're caught. And you can't arrest someone for a couple of tattoos." Medraut once again turned his gaze on the man. "If I ran into him on the road, he wouldn't be breathing afterward."

"Have the new bounty heads been posted yet?" the man asked of the clerk.

"Not today's" the clerk said. "It'll probably be another hour before they come down."

"*Sheet...*" the man said.

Medraut looked as if he might actually try to rip the man's throat out right there in the waiting room. While it might have been a nice change for Jamie to no longer be the sole focus of Medraut's anger, it wouldn't help either of them if it also endangered their mission. Hands still in his pockets, the man wandered away from the counter, completely heedless of how close he was to being killed. He glanced over the wanted posters for a moment without any real interest.

"Hey, where are the pissers around here again?"

"Out the doors to your right," the clerk said without looking up from his papers.

"Thanks," the man said, waving over his shoulder. Heading back out into the hallway, he had to sidestep around the titan-mecha pilot they'd seen earlier.

Entering the room with a flourish, he stood framed in the doorway for a moment before striding up to the counter. "Ah'm 'ere ta claim me bounties dere, sergeant major," he said with a broad smile as he dropped several rumpled papers smeared with blood on the counter in front of the younger of the two clerks. Next to those, he tossed down a pair of smaller slips of red paper.

"That's corporal, actually," the clerk said.

"Of course it is dere, sergeant major." The pilot flashed his pointed teeth with a grin.

The solider looked at the papers without making any move to pick them up. "These bounties specifically say that the reward is only valid if they are brought in alive. And those claim tickets are clearly not green."

The pilot turned, leaned his back against the counter, and propped his elbows up on the edge. He looked around the room, his self-satisfied smile growing bigger as if he were performing for an audience. "Well, dey put up quite a fight. Ya can't blame me if dey got a lil' banged up in da process."

"That's why the bounty says 'armed and extremely dangerous.'" The solider almost put his finger down on top of the stack of papers for emphasis, but stopped himself short, shying away from the blood.

Rolling his head on his shoulders, the pilot turned back around to face the soldier. "Well, if ya wanna run it by General Fiterasti, go right ahead. Ah can wait."

"General Fiterasti?" the soldier said dryly, raising a single eyebrow. "The commanding general of Fort Grassnar?"

"Yeah. Ya see, me an' him, we have us an understandin'. If Ah was you, Ah'd just go ahead an' pay dem bounties out." The pilot looked out across the room, as if to cue in any spectators to the upcoming punch line. "Dat is, unless ya want ta spend da rest o' yer time stationed 'ere scrubbin' latrines."

The clerk glanced to the other soldier working at the far counter. Frowning, the older man shook his head. The younger soldier took a deep breath and pulled the rumpled papers over to him, giving them a quick scan before finally picking them up. The pilot grinned so that all his sharpened teeth were visible once again.

"I'll take care of these for you right away," the soldier said, his tone measured. He went through a door behind the counter and disappeared.

With that, the pilot pulled a shiny silver flask from the inside of his coat and raised it in salute to the room before taking a triumphant gulp. He then offered it to the other clerk.

"Um, no," the soldier said as he shuffled some papers around. "There's really not supposed to be any drinking in here."

"Yer loss," the pilot said, taking another drink.

Leaning closer to Medraut, Jamie whispered, "Who is that guy?"

"I've never actually seen him before but he's pretty famous in mercenary circles," Medraut muttered. Still glaring out into the hallway, he'd hardly been paying any notice at all to the pilot's antics. "His name's Ironsides. He's a Thieradoonian mercenary and man-hunter. Supposed to be pretty tough."

"Thieradoonian? What's he's doing in Finttiranos?"

"Supposedly, Thieradoon kicked him out. But he's so good at what he does, he's got a license to operate here, even with his titan-mecha."

Jamie glanced at this Ironsides character as he tried to entice the soldier yet again to take a celebratory drink with him. It was starting to look like trouble might develop if the soldier continued refusing, but then the other solider returned with some more papers and a small leather sack that jingled with the sound of coins. His toothy grin broadening, the pilot turned back to the younger clerk.

"Do all Thieradoonians look like him?" Jamie said.

"Yeah, and some of them eat puppies, too," Medraut said with a sardonic twisting of the lip and a cheeky nod. "I'm gonna take a look around and see if I can find some way into the fort. Stay here and try not to make too much of a fool out of yourself."

"Hey, why are -- ?" Jamie began but Medraut had already stalked out of the room. Turning to see if anyone might take undue notice of him if he followed, Jamie came face-to-face with the mercenary titan-mecha pilot, Ironsides.

"So, we meet again dere, eh master chief?" he said, retrieving the flask from his coat and unscrewing the cap. Before taking a drink, he craned his neck around to get a better look at the two forms still laying on the table. "You an' yer friend 'ere ta sign up as man'unters? In such a rush seekin' glory and riches, ya couldn't bother ta spare even a minute ta 'elp out a fellow merc?"

His mind fumbling over what the man had said for several moments longer than it should have taken, Jamie finally managed to sputter, "He's not my friend."

"Oh, ma apologies," Ironsides said with mock sincerity and then took a long drink from his flask. "So, ya really tink ya 'ave what it takes ta be a merc?"

"I heard it's good money."

"Ha, if ya can stay alive, it is!"

Were these Heigelries rebels really so bloodthirsty that everyone felt the need to keep bringing that up?

"Do you need something, or...?" Jamie straightened the forms out in front of him, only then realizing that, even if he knew what they said, he didn't have anything to fill them out with. "I'm kind of busy here."

"Ya need someone ta read dat fer ya?" Ironsides said, slurring his words in what was no doubt meant to be an imitation of Jamie's own unique accent but was only making himself even less understandable. "Da way yer lookin' at dem papers makes me tink yer parents didn't teach ya yer letters before sendin' ya out inta da big scary world."

Jamie rolled his eyes. Being stuck on Terrarhea, he had actually started to entertain the notion that he'd never have to put up with the antics of high school jocks and bullies ever again. So much for that.

"Come on now master chief. None o' dese starched shirts is gonna tell ya dis because all dey do is file paperwork, but Ah will: ya ain't cut out to be a merc. Ah can tell dis just by lookin' at ya." He took another long swig from his flask and then returned it to his coat. "Ah don't have ta do dis, but Ah am, out'a da kindness o' ma heart."

Jamie paused to take a breath. This might not be Earth and he might make even bigger trouble for himself if he did start a fight with this man, but that didn't mean he had to sit there and be insulted either. "That," Jamie said, "or because you don't want the competition?"

"Yer a cheeky lil' bastard, ain't ya?" Ironsides laughed. "But why would Ah be worried 'bout competition from a scrawny lil' zit like you?"

"Scrawny? Look who's talking."

His nostrils flaring, Ironsides dropped his fist to the table with a bang. "Ah'm gonna let dat slide dis time, seein' as how ya just clearly been released from da bughouse an' all."

Shaking his head, Jamie met Ironsides' gaze. "Don't let that stop you."

He knew the smart thing would have been to shut up and take the insults, just like he always did. Starting a fight with some random guy who clearly had enough connections to endanger the entire mission was the sort of thing Medraut would have done.

But where was Medraut? At this rate, they'd run out of time before even making an attempt to get into the fort. Jamie doubted Doctor Calamestro would let something like that slide without consequence.

"Keep pushin' dere boyo," Ironsides said. "See if ah don't step on ya wit' ma titan yet."

"So, you're saying you'd need your titan to deal with scrawny little me?"

"Oh, ya 'ear dat?" Ironsides said, cupping a hand behind his ear. "Dat's me shakin' in ma boots."

"Well, it's certainly not me."

"Ya've got quite a pair on ya, Ah'll give ya dat. Ya wanna see 'ow far ya can push me before Ah rip 'em off?"

"And now you want to touch my balls," Jamie said dryly. "I wouldn't have taken you for that kind of guy."

Ironsides' eyes narrowed down to thin slits. Jamie didn't look away. He knew this conversation had now come within a hairsbreadth of turning into a physical altercation. Part of him actually wanted it. This posturing mercenary would have been a poor substitute for Medraut, or Doctor Calamestro, or Seth and his friends, or even the entire Finttiranos military, but it would be something tangible that he could actually triumph over.

The more rational parts of his brain, however, told him not to. Even if he could easily wipe the floor with Ironsides, the mercenary's connections would likely still result in Jamie taking the blame. His words alone might have already pushed things too far.

"I gotta take a leak," Jamie said, being very careful to use the exact Terrarhean phasing so as to avoid giving Ironsides any additional verbal ammunition that might yet tempt him into a fight. Heading for the door, he gave Ironsides a dismissive wave over his shoulder.

"Yeah, why don't ya run along dere boy!" Ironsides called after him. "Ah'd invite ya ta come along ta da brothel wit' me, but ah don't tink yer old enough ta get in!"

Once Jamie was back in the hall and had turned the corner, he stopped and took a deep breath. Back on Earth, his pulse would have been racing and his hands shaking, but not here on Terrarhea. Here, as his body remained perfectly calm, it was only his mind telling him that he hadn't wanted to be in that situation; that he should have been terrified; that he wanted more than anything to put Ironsides in his place.

Wandering the halls looking for Medraut had to be better than waiting back in that room. Jamie had walked about halfway to the end of the hall, passing a number of soldiers and lighted offices without making himself noticed, when he heard a muffled thump and raised voices from behind the door on his right. He couldn't read the text on the sign but the pictogram and the absence of a lock almost certainly indicated that this was the toilet room which the soldier had mentioned. There was another exchange of heated words followed by a sudden crash.

Jamie looked both ways up and down the corridor. No one came running to find out what the commotion was about but something was definitely going on in there, and as much as Jamie didn't want to investigate, he had a sinking feeling that he had no choice. Slowly he pushed the door open and peered around the edge.

The tiled room on the other side was outfitted with a surprisingly modern-looking array of porcelain toilets and urinals along one wall and a row of enameled lavatories and mirrors hanging on the other. None of the stalls had doors on them, revealing at a glance that there wasn't anyone else here besides the two at the far end of the room. There, Medraut had taken hold of someone by the arm and forced him to the floor with a boot heel on the back of his neck.

Jamie glanced hastily back into the hallways before rushing into the bathroom and pushing the door closed behind him. "Medraut! What are you doing!" Jamie said, sprinting across the room and pulling Medraut off the other man. Medraut struggled, still intent on going after his victim. It was only now that Jamie got confirmation of what he already suspected: that this was the same man Medraut had nearly attacked in the office. "You're gonna ruin everything!"

"Do we understand each other!" Medraut demanded of the man, his only interest in Jamie at the moment that he was preventing him from killing the object of his hate.

Indifferently, the man sat up on the floor, his back against one of the toilets as he glared up at Medraut with blood running from a cut on his lip.

"I'm really sorry about this," Jamie said. "I don't know what's got into him. We don't want any trouble."

"Do we understand each other?" Medraut said again.

The man's eyes narrowed and then he slowly climbed to his feet. "Yeah, I understand."

Finally, Medraut stopped his struggles enough that Jamie eased his grip. At that, Medraut shook Jamie off. He and the man continued glaring at each other as Jamie watched on, dumbfounded. Finally, the man stepped around them and walked out of the restroom, never taking his eyes off Medraut until the door closed behind him. The moment it shut, Jamie grabbed Medraut by the shoulder and turned the shorter boy to face him.

"What was that about! I get that you have reasons to hate those guys, but is that really worth it right now? What you just did is probably gonna get us killed!"

Medraut straightened his shirt with a jerk as he too turned and headed for the door. "We're fine," he said. Jamie didn't like that smile one bit. "And it was worth it; totally worth it. Now come on, I think I know how to get us inside."

Jamie shook his head. He really should have taken on Ironsides when he'd had the chance because his truce with Doctor Calamestro wouldn't allow him to do what he wanted to do to Medraut.

Chapter 54

When Medraut and Jamie arrived back at the doors to the waiting room, the man Medraut had assaulted was heading down the main stairs toward the exit. Jamie hoped that if he'd wanted to raise an alarm, he would have turned them in to the first soldier he saw. It would definitely be a good thing if he left without causing any trouble for them, but how could they be certain he would?

"What did you say to him?"

"I convinced him to give up his evil ways," Medraut said. Somehow Jamie doubted that was the case. Or that something like that would be so simple. Medraut slapped the back of his hand across Jamie's chest. "Now come on."

"No!" Jamie grabbed Medraut by the shoulder. "We're supposed to be working together here! What was that about? What's your big plan?"

"Don't worry, I got it all figured out. We just need a little distraction is all."

Jamie glanced down the stairs. The man had now left the building. "You convinced him to do something that's going to let us sneak in?"

Medraut's smile grew a little wider. "You're gonna love this."

With that, he strode back into the waiting room and right up to the counter in front of the younger clerk. At least Ironsides had left.

"I still can't sign up you and your friend until six," the clerk said.

"Hey, don't lump me in with him," Medraut said, leaning on the counter and pointing at Jamie with his thumb. "I may have seen some stuff, but this one is the real deal, ain't that right, Red?"

"What are you talking about?" The hairs on the back of Jamie's neck were standing on end. Something about this no longer felt right.

"Didn't you get into it pretty good with the authorities out east?" Medraut said. Jamie felt a hole open in his stomach. "Tavnic, wasn't it?"

"Hey, what are you talking about?" Jamie said, trying his best to laugh. What the hell was Medraut doing? "That's not funny at all."

"Where's Tavnic?" the clerk said as if even that wasn't worth his bother.

"A little village in the Coastal Territories," Medraut said, helpfully.

"Would you quit joking around," Jamie said. "You know I've never even been to Tavnic."

"Look, we have a lot of work to do here," the clerk said. "If you really want to sign-up, we can run the paperwork at six. Until then, just have a seat and don't bother us unless you have a question." Turning to the older clerk, he said, "Could you give me a hand with those 20-48's?" Both of them then disappeared through the door behind the counter.

The moment they were out of sight, Jamie grabbed Medraut by the front of his shirt. "What the hell do you think you're doing!"

"Hey," Medraut said with a shrug and a nonchalant smile, "I was only joking around."

"This is the last place we need to be joking around!"

"Come on, do you really think any criminal worth his salt would go around telling the authorities what he's done? Those guys just think we're a couple of kids who don't even know which way is up."

"That's not the point!" Jamie said giving Medraut a shake. "There's a difference between joking around and drawing attention to yourself! Whatever happened to 'low-profile'?"

"I think you've been drawing plenty of attention to yourself all on your own," Medraut said, still irritatingly smug.

"You think I'm drawing too much attention? Well what about you? How can you really know that guy you beat up is going to do what you want him to and not just turn us in?"

Medraut eyes narrowed a fraction of an inch and his smirk widened. "Oh, he'll do what I told him. Their kind is so predictable; makes them easy to manipulate."

"And just what is he gonna be able to do that'll make things any easier for us to get inside?"

"Patience," Medraut said with a chuckle. "Just give it a little longer. But when things start happening, we'll have to move fast."

"You don't really have any plan at all, do you!" Renewing his grip on Medraut's shirt, Jamie pushed him back against the counter hard enough that the young tracker gasped from the impact. "Well, I'm sick of this! I'm sick of you!"

"I think you better let him go," the clerk said from behind the counter. Jamie looked up and found himself staring across the top of a Finttiranos Military sidearm. The first time he'd seen one of those, it had been from the exact same angle.

"Red Rogue, huh?" the clerk said as he looked at a piece of paper in his other hand and spoke in the same monotone he'd been using since Medraut and Jamie had first met him. "Did you come up with that yourself?"

"I--I don't even know what that means!" Jamie said.

"Oh, they got you now," Medraut said, all but laughing to himself as he slipped out of Jamie's now slack grip. "I told you they'd figure you out."

"Why you -- " They could have found a way inside if Medraut hadn't gone and messed up everything. Truce or no, Jamie was going to wring his neck.

"Whoa there," the clerk said, pressing the pistol right into Jamie's temple and forcing him to retreat a step with hands raised. As he did, more soldiers filed into the room from each of the three exits. None of them had apparently had time to don any armor but several were armed with rifles and the rest were sporting handguns like the clerk. Jamie turned in a slow circle. In the confines of that room, it would be almost impossible for any of these soldiers to miss if they decided to start shooting.

"Hey, this is all just a big misunderstanding," Jamie said, trying again to laugh. "My friend was just joking. Go ahead and tell them..." And that's when Jamie noticed Medraut was gone, vanished from the room as if he'd never been there at all. "I'm gonna kill him!"

At that, three of the soldiers rushed in and took hold of Jamie.

"You've got me mixed up with someone else!" Jamie said, struggling with only a fraction of his strength. He could have thrown them off with ease, but that wouldn't exactly help his claim of innocence. "I'm telling you, I'm not a criminal!"

"I don't know about you, but I think that's a pretty good likeness." The clerk laid the paper he held down on the countertop for Jamie to see. He couldn't make out most of the printed Terrarhean letters, but right in the middle of the page was a large, hand drawn sketch of his face. For a moment, Jamie stopped his struggles and stared. It was actually a pretty good likeness. "I can't believe it took a whole platoon to bring you in the last time."

"Th-that's because that's not me!"

"Must have been hopped up on Devil's Root when he worked over those frontier grunts," the solider holding him in a headlock said.

"Either that or those guys were just a bunch of lightweights," one of the others added.

"What do we do with him now?"

"Process him and throw him into holding," the clerk said. "Coordinating transfers with other territories is always a pain in the ass. Could take weeks."

"You gonna split that reward with us?" one of the soldiers holding Jamie's arm asked as they dragged him toward the exit.

"You know soldiers aren't eligible for those," the clerk said. Once he was out of earshot to everyone, he added under his breath, "Not unless I file the paperwork under someone else's name."

"And ten-percent for me to look the other way," the older clerk said.

"Of course."

The soldiers dragged Jamie into the depths of the building where they forced him to strip out of his clothes and strapped him into a massive magesmith device with a chair at the center surrounded by sweeping panels behind and in front that made it look something like a giant, metal snail. With each ominous flashing light and clicking noise the machine produced, the military technicians manning it would jot down a note or ramble off some statistic to the officers supervising the operation. It seemed to go on forever, and since it didn't hurt in the least, Jamie had plenty of opportunity to realize it was some kind of scanner that was creating a description of him far more detailed than just mere fingerprints and a mug shot. He was actually a little disappointed when they finally finished and nothing from the results had garnered the least bit of extra scrutiny from the technicians. With all the things Reaver was capable of, it seemed inconceivable the machine wouldn't detect something abnormal.

After compiling the data, the jailers proceeded to question Jamie about his biographical information, along with his involvement in the events that transpired in Tavnic. He remained equally silent on both topics. Telling them about his past would have been just as confusing for them as it would have been dangerous for him. And as much as he wanted to correct the half-truths and outright lies his interrogators read from the wanted poster, it quickly became clear that the limited information printed on that sheet of paper was all they knew about the incident in Tavnic. So, rather than damage his claims of innocence, he simply held his tongue.

Eventually, after what seemed like hours, but he knew was actually much less, his clothes were returned to him and he was tossed down a large, round passage. He stumbled to the end where his foot dropped over an edge and he fell down a short incline of smooth concrete which deposited him onto a paved yard in the full light of day. Above, armored guards held rifles at the ready from within the protection of the fortifications built on either side of the chute Jamie had just entered through. The walls of Fort Grassnar towered directly overhead and the cut he'd seen from a distance now rose on either side of him. He stood in a narrow passage, lined on either side with chain-link fence made from razor-wire. It led past several more guard emplacements, tapering at the far end before ultimately emptying into a large yard of dirt. There, he could see orderly rows of simple wooden huts and crowds of people wearing civilian attire milling about.

"Go on. Proceed to holding," one of the guards said, his voice modulated through his helmet as he motioned with the muzzle of his rifle.

So far, Jamie's anger at Medraut's latest betrayal had been enough to counteract any embarrassment he might have felt at being naked. Even now, he cared little about his own exposure as he gave the fortifications and the guards manning them a slow glare before pulling on his leathers. Regardless of the reasons, this is where he now was, and he could at least confront it with some degree of dignity. After grabbing up the rest of his things, he strode into the prison camp beyond.

The fenced enclosure was huge, maybe covering a full third of that walled sector of the fort and containing enough huts to house thousands. On the other side of the barbed wire fences, the tall administrative buildings appeared surprisingly sleek with their vertical facades of thick concrete and orderly patterns of recessed windows.

Jamie's fellow prisoners watched him from a distance as they spoke amongst themselves in low voices. In their soiled and worn clothing, they had a desperate and calculating look to them, as if they were plotting some way to make Jamie's life even worse. Ignoring them, Jamie stepped into the relative privacy between two of the huts and finished pulling on the rest of his clothes.

Earlier, while searching his things, one of the soldiers had made a show of pocketing for herself the few coins he'd had on him at the time. However, she'd made no mention of the syringe, the one item which couldn't be replaced. Hoping that it might have miraculously been overlooked, Jamie instead found that it too was gone. Medraut might have succeeded at getting one of them into the prison, but without that injection, it would make it next to impossible for Jamie to escape with an unconscious Lord of the Wilds all by himself, if he could even find this Saexon person.

In the street beyond the alleyway, there were people everywhere; standing in doorways, walking along in small groups, playing improvised games, or just sitting on bare patches of dirt with their faces buried in their arms. It could take days for him to search his way through all of them.

The sound of heavy boots dropping onto the dusty ground behind Jamie sent him whirling on its source. With his luck, one of his fellow prisoners had probably decided to try and kill him for his boots. Or maybe a soldier wanted to test his mettle against the Red Rogue. The truth was only slightly worse than either of those two options.

"How's that for some teamwork?" Medraut said, laughing as he raised his hand in a close-fisted gesture that made Jamie suspect he was expecting some kind of reply, like a high-five. Even if Jamie knew the correct response, the only thing he wanted to do with his fist at the moment was put it into Medraut's face.

"You just got me arrested! Now they know who I am!"

"I'd call that the perfect motivation for you to get us out of here before they confirm that you really are the Red Rogue."

"And what are they going to think when I just up and disappear, along with one of their other prisoners?"

"Not my problem," Medraut said, slapping Jamie on the shoulder as he walked past. "Now come on. You're wasting time."

If not for Doctor Calamestro's insistence that they both had to return alive, Medraut wouldn't have made it much farther. "And just how the hell did you get in here anyway?"

"Everyone was so interested in you, I just slipped in right behind and they never even noticed me." Stopping suddenly, Medraut reached into his pocket. "Oh yeah, I almost forgot, you dropped this."

He passed Jamie the syringe Doctor Calamestro had given them earlier, suppressing a shudder the moment it left his hand and dropped into Jamie's.

"Great. Now they're gonna blame me for stealing evidence too."

"Don't worry," Medraut said, continuing on his way. "I knew they wouldn't let you keep it, so I picked your pocket before you even got arrested."

Jamie took a very deep breath and then slowly let it out. Nostrils flaring, he shoved the syringe into his own pocket once more and set off after Medraut. "So how do we find Saexon?"

The sarcasm thick in his voice, Medraut said, "We look for him?"

Jamie rolled his eyes. "Okay, fine, I'll ask if anyone's seen him." Jamie started toward a man leaning in a doorway. Medraut lashed out and grabbed him by the shoulder.

"What are you doing? This isn't just a prison camp, you know! It's all part of the interrogation. If we go around asking too many questions, the other prisoners are gonna think we're Finttie spies. Instead of finding Saexon, we're gonna get a knife in the back." Medraut swept his arm across the nearby prisoners. "Hell, for all we know, any one of them could be Finttie spies, and the last thing we want is to tip *them* off to why we're here! No one in here trusts anyone and the last thing they're gonna do is help us just because we ask."

"How do you get through life being so paranoid?"

"Being paranoid is what keeps me alive."

Jamie shook his head. "So do you know where the soldiers arrested Saexon?"

"In *Heigelries*, you moron."

"*Where* in Heigelries?"

Medraut blew out his breath and shook his head.

"What, you think I'm a Finttie plant too?" Jamie said.

Medraut's eyes narrowed. "*Sarantia*," he said at last.

"Was that really so hard?" Jamie once more approached the man, leaving Medraut sputtering in a futile attempt to stop him yet again.

"Hi there," Jamie said. The man didn't look much like a spy, just a shopkeeper or a bartender. Medraut held his distance.

The man's expression remained dour as he stood there, chewing on something and looking Jamie over. Finally, he spat a wad of brown leaves onto the ground and said, "Greetings."

"We just got picked up by the Fintties down around Sarantia," Jamie said. Even to his ears, the lie sounded casual enough to be convincing. "They brought in a bunch of people from there a few days ago, didn't they? Do you know where any of them are?"

"Sarantia, huh?" the man said. "You must know Gillis."

"I..." Jamie glanced to Medraut for help but the tracker didn't see, having turned away from the conversation in an attempt to make it harder for the man to see his face. They were supposed to be working together and all Medraut had so far done was make things harder. By getting Jamie arrested, he had also potentially ruined any chance Jamie and Alaida might have had at walking away from all this.

Feeling the fire of revenge welling up inside him, Jamie turned back to the man. "No, I don't really have any idea who that is. We live on a farm out in the middle of nowhere and we don't really get into town all that often. We're looking for someone named Saexon. He's the only person in here we might actually know."

The man eyed Jamie for a moment and then spit again. "I think most of the people they brought in from Sarantia the other day are back near Block Thirty-Four." He gestured over his shoulder, deeper into the camp. Just as Jamie was about to ask how to get there, he noticed that all the huts had a combination of a number followed by a letter painted on each door. The ones on this block all started with a 'Six.'

"Thanks," Jamie said, heading off in the direction the man had indicated.

Head down and shoulders stooped, Medraut fell in alongside him. "You gave that guy Saexon's name! Now they're gonna know what we were doing here."

"Not my problem," Jamie said, slapping Medraut on the shoulder as he picked up his pace and left the tracker a step behind. "Now come on. You're wasting time."

CHAPTER 55

Skirting along the perimeter of the camp, Jamie watched the numbers on the huts to their right quickly increase in value while the double row of twenty-foot high, barbed wire fences slipped past on their left. At one point, they passed a pair of fortified gates which were wide enough to allow vehicular access into the camp. Separated by a hundred feet or so of no-man's land between the inner and outer fences, each of the concrete and wood structures looked nearly identical, with a tower on each side of the gates and a fortified bridge above, all manned by multiple armored soldiers.

"Hmm, that's looks promising," Medraut said.

"Promising?" Jamie said. A second look at the gates did nothing to dispel his initial impression of them. "That looks like a death trap!"

Medraut did not bother to explain himself and it wasn't long afterward that they arrived at the row of huts labeled with a '34'. Near the southern edge of the prison camp, it sat directly in the shadows of the tall buildings on the other side of the fence. Jamie found it difficult not to keep looking up at them. From what Len had said, they housed the offices of the military's intelligence operations. The possibility that the soldiers up there were looking back down at him right now while they investigated the notorious Red Rogue sent shivers down his spine and hurried his pace.

As Jamie started down the path between the row of huts, Medraut caught him by the arm and hissed in his ear. "Let's try to keep a lower profile from this point on. I really don't want either the Fintties or these prisoners knowing any more about who we are or what we're doing here than is absolutely necessary. Okay?"

Jamie didn't respond right away, instead pursing his lips as he considered whether or not he should point out that since the Fintties already knew more than enough about Jamie, it was really only Medraut's own skin he was worried about. Ultimately, Jamie shook his head and said, "Fine." If Medraut now wanted to work together and use his head for a change -- as Jamie had been trying to get him to do from the very beginning -- who was he to argue?

"Good, now let's --"

"Medraut?"

He cut off abruptly at the sound of his name being spoken by someone behind them. Slowly, he looked over his shoulder at the speaker, a girl, maybe a few years younger than Jamie and himself with a dusky complexion and black hair that reached to her shoulders. Standing only an inch or two shorter than Medraut, her eyes were alight with a smile as she threw her arms around the dumbstruck tracker and hugged him tightly.

"It is you!" she said. "I never thought the Fintties would ever be able to catch Medraut the wolf-boy!"

"What's that you were saying about a low profile?" Jamie said.

Medraut seemed not to have heard him, however. Holding the girl at arm's length, he looked at her in utter disbelief as all color drained from his face. "Morgan? But what are you doing here? Don't tell me they got you too?"

Her smile dropped by a fraction but didn't disappear completely. "They rounded up just about everyone. I don't think there're enough people left in Sarantia to even call it a village anymore."

Medraut cursed under his breath and turned away from the girl, shaking his head.

"So, um, who's your friend?" the girl said after a moment.

"He's not my friend," both Jamie and Medraut said in unison.

"Jinx!" The girl laughed as the two boys stood glaring at each other.

Jamie was the first to pull himself away and turned to the girl with as much of a smile as he could muster. "My name's Jamie. I'm just here helping Medraut out with something that he couldn't handle by himself."

"I don't need your help! And this whole thing is *your* fault!"

"It's not *my* fault *you* decided killing me was more important than going after Saexon!"

"Wait, what're you talking about?" the girl said, her expression going slack. "Why are you here? You were arrested, right?"

"One of us was," Jamie said.

Medraut bared his teeth at Jamie before turning to the girl. "We're not working for the Fintties, if that's what you think. We came here looking for someone. His name's Saexon. He would have been picked up a few days ago near Sarantia."

"That's when they got us," the girl said. "They just came into town in the middle of the night and rounded everyone up."

"What were you doing in Sarantia in the middle of the night?" Medraut said.

"I live there now. I haven't stayed at the farm in a long time."

Medraut's face grew even more pale. Jamie had almost no idea what these two were talking about but seeing Medraut's discomfort didn't bring him any joy. Maybe Jamie could gloat after completing the mission, but until then, they needed to stay focused on the task at hand.

"Do you know anyone named Saexon?" Jamie said.

"No..." the girl said, shaking her head. "I don't think there was anyone in town by that name. And I haven't heard of any Saexons with the others who were brought in at the same time as us either."

"He might have been unconscious," Jamie said, "or sick."

"There were some old people who were sick," the girl said. "And a boy who's been in bed with a fever ever since they brought us in."

"That's probably him," Medraut said, his voice a low croak.

"Can you take us to him?" Jamie said.

"Sure," the girl said, "come on."

As Jamie moved to follow, Medraut stood rooted in place, staring into the distance.

"Medraut, we have to go," Jamie said.

Medraut sighed. "I'm coming." Listlessly, he followed a step or two behind the girl.

"Who is she?" Jamie whispered once they were underway.

"A friend," Medraut said, looking straight ahead. "Her name's Morgan."

"How do you know her?"

"I told you I'd spent some time in Heigelries."

"I didn't realize you were down there making friends. Or that you were even telling me the truth."

Medraut suddenly stopped and grabbed Jamie by the collar. "Look, I don't care what you think about me, but she doesn't deserve to be in here with the rest of these people. She's not a terrorist, she's just a girl who's had some terrible things happen to her."

Jamie could hardly believe it: someone who Medraut actually cared about besides his Wolf-Slaves. And he was probably right that she didn't belong here. Most of these people probably didn't. But there was nothing either of them could do about it, which was probably why Medraut was so upset.

"So how much does she know about you and Doctor Calamestro and your Wolves?"

"Oddly enough, even less that you. And I plan to keep it that way."

"Hey! Are you two coming?" Morgan cried back with a wave of her arm. "We're here."

Medraut let go of Jamie with a huff and stalked away. The hut at the end of the row didn't look much different from the others except for the extra windows down the side. Morgan led them inside without knocking or other preamble. The entire interior of the hut was a single narrow room with open rafters and stud walls, all painted a somber shade of gray. The wall on their right was completely blank while the one of their left was almost entirely windows. Just inside the door, a woman sat in a chair rolling bandages.

"Morning, Bonny," Morgan whispered to the woman.

She returned Morgan's smile but cast a wary gaze over her companions. A row of low, wooden beds lined the blank wall of the hut. Only the first three were occupied: two elderly women who appeared to be asleep and one man of a similar age who would periodically burst out into a fit of coughing before sinking back under the sheets with a moan. The thin mattresses on the other beds had been rolled up with a folded sheet and threadbare pillow placed neatly on top of each.

The bed at the farthest end of the room sat slightly askew of the others and its mattress lay diagonally across the top, its corners hanging nearly to the floor. In the corner of the room, someone huddled, shivering under a rough woolen blanket, his body completely hidden from sight but a string of fevered mutterings coming from beneath. Morgan stood to the side, allowing Medraut to go ahead but one look and he stopped dead in his tracks, looking like he might throw up. Had Medraut suffered through something similar after Doctor Calamestro had turned him into the Lord of the Wolves?

"Bad memories?" Jamie said to Medraut, pushing around him and stooping down next to the quivering bundle.

"What's he mean by that?" Morgan whispered.

"Nothing," Medraut said.

"Hey there," Jamie said, addressing the person under the blanket. "Are you Saexon?"

At the sound of that name, the blanket burst open and a pale, spindly arm swung wildly at Jamie. He stumbled onto his backside in avoiding it, but apart from the suddenness of the movement, there appeared to be little need for fear. It was just a boy who couldn't have been any older than Morgan. Being as thin as he was made him look even smaller. Wearing only a pair of dark pants, his ribs stood out sharply with each gasping breath and his cheeks were hollow within his face. However, gazing out from below his short-cropped, blond hair were a pair of dark, purple-on-purple eyes that flittered about like a caged animal's.

"His eyes," Morgan said with a gasp, "they're just like yours, Medraut."

"Hey, calm down, we're here to help," Jamie said as the boy retreated back into a ball. With those eyes, there could be no doubt he was the one they were looking for. "Doctor Calamestro sent us."

"Don't bother," Medraut said. "He could be like that for days yet. Just give him the injection and let's get on with this."

"What's that?" Morgan asked as Jamie pulled the syringe out of his pocket and unscrewed the metal cap from the end.

"Just something to make him well enough to travel," Jamie said, considering the sharp point of the needle. At least that's what he'd been told it was. If Doctor Calamestro had no qualms about doing this to a boy so young, might he just as easily have duped Jamie into acting as his assassin? "Are we sure this is safe?"

"Of course it is. Just get it over with," Medraut said. "You do know how to use that thing, right?"

Truth to tell, Jamie had never actually used a syringe before. All he really knew was that he didn't like them all that much -- not that he'd let Medraut know any of that.

In a single motion, Jamie jabbed the needle into Saxon's arm and pushed the plunger down. Medraut moaned softly and braced himself against the edge of the bed to steady his now shaky legs. Jamie meanwhile did his best to suppress a grimace as he extracted the needle with a sudden jerk.

"Did it--?" Medraut started to ask but cut off abruptly when Saexon's eyes snapped open wide with a prolonged gasp from deep in his lungs. A moment later he shot to his feet, knocking Jamie over once more.

"Oh wow!" the boy said, his pupils constricting down to tiny points and a giddy smile stretching his lips to absurd dimensions. A shudder passed through his thin body and he flexed his fingers rapidly before frantically jogging in place for a second. "That is...wow!"

"Yeah, I think it worked," Jamie said, picking himself off the floor.

"Hey, sorry about that," the boy said, giving Jamie a hand. "It's just that that was really, like, whoa! You know? Hey who are you guys anyway? What was that stuff you did to me?"

"A gift from Doctor Calamestro," Medraut said. "Now let's get out of here. No self-respecting Lord of the Wilds would ever let himself get captured by a bunch of Finttie losers."

Saexon gasped and stepped right up to Medraut, causing the Lord of the Wolves to recoil. "You're Medraut, aren't you! He told me about you! You're awesome! I need to get a pair of glasses like yours!" His head then whipped back and forth as he took in Morgan and Jamie. "You guys aren't Lords? Who are you?" Clenching his hands into fists, he dropped into a fighting stance. "Are you with Finttiranos?"

"Of course not!" Morgan looked honestly offended by the mere suggestion. "I'm Morgan and this is Jamie, we're friends of Medraut's."

"I'm not--," Jamie began but then threw up his hands. "We're here to get you out."

"Great! Let's go!" Saexon exclaimed, heading toward the exit. He stopped after a few steps and looked back at the others when they didn't instantly follow. "What are we waiting for?"

So as to not set the boy off once again, Jamie spoke with overly deliberate caution. "Do you *know* how to get out of here?"

"I don't even know *where* we are!" Saexon said.

Medraut shook his head. "This is gonna be fun."

"Um..." The woman sitting next to the door, who Morgan had called Bonny, cautiously approached the group. "Um, is everything okay? Should I get somebody? Is he...?"

"I'm great!" Saexon said. "I'm ready to get out of here and bust some Fintties up real good!"

"He's just a little over-excited," Morgan said. Taking him by the hand, she guided Saexon down to the edge of his bed. "Why don't you just sit down for a moment and take a breath."

"I'm going to get Tunios, just to be sure," Bonny said, backing away and then hurrying for the door.

"Who's Tunios?" Saexon said, looking about and rising halfway back to his feet before Morgan was able to sit him back down.

"He's a teacher. He knows about medicine. He helped people out in Sarantia when they got sick."

"I'm not sick. I'm ready to go. What are we waiting for?"

"Just calm down. I'm sure Medraut and Jamie have everything figured out."

"Yeah, do we?" Jamie said in a low voice to Medraut.

Medraut turned his back to Morgan and Saexon. "We got in easy enough. How hard can it be to get back out?"

"This is a prison, they're designed to keep people in," Jamie said. "But maybe you can just tell the guards that you were wrong about me being a criminal and when they release me with a hearty apology for the misunderstanding, you can sneak out right behind me."

"You're becoming a real jerk, you know that?"

"Pot. Kettle."

"No prison is completely escape-proof. We just need to take a look around for that one weakness in the perimeter that the four of us can use to slip through without being noticed."

"Four of us? We're only here for Saexon. This is already going to be hard enough without bringing along a kid who can't do what we can."

"You heard what that old man at the farm told us," Medraut said, his words firm, "getting sent here is as good as a death sentence. I'm not leaving her behind."

"What are you two talking about?" Morgan said from where she had kneeled down next to Saexon.

"We're just figuring out how to get you out of here with us," Medraut said.

Jamie threw up his hands, shaking his head.

Morgan's eyes grew wide as she stood. "You're going to get us out of here?"

Medraut grimaced. "Well, you and Saexon at least."

"But..." Morgan's shoulders stooped. "Everyone I know is in here with me. All my friends. My entire village! I can't just run away and leave them behind."

"Morgan, if you don't come with us, you are going to die."

"I don't care, I'm not leaving them."

"But Morgan, we can't rescue everyone," Medraut said, gesticulating with his hands. "It's just not possible!"

Morgan bit her lip. "Then...I guess you'll have to go without me."

Medraut looked to be on the verge of an outburst but stopped short when the door to the hut swung open and a small group of prisoners marched in. At their head was a tall man with lean, noble features and eyes that looked like they hadn't seen any sleep in quite a long time. His stride was confident and firm as he approached, the boots of the entire group clattering off the hollow floorboards.

"No one's going anywhere," he said.

CHAPTER 56

Despite the stark difference in their heights, Medraut stepped forward without any hint of trepidation to meet the man at the head of these interlopers. After having seen firsthand the things Medraut was capable of, Jamie knew his confidence was well founded

"And who the hell are you to tell me what I can do?" Medraut said.

"That's Luranc," Morgan whispered. "He's the leader of the --"

"We're the ones who make sure no one gets killed for doing something stupid," Luranc said, taking up position in front of Medraut and folding his arms across his chest.

Two others stood at his shoulders. One, a bearded man not quite as tall as Luranc who seemed to wear a perpetual scowl, and the other, a woman with long, crinkly, yellow hair who looked like she had more muscles than both of the men put together. Behind them, an assortment of random village types filed into the room. Most had the look of laborers or professions but none of them looked quite as intimidating as the three in front.

Meanwhile, a gangly man in glasses pushed his way through the others, followed close behind by a motherly-looking woman in a faded blue dress. Ignoring the confrontation in the middle of the room, they went straight to Saexon. As the woman put her hand to his forehead, the man asked him how he was feeling and took his pulse.

"There's nothing here that concerns any of you," Medraut said. "Just turn around and leave."

"From what I heard, there was talk of an escape attempt being planned," Luranc said. "Since the repercussions of any such activities effect the entire camp, all plans have to be cleared with us first."

"And don't hold your breath waiting for that to ever happen," the bearded man at Luranc's shoulder said.

"I don't really need your permission," Medraut said. "And I'm not going to ask for it either. If you want to stay in here and let the Fintties torture you to death, that's your decision, but you're not stopping me from leaving."

"You sound awfully confident about that," Luranc said.

"Cocky, I'd say," the woman on his left said.

Boxed into the back of the room as they were, Jamie began considering one of the windows for a hasty exit if things turned ugly.

464

Medraut, Jamie, and probably even Saexon could have managed such an escape, but what about Morgan? Would she even be willing to come with them? Would Medraut leave without her? This whole endeavor had quickly turned from difficult to impossible.

Medraut stood his ground against the rebel leaders. "I wouldn't have broken in here if I didn't have a way out again."

If Jamie hadn't known that Medraut was lying through his teeth right now, even he might have believed him. A ripple of murmurs passed through the gathered prisoners. Luranc glanced over his shoulder at them, but the whispers continued.

"You really broke into a prison on purpose?" someone in the crowd asked.

"Are you saying you're not actually a prisoner?" another said.

"Does anyone know him? When did he come in?"

Heads waggled back and forth as people muttered in the negative.

"His friend came in through admitting this morning, but I've never seen this guy before."

More mutters erupted. In addition to questions about them being Finttiranos spies, Jamie also picked out just as many desperate calls for escape and freedom.

"Look, I don't really care what you think I am or what you think I'm up to. If you hadn't decided to stick your noses into this, you never would have even known I was here. So why don't you just pretend like that's what happened. You'll never see me again and you can all go back to ratting out your friends or being sized up for body bags, okay?"

Luranc began to speak but someone in the crowd yelled over him. "Do you really have a way out?"

"Okay, that's enough of that," the bearded man at Luranc's right said, stepping toward Medraut.

Without warning, Medraut launched himself high into the air and dropped his fist across the bearded man's jaw. As the much larger man staggered from that first blow, Medraut landed solidly on the floor and kicked him across the back of the knees, sending him down hard. Another punch to the face and the bearded man landed flat on his back. Medraut then turned and brought his boot into the gut of the blonde woman who had also come at him. She crumpled but did not fall until he brought his other foot around in the high arc that drove her face-first to the floor right alongside her comrade.

The whole thing was over in an instant and Jamie readied himself to fend off an attack by the entire gathered mass of prisoners. Everyone else in the room merely stood rooted in place, however, staring in disbelief, Luranc included.

Medraut turned to face them. "Now I'm leaving, and no one is going to stop me. Understood?"

Even faster than Medraut had put down Luranc's two enforcers, the entire room suddenly became a cacophony of shouted pleas. Some begged Medraut to bring them with him, others unabashedly offered their assistance for whatever he might need.

Showing more trepidation than when he was ready to face off against them all in a fight, Medraut took a step back.

"Everyone be quiet!" Luranc cried out over the noise. It took him several attempts before he managed to reign the crowd in enough to be heard, but even then there were still murmurs and grumbling in the back. "Are you seriously that desperate that you'd be willing to put your fate in the hands of someone you don't even know -- someone who could very well be a spy sent here to get you killed?"

Several people actually voiced affirmation of their desperation and more than a few heads nodded in agreement.

"What reason would they have for staging something like this just to get us killed?" a young man called out. "The Fintties don't need any excuses for that!"

More agreement tore through the crowd.

"I agree that something needs to be done but we have to wait for the right opportunity to make our move," Luranc pleaded with the crowd.

Suddenly, Medraut stopped withdrawing and his lip twitched into that same smirk he'd put on right before turning Jamie into the authorities. Jamie didn't like the look of it any better this time.

"Okay," Medraut said, speaking in a voice loud enough to be heard by the entire room. "I didn't want to do this, but maybe I can change my plan a little to accommodate those of you who want to come along with me."

A hush fell over the room as those listening whispered between themselves. Meanwhile, Medraut's words had opened a pit in Jamie's stomach. What did he think he was doing? First Morgan, and now how many more of these people were they going to have to take with them? Jamie had certainly not agreed to any of this when Doctor Calamestro had wrangled him into this mission.

"Can you really get us out of here?" a woman with deep, sad eyes asked. She looked like she might actually be desperate enough to try climbing over the barbed wire fences bare-handed if Medraut didn't offer some alternative.

Medraut looked over at Morgan, his expression inscrutable. Jamie could only imagine what he was thinking. "Yeah," he said at last, again facing the others. "I can get out as many as want to come with me."

This was quickly getting out of control. Jamie stepped forward and grabbed Medraut by the arm. In a voice only loud enough for him to hear, Jamie said, "This isn't what we came here for!"

Medraut's smile returned as he pulled himself free and threw his arms out to the crowd. "I have mercenary forces who'll be attacking the intake facility as soon as I give them the signal. The bigger the distraction we can create in here, the easier time they'll have getting to us."

"Alright!" Saexon said, jumping to his feet. "Now that's a plan!"

"Young man, you shouldn't be up and about!" the man who had been attending to Saexon said, scuttling after him. "Just a little while ago you were delirious. You still have a fever, maybe even higher than before, and your heart is racing a mile-a-minute. You're going to kill yourself if you keep pushing yourself in this condition."

"Relax, I'm fine." Saexon did a back flip into the air and landed balanced on the foot of his bed. "We're breaking out of here, every last one of us!"

At that, the whole room erupted in a subdued cry of consensus.

"Are you crazy?" Luranc said, addressing the rest of the room as much as Medraut specifically. "Your plan is to have a couple of hired guns raid one of the most heavily guarded military bases in all of Finttiranos! You might have a death wish but I won't let you take the rest of these people along with you!"

Medraut laughed, his confidence with this outlandish lie quickly growing to the point of haughtiness. "I've seen it myself, the security is so lax down there, the Fintties are never gonna be expecting it. As soon as my team sees a commotion inside the camp, they'll sweep in with a surgical strike through the maintenance section of the intake facility, clearing a path for us to escape. We'll be out of here before anyone even realizes what's happening."

By that point, the excited energy sweeping through the room had built to infectious levels. Almost everyone present now nodded in agreement and clenched their fists in preparation for action.

"And what happens once we get out?" Luranc said. "What are we supposed to do once we make it into Tolfield? It's a long way from there back to Heigelries."

"The entire Boravian Highlands used to be part of Heigelries!" an older gentleman in the back of the room cried out. "This fort used to be our greatest magesmith town before those bastards took it from us and turned it into a prison! I say we're still in Heigelries and if we're going to die anyway, it might as well be fighting for our homeland, not locked away in a cell!"

The agreement to that was overwhelming, completely drowning out any plea Luranc might have voiced to the contrary. As the bearded man picked himself up off the floor, he helped the blond woman up as well. Still scowling, he said to Medraut. "You might be a scrawny little runt, but you know how to fight. I'll come with you!" The blond woman nodded as well.

"Maezro! Glaudiana!" Luranc said. "What do you think you're doing?"

"Hey, I'm all for keeping as many of us alive for as long as possible while we're in here," the bearded man said, "but I'd rather not be in here at all and I think this kid might actually know what he's talking about. If he can get us out of here, I'm going with him."

At that, Jamie could see Luranc's face cloud with defeat. As Medraut continued fanning the prisoner's passions and whipping them in the frenzy, the resistance leader was shuffled to the sidelines. Jamie tried telling himself to stay back and simply let Medraut run wild with this insane plan he'd just concocted, but he still found himself pulling the young tracker back from the adulation of the crowd once more.

"Mercenaries?" Jamie said, his words masked from the ears of the crowd by their own cheers. "We don't have any mercenaries! What do you think you're doing?

"What do you think I'm doing?" Medraut replied with mock innocence.

"I think you're using these people to create a distraction to help us escape!"

"Oh, it always surprises me when you show that you're not as stupid as you seem."

"But you're going to get them killed!"

"Remember, we only came here for Saexon. The rest of these people don't matter. They were gonna die anyway. At least this way, their deaths won't be wasted. Just meet me at the gate we passed on the way here!"

"The gate? Even if we could get through that, it just leads back into the fort! How is that going to help us any?"

"It's like you said: prisons are designed to keep people *in*. Forts, though, are designed to keep people *out*. Now take Morgan and Saexon out the back. I'll meet you there." Medraut turned back to the still cheering crowd and raised his fist to the air. "Now follow me, before those Finttie's spies tell them what's going on! We don't have any time to waste!"

"Out the back?" Jamie said as the crowd enveloped Medraut and began spilling out of the hut through the only doorway. "There is no...fine!" Already standing at the back of the hut, Jamie kicked a section of the wall, snapping a stud in half and buckling the clapboards outward.

"Alright! Now we're talking!" Saexon cried. He leapt at the opening Jamie had started and crashed through the boards, leaving a gaping hole behind him. Landing on the ground outside in a crouch, he looked about wildly. "Wow, where are we?"

"Come on," Jamie said, grabbing Morgan by the wrist and pulling her through after him. "We've got to go."

"But..." she said, pulling at Jamie's arm and pointing back toward the crowd. So swept away by the red haze which had descended upon them, only a few at the back of the room had even noticed Jamie's unconventional exit.

"Medraut's agreed to help them, but he's not going to let you anywhere near the fighting," Jamie said, spitting out his own lies to pile on top of Medraut's. "I'm going to keep you out of danger until it's safe for us to move."

CHAPTER 57

Making his way through the alleyways that cut between the huts, Jamie could feel that the energy of the entire camp had changed. Everywhere he looked, he saw prisoners on edge, aware that something was happening but not yet sure what. Others ran from one group to the next, quickly relaying news that Jamie suspected had already become greatly exaggerated. It never took long for both parties to run off, either to tell others or to join the steady flow of people headed north, no doubt to join Medraut's group. Jamie and those following him, however, made their way toward the main encircling thoroughfare that ran just inside the camp's perimeter fence, not stopping for anything.

Morgan followed without any further argument. Saexon, meanwhile, seemed to be under control for the time being, even if he was acting like a cartoon character with the way he kept hurrying on ahead to check each intersection with what looked like over-exuberant affection. Tunios and the woman who had been helping him, along with a few others, followed at a distance, saying nothing and merely watching with expectant curiosity.

As long as they stayed out of his way, Jamie didn't care what they did. He only had to get Saexon to that gate and wait. As tragic as it was, Medraut had been right when he'd said the rest of these people didn't matter. They weren't Jamie's responsibility, especially if they were foolish enough to let themselves be led into almost certain death by a few hastily uttered lies.

The jailors beyond the fence had noticed the change in the camp as well and could be seen nervously watching the proceedings within. Uniformed soldiers were running along with intent as more and more of their comrades, geared up in full armor and equipped with blaster rifles, were starting to congregate around the camp. So far, it only looked like Medraut's distraction had drawn greater scrutiny to the entire compound.

"Where are we going?" Morgan asked as Jamie brought them to a stop at the end of an alley about one block away from the gate he and Medraut had earlier passed. In the time since, additional soldiers had climbed into the battlements while a rather large group of fully armored troops were gathering outside the gates. The group of prisoners that Medraut had convinced to follow him could be heard farther north, their cries now sounding like a riot.

"Just hold tight," Jamie said, grabbing Saexon by the arm and pulling him back. "Medraut wants us to wait for him here."

"Why?" Saexon said, gazing at the fence and the soldiers on the other side. Then, turning to the rising voices from the north, he waved his thin arm. "It sounds like all the fun is happening over there."

"There's nothing fun going on there," Jamie said, "trust me."

Hopefully, this wouldn't take long. Even though the streets were now far more empty than they had been before, there were still a lot of people wandering around, looking confused. Two of them, a teenaged boy and girl, each with a similar shade of red hair and freckled skin, caught sight of Jamie's small group at the mouth of the alleyway and hurried over. Far from looking scared, he and the girl were smiling and bouncing on the tips of their toes.

"Morgan, Tunios," the boy said. "What's going on?"

"Kammie said something about an escape attempt," the girl said, not even trying to keep the excitement out of her voice.

Both of them took a critical look at Jamie and the boy said, "Is this the guy everyone's talking about?"

Before Jamie could even open his mouth to quash their erroneous identification, Saexon jumped forward to address them himself. "Nope, this ain't him!" he said. Jamie had been thinking that he would have to find the time for a private talk with the boy about keeping a lower profile, but maybe Saexon had actually realized just how precarious their situation was all on his own. But then, puffing out his chest, he added, "But we are working with him!"

The boy and girl both displayed near identical expressions of shock and drew back at the sight of the young Lord of the Wilds. Jamie just shook his head.

"Oh wow, your eyes!" the girl said, recovering quickly and leaning in for a closer look.

"That is so weird!" the boy added, just as curious.

"Yeah, it's pretty neat, isn't it?" Saexon said. "If you want to get out of here, just stick with us!"

"What? No!" Jamie said. "We're not here to rescue anyone else."

Unfortunately, some of the other prisoners within earshot of Saexon's exuberant statement now came running, all of them with the same question on their tongues.

"So what's the plan?" a serious-faced woman said. She had Asian features but dark skin and crinkly black hair. "What can we do to help?"

As the other prisoners pressed in, all of them speaking over each other until none of them could be understood, the red-haired boy and girl cheerfully began making introductions. "Hi, I'm Jorri and this is my twin sister Becka."

"That's Viellia, she's kind of a big deal around Sarantia," the girl, Becka, said, indicating the serious-faced woman.

Pointing to a burley man with a beard that hung all the way to his waist in intricate braids, the boy, Jorri, said, "That's her cousin, Kranskie. Looks like you've already met Tunios and his wife, Junliet."

"And of course, who doesn't know Morgan!" Becka said. "This is Forinom, Grovallic, Lirman, Yunus, and Goffry."

She pointed to two men who looked like farmers, one a shopkeeper, another young man who had a dead look in his eyes and didn't show any emotion whatsoever, and finally another bearded man wearing rugged wilderness garb with a watchful look to him who always stayed close to Viellia's side.

Jorri jumped in at that point to continue with the others who kept arriving, but Jamie had already stopped listening. The less he knew about any of these people, the less he'd have to think about them when he left them behind to their fate.

With all of them chattering away expectantly, Jamie couldn't even think.

"Quiet," he said.

When that didn't help, he raised his voice: "Would you all just be quiet!"

Finally, he fell back to: "Shut up!"

That, at least, brought the noise down to a constant din of dull murmurs. Unfortunately, it only heightened the sounds of the riot now fully boiling away at the intake facility. The distinct crack of a

Finttiranos blaster rifle going off suddenly joined in with the rest of the noise.

It was starting to look like Jamie would have to do *something* soon in order to take advantage of the distraction, but he still had no idea what Medraut next planned to do with this prison break of his. All these eyes boring into him, looking at him like he was their savior, wasn't making it any easier to figure out what he should be doing.

"Hey, look!" Becka said.

A rising commotion from the nearby gates drew everyone's attention to the armored soldiers who had been massing outside. Now they had moved into the no-man's-land between the double fences, waiting for the outer gates to close behind them and the inner gates to open.

"Is that why you were positioned here?" Viellia said.

"Positioned?" Jamie said, still no closer to a plan. "I don't ever know what you're --"

"Oh, I get it!" Jorri said. "You're here to cut off any Finttie reinforcements that try to outflank the main force at the front gates!"

"I..." was all the further Jamie got before Viellia started issuing orders to the gathered prisoners who instantly acknowledged her with nods of understanding and muttered agreement. "I don't think..." Jamie tried again but they were already in motion. He only just caught Morgan by the arm as she started following after the rest. "No," he said in reply to the indignant look she shot him. Then he had to restrain Saexon as well. "No, we're staying here! We're not getting involved in this!"

"But I thought we were staging a prison break," Saexon said, looking over his shoulder as the inner gate swung open and the armored soldiers began advancing through in neat rows. "Why are we just standing here doing nothing?"

"Yeah," Morgan said. "I know those people; we have to help them!"

The ground between the gate and the huts looked completely deserted, which had no doubt led the soldiers to believe that they were safe to enter the compound. Jamie had overheard enough of Viellia's orders to know that things wouldn't remain that way for long.

Should Jamie have tried harder to stop them? Or should he have encouraged them as Medraut had done so that he could take advantage of the distraction? He couldn't even reason out how either of those options would play into Medraut's plans.

While Jamie was still mulling over possibilities in his head, the prisoners rushed out of every hiding place within throwing distance of the soldiers and swarmed toward them. The soldiers reacted instantly, falling back into a defensive perimeter as their weapons came up.

This was just Jamie's luck. There would be no way to defuse this situation now. Everything was already moving too fast. By the time he realized the soldiers had opened fire on the advancing prisoners, some of those same prisoners had outflanked the formation and were engaging the soldiers with crude clubs and knives fashioned from bed frames. Before Jamie knew it, the soldier's formation had broken apart and the prisoners had intermixed with them so completely that neither the soldiers on the ground, nor the ones in the towers, could take a shot without the risk of shooting one of their own. Unfortunately, even though the prisoners outnumbered their opponents at least three-to-one, they had no means to do much harm to the soldiers encased in that magescript encrusted armor they wore.

Jamie knew he wasn't here to save any of them, but he also knew that he couldn't just stand there and watch them die either. If he didn't do something right now, they were all going to get themselves killed.

Cursing under his breath, Jamie stepped forward. "Stay here," he said to Morgan and Saexon as he launched himself toward the fray. "And keep your heads down!"

The first soldier Jamie came to was so engaged with the three prisoners who were trying unsuccessfully to drag him down that he didn't even notice until Jamie grabbed him from behind and threw him to the ground so hard his rifle fell from his hand. One of the prisoners had the weapon in her own hand before Jamie even stepped over the fallen man and knocked another soldier off his feet. He heard the gunshot behind him and the modulated cry of a dying soldier but didn't look back.

As more weapons were wrested away from the soldiers, gunfire from both the prisoners and soldiers increased, heedless of who might get caught in the crossfire. Jamie toppled another soldier before barely ducking out of the way of another's hastily fired blaster. There was a cry from the poor soul who'd been on the receiving end of that wayward shot, but Jamie had no clue which side the victim belonged to. He tore the blaster from the soldier's hands and drove his fist up into his chin. The soldier's already tenuous stance crumbled as his helmet flew from his head and he went over onto his back. The young face staring up at Jamie from within the armor was a mask of sheer terror.

That must have been the way people looked at the Red Rogue just before he killed them.

It turned Jamie's stomach. He had never wanted to be a part of any of this. But if he didn't act, he and Saexon and Morgan might very well end up just as dead as this soldier was soon to find himself.

The soldier cringed into a ball as Jamie dropped to a knee and punched him right across the face. As the soldier lay half-delirious from the blow, Jamie whispered, "If you want to live, just stay down and play dead."

He didn't wait for a reply before rising to his feet. All around him prisoners grabbled with soldiers as blaster fire crisscrossed the battlefield in every possible direction. Beyond the gates, more soldiers were running back and forth in a panic, shouting for someone to do something. Those stationed in the towers had apparently had enough and finally opened fire on the riot below them. Their shots were carefully aimed at first, dropping one prisoner after another, but as the volume of their fire quickly increased, the accuracy dropped, which only added to the chaos. Very soon, there wouldn't be anyone left alive on either side of this brawl.

Jamie took several long strides through the fray before ultimately launching himself in the air. The towers were high and the barbed wire encircling the edges meant his landing needed to be precise. Unlike the previous times he'd tried things like this, he now knew his capabilities and he had a clear goal in mind.

He dropped onto the platform at the top of the rightmost tower between two stunned guards who were both slow to turn their weapons on him after the impossible feat they had just witnessed. Jamie, however, wasted no time ripping away one of the blasters and shoving the other soldier over the side. Cries of warning and panic raced along the bridge connecting the two towers, drawing the soldier's attention away from the prisoners below and focusing it on Jamie alone.

The quarters here were even closer than down on the ground. It gave Jamie a brief advantage as he charged into the soldiers and knocked them aside with enough force than most would not be getting back up again any time soon. Several blaster shots burned through the air on either side of him, but it was only when Jamie toppled the last guard that he realized most of that fire was coming from the outer guard post on the other side of the no-man's-land; the guards there trying desperately to assist their embattled comrades.

Below, Jamie heard a loud creaking noise followed by a crash and the twang of barbed wire springing loose from its mountings. Through rifle slits in the floor, he saw the gate fall outward beneath a combination of gunfire and the raw muscle power of several dozen frenzied prisoners.

Shouted cries followed them through the breach into the killing ground beyond. With few friendlies remaining on the ground to temper the weapons fire of the soldiers on the far gate, they unleashed a solid wall of energy blasts that tore into the front ranks of prisoners, cutting every last one of them down. Men, women, and more than a few who were little more than children, all fell, their zealous war cries cut abruptly short. More and more prisoners, however, pushed forward right behind them. Most fell right alongside their friends.

It all happened so quickly that the bodies were already stacked three of four deep inside the gate by the time Jamie dashed down a covered spiral staircase that led back to the ground. It offered some protection from the gunfire, but when he reached the bottom, he found even more energy bolts streaking past than he had above.

Despite the death awaiting them, more prisoners kept surging forward. Some took refuge behind the bodies of their fallen comrades, others within the protection of the gate tower. Several, armed with commandeered rifles, stormed past Jamie and up the stairs, their leader urging them on with grim military professionalism. Just inside the gate, Jamie found the twins, Jorri and Becka, still smiling as they crouched behind the stairs, each armed with a rifle of their own.

"Oh, hey!" Becka said when she saw Jamie. "Quite the party you threw together here!" She then leaned around the corner and unleashed a barrage of fire at the opposite towers, along with a string of choice curses.

She kept it up far longer than seemed sensible, right up until her brother pulled her back under cover. He couldn't have been a moment slower because an energy bolt tore through the very spot where her head had just been.

"Hey, be careful!" Jorri said, leaning out to take a few shots at the soldiers as well, only to be pulled back a moment later by Becka when a new stream of weapons fire began ripping into the side of the stair tower.

"You be careful!" Becka said.

They both laughed and held their heads down as splinters of smoldering wood fell around them.

"This is just like that time in Vapagnia!" Jorri said.

"Except we actually had a way out of Vapagnia!" Becka shouted back.

The soldier's blaster fire lessened a moment later when the prisoners who had climbed the towers now used their elevated position to return fire and send the attacking soldiers scuttling for cover. It was only a temporary reprieve, however.

Becka and Jorri might have been completely insane but they were right about having no way out of here. Unless they breached that second gate, they would remain pinned down right where they were until the soldiers either managed to pick them off one by one or they were outflanked by another force from a different gate. If Medraut wanted to make any use of this exit, Jamie would have to make sure things didn't get bogged down before it was closed entirely.

CHAPTER 58

Peeking around the corner of the stair tower, Jamie took only a moment to confirm that the soldiers' attention had indeed shifted away from his position. The distance between the gates had to be at least a hundred feet. Even with his speed, he would be out there long enough for any of those soldiers to draw a bead on him. But if he waited any longer, he might lose any chance at all.

"Hey, can you two try to make them keep their heads down?" Jamie said to Jorri and Becka, indicating the soldiers in the other tower.

"You mean, can we cover you?" Jorri said.

"Um, yeah, whatever," Jamie said.

"Sure, we can try," Becka said, "But what are you gonna...?"

Her words trailed off as Jamie bolted from the relative protection offered by the stair tower and charged across the open ground as fast as Reaver's body would carry him. Jorri and Becka wasted no time unleashing everything they had on the distant towers. Even though the other prisoners needed little encouragement to join them, their combined firepower paled in comparison to what Jamie faced from the soldiers defending the second gate.

They had noticed his approach far quicker than he would have liked. Though the stress of the situation meant most of their shots were far off target, a few passed close enough to Jamie that he felt the rippling heat wave that followed each one. If he didn't have to keep dodging around and leaping over all the fallen bodies, he would have been a far easier target to strike.

Just as Jamie closed within range of the outer towers, one of the energy bolts finally found its mark. Though it only gazed his left shoulder, it hit with an explosive impact that twisted him around and nearly wrenched him off his feet. His nostrils were filled with smoke and other noxious smells that he wouldn't allow himself to consider the origins of. Like most times before, Reaver's body endured the injury without pain or apparent damage. So focused on his goal, Jamie simply ignored the sensation of heat and pressure smashing into him and rolled with the impact, quickly regaining his stride and jumping skyward.

Executed in haste, this leap had been less deliberate than the last. As he descended on the gate from above, he realized that he had miscalculated his approach. Instead of dropping amongst the soldiers like before and being able to capitalize on their confusion, this time he would land on the roof of the bridge that spanned above the gate.

Several soldiers who weren't quite as surprised by his move as the others managed to squeeze off a few shots at him in midair which blazed past without finding their intended target. Crashing down atop the roof temporarily removed him from their line of sight but not their wrath. The roof had been steeply sloped and stoutly built so as to prevent the prisoners from lobbing projectiles down upon the guards, but those thick wooden boards now exploded outward around Jamie's feet as the soldiers below tried their best to pick him off through the roof.

He scrambled down the length of the ridge, the gun fire following at his heels and joined by yet more from those soldiers who had gathered outside the gate. Quickly running out of roof, Jamie had few options left. Jumping down to the ground would put him right back where he'd been before, only with even less of an advantage. Turning back the way he'd just come would open himself up as an easy target.

As the end of the roof raced toward him, and still no idea where we was headed, Jamie's foot slipped on the smooth roof boards and he went tumbling back toward the inside of the prison camp. The gunfire that had been following him continued on its way unabated, the soldiers responsible obviously unaware their quarry was no longer traveling that path.

With the bottom edge of the roof rising up to meet him, Jamie scrambled for a handhold. He found one in the form of a splintered board which had been knocked loose by the soldier's reckless gunfire. However, that same damage had obviously cut through one of the rafters as well, because the moment the board took Jamie's full weight, the roof below him collapsed completely, sending him and a shower of debris down into the tower.

With their helmets shielding their eyes and mouths from the dust, the soldiers remained on roughly equal footing with Jamie, all of them merely shocked by what had just happened. But Jamie sprang into motion the moment his feet were once more on solid ground. If he wanted to capitalize on this happy accident, he couldn't waste the opportunity. Leading with his fist as he rose from the floor, he struck the nearest soldier with an uppercut that sent him over backwards right through one of the openings in the side of the tower. Another fell as Jamie turned and drove the soldier's own rifle back into his helmet.

Jamie had no plan or course of action, he just kept moving, lashing out with fist or foot at the nearest solider in whatever seemed like the fastest way to take them out of play. He remained in constant motion, letting none of them regain their footing or open fire in the close

479

confines of the guard tower. With cries of confusion and frustration, they fell one-by-one until Jamie found the path ahead clear of any further obstacles.

Surveying the fallen and groaning soldiers, he could hardly believe that he'd survived all that, let along come out triumphant. Just then, an energy blast ripped through the air from behind, passing dangerously close to his head. If the soldier responsible had not missed, Jamie would have been dead for sure. There never would have been any way for him to dodge it. But that's just what he deserved for getting cocky. They weren't anywhere close to getting out of Fort Grassnar yet and this particular fight wasn't even over.

Jamie turned, ready for whatever his next task proved to be, only to find himself staring wide-eyed as Saexon tackled the soldier around the neck and used the momentum of his own body to pull the much larger man right off his feet and drive his face to the ground with a loud crash.

"I told you to stay back!" Jamie said. "How did you even get up here?"

Saexon's head quickly twitched one way and then the other. "Same as you."

Face tight, Jamie shook his head as he headed past Saexon for the stairs. "Where's Morgan?"

Saexon delivered a kick to the face of the soldier he had just taken down, sending the armored man into unconsciousness and then hopped along to catch up with Jamie. "Morgan's fine, she's holding back with the civvies in the rear."

Civilians. Jamie almost laughed. As if there were any such designations in this brawl Medraut had instigated. Through the windows of the tower, Jamie could see fires burning in the northern end of the prison camp and hear near constant gunfire from all directions around him. Below, the outer gates had already been torn open and streams of prisoners were running through, descending on every Finttiranos soldier in sight. Those without weapons simply swarmed over the armored soldiers like ants, many of them falling from blaster fire, but an ever-increasing number dragging them down through sheer numbers alone.

Most of the prisoners lucky enough to be armed with stolen weapons concentrated their fire on key adversaries, if not killing them outright, then at least forcing the soldiers to keep their heads down. This allowed the other prisoners to spread out from the gate and into the streets of the fort. The way so many of them moved as disciplined units, coordinating with one another to maximize their efforts, made

Jamie realize just how many of these prisoners really were resistance fighters after all.

In the short time it took Jamie to reach the bottom of the stairs, the majority of the fighting had moved away from the gates and out into the streets that ran between the towering buildings of the fort. It gave Jamie a moment to stare at the utter death and destruction he had helped bring about. Fortunately, before he could consider it any more than that, he felt someone bump into him from behind.

"Morgan!" Saexon said. "Glad you made it!"

She was with Tunios and Junliet and a few others who all looked too terrified to even consider fighting the soldiers but also not willing to miss out on a chance at escape. Blank-faced, the young man named Yunus stood guard at the rear of the group with a rifle, ever watchful for danger. Jorri and Becka had already made it through the gate, having taken up defensive positions just outside. Meanwhile Viellia and Kranskie strode through the wreckage and shouted orders to the various nearby groups to keep everyone moving.

"I never thought..." Morgan said in a small voice as she shied away from the bodies of a prisoner laying alongside one of an armored soldier. "I mean, was this part of your plan?"

Jamie shook his head. "This was never part of the plan."

"Finttie reinforcements coming in from the north!" Goffry cried out, running through the gates. "I don't think we're gonna be able to hold this position much longer!"

Shaking her head, Viellia cursed under her breath. Turning to the camp and waving to the prisoners still rushing through the fallen gates, she called out to them. "Come on! Hurry up! As many of you as possible!"

"Make your way into the fort!" Kranskie said. "Try to find a way out and give these Fintties hell until you do!"

Within the crowds, Jamie saw one face in particular he knew, that of Medraut. The tracker saw Jamie as well and ran over.

"What the hell is all this!" Medraut cried out over the noise and stress of battle. He looked none the worse for wear, making Jamie wonder how soon after leading all those people to their deaths did he abandon them. "I told you to sit tight and wait, not bring even more heat down on us!"

"And how exactly was I supposed to do that? After you got everyone riled up with the Braveheart speech of yours, they did this all on their own!"

"But Jamie did help!" Saexon said, dropping down from the top of a battlement he had climbed just a moment before. "Where did you and Doctor Calamestro find him? He's incredible!"

"No, he's not! He's a bloody idiot!" Medraut shouted back. "Just how the hell are we supposed to sneak out of here now?"

As Saexon quailed under Medraut's scolding, Jamie stepped between them. "Hey, if you want to blame this on me for not being able to clean up the mess you created, then fine, I'll take full responsibility, but that's not going to change the fact that this is what we have to work with right here and right now!" Jamie pointed to the north. Escaped prisoners were running for their lives ahead of a fully armed squad of Finttiranos soldiers advancing up the street. "We've got to move, right now, or we're gonna find ourselves in another fight with them!"

Medraut bared his teeth and shook his fists. Falling back from the gate, Viellia and Kranskie cried out for everyone to head south ahead of the approaching formation. The resistance fighters neatly withdrew from their positions and fell in amongst the running civilians, instantly blending in and vanishing within the frantic crowds.

"Come on!" Morgan cried out, helping Yunus to get their little group of prisoners moving as well. Medraut let out a snarl and a cry of frustrated anger before following after Jamie and Saexon along with all the others.

CHAPTER 59

Filing down the street, surrounded by a growing mob of escaped prisoners, Jamie tried to keep Saexon, Morgan, and Medraut close while also trying to look in every direction at once. With stray shots still streaking overhead, he could practically feel a sniper's crosshairs on the back of his neck. Pressed on by the Finttiranos soldiers at their backs, the size of their group grew as they picked up more and more prisoners the farther they ran. The anonymity might have helped to conceal them, but the exuberance with which his new-found comrades gleefully gunned down every Finttiranos soldier they saw turned his stomach.

Regardless of whether their targets were wearing full armor and carrying a rifle or were simply clerks armed with nothing more dangerous than a clipboard and cowering in a secluded alleyway, they all met the same fate. As much as Jamie might have found himself sympathizing with the plight of these prisoners, he would never allow himself to condone such senseless violence. What they needed was a way out of the fortress, to get them all as far away from any Finttiranos soldier as possible.

"This is just great!" Jamie cried to Medraut. "Where are we supposed to go from here!"

"I've already got us this far, why do I have to do everything!" Medraut shot back. "You're the one who let all this get out of control! Why don't you start pulling your own weight!"

Morgan and Saexon looked on expectantly. Jamie clenched his teeth. If it weren't for all of Medraut's hastily conceived schemes, they never would have ended up in this death trap to begin with.

But all thoughts of punching Medraut left Jamie as he spied something at the end of a shadowy alley between two of the buildings they were passing. It was a squat metal cylinder about four feet across and maybe three high, rising out of the concrete pavement at the back of the alley and topped by a domed metal cap.

As he plodded to a stop, staring, the others nearest him drifted to a halt as well and began looking about to see what had grabbed his interest.

"What is it?" Morgan said.

"We don't have time for sightseeing, we need to keep moving!" Medraut said.

"Didn't somebody say that this place used to be a magesmith town?" Jamie said.

"Yes, it was once one of our greatest," Tunios said. "When it fell to Finttiranos, it was the first great loss of the war. It gave them control over all of the southern Boravian Highlands. Up until then, they had historically only controlled the northern half. And with the surest means of access the Cavadanian road, it meant they had to pass through Heigelries to get there. That was one of their main reasons for starting the -- "

"I don't need a history lesson!" Jamie said. "Come on, follow me, I think I might have an idea."

"Finally! It's about time you started doing something around here!" Medraut said, rushing after Jamie as they pushed through the escapees, most of whom were still moving down the street perpendicular to the alley. However, Jorri and Becka and a few others noticed the sudden urgency of the shift and followed them into the dead-end alley as well. The cap of the metal tube had been welded shut but the wheel on top was still in place and turned with a rusty shriek when Jamie gave it a try.

"What the hell are you doing!" Medraut said. "That thing is sealed! Even if we had a titan to rip it open, we don't know where it leads! You just trapped us in this alley with no way out!"

"Would you quit your whining!" Jamie said as he braced his feet again the base of the metal tube and secured his grip on the edge of the cap. "All magesmith towns are built basically the same. This should lead down into the storm sewers. We should be able to follow them right out of the fort."

"When did you suddenly become an expert on magesmith towns?" Medraut said.

"A friend told me," Jamie said.

"But won't they just follow us?" Tunios said. "Or cut us off once we're in there?"

"If this one is welded shut, then it's a good bet the others are too!" Jamie said. "Now leave me alone!"

The rebels who had followed them took up defensive positions at the mouth of the alley while encouraging their comrades still in the street to join them. A concentrated barrage of gunfire from down the street cut down several prisoners running past the mouth of the alley. One of the rebels who leaned around the corner to get a better look at what was happening had to quickly duck back as more wardcaster fire pelted the side of the building.

"We've got incoming!" he said. "Looks like they've finally got themselves organized."

"No pressure then," Jamie muttered to himself as he put all his strength into lifting the metal cap. He could feel the metal under his fingers buckle but the rest of the cap didn't budge.

"You must be crazy if you think you can open that with your bare hands!" Tunios said. Gently pulling him back, his wife tried her best to calm him. "This is crazy!"

The gunfire in the street had grown more intense and the prisoners defending the alley were now shooting back indiscriminately. So many of them had followed Jamie's desperate lead that the back of the alley was packed full of prisoners. Jamie bared his teeth and renewed his efforts. A rip began to form in the thick metal, running perpendicular to the welded seam. If he wasn't careful, he might only mangle things so badly that it wouldn't allow anyone through. Adjusting his grip while keeping a constant pressure on the cap, he tried again.

"Come on!" he muttered through clenched teeth.

This time, the metal cap creaked and groaned. Watching on in disbelief, Morgan's eyes grew wide. Even Tunios stopped his complaints and stared.

With a loud creak, and then a sudden snap, the cap broke lose from the base all at once. Stumbling forward, Jamie had to catch himself from falling into the dark hole it had exposed below. The other prisoners helped lift the cap back on rusty hinges which echoed down through the shaft. Jamie couldn't see the bottom but there was a ladder running down the side. He sure hoped Onorah had known what she was talking about.

"Come on!" he cried. With the gunfire becoming more frenzied, they didn't have time to be cautious about this. "Into the hole!"

"Morgan, you go first!" Medraut said, lifting her over the rim and all but tossing her down the black pit. She didn't seem to appreciate being the first to leave the fight, but she didn't argue, quickly descending the ladder. Medraut was close behind and Jamie ushered Saexon down next. Those prisoners without weapons or who weren't helping with the defense of the alley swarmed into the tunnel and began scurrying down the ladder as well, some of them nearly pushing Jamie out of the way to do so. Tunios and his wife were more polite about it, but no less insistent. Urged on by the increasing gunfire, all of the escaped prisoners surged into the shaft much quicker than Jamie would have thought possible. He did hear one panicked cry from below as someone lost their grip on the ladder, but otherwise the entire operation commenced with energetic precision.

Flanked by the twins and armed with only a Finttiranos sidearm, Viellia fell back from the mouth of the alley and took a quick look down the shaft before calling out, "Alright everyone: fallback! Covering fire!"

Kranskie saddled up alongside her as the twins slung their rifles and climbed into the hole, one after the other. "You first, Viellia."

"Dammit, Kranskie, just go, I need to make sure as many of us get out of here as possible!"

"Which is why you need to keep yourself alive!" the burly man said as several bolts of blaster fire streaked down the length of the alleyway, close enough that everyone at the shaft all ducked their heads. Kranskie raised the sizable Finttiranos rifle with one hand and fired back into the street over the heads of the retreating rebels.

"Go! Go! Go!" Jamie cried out, ducking down around the rim of the hatch as soldiers began storming into the mouth of the alley, their weapons blazing. Some of the defenders turned and fled while others backed away from their foes while returning fire. Viellia and Kranskie had climbed over the lip of the shaft and each of them hung off to one side of the ladder, pulling in those few remaining rebels who made it that far. The last one still on his feet took a hit to the back just as his hand found Viellia's, his face and body going slack as he fell to the ground.

Viellia cursed loudly and dropped down the ladder as the soldier's gunfire now concentrated on them, "Go! Close it up!"

Jamie didn't have time to think about the danger of the situation, he vaulted over the edge of the shaft and grabbed hold of the wheel on the underside of the domed hatch, letting his own weight and momentum pull it down on the base with a heavy metallic clang that echoed through the shaft and likely defended those nearest the top.

Blaster fire could be heard pinging off the metal hatch, causing spots on the inside to glow red. It took Jamie a moment of swinging from the bottom of the hatch before he managed to get his feet onto the ladder and give the wheel a powerful turn. He felt the bolts slam into their sockets so strongly that he knew it wouldn't be easy for a normal person to open it again.

However, the armor those soldiers wore would make that task considerably easier for them. The weapon's fire had already stopped, and he could hear their armored hands clamoring for a grip on the exterior wheel. After taking a second to brace himself, Jamie turned the inner wheel even farther. The shaft that connected it to its twin on the outside groaned and then snapped off, right above their connection to the bolts that held the hatch closed.

A clattering of armored bodies echoed off the top of the hatch as the wheel suddenly spun freely in their hands, sending them all falling over themselves. Now they'd need to cut their way through in order to follow. It might have gained Jamie and the other escaped prisoners a few extra minutes. After taking a second to listen to the muffled orders of the soldiers, Jamie quickly descended the ladder after the others.

At the bottom, he found himself in a domed chamber of gray concrete. Only a few of the illumination wards built into the walls had activated upon their arrival, leaving the entire place in murky twilight. Urgent chatter rang out from all the people crowded into the chamber. Medraut came at Jamie the moment he stepped off the ladder.

"Alright genius, where are we supposed to go from here! There are, like, twenty different ways out of here! This is even worse that up on the surface!"

Jamie could only see six tunnels radiating out from the chamber they had found themselves in, but Medraut's point was well taken. When Onorah had guided him and Alaida out of Tavnic, she'd taken them on a very specific route. Even if Grassnar was similar enough to Tavnic that this plan of Jamie's would actually work, the fort was far larger than that small frontier town. There was no way his limited knowledge would get them out of this. However, with all these people now looking at him for their salvation, he couldn't let them know that or panic would quickly become a bigger danger than those soldiers chasing after them.

"We just need to figure out which way to the discharge pipes," Jamie said. "Water flows downhill, so just have to keep going down."

"They all go down!" Medraut said. "You just got us buried under a Finttiranos fort! This is not how I ever wanted to die! You are just the worst luck ever!"

"Hey, calm down," Viellia said, stepping between them. "This isn't helping."

"And just who the hell are you to know what's going to help or not? Do you know how to get out of here? Does anyone!" His words echoed off the hard concrete walls and joined with the increasing number of escapees asking the same thing.

Saexon, however, seemed strangely calm for a change. Holding his nose to the air with his eyes closed, he pointed toward one of the six vaulted tunnels. "That way," he said. Everyone turned and looked at him in silence. He stared back for a moment before saying simply, "I smell fresh air coming from that one."

Medraut suddenly laughed. "Leave it to the Lord of the Stoats to find a way out of a rat's hole! I knew you scrawny bastards had to be good for something!" Medraut then pushed around Saexon and through the crowd of prisoners toward the tunnel indicated. "Come on, let's get out of here!"

Standing next to Jamie as they watched Medraut take the lead, Viellia said, "That kid is gonna get whiplash from those mood swings."

"Tell me about it," Jamie said.

"And I thought my daughters were bad," Kranskie said.

With a few words of instruction from Viellia and Kranskie, everyone began filing out of the chamber behind Medraut and Saexon, their hurried footfalls echoing off the walls. Of the hundreds of prisoners that had fled through the gates Jamie had helped to open, maybe only fifty or so had made it this far. Jamie didn't even want to think about how few on the surface were still alive. This was supposed to have been a quiet rescue mission and instead it had turned into a mass slaughter. As Jamie took up the rear with Morgan and the twins, he wondered how much worse it could still get before the end.

Compared to the tunnels under Tavnic, the ones they now traveled were bone dry, apart from a few shallow puddles where the condensation dripping from the walls collected in low spots on the floor. But their way was clear of debris, and despite the tight confines and the zigzagging route Saexon led them on, the prisoners made good time. Illumination wards were few and far between, usually spaced apart at the maximum distance one could see. Not much was said, and then only in soft whispers, every ear listening expectantly for sounds of pursuit. For the most part, all anyone heard where their own footsteps.

More than once the whole group froze at the sound of some distant clank or bang. For a few moments, everyone would hold their breath in silence until Viellia or Medraut would urge them on again when it became clear there wasn't any immediate danger. Even if the soldiers had already managed to descend into the tunnels after them, all the hard concrete would have turned the sounds of pursuit into nothing more than meaningless echoes coming from every direction at once.

The steady way in which Saexon never once seemed to doubt where they were headed certainly helped to keep everyone from growing more despondent than they already were. Jamie couldn't tell if the boy was just putting forward a confident front or if he actually knew where he was going, he was just happy no one was looking to him for leadership anymore.

At every new intersection or change in direction, the order of their column shifted and rearranged as those more able-bodied helped those who were not. As Jamie moved among the prisoners and became more familiar with them in general, he slowly became aware of two distinct types within the otherwise uniform group. The ordinary civilians, even those who currently carried weapons and looked no different from all the rest, now trudged along with heads down and shoulders stooped, their energy drained, if not from the physical exertions, then simply from the mental strain of what they had so far been through. Tunios, Junliet, and Bonny all fell into that category. On the other hand, the true rebels carried themselves just as alert and nimble as ever, despite the fact they had just endured the same pressures, if not worse, as all the rest. It came as no surprise that Viellia and Kranskie fell into that latter group, but to Jamie's eyes, it seemed others would have more appropriately belonged to the former, like Jorri and Becka, and even the grim-faced Yunus.

Morgan remained the only enigma to Jamie. Like the rebels, she hadn't let their situation get her down, but instead of turning her energies to outside dangers, as they did, she busied herself with the wellbeing of the others, lending a hand when needed, or just a simple word of encouragement at the right moment, all while still holding onto that effervescent smile of hers. Maybe she was just too naïve to realize how desperate things really where. Maybe she was just an optimist. Either way, if it weren't for her constant positivity, Jamie doubted most of the civilians would have remained as committed as they were.

In those blackened tunnels, time lost meaning. It quickly became hard to tell how long they had been underground or even how much ground they had covered. Jamie knew it probably wasn't even noon yet, but surrounded by the constant, murky darkness, he started to think that night must have fallen. Slowly, the fear of being discovered by the soldiers was masked by the weary drudgery of merely plodding from one tunnel to the next.

As they made their way down one particularly long and low tunnel, Bonny found herself walking beside Medraut. Talk amongst the escapees had almost completely ceased, so when she spoke, her words seemed especially loud, even though she kept her voice low. "What happened at the breech?" she said.

Medraut's boot scuffed on the ground as he missed a step. "Huh?"

"At the infirmary, you said you could get everyone out," Bonny said. She was unable to meet Medraut's gaze, but as she continued, her voice grew louder and started to waver. Even as Jamie started making his way closer, he noticed Viellia doing the same from the other end of the formation. "You said you had people on the outside who were going to help us get through the intake facility. Why are you here instead of there?"

"I, um, had to come back for Morgan," Medraut said. "By the time I got here, the Fintties had cut off my way back. Just bad luck really."

"So, the others made it out?" Junliet said as she and her husband gripped hands tightly. "How many?"

"Look, I, um, didn't really get a count," Medraut said, increasing his pace to leave these questions behind him. "Things were pretty crazy, especially after the guards opened fire."

"I was at the breech and I didn't see anyone make it out," one of the other prisoners, an older but still spry man, said. In the darkness, his tone sounded harshly critical. "We never even made it to the facility before things started going sideways. And by that point, almost everyone was running in the other direction."

Medraut turned on the speaker with a sneer. "Yourself included, obviously."

"You're damn right," the man said. "Those guards in their towers were cutting us down like grain and we couldn't even get to them. I saw Maezro and Glaudiana had managed to scale one of the towers with some others, but them guards shot every last one of them dead just a minute later."

"If you were really there then you remember me telling everyone to make a scene but don't attack until I gave them the word," Medraut said. The older man slunk back a step and held his tongue. Jamie watched Medraut closely but couldn't tell if his sharp words were spoken out of guilt at what he'd led those people into, or if this was just more of his typical blaming of everyone but himself. "Leave it to a bunch of farmers and villagers to go and jump the gun before we were ready."

"Maezro and Glaudiana were good, disciplined soldiers," Viellia said. "A lot of those people were. They wouldn't have acted unless they didn't have any other choice."

"I don't know which one of them made the first move, but my men on the outside weren't in position yet. Your *professional soldiers* likely got them killed."

And now Medraut was expressing sympathy for people who didn't even exist. Jamie had to bite his lip to keep from voicing his support for the escaped prisoners.

"Who cares about a few hired guns?" Bonny said. "You just got hundreds of our people killed with your stupid plan! Luranc was right, we never should have listened to you!"

"I didn't force anyone into anything!" Medraut said. "I gave you all a choice! Those people who died knew there was no guarantee but every last one of them willingly took that chance!"

"You sold them on a fool's gambit and then ran away at the first sign of trouble!" Bonny said, taking a swing at him as only someone who had never been in a fistfight could.

"Hey! Stop it!" Jamie said in a harsh whisper that cut through the yelling. "You guys can hash this out later. Yeah, it's terrible what happened to those people, but right now, we need to worry about keeping ourselves alive. All this yelling is only going to make it easier for those soldiers to find us!"

Bonny, close to tears as she glared at Medraut, didn't seem to care about the sense of Jamie's words. Medraut, meanwhile, looked like he would welcome the fight, even if it was from a woman who wouldn't last more than a few seconds against him. Viellia appeared conflicted between siding with Bonny or ceding to Jamie's logic. In the end, she sighed and shook her head.

"The kid's right, we can't do this here," Viellia said. Then, turning to Medraut, she said, "But when this is over, there's gonna be some things you'll have to answer for."

Lip curled back, Medraut leaned forward to offer his rebuttal, but Saexon called out from further down the tunnel before he could. "Hey! I think there's a way out down here!"

Medraut's eyes narrowed as he continued glaring at Viellia for a moment and then broke off and stomped away to the head of the now halted line of refugees. Viellia took a deep breath, placing hands on hips as she watched him leave.

"Once we're out of here, I'm gonna skin him alive," she said.

"The line starts behind me," Jamie said, following after Medraut.

CHAPTER 60

Viellia, Kranskie, and Jamie found Medraut with Saexon some distance beyond where the rest of the escapees had stopped. The tunnel they had been following ended abruptly, dropping straight down some ten or so feet before continuing on in roughly the same direction as before. Laying on their bellies to look over the edge, there was no mistaking the sunlight and fresh air filtering in from farther on. However, they could also hear the echoes of voices and equipment. From the sharp bend in the tunnel, is was impossible to see how far away the end was or what might await them there.

"I'll check it out," Saexon said, dropping himself over the edge before anyone could even try to stop him. There was a slight bend at the bottom of the drop, and he landed without a sound, skittering to one side of the tunnel and staying low. With eyes fixed on the route ahead, he crept forward and quickly disappeared from sight.

"I better go too," Kranskie said, pushing himself up off his stomach. "I don't think I want to leave my intelligence to that kid."

"He'll be fine," Medraut said. "This is what he was designed for."

Kranskie turned to Viellia who merely shrugged. With a huff, the bearded freedom fighter lowered himself back down, muttering something about not waiting forever. After having come this far, Jamie could practically feel the restlessness of the other escapees as well. With their potential freedom just around that bend, they wanted to make a run for it, regardless of what awaited them. However, Jamie knew the military wouldn't have spent so much time fortifying the hill surrounding Fort Grassnar but overlooking a gaping hole in their security like this tunnel. There was absolutely no way they were out of danger just yet.

Kranskie and Viellia whispered between themselves, speculating about the types of equipment they were hearing based solely on the sounds. Maybe it was just Jamie projecting his own imagination onto the sounds coming from the end of the tunnel, but to him, the indistinct voices still carried with them an edge of that crisp military professionalism.

"Alright, I've waited long enough," Kranskie said as he once again pushed himself off the ground.

He nearly dropped back down again when Saexon suddenly reappeared in the tunnel and hissed to catch their attention. "Come on," he said, waving them down. "It's clear for a little ways yet; but then, well, come on and see for yourselves."

Medraut and Kranskie both vaulted over the edge as if trying to beat the other to the bottom. Viellia instead turned back to the column of prisoners and called Goffry forward. After quickly telling him to keep everyone calm a little longer, she stood to follow after Kranskie and Medraut.

"Want a hand?" Jamie said. The drop wasn't that far but it was still high enough that it would give most normal people pause. Viellia considered his offer for a moment before finally nodding. Jamie took her hand and lowered her over the edge, reducing the distance she had to fall to only a few feet. She scrambled over the curve in the floor and quickly found her footing once more. Jamie dropped down in a single jump and landed next to her. She eyed him curiously but said nothing as she skulked toward the bright light shining in through the vertical bars at the end of the tunnel.

The mouth of the tunnel was shaped like an oval, maybe twenty feet wide and ten high. The others were crouched down behind the thick steel bars at the end, gazing out at the view beyond. Where Jamie had been expecting the absolute worst-case scenario, what he saw was only slightly better.

The tunnel emptied into a small pool which then drained into a concrete flume that flowed away to their right alongside a well-traveled gravel path. On the other side of the path was an oblong enclosure about five or six hundred yards wide filled with Finttiranos soldiers bustling about as vulcan-mechas hurriedly unloaded supplies from a whole fleet of those floating transports. Similar to the ones Jamie had seen in Tavnic, they had the same teardrop shape and flat deck of a sailing ship but with two faintly glowing glass orbs in each corner which kept them floating several feet off the ground. In addition, they also had a mounted gun on the elevated front and rear decks and a series of shoulder-high, armored panels fixed around the edge of the main deck. Pointed at the top and bottom, the armor overlapped like giant scales, making the transports look a little bit like ancient Roman war galleys or Viking longboats, just without the oars or sails. Beyond the yard was a high concrete wall interspersed with four hulking towers, above which only blue skies could be seen. These fortifications weren't as tall as the ones around the fort but they were still too high to scale without anyone noticing the attempt.

From their vantage point, Jamie and the others couldn't see much of what lay on either side of the tunnel, but the curve of the landscape did offer them a glimpse. They appeared to be about halfway down the side of the hill upon which Fort Grassnar had been built, this smaller fort nestled into a saddle on the southern face. All the supplies that were being unloaded from the transports eventually made their way out of view to the left, which made Jamie suspect there had to be some kind of route over there that connected this place to the rest of the fort.

In a lot of ways, it was much like the Annex Yard in Tavnic, only bigger and better fortified. Apparently, all magesmith towns really were quite similar.

"This has got to be the southwest sally port," Viellia said.

"Great," Kranskie said with a shake of the head. "That means there's nothing but five miles of no-man's-land between here and the nearest piece of cover."

"At least we don't have to circle all the way around Grassnar and through Tolfield before starting on our way back to Heigelries."

"There's no way we're gonna be able to sneak everyone out of here past those gates without being noticed," Kranskie said. "Maybe we could stow away on one of those barques."

"None of them are leaving, they're just being staged over there once they've been unloaded," Viellia said. "What with the prison escape, the entire fort is probably on lockdown. No one's going to be allowed in or out until things are back under control. And with the huge breech we just caused, they're probably going to be instituting some serious new security procedures."

"Then we're gonna need to take one of those barques and shoot our way out," Kranskie said.

"We'll have to get those gates open first."

As they continued talking, Medraut nudged Jamie over to the side of the tunnel. "My wolves are near," he said as soon as the others were out of earshot.

"What are you talking about? They've got to be miles away from here." Jamie didn't know how, but he had the impression that the bluff

Doctor Calamestro had indicated on his map lay quite some distance to the east of their current location.

"You really are an idiot, aren't you? I know how they think. When they realized things had started happening inside the fort, they would have sent out scouts. Even they wouldn't risk coming in after me but they're out there, right on the other side of those walls. I know it."

Jamie remembered well that last time he'd just crawled through a sewer and had been looking at freedom on the other side of a fortified wall. That time, the wolves lurking beyond had been there to kill him.

"Can they help us?"

"Listen," Medraut hissed, "once we're out of this tunnel, we go over that wall with Saexon and Morgan and forget about the rest of these people, you got that?"

Jamie should have been shocked by what he'd just heard, but he'd come to expect this from Medraut. "You got these people into this situation! Now you're just going to abandon them?"

"Yes," Medraut said, "I am." Jabbing Jamie in the chest with his finger as he walked away, he added, "And so are you."

"We're going to need someone to open those gates," Viellia was saying as Jamie and Medraut returned. Both she and Kranskie glanced at the two boys.

"What?" Medraut shrugged. "Why are you looking at me?"

"I'll do it," Jamie said. If the simple sense of knowing he was doing the right thing wasn't reason enough to volunteer, hearing Medraut's startled yelp would have been.

Medraut's lip twitched and his hands flexed into claws, but he must have realized he couldn't do anything to Jamie right here in front of the others. He probably still had plans to use them as a distraction while he made his own escape. But Jamie wasn't about to let that happen, not again. He was going to do everything in his power to make sure as many of these people as possible made it out of this place alive, regardless of what Medraut intended. As Jamie met Medraut's gaze, Saexon looked quizzically between the two of them.

"Such a stand-up guy," Medraut said through clenched teeth.

"I'll go," Kranskie said. "And we should bring Lirman too. There will probably be security locks on the gates, and you know how good he is at breaking those codes."

"Good. We'll start bringing everyone down and getting them ready to move," Viellia said.

While she busied herself with that, Kranskie tested the small access gate set into the larger steel bars covering the end of the tunnel. There was a latch, but no one had bothered to close the lock which hung open on the end of the hasp. Kranskie pushed the gate back just enough to allow a man to slide out. The rusty hinges produced a shrill cry, but with all the soldiers far away and busy with their heavy equipment, none of them would have been able to hear.

Of greater concern was being spotted by one of the four guard towers along the perimeter wall. The gravel path outside the tunnel followed the concave arc of the hillside for about a hundred yards before passing beneath one of those perimeter towers which also acted as a fortified gatehouse. The windows above were dark, so it would be impossible to know if anyone up there was even looking in their direction. They would just have to start moving and hope for the best.

Viellia ensured Lirman was one of the first of the escapees brought down and Kranskie wasted no time once their team was complete. Lirman was a thin man with a shifty look in the pale eyes behind his wire-framed glasses. He looked more like an accountant than a rebel but he carried his rifle with familiarity and purpose, never once questioning Kranskie as their task was explained to him.

"Well then, shall we get underway?" he said, as if the undertaking ahead was no more challenging than the balancing of a checkbook and not very likely a suicide mission.

"I'll go first. Once we know it's safe, you two follow." Though Kranskie addressed his instructions to both of them, he only looked at Jamie. "Keep your heads down and stay quiet."

With that, Kranskie slid through the opening and dropped to the jagged rocks lining the pond below. Somehow, he skirted around to the concrete flume without making a sound. He remained crouched in the shoulder-deep channel for only about thirty seconds before waving toward the tunnel. Jamie went next, followed by Lirman.

Knowing that it would be far too easy to miss a step when scrambling across the uneven boulders in the heavy boots he wore, Jamie simply focused on putting one foot down in front of the other. It also kept him from thinking that if a single eye fell upon them, it would be over for every escapee in the tunnel as well.

He and Lirman made it to Kranskie's side without incident but that was of no comfort whatsoever, since their current position now made them perfectly visible from the towers above. The open dome of the sky overhead only made them feel even more exposed. Plus, now that they were free of the protection of the tunnel, they could also see the rest of the hillside that reached back up toward Fort Grassnar. The towering walls of the main fort were closer than Jamie had been expecting, looming malevolently right at the top of a steep cliff face. Any guards up there would likely be able to see them as well.

At least the attention of the soldiers in the yard didn't waver from their work. Each load of cargo they removed from the barques was quickly loaded into the massive hoppers of a vertical conveyer that carried the supplies up to the main fort. The mechanism that ran the conveyor never stopped, but each hopper paused for a few moments at the level of the yard, giving the soldiers a short span of time to load it before it began moving again. The hypnotic rhythm of the operation was so perfectly choreographed Jamie didn't see anyone miss a single step. He might very well have kept staring for quite some time had Kranskie not slapped him on the shoulder, indicating that they were moving once more.

With only a trickle of water in the bottom of the rounded flume, the three of them dashed along the sides to avoid making any more noise than necessary, all the time keeping their heads down. Jamie could have covered the ground faster than either of the other two men and he found himself wishing that he could have. The longer they were out in the open, the more risk they were in. At this point, it was only a matter of time before someone in the yard or the towers saw them. Or those in pursuit finally caught up.

When they finally passed into the long shadows cast by the gatehouse without any alarms having been sounded, Jamie allowed himself a tiny sigh of relief. Between the base of the tower and the rock of the cliff, the water flowed out onto the hillside beyond through a culvert that was barred at both ends by heavy steel grates. These looked to be fixed, cast right into the concrete, and offering no option for escape. Not that it would have helped them if it had. As Kranskie had said, the hillside outside the walls had been scoured clear of all vegetation and the landscape itself had been smoothed off to offer no dips or boulders to hide behind. The only way they had left to them was through the massive gates which currently sat closed and sealed tight.

The gatehouse itself was solid concrete and the base on each side of the gate had a footprint as big as a house. On the inside of the gated passage which passed below the fortifications above, they could see a small man door in the opposite side.

"Come on," Kranskie said, levering himself out of the flume. "Move! Move! Move!"

He dashed to the edge of the gatehouse and peered around the corner into the gated tunnel. His fingers flicked with some kind of silent order that Lirman apparently understood because he darted around the corner to check on the man door. While it remained barred and would not open, Lirman indicated another door on the other side of the tunnel which currently hung ajar and didn't even appear to be guarded.

Kranskie turned to Jamie and waved him toward the other door. "Go, get inside!"

"Right," Jamie whispered under his breath, sprinting around the corner. Not knowing what to expect on the other side of the door, he quickly formulated a plan to first peek inside before barreling through.

Just as he reached it, however, his preparations were rendered moot when the door swung open at his approach and a fully armored soldier stepped outside. With his face visor raised and lifting a wardcaster lighter to the cigarette hanging from his lips, he froze upon seeing Jamie and his eyes bulged.

Jamie reacted without even thinking, clapping one hand over the man's mouth and slamming his head against the concrete doorjamb several times. The guard's body went limp and Jamie pushed him through the doorway. Kranskie and Lirman followed right on his heels.

Inside was only a single small room with a desk and a chair and an assortment of official-looking forms hanging from clipboards on the wall. A quick glance from the doorway would have revealed nothing more, but once all three of them were inside with the unconscious guard, they could see a niche tucked away behind the desk which concealed a flight of stairs spiraling upward through the solid concrete core of the tower. Kranskie threw himself against the wall, pointing his rifle up through the opening as he scanned above for potential danger.

"Clear!" he said, his whisper cutting through the silence of the tomb-like guard chamber. "Take care of that guard and seal the door! I don't want anyone coming up on us from behind!"

As Jamie went to latch the door, Lirman bent and unplugged a large, flat power cell from the guard's back which caused the armor's magescript to instantly go dark. Looking back through the door before closing it, Jamie caught a glimpse of the other prisoners slipping from the tunnel and staging at the edge of the pond before sneaking across the road toward the nearest parked barque. He threw the latch closed on the door, sealing the three of them inside the tower. There would certainly be no going back now. If they didn't get those gates open, it wouldn't matter if the others managed to secure transport or not.

While Kranskie stood guard at the stairs, Lirman also took the soldier's rifle and extra power cells. Of the latter, he passed half to Kranskie and kept the others for himself. The rifle he handed to Jamie.

Jamie hesitated for a moment but ultimately put up his hands and shook his head. He knew that it might prove to be a useful tool in other ways than shooting people, but he'd been thinking much the same thing about Reaver's titan-mecha that night the Wolf-Slaves had attacked him and Alaida after fleeing from Tavnic. The last thing he wanted at the moment was to put himself in a situation like that again.

Kranskie merely shrugged, taking the rifle for himself and slinging it across his back. With no further use for the room or its contents, Kranskie began moving up the stairs, his weapon trained constantly on the curving passage ahead. Jamie followed. Lirman did as well, but only after also pocketing the guard's cigarettes and lighter.

Evenly spaced wards set into the walls of the stairway illuminated as they approached and darkened once they were past, creating a pocket of light rising through the tower with nothing but darkness ahead and behind. The stair maintained the same tight corkscrew shape, the walls on each side always close enough that Jamie could have touched them both if he stretched out his hands. Though they all stepped lightly on the concrete treads underfoot, each footfall still echoed loudly in Jamie's ears.

The climb lasted long enough that it seemed they should have run out of tower long before they finally saw light above them, and not the artificial illumination of a gloworb, but the warm light of the afternoon sun. Kranskie motioned them both to hold their tongues, reiterating what they had already been doing the entire time, and then advanced at a more cautious pace. The stairs deposited them into an empty, dome-shaped room completely devoid of windows. The light they had seen was coming through a heavy, steel door which hung open and offered a glimpse into the guard room beyond.

Kranskie peaked above the topmost step, quickly confirming that they had not yet been noticed, and then stepped quickly and quietly to the side of the room. Leaning one eye around the doorjamb, he motioned Jamie and Lirman up as well. They pressed their backs to the wall on either side of the door.

The guard room spanned from one end of the tower to the other with the gates directly below. A continuous bank of windows lined both the front and back walls, offering clear views of the road running away from the gate down the side of the hill and of the yard encircled by the walls. A long, narrow console in the center of the room held all manner of magesmith-conceived instruments, several of which chirped periodically with reports from different portions of the fort.

Only two guards could be seen and neither had his helmet on. One of them sat in a chair with his feet up on the windowsill as he ideally flipped through a magazine. The other paced at the far end of the room, listening to the relay nets and occasionally trying to bite his fingernails, only to realize each time that his armored gauntlets wouldn't allow it.

From what little Jamie could make out of the transmissions, the soldiers in Fort Grassnar had not yet gotten all the chaos caused by the prison break under control. Numerous fires were burning in the prison district and reports were still coming in of combat with isolated groups of escaped prisoners. Maybe Jamie's group had been overlooked in the midst of all that.

Despite the relative lack of manpower stationed here, the situation remained far from simple. Maybe it was possible that gunning down these two guards would go unheard by their comrades down on the ground, but there was also a metal stairway on each end of the room that must have led up to what were likely more guard posts at the very top of the gatehouse. How many more soldiers were currently stationed up there?

CHAPTER 61

Kranskie mouthed a silent curse, likely having come to the same conclusions as Jamie. He turned to Lirman, making a quick series of hand motions. The other man nodded and drew a long stiletto knife from his boot. Likewise, Kranskie pulled out a large pocket knife and quietly unfolded the blade. He turned to Jamie and indicated that he was to stay where he was.

That was just fine with Jamie. He'd agreed to help get the prisoners out of here, and he wasn't so naïve to think that they could do that without anyone else dying, but he wasn't going to do it himself if he could help it. Kranskie nodded to Lirman and then the two men slipped into the control room.

"What the -- " he heard one of the guards say before being cut off by a series of muffled thumps and bangs. The clattering of a armored body falling to the floor echoed from the other room. Jamie waited another moment before heading inside. Lirman crouched over the body of the young guard, pulling his knife from the many lacerations in the soldier's neck. On the other side of the room, Kranskie stood with hands covered in blood as it fell in sheets from the other soldier's neck. He took one last frantic grasp at Kranskie before collapsing to the floor with a gurgling moan.

Lirman had already made his way to the center console, though his stride was hindered by a significant limp that hadn't been there before.

"You okay?" Kranskie asked.

"Bastard kicked me in the shin," Lirman said as he searched for the control that would operate the gate.

"What was that noise?" a voice called down from one of the two metal stairs. "Are you guys okay down there? I think something's going on down in the loading yard."

The voices coming through one of the relay nets suddenly took on a more frantic tone as the frequency of the transmissions rapidly increased. Through the windows, Jamie could see that a commotion had erupted in the yard around one of the barques as people clad in civilian garb ran from a group of confused-looking soldiers, none of whom were wearing any armor or even appeared to be armed. He couldn't hear what was being said, but he jerked back at the flash of a blaster cutting down one of the soldiers. Heads low, the rest scattered as the last of the escaped prisoners broke from cover at the edge of the pond and ran for the barque. The transport lurched and the glass orbs on the underside of its hull glowed a little more brightly as it rose and slowly began turning, bringing its nose around to face the gate tower.

A clattering of boots on the metal stairs to Jamie's left pulled his attention away from the chaos quickly breaking out below. A female voice accompanied the armored figure that descended the stairs with rifle in one hand and helmet in the other. "Hey, guys, I think some of those prisoners might -- !"

The moment she saw Jamie and the others, she brought her blaster up. Being the closest, Jamie charged forward, ducking under the flashing muzzle of her weapon as a burst of wild shots knocked out several windows in the back of the room and tore smoldering holes in the instrument console. Jamie crashed into her and knocked her back against the stairs.

Crying out through clenched teeth, the woman slammed her helmet into the side of Jamie's head as hard as she could and then tried to throw him off. The armor made her strong, but she was on her back and Jamie was even stronger. He managed to pin her gun arm and was just a moment away from immobilizing her entirely when Kranskie pressed his own weapon under her jaw and pulled the trigger.

Sputtering nonsensically, Jamie jumped back from the dark cloud that had suddenly replaced the woman's head. "What the hell! How could -- I mean, she was -- what the hell!"

"She was tryin' to kill us," Kranskie said flatly. "And we got more on the way!" He turned his rifle on the staircase across the room and unleashed a full barrage into the chest of another armored soldier who promptly dropped. Lirman, meanwhile, lay on the floor, grunting in pain as he clutched a large burn on his side. He must have been winged by one of the shots that woman had gotten off before Jamie had taken her down.

Kranskie rushed to Lirman and helped him to his feet. From what little Jamie could see of the wound around the scraps of burned fabric and skin, it looked bad. "You okay?"

"Yeah," Lirman nodded, his jaw tight. He dropped his hand on a large lever in the middle of the console. "This is the gate release. It's got a three-tier security lock. It's gonna take a minute to crack."

"I think a minute is all you got," Kranskie said.

Down in the yard, the barque had gotten underway, heading toward the gate, though moving far too sluggishly for Jamie's liking. Those escaped prisoners without weapons huddled on the deck behind the armored plates while the rest fired over the sides at the armored soldiers who had started spilling into the yard. Most of the soldier's return fire bounced harmlessly off the barque's armored plates with little more than a flash of magescript. Those shots that found unprotected flesh were far more destructive. In just the few brief seconds Jamie watched, he saw at least three rebels fall back from the defensive armor in clouds of vaporized blood. Even taking into account the prisoners still on the ground, scrabbling to intercept the now moving barque, their numbers had already been significantly reduced.

The relay nets were now screaming with activity from all points. Several demands were directed toward "Tower 1" but when no reply came, an order was given to switch channels. After that, all the relay nets went eerily silent.

"They'll be comin' for us now," Kranskie said, leaning out one of the broken windows to try and get a look at the perimeter wall beyond the gate tower. "Our ride's getting awfully close, Lirman. We might want that gate open about now."

"Getting there," the other man replied, completely focused on the brass and crystal switches below the large gate lever.

As the two of them talked, Jamie turned towards the doorway at the other end of the room. Much like the one they had entered through, it opened into a small, domed chamber with the top of a spiral stair protruding through the center of the floor. However, this chamber also had a second door which sat directly opposite from the one leading into the control room. It was from that door that Jamie could hear the armored footsteps of multiple bodies quickly approaching.

"Hey, guys," Jamie said, rushing into the chamber, "I think we got company." No sooner had the words left his mouth than he saw the first glowing traces of yellow magescript on the armor of the soldiers rushing down the darkened tunnel. The leading soldier caught sight of Jamie a split second later and raised his rifle. Jamie had already thrown himself at the armored door at the end of the tunnel, crashing into it with his shoulder and pressing it closed as a spattering of blaster fire rang off the other side. With no latch that he could see on this side of the door, Jamie could do nothing but put his back to the door and dig in his heels to keep it shut.

"Got it!" Lirman cried, throwing the gate lever at last. A deep rumble reverberated through the concrete structure all around them.

"Not a second too soon!" Kranskie said. "Come on, everyone downstairs!"

"I think I'm gonna need a hand with that," Lirman said, taking a step toward the exit and nearly collapsing.

A bang against the door at Jamie's back pushed it open a fraction of an inch before his efforts sent it closed once again with a crash. As the soldiers pushed from the other side, his feet began slipping across the floor. Another powerful bang almost unseated him entirely. Digging his fingers into the steel jamb, Jamie used his hands to clamp the door shut.

"I think you guys better get moving!" Jamie called out over his shoulder. "I can't hold these guys forever!"

"You sure?" Kranskie said as he threw an arm around Lirman.

"Go!" Jamie said. "I'll catch up!"

Before leaving the room, Kranskie lifted his rifle and sent several shots into the center console, paying special attention to the lever that operated the gate, and reducing it to nothing but a mangled heap of smoldering metal.

"Good luck," he said as the two of them disappeared down the stairs.

Several repeated crashes from the other side of the door bent the metal around Jamie's fingers. His grip remained secure but at this rate, the frame was going to give way before the door. And then they started shooting, concentrating their fire on a spot not too far from Jamie's hands. They must have noticed the weak point as well. He could feel the metal heating up, and as the barrage continued, it started to glow red. Would the metal eventually start to melt or would it simply explode into razor sharp pieces of shrapnel when it finally reached it breaking point?

Kranskie would be slowed by Lirman's injury but they must have been getting close to the bottom of the tower by now. It would have to be enough. Jamie wasn't sure he'd be able to make it out if he waited any longer. He shifted one of his hands to a new spot, crimping the door's edge around the frame. He did the same in several other places and then bent each hinge with a solid kick. It probably wouldn't keep the soldiers from opening the door, but it should at least slow them down a little.

As the blaster fire continued against the door, Jamie backed cautiously away, hoping his handiwork would hold. A moment later, the gunfire ceased, and a powerful kick slammed into the door, causing it to buckle and crash open about six inches. Jamie retreated to the control room just as a second kick increased the gap to the point that two blaster muzzles were stuck through and began firing indiscriminately at anything on the other side.

Jamie had to duck around the corner to avoid being shot in the back. The blaster fire wasn't very accurate but there was so much of it that he wouldn't be able to make it to the stairs at the opposite end of the room without getting hit. Had he been paying more attention to his surroundings, he would have closed the door to the control room behind him. It latched from the inside, but it also swung outward, currently placing it beyond his reach.

He could now see that the commandeered barque had started to pick up speed and was just about to pass beneath the gate tower. If Jamie didn't get out of there now, he'd miss his chance.

"What the heck," he muttered to himself, eyeing the broken windows in the back of the control room. "I've survived worse."

Without letting himself think any further about the fall that awaited him, Jamie vaulted himself up and through one of the broken windows. He dropped like a stone, the wind rushing past his ears canceling out all other noise. He barely even had time to look down before the edge of the moving barque raced up to great him. He hit the deck and his legs collapsed beneath him, sending his forehead ricocheting off one of the armored panels.

The escaped prisoners around him looked back in shock; a shock which only grew when he picked himself off the metal deck. The blaster fire lancing over the tops of the armored plates was intense and everyone seemed to be screaming. Nearby, a gap in the armored plates that had been used for the off-loading of supplies now offered the only way for the handful of rebels still on the ground to get aboard.

Junliet was running alongside the barque, reaching out for a handhold as Tunios gave her a boost onto the deck. Jamie lunged to meet her and grabbed her hand, pulling her aboard in one jerk. In the same instant, he felt the tendons in her hand go limp. Jamie fell over onto his back as her body crashed heavily to the deck, some random energy bolt having burned a hole in her side just as she boarded. Tunios's howl cut through the chaos of the moment like a razor blade. Jamie sprang back to his feet and grabbed Tunios by the back of his shirt as he madly scrabbled onto the barque and lifted him onboard. Jamie likewise hauled two more onto the deck until only Viellia, still running alongside the barque, had yet to board. As they finally passed through the opened gates, Kranskie and Lirman emerged from the side door at a hobbling sprint. Viellia ushered them toward the barque and Jamie pulled each of them onboard in turn.

"That's everyone!" Viellia cried, the last aboard as she threw her back against the armored plates. "Now get us the hell out of here!"

In the middle of the raised front and rear decks stood a large wheel, like one might expect to find on an old sailing ship. Each one was manned by an escaped prisoner and they both apparently had to be operated in coordination with the other to maneuver the barque, something the current pilots only now looked to have started getting the hang of. At Viellia's command, they both stomped their foot down on a large paddle set into the deck and the barque sprang forward with a new-found velocity as the magescript etched into the sides of the hull buzzed excitedly.

The transport shot out through the gate tower and onto the gravel road beyond. The levitation wards that kept the craft aloft automatically adjusted to the changing terrain, constantly keeping the bottom of the barque no more than a foot or so off the hard ground. The road, however, descended down a series of switchback turns which required them to go back-and-forth along the length of the loading yard's walls and leaving them exposed to the blaster fire that rained down on them from above. The mounted cannons at the front and back of the barque had already been pressed into service while crossing the loading yard, but now the gunners rotated them around and fired randomly at the tops of the wall where the soldiers were taking up new positions.

Each new turn took them a little farther from the walls, which meant the gunfire at their back became less accurate. Stray shots still splashed off the armor and the deck, each time causing everyone onboard to flinch in the opposite direction. Just as they were starting to pass beyond the range of the walls defenses, one such shot struck the already injured Lirman, cutting him down where he sat slumped against the armor plates with one of his stolen cigarettes hanging from his mouth.

"Where to, Viellia?" the man at the front wheel called back over the wind once they broke into the open terrain at the bottom of the hill. A few desperate soldiers were still shooting, but at that range, their weapons didn't appear to have enough power to do any damage even if they were able to hit something.

With a groan, Viellia picked herself up off the deck and made her way forward, her legs shifting to account for the sway of the transport. "South: to Heigelries, as fast as you can." An exhausted cheer started to rise up from the survivors, but she cut it off short. "We may have made it out, but they're not going to just let us go. They probably already have titans out in pursuit. I want half of you on guard at all times. The other half, take a rest if you can."

Jamie glanced around the deck. Of the fifty or so who had made it into the tunnels, he saw no more than thirty here now. In the front of the transport, Medraut crouched with a rifle over Morgan who huddled in a ball. Saexon kneeled nearby, holding onto a railing as he looked around with his big purple eyes, strangely indifferent to the situation they had found themselves in. Kneeling over Junliet's body, Tunios wailed as he clutched his hands into fists and buried his face in her pale blue dress. Jorri and Becka sat on the edge of the rear deck, both completely unscathed and still smiling, though neither appeared willing to make any jokes at the moment. Bonny had made it as well, but from the multiple burns on her arms and back, she didn't look very well. Kranskie, meanwhile, cursed to no one in particular as he picked up Lirman's body and placed it in the center of the barque along with all the others who had fallen in their flight.

While Viellia organized the shifts for keeping watch, Kranskie gathered up a few of the others to procure tarps and ropes from one of the utility holds below the barque's deck to cover and bind the fallen in makeshift burial shrouds. The landscape which flew past the barque remained bleak and nondescript. As Kranskie had said, it had all been scoured clean, leaving nothing but the major topographical features behind.

Back to the north, a thick column of grey smoke rose up from within the western walls of Fort Grassnar, drifting high into the blue sky. For the moment, things were quiet. However, they weren't out of danger just yet. With all this open terrain, someone back in Fort Grassnar was likely still following their escape through a pair of binoculars and relaying their position to those titan's Viellia had mentioned.

"Um, Viellia, I think we may have incoming..." one of the rebels who had taken up position at the left side of the vehicle said. Everyone on the barque suddenly tensed. Jamie and a few others shot to their feet. Looking uncertainly over the armored plates, the one who'd raised the alarm lifted his rifle and sighted at a pair of figures running across the barren landscape on a course that would shortly intercept the barque.

Medraut was at his side in a flash, pushing his muzzle skyward. "Hold your fire! They're with me!"

A pair of thumps sounded from the other side of the armored plates and then two of Medraut's uniformed Wolf-Slaves climbed over the top and dropped to the deck, one male and one female. They were the same two who acted as Medraut's lieutenants. The rebels all shied away from these civilized Wolf-Slaves, but at least no one started shooting. Jamie and Saexon, along with Viellia, crept near.

"What's the situation?" Medraut said.

"Due to all the commotion within the fort, our rally point has become untenable," the female said. "The doctor has moved south and will link up with us farther on."

"The fort has already scrambled several companies of titans and artemis-mechas which have been patrolling the perimeter," the male said. He handed Medraut the pack which contained his carbine and machete. "We managed to draw their attention and create an opening for your craft's escape but there are more of them out there."

"Alright," Medraut said. He tossed aside his stolen Finttiranos rifle, slung the pack across his back, and pulled out his carbine. "Bring the troop around. We're gonna run distraction for this barque; see if we can't keep the Fintties off their back."

The two Wolf-Slaves nodded and then vaulted over the side of the still-moving vehicle, drawing more than a few stares from the escaped prisoners. Medraut put his hand on the nearest armored plate and began lifting himself up when Jamie stepped forward and grabbed him by the shoulder.

"What are you doing?" he said. "You're going with them? We're supposed to be working together!"

"I am. I'm helping you escape with all your new friends here," Medraut said with a sneer. "Keep Morgan and Saexon safe. I'll be back. Just don't get yourself killed before then."

"I didn't know you cared," Jamie said with a roll of the eyes.

"I only care about what Doctor Calamestro would do to me if you don't come back alive." With that, Medraut followed the Wolf-Slaves over the side of the barque. Jamie watched the three figures running across the landscape, quickly vanishing from sight.

"Think he'll actually come back?" Viellia said.

Jamie shook his head. "Probably." He glanced over at Morgan who had been helping tend to the dead but now gazed at the spot where Medraut had just left them.

CHAPTER 62

Jamie took off the thick black coat he'd been wearing all day and dropped back heavily against the barque's armored plates, sliding down to the deck. It seemed like days ago that Alaida had given him that coat to wear, but it had just been that morning. And with the sun only just starting to dip near the tops of the western mountains, the day wasn't even over yet. With luck, it wouldn't be too much longer before he could return the coat. The tired and ragged group of escapees had been traveling south for several hours now and they had yet to see any sign of Finttiranos patrols. Medraut's Wolves must have been doing their part.

Once they'd made it beyond the no-man's-land south of the fort, the landscape turned greener once more, though it remained a dusty and rocky terrain with most of the vegetation dominated by tough grasses and compact evergreen trees that mixed wicked-looking thorns in amongst their scaly leaves. It might have left them feeling exposed if it weren't for the steep hills and frequent gullies which made observation beyond a mile under the best of conditions impossible.

Viellia and Kranskie were somewhat familiar with the area, though Jamie didn't want to know why. They had the pilots veer off the main road as soon as they were able and ever since had them following back roads that looked like little more than game trails. However, with the openness of the countryside and the suspension of the barque, they were still making good time. The craft did dip and sway somewhat suddenly at times, leaving the passengers scrambling for a handhold or clutching their stomachs, but no wheeled vehicle ever would have been able to maintain such a smooth ride at such a speed over that terrain.

Tunios still lay next to the body of his wife, now bound in a pale beige tarp and tied to the deck to keep her from disrespectfully shifting during sharp turns. Occasionally, Jamie would think that Tunios had finally fallen asleep but then he'd unexpectedly break out into a new fit of soft tears. The others had stopped trying to comfort him long ago. Those escapees who weren't currently on watch lay slumped against the deck as Jamie was. No one talked and few slept. They just stared straight ahead without seeing anything, a few holding tightly to someone's hand in silence reassurance that they were still alive.

Jamie had heard the rebels talking amongst themselves and learned that they would eventually come to the official border between Finttiranos and the Heigelries Control Zone. Crossing would be a challenge, since it was always heavily guarded, even when Fort Grassnar hadn't just had a massive prison break, but Jamie hoped to part ways with these people long before that. He'd already helped them regain their freedom. Keeping it was going to be up to them, as Jamie would now have to do for himself. Not only had the authorities gotten a thoroughly detailed description of him after Medraut had sold him out, but they had now also linked him to the Red Rogue. The sooner Medraut returned and Doctor Calamestro took Saexon off their hands, the less ground Jamie would have to cover to get back to Len and Emma's farm, but also the fewer Finttiranos patrols he'd have to avoid along the way.

Jamie knew the odds of any trouble finding Alaida at the farm were dim, but he still wished he hadn't needed to abandon her back there. The farm was far from Fort Grassnar and in the opposite direction any of the escapees would be headed. Even if a random patrol did happen past the farm, what reason would they have to take notice of a single Raven-Slave? With Jamie's track record, she was probably safer on her own than anywhere near him. Still, he wanted to get back to her as soon as possible so they could finish that conversation they'd started in Len's barn that morning. Every moment sitting in this barque only carried him a little farther in the opposite direction.

As Jamie sat lost in thought, Morgan made her way over and handed him a canteen.

"Would you like some water?" she said. After the initial excitement of their escape, they'd spent some time going through all the supplies that had been aboard when they'd commandeered the barque. Rations might have been limited but they had come up with quite a bit of drinking water. With the number of their fallen, the only other commodity they had a bigger surplus of was guns.

"Thanks," Jamie said. Even with Reaver's iron constitution, a drink of water actually sounded quite good at the moment. The canteen was shaped like any Jamie might have imagined but this one had magescript etched all over the surface. Was it meant to cool the water inside and keep it fresh, or just stop it from making noise when sloshing around on a silent patrol? Maybe the wards even collected water vapor out of the air to keep the canteen full. Whatever the case, they remained dark as Jamie took a drink of the stale and lukewarm water inside. Still, he drank it down in deep gulps, completely draining the canteen. He couldn't remember the last time he'd eaten or drank anything on Terrarhea that had actually left him with such a sense of satisfaction afterward.

Turning the canteen over in his hand, he saw stenciled letters painted on the back, probably the name of the owner. Would he ever get his property back or had he been one of those soldiers who had fallen at the gates? Jamie handed the canteen back to Morgan. "Thanks. I think I really needed that."

"Saexon was right about you: you really are incredible," she said. "I can see why Medraut trusts you."

Jamie couldn't even work up the energy to try and correct her. "How do you and Medraut know each other?" he said instead.

Morgan pulled her knees up to her chest and wrapped her arms around them. Resting her chin on her wrists and staring into the distance, she said, "It was a few years ago, during one of the worst winters I can remember. It had been snowing for weeks, no one could get anywhere. Me and my father were completely snowed in on our farm. The cold had been so bad we lost three noxards and then something started stealing chickens from their coop too."

Jamie raised an eyebrow, remembering how big the chickens were in Tavnic and imagining what sort of creature would even be capable of making off with one of them.

"One night when I was checking on them, I found out who was responsible: a boy, not much older than me, with strange, purple eyes. It was Medraut, but he wasn't like he is now. He didn't talk and he was only wearing scraps of clothes, without even mittens or shoes. He acted more like a wild animal than a boy and he ran off at the first sight of me."

Would Saexon be turned loose to fend for himself once he was reunited with Doctor Calamestro? The Lord of the Stoats didn't seem to be nearly as feral as Morgan described Medraut, but he remained unbalanced in his own ways. Now that the drugs they had given him had started to wear off, he had become lethargic, barely able to stay awake but determined to do so no matter what.

"My dad didn't believe me at first, so I left some food out for Medraut, hoping to coax him back," Morgan continued. "I almost fell asleep waiting, but when he did eventually return, he just took the food and ran away again. Each night after that, me and my dad would leave food for him and each night he'd come and take it. Eventually, he even stayed long enough to eat it before running away, but he'd never let us get too close to him. After that, he started sleeping in one of the hay lofts. I don't even know if he had really accepted us or not, but I started to think of him a little like a pet; my very own wolf-boy.

"Were you the one who brought him back to his senses?" At least back to as much sense as he had.

"No, it wasn't me," Morgan said distantly. "When the first storm started, a Finttiranos patrol had gotten snowed in at Sarantia. They hadn't been able to get back to their unit, but they still went on patrols as far as they could every day. Our farm wasn't anywhere near the village, but the soldiers found my dad one night when he was going out to leave food for Medraut and they..." Morgan stopped to swallow hard, her eyes still fixed on nothing at all. "My dad had never done anything wrong. He had never supported the resistance. He had never even hurt anyone before in his whole life, but there in the woods that night, they hurt him. Just to be cruel, they tortured him, cutting him with their knives, over and over again. I was right there in the house the whole time and I didn't even know."

As much as Jamie wanted to think that something like this could not have happened, he'd seen enough to know it probably did all the time on this world. "You don't have to keep going," Jamie said. "I understand."

Morgan took a very deep breath and then let it out as a long sigh. "When my dad didn't come back, I went looking for him, but I couldn't find him anywhere. I probably would have frozen to death looking in the dark if Medraut hadn't found me instead. It was the first time I ever heard him speak. He was covered in blood and he told me what had happened: how the soldiers had cut my dad's throat and left his body in the snow to freeze. Medraut had been too late to save him, but he had tracked down those soldiers and he had killed every last one of them."

Jamie looked over at Morgan, still so wrapped up in her memories of the past she probably wasn't even aware of the present at the moment. Questions were starting to swirl in Jamie's mind, but he knew this wasn't the time to ask them.

"Medraut stayed with me on the farm the rest of that winter," Morgan said, her voice still flat. "He helped me tend to the livestock and would go hunting for jackelopes and rallore that he'd cook for me."

"No goplisams?" Jamie said. "I hear they're his specialty."

Morgan grimaced. "Gross! Nobody eats those things. They're disgusting."

Jamie managed a meager smile as he shook his head. Apparently, his opinion of Medraut's intentions when he'd cooked for Jamie and Alaida hadn't been too far off the mark after all.

"When the spring came, a pack of Wolf-Slaves came through the area and he went away with them. He knew there were people coming, villagers who wanted to check in on me and my father since they'd not heard from us in so long. They didn't believe me about Medraut, and they all said that I had been so brave and that I was quite an extraordinary young girl to have survived on my own for all that time. I've seen Medraut a few times since then. I know he's busy, but he always stops in to check on me whenever he's in Heigelries."

Once Morgan finished her story, Jamie sat for a time just listening to the breeze swirling over the tops of the armored plates. Time and again, Terrarhea had no trouble proving that it was just as cruel as his own world. "You are very brave," Jamie said at last. "I lost both my parents not too long ago and I don't think I would have been able to do what you did if I had been in your situation."

Morgan reached over and placed her hand on his forearm. Giving it a squeeze, she smiled. "Things always work out in the end. You just have to be patient and you can't ever give up."

Jamie couldn't help but smile back at her. For such a young girl, she was awfully wise.

In that same moment, a loud, crackling noise filled the air and the entire barque suddenly lurched to the side, throwing everyone who wasn't already holding onto something rolling across the deck. Jamie and Morgan both found themselves thrown against the armor at their backs.

Looking about for the cause of this unexpected chaos, Jamie saw a thick plume of black smoke billowing from the front left side of the barque. Just then, a bright stream of energy tore through the air and slammed into one of the armor plates on the other side of the deck.

The magescript etched into the armor flared brightly but the edge of the metal plate burst apart like shattered ice, spraying the deck with razor-edged shards of burning shrapnel. Cries rang out from multiple people as the deadly projectiles buried themselves in soft flesh.

The barque began pulling madly to the left and the escapees at each of the two wheels spun them frantically in the opposite direction to counter. It only worked to a small degree. The vehicle had just started to climb the side of a tall ridgeline and it now veered off the road and into a shrub-filled ditch. As the deck canted to follow the roll of the terrain, Jamie caught a glimpse back at the road they had just traveled. Far in the distance, he could make out the form of a golden-olive titan-mecha, one with long, multi-jointed limbs and an insect-like head. Just as the barque dropped behind a small grove of trees, the cannons mounted on the titan's shoulders let loose with a full salvo that ripped through the air overhead and sent leaves showering down on them torn from the branches of the trees.

Jamie felt his stomach drop. Not only had they been found, even with their substantial lead and Medraut's distractions, but it was by none other than the notorious man-hunter, Ironsides. A moment later Jamie felt the deck drop out from under him and then quickly rise back up to slam him down once more. The ground rose up a gentle incline beyond the ditch and the barque rebounded off the grassy meadow which covered the sloped side of the ridge.

"We can't keep it up!" someone cried. "We're losing elevation fast!"

"We lost one of the front lifters! Hang on!"

The front left corner of the barque dipped dangerously low and then the whole vehicle shuddered from the impact of the hull with the ground. Refugees were thrown across the deck, scrambling wildly to find anything at all to hold onto. With one hand, Jamie somehow grabbed onto a handle welded to the back of a nearby armored plate while holding Morgan's hand by the other.

The next thing he knew, the barque came to a jagging stop. Clods of soil and grass flew up over the prow and showered down across the passengers who suddenly found themselves thrown toward the front of the craft, rolling and sliding across the deck. Cries of terror mixed with those of pain as bodies rebounded off every solid protrusion along the way.

Jamie picked himself off the now sharply pitched deck, a broken metal handle in his left hand and Morgan still in his right. "Are you okay?" Jamie said, helping her to her feet as she clutched her head. She nodded even as others cried out and groaned all around them.

"We have to get out of here!" Jamie said, standing in the middle of the wreckage. "That was a bounty hunter who just shot us down and he's going to be on top of us in no time at all!"

Tunios picked up one of the many blaster rifles laying scattered across the deck and threw himself against the armored plates. Between the lay of the land and the grove of trees blocking their view, they could see no sign of Ironsides.

"I know where we are," Viellia said as she climbed shakily to her feet with the help of Kranskie. A large gash to his forehead had already painted half his face with blood but he didn't seem to be the least bit stunned. "The Forinagrei Monastery is only about a mile straight ahead. It's been abandoned since before the war, but it's got thick, stone walls. If we can get there, it might give us a chance."

"We'll never make it!" Tunios said. "There's nothing but open ground between here and there! We'll be picked off one-by-one in that grass! If we stay here, at least we have some armor and those mounted cannons!"

"Did you see what his guns did to that armor!" Kranskie said, pointing at the charred remains of the armor plate which Ironsides had hit. "And even if we hadn't lost all power in that crash, our cannons aren't big enough to scratch a titan-mecha!"

Looking at the route ahead, Jamie could see little beyond the crest of a grass-covered ridge besides the tops of a few dark green trees swaying in the breeze. Tunios was right about having a lot of open ground to cover. Unfortunately, as Kranskie had just pointed out, they didn't have many options. Jamie had gone up against titan-mechas unarmed before, even two at a time, but those had been piloted by trigger-happy filing clerks, not a notorious mercenary who even Medraut had tried to avoid.

Saexon stood at the front deck, looking about with purple eyes squinting in the light. Jamie couldn't tell if he was dazed from the crash or this was still a side effect of Doctor Calamestro's drugs. Jamie went over to him and pushed him into motion. After everything they'd been through, Jamie couldn't afford to lose him now. Once moving again, Saexon seemed to regain a little of his energy, but only a little. He hopped down the five foot drop to the ground and began helping others down as well.

As the twins began getting everyone else back on their feet and ushering them off the barque, Tunios remained steadfast at the armor, unwilling to leave and loudly voicing his intent in shrill tones. With the other escapees looking on uncertainly, Kranskie stalked over to Tunios and lifted him with a single hand before tossing him over the edge to join the others.

"Less talking, more running," Kranskie said.

At that, those survivors who had already evacuated the barque now set off at a breathless sprint toward the top of the ridge, some of them helping to carry those who couldn't walk on their own. The twins disembarked simultaneously while Jamie helped Viellia down to Saexon below. As Jamie turned to give Morgan a hand as well, Kranskie retrieved two of the dropped blasters from the deck, checked their power cells, and handed them to Jamie.

"No," Jamie said, holding up his hands. "Killing is what got me into this in the first place."

"It's not just for you," Kranskie said, indicating Morgan with one of the weapons. Biting her lip, she eyed it for a moment before finally taking the large rifle awkwardly in her small hands. Jamie frowned but he wasn't about to stop her. It would be a miracle if any of them made it out of this alive and she didn't have Jamie's abilities to help her cheat fate. He only hoped she wouldn't have need to use the weapon.

"Last chance," Kranskie said.

Jamie simply shook his head and lowered Morgan down to Viellia.

Kranskie shrugged and slung the weapon over his own back, along with a bandoleer of power cells, and then took up another weapon in his hands. He followed Jamie off the barque a moment behind. Tunios lingered as if being pulled back toward the vehicle, his eyes fixed on the tarp which still covered his fallen wife.

"We can't just leave her like this," he said, his eyes full of tears.

Morgan tugged at his arm. "If we don't get out of here, there won't even be anyone left to morn Junliet!"

"Or any of the others!" Viellia said, spinning Tunios around and pushing him into motion. "Let's go!"

CHAPTER 63

Running through the chest-high grasses, Jamie kept stealing glances back over his shoulder. Keeping pace with the others, he felt like he was running in slow motion and thus had plenty of energy left over to spend on something that was probably only going to make him more nervous. So far, there had been no further sign of Ironsides. But with a wispy trail of black smoke still trickling from the downed barque, it shouldn't have been hard for him to find them. He had to be close.

The first of the escapees to set off from the barque had just reached the top of the ridge and were starting to disappear beyond it. Jamie, along with the others in the rear of that running mob, were getting close. Saexon was loping along ahead of Jamie to the left, with Morgan just a short distance behind the Lord of the Wilds. Immediately to Jamie's left, Kranskie barreled along like a freight train, seemingly crashing over the prairie vegetation rather than through it like everyone else. Viellia was far to Jamie's left with the twins and Yunus just ahead of her. Goffry was the farthest along of the rear guard, pulling Tunios along by the sleeve and accepting no rebuke from the schoolteacher. All of them were running as fast as they could, their ragged breath ringing in Jamie's sensitive ears as wheezing and gasping started to replace disciplined breathing.

Jamie took a another look down the hillside. The swaying grasses rolled down the side of the ridge, marred only by the numerous trails the running survivors had cut through them, each one tracing directly back to the barque. When one was running up that incline, it didn't seem nearly as gentle as it looked. The small stand of trees the barque had veered around before crashing blocked much of the view farther on, but as they climbed higher, they were starting to be able to see over the treetops. However, even then, there was nothing there but more prairie flowing all the way down to a stream at the very bottom. Jamie stamped down the thought that maybe, through some great fluke, they had actually escaped from the notorious man-hunter. This wasn't over yet and he knew it.

"Look out!" Saexon cried and pointed into the air. Jamie cast his gaze skyward to see what appeared to be a boulder dropping from above. The sun glinted from its metallic surface right before it crashed to the ground near Goffry and Tunios, missing them both but producing enough of an impact that they stumbled and fell. Even at a distance, Jamie felt the shock ripple under him.

He paused just long enough to look back down the hillside once more. The view looked exactly the same as it had just a moment before except that Ironsides' distinctive titan-mecha had somehow appeared from behind the stand of trees. It couldn't have been more than half a mile behind them. As Jamie started to head for Goffry and Tunios to check on them, the titan-mecha drew back one of its long arms and rotated at the waist before quickly untwisting and letting its arm swing wide. Another boulder shot from the end of its hand, sailing through the air at a lower trajectory than the last. It crashed to the ground about fifty feet behind them and then proceeded to bounce across the grassy field like a stone skipped on a pond, leaving a shallow crater of torn-up earth with each impact.

Kranskie and Jamie both dove out of the way in opposite directions. Pressing themselves down flat, they could feel the boulder skim the tops of the swaying grasses just overhead. With a thud, it came to rest not far away.

"That bastard's toying with us!" Kranskie said, slamming his fist into the ground. Gripping his rifle tight, he shot to his feet and began firing from the hip at the distant titan-mecha, screaming with unleashed anger and frustration.

At a crouch, Jamie sidestepped toward the bearded man, keeping his head below the top of the grasses. "Keep down! You're not gonna do anything to him with that! We've got to keep moving!"

Just as Jamie reached out to pull him down, Kranskie's chest exploded outward in a cloud of red vapor and steam. His eyes opened wide in disbelief as he crashed to his knees, staring at the gaping hole that had just been torn through his body. He remained like that for a brief moment as Jamie stared on, not really certain what had just happened. Then he fell face-first to the ground and remained motionless, the charred hole in his back still smoldering.

More blaster fire lanced across the prairie as the cries of the escapees rang out in panic and shock. Jamie tore his eyes away from the fallen man at his feet. He didn't have time to dwell on that. He couldn't let himself even consider that he might be the next to fall. Something wasn't right here. Kranskie had been shot in the back. The blaster fire crisscrossed overhead in all directions at once. Had they been outflanked? Was this a trap? Out here in the open, they were completely exposed.

Jamie peeked above the grass, quickly scanning the hillside for some sign of whoever it was who'd shot Kranskie. Expecting a distant firing position or a sniper's nest, Jamie couldn't believe his eyes when he saw the source quite near. Right in the spot where the boulder had come to rest there now stood a machine of some kind, roughly in the shape of a man but clearly not. Cast of metal in a shade of weathered brass similar to Ironsides' titan and far too thin to be an armored person, it must have been a drone of some kind.

The moment Jamie's head appeared above the grass, the machine's face, nothing more than a blank mask of angled metal covered in rows of glowing yellow magescript, turned in his direction. Instead of hands, its lower arms were a pair of massive blaster rifles. Based purely on size alone, the destructive power of each one was likely more in line with the guns mounted on the barque than the commandeered rifles the rebels carried. With deliberate and unhurried precision, it now turned those guns on Jamie.

He ducked just as rapid-fire bolts of energy began crashing through the air above his head, each one pounding in his ears like the bass of a drum. The machine tracked his movement, always with the same soulless exactitude, following him down into the grass. Frantically, Jamie rolled to the side, not realizing where he'd ended up until he collided with Kranskie's corpse.

Just as Jamie began considering using the fallen man's body as a shield, the weapon's fire from the machine stopped. Not far away, Jamie could feel the faint clomp of its footsteps through the ground as it turned, apparently having lost interest in him, its focus now shifting to some new target farther uphill, right about where Jamie had last seem Morgan and Saexon.

Jamie tore the spare rifle from Kranskie's back and flipped the selector lever to one of the most powerful settings he remembered Onorah having shown him long ago. Killing people or Wolf-Slaves was one thing, but these machines were something else entirely.

When he rose above the grass this time, the machines' back was to him and its focus was on Saexon and Morgan, running side-by-side away from the thing as fast as they could. Jamie raised the rifle to his shoulder and pulled the paddle-like trigger. He had never used one of them before but up until the disk of projected magescript appeared in the air around the muzzle and the blazing pulse of energy tore into the machine, he had simply been hoping it would work. The machine staggered; the weapons fire it had intended for its targets ripping into the ground at their heels. Morgan looked back, her eyes wide with fright.

"Keep going!" Jamie shouted over his own blaster fire as he continued shooting the machine. Each pull of the trigger sent another bolt home, but the thing just would not fall. He could feel the weapon pulsing in his hand with each shot. The glowing display on the side indicated how many shots remained in the magazine but he didn't need to look, instead feeling the drain of the power cell with that strange sixth sense

Onorah had first introduced him to. Even before he pulled the trigger the last time, he knew the weapon wouldn't fire again.

No longer distracted by Jamie's best attempt to gun it down, the machine straightened itself and swung its own guns back in his direction. He had blackened and deformed some of its armor with his barrage, but the machine's movements did not appear to be the least bit impaired.

Jamie needed a fresh power cell.

Kranskie had had a whole bandoleer of them on his back.

Jamie knelt and reached for one as he simultaneously fumbled with the latch on the weapon's magazine cover. He couldn't do both at the same time and the second was proving to be more difficult all on its own. In the corner of his eye, he could see the machine draw a bead on him. He dropped the weapon and grabbed the one Kranskie had been using when he'd fallen. It only had a few shots left in it, but that hardly mattered since he'd never bring it to bear before the machine opened fire.

Looking down the length of the machine's cannons, Jamie saw the magescript on them flare just as Saexon collided with it from behind, his foot on the back of its head knocking it forward and causing its guns to fire into the ground. One of the shots actually hit the machine in its own foot, blowing the appendage to shrapnel. It fell to a knee but stayed upright, its cannons calmly reacquiring their target. Saexon kicked the machine again, staggering it and throwing off its aim just long enough to give Jamie the opportunity to walk up and stick the barrel of his rifle between two of the armored plates where neck met torso.

He pulled the trigger, emptying the power cell into the machine. The first shot appeared to do little but the second produced a small explosion inside the machine's chest and the third caused all its magescript to go suddenly dark.

"Alright!" Saexon said, throwing a fist into the air. "Now that's how it's done!"

"It's not over -- " Jamie began to say just as a shot from across the prairie ripped into Saexon's side, blasting him right off his feet amidst a cloud of black smoke.

As Jamie saw the young boy fall into the swaying grass, he felt his whole world collapse around him. Morgan was running back down the hill toward the fallen boy, kicking her knees high and screaming something at the top of her lungs. Jamie couldn't hear her. He couldn't hear anything. Without Saexon, he had no way of escaping from Doctor Calamestro or Medraut and his wolves.

Where was Medraut? He and his wolves should have been here helping. Instead they'd left Jamie to take care of all this by himself. He wasn't a solider. He didn't see how any of them could possibly get out of this. So far, his best attempts at survival had barely been enough to keep himself alive. Now his ineptitude was going to get them all killed. How had he even let himself get involved in all this?

Not far away, Yunus had risen out the of the grass, screaming with bloodlust as he charged another of the machines. The rapid fire of his rifle did little damage and was only just enough to keep it off balance enough that it couldn't get a clear shot at him in return. It must have been the one that had gotten Saexon, and from the look of it, Goffry as well. Tunios kneeled on the ground next to the fallen man, fumbling with his rifle as he tried in vain to make it work. Just as Yunus was right on top of the machine, it managed to get off a single shot which struck the rebel in the arm. Yunus's arm fell limp but the man did not stop, throwing the whole weight of his body against the machine. Both of them kept firing their weapons even as they went over into the grass.

A little farther downhill, Viellia and the twins were hunched down, all three back-to-back as they did their best to keep a second pair of those machines off balance with a constant stream of weapons fire. However, they were pinned down and it would only be a matter of time before they ran out of ammo.

This really was hopeless. Even if they could deal with all of these drones, how many more did Ironsides still have to throw at them? Even if they could somehow deal with all of them, the man still had a whole titan-mecha to gun them down with.

"Oh my god!" Morgan cried out, kneeling down next to Saexon. "No!"

How would that young boy be remembered here? As just another casualty of a failed escape attempt, his name and unique origins unknown and ultimately forgotten? All Jamie had needed to do was keep him alive, but he hadn't even been able to manage that. Now it was all over. What reason did he even have to keep fighting?

"M'fine," Saexon bit out, clenching his teeth as he tried and failed to sit up. Jamie felt his chest constrict. He'd thought for sure Saexon had been done in by that hit he'd taken. Apparently, he was even tougher than Jamie had so far seen. "Just give me a second to catch my breath and then I'll help you finish these bastards off."

"No," Jamie said, his focus shifting to the other survivors. He retrieved the bandolier from Kranski's body. This time, forcing himself to remain calm, he replaced the power cells in both rifles smoothly and quickly, and then rose up with one weapon in each hand. "Morgan, get him out of here. I'll deal with these things."

He didn't wait for a reply. He was already in motion, targeting each of the two remaining machines with one of the rifles he carried. He'd been a fool to even consider giving up just because he'd thought Saexon was dead. Viellia, Jorri, Becka, Morgan, and all those who had already made it over the hill still needed him. He'd never wanted to be in this situation, but he was here now, and he wasn't about to let any of these people die just because it wasn't part of the task he'd been given.

Firing on the run, Jamie's aim was better than ever before in his life. Even before he pulled the trigger, he knew exactly where each shot was going to go. It was like the connection between his eyes and his hands knew every angle involved and instantly accounted for every possible variable. The rifles blazed again and again as Jamie continued advancing, veering toward the machine which was farther downhill. Viellia and the twins, amazed at what they were seeing but also aware of Jamie's intent, shifted their fire fully to the other machine just as Jamie launched himself into a particularly long stride directed at the one right in front of him.

He collided with the thing full force, carrying it to the ground as he dropped the rifles and reached for the machine's neck with his bare hands. His fingers found purchase against the edges of the armor, digging into the workings below. The magescript across the machine's face flashed, as if in panic. It didn't last more than a second before Jamie tore the whole head free from the body. As he rose up, he cast it back down with the rest of the machine. Nearby, the three resistance fighters had managed to take down the last one through a concentrated barrage which had left their weapons exhausted.

Directly downhill from them, Ironsides was now in motion, his titan-mecha bounding forward with a long, flowing stride that only increased in speed with each step he took. Jamie replaced the power cells in both of his rifles and then tossed the bandolier and its few remaining cells to the others.

"Get out of here," he said, now focused completely on the charging titan-mecha. "I'll deal with him."

"Are you crazy!" Jorri said.

"That's a bloody titan!" Becka added.

"Go!" Jamie said. This time, Viellia pushed the other two into motion, all three of them setting off once more with all due haste.

Ironsides was now close enough that Jamie could feel the pounding of his feet as he barreled straight toward him. His amplified laughter echoed from the titan-mecha, carrying with it a tinny resonance that did nothing to diminish the lilting character of his words. "Ha, ha, ha, it *is* you! Ah told ya da last time we met Ah was gonna step on ya wit' ma titan if ya ever got in ma way!"

Jamie didn't move from where he stood, instead staring down the giant machine. With long arms swinging in great arcs that could level a house with one swipe, the machine's loping step had carried it to within a single pace of Jamie. It was certainly agile and well-armed, but the swivel cannons mounted on its shoulders weren't tracking anything at the moment. It appeared Ironsides was intent on following through with his threat quite literally.

"Ya really tink them teeny lil' guns is gonna do sheet 'gainst me!" Ironsides voice now boomed, vibrating from every plate of the titan's armor. "Dis is a mecha fight, ya moron!"

"I don't need a titan to deal with you," Jamie said.

He barely felt the toe of his boot push off against the ground, launching himself into a headlong stride. Like a rocket, Jamie cleared a full ten feet with his first step, bringing him well within reach of the machine's long arms. Continuing in the same direction would only result in him being trampled, just as Ironsides had promised, but Jamie's foot only tapped the ground long enough to send him skyward. The forward momentum of the titan now brought the machine right to Jamie. With a thud, he alighted on its shoulder alongside one of the swivel cannons, his legs compressing to absorb the considerable impact.

"Wha' da bleedin' 'ell!"

As much as he heard the words, Jamie also felt Ironsides' voice vibrating up through his boots. The cannon rotated in his direction, but Jamie was too close for it to actually aim at him. He took the opportunity to press the muzzles of both rifles into the flexible joint at the base and pull the triggers.

The cannon must have been better protected than the robotic drones because Jamie's onslaught didn't appear to do much of anything. The way the surrounding magescript flared brightly must have meant it had been hardened with wards to make up for the lack of physical armor. Jamie would have emptied both rifles into the cannon if one of the mecha's hands hadn't been thrust in his direction. With the four needle-thin fingers sticking from the front of the hand, it made the appendage into a multi-headed spear. The pilot was also far more precise with his attack than those Finttiranos soldiers had been. As Jamie jumped backward over the titan's shoulder, the giant machine's hand followed him exactly, missing the cannon by only inches.

Jamie landed on the ground at the base of the massive cargo pod the titan-mecha carried on its back. Up close, he could see a single hatch at the base just about big enough to fit one of those drones through when folded into their boulder-sized configuration. How much longer before Ironsides decided to send them after the rebels while he finished dealing with Jamie?

As the mecha spun to reacquire its foe, the cargo pod swung in Jamie's direction, threatening to swipe him right off his feet. Instead, Jamie quickly passed both rifles to his left hand and drove his right fist into the cargo hatch. Combining his own strength with that of the moving titan, his hand tore right through the seam at the edge, completely mangling both halves of the sliding hatch. Ironsides would have a hard time getting that open again any time soon.

Jamie had to sidestep quickly in order to avoid the rest of the cargo pod as well as the huge, clawed feet of the titan itself. Stopping Ironsides' machine would be no easier than Jamie had first figured, but if he could stay alive long enough to take him apart one piece at a time, he might just have a chance.

Jamie sprang off his rear foot and leapt onto the back of the cargo pod, his free hand grabbing onto one of the ladder-like rungs which ran up the outside of the pod. Even with Ironsides' impeccable control of the titan and its long, multi-jointed arms, he couldn't quite reach Jamie there. Unfortunately, as the titan thrashed back and forth trying to dislodge him, Jamie could do little but hold on tight.

"Yer like a bleedin' tick, you are!" Ironsides' voice rang out. "Well den, dis might just call for a wee lil' change o'..."

Below Jamie, the hatch which he had damaged suddenly made a tortured wrenching sound and something deep inside the cargo pod groaned uncooperatively. Ironsides' answering curse was livid, echoing across the surrounding valleys.

"Fine, ya wanna play games? Let's play!"

Jamie heard an explosion somewhere above him and looked up to see the connection between the titan's upper back and the cargo pod sheer away in a blaze of sparks. The base of the cargo pod dropped to the ground with a crash and the whole thing slowly began to topple over backward. As the prairie grass quickly rushed up toward him, Jamie frantically dove clear.

With the cargo pod crashing down mere feet away, Jamie hit the ground on his shoulder and rolled some distance downhill before finding his footing. Just as he shot back to his feet, one of the mecha's hands slammed into his chest and carried him off the ground. Its thin fingers closed tightly around him, constricting his ribs. Any normal person probably would have been crushed to death.

"Now Ah've got ya, ya annoyin' lil' git!" Ironsides said, his voice cackling with glee. He held Jamie up before the titan's insect-like face and laughed. "Ah knew dere was somethin' odd about you back in Grassnar but Ah didn't tink ya were a bleedin' rebel! Where dey been hidin' you all dis time? Maybe if ya bastards had a few more like you, dis gig might be a bit more fun."

Jamie strained against the titan's metal fingers but he couldn't even make them budge. They might have been powerful, but if he had a little more leverage, he just knew he could have torn them apart with ease.

"So much fer dat. Yer just a bug, an' Ah squash bugs!"

Still holding tight to Jamie, Ironsides swung him through the air and smashed him into the ground. With the entire force of the titan behind that swing, Jamie sank into the ground, leaving a crater behind when Ironsides lifted him overhead in a great arc that ended once again by smashing him down on the other side. Again and again Ironsides whipped Jamie's flailing body down with a tangible sense of ire in his every movement.

Though Jamie remained conscious through it all, he couldn't focus on much of anything. His senses remained clouded by bits of flying dirt and shredded grass during each impact and then by a frantic sense of vertigo and wheeling images of blue skies and green hills as he was carried through the air. Even if he had more awareness of his situation, the titan's hand still gripped him tight. He didn't know how much more punishment Reaver's body could take. As he'd learned while facing off against Medraut in single combat, he wasn't invulnerable. And if he could be injured, he could probably also be killed.

Jamie lost track of how many times he collided with the ground by the time Ironsides finally stopped.

"Now ta deal wit' da rest o' ya," the manhunter said as he drew the titan's arm back as he did when launching his drones. The machine twisted around, unleashing all its power in a single split second. The centrifugal forces pulling at Jamie felt as if they might rip him in half. But then, at the peak of acceleration, Ironsides released him, sending Jamie soaring high overhead.

For a moment, he drifted, weightless, like flying in a dream. With the air rushing past, he could see over the peak of the ridge and down the hillside on each side. The grassy prairie continued across the flat peak of the ridge for some distance. He could also see figures running through that grass. To their right, the prairie rolled away down into a series of valley and hills. To their left, the side of the ridge dropped away more steeply and was covered with tall, spindly evergreen trees and large boulders. Farther on, where the ridge curved off to the west, that same southern slope became a sheer cliff face. Above it, the grasses gave way to a high spot dominated by a full stand of large trees. Jamie thought he might have caught glimpses of thick stone walls mixed in amongst the trees. That must have been the monastery Viellia had mentioned but his view was quickly shrinking as he rapidly fell back to the ground.

He landed just beyond the edge of the peak, tearing into the hard topsoil and leaving a long furrow in his wake as he tumbled end-over-end through the grass. Regaining control of his flailing limbs from the chaotic forces acting on them, he dug his feet into the ground and finally brought himself to stop, kneeling in the loose earth.

He heard a number of curses from not far away. When he rose to his feet, he found Becka and Jorri off to his left, training their rifles on him. Once they saw he wasn't another of Ironsides' drones, however, they stopped dead in their tracks and their mouths both fell open.

"How in the hell did you survive that?" Becka said.

"Keep moving," Jamie said. "This isn't over yet."

Beyond the edge of the hill, Ironsides was just coming into view, the long antennas from the top of his titan swaying back and forth as he sped up the hillside, now even faster and more nimble without the cargo pod on his back. As the twins got underway once more, Jamie looked down at his hands. He'd lost one of the rifles entirely while being rough handled by Ironsides. The other had broken in half and all Jamie still held onto was the grip and part of the stock. He tossed it to the ground. Apparently, he was going to have to do this without guns after all.

CHAPTER 64

Jamie ran at full speed toward the monstrous titan which had gained a considerable amount of speed itself. When the two of them met right at the edge of the ridge, they collided with a thunderous clash. Ironsides had been ready for his foe, thrusting one of those blunted hands at Jamie with the intent of skewering him on the ends of its spiked fingers. Jamie had also been expecting something like this. He also knew that Ironsides was still underestimating him.

Jamie saw the hand coming and he altered his approach ever so slightly, just the faintest twist of his toe as it made contact with the ground. He slid along the length of the speeding hand, feeling the swirl of the air in its passing. Leading with his own fist, Jamie streaked right toward the angled slits along the front of the titan's body. From what he had seen earlier, Ironsides would be right on the other side of them. If he couldn't take down the whole machine, then taking the pilot out of the equation would be the next best thing.

With Jamie's full weight behind the blow and the combined speed of them both moving in opposite directions, the thick armor plating buckled between two of the slits, giving Jamie just enough of a opening to get a grip at the edge with his other hand. Hanging from the front of the still moving titan, Jamie swung his legs around and braced them against the titan's chest as he wrenched at the armor with his hand. It was far tougher than the Finttiranos machine he had done the same to so long ago, but he could feel the metal creaking and the wards that reinforced the bonds between each atom of steel straining to hold them together. The gap that his punch had started now opened to the width of a single hand. Jamie could see Ironsides' eye glaring back at him through that tiny hole, alight with a rage more intense than he ever could have imagined.

"Dat's impossible!" Ironsides words came to Jamie both from his own lips within the machine and from the vibrating of its armored plates.

Again, a swipe from one of the titan's long arms forced Jamie to disengage from his perch. Pushing off with his legs, Jamie launched himself over the top of the speeding arm, twisting his body in midair to land on the ground just ahead of the machine. The instant he landed, he was already in motion once more, throwing himself out of the way of another swipe by the other arm. It seemed impossible that a thing so large could move so quickly. Jamie had to call on every ounce of his reflexes just to avoid each swing Ironsides took at him.

The latest attack was another thrust at Jamie with those needle-like fingers, but this time they extended from the end of the hand, as if on hydraulic rams that tripled their reach in a fraction of a second. Jamie twisted out of the way, barely avoiding them but two of the fingers still sliced through the trailing end of his poncho and put a few new rips in it. Jamie dropped his fist on one of the extended appendages and it quivered as it retracted back into the hand, not nearly as smoothly as the others.

When Jamie jumped back, Ironsides did not pursue him, instead experimentally flexing the fingers of the hand Jamie had just struck.

"Ya really are quite a pain in da arse fer bein' such a scrawny lil' git, ain't ya?"

Before Jamie could reply, a pair of energy blasts streaked over his shoulder and splattered harmlessly off Ironsides' armor. The gun turrets on the mecha's shoulders swiveled at the distant origin of the weapon's fire.

"Hey! Leave them alone!" Jamie cried, waving his arms and placing himself between the mercenary and the twins. "If you want to fight someone, fight me!"

"Oh, Ah'm gonna fight ya, don't ya worry 'bout dat," Ironsides' voice came rattling out of the machine, "but Ah don't want no lowlifes takin' advantage o' da situation! I left dose Finttie pups so far behind dey'll never be able ta catch up, even if dey could follow a trail half as well as Ah can. Ah wanna personally be able ta take ma time wit' da lot o' ya!" Both cannons fired. Jamie stole a glance over his shoulder, catching sight of Jorri and Becka fleeing through the grass just as the energy bolts ripped into the ground almost twenty feet to their right. "Wha' da bloody -- " Ironsides said before his voice cut off abruptly.

The guns now swiveled in Jamie's direction, but he was already dashing perpendicular to what he guessed would be Ironsides' line of fire. He heard the guns open up with a rapid fire barrage, but instead of feeling the heat of the bolts tearing into him, or at the very least passing dangerously close, Jamie heard them impacting far off, harmlessly cratering the landscape. Zigzagging to keep from moving in one direction for too long, Jamie could see the cannons tracking a smooth line in relation to their target, but far off their mark. Maybe Jamie's attack against them hadn't been completely useless after all.

"Fine!" With its guns cutting off, the titan rose to its full imposing height once more and began swaggering in Jamie's direction. "We do dis da ol'-fashioned way!"

This time, Ironsides was even faster on his feet. Jamie saw the titan's gigantic hand slicing in his direction. It was impossible to tell if Ironsides was trying to grab him, skewer him, or simply punch him;

Jamie only knew he barely had time to try and jump clear. Even as he did, thwarting Ironsides' intended attack, the metal arm smashed into his side, sending him airborne once more.

The trajectory was lower this time and Jamie spun slowly through the air as he saw the trees on the southern slope of the ridge rushing toward him. He crashed through their upper branches, trying futilely to grab hold of one as they whipped against him. He never came close enough to be stopped by any of the trunks either, instead falling quite far down the side of the narrow valley before skipping off the ground about halfway down. He rebounded into the air and then crashed down again and continued rolling, ricocheting off trees and boulders alike.

Unable to even see anything he might latch onto until it passed beyond his grasp, Jamie had little choice but to let gravity have its way with him until he reached the bottom. However, he couldn't afford to wait that long. With no one else for Ironsides to focus on, the mercenary would turn his attention back to the rebels once more. Jamie needed to get himself under control and get back up to the top of the ridge.

Before he could formulate a way to do that, he smashed into a man-sized boulder protruding from the side of the slope. It checked his movement just enough to stop him from tumbling. Now only sliding, Jamie splayed out his arms and legs to try once more to arrest his fall.

The slope flattened out a short distance lower and he went skittering across a slab of stone which formed a rather broad ledge that ran parallel to that side of the valley. Pits and grooves within the folded surface had been filled by many years worth of fallen leaves and pine needles, giving root to further vegetation and also presenting numerous hand holds. Jamie finally came to a stop in the middle of that stone slab, more due to his loss of momentum than because of anything he had actually done. However, the ledge where he now found himself was almost all the way at the flat, tree-filled bottom of the valley. The way back to the top looked steep and far. He'd have to hurry to get back into the fight before it was too late.

As he picked himself off the ground with all due haste, he suddenly froze. He wouldn't need to go after Ironsides after all. The mecha was currently barreling down the steep hillside, headed straight toward *him*. Ducking around trees and stepping nimbly around boulders, it looked less like a machine and more like some living creature, a true physical extension of the pilot's own body.

Jamie stared, unable to look away as the mecha launched itself into the air. Seeming to defy all gravity, the gigantic machine drifted overhead, twisting itself in midair so that it would land on its feet. It came crashing down at the head of the stone ledge, alighting atop a small pinnacle of rock that didn't look big enough to support the entire machine, let alone absorb the impact of its landing without breaking. However, the machine's legs and body folded in on themselves, almost completely negating the force of the impact.

If Ironsides was that skilled with his mecha, maybe it hadn't been such a good idea to go up against him after all. Eventually, Jamie might be able to defeat him, damaging one system after another until the entire machine could no longer keep going, but at this rate, he'd end up dead long before he could ever get to that point.

"Ya certainly are a persistent lil' gnat, ain't ya?" Ironsides said, his mecha rising upright, still perfectly balanced on that small outcropping. "Why don't ya just stop movin' 'round so Ah can finish ya off. Ah'd really like ta collect da reward fer you and all'o yer friends before dey close da office tonight."

Without the slightest twitch or shift in stance to betray what was coming, the mecha sprang forward, its long arms whipping huge arcs overhead and tearing jagged furrows through the pine needles covering the ground. Each swipe threw up a billowing cloud of debris that all but hid the entire mecha from view.

Shaking himself from his stupor, Jamie ran for the trees covering the near side of the valley. They probably wouldn't offer much of a deterrent against Ironsides, but they might at least give Jamie something to hide behind. His long strides carried him far with each step but the violent whirlwind thrown up by the mecha was upon him before he even made it to the edge of the stone slab. The sound of howling winds and metal claws scraping on rock surrounded him as he was pelted by flying debris, throwing off his stride and driving him away from any protection the tree-lined slope might have offered.

Just before the full rush of the vortex enveloped him, Jamie caught sight of a wide crack in the exposed bedrock, half-filled with dirt and loam. One of the mecha's whipping claws ripped through the ground right at his heels just as Jamie dove headlong into the crack. Covering his head, he heard the scrape of metal on stone and felt himself buried under a wave of debris.

"Eh, not bad, but you'll 'ave ta do better'n dat ta outsmart dis man-'unter!" Ironsides' voice boomed down from directly overhead.

Jamie looked up to see one of the mecha's claws descending through the still swirling cloud of dust and earth, right toward the crack where Jamie had taken refuge.

He scrabbled to his feet, throwing off the blanket of dirt on his back, and lunged down the length of the fissure. Right behind him, the mecha's talon ripped through the thick layer of dirt in the bottom without slowing. The crack ended abruptly just ahead, its end dropping off into space. Jamie didn't have time to see what lay beyond, he leapt from the end as an explosion of dirt billowed out at his back.

He dropped maybe five feet, maybe thirty, it was difficult to say for sure, but he crashed down with a splash in the thigh-deep stream that cut its way through the very bottom of the valley. The otherwise smooth waters were no more than twenty feet wide but flowed with enough force that Jamie had a hard time staying on his feet after his hasty landing. Ironsides' mecha crashed down alongside him, creating a surge of water and river stones that lifted Jamie off the bottom and carried him farther downstream in a rushing wave. Ironsides' clawed fingers raked across the surface of the wave, missing Jamie by mere inches. That had been far too close. And now that Jamie was at the mercy of the water, he could no longer evade Ironsides' attacks.

As he crashed back down again, water swirling around him, he briefly felt his feet touch bottom and he instantly pushed himself toward the far shore. The turbulent waters wrenched at him, trying to pull him back under, but Jamie wouldn't allow them. Another wave struck him, this one pushed by the mecha as it took a step through the water.

Again, Jamie felt himself washed backwards, his feet slipping away from solid ground as the water rushed around his head and filled his nose and mouth. Riding the wave, sputtering and thrashing his arms, he kicked off against the bottom once more just as the wave from Ironsides next step propelled him even farther beyond the mecha's grasp.

Though the water might have completely knocked Jamie off his feet, it had also slowed the mecha, dragging at its feet with each step. Jamie lost sight of the machine a moment later as the water surged around him and pulled him under once more. This time, his neck struck a large, submerged boulder that raked across his back as he was pulled on by the current. The flow of the water had definitely gotten stronger now, and not just because of Ironsides' thrashing about. There was also a roaring sound, as if rapids lay ahead. If he got caught up in that, he'd be fully at the mercy of the river without any chance of fighting back.

Jamie kicked out against the boulder that he'd just struck. His foot almost slipped off the slick layer of clinging river weeds, but his heel caught on a sharp edge and pushed him toward what he still hoped was the opposite shore. As the latest wave receded, Jamie felt a stony riverbed press against his back. Clawing at the ground, Jamie scuttled out of the water.

Ironsides, however was not far behind. Lunging forward, the mecha thrust its spiked hand forward, overextending itself and nearly loosing its balance in the process. Jamie still had to duck, barely avoiding the claw as it ripped through the trunk of a sizable tree growing right on the edge of the river. It swayed precariously and creaked, but Jamie didn't have time to stick around. Ironsides was still coming, undeterred by a little water or the luck of his prey. Beyond, the river did not turn into a roaring path of whitewater, but instead seemed to vanish completely, leaving nothing but a panoramic vista of the countryside for miles and miles to the south in its place.

Only as Jamie scrambled out of the water, dashing along the edge of the river, did he realize it was a waterfall. With the roar of the water crashing down at the bottom sounding distant and the mists not quite reaching back to the top, it must have been a tall one too.

There would be no going any farther that way and Ironsides would never allow Jamie to go back the way he had just come. The valley sloped up much more steeply on that side of the river, which meant Ironsides would find it easy to knock Jamie back down if he tried to scale it.

The only other place to go was back across the river, hopping from one of the few stones protruding above the surface to the next. One wrong move would likely send Jamie over the waterfall, but if he could manage it, it would force Ironsides to follow him through the water again, preventing his pursuer from using quite so much of the mecha's terrifying speed. Without any other option, or time to think of one, Jamie leapt for one of the rocks about a quarter of the way across the river.

His feet landed squarely on top, but the rock was slick, and the boxy soles of his boots did not conform well to the angular surface. Waving his arms as Ironsides crashed through the water after him, Jamie again threw himself at the next nearest stone. He landed firmly with his left foot, but his right slipped out from under him, forcing him to take a moment to regain his balance before making any attempt for the next stone in the chain.

As Jamie twisted his body to keep from falling, he stole a glance over his shoulder. The current was indeed much stronger here and the water deeper. The mecha was in nearly up to its waist, and though it was defiantly being slowed by the rushing waters, it was still pushing its way through unrelentingly.

"Nowhere ta run now!" Ironsides called out. He dragged one of the mecha's arms through the river and came up with a small boulder that dangled long strands of slick river weeds. He tossed it in Jamie's direction without any of the same force he'd used before; no doubt just toying with him. The rock crashed down alongside Jamie and threw up a huge splash of water which drenched him and nearly unseated him from his already tentative perch. Ironsides' laugh boomed across the waters.

The next rock in the chain Jamie had been jumping between was farther away than the previous two. His footing was also less sure, especially now that he suddenly felt an odd feeling of vertigo wash over him. It took him a brief moment to realize that one of the trees behind Ironsides was listing precariously, causing Jamie to feel like he might be the one falling over instead. Finding his center once more, he could now see that this tree was the same one that Ironsides had nearly cut in two. What little there was left of the trunk could no longer support its own weight. Any moment now and it looked like it might topple over completely.

Holding out his arms to keep his balance, Jamie turned to face Ironsides and said, "You know, you sure talk a lot!" With a lurching motion, the tree swayed and its truck let out a loud crack. "But I'm still here! I thought you were supposed to be some kind of incredible man-hunter!"

"Dat's right; a man-'unter, not pat'etic lil' fleas like you!" Ironsides shot back, taking another step through the stiff current. So focused on Jamie, he didn't notice the tree finally give way until it was already on top of him. The whole mecha turned at the last second, a somewhat clumsy movement in the rushing water, but there was no avoiding the tree.

Its trunk struck the mecha high on the shoulder and threw the machine even more off balance than it already was. As it stumbled toward the waterfall, one of its arms shot for the riverbed to find an anchor, but the action looked like one of desperation. Now hanging right on the edge of the waterfall, the huge machine teetered mere inches away from going over entirely. Even for a pilot as skilled as Ironsides, there would be no easy way to survive a fall like that. Unfortunately, a pilot as skilled as him could yet save himself from going over at all.

"I'm gonna regret this," Jamie muttered, shaking his head as he leapt back toward the first stone he'd used to make his crossing. His foot touched down and then he launched himself forward with all the strength and speed he could summon.

Leading with the soles of his boots, he collided with the side of the mecha's head, producing a reverberating thud. His knees folded and then pushed him away once more. Jamie's weight wasn't much compared to that of the entire titan-mecha, but when propelled at such velocity, it proved to be just enough to break the tentative balance the machine had managed to hold onto.

As the mecha began to topple, its movement stole most of Jamie's own momentum. The rock he had launched himself from was now well out of range. It even looked dubious that he might be able to reach the churning waters where the river crashed over the top of the waterfall. Sailing through the air with nothing but a hundred foot drop and an angry titan-mecha below, Jamie stretched his arms as far as they would go, reaching for anything at all that he might grab hold of. Though the trunk of the fallen tree had snapped, it hadn't completely broken free from the stump quite yet. Maybe if he could reach one of its branches, he might yet be able to save himself from the fall.

As the mecha slowly tipped over the edge of the waterfall, Ironsides let out a profane curse and lashed out with the mecha's long arms. One of them tore into the bedrock behind the lip of the waterfall but the machine's weight was too much for the rock to bear and it immediately came away in a landslide of crumbling boulders and mud. The other hand swung high overhead, and just as Jamie's own hand grasped one of the upper most branches of the fallen tree, the mecha's clamped around his ankle.

One moment Jamie had merely been hoping the branch might be able to hold his weight, and the next, he found himself falling through a shower of rocky debris and water with nothing more than a tattered clump of leaves in his hand. Below, Ironsides' mecha continued to reach for something to arrest its fall but it had already drifted beyond reach of the waterfall. At least it released its grip on Jamie's leg, but not before tossing him even farther away from the edge of the cliff.

Falling, Jamie could see the rolling hills of Heigelries stretching out for miles and miles as the late afternoon sun illuminated the treetops in blazing shades of yellow and orange. He supposed there were worse views one could have in his last moments.

CHAPTER 65

The titan crashed down into a wide pool at the bottom of the waterfall and struck a protruding stand of rocks squarely on the back. The whole machine crumpled from the impact and then one of the boulders torn loose from above crashed into its chest which caused the titan to roll off the rocks and slump beneath the surface.

Jamie landed a second later. Though he hit water, it felt like concrete. His feet parted the surface of the pool and dragged him under as the swirling waves surged around his head and rushed into his mouth and ears. His feet struck the pool's rocky bottom and his knees crumpled as his body crashed down above them.

And then he was briefly weightless as the air bubbles that had filled the water and rendered him blind quickly rushed back to the surface, leaving him on the bottom. He could barely believe he was still alive. He was even pretty sure he was still in one piece. But what of Ironsides?

In a frantic thrashing of limbs, Jamie pulled himself up through the water toward the shimmering sunlight above. He broke through and treaded in place until he could blink the water from his eyes and orientate himself once more. Though the roar of the waterfall was nearly deafening, the flow of the river had already carried him some distance from his initial point of impact. The somewhat flattened pinnacle of rock that had been Ironsides' unfortunate landing spot was not far away. Jamie kicked out and swam closer.

If the landing hadn't already killed the mercenary, he would almost certainly drown if he stayed in his titan-mecha much longer. That might not be a bad thing, but without his war machine, Ironsides was just a man and hardly any threat at all.

The water near the pinnacle of stone was shallow enough that Jamie could see the mecha laying on its back at the bottom of the pool. The front hatch suddenly burst open with a cloud of bubbles and the machine's pilot shot to the surface gasping and kicking wildly.

"Ya bleedin' lil' dodger!" Ironsides cried, his lilt and his anger making the words almost completely unintelligible. Baring his filed teeth, he lifted a short carbine rifle to his shoulder and pointed it at Jamie. Without the use of his arms to steady himself in the water, however, he was only able to squeeze off a single wild shot before sinking back under the surface.

Jamie was on him before he could come back up, wrenching the weapon out of his hand and pulling him up onto the tiny island of rock in the middle of the pool. Even as he sputtered and gasped for breath, Ironsides drew a wide-bladed dagger from a sheath on his back and lunged at Jamie.

Jamie didn't even flinch. After everything he had put up with that day, a single man with a knife hardly even registered as a threat. Jamie batted the knife out of his hand with the carbine, the glowing magesscript on the blade putting a long gouge in the side of the firearm. The knife fell into the water and promptly sank out of sight. Jamie tossed the rifle in after it and then grabbed Ironsides by the front of his long coat, looking him directly in the eyes.

"Are you finished?"

"Ah ain't never gonna be finished wit' you!" Ironsides said, a smile creasing his thin lips. "Ya might tink ya get ta walk away today, but after what ya did ta ma titan, yer a dead man! Ya 'ear me: a dead man!"

Jamie chuckled and shoved Ironsides down to the ground. "So, I am a man now, not just a little flea, huh?"

"Yer dead is what you are!" Ironsides said, lunging to his knees.

"Good luck with that." Planting his feet, Jamie quickly gauged the distance to the western shore of the river and then jumped. He didn't quite make it all the way, crashing down in the knee-deep water and reeds at the edge, but the current was calm there and he stepped out onto the shore.

He ignored the insults Ironsides continued throwing at his back and pushed through the shoulder-high marsh weeds growing in the soggy earth along the edges of the river. The cliff he had just fallen down was indeed steep, and just as high as it had looked from above, but it was also rough and pitted with many ledges and steps which wouldn't have made the climb all that challenging even if he didn't have Reaver's strength and speed.

When he reached the top, pulling himself over the last sharp outcropping of bedrock, he wasn't too surprised to find himself greeted with the muzzle of a Finttiranos blaster rifle pointed in his face. After what he'd just been through, he merely sighed.

"Holy crap! Jamie, it's you!" the person on the other end of the weapon cried, promptly dropping the muzzle. Rolling the rest of the way over the edge on his belly and sitting down on the stony ground, Jamie looked around to see Morgan and both of the rebel twins, all three of them looking at him like they'd just seen a ghost.

"I thought I told you guys to keep going," Jamie said. If he'd been in his real body right then, he probably would have been ready to pass out from exhaustion. As it was, he still felt fine. But if he could just sit for the next five minutes and not have to worry about staying alive the whole time, that would have been very nice as well.

"Morgan was hell-bent on coming to help after we saw that mecha toss you into the trees," Becka said. Standing at a distance, she kept her rifle at her shoulder as she periodically swept her eyes over their surroundings.

"It kinda looks like you don't need any help, though," Jorri said, creeping toward the cliff edge with his weapon also at the ready. "Where *is* the other guy?"

Jamie pointed over his shoulder with his thumb. "Down there. His titan's out of commission. At least for the time being. I don't think we should stick around any longer than we have to, though."

"The others all made it to the monastery," Morgan said. "They should be waiting for us there."

"Good," Jamie said, slowly pulling himself to his feet. They might have been able to deal with Ironsides, but how many more just like him were not far behind. If any of the rebels wanted to make good on this prison break they'd engineered, they couldn't let their guard down for even five minute's rest. "Let's get moving."

The four of them climbed out of the narrow valley, Jamie helping Morgan over some of the steeper portions. The afternoon light angling through the trees made the day seem later than it really was, so that when they broke through to the top of the ridge and set out again across the field of prairie grasses there, it felt like a whole new day. They moved quickly through the grass, keeping their heads down and remaining alert.

As the distant stand of trees which surrounded the pinnacle at the very top of the ridge grew closer, Jamie could see that the rock walls he'd glimpsed earlier hadn't just been a figment of his imagination. Interspersed among the gigantic trees, the walls had been constructed from equally large boulders, some as big as a car, but all of them tooled just enough to fit together like a jigsaw puzzle. Despite the incredible size of the stones, large portions of the wall had been knocked down or were simply gone, as if blown to dust by explosives. When new, the wall must have formed a complete ring at least half a mile or more in diameter. Where it remained intact, its edges were perfectly straight and square, with its outer face marked at even intervals by massive stone pilasters standing proud of the wall.

Passing into the trees, gloom once more overtook them. A well-defined path wound its way between the fallen stones, blackened by countless years of weather and slick with the humidity under the trees. They'd only gone a short way when two figures stepped into their path.

Jorri and Becka both drew back, lifting their rifles halfway, not entirely sure what to think of the two uniformed Wolf-Slaves who also held rifles of their own. Jamie wasn't quite sure what to think himself after the last few times he'd seen these two.

"Enide and Kaius, am I right?" Jamie said. The Wolf-Slaves gazed back at him but said nothing. "I hope this isn't going to be a repeat of the last time you guys ambushed me in the middle of an abandoned ruin."

"Why?" Jorri whispered. "What happened last time?"

"Yeah?" Becka said, the grip on her rifle tightening.

Kaius propped his rifle across his shoulder and nodded farther down the path. "Come on," he said, leading the way.

"Um, okay," Becka said as she and her brother followed, fingers still resting near the triggers of their rifles.

Morgan took a few steps but then turned back, waiting for Jamie. Enide had continued staring at him and he met her gaze, wondering if he would ever truly be free of them. When Jamie finally turned and followed, the Wolf-Slave slung her own rifle and brought up the rear of their little formation.

They marched on in silence, winding their way under giant arched tree roots and over piles of fallen stones. The trees grew so thick inside the walls of the monastery that it was impossible to get a feel for what the place must have looked like when it was still inhabited. The remains of buildings that Jamie could make out had been built using the same construction as the perimeter wall and were just as imposing.

"So..." Jorri said after they'd gone a short distance, "Are you guys really Wolf-Slaves?"

"We've never seen anything like you before," Becka added. "But you must be pretty good in a fight to have made it this far on foot."

Neither Kaius nor Enide said a word.

"I don't suppose you'd be interested in fighting for the resistance?" Jorri offered.

Again, silence.

A little farther on, they broke into a clearing created by a wide slab of flat bedrock that sat right at the edge of the cliff running along the southern face of the ridge. A narrow spire of rock jutted out from the edge of the cliff, no doubt offering spectacular views of the same countryside Jamie had seen from the top of the waterfall; if one was so inclined to make the harrowing walk out to the end. At the opposite edge of the clearing, back amidst the trees, a high step in the stone formed something of a natural stage overlooking the lower portion of the clearing. Most of the rebels were gathered in that natural plaza, sitting on the ground or tending to their wounded.

Almost everyone who'd made it out of the barque was there, even Yunus, though one of his legs, both his arms and half his face had been hastily bandaged. Jamie also saw others he recognized, but their presence did not fill him with the same sense of relief.

More of Medraut's Wolf-Slaves were moving among the rebels, offering them food or first aid supplies. Their master was there as well, just stepping down from a set of stairs carved into the side of the stone stage. Sweat dripped from his hair and he still looked winded. He caught sight of Jamie as his foot touched down and he stopped for a moment, his eyes narrowing, before continuing on his way.

Enide and Kaius, their presence no longer needed, moved off after Medraut. Jorri and Becka excused themselves as well but they remained captivated by the two Wolf-Slaves and kept stealing looks at them as they checked on their fellow rebels.

"Jamie!" Viellia came out of the gathered rebels and clapped him heartily on the shoulders. "I can't believe you're still alive! What you did back there is easily the most incredible thing I've ever seen!"

"He even took care of that mercenary," Morgan said, "pushed him right off the cliff!"

"Not quite. Mostly, it was just luck." It felt strange to be praised rather than attacked for something he'd done. Jamie didn't quite know what to make of it. "How's Saexon?"

"He's up there with some creepy old man," Viellia said, glancing up toward the top of the rock stage.

"Doctor Calamestro's here, too?"

"He wasn't exactly keen on introductions, but whoever he is, he at least put that friend of yours in his place for a little while."

Jamie actually allowed himself a surprised chuckle. Finally, for the first time today, some good news. With Doctor Calamestro, Saexon,

Medraut, and himself all in one place, they wouldn't have to track anyone down to finally bring this insanity to a conclusion.

"So what's next for you?" Jamie said.

"The wolves say they were able to throw the Finttiranos search parties off our trail," Viellia said. She paused and shook her head. "I can't believe I'd ever be indebted to a slave. I'd like to stay here for the night but its way too close to the crashed barque. We'll rest for a while, bury our dead, and then try to push on cross country a little farther before night fall. What about you? Want to come with us? We could use someone with your talents in the resistance."

Jamie shook his head. "I can understand why you guys want to fight for your homeland and I respect that, but Heigelries isn't my home. There, I'd just be another hired mercenary, same as Ironsides."

"Well...actually, you wouldn't even be that," Viellia said with a smile. "We're pretty much broke so you'd just be a volunteer. But I can guarantee that we're a lot more fun than these Wolf-Slaves you're running with.

"I don't doubt it," Jamie said with a chuckle. "But with any luck, I won't have to worry about these guys anymore. Besides, I left someone back near Tolfield that I really have to get back to."

"After what happened in Fort Grassnar, it's going to be dangerous for you back there."

"Yeah, I know, but I can't leave her." Only half-joking, Jamie added, "You wouldn't happen to know what Secotia's extradition laws are like, would you?"

Viellia laughed. "Despite the alliance, Secotia and Finttiranos don't exactly go out of their way to cooperate with each other. I actually know of a few former resistance members who've relocated there and built new lives for themselves. As long as you don't get into any trouble, you should be just fine."

"Thanks," Jamie said, offering his hand.

"No," Viellia said, shaking it. "Thank you. I know we weren't exactly the reason you and that other one went into that prison, but you saved us. We owe you our lives, and I don't mean that lightly. If it weren't for you, none of us would have made it out of there. If you ever do find yourself in Heigelries, drinks are on me."

"I'll hold you to that."

"I've got to go check on my people now, but it's been a pleasure to have fought alongside you."

Jamie was pretty certain he wouldn't have chosen to describe anything they had been through together as a pleasure, but these *were* good people. At the moment, however, there was only one person on that entire planet he wanted to be with.

"Are you really going?" Morgan said.

"I have to." As long as Medraut and Doctor Calamestro held up their end of the bargain, this was Jamie's chance to start a life for himself here on Terrarhea, with Alaida. Allying himself with the rebels would only put him in an even more precarious position than he'd been in before. "Are you going to be okay?"

"I think so. None of us can really go home after having been arrested like that, but the resistance will take care of us. They always do."

Jamie suddenly felt a presence behind him. Somehow, he knew it was Medraut.

"You don't need the resistance for that," he said. "Me and my Wolves will help you get set up somewhere far from here where you'll never have to worry about Finttiranos ever again."

Morgan turned to him, her eyes sad. "Medraut, I'm not leaving Heigelries."

"Are you crazy? After what happened in Grassnar, your face is going to be on wanted posters from here all the way to Kjiram!"

If only he'd had the same concern for Jamie's face ending up on wanted posters.

"But this is my home," Morgan said. "These are my people."

"Still..." Jamie said. As much as he disliked agreeing with Medraut, the tracker did have a point. "It might not be such a bad idea. They *are* fighting a war."

"They're fighting it for people like me," Morgan said. "Should I really just go away with you to Secotia until it's all over and then come back once everyone's died?"

"You'd be safer with the rebels than with me," Jamie said without even a hint of sarcasm. "But would letting Medraut help you really be so bad?"

Medraut looked torn between yelling at Jamie for interrupting or thanking him for trying to help convince Morgan of this action. Regardless of Jamie's and Medraut's feeling about each other, Jamie knew there was no one else who would try as hard as Medraut to keep Morgan safe.

"I know it's dangerous," Morgan said, "but I can't leave. Someday, Heigelries will be free again and I want to be here when that happens."

She spoke with such conviction, Jamie actually believed it might be possible for this battered resistance to one day drive out one of the most powerful nations on the entire planet.

Medraut ground his teeth together as he growled from deep in his throat. "We'll talk about this later," he said to Morgan. Then to Jamie, "The doctor wants to see us."

"The old man?" Morgan said. "Is he your boss? I want to meet him."

"No, you don't," Jamie said, a chill running down his spine at the memory of the previous times he'd spoken to the doctor.

"Yeah, I don't think that's a good idea," Medraut added.

"Well, I want to make sure Saexon's okay." Defiantly, Morgan started up the stairs. "He might not have taken out a whole titan-mecha by himself or run the entire Finttiranos army on a wild goose chase, but he did save me back there when those things were attacking us."

Medraut growled again.

Jamie just shook his head and said to Medraut, "Yeah, thanks for all the help with Ironsides, by the way."

Medraut's lips curled back from his canines. "I just got here! Besides, it looks like you did just fine all on your own. Now let's get this over with. I've already been around you about three days too long as it is." He pushed around Jamie and the two of them made their way up the curving stone stairs behind Morgan, the scuffing of their boots on the damp grit underfoot the only sound to be heard all the way to the top.

CHAPTER 66

The crown of the stone platform really was like a stage overlooking the plaza below, complete with a dense stand of thick trees forming a semicircular backdrop on three sides. Several of Medraut's uniformed Wolf-Slaves stood guard around the edges while the robed form of Doctor Calamestro bent over a tiny body laid out of an alter-like slab of stone toward the center of the rock formation. Morgan strode right on ahead without pause but Jamie had to take a moment at the top of the steps to gather himself before going any farther. This time, he swore he wasn't going to let that man unnerve him the way he had before. Jamie walked up alongside Morgan while Medraut stood off to the side, trying to look indifferent about the whole meeting as he scowled at the ground.

Saexon lay motionless on the stone with eyes closed. His ribs seemed to stand out more sharply though his pale skin than ever before. If it weren't for the slight rise and fall of his chest under the pure white gauze that had been used to bandage his side, he would have looked dead. As Doctor Calamestro examined his patient, Jamie made several attempts to speak but Morgan beat him to it.

"Is he going to be okay?" she said.

"I should think so," Doctor Calamestro said without looking up, "which is rather surprising." He lifted one of Saexon's arms and bent it experimentally at the elbow. Laying it back down gently, he turned and rose up once more, almost causing Jamie to retreat, regardless of any intent he had to the contrary. Even a little of Morgan's unflappable determination slipped from her face. "After receiving word of all the chaos inside Grassnar, I had not expected any of you to make it out alive. Yet here you are, all three of you." Frowning, he took in Morgan with a glance. "And some others besides."

"I...I know it wasn't exactly a clean getaway but, like you said, we did make it," Jamie said, forcing himself to stand his ground. Doctor Calamestro stared down at him, his head canting slightly to the side. Meanwhile, Medraut's attention seemingly remained elsewhere. Jamie cleared his throat. "You didn't say that we needed to do it a certain way. And they still have no idea who Medraut or Saexon are. As far as the military knows, everything that happened there is the resistance's fault."

Doctor Calamestro's head drifted back and forth at the end of his crooked neck in what appeared to be a disapproving shake of the head. "No, I'm not upset. But, as you yourself say, a cleaner exit would have been preferable. However, by involving the resistance as you did, it does help to conceal the true purpose of what you were doing there."

"You're not going to do anything to them, are you?" Jamie said.

It was only now that Medraut looked up with interest, his body tense. Would a monster such as Doctor Calamestro even give a second thought to killing all the survivors, including Morgan, just to keep his existence a secret? Morgan looked on quizzically.

"I have no interest in them whatsoever," Doctor Calamestro said. He then took in Morgan again, a thin smile creeping across his gray lips. "Morgan, is it? I have heard interesting things about you, however. It's a pleasure to meet you."

Jamie shifted his feet slightly so that he could throw himself between the doctor and the girl if necessary. As Doctor Calamestro extended one of his bony hands from within the folds of his robe and offered it to Morgan, Medraut's jaw tightened and he began fidgeting from one foot to the other. Morgan considered the doctor's offered hand for no more than a second or two before she reached out and shook it.

"It's...it's nice to meet you as well." Somehow, Morgan actually managed a smile. "I wouldn't think that anyone would ever be interested in me, though."

"As Medraut and Saexon well know, I'm always on the lookout for new talent," Doctor Calamestro said, releasing her hand, "and you intrigue me."

Medraut suddenly stepped forward. "What? Why?" he said, any reverence he might have had for this man completely forgotten. "Don't you dare think about turning her into a Lord! This life...there's so much bloodshed and death. It's not for her!"

Doctor Calamestro swung his gaze in Medraut's direction. Much to his credit, the Lord of the Wolves did not back down from his master. "Even if I were to extend such an offer, which I have not, the decision to accept or not would be up to Morgan herself. You know I do not force this upon anyone."

"But she's not like us! She's led a peaceful life! She's not even with the resistance, she just got caught up with them when the soldiers started arresting everyone! Tell him, Morgan!"

She looked away, unable to meet his gaze.

"Morgan?" Medraut said, his voice a creaking whisper.

"I...Medraut, I'm sorry, but I am with the resistance. I have been for over a year now. I've been running messages for them and helping them get supplies in Sarantia."

"What? No. No! Why would you do that! I've always kept you safe so that you wouldn't need to."

"Finttiranos killed my father, Medraut! Why shouldn't I do what I can to avenge his death?"

"But...that's not..." Medraut looked to be at the end of his rope, grasping for some argument to use against her. Jamie suspected he knew the root of Medraut's dilemma, but this was a personal matter between the two of them and he wasn't about to get in the middle of it. "You can't go back with them!" Medraut said at last. "I won't allow it!"

Morgan set her jaw firmly as she stared back at Medraut. "I appreciate the things you've done for me all these years, Medraut, but that doesn't give you the right to tell me what I can and can't do. Now I'm going to go help the wounded. If you want to talk more sensibly before you leave, that's where you can find me." As she passed Jamie on her way back to the stairs, she stopped and hugged him. "Don't leave without letting me say goodbye."

"Don't worry. I'll be sure to stop by after I finish up here."

Watching her leave, Doctor Calamestro said, "She has spirit, that one. But seeing as how it appears Saexon will pull through, I have no need of a new Lady of the Wilds at the moment."

"Speaking of Saexon..." Jamie said. "You've got him back now. Does that mean..."

"Yes," Doctor Calamestro said. "The terms of our agreement have been satisfied. You are now a free man. Medraut and his Wolves will no longer trouble you." He paused to lift a single bony finger. "Provided you do not antagonize them ever again."

"That shouldn't be a problem," Jamie said, breathing a deep sigh of relief. From the very beginning of his association with Doctor Calamestro, he'd wanted to believe him when he'd said that he would honor his word, but Jamie had never been completely convinced he actually would in the end. Medraut didn't even seem to have heard half of what the doctor had said, still dwelling on Morgan's exit.

Turning to Saexon, Jamie set his hand on the boy's shoulder. "You did good out there today. Be safe, and whatever you do, try not to turn out like Medraut, okay?" Even though he was pretty sure Saexon couldn't hear him, the young Lord of the Wilds shifted in his sleep and smiled, his lips mumbling some incoherent rambling from the edge of consciousness. "Take it easy, kid."

Returning to the boy's side as well, Doctor Calamestro began adjusting his bandages. His long bony fingers worked delicately yet with great speed and precision. It reminded Jamie of a spider checking on an ensnared fly. "If you will excuse me, I must prepare Saexon for departure. I do not wish to be caught up by any more random Finttiranos patrols."

"Sure." Jamie backed away but then stopped. Now that their business had been concluded, Doctor Calamestro had seemingly lost all interest in him. "Can I ask you something?"

"You still wish to know how I am able to speak your language," the doctor said without looking up from what he was doing. It wasn't a question, but a statement, and he was entirely correct. "But I have already given you my answer."

Which was to say Jamie wouldn't be given any answer at all. But Jamie needed something more. After all he'd put up with for this person, he deserved it. "Do you know anything about a planet called Earth?"

"Again with this trivia," Doctor Calamestro said, shaking his head. "You are a strange one. What is your interest in these antediluvian concepts?"

"If I tell you that, will you tell me where you learned English?"

"You wish to enter into another bargain with me?" The doctor's eyes narrowed as he examined Jamie. Then he smiled. Jamie wanted to back away, but he stood his ground. "Very well. Why are you interested in these things?"

What had Jamie gotten himself into now? Could he really tell this monster something that only Alaida was so far privy to? What kind of new troubles might this single piece of information create for him if it were to get out? Could he even trust Doctor Calamestro to tell him anything at all in return?

"This stays just between the two of us?" Jamie said.

"You have my word," Doctor Calamestro said without any hesitation.

Jamie took a deep breath. In the end, what would it matter? Maybe it was illegal to be from another planet here, but Doctor Calamestro was not exactly one for following the laws himself. "Earth is my home. It's where I'm from."

"And you do not mean this in a purely figurative sense, do you?" Doctor Calamestro's head tipped first one way and then the other as he stared at Jamie with those jaundiced yellow eyes of his. "I find that hard to believe. Yes, very hard to believe. But I see that you do believe it. As to where I learned to speak English, if I were to tell you that it was on a planet called Earth, very long ago, would that answer your question or merely create more?"

"You're saying you've been to Earth? How? Why? Have others been there? Has Lareed?"

"That would require many more bargains, but I am afraid we do not have time for that at the moment, nor do you have anything of value left to trade." With that, Doctor Calamestro returned his attention to Saexon.

Jamie's head was a swirl of questions. If what the doctor was telling him was true, he needed to know more. He took a step forward, ready to demand answers if necessary. Without looking up, the doctor held up a single thin finger. Jamie froze, remembering how easily he had been batted aside the last time he'd been attacked by this creature. "Be satisfied with what you've already gained here. Don't let greed cloud your judgment. There are other avenues for investigation that do not involve me divulging my entire life's story to you. I suggest you seek them out instead."

"But where?"

Doctor Calamestro merely shook his head and dismissed Jamie with a flip of the wrist. The last time Jamie had confronted him, he'd been wounded and had been thrown off balance by the perpetual sense of dread that seemed to follow the doctor like a dark cloud. He might have better luck this time. Maybe the rebels might even be able to help. But the Wolf-Slaves were far better armed at the moment and also in better fighting condition. Medraut would also welcome any chance at all to have another opportunity to take Jamie apart.

Grinding his teeth, Jamie turned and headed for the stairs. Maybe Doctor Calamestro wasn't entirely wrong. He did know things, but even if he were to tell Jamie everything, how much of it would actually be of any relevance to what he really wanted to know? This Lareed person that had been mentioned seemed like a far better source of information more directly pertinent to Jamie's own situation. Once he and Alaida were reunited, they could then start pursuing this new lead with all their energy and maybe finally get some real answers.

"You really are a moron, aren't you?" Medraut said as Jamie walked past.

Since Morgan's departure, the tracker had retreated to the edge of the stone formation in order to brood in silence. Now he looked up at Jamie, his eyes filled with just as much hate as ever. Instead of punching Medraut in the face as he wanted to do, Jamie took a deep breath and held out his hand.

"Are we good?"

Medraut looked at Jamie's hand and merely scoffed. "We'll never be good. But since you did manage to keep Morgan out of harm's way, I suppose I'll honor Doctor Calamestro's agreement. From this moment forward, me and my wolves won't lift a finger against you."

Despite Medraut's pledge, there was something about the way he said it that made the hairs on the back of Jamie's neck stand on end. He considered Medraut's words a moment longer and then finally dropped his hand. "Better than nothing I suppose." He turned to head for the stairs but stopped after taking several steps. "There is one thing, though. You really should tell Morgan the truth about her father."

Medraut retreated a step and glanced down at the open plaza where Morgan was currently helping to treat the wounded. "What are you talking about?"

Until now, Jamie only had suspicions about how Morgan's father had died, but seeing Medraut's reaction to his claim, he knew those suspicions were correct. Jamie turned around and walked back up to Medraut. "Morgan told me about that night when her father died."

"Yeah, he was killed by a Finttiranos patrol!"

"In the dead of winter, in the middle of a blizzard that had kept everyone snowed in for weeks?" Jamie shook his head. "But during all that, for some reason, a lone Finttiranos patrol went out in the dead of night just to cut up some poor farmer in the middle of nowhere who didn't have anything at all to do with the resistance?"

"What are you getting at?"

"You killed him, didn't you?" The grimace that flashed across Medraut's face told Jamie that he had. "And even though the truth is right there in front of Morgan, she doesn't want to believe it."

Snarling in a low whisper, Medraut leaned in close to Jamie. "It wasn't my fault! After Doctor Calamestro made me Lord of the Wolves, I let myself become an animal! That winter I was just as snowed in as everyone else and Morgan and her father were kind to me. I never wanted to hurt either of them but that night when he came out to give me some food, I was asleep and when I woke up, I reacted without thinking! He was dead before I even knew what I was doing. It was an accident. Since that moment, I've done everything I can to try and make up for that mistake by watching out for her."

"And you think the best way to do that is by letting her believe Finttiranos soldiers killed her father?"

"Even if they didn't actually do it, none of them deserve any sympathy!"

"But it's a lie. If you'd told her the truth, would she be in this situation now? Would she have gotten picked up in that raid with the rest of the resistance members? Would she have even joined them in the first place?"

Medraut looked away. "Are you going to tell her?" he said in a small, almost pleading, voice.

"It's not my place. But you should. She's a good kid and she's going to get herself killed if she stays with the resistance. It's only a matter of time. Finttiranos isn't going to be pulling their punches with Heigelries anymore, not after that mess you created in Fort Grassnar."

Medraut's breathing had increased and his shoulders had tensed, as if getting ready to attack. However, he couldn't bring himself to meet Jamie's eyes. In his heart, he must have known Jamie was right.

550

Jamie waved flippantly over his shoulder as he started down the stairs. "I'd say 'see you around' but I hope we never meet again."

Below, Jamie said his goodbyes to the rebels. Most of them were understanding of his decision to leave, but even those that did not agree were merely a little gruff in shaking his hand. Still in shock from the loss of his wife, Tunios rambled on at length with tears in his eyes about the Forinagrei Monastery's history and how it had once been a place for holy people of all faiths to come and discuss their beliefs in spirited yet peaceful debate and that they never would have stockpiled weapons for the Heigelries military as Finttiranos had said when they attacked and destroyed the place in the years leading up to the war. Viellia pulled Tunios away before he could go much further, promising that he would be looked after. She also voiced her continued desire to make Medraut pay for his duplicity during the prison break, but admitted the rebels didn't have the manpower or resources to carry out any such judgment at the moment. Since Medraut had finally helped in the end, she was willing to grant him a temporary reprieve, but certainly not a permanent one. Jorri and Becka, meanwhile, made a final attempt to get Jamie to stay with the resistance. He wished that he could have known those two under different circumstances. They seemed like the sort of people he would have liked having as friends back on Earth.

Morgan hugged him so tightly he thought she might be trying to break his ribs. It was only then that she cried. After everything they'd been through in the prison and during the escape and then being chased by Ironsides, she'd never once shed a tear or let herself be overcome with hopelessness or doubt. Maybe she could yet find a way to survive all this. If anyone could, Jamie believed it would be her.

The departure of Doctor Calamestro and his subordinates came as bittersweet. With them no longer looming over the rebels, it helped to further solidify Doctor Calamestro's word that he would not harm them. However, without them standing guard, the ruins suddenly became much colder and foreboding. Medraut had gone too, without once stopping to speak with Morgan. Jamie had hoped the two of them could have come to an understanding, but as he'd told Medraut, he wasn't going to get involved. He'd already gotten far more involved with matters that didn't concern him than he ever would have liked.

Jamie left as the rebels were starting to pick up what little they had in preparation to move on as well. They might have been safe for the moment, but just knowing the Finttiranos military was out in force made everyone a little anxious to get moving again. They nodded to Jamie as he passed them, smiling and wishing him good luck or their thanks. The sentries they'd posted at the entrance to the woods even stood up straight and raised their hands in salute. Jamie merely replied with a wave before setting out at a jog across the grassy top of the ridge. The sun had nearly dropped below the horizon. It was a beautiful sunset, but Jamie barely spared it a glance. Soon, everything would be dark, and he still had a long way to go in order to get back to the Burke Farm.

Jamie tried to tell himself the odd sense of unease he felt was just the anticipation of being reunited with Alaida and his expectations for what lay ahead for them. Somehow, he knew exactly which way he needed to go in order to get back to her, so he wasn't concerned about that. There would be Finttiranos patrols that he'd undoubtedly have to avoid, but he knew even those wouldn't pose much threat to a single traveler with his abilities moving on foot.

No, this was something else. Up until recently, most of his time on Terrarhea had been spent by himself, or just with Alaida. Even when he had been around others, he'd seldom felt like he belonged. Now he simply found it strange to be alone again.

He moved as fast as he could, but the way the terrain had been folded back on itself, time and time again, sometimes made it difficult for even Jamie to follow a straight line. The roads that they had used to make their getaway might have offered a more manageable, if less direct, route, but that same path would be the one where Finttiranos trackers would eventually concentrate their searches. Wide rivers couldn't be forded without careful planning and it took time finding routes into and out of all the steep valleys he came across.

It was nearly midnight when he saw the first signs of the military. They weren't exactly going out of their way to remain inconspicuous either. Jamie saw the lights several miles off and quietly approached until he could get a better feel for what they were doing. As much as he wanted to avoid them completely, he didn't want to walk right through a patrol if he could help it either.

From across a narrow valley, Jamie could see an armored military barque, just like the ones the rebels had used to make their escape, parked at the top of a bald hilltop. Tarps and netting had been strung up over and around it to create a make-shift encampment, while floating gloworbs had been tethered around the perimeter. The three or so armored guards he saw patrolling along the edge of the light did so mechanically and without any real enthusiasm. From the very center of the barque rose a short pylon of some kind. Maybe it was a relay point for their communications. Onorah had once mentioned that whatever method they used only worked over line-of-sight for relatively short distances. They had probably set up many of these stations throughout the whole area. If they were all this conspicuous, they would be easy to avoid. The soldiers performing the actual searching, however, would probably be keeping a much lower profile.

As if to confirm Jamie's suspicion, a pair of mechas emerged from the darkness and stepped into the light of the distant camp. Jamie couldn't get a clear look at them, but they definitely weren't the titan-mechas he was familiar with. Their lines were somewhat similar, but they were sleeker and closer in size to a vulcan-mecha. Perhaps these where the artemis-mechas he'd heard mention of.

Jamie was too far away to hear anything said between the guards and the pilots when they disembarked from their machines and headed into the tents. Whatever words were exchanged, it seemed clear that this search wasn't going to be called off anytime soon. With this much effort still being exerted, he wondered if more rebels than just the group he'd helped had made it out of Grassnar. He'd have to be even more careful going forward so as to avoid whatever waited for him out there.

However, as he crouched behind a bush on that neighboring hilltop, his head suddenly filled with a feeling that crashed into his skull and seemed to set his ears ringing. He shook his head, trying to dispel it. He tried to tell himself it wasn't what he thought it was but there was no denying that the nagging sensation that had always marked his time on Terrarhea had returned with a vengeance.

It was far louder than ever before and ticking along at a ferocious rate. This time, it wouldn't be easily pushed aside or ignored. In fact, when he tried to drive it away like he had the last time, it merely came roaring back even louder than before, threatening to intrude into his conscious thoughts.

He thought he'd been done with all this. He'd been ready to give up on Earth and call Terrarhea his home. Now it felt as if he might not even have enough time left to make it back to Alaida before the end. Springing to his feet, he dashed off into the night.

CHAPTER 67

The eastern sky was just begging to show the first hints of light when Jamie saw the steep driveway leading up to the Burke's Farm. It had been almost exactly a day since he'd left this place -- so much longer than it should have taken to get back here.

The patrols had become more and more frequent the closer he got to Fort Grassnar, requiring him to make wide detours or simply hunker down until they moved on. No matter what he did, however, that incessant niggling was always there, monopolizing his thoughts like a whisper in his ear reminding him that he didn't have time to waste. Somehow, he kept his wits about him and didn't just go storming straight through. He'd been careful, even altering his course far to the east when it became clear there was simply too much of a military presence south of the fort.

When he'd crossed one of the roads he remembered from his journey into the area with Doctor Calamestro, it had filled him with a new sense of urgency. He was close, and he'd made it with time to spare, but he still had a fair amount of ground to cover. There was also nothing but farms and roads and houses between him and Alaida. Much like the previous morning, there hadn't been enough people out to notice him, but a single person running more quickly than the fastest barque would certainly draw more attention than a Custom titan-mecha cruising along in the pre-dawn light.

He tried walking for a while but soon found himself jogging. It wasn't long after that he was running. He told himself that if he simply kept his pace at something close to a normal person's, he wouldn't draw any undo notice. But just knowing that he could go faster made him want to, and before he even knew it, he was tearing down those deserted farm roads as fast as he could. Periodically, he'd catch himself and force himself back down to a trot, but it never took long for his pace to pick up once more.

In the end, the only close call he'd had was when he'd rounded a corner at top speed and nearly ran headlong into a noxard-pulled cart heading the other way. Jamie sidestepped around it and was gone in an instant, but he'd heard the bleating of the animal and the cry of its master as he struggled to get it back under control. Neither had likely seen enough to know what had caused the fright, but it did help convince Jamie to maintain a less conspicuous pace from that point onward.

Jamie ran up the Burke's driveway but jogged to a stop as he crossed the farmyard. He could tell right away that something wasn't right.

The door to the house hung open halfway and there weren't any lights on inside.

He hurried to the door and called inside, "Alaida?"

The neatly hung coats he'd seen earlier were scattered across the floor and several chairs in the dining room had been overturned. Something was definitely very wrong. From around the corner of the house, a heavy wooden post fell with a thud.

"Alaida!" he said, setting off at a run.

Just as Jamie reached the corner, Emma stepped into view, her eyes wide and frantic. Len held tight to one of her shoulders, a bloody bandage tied around his head and a glassy look in his eyes. In her hands, Emma carried an old rifle which she pointed right at Jamie's face.

"Now you get back you -- !" Seeing it was Jamie, she dropped the weapon from her shoulder with a heaving sigh of relief. "Oh, Jamie, it's you! I'm so sorry!"

"What happened here?" Jamie cast his eyes around the farmyard. "Where's Alaida?"

"He took her," Emma said, tears in her eyes as she shook her head. "I'm so sorry Jamie. We tried to stop him, but they have her."

Jamie shook his head. He suddenly felt frozen and empty inside. What was Emma even talking about? Of course Alaida was here. He'd left her here so she would be safe. How could anyone have taken her? He must have misunderstood Emma's frantic babbling. "What do you mean?" Jamie finally managed. "Who took her? Where?"

Len shook his head somberly. "It was that Enlightened Path twat, Casper Jansion."

"What? No. No!" This couldn't be happening, not now of all times. He wanted to rip someone apart with his bare hands. Len and Emma had sworn they'd look out for Alaida, but apparently they hadn't tried very hard. "The Enlightened Path? How would they even know she was here!"

"I don't know," Emma said. "We hadn't talked to anyone all day. Alaida stayed inside most of the time. She was such a pleasure to have around the house. But then, early this morning, he showed up."

"We told him to get lost, that we didn't have any Raven-Slaves, but he knew she was here," Len said. "Somehow he knew. He even knew her name. When I tried to send him packing, he hit me in the head with one of those little billyclubs they like so much."

"It nearly cracked Len's skull open and then he tore the house apart," Emma said. "By the time I was able to get the gun, he'd already taken her. I would have gone after him, but Len was unconscious, and I couldn't leave him."

"I'm fine," Len said, leaning heavily on Emma's shoulder. "We have to get her back before it's too late."

"You're not going anywhere but the hospital," Emma said. "You have a concussion."

Jamie shook his head. This didn't make any sense. How could anyone have possibly known Alaida was here? How could they have even known her name? They hadn't talked to anyone in town and he believed Len and Emma when they said they'd kept Alaida's presence on the farm unobtrusive. Jamie hadn't even crossed paths with anyone from the Enlightened Path except for that guy Medraut had attacked at Fort Grassnar.

Jamie's eyes grew wide and his jaw tightened as realization suddenly dawned on him. He'd never understood why that man had left so peaceably after getting rough-handled by Medraut. Now it suddenly made sense.

"Medraut!"

"Jamie, what is it?" Emma said.

"What did this guy look like?" Jamie said. "Tall and skinny, long greasy black hair, walked with a slouch, a bunch of Raven and Wolf tattoos on his neck?"

Len nodded. "Yeah, that's Casper alright."

Jamie turned and screamed into the night, his howl echoing through the dawn's light. Medraut had told this Casper person where Alaida was. Jamie had thought his wording when they'd parted ways at the monastery about not lifting a finger "from this moment on" had been a little odd. He'd also told Jamie that there were other ways to hurt him without violating Doctor Calamestro's order, and apparently, he had found one. Truce or no, Jamie was going to hunt Medraut down and kill him. But first, he had to find Alaida and get her away from those people.

"You said you were going after her?" Jamie said. "Is she...? Is there a chance she's...?"

"They usually hold their twisted little lodge meetings at night so people won't see what they get up to," Len said. "Casper only came a few hours ago and he was alone so there's still a good chance he'll wait until tomorrow night to get all the others together."

Jamie clenched his fists and cursed under his breath. If he'd been just a little quicker in getting back, he could have stopped all this from happening. Damn Medraut for making such a mess of their rescue operation in Fort Grassnar. Damn the rebels for letting them convince Jamie to help them. Damn Ironsides for coming after them like he had. And damn Jamie most of all for having set this whole chain of events in motion in the first place. The only solace he had was that it had taken that cowardly Enlightened Path scum a full day to work up the courage to come for Alaida.

"Yes, you have to be right," Jamie said, already heading for the barn. "Alaida still has to be okay." He couldn't let himself even stop to consider any other option. "I'll get my titan!"

Even with the urgency of the situation and the nagging in his head taunting him with its relentless countdown, Jamie maintained enough sense to roll back the barn doors and carefully pilot the titan outside without smashing the whole building down. He needed something to vent his frustrations on but that would have to wait until he got his hands on this Casper Jansion person. He easily lifted Emma and Len into the passenger compartment and then set off at a run toward Tolfield. On his way back to the farm, he'd considered a number of routes he and Alaida might take when they left this place, but he'd never once thought about heading back toward Fort Grassnar.

At Emma and Len's instruction, Jamie veered further north of the city as they approached. Against the lightening sky, a thin trail of smoke could still be seen rising from the northern sector of Fort Grassnar.

"There was quite a bit of excitement down in the fort yesterday," Len said, his voice still sounding tired, "but then I assume you know a bit more about that than we do."

Without turning around, Jamie clenched his jaw. The last thing he wanted now was small talk, especially if it might lead these people to change their minds about him. If they hadn't heard any details about what had happened, they probably didn't yet know how many had died either. "That was mostly Medraut," Jamie said, his voice tight.

"I can tell you right now that I don't miss that one even a little bit," Len said. "I knew he was trouble the first time I saw him. Most of the doctor's purple-eyed kids are. But you, I can't quite figure out. I do know that Alaida's lucky to have you, though."

"She was so worried about you," Emma said, "but she said she knew you'd be okay. She's a brave girl."

Jamie swallowed down the quivering in his chest. So far, the only way he'd held himself together was by channeling his rage. He couldn't let himself fall to pieces now. He felt a hand on his shoulder.

"She'll be okay," Emma said.

Jamie nodded, unable to speak without knowing if he might break down into sobs.

In contrast to the eastern parts of Tolfield, the buildings in the northern portion seemed more permanent and not quite so antiquated, many of them possessing what could even have been described as an almost municipal character. The streets also transitioned more quickly from dirt to cobblestones. Though things didn't seem quite as busy, that might have had more to do with the sense of brooding that filled the streets. Everywhere Jamie looked, he could see a town guardsmen or two, armed with stun-spears and wearing their distinctive green jackets and steel helmets. Completely absent, however, were any of the once omnipresent soldiers.

"The whole fort must be on alert," Len said. "Everyone's at their posts. The Enlightened Path lodge is just a little farther that way." He pointed down one of the city streets that ran parallel to the hill upon which Fort Grassnar was built.

"The hospital is just another block this way," Emma said, indicating the street they currently traveled and which led deeper into town. "We can drop off Len and then I can show you the way to the lodge."

Len stood but had to grab the side of the roll cage to keep from falling. "No. Emma, you stay here. I'll go with Jamie."

"No, you won't!" Emma quickly grabbed his arm. "You need a physician right now!"

"I'm fine," Len said, though Emma was able to pull him back with ease.

"No, she's right," Jamie said, bringing the titan to a stop and raising one of its hands alongside the passenger compartment. "But neither of you are coming any farther. Both of you have already suffered enough because of me. Just tell me how to get there. Emma, you get Len to the hospital, okay?"

"I...okay," she said, helping Len over the side and into the titan's hand. More than once, Len threw off her protective hands and voiced his disapproval of this plan, but at least he didn't resist.

"The Enlightened Path have a place on Lowden Street, just outside of town," he said.

Jamie looked up at one of the street signs hanging from the nearest intersection, but he couldn't read the words any more than he could anything else on this world. "I don't know where..."

"Head west on this street and it will be the third intersection you come to after this one," Emma said, pointing as she climbed into the titan's hand after her husband. "Then take a right."

"There's a little grove of trees, just past the edge of town," Len added, slumping somewhat more heavily against Emma. "They have an old grain bin out there they use as their lodge. It's a big, eight-sided building with a domed top. You can't miss it."

"How do you know where it is?" Jamie said.

Emma shook her head. "Everyone knows."

"And they all know what they do there too," Len said. "But no one ever does anything about it."

And now this whole town's silent compliance with genocide might have cost Jamie his best friend, a woman who meant more to him than anyone else. And he'd never even had a chance to tell her just how much.

As the two elderly farmers stepped down from the titan's hand at the edge of the busy street, several pedestrians who had been watching the strange titan now rushed over when they saw who its passengers were. At least one of them knew the couple and all of them offered to help get Len the rest of the way to the hospital.

"You be careful!" Emma called up to Jamie. "I'm sorry about what we let happen to Alaida. I'm sorry we couldn't do more."

"It's not your fault," Jamie said, "and you've already done more than enough. Just make sure Len is okay."

"I'm fine!" Len called back. "Now you go get Alaida."

Jamie nodded as he brought the titan around and set off down the street.

CHAPTER 68

Jamie wanted to hurry through the busy streets, but he didn't want to miss his turn either. Alaida would be fine until this evening and Jamie still had plenty of time to find her before he was dragged back to Earth. He didn't need to rush this and mess things up even worse. He counted off the first three intersections and then set off to the right, his pace restrained yet urgent.

Fortunately, he wasn't left wondering for very long if he'd taken the correct turn or not. The city quickly tapered away and the street became nothing more than a seldom-used dirt road that made its way around a small stand of trees no more than a block beyond the last house on the street. Tucked in within those trees stood a building which aligned exactly with Len's description of the lodge.

With eight walls and a domed top, it did look something like a squat grain bin. However, the whole thing was made of concrete and its hulking form was only amplified by the thick ribs of concrete that wrapped the structure in vertical bands at each corner, from base all the way to the apex of the dome. Some time after its initial use had come to an end, glass windows had apparently been punched into the thick walls at various levels, suggesting at least three spacious stories inside. A well-walked path through the grass led around to a door in the side of the building.

Jamie stopped his titan short and parked it alongside the road in a weed-choked field sitting fallow on the opposite side of the road. As much as he wanted to rip that whole place down with the titan-mecha's hands, he first had to get Alaida out.

He jumped out of the seat, jogged across the road, and made his way along the path, all the time careful to keep his footfalls as silent as possible. He didn't know what kind of security they might have in there or how vigilantly they might be keeping watch for intruders. He reached the door without any alarms being raised and when he placed his hand on the handle, it turned without effort. Either they were just that cocky or the city's silent acceptance of their activities had made them complacence.

The door opened into a large foyer with a high ceiling. A set of stairs rose up to the left while two doors stood directly ahead and to the right. The scale and shape of the rooms looked grand, but everything was made of bare concrete and unfinished wood, as if the previous owners had been in the process of turning it into a palace but had abandoned the project halfway. Now there were random coats hanging from a mismatched assortment of hooks and nails around the perimeter. A dusty rack held several equally dusty umbrellas and one highly polished walking stick with a brass head. Meanwhile, several pairs of boots laying on the floor and two shovels propped in the corner were covered with fresh mud.

Jamie heard voices drifting down from upstairs and footsteps on the wooden floorboards. He stood just inside the doorway for a moment, listening to the masculine voices, but he couldn't quite make out any of what was being said. A loud guffaw of laughter seemed to indicate that they weren't yet aware of him. Maybe he could just sneak in and get Alaida out of here without even having to face any of these people.

With a floor of cracked concrete, there seemed to be little chance of a basement. Jamie started his search by checking each of the doors opening off the foyer. One was a short hallway that led to a bathroom, which was in dire need of cleaning, and a darkened kitchen with another set of stairs going up. Behind the other door was a dank room of domed concrete that sat empty except for a bit of straw scattered across the floor and several steel shackles hanging from the walls.

They must have been holding Alaida upstairs. If that laughter he could still hear was being directed at her, they would be in even greater danger than they already were. With a tensing of his fists, Jamie actually started hoping the men upstairs would discover his presence in their lair.

The stairs followed the outer curve of the building as they took Jamie to the second floor. There, a wide hallway continued around the perimeter while a grand doorway on Jamie's right opened into a huge room that dominated that entire floor. A gallery of columns encircled the room and supported a wide balcony above, leaving the center of the larger room open all the way to the underside of the dome. Between the windows and skylights, the roaring fireplace, and the hanging gloworbs, the room was warmly lit and sheltered few shadows.

A long trestle table in the center of the room held a mismatched collection of candleholders, stacks of unused serving platters, and what looked like several random boxes of junk. Elsewhere, an assortment of upholstered chairs had been arranged around the fireplace. Tattered tapestries hung from the balcony above, creating semi-private niches around the perimeter. Off to one side, a large sideboard stocked with all manner of bottles seemed to be the center of activity for the five current occupants, each one with a drink in hand and laughing heartily.

Most were of a similar ilk to Casper Jansion, dirty and crude and dressed like day laborers who didn't take any pride at all in their appearance. Four of them also wore prominent tattoos of feathers and claws and fangs. The fifth was an older man dressed in nicer clothes and sipping from a small glass of cut crystal instead of gulping down shots like the rest.

Jamie watched them through the open doorway for several moments. He could see no sign of either Casper or Alaida, but if any one of those five had simply turned around, they would have seen Jamie. He continued on before any of them did, however.

The hallway ended with another set of stairs going up and the top of the flight that went back down to the kitchen below. Jamie went up to the balcony above. Open crates and broken furniture had been stacked haphazardly around the edges and all of it was covered in a thick layer of dust and grime, just like the long-abandoned junk hidden away in someone's attic. Again, he saw no trace of Alaida.

As he stood there, listening to the men below laughing while feeling the tension between this world and his own growing ever stronger and more insistent, he found he could barely think. Alaida had to be here somewhere but he'd already searched the entire place. Where else could she be? With these people's overconfidence for the things they obviously did here, secret rooms or chambers seemed unlikely. Did they have her bound in the woods somewhere where the authorities couldn't connect them to any crimes if she was discovered before this evening when they returned for her?

Or had they already...

No. She was still okay. She had to be.

"How long do you suppose Grassnar's gonna stay locked down?" one of the men said. He was a stocky man with a full beard who didn't sound quite as dim as the others. "That could make things harder for us with all the extra security."

"It all depends on what the commotion is about," the old man said. "But it could work to our advantage. I remember back during the war, the soldiers were so busy with the enemy, my father went out just about every night and culled a slave or two. Never once came close to getting caught and every time it just got blamed on the Heigelriesians."

"Those must have been the days," the other man said.

"Aye." The old man nodded and sipped wistfully at his drink.

Jamie's hands clenched around the railing at the edge of the balcony.

"Did you see the way she was looking at me?" one of the other men said with a bellow of laughter. He was a thin man with a beard that looked more like the result of several weeks not shaving rather than any intentional attempt at style.

The man he was talking to, who Jamie only now realized was actually a woman, laughed and said in a voice more gruff than some of the men, "I'm surprised you could see anything at all with the way she nearly scratched your eyes out."

"Oh, but she was into me, I know it! If we hadn't had to cut things short last night, I coulda' made my move."

"I'm sure Casper would have enjoyed watching that," the fourth man said.

"Where the hell is that bastard anyway?" the woman said. "I thought he said he was gonna meet us back here."

Jamie vaulted over the railing and crashed down on top of the trestle table before he even realized he was in motion. "Where is she!" he cried as he stepped off the table and strode toward the gathering at the edge of the room.

"What the -- ?" was the expression uttered by all.

"Hey, this is private property!" the fourth man got out right before Jamie punched him in the gut and sent him crumpling to the floor.

The woman came at Jamie with a small, magescript encrusted rod of brass and wood which she wielded overhead like a bludgeon. Jamie caught her by the raised forearm and twisted, inciting a cry of pain as she dropped her weapon. Jamie caught it in his other hand. He could feel that it was charged and ready to fire. He pressed the end against her sternum, and she flew backwards as if hit by a car.

"Where is she!" Jamie demanded again as he bore down on the man with the scraggly beard.

He took a swing at Jamie and Jamie intercepted his fist with the wardcaster. The cells had almost been depleted from that first strike, so it now merely threw the man's arm back. From the way he howled in pain, he'd likely broken a few fingers. Jamie tossed the now useless weapon aside and grabbed the man by the throat, lifting him off the ground.

""Where's Alaida!" Jamie said. "What did you do to her!"

"Who?" the man choked out.

"The girl you were just laughing about!"

"That was Susan, the barmaid down at the Crawler, you stupid twit!"

Jamie's brow furrowed as he tried to cast his muddled thoughts back over what these men had just been talking about. Maybe it was possible they hadn't been talking about Alaida after all. It was hard to stay focused with that dogged nagging sensation intensifying by the minute. The man didn't appear to be lying. But if he didn't know what Jamie was talking about, where was she?

"Where's Casper Jansion!" Jamie tried again.

"We don't sell out our own!" the stocky, bearded man said as he came at Jamie from behind and drove a knife into his back. Without any wards to empower it, the blade cut through Jamie's tough leathers but skipped off his skin. With a flip of the wrist, Jamie tossed aside the man he held and sent him crashing into the bottles arrayed across the top of the sideboard.

Eyes wide and knife still in hand, the other man backed away. Jamie lashed out, grabbing him by the wrist and twisted his arm backward. He felt a bone snap and the man instantly dropped to his knees, screaming in pain. It had been so easy; Jamie hadn't even tried. Nor did he care. These people deserved far worse than just a few broken bones.

"Where's Casper?" Jamie said, still holding tight to the man's wrist and pressing the fractured arm a little farther out of alignment.

"I don't know!" the man said, frantically trying to twist himself so as to lessen the pressure on his arm.

Jamie pushed a little harder. He could feel the bone splintering.

"I swear!" the man cried. "We haven't seen him since we left the bar last night at midnight curfew!"

He sounded sincere. But Casper had gone to the Burke Farm several hours after that. If he hadn't brought Alaida back to his confidants, what would he have done with her?

"Hey, you guys see the sweet titan parked across the street?" a slow, lazy voice said from the hallway. "Don't tell me Craine's back in town with some Ravens for us to play with. Sure sounds like one hell of a party going on up here..."

Jamie and the bearded man both turned their gazes to the hallway. Into the doorway stepped a tall man with greasy black hair and tattoos on his neck. Slouched, with hands in his pockets, he stood for a moment looking around the room at his fallen comrades and the broken bottles. His breathing increased, and after staring at Jamie a moment longer, he nearly fell over himself scrambling back into the hall.

Jamie released his current prisoner and was on Casper before the man even made it three steps. Grabbing him by the shoulder, Jamie yanked him back into the room and threw him to the floor. He slid on his side until he collided with one of the wooden columns supporting the gallery above. Clutching his ribs, he squirmed on the floor as Jamie stalked over and seized him by the throat, lifting him off the ground and slamming his back against the post. He thought he might have heard something crack but he couldn't be sure it was the man's bones or the post. He didn't really care either.

"Where's Alaida?" Jamie said. "What did you do to her?"

"Who?" Casper sputtered, clutching at Jamie's wrist.

Jamie tightened his grip. "The Raven-Slave you took from the Burke farm last night. Where is she?"

"The Burkes?" the man kneeling on the ground with a broken wrist said. "They ain't got no Raven-Slaves."

Casper choked out some incoherent string of words that were no doubt meant to be speech. Jamie eased off just enough so he could breath.

"Man's right!" Casper said though a fit of choking. "Never been to the Burke's! Ain't got no Ravens!"

"You remember who I am, don't you?" Jamie said, leaning in close to the man's face. "We crossed paths in Grassnar. My friend told you about Alaida and where to find her. You attacked the Burkes last night and took her. I know it was you so I'm only gonna ask you one more time: what did you do with her?"

"I didn't take no filthy Raven -- !" Casper got no further because Jamie threw him across the room. The man soared through the air for a few brief moments and then crashed down atop the heavy trestle table. Casper landed hard, a candle holder jabbing him painfully in the stomach. The table legs shuddered and groaned but did not break. The other men cringed to the edges of the room as Jamie walked over to the table and grabbed Casper by the back of the neck. Wrenching him off the tabletop, Jamie drew back his fist.

The first blow sent a fountain of blood gushing from Casper's nose. The second crushed his nose flat.

Before Jamie could deliver the next, Casper barked out through the blood running into this mouth, "I sold her!"

"You what?" the bearded man with the broken wrist said. The energy of the room had suddenly changed. The men who had been cowering now bristled with anger, but not at Jamie, at Casper.

"I took her to Boravian!"

"You *sold* her, to the slave farm?" the big, bearded man said as he picked himself off the floor.

Jamie held his fist. He didn't know whether to be giddy with relief or outraged all over again. If Alaida had been sold to the slave farm, she was still alive. Unfortunately, from what she had told him about such places, it wouldn't be much better than death.

"There's a man I know there," Casper said, now tripping over his words in order to explain. "He pays me five sorin a head, cash, under the table!"

"You've done this before?" the man Jamie had thrown into the sideboard said as he got up, soaked with spilled alcohol and bits of broken glass sticking out of his face.

"It's easy money!" Casper said. "Good money! Better than any of us can make doing anything else around this town! "

"You know that goes against our creed," the woman said, sitting with her back to one of the columns, her breathing ragged.

"Who cares if we kill them or sell them back to the market?" Casper said. "It still takes those filthy creatures off the streets."

"That merely propagates the whole unholy cycle!" the old man said, nearly screaming with righteous indignation as he stepped away from the hiding place he'd taken up during Jamie's attack. "We cull them so as to eventually eradicate their kind from the face of Terrarhea for all time, not just so they are removed from your delicate sensibilities today!"

As much as Jamie would have liked to see Casper torn apart by his own friends, he didn't have time for that. Alaida didn't have time. He needed to get to her before Reaver returned or she might get left behind entirely. Jamie pulled Casper's attention back with a twisting of the man's neck.

"What man did you sell her to?" Jamie said. "How do I find him?"

"He won't just give her back to you," Casper said. "Buying stolen Slaves is against the law. That's why he pays me in cash!"

"Do you really think I'm just going to ask him?"

"He's an Executive Director! Do you really think he's going to be intimidated by some foreign drifter hopped up on Devil's Root? If he admits to buying stolen slaves, he can kiss his career goodbye! Your precious little Raven is gone and there's nothing you can do about it!"

Jamie drew back his fist yet again but stopped just short of unleashing it when the bearded man spoke.

"An Executive Director?" he said, taking another step closer. "Falco."

The man with the glass sticking out of his face shook his head and he too came nearer. "That's why you're always so chummy with that flesh merchant."

"Okay, yes. It's Falco," Casper said, his eyes wide as they darted back and forth between his friends and Jamie. "I was talking with him down at the Minaret right before I came here. He'd just ordered breakfast, so he'll be there for a while yet. If you really want to see how far you can get with him, go right ahead!"

"I've seen that grubber down there myself," the bearded man said. He had now come close enough that he was looming over both Jamie and Casper but his stony expression took in only the other man. "He always has breakfast there, every morning about this time."

"It's about a block outside the main gates to the market," the man with the glass in his face said, also glaring at Casper. "A big two-story building with a little tower on the front corner."

"Why don't you go talk with Falco?" the bearded man said, addressing Jamie but focused on Casper.

The other man flexed the fingers of his unbroken hand and formed a fist. "We can take care of this for you."

As much as Jamie wanted to deal with all of them himself, he couldn't. The niggling in his mind had grown stronger, pounding like a bass drum at a speed-metal concert. If he didn't hurry, he wasn't going to get anywhere near Alaida before his time ran out.

Jamie took one final look at Casper, gagging and squirming in his grip, and then released the man, letting him fall gasping to the tabletop. As Jamie headed for the exit, Casper cried after him, "Wait! He knows me! I can help you talk to him!"

Casper's next words were drowned out by the sound of a fist colliding with flesh. Jamie didn't look back.

CHAPTER 69

The look of the buildings changed the closer Jamie got to the slave farm. The streets became wider and none of them were paved. The buildings were spaced farther apart, and all seemed to be made from heavy timber and stucco. The walls of the farm were likewise constructed from timbers, a single palisade wall of logs driven into the ground all around the perimeter of the entire sprawling complex. The gate sat at the end of the main thoroughfare, a blocky structure of looming timbers with a titan-mecha-sized gate running through the middle.

The Minaret proved to be just as conspicuous. It looked like a tavern or a restaurant, the yellow color of its timbers suggesting that it was newer than most of the other buildings surrounding it. The spindly tower at the corner did look something like a minaret, complete with an elongated onion-shaped dome on top, but it looked more like an architectural flourish than something actually functional.

The smells of cooking wafted out into the street and must have been the main draw for the many people going inside. The massive, two-story façade fronted tight to the street with only a western style hitching post and water trough separating the two. Several creatures that looked like a strange cross between a horse and a deer were tied up there but a number of vulcan-mechas and even two titans had been parked in the wide open spaces on either side of the building. Jamie found a spot near the street and disembarked from his own mecha as soon as the seat restraints unlatched.

He stalked past the hitched mounts, up the three steps to the small front porch, and through the large double doors. The inside was mostly dominated by a single large room that stepped down several levels to a huge, u-shaped bar that reached out from one of the side walls into the center of the room. Above, a balcony with additional seating wrapped around the other three walls. The whole place was filled with tables and chairs, most of which were in turn filled with early morning diners who had apparently come from all walks. There were farmers, woodsmen, townsfolk, businessmen, and also a fair number who all wore some kind of light blue uniform Jamie had never seen before. Though somewhat similar to the ones worn by the military, their jackets were shorter and had been styled to look less authoritarian and more business-orientated. Like the streets, there were no soldiers to be seen, but also absent were any of the town guard.

Standing at the head of the highest terrace, Jamie called out to the entire room, "Where's Executive Director Falco!"

An uneasy silence instantly fell over the room and all eyes turned on Jamie. Some of the diners chuckled amongst themselves, others began glancing about for the nearest exit, while others merely looked on curiously. No one, however, spoke up.

"Executive Director Falco!" Jamie tried again, taking a farther step into the room. Those Enlightened Path people had better not have lied to him.

A burley man stepped out from behind the bar and met Jamie in the middle of the room. "Hey, now that's enough of that. People are trying to enjoy a meal here. Why don't you just head back outside."

When the man went to put a hand on Jamie with the intent of pushing him toward the exit, Jamie swatted the hand away, grabbed the man by the back of the neck, and slammed his head through the top of a nearby table. The table cracked in two, scattering the occupants' meal and sending the people sitting nearby scrambling for cover. Jamie didn't have time for niceties. The room now became utterly quiet except for the screeching of chairs being pushed back as a few of the men and women in the blue uniforms rose to their feet. Unarmed as they were, however, they didn't look like much of a threat.

"Falco!" Jamie said. "Where is he!"

The silence lingered as Jamie swept his gaze across the room. If no one gave up this Falco person, he didn't know what else he could do. Would he have to start interrogating everyone who looked the least bit official?

Just as he was about to start shouting again, Jamie saw a man wearing one of those blue uniforms rise from his table and motion Jamie over with a flip of two fingers. Jamie glanced around the room but no one else seemed the least bit interested in doing anything more. Keeping a watchful gaze, Jamie crossed the room to the man who had signaled him.

He was a tall man, with a thin face and pale skin. His anxious expression told Jamie that someone like him probably didn't have the nerve to take part in the illicit buying and selling of slaves. There was another man, however, in the same uniform, still sitting at the table, meticulously wiping his lips on a napkin. His dark hair had been neatly combed and oiled and the thin moustache on his upper lip seemed almost artificial in its perfect symmetry. Without even looking up from his meal as he took a drink, he motioned for Jamie to have a seat across from him.

Jamie eyed the standing man who clutched a sheaf of papers to his chest. Slowly, Jamie, lowered himself into the chair facing the other man.

"Falco?"

"Yes, now what's this about?" the man said. He sounded bored. His blue eyes remained cold and devoid of any emotion. "I don't usually make a habit of conversing with drunken troublemakers, but to spare all these people any further stress, I'm willing to humor you for a few moments."

"You bought a stolen Raven-Slave from Casper Jansion last night," Jamie said. "I want her back."

"Casper Jansion?" Falco said. Slowly and deliberately, he set down his glass. "I don't believe we have any registered brokers by that name on file."

Jamie slammed both his palms down on the tabletop and leaned forward. The tall man still standing next to the table flinched backward and nearly stumbled. "You know he's not a broker. He's with the Enlightened Path. At least he was. Now that they found out what he was up to, I don't think things are going to turn out too well for him. Do you want to see how long you last if your superiors find out about this?"

Staring dispassionately at Jamie, Falco's mouth twitched in thought. Finally, he said, "Davide, give us a moment."

It took the tall man a moment before he replied. "Um, Sir?"

"Now," Falco said.

Brow furrowing as he looked from the Director to Jamie, the other man frowned and scurried away to the edge of the bar. Many of the other patrons in the room were keeping a close eye on the conversation but most wouldn't be able to hear what the two of them said.

Interlocking his fingers above the table, Falco leaned forward a few inches. "Now, just for the sake of argument, let us assume that someone such as myself were in the business of illegally buying slaves from unregistered sellers. Any slave obtained in such a manner would have to be processed into the general population of the farm as contraband in order to avoid raising any suspicion. Once a slave has been designated as such, it can not simply be changed back."

Jamie dug his fingers into the edges of the wooden tabletop. The last thing he wanted right now was to debate the situation with this lowlife. However, if he could talk Alaida out of this mess he'd gotten her into, it had to be better than going in guns blazing. "Tell them you made a mistake; that she was just being transferred and got mislabeled."

"I'm afraid that's not possible. I'm in charge of outside acquisitions, not transfers. Even if a transfer were somehow mislabeled, it would never end up in my department."

"Then just go in and get her out," Jamie said. "You've already broken the law to put her in there, what's once more?"

Falco shook his head. "It's easy to add an extra head here or there to the inventory. Once they're on our roles, though, it's impossible to get them off without following the proper procedures."

Jamie took a very deep breath. "Then what's the proper procedure to get her out?"

"There isn't one. Once an outside acquisition has been processed, they'll be cycled into the breeding stock with the rest of the contraband and wilders. Those are not for sale to anyone. They can't even leave their home farm without very explicit transfer orders, and then only to another farm."

"I don't care about your orders and your rules! You're going to go in there and you're going to get her back!"

Falco sat back, shaking his head and shrugging as if unable to get through to a sullen child. "Perhaps I could talk to someone and get you a discount on a new Raven-Slave for all your troubles."

Jamie swept his arm across the table, spilling the plates and cups to the floor and causing a collective gasp to rise up from the rest of the room. Standing and leaning over the table, he said, "You're not listening! One way or another, you're going to make this happen!"

"No, you're not listening. What you're asking is impossible."

"I'm not asking," Jamie said, grabbing Falco by the back of his coat and pulling him out of his chair. "Now, come on, we're going to figure this out."

"Are you crazy!" Falco cried, flailing about and trying unsuccessfully to break Jamie's grip. "Just what do you expect to happen here? Do you really think that if you just march in there with me as a hostage, they'll give you whatever you want?"

"Actually, I hadn't really thought that far ahead," Jamie said, pulling the man across the room. Still struggling, Falco rebounded off tables and customers as he passed. Twitching, Davide sprang to his feet and followed at a safe distance, trying several times but unable to work up the courage, or even a plan, to free his boss. "Maybe I'll just break the front gate down with your head and find her myself."

By this point, the other witnesses in the room could no longer stand by without doing anything. Several of the diners, nothing more than common citizens, stepped into Jamie's path, offering words to discourage him from his chosen course, but he pushed right past them without slowing. Others, wearing the same blue uniform as Falco and Davide, rallied themselves to the defense of their comrade and now came at Jamie, some of them armed with short batons that crackled with the same white electrical arcs as the stun-spears used by the guardsmen. Jamie only let go of Falco when his attackers finally got close enough to take a swing at him.

Jamie didn't think about any of what he did next, he simply reacted, swatting aside their clubs, turning them against their own users, or simply rendering them unconscious with a sharp blow from his own fist. Before Falco had even had a chance to scuttle to safety, eight Slavery Affairs Agents lay senseless on the floor.

A young woman with distinctly Asian features and wearing the black leather garments of a traveler, looked on from one of the nearby tables as if torn between hiding under her chair or making use of the gun that hung from her hip. Jamie pushed the last agent still standing through the empty chair on the opposite side of the table from her and met her terrified gaze. She jumped as he slammed his hands down on the tabletop.

"Don't even think about it," Jamie told her. "I'm just here for this guy. The rest of you don't need to get involved." With that, he once more grabbed Falco by the collar and dragged him to the exit.

CHAPTER 70

Jamie pushed Falco on ahead of him as they approached the gates to the slave farm. He would have preferred the security offered by his titan-mecha but the logistics of bringing it that short distance with an unwilling prisoner in tow were just too complicated. It also would have taken too much time. He could already feel that the nagging sensation was stretched thin and ragged. It felt more fragile than ever before. This time, he knew he wouldn't be able to fight back against it and win. There was also no reason to think that the people who'd seen what he'd done at the tavern hadn't already alerted the authorities. If he didn't act right now, he'd lose whatever tenuous head start he currently had.

They passed other Slavery Affairs Agents on the street who eyed Jamie and Falco strangely. A few nodded. Had word already reached them? Or was it just the fact that their suits weren't rumpled like Falco's? Most of them probably knew the man, and from the way he'd looked before Jamie got his hands on him, this was probably quite out of character.

"Straighten yourself up," Jamie said to Falco in a low voice as he cast his gaze across the other SAA personnel arriving at the main gate for work that morning. All of them were wearing caps which matched their uniforms and most carried briefcases as well. In this crowd, Falco stood out almost as badly as Jamie.

To get to the gates, he and Falco had to enter into the covered tunnel that cut through the center of the gatehouse. If this structure had been made of concrete instead of wood, it would have looked quite similar in concept to the one Jamie, Kranskie, and Lirman had raided less than a day ago. Jamie pushed aside the thought that both of those men were now dead. Just how much further could he press his own luck before it ran out as well? The big doors were sealed tight at the moment but a smaller pair of man doors in the bottom of each door stood open wide. The agents gathered themselves into two neat lines in order to pass through, presenting their ID's to the agent standing guard at each one.

"Don't try anything smart or I'll break your neck," Jamie whispered as they approached the doorway. Under other circumstances, it would have been an empty threat, but this time, he wasn't so sure. "And you know I'm capable."

"And how exactly do you expect this to play out?" Falco said over his shoulder as he did his best to finish smoothing out his uniform.

"Tell them I'm an old friend. Tell them you want to give me a tour. Tell him whatever you want. I don't care. Just get us through that gate."

"Good Morning, Executive Director," the agent said as Falco stepped up to the doorway. Falco offered no ID and the agent didn't ask for one either.

"'Morning, Brock," he replied, his voice quavering only slightly as he stepped through the doorway.

When Jamie followed him, the agent stepped forward and held up his hand. "ID, sir?"

"Oh, don't worry, he's with me," Falco said. "I'll vouch for him."

"Sir?"

"He's...an old friend," Falco said, barely stumbling over the lie. "I'm going to give him a tour of the market."

"I still need to see an ID."

Jamie eyed Falco with a narrowed gaze. The Executive Director swallowed hard. "Brock! Just let him through," he said, his words rising in pitch. He then put on a hasty smile and attempted a laugh. "It's fine. I said I'd vouch for him."

"Sir, I don't think..."

"Now, Agent Brock," Falco said. Though his voice cracked a little, it still carried enough authority to make the other agent step back and let Jamie through. "Thank you," Falco said as they continued on their way. Jamie tried his best not to notice all the strange looks they were getting from everyone who'd just seen that. Still, it could have gone worse.

The tunnel continued for quite some distance inside the gates, looking almost like a domed hanger with the far end hanging open. Built into the walls on either side were several doors, nearly as big as the main gate. One of them hung open a few feet, giving Jamie a glimpse of the titan-mecha parked inside. It looked like the Mk-4s he had seen in Tavnic, only this one had been painted the same shade of light blue as the SAA uniforms. From what Alaida had told him, a slave would never think about revolt so those machines must have been there for use in fending off attacks from outside forces: kind of like himself.

"Now where?"

"Contraband is taken to the holding facility to be in-processed," Falco said.

"Then let's go." Jamie nudged Falco on. He hated to be walking so slowly. The persistent buzz invading his mind told him he should be running as fast as he could.

Beyond the gatehouse, there was a wide street that ran perfectly straight between a twin row of tall, wooden buildings with tiled roofs and surrounded by precisely arranged yards. Small, ornamental trees which had been trimmed like bonsais were scattered about the buildings in artistic arrangements. It would have looked flawlessly serine, like some old Japanese painting, if not for the handful of pale-skinned women with long black hair and yellow eyes, carefully trimming the grass on hand and knee with hand sheers. The SAA personnel walking about on business of their own passed the Raven-Slaves by without even sparing them a glance.

"This way," Falco said, leading Jamie northward, away from the administrative buildings.

They climbed a set of exterior stairs which brought them to an elevated walkway. This circled around the back of the gatehouse and looked like it would eventually link up with the battlements at the top of the farm's main wall. For as busy as things had been at the gate, this place looked absolutely deserted. It also gave Jamie a better view of the farm as a whole.

Its perimeter wall extended from Tolfield's western edge all the way to the base of the foothills spilling down from the northern mountains. Lush green grass covered the gently rolling land inside these walls and neat wooden fences divided the interior into straight geometric zones, each one with its own little cluster of buildings. Most appeared to be tidy rows of low barracks, but others were larger, multistory affairs.

Wherever Jamie looked, he saw Raven-Slaves of every age, from mere babies all the way to the elderly. They were all female and all of them were dressed in their typical gray and black garb as they went about their duties. In one grassy field he saw a group of adults performing calisthenics. On a neighboring path, a throng of laughing girls was being led along by an older Raven. Elsewhere, he saw what looked like an outdoor class with the young students sitting on long benches. It must have been its own little city down there, complete with hospitals, cafeterias, and training facilities so that young Raven-Slaves would be ready to perform all the duties expected of them when they were inevitably purchased by some new owner.

Just north of the gate building, one section of the interior had been separated from the others with chain link and barbed wire instead of wooden fences. The six buildings within were also bigger and more ominous, built from stark concrete with few windows or doors to be seen. These long, thin structures ran parallel to the farm's main wall, and at three stories high, stood just as tall. A grid of elevated walkways hung above the spaces between them and sheets of metal mesh had been strung from the top of each building to the next, completely sealing that entire sector off from above as well as the sides. If the rest of the farm looked like a military base, this section looked like a prison.

"Is that where she is?" Jamie said as the walkway they followed took them closer to that miserable-looking place. "Is she in there somewhere?"

Falco looked back over his shoulder. "Yes," is all he said.

"Why?" Jamie said, shaking his head.

"Why? What do you mean? It's standard procedure. All outside acquisitions are held in quarantine for three weeks at a minimum before being cycled into the general population."

"No, I mean, why...all of this?" Jamie motioned to the farm as a whole. It would have been hard enough to put all this depravity into words without the pressure building in his head distracting him as well. "Why do you treat them like this? Why do you keep them as slaves in the first place? Why put yourself out on a limb just to buy Alaida from the Enlightened Path when you already have all of them?"

"Economics," Falco said, his voice tight. "The equation isn't difficult. Since natural distributions still hold true for the slave races, half of all Rave-Slaves born are male, which have no economic value. That instantly cuts our potential supply in half. Next, slaves are most valuable in their prime, which is also the same span of years they are cable of bearing offspring. Since breeding can only be conducted at slave farms, it means we are always in short supply of mothers."

Falco stopped to unlock a chain link gate which allowed access out onto the elevated walkways that ran between the holding buildings. Once it was open, Jamie pushed him through and followed close on his heels.

"The rules concerning contraband are kept intentionally strict in order to ensure that we always have fresh stock coming back into the farms," Falco continued. "And when it comes to conducting deals under the table, everyone is willing to turn a blind eye if it helps keep things running a little more smoothly."

"So, all this is just a business to you?" If Jamie didn't need this man to show him the way to Alaida, he would have tossed him over the side of the walkway into the steel mesh below. "Don't their lives mean anything to you?"

"Of course, they do," Falco replied flatly. "Dead slaves aren't worth anything."

"You're not really saying anything to help your case."

Falco stopped to unlock another gate, this one leading out onto one of the building's flat roofs. As he did, he turned to Jamie and opened his mouth as if to speak, but then closed it again. He led Jamie down a short ship's-ladder and then across the gravel-covered roof. "I use the upper level of this building to hold special acquisitions…that is to say…I mean…" he paused, considered Jamie's stony expression, and then said simply, "She's in here."

A small penthouse sat at each end of the long building, each with a single door in the side. Falco unlocked the nearest one and descended ahead of Jamie down a dark flight of stairs. At the bottom, a small vestibule contained a shelf that held several handheld gloworbs, a stun baton like the one used by the guards at the tavern, and a large keyring. Falco took one of the gloworbs and the keys and then threw open the inner door.

In the darkness beyond, Jamie could make out a long corridor with barred cells on either side. It must have run half the length of the entire long building. Only two equally spaced gloworbs hanging from the ceiling provided any illumination. One was dim, barely any brighter than the light from a single match and the other flickered sporadically, never staying fully lit for more than a second at a time. The air smelt damp and humid but not all together unclean. Over the harsh tread of Falco's boots echoing off the concrete walls, Jamie's ears could just barely make out the sound of bare feet on hard floors and a rustling of fabric.

"Alaida!" Jamie called out, rushing past Falco and running down the center of the corridor. Save for a single floor drain in the back of each cell, all those he passed were empty, swept clean and scrubbed down to the bare concrete walls and floors. Jamie went to a rustling of movement from one of the cells near the flickering gloworb. "Alaida!"

A looming shape of pale white rose out of the shadows in the back of the cell and threw itself against the bars. Jamie stumbled backward, colliding with the bars on the other side of the corridor. Inside the cell, a pair of gold-on-gold eyes glared back at him from beneath a head of shoulder-length, black hair.

Though Jamie had never seen a male Raven-Slave before, the prisoner's pale skin and the bluish cast to his matted hair suggested he could be nothing else. Wearing only a pair of black leather pants, he stood tall and thin with the tight muscles of a dancer and a face that was eerily handsome in the same way the females of his kind were beautiful. As he leaned against the bars of his cell, he glared at Jamie as if he might try to rip out his throat if he got too close.

"Jamie?" a quiet voice came from the cell to his right.

"Alaida!" Jamie ran to the door of the cell and grabbed hold of the hand grasping the bars from inside. He knew it was her even before he saw her standing on the other side. It seemed like they'd been apart for so long, but Jamie had to remind himself it had only been a little over a day. Though her hair was a little frazzled and her dress more worn, she looked almost exactly as she had the last time he'd seen her. That is, except for the strange mark that now crisscrossed the skin around her right eye.

It stood out darkly black against her otherwise pale skin and looked something like a backwards "C" that passed vertically through the center of her eye while a second stroke extended horizontally in much in the same fashion.

"So this is your Jamie, eh, Alaida?" the male Raven-Slave said, his voice taunting. "And he really did come for you, just like you said." Neither Alaida nor Jamie heard much of what he said though.

"My god, Alaida, are you okay?" Jamie said. When he touched the mark on her face, she winced back. He could feel that it hadn't just been painted on her skin but had actually been etched into it like an old scar. "What did they do to you?"

"It's a brand," Alaida said. "I'll be fine. It just stings a little right now."

"A brand!" Jamie turned on Falco with murder in his eyes. "What the hell did you do to her?"

However, the Executive Director was no longer there. At the end of the hallway, the door Jamie had just entered through rang out with a clang as someone slammed it shut from the outside.

"That brand marks her as contraband," the male Raven-Slave said. "Now that she's been blemished, I suppose you're regretting all the trouble you obviously went through to get to her."

"I don't care about that!" Jamie whirled on the man. "I care because they hurt her!"

"I'm sure," the Raven-Slave said, casting his eyes toward the ceiling. "That honor alone goes to you, her master, correct?"

"Corbin, stop it!" Alaida called from her cell. "I told you Jamie isn't like that!"

Jamie barely even knew this Corbin person and he already didn't like him. Maybe it was the way Alaida seemed friendly with him, or just the way his supermodel looks weren't disfigured the way Alaida had been. "If you're locked up in here too, where the hell is your brand!" Jamie said.

Corbin threw out his hands and looked down at his body. "I was born with my brand."

"You know what? I don't care," Jamie said. He was letting himself get distracted. It felt like he only had minutes left on this world. "Alaida, we have to get out of here."

"Good luck with that," Corbin said. "Looks like you let yourself get locked in with the rest of us.

Ignoring Corbin's taunts, Jamie took hold of Alaida's cell door and pulled, tearing the metal hinges in half and twisting the lock until it sprang loose. He tossed it aside and it crashed down on the concrete floor with an echoing clank. "Reaver's coming back."

Alaida's eyes flashed open wide in the flickering light. "Reaver? But I thought he was gone for good."

"I thought so too," Jamie said. At least that's what he'd hoped. "But it came back, stronger than ever. I don't think I can fight it this time. Come on, we don't have much time."

Taking Alaida's hand, Jamie started for the door that led back up to the roof but Alaida pulled herself free and went to Corbin's cell. "Jamie, you have to let Corbin out too."

"Alaida, we can't rescue everyone!" Something about the way Alaida sounded so eager to set him free made Jamie want to leave him locked up right there in his cell.

"I know, but Corbin doesn't belong here!"

"None of you belong here! But we don't have any time!"

"But he needs your help!"

"I don't want help from any Human," Corbin said, even as Jamie wrenched his cell open. With a tip of the head he added, "But then maybe you aren't exactly Human, are you?"

"Anyone else?" Jamie threw up his hands and shook his head. After a quick glance around the rest of the cell block, it looked like Alaida and Corbin were the only ones being held here. "Can we go now?"

"Yes!" Alaida said as she set off after Jamie. "Thank you."

"Don't thank him yet," Corbin said, a single step behind Alaida. "We're still locked in and the alarm has probably been raised by now."

Jamie shook his head to try and keep the nagging from intruding any farther into his consciousness. "If you want to go back to your cell, feel free!"

Reaching the door at the end of the corridor, Jamie unleashed his frustrations on it instead of Corbin. His first kick buckled the metal door. His second caused the hinges to groan. On his third, the latch snapped open with a loud ping and the door crashed back, rebounding off the wall behind it. Falco hadn't bothered to close the outer door to the vestibule or the one at the top of the stairs either. As Jamie burst through onto the roof of the prison and back into the bright light of day, he heard a chorus of cries rise up in the distance.

Chapter 71

On the same catwalk that Jamie and Falco had come in on, at least ten SAA agents armed with stun spears, batons, or handguns were all hurrying in Jamie's direction. The moment they saw him, several took aim and fired. Jamie ducked around behind the penthouse, pulling Alaida with him. Corbin joined them only a second later. Already, some of the SAA agents were moving along the other catwalks in order to outflank them.

"Wonderful escape," Corbin said. "Now how do you plan to get past them?"

Jamie gauged the distance between this building and the next. It would be about as far as he'd ever jumped before. Carrying Alaida, he didn't know if he'd be able to make it. To bring Corbin as well, it would almost surely prove disastrous.

"I'm pretty sure I can get Alaida out of here but..."

"Don't worry about me, I don't want any more help from you anyway," Corbin said. He then held out his hand to Alaida. "But if you really want to be free, Alaida, come with me. I can get us both out of here. You just have to trust me."

"And what about Jamie?"

"He's a Human, he doesn't matter. Forget about him."

"We cannot leave him!"

"The only one you have to worry about is yourself. Now, last chance. Are you coming with me or not?"

Alaida shook her head. "No, I am not leaving Jamie."

Corbin blew out his breath. "I'm disappointed, Alaida. I really thought you were better than this." With a final shake of the head, he turned and broke from cover, running across the length of the rooftop in the opposite direction from the approaching agents.

Jamie had no idea how Corbin planned to get out, and he didn't really care either, but he did have the right idea. They had to get moving right now. Lifting Alaida into his arms, Jamie planted his feet and set off across the short distance between him and the edge of the roof, accelerating like a speeding car. Alaida's arms tightened around his shoulders. After only a few long strides, his foot came down on the edge of the roof and he pushed himself out across the space beyond with all the strength at his disposal.

The two of them soared through the air above the hanging sheets of mesh and over the narrow catwalk which hung equidistant between the two buildings. The agents who had already made it that far took aim and fired as their quarry passed overhead. Bolts of crackling energy streaked by on either side of them.

Jamie barely noticed, instead focused on the quickly approaching edge of the far building. It didn't look like he was going to make it. He'd have to throw Alaida farther on and hope she at least might avoid the fate of falling into the jagged metal mesh below.

But then the toe of his leading foot touched the roof's parapet and he pushed himself over the edge, stumbling as he broke out across the next roof top but quickly regaining his stride. This time, he had more ground to build up speed before attempting the next jump and he made sure to use every inch of it. Alaida let out a whimper as she buried her head against his shoulder.

By the time Jamie threw himself and Alaida off the next rooftop, he had no doubt they would clear the gap with ease. And this leap would take them right to the walkway built along the top of the farm's outer wall. Most of the agents in pursuit had now been left far behind. After this, it would be a simple matter to hop over the wall and make their way back to the titan-mecha.

If only Jamie could hold on that long. He could already feel the pull of Earth had been stretched to its breaking point. "Alaida! If I don't make it, tell Reaver the titan's just ahead, parked outside a Tavern called the Minaret!"

He felt the nodding of her head but heard no other reply. Words suddenly failed Jamie too as he realized he might have been a little too exuberant with that last jump. In now looked like he was going to overshoot the farm's outer wall entirely. His eyes grew wide as the edge of the wall came into view and then passed beneath him, the tips of his toes just brushing against the top. Then it was gone, and they were falling, straight down a three story drop.

Alaida's grip on his neck grew even tighter and he felt her whole body turn rigid. Jamie knew he would survive this fall, and after all he'd gone through to get to Alaida, he forced himself to believe that he could protect her as well.

Below, running between the base of the wall and the dirt road which encircled the slave farm, was a grass-covered berm that sloped sharply away from the wall. Jamie had only an instant to take it all in, his mind calculating where they would land and how he would have to respond to the terrain at the moment of impact.

That moment came only a split-second later. His feet smashed into the side of the berm about halfway down and his knees buckled, absorbing only a small bit of the impact. For Alaida, the shock of stopping that suddenly after such a fall, even cushioned in his arms, could still be fatal.

Jamie threw himself into a roll, using the angle of the slope to help further slow their descent. They spun down the side of the berm, Jamie holding tight to Alaida and doing his best to shield her from the ground with his own body.

At the very bottom, they hit hard-packed earth and the impact finally tore Alaida away from Jamie's grasp. They both went rolling out into the road, only coming to a stop right in the middle. Some ten feet away, a startled noxard pulling a cart reared back and bellowed.

Jamie scrambled around on hands and knees to Alaida's side. Her hands and arms were skinned, and she'd gotten a cut on the cheek, but otherwise looked fine. Helping her up as he too stood, Jamie didn't have time to ask for confirmation.

"Come on, can you run?" he said, already pulling her into motion.

"Yes," she said with a nod, moving as fast as she was able just to keep up with Jamie. If he'd had the time to assess their injuries, he would have, but he didn't. Only through sheer force of will had Jamie so far been able to stave off his inevitable return to Earth.

They dashed past the noxard and the cart, ignoring the calls from the driver as they made their way back toward the slave farm's main gate. The Minaret lay directly to their left but the land dropped off steeply past the edge of the road and the embankment was covered in a dense mix of various thorny plants. The road would be the quickest and surest route back to the titan. Hopefully, no one at the gate would yet be expecting the escapees to have made it that far.

Jamie and Alaida both skidded to a stop in the dusty road as they saw one of those blue Mk-4s step out from around the corner of the gatehouse. A cluster of uniformed SAA agents were gathered below, screaming hysterically and pointing right at Jamie and Alaida. The machine stepped into the street hefting a gigantic sword and began advancing toward them.

"This way!" Jamie said, turning off the road and running down the weed-covered embankment. A dense growth of vines creeping close to the ground nearly tripped him more than once. He didn't even want to think about what the thorny little shrubs they trampled over were doing to Alaida's bare feet. At the bottom, they scrambled across a muddy ditch and into an open field that ran behind the first several buildings on that street. Jamie could feel the tremors of the titan's footsteps, increasing in pace and growing nearer.

Despite Alaida's gasping breath, she let out a dry chuckle. "It's just like Tavnic, isn't it?"

"At least no Wolf-Slaves this time," Jamie called back, not quite able to share in the lunacy of the situation as she was.

Beyond the next building stood a wide-open yard, partly filled with vulcan-mechas and hitched noxards. Beyond that was a building sporting a thin wooden turret on its opposite corner.

"Hurry!" Jamie said. "We're almost there!"

As they reached the rear of the tavern, Jamie looked back over his shoulder, catching a glimpse of the SAA titan rushing down the street. A second later, he lost sight of it behind the corner of the building. He and Alaida rounded the next corner and hurried toward the street, past all the parked vehicles and hitched animals. With that SAA titan closing in, this was going to be close.

Apparently, no one had been paying much attention to Jamie's arrival at the Minaret because his titan still sat right where he'd left it, completely unmolested and unguarded. Alaida darted up the side and into the passenger compartment the moment it was within reach. Jamie meanwhile threw himself into the pilot seat. The footfalls of the approaching titan were far too close now. It must have just been around the corner of the building.

Jamie's slow assent into the belly of the machine was made even more ponderous by the relentless force trying to sweep him away from this world. With eyes pinched shut, Jamie flung his head side-to-side as the seat snapped into place. He couldn't leave this for Reaver to solve. He'd gotten Alaida into this situation, he'd rescued her, and now he had to get both of them out of here. He just needed a little more time.

"It's good to be home," Alaida said, hunkering down behind the front bulkhead.

"Hold on tight!" Jamie said as he brought the titan to its feet in a burst of movement. "This is gonna get rough!"

The titan's joints groaned as it lurched off the ground and sprang into the street beyond. Leading with one of the machine's giant fists, Jamie broke around the corner of the Minaret just as the SAA titan charged into view. His fist struck the other machine squarely in the face and rattled back down through the arm, shaking Jamie's machine violently. The SAA titan stumbled to a jarring stop, the metal plates around the point of impact buckling and cracking.

Jamie followed through by throwing the whole weight of his machine against the other titan, pushing it backward. He had hoped to topple it entirely onto its back, but the other machine somehow recovered and managed to brace itself, large berms of earth being pushed up behind its heels as Jamie drove it out into the street. The massive sword it still held, lined tip to hilt with glowing magescript, came swinging down directly at Jamie in his open-air roll cage.

He pushed himself away, raising a hand to deflect the blow, and struck the other titan's forearm, sending the tip of the sword blade streaking through the air mere feet above his head. The arc of the blade passed right through the Minaret's namesake feature, leaving a neat diagonal slash along which the top half of the turret fell away from the rest, trailing dust and throwing up a billowing cloud as it crashed to the street below, breaking apart into splintered debris.

Before the other titan could recover, Jamie seizing the hand holding the sword and twisted. The armor plating down the length of the forearm cried out as it deformed and its magescript wavered and then blinked out entirely. The fingers of the hand went suddenly limp and the sword dropped free, clattering down into the street and sending pedestrians scrambling for safety.

Jamie shoved the other titan once again, this time spinning into the street and grabbing hold of the dropped sword. As the SAA titan struggled to regain its footing, Jamie brought the sword crashing down from above. The blade ripped into its right shoulder, slicing through its armor and tearing a jagged gouge diagonally down to its armpit. The whole arm and shoulder slumped away from the torso, now hanging on by only a few frayed pieces of metal.

The SAA titan staggered in the middle of the street, its left arm now behaving sporadically as it tried to shield itself from Jamie's next blow. This time, Jamie swung at the level of the machine's knees. It only ripped part way through one of the knees before getting snagged by all the intricate mechanisms inside. It was still enough to bring the machine down and the whole thing fell with a crash. Jamie had to brace one of his feet against the fallen titan in order to pull the sword free.

"You okay back there?" Jamie called over his shoulder.

"Y-yes," was all Alaida said in reply.

Jamie knew they needed to get out of the area as quickly as possible, but he hadn't really had any time to give it any more thought beyond that. East would take them back through Tolfield and deeper into Finttiranos. South meant they'd have to go past Grassnar and then into Heigelries, a place he'd just barely escaped from the last time. To the north were only treacherous mountains which would slow their escape to the point that it would make capture almost certain. West, the only other option available, would take them into the heart of the Boravian Highlands. It was still Finttiranos territory, but beyond that was Secotia, and potentially, freedom as well. Jamie had hoped to talk with Alaida about absconding to a foreign country before doing so, but their reunion hadn't exactly gone as he would have liked. The start of that journey would require them to head back toward the slave farm and retread the same road they'd just crossed after escaping from the farm's walls.

Jamie put the titan into a dead run. He needed to set them firmly on this course so that it would be the only one Reaver had left to him upon his return. If Jamie let that maniac set their destination, there'd be no way of knowing where they might find themselves the next time Jamie came to Terrarhea. Just a little farther. That's all he needed.

Since the streets had become largely deserted in the wake of the titan-mecha battle, Jamie was able to unleash his machine's full speed. However, just as he started to round the sharp turn outside the slave farm's gatehouse, a second sword-wielding SAA titan emerged from within.

Using the momentum of the speeding titan under him, Jamie brought his commandeered sword around in a huge arc. The other titan raised its own blade in time to parry, but caught the impact fully on the flat of its blade. Having already been on its back foot, the SAA titan stumbled backward into the side of the gatehouse. In a snapping of timbers, one of the massive jambs that held up the gate gave way and collapsed.

As Jamie followed through with the swing of his sword, the tip ripped through the battlements on the opposite side of the gatehouse. It wasn't enough damage to completely level the structure, but the whole front corner now slumped forward at a peculiar angle and all the SAA agents who'd taken up position behind the hoardings in the hope of sniping the titan as it passed by now found the need to hold on for their lives a far more pressing concern.

Jamie left it all behind him, powering the titan down the road that wrapped around the northern edge of the slave farm and began climbing into the hills to the northwest. With the wind rushing through the front of the titan's roll cage, Jamie threw back his head and laughed at the sky, a maniac cackle of unrestrained joy and triumph. Alaida peaked over the top of the bulkhead with a quizzical expression on her face.

"Alaida, we did it!" Jamie shouted over the roar of the wind. And they'd done it all without Reaver. "I got you out of that place and the Wolf-Slaves won't bother us anymore! We're free!"

"Free?" Alaida said, her voice flat as she lightly traced the edge of the mark over her eye with the tips of her fingers. "I have been branded. Even if we can escape repercussions for what just happened back there, the authorities will confiscate me on sight the next time we go near civilization and you will likely be arrested for being in possession of a contraband slave. Perhaps it would have been better had you not come back for me. Then you at least might have had a chance to start a new life."

"Alaida, don't say that," Jamie said, speaking in a rush to beat the inevitable snap that he knew would pull him away. "I'm so sorry I let this happen to you, and I wish I didn't have to leave you right now, but even with all that's happened, I'd still choose this world over mine. I haven't changed my mind about that, and I never will. I'd chose you every time, no matter what!"

Alaida opened her mouth to reply, but Jamie never heard what she said. The pull could no longer be held back. Despite his best efforts to keep it from doing so, it broke once more, and Terrarhea vanished.

CHAPTER 72

Jamie clenched his fists.

That sky overhead was dark, the air crisp. Jamie stood alone on a recessed patio looking out at a grassy backyard illuminated by strings of orange and green lights hanging from the eaves of a house and the branches of the trees. A tall wooden fence, mostly obscured by ornamental vines and shrubs, enclosed the back end of the yard while most of the space between it and the house was filled with kids Jamie recognized from his school. A large throng in the middle of the yard was dancing to the throbbing pop music coming from two huge speakers someone had lugged out onto the wooden deck. Many of the partygoers were wearing either broad-shouldered pin-stripe suits or slutty flapper dresses. Others were dressed in ironically comedic versions of the same or simply just regular street clothes. Regardless of what they wore, nearly everyone held at least one plastic cup filled with beer.

Jamie's own corner of the yard, tucked in below a rearward reaching wing of the house, remained in relative quiet and shadow, unoccupied except for himself. A series of terraced retaining walls, stairs, and paths, interspersed with thin ribbons of planting beds, all stepped up to the level of the main yard. Several pieces of patio furniture surrounded him while a number of potted plants in highly decorative containers had been placed atop the retaining walls, though most of them were badly wilted from a cold snap and well on their way to turning brown. Behind him, a pair of wide patio doors looked into a darkened room on the other side. The dim accent lighting built into the landscaping provided just enough illumination to turn the glazed doors into a huge mirror.

It took Jamie a brief moment to realize that the reflection staring back belonged to him. The only article of clothing he recognized was the flat cap pulled low over his eyes: the same one April had gotten for him that one night they'd almost been killed by Seth and his friends. The rest of his costume consisted of a pair of pleated khaki slacks with a high waist and suspenders, a band collar shirt unbuttoned to the middle of the chest over a plain white tank top, and a fashionably scuffed, tweed blazer that almost matched the flat cap. Compared to all the ubiquitous mobsters at this party, he looked like nothing more than a roustabout.

He might not have recognized this place or his clothes, but he could guess it was the night of the Halloween party that Derek and Alex had been so eager to take part in. At least he'd been able to get Alaida out of danger before leaving Terrarhea. Reaver would keep her safe just like he had before. He was actually better at that than Jamie. Now Jamie just had to wait until they switched places again. With the way things had been progressing, he probably wouldn't have long to wait.

Jamie turned at the sound of soft footsteps coming down the garden stairs. There he saw April, carefully holding a full cup in each hand and wearing a shimmering gold and pink dress. Overlapping layers of translucent gold lace above a base of rich pink created flamboyant angular shapes which were further accentuated by the glittering sequins that raced in intricate patterns all the way from the lace sleeves to the diagonal hem of tassels that swayed rhythmically as she walked. Her blonde hair had been pulled up tight and done in curls. Crowned with a matching, feathered headband, she didn't just look like a flapper, she looked like flapper royalty.

The only flaw in the entire ensemble was the heavy bulge in her matching handbag. She swayed slightly as she handed Jamie one of the two cups. Unlike her own, which was bubbly yellow and had a frothy head on top, his was clear and smelled faintly of chlorine.

"It doesn't look like Seth has any soda left so I just got you some water," April said, taking a sip from her cup.

"We're at Seth's place?"

"Hey, you're the one who wanted to come, remember!" April said, a few of her words slurring one into the next. Why did Reaver have to keep pushing his luck with that guy? "You even insisted on bringing those two losers with us. I wonder if they've gotten their asses kicked yet. I haven't seen them since they helped me break into Seth's parent's liquor cabinet. Knowing those two, they're probably the ones who drank the last of the soda." She pulled a brown bottle from her handbag and held it up, noisily sloshing the inch or two of alcohol in the bottom. "How am I supposed to make a rum and coke now?"

From the look of things, it was probably for the best that she couldn't. Jamie on the other hand felt perfectly clear-headed. After the breakneck insistence of that nagging sensation he'd been putting up with, his mind now felt perfectly still. He didn't know if Reaver had something against alcohol in addition to his other personality quirks, but right now, he was just grateful he didn't have to deal with drunkenness while trying to figure out what that maniac had gotten him into this time.

"This is a nice little place you've found here," April said. She set both her beer and the bottle of rum on the patio table and put her arms around Jamie from behind. "Very cozy. Very romantic."

Jamie barely noticed her touch. Something about this just didn't feel right. Reaver had never seemed like much of a partygoer, so why would he insist on going to one hosted by their enemy and then spend all his time lurking in the shadows? Though cold, the water April had given Jamie tasted lifeless and didn't help much to alleviate the dry, pasty feeling in his mouth. Even a drink from a stolen Finttiranos military canteen would have tasted better that this.

"Oh great," April said, looking over her shoulder and disengaging from Jamie. "I shouldn't have said anything, they found us." She retrieved her beer and took a long drink.

From the yard above, Derek and Alex descended the stairs, each with a beer in one hand and Derek carrying his coveted violin case in the other. Both were wearing black fedoras and dressed in what looked like period suits that had been tailored just for them.

"I can't believe she slapped me just because I asked her if she wanted to see what's in my case," Derek was saying.

"Nikki is way out of your league," Alex said. "Just because she's Asian doesn't mean she likes anime. Besides, I told you not to bring that thing. You look like a complete loser carrying it around. That's why I left mine at home. Now shut up and drink your beer."

"It tastes like crap," Derek said, taking a sip from his cup and grimacing.

"It's supposed to taste that way," Alex said, nearly choking after a long gulp from his own.

"Hey Jamie, let's head back up," April said, tugging at his elbow. "I wanna dance."

As Jamie stared at their reflections in the patio doors, a light on the other side suddenly came on, turning the glass transparent once more. Inside stood Seth and five of his nameless compatriots, all of them glaring at Jamie from the other side of the glass. Two of them were wearing flat caps and one, a fedora, but none looked to have put a great deal of effort into their costumes. Seth and that Freckled Skeleton who'd broken into Jamie's locker were just wearing regular street clothes. Jamie heard Alex mutter a curse under his breath.

Seth rolled back the patio door and stepped through, followed by the others. A few of them still held cups of beer and all of them swayed slightly as they took up positions on either side of their leader.

"What the hell are you doing here?" Seth said, stepping forward. "No one invited you. Looking for a repeat of last time?"

Once again, Reaver had left Jamie to clean up his mess. That was fine. Jamie could handle this just like he had everything on Terrarhea. As Seth approached, looming over Jamie and smelling of beer and vodka, Jamie stood his ground and met the other boy's gaze. Though Seth was trying hard not to show it, he was even less sure on his feet than April was. Jamie, meanwhile, could feel his own heart trying to pound its way right out of his chest.

"Well? What's --" Seth cut off abruptly when Jamie promptly brought his knee up into the larger boy's groin with all the force he could muster. Seth let out a high-pitched shriek and crumpled at the waist. Jamie wasted no time bringing his other knee up into the bottom of Seth's jaw on its way down. He felt the clatter of teeth crashing together and the sting of Seth's jawbone impacting the fleshy part of his knee. That was probably going to leave a bruise. The other boys stood dumbstruck, merely staring in shock as Seth fell over onto his back, a few of them actually quailing back from the stony look in Jamie's eyes.

Unfortunately, their bewilderment only lasted a moment. The first one to break ranks charged Jamie and caught him across the jaw with his fist. Jamie spun and staggered backward into one of the retaining walls but the blow hadn't really hurt. The coordination of the boy who'd thrown it had been badly affected by the alcohol and the punch didn't have nearly as much power as it should have. With all the adrenaline surging through his body, Jamie probably wouldn't have felt much of anything regardless.

Seizing hold of a small concrete planter shaped like a vase, Jamie spun on his attacker. The planter crashed into the side of the other boy's head and split in two, showering them both in a cloud of potting soil and dry flower petals. The other boy instantly dropped to the ground, blood already flowing from the wound on his head.

Blood trickling from his own lips, Seth had pushed himself up to his hands and knees and was shouting something to his comrades about taking Jamie apart, but he never finished because Jamie kicked him in the face and sent him back to the ground.

The four remaining boys surged forward en masse, eager to follow through on Seth's demand. Jamie smiled a toothy grin even as their fists clumsily rained down on him. Though he was weak and slow by comparison to Reaver's Terrarhean body, and his senses weren't nearly as sharp, here he felt the sting of every blow against him. That was the greatest motivation ever not to lose this fight. Even the desperation of taking Ironsides down hadn't made Jamie feel as alive as he did right now.

He lashed out at the nearest boy, heedless of how it might leave him exposed to the others. His fist struck one of the flat cap attired attackers in the ribs and sent him staggering backward. It was only then that Jamie realized he still held the broken base of the concrete planter in his hand. Turning on the others, Jamie caught a flash of movement from the corner of his eye.

With a cry of "Spoon!" Alex launched himself off the retaining wall and right into the face of another of the attackers. Derek meanwhile advanced from the other side with his violin case raised high overhead. "Goongala!" he cried as he brought it down over the back of the fedora-wearing boy's head, splitting the case open and spilling out a random assortment of half-empty liquor bottles. Of the two combatants left facing off with Jamie, the Freckled Skeleton received a thump to the back of the head from April wielding an expensive bottle of rum as the gold tassels of her dress flared around her. The bottle remained intact and the boy it had struck turned on April with a snarl, his fist raised and ready to strike.

A bloodthirsty howl peeling from his throat, Jamie leapt at the freckled boy, hooking an arm around his throat and pulling him back. As the two of them thrashed about, stumbling backward, Jamie's foot came crashing down on top of Seth's hand which incited another howl of pain.

The boy wearing a flat cap who Jamie had previously struck in the ribs with the planter grabbed him from behind, managing to break his friend out of Jamie's improvised chokehold. Now freed, the Freckled Skeleton tried once more to punch Jamie. However, his blow lost most of its power from the way Jamie thrashed about madly in the hands of his captor, throwing elbows, knees, fists and feet at anything he could reach.

Nearby, as Seth climbed back up to his hands and knees, the random flailing of Jamie's foot caught him right in the gut and sent him rolling over onto his side. When Jamie's attackers tried yet again to strike him, Jamie unintentionally jerked out of the way at the last moment and the fist intended for him ended up striking Flat Cap instead. That slackened his hold just enough that Jamie was able to twist around and bring his elbow into the side of his captor's throat. In a fit of coughing, Flat Cap released Jamie entirely.

The Freckled Skeleton now came at Jamie once more, again leading with his fists. His nerves buzzing, Jamie just barely managed to sidestep the attack, but rather than retreat, he charged forward and delivered a counterpunch of his own to the boy's face. Jamie's knuckles cried out from an impact with something hard and sharp. The boy stumbled back, the bright red blood running from his nose standing out vividly against his pale skin.

Just as Jamie turned his attention back to Flat Cap, Seth pushed himself off the ground and threw his arms around Jamie's feet, pinning him in place. As the other boy charged with a snarl on his lips, April stepped forward with her bottle once more and knocked Seth over the head, actually laughing as she did so. Seth dropped flat to the ground, shielding his head with his hands and unintentionally releasing Jamie. However, it wasn't soon enough for Jamie to evade Flat Cap, who now tackled him.

April jumped back with a shriek and Jamie backpedaled desperately, right across Seth's back, struggling to stay on his feet. He would have fallen completely if the backs of his shins didn't collide with one of the retaining walls. Twisting as his knees bent, Jamie fell into a soft planting bed while Flat Cap ran headlong into the masonry wall below. He instantly fell to the ground, moaning and clutching his head.

Not far away, Derek clung to the back of his opponent as the larger boy spun wildly in a effort to unseat him. Meanwhile, Alex brandished a misshapen patio chair and left his own foe laying unconscious on the ground as he charged to Alex's aid. The chair broke completely in half as he crashed it across the jock's hips. As he went down to his knees, both Derek and Alex instantly descended on him. April, meanwhile, stood over Seth, kicking and stomping on his back, yelling at him to just leave them alone.

Standing with legs akimbo and swaying as he bared his teeth, the Freckled Skeleton wiped the back of his hand across his nose and spat blood. "I am so gonna kill you," he said.

With a determined look in his eye, Jamie advanced. The Freckled Skeleton threw the next punch but Jamie only registered it in passing, his vision having narrowed to a dark tunnel straight ahead. He wasn't going to let this end any other way than total and absolute victory. Jamie couldn't match Reaver's speed or power, but he drove his fists into the Freckled Skeleton as fast and as hard as he possibly could.

Already off balance from the drinking and the previous blows, his foe reeled under Jamie's onslaught. An elbow to the face, a knee to the groin, a kick to the shin; Jamie had no plan or technique, his only goal was to take the other boy out of this fight for good. As the redhead bent at the waist from a punch to the kidneys, Jamie brought his interlocked fists down right on the back of his neck. His foe went down, and Jamie finished by cracking the heel of his shoe across the boy's jaw, leaving him a moaning ball quivering on the ground.

Having finally batted off April, Seth had once more begun pushing himself off the ground. However, as Jamie stepped in front of him, he stopped in mid-kneel and swept his gaze across the combined force now arrayed against him. April stood at Jamie's shoulder while Derek and Alex had taken up flanking positions on each side.

"Just stay down," Jamie said, glaring down at the much larger boy.

Seth's lip curled into a snarl and his shoulders shifted as he began to rise. Jamie didn't hesitate. Stepping forward, he drove the full weight of his body through his fist and right into Seth's face. Seth dropped like a stone, his head falling with a thud to the pavers below. Jamie stood staring for a moment, certain that Seth couldn't yet be out of the fight, but he remained motionless, a small pool of blood forming around his mouth.

Even as Derek and Alex descended on Seth's lifeless form, kicking him repeated and cackling madly, April grabbed Jamie from behind and frantically pulled him away.

"Come on, we gotta go!" she said. "Someone called the cops! We gotta get outta here, now!"

Even if the importance of her words hadn't quite registered with Jamie, the urgency in her voice spurred him to turn away from the carnage he'd just inflicted and fall in behind her at a trot as they climbed the garden stairs and then at a sprint as they crossed the quickly emptying backyard.

CHAPTER 73

Being jostled by the crowd of other frantically departing underage party-goers, Jamie followed blindly through a gate in the back of the grassy yard and out into a narrow alleyway lined on both sides by sealed garage doors and only dimly illuminated by a spattering of yard lights.

A siren sounded in the distance and a flashing red and blue light crossed the street at the end of the alley just as April pulled Jamie into another yard on the other side. They ran past a house whose residents looked out from the brightly lit interior at the flash of movement outside their windows. They crossed an all but deserted street and kept running for nearly two blocks until they drifted to a stop below the trio of streetlights which lined the path cutting its way through Serrano Park.

Gasping for breath and still holding the bottle of rum she'd liberated from Seth's house, April doubled over with hands on knees while Jamie dropped onto one of the adjacent park benches. On the nearby playground, four girls several years their junior and dressed in superhero costumes, stopped their idle chitchat at the sight of them.

Jamie's heart was still pounding in his ears and his hands were quivering. It would probably take a while for his body to return to normal with all the adrenaline currently surging through it. His mind, however remained clear. He couldn't find even a shred of remorse for what he'd just done; probably the same way Reaver felt after the things he did.

When April sat down next to him and rested her head on his shoulder, he didn't even try to push her away. Were the police going to be coming for him now? He couldn't seem to care about that either. He just felt indifferent about it all. In that moment, the only thing he really wanted was to go back to Terrarhea.

Alex and Derek emerged from the shadows about thirty seconds later, plodding along at an ungainly clip and laughing as they sang a horribly off-key rendition of *Ding-Dong the Witch is Dead*.

April sat up a little straighter and looked at them sharply. "Dead?"

"Well, not dead exactly, but I did give Seth's balls a good stomp before the EMTs got there," Alex said, puffing out his chest.

"Yeah, he was still down on the ground when we left but he was groaning," Derrick said, "and I've seen enough dubbed anime to know that means he's still alive."

"Jeeze! That was completely crazy!" Alex said. "I can't believe somebody actually called the cops."

"Not that anyone's left for them to question," Derrick said. "That place was completely empty before we even made it out. You don't think Seth will turn us in, do you?"

"I think he might have more important things to worry about at the moment," Alex said. "Like where he got all that beer and why he's completely drunk."

"Serves that asshole right," April said. "I never even got to dance. At least I got this." She twisted the cork out of the rum bottle with a pop and took a long drink. "That's good," she said, handing the bottle to Jamie.

He considered it a moment and then accepted and took a drink himself. It was sweeter than he was expecting, and spicy, with a buttery taste of cloves and vanilla. It still burned his throat on the way down but he didn't cough more than a tiny sputter. April retrieved the bottle and took another gulp for herself. After staring at Derrick and Alex for several long seconds, she finally offered the bottle to them as well. Derrick's eyes went wide and Alex's mouth dropped open but he still snatched the bottle away and took a long drink. As he handled it to Derrick, he nearly doubled over coughing. April, meanwhile, kicked up her feet, laughing. Though he coughed as well, Derrick held his composure better than his friend, nodding with a grimace as he passed the bottle back to April who took yet another drink.

As Jamie sat staring into the darkness at the far end of the park, a fast-tempo jazz number suddenly started blaring from nearby. All eyes turned to Derrick who was holding up his cell phone.

"What do you think, April?" he said. "Care to dance?"

"Alright!" she said with a laugh and jumped to her feet. Pulling Jamie off the park bench, she said, "I knew you guys had to be good for something. Come on, Jamie, let's dance!"

Completely missing Derrick's frown and the stoop of his shoulders, April immediately started into some stumbling rendition of what she might have intended to be the Charleston. Sober, she might have pulled it off. As she was, she tripped over her own feet twice before finally falling against Jamie.

"Maybe something a little slower," Derrick said with a sigh as he scrolled through his playlist and selected another period number that was considerably more down beat than the previous track.

April leaned against Jamie, swaying to the music. "Yeah, this'll work."

Jamie would have been perfectly happy passing her off to Derrick, but the way she clung to him, she probably wouldn't allow it. April certainly wasn't Alaida -- she wasn't even close -- she was Reaver's girlfriend, but that didn't mean Jamie couldn't at least do the gentlemanly thing and let her have a dance or two. He shrugged to Derrick over April's shoulder as they slowly turned in a circle. Derrick shook his head in resignation and waved for Jamie to forget about it. Meanwhile, Alex had begun pacing from one foot to the other.

"Man! I'm starting to feel like a fifth wheel around here," he said. Turning to the girls gathered around the merry-go-round, his eyes narrowed. He walked up to one of them dressed as Supergirl and bowed, holding out his hand in a princely gesture. "Kara Zor-El, would you give me the pleasure of this dance?"

The girl quailed away from him with a bemused smile. "My name's not Kara."

Smiling the whole time, Alex clenched his fists in an overly theatrical manner. "Don't ruin it for me!" he cried into the sky.

"Dude, what are you doing?" Derrick said. "She's still, like, in junior high."

"I'm not asking her on a date, I just want someone to dance with," Alex said, shuffling his feet and rotating his shoulders in what could only be described as the most ham-fisted interpretation of dancing ever. "Unless you'd like to volunteer?"

"No," Derrick said, waving both his hands in front of his face.

Two of the other girls called out for Derek to reconsider, while the one dressed as Supergirl merely shrugged and said, "Okay."

As she and Alex awkwardly began dancing, the three remaining girls, all laughing, swarmed around Derrick and began dancing as well, each in their own style. Derrick cringed as if he'd unexpectedly discovered a raccoon in his trash can while taking out the garbage.

April laughed and pressed the side of her face to Jamie's chest. "I guess even those two were bound to have some luck with the ladies eventually."

"I don't know if they look all that lucky but it's better than nothing, I suppose," Jamie said. "I don't know if I mentioned this yet, but you look really nice. Your mom outdid herself on that dress."

"I was wondering when you were going to notice," April replied. "You haven't said a thing about it all night."

"I know I've been a little off the last couple of days..."

"You're here now," April murmured, snuggling a little tighter to Jamie, probably because she was barely able to stay on her feet any longer.

If only Jamie and Alaida had been able to finish that conversation they'd started in the barn. She'd told him that she felt the same way he did, but the same way about what? Jamie hadn't quite been able to say that he loved her. Did she truly feel the same way about that?

Fortunately, he only needed to wait a little longer before they could talk again. He knew it. With every changeover between worlds, his time on Earth grew shorter while his time on Terrarhea kept increasing. As that old man had said, not far from where they currently stood, this cycle had not yet run its course.

By the time the bottle of rum had been emptied, most all of it by April herself, the four girls dressed as superheroes had departed and Alex and Derrick had gone their separate ways as well, leaving only Jamie with a semi-conscious April. If the bottle had had any more in it when they'd started, she likely would have been completely comatose now.

"Come on, can you walk?" Jamie said, holding on to April by the shoulders. His own buzz seemed to make things move more fluidly than normal but at least he had retained enough coordination to keep April on her feet. "I think we should get you home."

"No. No, no, no," she slurred, feebly pawing at Jamie's chest. "No. My step-dad is home and he'd kill me if he saw me like this. No."

"Well, I'm not just gonna leave you here in the park all night." It must have been getting late. If they didn't get moving, they might get arrested for vagrancy. "Think you can make it to my place? It's only a couple of blocks."

"Jamie. Jamie." April laughed as Jamie led her out of the park, holding tight to him as she dragged her toes. "Oh Jamie, you're not trying to take advantage of me, are you?"

Jamie rolled his eyes and shook his head. She may have been playing the part of an uninhibited flapper-girl to perfection, but that didn't exactly make her all that attractive at the moment. In her current condition, she was liable to throw-up on him just walking her home. "I'm going to let you crash on my couch, okay?"

She merely mumbled something unintelligible. Tomorrow, she probably wouldn't even remember any of this. About a block later, she threw-up in someone's bushes, afterward declaring that she felt much better, but not displaying any signs of improvement as far as Jamie could see. The house was darkened when they arrived, as were most of the others on the block. Though he still felt a little light on his feet, the walk home had burned away the worst of the alcohol's lingering effects on his own body. He led April in through the side door and across the deconstructed kitchen and living room.

The place seemed awfully quiet. Jamie's heart began beating up into his throat, once again wondering what Reaver could have done to Heather. She was just probably out with friends. It was a Friday night after all and

Halloween to boot. Or maybe she'd turned in early after a hard day at the office. There was no reason to get worried until he put April down on the couch and could confirm one way or the other if anything had happened to Heather.

"Come on, we're almost there," Jamie said. "Just through here."

When he opened the door to the makeshift living room, he discovered any concern for his sister to be completely unfounded. In the dim light of the room, Heather sat on the couch wearing a skimpy nurse's uniform as she kissed the man next to her. Appropriately, he was wearing a doctor's white lab coat over his stylish, skinny-fit suit. The two of them sat up straight at Jamie's intrusion, both hastily trying to look as if they hadn't just been doing exactly what Jamie had just seen them doing.

"Jamie!" Heather said. "I, um, wasn't expecting you!"

"Obviously," Jamie said, glancing back out into the darkened hallway. He hadn't been expecting this either. Now what was he supposed to do with April? He wasn't about to give up his own bed for her. If she were going to throw up again, maybe it wouldn't be such a bad idea to leave her in the bathtub.

"Or...is that April?" Heather added, rising to her feet.

"Is she okay?" the man said. It was only then that Jamie finally recognized him.

"Mister Clark?"

"Um, Jamie, hi," Mister Clark said, offering a halting wave. "Me and your sister, we got back early from the party and were just, um..."

"No, don't say anything else," Jamie said. "I know what you were doing and that's already more than I want to know."

"What happened to April?" Heather said, stepping forward to ease her down onto the couch.

"She's, um..." Jamie eyed Mister Clark out of the corner of his eye. "She's just a little tired."

"Yeah, alcohol can do that to a person," Mister Clark said. "Heather, we should really drive her home."

April moaned and pulled herself into a tight ball.

"She doesn't really want to go home right now..." Jamie said. "And, for the record, I never said we were drinking."

"Yeah, I get it. I've been there before." Heather said. "I'll call her parents and see if I can convince them that she...that she fell asleep on her boyfriend's couch and she's going to spend the night at his place? Yeah,

I'm sure they'll be fine with that, especially coming from her boyfriend's older sister." She sighed and shook her head.

"Why don't I give them a call?" Mister Clark said. "After all, what's the point of dating a school administrator if you can't call in a favor once in a while."

"Steven, you know that's not why I'm dating you."

"But because we *are* dating, I'm going to do it without you even needing to ask."

"This is just too weird," Jamie said. He was used to putting up with Heather's boyfriends but not when this one was his teacher as well. "You two really need to get a room."

"We had a room, right until you dropped sleeping beauty here into our laps," Heather said. "So just what *were* the two of you up to then if you 'weren't drinking'?" She added that last part in finger-quotes.

"We kicked Seth's ass!" April, her face half-buried in the couch cushions, exclaimed before Jamie could even think up some lie to tell instead.

"You kicked -- ?" Heather cut herself off abruptly when she noticed how intently Mister Clark was listening. She ran her hand through her hair and pressed her palm against her mouth. "Steven, could you maybe give us a minute?"

"Um..." He looked from April to Jamie and then to Heather. "Sure," he said, stepping around them and into the hall.

Heather and Jamie watched him leave. As soon as the door closed with a soft click, Heather leaned forward and said in a whispered hiss, "What did you do? Did you jump Seth?"

"What, you think I planned this?" Jamie said. Although now that he thought about it, that did sound exactly like the sort of thing Reaver would have done. What better way to get revenge on his nemesis then by utterly trouncing him at his own party? "Look, we were just hanging out at the party and he came at us."

"We? Us?" Heather said. "Are you crazy! That's not a fair fight, that's like, assault, or something! How many of you were there?"

"There were just four of us," Jamie said, and then quickly speaking over Heather's gasp, he added, "but there were six of them, so no, it wasn't a fair fight!"

Heather opened her mouth to retort but nothing came out. After several attempts, gesticulating with her hands, she said, "Have you been drinking?"

"Really? You, of all people, are going to get on my case over something like that?"

"I just want to get my facts straight. Since you don't look anything like you did after the last time you and Seth got into it, I assume you won this time?"

"Yeah, I don't think I'll have to worry about Seth for a while." Yes, there was little doubt it had been a decisive victory, but Seth probably wouldn't let his feud with Jamie end here. But by the time he was well enough to come after Jamie again, Reaver would be the one who'd have to deal with him.

"And if he did come after you tonight, it sounds like you were justified," Heather said. If only she knew about all the other times Seth or his friends had come after Jamie. "But you know how those entitled rich people can be. We'll have to get our story straight if anyone decides to press charges. So: were you drinking?"

Jamie bobbed his head side-to-side as he considered the question. "Okay, yeah, I was drinking, but only a little." He held up his thumb and forefinger. Eyes still closed; April giggled. "And only after the fight."

"What was it?" Heather said. "Beer?"

"Is that important?"

"Not really, I'm just curious."

Jamie shrugged. "Rum, I think. I'm not really sure because the label was in Spanish. It looked expensive though."

The corner of Heather's lip turned up into a smirk as she shook her head. "Who'd'a thought: underage drinking with imported booze, bringing home girls to spend the night, getting into fights with the school jocks? I gotta admit, that's kind of impressive." She held up her hand for a fist bump. Jamie just stared at it with a lopsided grin. "Come on, don't leave me hanging here. It's not often I can relate to the things you get up to."

Shaking his head, Jamie tapped his own fist against hers, but only half-heartedly. "Shouldn't you be grounding me or something?"

"Oh, trust me, if this happens again, you're gonna regret it. But for the moment, just let me have a bit of pride in my little brother, okay? Besides, it's not exactly like you got away with any of it. We'll have to wait and see how things play out with Seth, but as for the rest, you were caught by the school's *guidance counselor* of all people."

Jamie rubbed his face. "Okay, you're right. I'm not nearly as good at this stuff as you were. And personally, I'd rather not get any more practice."

"I'd rather you didn't either. It's only making my job harder." Heather pulled a blanket over April. "So, what's with the accent? I thought this party was supposed to be a 1920's theme, not -- what is that supposed to be anyway? British? South African?"

"Accent? Oh...sorry." Over the last few days on Terrarhea, Jamie had gotten so used to mimicking the natives that he hadn't even realized he'd reverted back to doing so here. He cleared his throat, and when he spoke again, he was very careful to keep all trace of Terrarhean dialect out of his voice. "It was just something some of us were doing. I kinda forgot."

"See, that's what I mean: most of the time I just don't get you."

"Then I suppose I should apologize for the last couple of days in particular."

"What do you mean?"

Jamie's stomach roiled. "You mean I haven't been acting a little...weird?"

Heather raised an eyebrow. "A little more quiet than usual, but no, not really. You haven't really been around much to be honest. Is there something I should know about?"

Why should it surprise Jamie that Reaver could fit into Jamie's own life without raising any concerns for those who knew him best? April and Alaida had both said Jamie and Reaver weren't all that different. To hear it confirmed by the one person who probably knew him better than anyone else on either of those two worlds came as more than a little bit of a shock.

"Um, no, I mean, I've just been thinking a lot recently, you know, keeping to myself; quiet. I'm just sorry that I wasn't there if you needed anything."

"Come here!" Heather said throwing her arms around him and hugging him tightly. "Even as weird as you are, I still love you."

Jamie hugged her back, and for those few moments, he almost regretted that he'd eventually have to leave her again. She was the only family he had left but Terrarhea was becoming his home now. This place, these people, they were just a temporary stop along the way. Heather was moving on too, getting back on with her old life.

"So..." Jamie said as they parted. "You and Mister Clark, huh? How long has that been going on?"

"Since about the time you suggested he should look me up," Heather said. "And here you were the one giving me crap about playing matchmaker."

"I wasn't actually serious when I told him that, you know." Jamie opened the door once more. In the hallway, Mister Clark was talking on his phone and turned at the light spilling out of the room.

"Yes," he said to the person on the other end of the line. "Mm-hm. Sure, just a second." He held up his phone and snapped a picture of April laying on the couch with her face mashed up against the cushions. Even if she'd been staging the scene to convince her parents of her innocence, April never would have allowed anyone to take a picture of her looking like that. "Did you get it?" Mister Clark said a moment later. "Yes. Yes, first thing in the morning. Okay. I'll see you then. Bye."

Ending the call and putting the phone away, Mister Clark blew out his breath. "So that's taken care of. I managed to convince her dad that she and Jamie were here hanging out with me and Heather after the party and that she fell asleep on the couch and won't let us move her."

Heather laughed and draped her arms around Mister Clark's neck. "Where were you when I was in high school?"

"Probably still in school myself," Mister Clark said. The way the two of them were staring into each others eyes made Jamie want to be just about anywhere else at the moment. "But just so you both are aware, I'm now an accessory to...to whatever it is that just happened here."

"Don't worry," Heather said, "I won't tell anyone."

"Oh, I trust you," Mister Clark said. "But I did promise that I'd keep an eye on April until we take her home in the morning, so I am going to have to spend the night."

"Oh really?" Heather said with mock innocence. "You're gonna have to spend the night, here, with me?"

"It is my duty as an educator."

"Have I ever told you how much I admire your work-ethic?"

"No, but I'd love to hear more."

"Now that is just about enough of that," Jamie said, stepping out of the room. "I'm going to bed now. I'll be in my room, but I sincerely hope you don't need me for anything because all of this is about to make me throw up."

The adults laughed as Jamie crossed the hall to his room and closed the door behind him. Alone, finally. His knuckles were bruised, and he'd probably be sore in the morning. He was just about to drop back onto his bed when a chill went through him as he remembered that was the exact same thing he'd done the last time he'd gone to Terrarhea.

How long ago had that been. Four days? Five? It was hard to keep track. It seemed like ages since Seth and his friends had chased Jamie and April through the streets that one night. In the meantime, Jamie had been away making deals and trying to clear debts, but his life here on Earth, even with a sociopath like Reaver in control, hadn't seemed to have changed much at all. Although, after the way Jamie had behaved, first while freeing Alaida from the slave farm, and later when confronting Seth, maybe the two of them weren't really all that different.

He knew there was no trigger that would send him back to Terrarhea, but he still took a seat on the edge of his bed with a bit more deference than usual. On his nightstand sat a pile of homework which had been completed over the last few days. So Reaver had been going to school in Jamie's place? From the look of the grades he'd received, he was an even better student than Jamie himself. Probably just his way of gathering more information about Jamie's life and this world. Under the papers, Jamie found the notebook he'd used to catalogue his experiences on Terrarhea.

Jamie could have sworn he'd left it in one of his desk drawers. Pulling it free and flipping it open, Jamie's eyes grew wide. Whole pages of writing had been added since the last time he'd looked at it. Some sections had been heavily edited to offer corrections or clarifications to Jamie's observations, while others had simply been crossed out entirely. Most of the new entries had been written in Terrarhean but some of it was in a poor version of English, scribbled out in an unsure hand.

Jamie's heart was nearly beating into his throat as he hurriedly flipped through the notebook to the section where he'd speculated about causes for his and Reaver's shared situation. However, his notes there were barely changed. In fact, the only contribution Reaver had made was to offer up several new theories in addition to Jamie's own.

Jamie sat back with a sigh. Elsewhere, Reaver had added a lot of information. Most of it appeared to deal with the world of Terrarhea as a whole but little about Reaver himself. One strange irregularity, however, was a single name which had been added to the list of people Jamie had encountered on his Terrarhean adventures: Heather's own. Next to it were several aborted attempts to write another name, one that started with a Y or an I, but each time had been crossed out. Did Reaver have a sister too, one he couldn't quite remember the name of? Was she as much like Heather as Jamie was like Reaver?

It also looked like Reaver had completed Jamie's attempt to compile an inclusive Terrarhean alphabet, complete with pronunciations for each of its two-hundred and eighty-three letters. Given the similarities Terrarhean shared with English, Jamie might actually be able to use that information to decode the new text. It would take time, but he suspected he could do it.

Jamie might very well have stayed up all night doing just that if he hadn't next turned at random to a page where he'd previously noted the times and durations of the changeovers between worlds. When he saw the mathematical calculations and graphs that Reaver had filled the page with in attempting to discover a pattern to their situation, Jamie went no further. It looked as if Reaver had actually arrived at a formula which came quite close to predicting when each changeover would occur. But when his last prediction had not come to pass, he had grown frustrated, at least if all the corrections and revisions which followed that point were any indication. However, the day and time of that one calculation corresponded exactly with the moment Jamie had been facing off with Doctor Calamestro and had broken the link for a few days. Assuming that Jamie hadn't irreparably ruined the situation and things would once more return to the oscillating curve Reaver had mapped out, the next changeover would occur in just a few days and give Jamie maybe as much as a whole week on Terrarhea.

The thought of seven days with Alaida and free of the Wolf-Slaves and the Lords of the Wilds almost made Jamie laugh out loud.

When he looked up from the notebook, he saw his reflection staring back at him in the wall mirror. Even after everything he'd been through, he still looked like the exact same person he'd been before the death of his parents had started to send his life off the rails. Both he and Reaver each seemed to exist in their own static and unchanging ways, just another similarity they shared. Had Reaver stared at that same reflection, thinking similar thoughts?

Jamie turned to a blank page of the notebook and picked up a pen. At the top of the page, in bold letters, he wrote a single word: "Truce?"

It wasn't just that the two of them were tied to each other: they seemed to be in the exact same situation; both trapped between worlds, both looking for answers. Reaver seemed to be doing just fine here on Earth and, even with all the troubles Jamie had encountered on Terrarhea, if the last few days had shown them anything, he could get by there just fine on his own.

Let Reaver have Earth.

Jamie would take Terrarhea.

Together, they might just figure this whole thing out.

CHAPTER 74

EPILOGUE

Captain Rossack strode across Cavarinov's village square as the sharp crack of five nooses stretching tight rang out from the far end. This was the third batch of bandits to meet their end this morning and yet the gathered crowd still cheered. They had reason to applaud. Those criminals had been terrorizing this remote village for nearly a year and the government had done little to help until now.

When Rossack's team had first brought them in, it had been all they could do just to keep the villagers from lynching every last one of those criminals on the spot. They'd allowed themselves to be held at bay for the duration of the trial but if it had stretched on any longer than the four hours it had, there likely would have been a riot. Now that the result of those guilty verdicts was being meted out, the villagers seemed content simply to watch.

Regardless, Rossack's men still stood guard around the gallows just in case someone decided to try extracting some revenge in person. Dressed in their crisp garrison uniforms and standing at ease, they must have looked like an impassive and unyielding bulwark. But Rossack had served with them long enough to notice the subtle traces of satisfaction the executions brought them as well.

Even if the villagers were observant enough to notice, they wouldn't have dared move against the soldiers. Most in the village had likely seen Finttiranos soldiers in their green uniforms but every one of Rossack's men wore the black and grey of the Finttiranos Special Operations Group. Not only did it visually set them apart from the rank-and-file, there were few who had not heard tales of the SOG's prowess in a fight.

When the ceremony eventually concluded and Gracchus dismissed the team for a little R&R, few of those clean, black uniforms would likely make it through to morning without some memento of the night, but that was an entirely different matter than ruining them in a fight.

Like his men, Captain Rossack's black uniform was also accented with gray and decorated with silver pins instead of the brass of the regular forces. As the commander of this rapid response team, he was also issued a tactical operations visor which covered the top half of his face behind an angular black mask with glowing red eyes. If the SOG uniform didn't bring people into line at the sight of it, the visor always did. It was mainly for this reason that he wore it now, even though they were technically no longer in a tactical situation that would require all the scanners and sensory enhancements it provided.

It also helped to keep the ladies at a distance. Rossack had always been amazed how quickly they came writhing out of the woodwork whenever he took the visor off around civilians. On the many occasions he'd been approached by eligible young women or their proxies, they never failed to mention how handsome he was with his athletic frame and wavy blond hair, or his fair features and pale blue eyes.

Romance of any kind, however, did not appeal to him. He could appreciate the subtle moves and countermoves that the various parties in a courtship employed against each other. They weren't very much different from the tactics of warfare. However, unlike war, where the victor would ultimately stand triumphant over his defeated opponent, a courtship could only end with the winner shackled to that same foe. When Rossack entered into any type of competition, it was always with the sole intent of emerging victorious and nothing less.

As he walked, Rossack tapped the side of the visor to select his First Sergeant's personal communication channel. "Gracchus, keep an eye on things for a while. I just received a ping from headquarters."

Over by the gallows, the tall soldier with a bald head and a long scar crossing his one milky white eye, looked across the square at Rossack and spoke into his relay set. "That didn't take long," his voice rumbled in Rossack's ear. "Want me to hold off on cutting the team loose after we wrap up here?"

Rossack shook his head, sending his long hair swaying. "Probably not a bad idea."

He climbed the three steps to the team's mobile operations center; essentially a small, armored fortress, maintenance facility, mess station, office, and communications center all squeezed onto the back of a single military cargo barque. At the moment, the outriggers had been extended, expanding the rooms inside to almost comfortable proportions. Removing his visor, Rossack fell into the folding chair beside his desk. It was really little more than a narrow board mounted to the wall on a hinge, but he'd learned to make due without luxuries when in the field.

The codex box, with its flat disk of brushed chrome surrounded by an intricate array of cut crystal and brass switches, sat dark and silent in its niche over his desk, as it had for most of the last several weeks. That's how Rossack liked it best. At the moment, there were a whole host of things he'd rather be doing than dealing with this device that tethered him to the rest of the world. Unfortunately, his duties placed other requirements on his shoulders.

He ran his fingers over the crystals in a very specific order, one that changed periodically and was known only to him. Immediately, the magescript etched into the housing began to glow and the central disk seemed to take on an almost ethereal translucence as a soft hiss emanated from somewhere inside the box. Lines, similar in appearance to those of a charcoal sketch, began to rise to the surface of the metal disk. After a moment, the lines sharpened somewhat into the face of an older man with a balding head, a pale mustache, and wearing the same black uniform as Rossack and his men. Instead of the two bars on his shoulder which marked Rossack as a captain, this man wore the three stars of a general.

"General Peraku," Rossack said. He'd been in the military long enough to keep his voice level despite the fact the hairs on the back of his neck were starting to stand on end. The Special Operations Group were known to be somewhat more flexible with the chain of command than their regular forces brethren, but even then, a general seldom had reason to contact a captain directly. Something big was up. "You wanted to speak with me."

The image on the disk moved in response to the man it portrayed but it didn't have the fluidity of real life, seeming more to shift and melt from one still likeness to the next. When the man spoke, the disk itself vibrated, conveying his words. "Captain Rossack." General Peraku's tone was not at all friendly but typical of the man even on his best days. "How goes the mission?"

Small talk? Clearly that's not why he'd called. "Successful, sir. I'll be relaying a full report this afternoon, but the bandit enclave here has been completely neutralized: thirteen hostiles killed in the assault on their stronghold and another twenty-four taken into custody who are currently being dealt with by the village magistrate."

"That didn't take long." General Peraku glanced down at his desk to read a memo. "Casualties?"

"Koberaty, Amnatash, and Trang suffered minor injuries in the assault. They've all received treatment and should be back on duty in a few days. Lieutenant Hanley, however, was killed in action."

"Hanley?" The general looked back out of the disk. "That old fool should have retired years ago."

"He was an excellent soldier, General, and his age had never been a liability." Rossack kept his voice a monotone. That 'old fool' had indeed been the best magesmith Rossack had ever served with. It was also guaranteed that the rest of the team would be drinking more than one round in his honor tonight. "He had always been eager and capable of carrying his share of the work, and more besides, right through to the end. His death was no fault of his own. Those bandits had more firepower in their possession than a fully outfitted combat battalion. They'd also dug themselves into a network of caves and gullies which wouldn't allow us to bring our titans and Artemis's into play. We had to go in on foot. If they'd had just a bit more luck or training, a lot more of my team would have ended up just like Hanley."

"Were they really that well equipped?"

"Their armory was like a catalog of every independent nation that's fallen to one of the Biregeth Nations in the last thirty years. You know this isn't the first time we've seen this. It's becoming more and more common all the time. Bandits like this used to be freedom-fighters and resistance cells. Now they're just thieves and murderers."

"Hmm, a sign of the times, Captain," General Peraku said, lifting a pair of reading glasses to his face and scanning another memo.

Rossack suppressed a scowl. "Command needs to start being more proactive with the gangs that smuggle these weapons instead of just sending us in to deal with the aftermath."

"All of us here at headquarters have read your reports, Captain, and most of us fully agree with them. And while no one is doubting the tactical prowess of the renowned Captain Rossack, our forces are simply stretched too thin."

Behind the impassive expression on his face, Rossack bristled, and not just at being called "renowned". He knew the moniker wasn't meant in scorn, but if being able to see the obvious and leading men to victory more often than not was all it took to be so highly regarded, then he failed to see why anyone couldn't achieve the same. Never mind the fact that Rossack had specifically addressed his concerns of limited manpower in dealing with the smugglers in the last memo he'd posted. What the general really meant to say was that politics were getting in the way once again, just like they did every time military operations started to fall apart.

As General Peraku once more became distracted by the papers on his desk, Rossack paused to take a breath. "I'd like to put him in for a commendation, sir."

"Who's that then?"

"Hanley." It took an effort on Rossack's part not to raise his voice.

"Yes, of course, I'll see that's it's taken care of," General Peraku said as if he'd only half-heard Rossack.

After a moment of silence from the codex box, Captain Rossack's eyes narrowed by a faction of an inch. "General, would you mind telling me the reason for this communication?"

General Peraku looked up, his eyes gazing out of the codex box, studying Rossack. "There's been an incident at Fort Grassnar. Your team will need to go there immediately."

If the military wasn't so predictable, Gracchus would have seemed like a seer. "General, my team has been in the field for nearly three months straight without any R&R to speak of in all that time. Surely, there must be other teams who can handle this."

"Yours is the closest. We also need the best."

"What kind of 'incident' could be that important?"

"There was a prison break from the fort's insurgent holding facility. Numerous suspected terrorists escaped. Most have been recaptured or killed but many are still at large. They still don't have solid numbers on how many of our own people were killed. A well-known mercenary, who I think you know, Ironsides, was also defeated in combat and his titan-mecha destroyed. Shortly thereafter, the Boravian SAA facility was attacked, several of its personnel were injured, and contraband slaves were stolen. There are also reports of several civilians having been attacked and at least one killed."

Captain Rossack shook his head. "Tragic, but I fail to see why any of that would require my team's involvement. Surely, even the local forces are capable of rounding up a few escaped rebels."

"Normally, I would agree with you, but in this case we don't need you to round up any of the terrorists. As hard as it may be to believe, the facts would seem to suggest that all these incidents were perpetrated by a single individual who is currently at large."

"One man did all that?"

"In a single day no less -- if the reports are to be believed, that is. At this point, a lot of the information is still sketchy. However, all of it so far seems to corroborate that conclusion. Everything also seems to indicate that he is still in Finttiranos and has not yet passed beyond our purview."

As a rule, any intelligence coming out of Fort Grassnar would be taken with a grain of salt. That place was notorious for its corruption. However, if there were really enough cross-verified reports to get the SOG involved, there might actually be something to this.

"There is one more thing," General Peraku said. "As I indicated, reports are still somewhat imprecise, but there is evidence here to at least suggest human augmentation may have been involved."

Could there really be that much evidence to support such a wild claim? The very notion was almost laughable. Still, it would begin to explain how one man might have been capable of doing all those things and still escape. And even as outlandish as such a claim was, the original Biregeth Alliance Treaty had even included language to address this exact possibility, to ensure cooperation between the three nations should it ever occur.

"Does that mean high command will be initiating Directive Thirty-One?" In all Rossack's years of military service, he'd never once even heard rumors of that obscure amendment ever being utilized.

"No. That would require us to inform Secotia and Thieradoon -- and possibly even request their assistance. At this point, we still don't know what we're dealing with. You need to apprehend this person and bring him in, preferably alive, so that we can make that determination. For the duration of this mission, you will be operating under the strictest of confidentiality and will report directly to me and me alone. Is that understood?"

"Yes, sir," Captain Rossack said. Even with as many problems as Finttiranos had, it was still his country and the last thing he'd ever want was to involve either of those other two nations in Finttiranos business. The three of them may have been allies on paper, but that only meant none of them had yet been caught betraying the others. "My team can depart immediately."

"Excellent," General Peraku said. "I'll forward you everything we have on the situation so you can get up to speed en route. Good hunting, Captain Rossack."

www.ingramcontent.com/pod-product-compliance
Lightning Source LLC
Chambersburg PA
CBHW070537030726
47505CB00001B/63